More praise for *The Last Full Measure*

"Exhaustively researched, infused with a profound understanding of the great issues of a nation and the small quirks of the human heart and ego, *The Last Full Measure* is fiction that brings history brilliantly to life."

—*Newsday*

"*The Last Full Measure* primarily follows three men—Lee, Ulysses S. Grant and Joshua Lawrence Chamberlain, a Union hero at Gettysburg—through the last two years of war. Shaara picked them because 'each, in his way, rose to a higher level, not just as a war hero, but as a man of character and dignity and honor.' Shaara's work similarly rises. His achievement in *The Last Full Measure* is showing us through these three characters how a nation was forever changed."

—*Detroit Free Press*

"After reading *The Last Full Measure*, I know Michael Shaara is smiling in Heaven."

—Gabor Borritt
Director, the Civil War Institute
Gettysburg, PA

"Jeff Shaara's prose is clear and even vivid . . . executed robustly, with [an] expert command of detail and compassionate eye for emotion and disillusionment. . . . He is at his best in showing the near unraveling of Lee's religiosity, a stubborn faith that God was on his side, contrasting it with the flinty doggedness of Grant, who trusted in his cigars and his unbroken lines of supply more than he did a Supreme Being."

—*Chicago Sun-Times*

"Ideally, the Homeric Civil War Epic that Americans have longed for depicts both sides even-handedly and compassionately, encompasses major battles led by major leaders, and appeals to all readers, North and South, young and old, men and women—the trilogy begun by the father and finished by the son is that epic, and Jeff Shaara's *The Last Full Measure* brings the monumental trilogy to a triumphant conclusion. The Shaara vision of its origins in blood and courage illuminates America's future on the threshold of the new millennium."

—David Madden
Director, The United States Civil War Center

"*The Last Full Measure* brings a unique and monumental father-son trilogy to a triumphant conclusion. . . . Shaara sustains a major achievement that distinguishes this trilogy from most other Civil War novels: He gives a balanced experience of the temperament, sensibility, and character of generals on both sides of the battle lines. Shaara also proves once and for all that, though influenced by his father, he has a voice and talent all his own."

—*BookPage*

Please turn the page for more reviews. . . .

THE LAST
FULL
MEASURE

JEFF SHAARA

THE RANDOM HOUSE PUBLISHING GROUP
NEW YORK

To my friend Ron Maxwell,
who has taught me to never lose sight of the dream

TO THE READER

THIS STORY IS THE THIRD PART OF A TRILOGY, FOLLOWING THE lives of key characters of the Civil War, from the aftermath of the Battle of Gettysburg, through the surrender at Appomattox, and beyond. While the cast of characters of that momentous event was huge, this story follows primarily three men: Robert E. Lee, Joshua Lawrence Chamberlain, and Ulysses S. Grant.

This is neither a history book nor a biography, but a story told from the points of view of the characters themselves, through their own eyes and their own experiences. In many ways these are ordinary people caught up in extraordinary times. These particular characters stand apart because each, in his own way, rose to a higher level, not just as a war hero, but as a man of character and dignity and honor. To some these characteristics are quaint and out of date. To many others they are qualities that our modern world is sorely missing.

In some ways this is a very different story from the first two parts of the trilogy. After Gettysburg there is a change in the way men see the war, and in the way they fight it. There is little enthusiasm now for the traditional assault, sending dense lines of men across open ground into the massed guns of a heavily fortified enemy. Gettysburg has badly wounded both sides, and though it is clearly a defeat for Lee's army, neither side is quick to pursue another fight on such a huge scale. In the West—Tennessee and Mississippi—the war still rages, but in Virginia there is now a lull, a time for both armies to heal their wounds and plan the next great strategy to bring the awful war to an end. What no one can know is that Gettysburg is not the final battle, and that for nearly two more years there will be no peace.

It is the job of the historian to tell us *what* happened, to provide the dates and places and numbers, all the necessary ingredients of text-books. It is the job of the storyteller to bring out the thoughts, the words, the souls of these fascinating characters, to tell us *why* they should be remembered and respected and even enjoyed. While this is a novel, it is not false history. The time line, the events, and the language are as accurate as I could make them.

It has been my great privilege to become close enough to these marvelous characters to tell their story, and so, to bring them to you.

JEFF SHAARA

ACKNOWLEDGMENTS

For the considerable assistance I have received in the writing of this book I must thank the following:

Gabor Boritt, The Civil War Institute, Gettysburg, Pennsylvania, for generously providing information and materials and insight on the character of Abraham Lincoln.

Chris Calkins, Chief Historian, Petersburg National Battlefield, Petersburg, Virginia, for the generous gift of his time, his singular knowledge of those special hidden places and his enthusiasm for sharing them.

Dr. John Elrod, President, Washington and Lee University, for his extraordinary graciousness and hospitality, making available the Lee and Junkin residences, occupied still by the university president and dean, thus allowing prying eyes into the privacy of his own home.

Patrick Falci, of the Civil War Round Table of New York, who is a tireless source of information and research material, and who sacrificed a large chunk of his vacation time to serve as guide for much of the field research.

Beth Ford, Cincinnati, Ohio, who generously provided a marvelous collection of original published works from the postwar era, including the published battle reports of every Confederate general.

Keith Gibson, Director of the VMI Museum, Lexington, Virginia, and his wife, **Pat Gibson,** whose hospitality and friendship continue to provide insight and direction, and whose talent and enthusiasm for the music of the period always remind us that there is more to our history than the written word.

Cory Hudgins, and all the staff of the Museum of the Confederacy, in Richmond, Virginia, for their enthusiastic cooperation, and knowledge of details otherwise lost to history.

Joan McDonough, President, the Civil War Round Table of New York, for her own suggestions of source materials; her tireless energy and assistance in fact-checking are always appreciated.

Len Reidel, the Blue and Gray Educational Society, Danville, Virginia, for providing difficult to locate documents and material on several of the characters.

Gordon Rhea, Charleston, South Carolina, author of *The Battle of the Wilderness* and *The Battle of Spotsylvania Courthouse and the Road to Yellow Tavern,* for not only having produced the two finest accounts of these events that I have come across, but for his generosity and support of this project by providing additional research materials.

Diane Smith, East Holden, Maine, whose own research into the lives of Joshua and Fannie Chamberlain provided insights into and discussion of aspects of their personal relationship not readily available.

Michael Wicklein and **Susan Saum-Wicklein,** of the Association for the Preservation of Civil War Sites, Hagerstown, Maryland, for their generous assistance with biographical material I simply couldn't find.

It is also my privilege to acknowledge the continuing friendship and support of **Clare Ferraro,** the former publisher of Ballantine Books in New York, without whose faith and confidence I would not now be nor probably ever have been a writer.

Every writer needs guidance, and for that I must thank **Doug Grad,** editor, Ballantine Books, who has been a patient sounding-board, and has always supported my ideas. He is one of the few who seem to understand the magic of this amazing process, how the story flows from the mind to the page, a process that is baffling to me yet.

This process never could have been completed without the constant support and tolerance of my wife **Lynne.** She reads every word, offers welcome insight into what I am doing right, and what I am doing wrong, but more, she has endured my journey through stress, euphoria, aggravation, fear, exhaustion, and, when the work allows, laughter.

The positive attention that *Gods and Generals* received was a wonderful surprise, and something that has pointed me in a direction I will follow for the rest of my life. My brief writing career has already provided me many positives, and a great deal of fulfillment. I did not start this journey, I merely continue it, and I am following enormous footprints. I will never stand before an audience, or dedicate a book, without acknowledging the man who opened the door. Thanks, Dad.

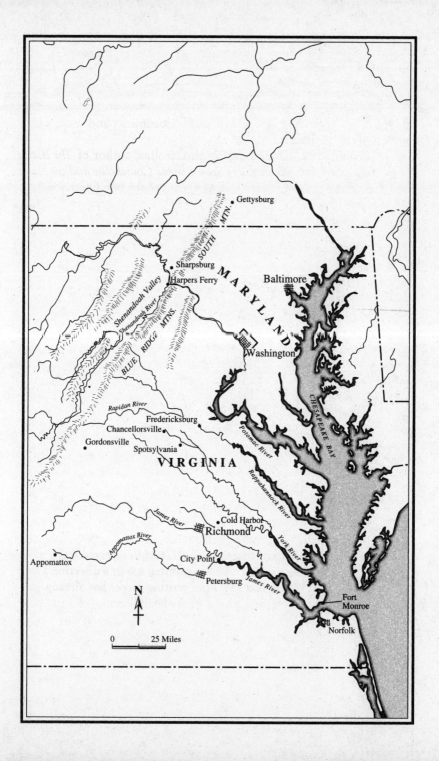

Gettysburg

SOUTH MTN.

Sharpsburg

Harpers Ferry

MARYLAND

Baltimore

Shenandoah Valley

Shenandoah River

BLUE RIDGE MTNS.

Washington

Rapidan River

Fredericksburg

Chancellorsville

Gordonsville

Spotsylvania

VIRGINIA

Potomac River

CHESAPEAKE BAY

Rappahannock River

James River

Appomattox River

Cold Harbor

Richmond

York River

City Point

Appomattox

Petersburg

James River

Fort
Monroe

Norfolk

N

0   25 Miles

INTRODUCTION

B
Y JULY 1863 THE CIVIL WAR HAS BEEN FOUGHT OVER THE FARM-
lands and seacoasts of the South for better than two years, and is
already one of the bloodiest wars in human history. It is a war
that most believed would be decided by one quick fight, one great
show of strength by the power of the North. The first major battle,
called Bull Run in the North, Manassas in the South, is witnessed by a
carefree audience of Washington's elite. Their brightly decorated carriages carry men in fine suits and society matrons in colorful dresses.
They perch on a hillside, enjoying their picnics, anticipating a great
show with bands playing merrily while the young men in blue march
in glorious parade and sweep aside the ragged band of rebels. What
they see is the first great horror, the stunning reality that this is in fact
a *war*, and that men will die. What they still cannot understand is how
far this will go, and *how many* men will die.

In the North, President Lincoln maintains a fragile grip on forces
pulling the government in all directions. On one extreme is the pacifist
movement, those who believe that the South has made its point, and
so, to avoid bloodshed, Washington must simply let them go, that
nothing so inconsequential as the Constitution is as important as the
loss of life. On the other extreme are the radical abolitionists, who demand the South be brought down entirely, punished for its way of life,
its culture, and that anyone who supports the southern cause should be
purged from the land. There is also a great middle ground, men of reason and intellect, who now understand that there is more to this war
than the inflammatory issue of slavery, or the argument over the sover-
eign rights of the individual states. As men continue to volunteer,
larger and larger numbers of troops take to the fields, and other causes

emerge, each man fighting for his own reason. Some fight for honor and duty, some for money and glory, but nearly all are driven by an amazing courage, and will carry their muskets across the deadly space because they feel it is the right thing to do.

From the North come farmers and fishermen, lumberjacks and shopkeepers, old veterans and young idealists. Some are barely Americans at all, expatriates and immigrants from Europe, led by officers who do not speak English. Some are freedmen, Negroes who volunteer to fight for the preservation of the limited freedoms they have been given, and to spread that freedom into the South.

In the South they are also farmers and fishermen, as well as ranchers, laborers, aristocrats, and young men seeking adventure. They are inspired first by the political rhetoric, the fire-breathing oratory of the radical secessionists. They are told that Lincoln is in league with the devil, and that his election ensures that the South will be held down, oppressed by the powerful interests in the North, that their very way of life is under siege. When the sound of the big guns echo across Charleston harbor, when the first flashes of smoke and fire swallow Fort Sumter, Lincoln orders an army to go south, to put down the rebellion by force. With the invasion comes a new inspiration, and in the South, even men of reason are drawn into the fight, men who were not seduced by mindless rhetoric, who have shunned the self-serving motives of the politicians. There is outrage, and no matter the issues or the politics, many take up arms in response to what they see as the threat to their homes. Even the men who understand and promote the inevitable failure of slavery cannot stand by while their land is invaded. The issue is not to be decided after all by talk or rhetoric, but by the gun.

On both sides are the career soldiers, West Pointers, men with experience from the Mexican War, or the Indian wars of the 1850s. In the North the officers are infected and abused by the disease of politics, and promotion is not always granted by performance or ability. The Federal armies endure a parade of inept or unlucky commanders who cannot fight the rebels until they first master the fight with Washington. Few succeed.

In the South, Jefferson Davis maintains an iron hand, controlling even the smallest details of governing the Confederacy. It is not an effective system, and as in the North, men of political influence are awarded positions of great authority, men who have no business leading soldiers into combat. In mid-1862, through an act of fate, or as he would interpret it, an act of God, Robert Edward Lee is given command of the Army of Northern Virginia. What follows in the East is a clear pattern, a series of great and bloody fights in which the South prevails and the North is beaten back. If the pattern continues, the war will end and the Confederacy will triumph. Many of the fights are won by Lee, or by his generals—the Shenandoah Valley, Second Manassas. Many of the fights are simply lost by the blunders of Federal commanders, the most horrifying example at Fredericksburg. Most, like the catastrophic Federal defeat at Chancellorsville or the tactical stalemate at Antietam, are a combination of both.

By 1863 two monumental events provide an insight into what lies ahead. The first is the success of the Federal blockade of southern seaports, which prevents the South from receiving critical supplies from allies abroad, and also prevents the export of raw materials, notably cotton and tobacco, which provide the currency necessary to pay for the war effort. The result is understood on both sides. Without outside help, the Confederacy will slowly starve.

The second is the great bloody fight at Gettysburg. While a tragic defeat for Lee's army, there is a greater significance to the way that defeat occurs. Until now, the war has been fought mostly from the old traditions, the Napoleonic method, the massed frontal assault against fortified positions. It has been apparent from the beginning of the war that the new weaponry has made such attacks dangerous and costly, but old ways die slowly, and commanders on both sides have been reluctant to change. After Gettysburg, the changes become a matter of survival. If the commanders do not yet understand, the men in the field do, and the use of the shovels becomes as important as the use of muskets. The new methods—strong fortifications, trench warfare—are clear signs to all that the war has changed, that there will be no quick and decisive fight to end all fights.

As the Civil War enters its third year, the bloody reports continue to fill the newspapers, and the bodies of young men continue to fill the cemeteries. To the eager patriots, the idealists and adventurers who joined the fight at the beginning, there is a new reality, in which honor and glory are becoming hollow words. The great causes are slowly pushed aside, and men now fight with the grim determination to take this fight to its end; after so much destruction and horrible loss, the senses are dulled, the unspeakable sights no longer shock. All the energy is forward, toward those men across that deadly space who have simply become the enemy.

ROBERT EDWARD LEE

Born in 1807, he graduates West Point in 1829, second in his class. Though he is the son of "Light-Horse" Harry Lee, a great hero of the American Revolution, late in his father's life Lee must endure the burden of his father's business and personal failures more than the aura of heroism. Lee is devoutly religious, believing with absolute clarity that the events of his life are determined by the will of God. On his return from West Point, his mother dies in his arms. The haunting sadness of her death stays hard inside him for the rest of his life, and places him more firmly than ever into the hands of his God.

He marries the aristocratic Mary Anne Randolph Custis, whose father is the grandson of Martha Washington, and whose home is the grand mansion of Arlington, overlooking the Potomac River. The Lees have seven children, and Lee suffers the guilt of a career that rarely brings him home to watch his children grow, a source of great regret for him, and simmering bitterness in his wife Mary.

Lee is a brilliant engineer, and his army career moves him to a variety of posts where his expertise and skill contribute much to the construction of the military installations and forts along the Atlantic coast. He goes to St. Louis and confronts a crisis for the port there by rerouting the flow of the Mississippi River. In 1846 he is sent to Mexico, and his reputation lands him on the staff of General-in-Chief Winfield Scott. Lee performs with efficiency and heroism, both as an engineer, a scout, and a staff officer, and leaves Mexico a lieutenant colonel.

He accepts command of the cadet corps at West Point in 1851, considered by many as the great reward for good service, the respectable job in which to spend the autumn of his career. But though his family is now close, he misses the action of Mexico, finds himself stifled by administrative duties. In 1855 he stuns all who know him by seizing an opportunity to return to the field, volunteering to go to Texas, to command a new regiment of cavalry. But even that command is mundane and frustrating, and there is for him nothing in the duty that recalls the vitality and adventure of the fighting in Mexico. Throughout the 1850s Lee settles into a deep gloom, resigns himself that no duty will be as fulfilling as life under fire and that his career will carry him into old age in bored obscurity.

As the conflict over Lincoln's election boils over in the South, his command in Texas begins to collapse, and he is recalled to Washington in early 1861, where he receives the startling request to command Lincoln's new volunteer army, with a promotion to Major General. He shocks Washington and deeply disappoints Winfield Scott by declining the appointment. Lee chooses the only course left to an officer and a man of honor and resigns from his thirty-year career. He believes that even though Virginia has not yet joined the secessionist states, by organizing an army to invade the South, Lincoln has united his opponents and the southern states, which must eventually include Virginia. Lee will not take up arms against his home.

In late April 1861 he accepts the governor's invitation to command the Virginia Militia, a defensive force assembled to defend the state. When Jefferson Davis moves the Confederate government to Richmond, the Virginia forces, as well as those of the other ten secessionist states, are absorbed into the Confederate army. Lee is invited to serve as military consultant to Davis, another stifling job with little actual authority. In July 1861, during the first great battle of the war, Lee sits alone in his office, while most of official Richmond travels to Manassas, to the excitement of the front lines.

In June 1862, while accompanied by Davis near the fighting on the Virginia peninsula, commander Joe Johnston is wounded in action and Davis offers command of the Army of Northern Virginia to Lee. Lee accepts, understands that he is, after all, a soldier, and justifies the decision with the fact that his theater of war is still Virginia. Defending his home takes on a more poignant significance when Lee's grand estate at Arlington is occupied and ransacked by Federal troops.

Lee reorganizes the army, removes many of the inept political generals, and begins to understand the enormous value of his two best commanders, James Longstreet and Thomas Jackson, who at Manassas was given the nickname "Stonewall." Using the greatest talents of both men, Lee leads the Army of Northern Virginia through a series of momentous victories against a Federal army that is weighed down by its own failures, and by its continuing struggle to find an effective commander. Much of Lee's war is fought in northern Virginia, and the land is suffering under the strain of feeding the army. The burden of war and of the Federal blockade spreads through the entire Confederacy and inspires Lee and Davis to consider a bold and decisive strategy.

In September 1862, Lee moves his army north, hoping to gather support and new recruits from the neutral state of Maryland. The advance results in the battle of Sharpsburg—known as Antietam in the North—and though Lee does not admit defeat, the outrageous carnage and loss of life force him to order a retreat back into Virginia. But his army is not pursued by the Federal forces, and with new commanders now confronting him, Lee begins a great tactical chess game, and accomplishes the greatest victories of the war.

In December 1862, at Fredericksburg, Virginia, his army maintains the defensive and completely crushes poorly planned Federal assaults. In May 1863, at Chancellorsville, Lee is outnumbered nearly three to one, and only by the utter audacity of Stonewall Jackson does the huge Federal army retire from the field with great loss. But the battle is costly for Lee as well. Jackson is accidentally shot by his own men, and dies after a weeklong struggle with pneumonia.

Lee and Davis continue to believe that a move northward is essential, that with weakened confidence and inept commanders, the Federal army need only be pushed into one great battle that will likely end the war. In June 1863, Lee's army marches into Pennsylvania. He believes that a great fight might not even be necessary, that just the threat of spilling blood on northern soil will put great pressure on Washington, and the war might be brought to an end by the voice of the northern people. The invasion of the North will serve another purpose: to take the fight into fertile farmlands where Lee might feed his increasingly desperate army.

Some in Lee's army question the strategy, raising the moral question of how to justify an invasion versus defending their homes. Others question the military judgment of moving into unfamiliar territory, against an enemy that has never been inspired by fighting on its own ground. There are other factors that Lee must confront. Though he is personally devastated by the death of Jackson, Jackson's loss means more to his army than Lee fully understands.

As the invasion moves north, Lee is left blind by his cavalry, under the flamboyant command of Jeb Stuart. Stuart fails to provide Lee with critical information about the enemy and is cut off from Lee beyond the march of the Federal army, an army that is moving to confront Lee with uncharacteristic speed. The Federal Army of the Potomac has yet another new commander, George Gordon Meade, and if Lee knows Meade to be a careful man, cautious in his new command, he also knows that there are many other Federal officers now rising to the top, men who are not political pawns but in fact hard and effective fighters.

The two armies collide at a small crossroads called Gettysburg, a fight for which Lee is not yet prepared, and the fight becomes the three bloodiest days in American history. As costly as it is to both armies, it is a clear defeat for Lee. He had believed his army could not be stopped, and begins now to understand what Jackson's loss might mean—that as the fight goes on, and the good men continue to fall away, the war will settle heavily on his own shoulders.

JOSHUA LAWRENCE CHAMBERLAIN

Born in 1828 near Brewer, Maine, he is the oldest of five children. He graduates Bowdoin College in 1852, and impresses all who know him with his intellect, his gift for words and talent for languages. He is raised by a deeply religious mother, whose greatest wish is that he become a man of the cloth, and for a short while Chamberlain attends the Bangor Theological Seminary, but it is not a commitment he can make. His father's ancestry is military. Chamberlain's great-grandfather fought in the Revolution, his grandfather in the War of 1812. His father serves during peacetime years in the Maine Militia and never sees combat. It is family tradition that his son will follow the military path, and he pressures Chamberlain to apply to West Point. When Chamberlain returns to the academic community, a career for which his father has little respect, the disappointment becomes a hard barrier between them.

He marries Frances Caroline (Fannie) Adams, and they have four children, two of whom survive infancy. Fannie pushes him toward the career in academics, and his love for her is so complete and consuming that he likely would have pursued any path she had chosen.

Considered the rising star in the academic community, Chamberlain accepts a prestigious Chair at Bowdoin, formerly held by the renowned Calvin Stowe, husband of Harriet Beecher Stowe. Her controversial book, *Uncle Tom's Cabin*, inspires Chamberlain, and the issues that explode in the South, so far removed from the classrooms in Maine, reach him deeply. He begins to feel a calling of a different kind.

As the war begins in earnest, and Chamberlain's distraction is evident to the school administration, he is offered a leave of absence—a trip to Europe, to take him away from the growing turmoil. Chamberlain uses the opportunity in a way that astounds and distresses everyone. He goes to the governor of Maine without telling anyone, including Fannie, and volunteers for service in the newly forming Maine regiments. Though he has no military experience, his intellect and zeal for the job open the door, and he is appointed Lieutenant Colonel, second-in-command of the Twentieth Maine Regiment of Volunteers.

After a difficult farewell to his family, Chamberlain and his regiment join the Army of the Potomac in Washington, and in September 1862 they march toward western Maryland, to confront Lee's army at

Antietam Creek. The Twentieth Maine does not see action, but Chamberlain observes the carnage of the fight and, for the first time, experiences what the war might mean for the men around him. Three months later he leads his men into the guns at Fredericksburg and witnesses firsthand what the war has become. He spends an amazing night on the battlefield, yards from the lines of the enemy, and protects himself with the corpses of his own men.

In June 1863 he is promoted to full colonel, and now commands the regiment. He marches north with the army in pursuit of Lee's invasion. By chance, his regiment is the lead unit of the Fifth Corps, and when they reach the growing sounds of the fight at Gettysburg, the Twentieth Maine marches to the left flank, climbing a long rise to the far face of a rocky hill known later as Little Round Top. His is now the last unit, the far left flank of the Federal line, and he is ordered to hold the position at all cost. The regiment fights off a desperate series of attacks from Longstreet's corps, which, if successful, would likely turn the entire Federal flank, exposing the supply train and the rear of the rest of the army. Low on ammunition, his line weakening from the loss of so many men, he impulsively orders his men to charge the advancing rebels with bayonets, surprising the weary attackers so completely that they retreat in disorder or are captured en masse. The attacks end and the flank is secured.

During the fight, he is struck by a small piece of shrapnel, and carries a small but painful wound in his foot. As the army marches in slow pursuit of Lee's retreat, the foul weather and Chamberlain's own exhaustion take their toll, and he begins to suffer symptoms of malaria.

Though he is unknown outside of his immediate command, this college professor turned soldier now attracts the attention of the commanders above him, and it becomes apparent that his is a name that will be heard again.

ULYSSES SIMPSON GRANT

Born in 1822 in Point Pleasant, Ohio, he graduates West Point in 1843. Small, undistinguished as a cadet, it is his initials which first attract attention. The U.S. becomes a nickname, "Uncle Sam," and soon he is known by his friends as simply "Sam." He achieves one other notable reputation at the Point, that of a master horseman, seemingly able to tame and ride any animal.

His first duty is near St. Louis, and he maintains a strong friendship with many of the former cadets, including "Pete" Longstreet.

Grant meets and falls madly in love with Julia Dent, whose father's inflated notion of his own aristocratic standing produces strong objection to his daughter's relationship with a soldier. Longstreet suffers a similar fate, and in 1846, when the orders come to march to Mexico, both men leave behind young girls with wounded hearts.

Grant is assigned to the Fourth Infantry and serves under Zachary Taylor during the first conflicts in south Texas. He makes the great march inland with Winfield Scott and arrives at the gates of Mexico City to lead his men into the costly fighting that eventually breaks down the defenses of the city and gives Scott's army the victory. Grant leads his infantry with great skill, and is recognized for heroism, but is not impressed with the straight-ahead tactics used by Scott. He believes that much loss of life could have been avoided by better strategy.

He returns home with a strong sense of despair for the condition of the Mexican peasantry, which he sees as victims of both the war and their own ruling class. It is an experience that helps strengthen his own feelings about the abominable inhumanity of slavery.

Returning to St. Louis, Grant receives reluctant consent to marry Julia, and eventually they have four children. He receives a pleasant assignment to Detroit, but in 1852 he is ordered to the coast of California, an expensive and hazardous post, and so he must leave his family behind. The following two years are the worst in his life, and despite a brief and enjoyable tour at Fort Vancouver, he succumbs both to the outrageous temptations of gold-rush San Francisco and the desperate loneliness of life without his young family. Shy and withdrawn, he does not enjoy the raucous social circles of many of his friends, and the painful isolation leads him to a dependency on alcohol. His bouts of drunkenness are severe enough to interfere with his duty, and his behavior warrants disciplinary action. Because of the generosity of his commanding officer, Grant is afforded the opportunity to resign rather than face a court-martial. He leaves the army in May 1854 and believes his career in the military is at a painful conclusion.

He returns to his family unemployed and penniless, and attempts to farm a piece of land given him by Julia's father. With no money to provide the beginnings of a crop, Grant attempts the lumber business, cutting trees from the land himself. He eventually builds his own house, which he calls, appropriately, "Hardscrabble."

He is generous to a fault, often loaning money to those who will never repay the debts, and despite a constant struggle financially, he is always willing to help anyone who confronts him in need.

In 1859 he is offered a position as a collection agent for a real estate firm in St. Louis, and trades the small farm for a modest home in the city, but the business is not profitable. Though he is qualified for positions that become available in the local government, the political turmoil that spreads through the Midwest requires great skill at intrigue and political connections, and Grant has neither. He finally accepts an offer from his own father, moves to Galena, Illinois, in 1860, and clerks in a leather and tanned goods store with his brothers, who understand that Grant's military experience and West Point training in mathematics will make for both a trustworthy and useful employee. But the politics of the day begin to affect even those who try to avoid the great discussions and town meetings, and Grant meets John Rawlins and Elihu Washburne, whose political influence begins to pave the way for an opportunity Grant would never have sought on his own.

As the presidential election draws closer, Grant awakens to the political passions around him, involves himself with the issues and the candidates, and finally decides to support the candidate Abraham Lincoln. When Lincoln is elected, Grant tells his friend John Rawlins that with passions igniting around the country, "the South will fight."

Persuaded by Washburne, Grant organizes a regiment of troops from Galena and petitions the governor of Illinois for a Colonel's commission, which he receives. After seven years of struggle as a civilian, Grant reenters the army.

Serving first under Henry Halleck, he eventually commands troops through fights on the Mississippi River at Forts Henry and Donelson, each fight growing in importance as the war spreads. Promoted eventually to Major General, Grant is named commander of the Federal Army of Tennessee, but still must endure Halleck's fragile ego and disagreeable hostility. On the Tennessee River at a place called Shiloh, facing a powerful enemy under the command of Albert Sidney Johnston, Grant wins one of the bloodiest fights of the war, in which Johnston himself is killed. Here, Grant's command includes an old acquaintance from his days in California, William Tecumseh Sherman.

In July 1862, when Halleck is promoted to General-in-Chief of the army and leaves for Washington, the army of the western theater is a confused mishmash of commands under Grant, Don Carlos Buell, and William Rosecrans. While the focus of the nation is on the great battles in Virginia, Grant gradually establishes himself as the most consistent and reliable commander in the West. He finally unites much of the Federal forces for an assault and eventually a long siege on the critical river port of Vicksburg, Mississippi. In July 1863, the same week Lee's army confronts the great Federal forces at Gettysburg, Grant succeeds in capturing both Vicksburg and the Confederate force that had occupied it.

Now, Lincoln begins to focus not just on the great turmoil of Virginia, but toward the West as well, and it is Grant's name that rises through the jumble of poor commanders and the political gloom of Washington. After the disasters of leadership that have plagued the army, Lincoln's patience for the politics of command is at an end. He begins to speak of this quiet and unassuming man out West, a general who seems to know how to win.

PART
ONE

Four score and seven years ago our fathers brought forth, upon this continent, a new nation, conceived in liberty, and dedicated to the proposition that all men are created equal. Now we are engaged in a great civil war . . .

PART
ONE

1. LEE

JULY 13, 1863

I T WAS A HIGH BLUFF, OVERLOOKING THE DARK VIOLENCE OF THE
swollen river. He sat alone, watched as the men fell into line and
the columns began moving slowly through the steady rain. He felt
the coolness run down his neck, the water soaking every part of him,
his hat, his clothes. A vast sea of mud surrounded them all. The Potomac was rising again, was well beyond their ability to ford, as they
might have done before the rains. Now, it was angry and swirling. In
the darkness, the motion was accented by the small fires that lined the
riverbank, a flickering protest to the misery of the weather, the only
guiding light the men would have to reach the crossing.

Lee straightened his back, stretched, pulled at the miserable wetness in his clothes. He reached down, patted Traveller gently, said quietly to the horse, "He has given us one more night . . . he has not come."

He was thinking now of George Meade, the commander of the
vast Federal army he knew was encamped out there, somewhere, deep
in the thick darkness. He had expected them to come at him well before now. It had been ten days, and Lee's army had been strung out for
miles, moving southwest away from Gettysburg. The army had begun
the march away from the bloody fields in a terrible downpour, led
away by the wagons of the wounded, and Meade had not pursued. But
they reached the Potomac to find the river swollen nearly out of its
banks, their one good bridge swept away, and so they would have to
try to build another, or wait longer for the river to drop.

When Meade had finally moved, he pushed his army in a more
roundabout way, to come at them from downriver. But there was too
much time, Lee's men had fortified into a strong defensive line, and so
Meade waited again. Lee had known the risk was enormous, and he

feared the attack at any time. There was some skirmishing, small out-
breaks of musket fire, the feeling out of two great armies close together. The only real assaults had been with cavalry, all along the
march, the Federal horsemen thrusting and jabbing, while Stuart held
them away from the main lines. When the skies finally cleared and the
roads began to dry, Meade moved his army close, and Lee was backed
hard against the high water. Now they had dug in, the quick work of
men with shovels, because even the foot soldiers knew that they were
trapped and a strong push from a healthy enemy could crush them. But
Meade did not come.

It was Major Harman, the foul-tempered and foul-mouthed quartermaster of Jackson's old Second Corps, who saved the day. Lee smiled
now, remembered Jackson's embarrassment as Harman would ride by,
screaming profanities at a line of slow moving wagons. Jackson would
glance at Lee like a small boy expecting an angry response from a stern
parent, and Lee would look away, would make no issue of it, knew
well that Jackson would tolerate the man's harsh outbursts because he
was very good at his job. Now Harman was serving new commanders,
and still did his job. He'd scouted the countryside, found the abandoned houses and barns, the people far away from this invading army.
Harman ordered the houses dismantled and the wood planking thrown
into the river, swept downstream to where the engineers waited. The
wood was collected and strung together into a snaking mass of ragged
timber. They had laid tree branches across the planks, muffling the
sounds of the wagons' wheels, and now the ambulances and the guns
and the weary soldiers were finally crossing the river.

Lee still watched them, the glow from the fires throwing light and
shadows on the faces, some looking up toward him, seeing him on the
high knoll. But most stared straight ahead, looked silently at the back
of the man in front, or down at the slow rhythm of bare feet, moving
slowly, carefully, and they all knew they were marching south.

He thought of Jackson again, closed his eyes and saw the sharp
face, the brightness in the clear blue eyes. We miss you, General. No,
do not think on that. He opened his eyes, looked around to his staff,
saw Taylor, sitting with the others, a cluster of black raincoats.

"Major, have we heard from General Ewell?"

Taylor moved up, pushed his horse through the mud close to Lee.
"Yes, sir. He reports his men are crossing well. They should be south
of the river by daylight."

Lee nodded, wanted to say more, to break away from the
thoughts of Jackson, but the image was still there, would not go. Lee

turned back toward the march of the men, felt the wetness again. Taylor waited, watched Lee, could sense his mood through the darkness, backed his horse away.

Below, along the river, a group of horsemen moved out of the woods, and Lee saw the flag of the First Corps. They rode slowly toward the knoll, then one man moved out in front and spurred his horse up the hill, broad thick shoulders slumped against the rain. The wind suddenly began to blow, the rain slicing across them, and the big man leaned into it, held his hat in place with a gloved hand.

"General Longstreet . . ."

Longstreet looked up, peered from under the wide wet hat, nodded, saluted. "General Lee. We're moving pretty quick, considering the conditions. The bridge may not hold. We're watching it pretty close . . . both sides of the river."

"It is a blessing, General." Lee looked to the water again, the slow march of the troops. "Major Harman may have saved this army."

Longstreet followed Lee's look, and for a moment the wind stopped and there was just the quiet sound of the rain. Suddenly, beyond the trees, there was a rumble, one sharp blast from a big gun. They waited for more, but the silence flowed back around them. Longstreet looked that way, said, "Damned fools . . . save your ammunition."

He looked toward Lee, lowered his head, did not like to swear in front of Lee, but Lee did not seem to notice, was again staring at the marching troops. Longstreet saw now that Lee was counting, nodding to the regimental flags as they caught the brief flickers from the fires.

"We'll make it all right, sir. If Meade hasn't hit us by now, he isn't coming at all. Ewell is making good time down below, and the First Corps is nearly all across. Hill's corps is right behind us."

Lee nodded, looked now out in the darkness, to the far trees. "He should have hit us here. We gave him an opportunity. God . . . gave him an opportunity. The rains slowed us, kept us here. Now, God has taken his opportunity away."

Lee paused, and Longstreet waited.

Lee said, "I don't understand His ways. . . . I thought it would never be like this. The Almighty was with us, the fight was ours . . . we should have won the day. But it was not to be. I thought . . . I understood. But now, He is allowing us to go back home."

Longstreet looked at Lee for a long moment, said, "I thought Meade would end it. He is making a mistake letting us escape. I suppose . . . there will be another day."

Now there was the sharp sound of another gun, a brief flash of light in the trees far downriver, then another gun, closer, the reply. Lee watched, sat up straight.

Longstreet said, "No musket fire. They're just playing . . . probably firing at the wind. Meade's cavalry is moving around, but no infantry. They're still in place."

Lee shook his head. "He dug trenches. He came right at us, and then dug trenches."

Longstreet said, "The scouts have been bringing in some numbers. . . . Word is, he's pretty beat up. Maybe worse than us. They lost some good people. . . . John Reynolds is dead, that's for certain. I heard Hancock was down, and Dan Sickles. Meade's still new to command, doesn't want to make any mistakes. He won the fight, he knows it. Let those folks in Washington absorb that. They haven't had much to cheer about."

Lee looked at Longstreet, ran the names through his mind. "General, he has not lost what we have lost. We cannot replace what has been taken from us, and this fight has taken too much. I do not understand why we have been . . . punished so. We could have ended the war, right over there, if we had prevailed on that ground. The pressure on Washington . . . we took the fight to *them*, it was the only way. And we have paid a terrible price." He paused, said quietly, to himself, "I would have thought . . . surely God does not want this to go on."

Longstreet watched the troops again, said, "There were many mistakes."

Lee did not answer, thought again of Jackson, closed his eyes, fought the image. But it would not go away. The image stared hard at him, and Lee knew that Jackson *was* there, had *seen* the great fight, the great bloody disaster. Lee thought, If you had been here . . . if you had led them . . . it would have been very different.

From down below, one of Longstreet's staff moved up the hill, said, "General, excuse me. The last of the corps is on the bridge, sir. General Hill's column is forming on the road, behind those woods."

Longstreet turned, nodded. "Thank you, Major. We'll move across in a minute." He turned to Lee, paused, saw Lee's eyes closed, said quietly, "General Lee? With your permission, sir, I will take my staff across the river. I expect General Hill should report to you soon. I'm sure he wants to get across this river as much as we do."

Lee looked at him now, and Longstreet suddenly felt foolish, knew it was the wrong thing to say.

Lee looked into the shadow of Longstreet's face. He felt a small tug of anger, but he would not say anything of it, would not lay blame on anyone. "General Longstreet, you may accompany your corps."

Longstreet bowed slightly, saluted, pulled the horse away. Lee watched him, the staff gathering together, the horses moving in slippery steps down to the bridge head.

Longstreet was right, there were many mistakes. But he would not think on that now, would not see the faces, the commanders who had not done the job, would not think on troop movements and poor cooperation, could not even recall his own orders, the horrors of what he had seen, what they had all seen in those three days. He had tried to understand it, to sort it out, but it was too soon, and he knew the memories would come back in time, and the images would be as sharp and painful as so many of the memories he carried from the fights long before.

Even the great victories held vast horror, but he could not even recall those, the days when you knew you had beaten those people, had driven them from the field, commanders like Pope and Hooker, who by their bluster and profane arrogance invited nothing less than total defeat. And the incompetence of Burnside, who threw his very good army against an impossibly strong position, and so sent his own men to a senseless slaughter. Lee tried to recall the feeling, standing on his hill behind Fredericksburg, hearing the bright yells and joyous shouts from below, his men looking out at the bloody fields in front of them, understanding how utterly complete their victory had been. He tried to remember the chaos at Chancellorsville, the complete destruction of the Federal flank, how Jackson had nearly crushed the Federal army in a panic so complete that had the daylight not run out . . . it could have ended the war right there. But Jackson would not be stopped by nightfall, kept moving forward, even when his men could not, and in a dark and terrifying night his own men had panicked at the sound of horses, had fired at silhouettes in the moonlight.

Lee saw the face again. He had not been to see Jackson after he was wounded, but the reports from the doctors, from the staff, were optimistic, just an arm, he would recover. Then suddenly the bright blue light was gone, and not from the wounds, but from pneumonia. And it was only . . . He tried to think. Two months ago. Or an eternity.

Already now there were letters, reports beginning to move through the army, commanders deflecting the blame they knew was yet to come. There would be the newspapers, of course, and the letters

from home, questioning. Some of the officers had already made protests, angry challenges, hot criticisms of the generals Lee trusted so
much, men he *had* to trust. But those men had not performed, and in
the maze of faces and names and mistakes, he knew that ultimately no
one could be held responsible but him.

Now there was fresh motion on the road, reflections from a new
line of troops. It was the Third Corps, A. P. Hill's men. They moved
out of the woods, marched down toward the angry water, and again Lee
watched, sat quietly on Traveller as his army moved silently through
the wet misery of the retreat, knowing once again the war would roll
on in a bloody wash of men and machines back into Virginia.

AUGUST 1863

H E HALTED THE ARMY SOUTH OF THE RAPIDAN RIVER, NEAR
Orange Court House, and as they slowly gathered together,
many of the stragglers and men with light wounds began to
return. In the weeks since the start of the retreat, it was the first time
Lee could see his army for what it had now become, how badly the impact of Gettysburg had changed the strength, how deep were the
wounds.

The fields around the Rapidan were bare now. No farmers worked
the land, the homes and barns were empty, most of the big trees were
gone. The war had long since claimed this part of Virginia, and Lee
hardly recognized this countryside. He stood at the edge of a wide field
of dried mud, knew that this land, this fertile and beautiful ground, had
once borne the bounty, the tall corn, the vast green oceans of grain.
Now it was gray and barren, wagon tracks cutting through in all directions, the former campsites of both armies, and for now it was his
again.

The men were spread out around him, secure in the new camp,
and Lee rode along the hard road, away from his own tents, where the
staff worked with the papers, sorting out the problems in the regiments, the brigades, the endless fight for supplies.

Taylor had encouraged him to slip away, and Lee was grateful,
knew this young man with the boundless energy could handle the business of headquarters, the vast clutter of details. He rode slowly away,
did not look back, did not see Taylor watching him, peering past the
lengthening line of soldiers, officers, men with complaints or "urgent"
business.

He moved down the hard road, past the troops who now stopped to watch him. There were shouts, calls of greeting, and even now, even with the hard wounds of the great defeat, the men still rose up and gathered, still called his name. He reined the horse, lifted his hat, a small salute, looked at the faces and then beyond, saw the numbers, the wide field spread with the men who were still there, still with him. They did not look to him for comfort or pity, and he did not see pain or defeat. They still made the cheerful calls, faces bright with the look that says, We are still your army, and we will fight again.

There had been desertions, many stragglers who were captured or simply disappeared. The muddy roads out of Pennsylvania had swallowed up many who had lost the strength, the energy, for the fight. The casualties were staggering, over twenty thousand men, nearly a quarter of his army gone. But as much as he mourned the loss of the fighting men, it was their commanders, the brigade and regimental officers, who would have to be replaced. As the war flowed into its third year, the men who knew how to lead, the capable commanders with an instinct for battle, were becoming more and more scarce.

He thought of the names, saw the faces: Lew Armistead, Barksdale, Pender, Garnett, Pettigrew. They were gone, and there were none better. He thought of young John Bell Hood, the huge blond-haired man from Texas whom he had known so well in the old cavalry, the man who loved chasing Comanches all through the misery of the frontier. Lee had always thought Hood was indestructible, but he was down too, a severe wound, might still lose an arm. And old Isaac Trimble, the man who brought him the news of Ewell's failure to take Cemetery Hill, a catastrophic mistake in a fight with many mistakes. Trimble was a fierce and disagreeable man whom Lee knew he could trust absolutely, but Trimble had been wounded as well, had to be left behind, and so was captured.

You could not train new leaders, you could not replace what a man had brought with him from the battlefields in Mexico. There was no fresh class from West Point or VMI. The new officers were young, very young, and if a man did not have the gut instinct, could not take his men forward with absolute command of himself and his situation, there was no time to teach him, to show him his mistakes. Now, when mistakes were made, the men did not come back.

He spurred the horse again, moved beyond the camp, saw the road turning through a small grove of thick trees. It was hot, growing hotter, and he looked to the shade, moved that way. He heard the sound of water, saw a small stream snaking its way in the dark coolness, flowing close to the road. He reined the horse, watched the thin stream of water rolling over polished rocks, was suddenly very thirsty. He climbed down, and Traveller moved to the water with him. Lee bent low, cupped his hand and took a deep cold drink. He stood, wiped at his face with a wet hand, watched the horse now nosing the edge of the stream. He could still hear the men, the sounds of the camp carrying beyond the fields, and there was even music, a banjo, and he smiled at that, felt a sudden pride. Yes, he thought, they are not beaten. I should take a lesson from that.

He reached into his pocket, felt for the letter, pulled it out. It was the reply, the inevitable response from Jefferson Davis. Lee understood that in this army, in any army, it was the commander who must bear the responsibility. If he did not dwell on that, the newspapers did, great ponderous prose from the fat men in their clean offices in Richmond, Charleston, Atlanta, the men who had built up the expectations of their nation with the move northward. They gave their readers the first reports of the glorious invasion of the North, reported outrageous rumors as fact, the defeat of Meade's army, the imminent capture of Washington.

Lee had not seen the papers until after the battle, then read the absurd reports with deep dread, because he knew that when the truth came out, when the reports of the fighting became real, the impact would be far worse. So with the first major accounts from Pennsylvania, the papers that had given the people grand headlines of their mythic victory, the victory that would surely end the war, now gave them the story of crushing defeat. The papers had provided the power behind the myth, and many had come to believe that his army was invincible. Now they had to accept that it was not always so, and many would not accept it. Even the reasonable, moderate voices could not temper what many were saying. Lee had lost the fight. As he absorbed the anger, the reckless calls from the papers, the voices of those quick to place blame, to seek the simple explanation, he responded in the only way he could. In early August his letter of resignation had gone to the president.

The letter had been as much a response to the papers as to the president personally, an effort to relieve any criticism of the army, the men who had done the fighting. And if Lee accepted responsibility for the failure, he also began to accept that his health was becoming an issue, and for the first time he had wondered if his heart problems might have clouded his judgment. So, at least he had provided Davis with an excuse, a reason for accepting his resignation, which would preserve his honor.

Now, as Lee stood beside the big horse in the cool shade, he held Davis's reply in his hand. He opened the letter, read it again. If Davis had become fragile, even suspicious and secretive in his dealings with his other commanders, he could still show Lee the warmth that many never saw, that Lee had often forgotten. He scanned the page, paused at the words "my dear friend," smiled, then read silently.

> To ask me to substitute you by one in my judgment more fit to command, or who could possess more of the confidences of the army, or of the reflecting men of the country, is to demand an impossibility.

He looked back toward the sounds from the field, thought, The confidences of the army. He knew Davis was right, he had just seen it again in the faces of the men. He put his hand out, touched Traveller's neck, said aloud, "Well, if they want me to lead them still, then I will lead them. After all, my friend, what else can I do?"

He climbed up, considered moving farther away, exploring the road deeper into the shade of the trees, but before he could tug at the reins, the big gray horse turned its head and began to carry him back to his men.

2. CHAMBERLAIN

BRUNSWICK, MAINE, AUGUST 1863

H E HAD SEEN HER FROM THE WINDOW OF THE TRAIN, MOVED
toward the doorway, and when the train slowed enough he
jumped down to the platform. The pain from the wound in
his foot shocked him, and he staggered, fell forward, caught himself
with one hand, then stood again, and the twist in his expression told
her he was hurting.

Fannie moved toward him now, and he reached for her, and
the pain was gone. She lifted her hands to him, and he saw the look,
that same dark sadness, the look she had when he'd left her a year ago.
He hugged her, and they stood for a long moment, said nothing. He
could feel her arms pulling hard at him, and he did nothing to end it,
would feel her pressing against him as long as she would have it go
on. As people moved from the train, filling the platform, there were
glances, discreet stares, a few children began to point, hushed by embarrassed mothers. As she kept him tight to her, he began to sag, to feel
the weakness, leaned against her more, and still she held him, said quietly, "Oh God . . . oh God . . ."

She was crying now, and he moved slowly, lifted her away and
saw the tears. She smiled then, said, "How do you feel?"

"Not very well. It was a rough trip. I feel like . . . bed."

They began to walk. She held his arm as they moved away from
the train. He still leaned against her, and they climbed down the short
steps. As she guided him toward the carriage, people began to recognize him, saw more than just the blue uniform, saw the familiar face of
the professor, the man many of them had known before. People began
to move closer, there were greetings, hands came toward him. He tried
to smile, to be gracious, but the weakness was overwhelming, and the

smile faded and he could only nod. He climbed slowly up into the carriage, and Fannie moved around, sat beside him.

Chamberlain saw now the young man sitting up in front, watching them, holding the reins, and he looked at the smiling face, thought, Yes, it's . . . He tried to clear his head, staggered through names, said, "Yes, Mister . . . Silas. The rhetoric class."

The boy was beaming now, flattered at the recognition. "Yes, sir, *Colonel* Chamberlain. Welcome home."

Chamberlain remembered he was in uniform, had forgotten all about that, how the people here saw him, what it was like for him to come back home from such a different place. And he knew now what they all knew. He was not a professor anymore.

Chamberlain looked at Fannie now, who was watching him, questioning him silently with hard concern.

"We should get you home. Mr. Silas asked if he could drive me to the station. Many of your . . . the students have been calling on me every day. The word did get out, I'm afraid . . . that you were coming home."

He glanced out toward the small crowd, saw the people staring at him with a look of sorrow, dread. She waved a hand and said, "Thank you, he's all right. We're taking him home now."

Chamberlain looked at the faces, the sadness, did not understand. He saw a man, familiar, and the man removed his hat, gave a small bow, said, "God bless you, Colonel. We pray for you, sir."

Chamberlain looked at the man, the others, suddenly wondered if they expected a speech. He said, "Thank you. I'm only here for a while . . . please, do not be concerned for me." He looked up at the boy, who was staring at him intently, and he suddenly felt confused, embarrassed.

Fannie said, "Mr. Silas, we should proceed."

The boy slapped at the horse, and the carriage rolled into the wide street, the boy holding the horse to a slow walk. People were still gathering, pointing, but Chamberlain began to sag again, leaned weakly against Fannie, closed his eyes, heard his name in small faint voices. He was suddenly very sleepy, and the gentle lurch of the carriage rocked him against her side, his head resting against her shoulder. Fannie put her hand softly against his face and felt the hot sweat of the fever.

The malaria had been coming on slowly, during the weariness of the long marches, the summer heat beating him down. What the marches had not taken from him, the battlefield had—the small wound in his foot, the shock of the fight on Little Round Top. But it was afterward, the slow and miserable march, the sluggish pursuit of Lee's army, the mud and the wet chills, that had weakened him, left him prone to the sickness. And since there had been no fight, with Lee escaping across the Potomac, he'd been granted leave, two short weeks, much of it in a long train ride home to Maine.

H E HEARD A CHILD'S VOICE, AND THEN FANNIE, A STERN WHISper, and he looked toward the door. He saw her gently guiding the small boy out of the room, but the child saw Chamberlain looking at him over the thick bed covering, called out, "Daddy!" spun free of Fannie's grasp, ran to the bed and jumped up.

Chamberlain wanted to reach out, catch him, but the weight of the covers and his own weakness would not let him move. He did not fight it, smiled weakly, said, "Good morning, Wyllys. Are you helping your mother this morning?"

With a small groan, Fannie lifted the boy, and Chamberlain saw now how much bigger he was, tried to remember, fought through the fog in his mind, thought, He is *four*. The boy protested, but Fannie carried him out of the room, and Chamberlain heard her in the hallway, scolding him.

Now she was back, moving quietly to the bed. "I'm sorry. I've tried to keep them quiet. Daisy was in here earlier. She just wanted to look at you, but Wyllys . . . he doesn't understand why you're not up playing with him."

"Neither do I." Chamberlain tried to sit, to slide up from under the blanket, but there was no strength, no energy. He closed his eyes, frowned, then looked up at her. "This is ridiculous. I'm supposed to be a soldier, a man of action." He tried to laugh, watched her eyes, and she smiled, could not help it.

She sat on the bed, put a hand on his forehead. "Well, my soldier, you still have some fever. So, you will not be seeing much action of any kind for a while."

He reached up for her hand, held it for a brief moment. She stood, and he tried to hold on to her, to keep her from leaving, but she was away now, at the door. "I'll bring you something cool to drink. And, you should eat something. I have some breakfast."

She was gone, and now he let himself relax, felt the weight of the blanket again. He stared up at the ceiling, then over toward the window, but there was no sunlight, the curtain was down. He flexed his foot, felt the small stab of pain, but knew it was improving. He'd been walking with less of a limp before he stopped walking at all.

He had always been a miserable patient, had no tolerance for being ill, fought it angrily, thought of the disease, went through this every time he was sick: What right do you have to invade me? It was a rhetorical question, it never seemed to make the sickness go away. He never did understand why he got sick in the first place. Punishment? Was this the hand of God, slowing you down from your own work, telling you, "Stop, you're not doing it right"? But what if your work was good, of benefit to others? Even doctors got sick. He thought of the bizarre illogic of that. How can You punish a doctor when he is helping cure the illnesses of others?

He thought of his mother: This was a question for her. He smiled, pictured the stern devout face, the faith of the pious optimist. She would say the malaria is a sign from God, a message: give up this foolishness, this soldiering, and come home and accept the life she had always insisted was his destiny; take up the cloth, preach the word of God. And here he was, at home. Maybe she was right. He felt the impatience again. Maybe this was *her* doing, maybe she had talked God into giving him this disease. But I won't take this lying down, Chamberlain thought. It won't work. Now he relaxed again, felt guilty. No, his mother just wanted what was best. That's what mothers did. She had never seen him as anything but her gift from God, and the gift had to be repaid. But there were other ways. God did not need everyone to be a preacher.

He smelled food, was suddenly very hungry. Yes, I am better, he thought. I will fight this thing. He suddenly felt Shakespearean. Plague, be gone! Out, damned spot! He tried to focus, sort out the smells, an exercise. What food is that? Bread, yes, and something burnt; when Fannie cooks, there is always something burnt. He wanted to get up, push away the covers, but his body did not respond, and he suddenly felt depressed, his mind slowed, quieted. I cannot stay here, he thought. And he knew he would not stay here, that this was only a short break, the inconvenience of illness, that when his strength came back, the uniform would be there.

He closed his eyes. I should rest, sleep, he thought. But there was no sleep, because now he began to think of his men. He thought of the mud, the deep mire of the roads. Still, they had moved eagerly through the rains, always believing they would catch Lee's army, that there would be another fight, possibly the last fight. Each man had moved as quickly as the man in front of him would allow, and they did not take the time to see the numbers, what was left of the regiment, how many were no longer there. There were no official reports yet, the men did not know how badly their army had been bled. They only saw the men beside them and the man who led them. They looked at him differently now; every one of them carried the memory of the colonel who had stood out in front of them on that bloody rocky hill, and they all had written of it, letters home, had remembered that place, Little Round Top. They would never forget that he'd ordered them to do the unbelievable, the wild bayonet charge through those men from Alabama, the shock so complete that the rebels had simply stopped fighting. Those who could not run had given up, had nothing left inside to resist the small wave of screaming blue troops that suddenly rolled down into their lines.

For a moment he was there again, running wildly through the rocks and trees. His heart was racing, and seeing the raw shock in the faces of the enemy, he opened his eyes, stared up at the ceiling of his room, clenched his fists under the covers of the bed.

To do it again . . . another fight, he thought, How can there be another fight like that? Was it not enough? It should have been, we should have hit them again, and on the march, finally, there had been hope, maybe Lee would just . . . surrender? Surely, with his back to the river . . . but then it became familiar, and the veterans understood, had been through this before. There would be no attack, they had waited too long, and Lee had prepared, was ready for it. And so they were brought to a halt from behind, from their own commanders, the men under the great tents who alone knew how badly hurt this army had been.

They had seen bits of Lee's lines, small skirmishes, often at night, firing only at brief flashes of musket fire, firing back at the brief glimpses of them. Chamberlain stayed close to his men, and they spoke of it, that even if the fight was not to happen then, they realized what Gettysburg had meant, that Lee's invasion was stopped, that the Army of the Potomac had finally put the right people in the right place. The hard power of the good guns and the good soldiers had been put to the test, and they had prevailed. It was the test they'd always wanted, especially the veterans, the men who had been there from the beginning, from the early disasters at Bull Run, at Fredericksburg, men who carried the fight as well as any soldier could. They never felt they had been beaten by the enemy, by that man over there who pointed his musket at your heart. Their aim was as sharp and as clear as his. Chamberlain knew his own men well, knew they all shared something new, the feeling that this time they had been led by men who knew how to command, the men who let the soldiers decide the battle. On Little Round Top they'd seen the faces of those other fellows, those men in the ragged clothes, faces the generals never saw, and they learned that when the fight came to the bayonet, when there were no trenches and no lines and the enemy looked you in the eye, the uniform made no difference. It was the heart of these men, his men, that had won the fight. And they were ready to do it again.

H E PULLED THE BELT TIGHTER, KNEW HE'D LOST SOME WEIGHT. But at least he was out of bed, had even gone outside, taken a short walk with the children. He was still weak, and had considered asking for a longer leave. The two weeks had expired, but the army was moving again, and so he would go back and join his men in Virginia.

He stood in front of the long mirror, looked at the navy blue of the jacket, the light blue pants, saw no dirt. Fannie had cleaned the uniform, and except for the small frayed areas along the cuffs, it looked nearly new. He frowned at that, thought, This is not quite right. He had gotten used to the dirt. It was good dirt, the dirt of the fields, the muddy ground, the spray from the impact of the incoming shell, the close shudder of death. He stared at clean knees, elbows, wondered, What will the men say?

She came into the room, carrying a stack of bed linens, saw him staring at himself, smiled. "There, now isn't that better? You were quite a mess, you know."

He had not asked her to clean the uniform, but nodded, tried not to show his disappointment. "Yes . . . much better. Thank you." There was no enthusiasm in his voice.

She put the linens on the bed, moved beside him, looked at the both of them in the mirror, said, "I have actually . . . gotten used to this. I never thought I would. My husband, the soldier."

He put his arm around her waist, stood tall, posing. "We are a respectable couple." He coughed, let her go, moved away and sat on the bed.

"And you, my dear colonel, are still sick."

He did not look at her, knew she was right, the weakness was still there. He had tried to make a good show, playing with the children, making preparations for the trip south.

"They need me. The orders . . . I have no choice."

She folded her arms, said sternly, "I don't recall hearing the war had stopped because you were ill. My guess is they will go on fighting whether you are there or not."

He did not want the argument, felt the energy draining out of him. "They do need me. I've been called back. I tried to extend the leave. . . ."

"Oh, yes, I know. But Mr. Lincoln's army cannot stand for one of their heroes to be idle."

He knew this was coming. She had nursed him with joyous energy, had truly enjoyed his being home, even if he was mostly in bed. They had not argued, she did not show the anger of a year ago.

He never knew he would be a soldier, had never thought much about causes and patriotism. There had always been the expectations, the pressure from his father. Chamberlain always resisted, had always believed that his greatest gift was his mind, that teaching was his destiny. But the war had changed that, the causes, the talk of politicians became bloody action, the men with powerful ideas and the force of will and guns that this country had never seen before.

When it all began, he tried to understand the dangers, felt the new frustration of being far from the loud voices, and then from the fight. Then the young people, the quiet faces he spoke to every day, began to speak back, and soon many of them were gone, had put on the uniform and taken the trains south. That shocked him most of all, the passion of the students, the young men who many of the faculty at Bowdoin considered to be but children. But they had become educated, were listening, hearing all the talk, the rhetoric, the voices of reason and the voices of outrage.

Chamberlain found himself speaking of it as well, his prepared lessons fading from his mind, losing their importance in the face of the spreading violence. He had never been political, did not understand much about what drove men to become politicians. The politicians were dangerous; the strength and the passion of their voices had pulled the people on both sides toward this brutal fight. The other professors had accused him of undermining the school, encouraging these boys to join the army, would not see beyond the dark halls of Bowdoin. His anxieties were seen as contagious, and so he had been offered a leave of absence, two years, a trip to Europe perhaps, a tonic for his stress. Instead he had gone to the governor and volunteered to join the army, because he knew it was the most important thing he would ever do. But he hadn't discussed it with anyone, didn't tell them he was going. And he had not discussed it with Fannie.

She left the room now. He heard her moving down the stairs, and he let out a breath, thankful. He knew she was still angry about that, and he would always regret that he did not trust her to support his decision. He had been certain she would object, would not allow him to enlist, and when he finally told her what he'd done, she *was* angry, but it was the anger of love, of fear. Now he would leave her again, and he knew the emotions would be the same.

He heard voices now, from the front of the house, the unmistakable cries of the children for their "Grampa." Chamberlain stood, felt his way along the bed, straightened, took a deep breath, tried to find the energy. He heard his father's voice now, the booming sound he only seemed to make around the small children. Chamberlain glanced in the mirror, checked the uniform, then moved toward the stairway.

He heard the sounds moving into the parlor, the children still bouncing around their grandfather, and the subdued voices of the women.

He paused, listened, heard his father ask, "So, when is he leaving?"

Fannie hushed the children, said, "Tomorrow morning, the first train."

"Oh my dear. So soon . . ." It was his mother, and Chamberlain smiled, had mouthed the words exactly as she spoke them. He moved down the last step, went to the parlor, and his father rose, had a child on either side of him, holding tight.

Fannie reached for them, said quietly, "Not now . . . let Grampa be for now." There were mild protests, and then his father was free of the small hands, and Chamberlain looked into the old face, and his father moved beside him, past, went into the hall. Chamberlain knew what this meant, knew to follow, that the men would be alone now. He followed his father out to the front porch, and there were no words.

They sat in the creaking chairs, and Chamberlain waited, would let his father have the first word. There was a long minute, and his father rocked the old chair slowly, then said, "Tomorrow morning?"

"Yes. The leave's up. They called me back."

"I hear there might be a fight . . . Lee's on the move."

Chamberlain nodded, had not heard anything that specific, wondered, How does he always seem to know what is happening?

"The regiment holding up? The boys doing all right?"

Chamberlain said, "None finer in the army. Just . . . not as many of us now."

"Part *of* it. Always has been." The old man stilled the chair, stood, walked to the porch railing and stared out across the green yard.

There was a pause, and Chamberlain said, "Tom's fine. He's a good officer. He'll command his company soon."

The old man said nothing, and Chamberlain could not see his face, knew he would not say much about his youngest son, had never expected Tom to volunteer.

Chamberlain stood now, moved to the railing, waited, sorted the words, then said, "In the last fight . . . we were in a bit of a jam. I had to use him." He paused, had been thinking of this moment for weeks. "There were men going down, the line was weakening. I sent him in, ordered him to fill a gap in the line. Didn't even think about it . . . until later. If something had happened to him—"

"You won the fight." The old man did not look at him, and Chamberlain wanted to say more, to explain.

"I'm sorry . . . it would have been hard to tell you that, if he had—"

"You won the fight." The old man looked at him now, a sharp hard stare. "You did what officers are supposed to do. You would have learned that at the Point."

Chamberlain sagged. He'd heard this before. That he had not gone to West Point, but stayed in Maine to finish his schooling, was something his father had never understood, had never seen the value in. Even when he was young Chamberlain had heard this, great stories of his ancestors. His father believed the military was the only way a man could measure himself, could find the respect, something to carry with you all your life. They did not argue; his father's disappointment was subtle, quiet. But Chamberlain had always known it was there, and after his graduation, when the first teaching appointments came, when Chamberlain accepted the position at Bowdoin, there was little pride from his father.

His mother had dreamed of the glorious day her oldest son would serve God, seek the ministry, and she still hoped. But his father never spoke of that, the ministry would not bring honor to the family, no matter how devoutly his wife disagreed. When Chamberlain had volunteered for the army, there had been few words between them, but he could feel the quiet attention, that his father was suddenly interested.

By now the people had learned of Gettysburg. Word had spread all over Maine, through letters and newspaper stories, that Chamberlain had done something truly extraordinary. Fannie had written him that his father had begun to take long walks through Brewer, even went across the river, to Bangor, the town he never cared to visit, because now he could talk of his boy the soldier, and the people would come to him to hear all they could of this man's son, the hero of Little Round Top.

The old man stared out again across the yard, said, "This Meade fellow . . . you expect he's ready to wrap this up?"

"General Meade is a good commander. He's finding his way, learning what his army can do. He'll be fine."

"Damned well better be. Gone on long enough. Lee's given all he's got. Time to finish the job."

Chamberlain said nothing, thought, Lee is not whipped, not yet. The old man glanced at Chamberlain's shoulder strap, the silver eagle. "Full colonel. What do you hafta do to be a general?"

Chamberlain smiled, said, "Not sure . . . it would take a few more good fights, I suppose."

The old man said nothing, and Chamberlain watched him, waited. After a minute the old man turned, looked past him toward the front door, moved that way, said, "I better check on those youngsters. . . ." He moved past Chamberlain, then stopped, and Chamberlain waited, felt the old man struggling silently. The old man stared down at the floor, then reached out his hand, touched Chamberlain's arm, still did not look at him, but wrapped his hard fingers around the blue cloth, a tight sharp squeeze. He held it for a brief moment, then moved away, to the door and into the house.

Chamberlain still felt his father's grasp, smiled, felt something move inside of him, knew it was the first time; that if the words were not there, if the old man did not know how to tell him, Chamberlain knew now the barriers were behind them, that finally he had made his father proud.

3. CHAMBERLAIN

AUGUST 1863

H E WOUND HIS WAY AMONG THE CAMPSITES, PAST GROWING fires, the end of a peaceful day, the men relaxing from a slow, easy march. The smells were drifting by him, coffee and bacon, and he felt a rush, the excitement. He was back with the army, back in northern Virginia.

The return trip had not been too rough, but he felt the weariness, a dull throb in his head. As he moved through the camps, he already felt stronger, the remnants of the illness fading away. Officers noticed him as he passed their units, men Chamberlain had never seen. Some spoke to him, nods, casual greetings. The soldiers ignored him, it was their own private time, and unfamiliar officers did not attract attention. The daylight was nearly gone, but he could see the red Maltese cross in the distance, the flags of the Fifth Corps, and then the flag of the First Division. Near the flag were the larger headquarters tents, and he saw many officers now, sitting in a circle, some standing behind. There was laughter, a brief glimpse, the passing of a bottle. Beyond the big tents he saw the brigade colors, saw finally the Third, moved that way. Now some men began to call out, he was recognized, and he saw a few familiar faces, the cordial greetings, then heard a voice behind him.

"Colonel Chamberlain . . ."

He turned, saw a tall man, lanky, long strides, moving from the cluster of officers, and he stood straight, saluted.

"General Griffin. I have returned, sir. I was going to report as soon as I found my men, sir."

Griffin returned the salute, briefly patted Chamberlain on the shoulder. "No matter, Colonel, no urgency. Might I walk with you?"

It was an unusual request, generals walked wherever they pleased.

"Certainly, sir. I was headed toward the Third Brigade over that way, unless you want to go . . . elsewhere." He felt awkward, self-conscious, waited for Griffin to move, fell into step beside him.

"Colonel, I don't believe we've spent much time together. Not since Gettysburg. The men . . . my staff tells me they hear your name every day."

"Thank you, sir."

"You back for duty? You . . . fit?"

"Oh yes, sir. It was a touch of malaria." He made a face. Don't explain, he thought. Never give the generals a reason to doubt you. He looked toward the flags, began to move a bit faster. Where was the regiment? He was beginning to feel the familiar rumble in his gut, thought, Generals do that, they make you think too much.

Griffin stayed close to him, and men were now standing as they moved past. There were salutes from low-ranking officers, a few voices. Griffin was not often among the men, was rarely sociable, except around his staff and other officers of high rank. Chamberlain had first met him at Fredericksburg, after the long and horrible night on the cold ground, the night spent close to the enemy. Chamberlain would always recall that meeting, Griffin holding out his hand to him, a ragged, exhausted man who had slept behind the cover of the bodies of his own men. Griffin had simply told him, "Good work."

Chamberlain had not understood that, had not thought there was any good work in that horrible assault, the pure stupidity of marching up against the stone wall, straight into the massed fire of Lee's strength. It had been his first real fight, leading his men forward into the smoke, the first time he heard the screams and the sickening sound of the lead ball cracking the skull of the man beside you. All of that was a fog, a cold blur. He did not try to remember, did not pick out the details. But he did remember Griffin, and his words.

Chamberlain had always heard that Charles Griffin was not anyone's friend, but a man of great temper, quick to bring down his wrath on the man, private or colonel, who did not do his job. And Griffin demanded more than a good job. Chamberlain did not mind that, had been taught and trained by another manic disciplinarian, Adelbert Ames, knew that no matter how much the men grumbled, the low curses behind the commander's back, the training would save their lives. The men knew it too, were veterans now, had marched into the deafening roar of the fire, felt the lightning flash of fear, that small edge of panic, and they understood that it was that cursed discipline, inside each of them now, that kept the panic away.

Chamberlain saw his own regimental colors, changed course slightly, pointed. "The Twentieth Maine . . . my unit."

They walked closer to the fires, and now more men rose, and the salutes gave way to shouts, the men gathering, emerging from tents, all moving toward Chamberlain. Chamberlain smiled at the familiar faces, then saw Tom.

The young man jumped up, ran forward. "Lawrence . . . Colonel! You're back!" Tom moved close, put his hands on Chamberlain's arms, a wide boyish grin on his face. "We been waiting for you . . . we knew we weren't going nowhere till you got back!"

Chamberlain had shut off his own smile, stared at his brother with a silent scolding, motioned with his eyes toward Griffin and said stiffly, "Lieutenant Chamberlain, thank you. General Griffin, this is Lieutenant Tom Chamberlain . . . my brother, sir."

Tom's smile vanished and his mouth opened as he looked at Griffin with wide startled eyes. He remembered to salute now, stepped back, snapped his arm in place. "Sir!"

Griffin returned the salute, did not focus on Tom, said aloud, to the gathering crowd, "Gentlemen, I share your enthusiasm for the return of your colonel. And I am sure he is equally anxious to see you. However, if you will excuse us, we have a matter to discuss. He won't be long."

There were small murmurs from the men, quiet questions. They rarely saw the division commander, knew something was up. Even the officers traded glances. Chamberlain looked at Griffin, surprised, and suddenly nervous, said, "Certainly, General. Always at your disposal, sir."

Griffin turned, moved away from the light of the fires, and Chamberlain followed. They moved down a long hill, a clearing between short pines. Griffin stopped, stared out into the darkening woods. "Did you hear about Colonel Rice?"

Chamberlain had a sudden dark dread; his stomach turned. Jim Rice had replaced Strong Vincent as brigade commander, Chamberlain's immediate superior. Vincent was a popular commander and a very good soldier, the man who had seen the value of the ground and so placed the Twentieth Maine on Little Round Top. Vincent had been badly wounded on that same day, and died a few days later, and it had deeply affected the men. Chamberlain thought, What has happened now, to Rice? "Is he . . . all right?"

Griffin heard the hesitation, looked at Chamberlain, laughed. "Oh, yes, Colonel, he's quite all right. He's been promoted to brigadier general, they moved him to the First Corps."

Chamberlain let out a breath. "Thank God. That's wonderful . . . well deserved."

"Well deserved." Griffin shook his head. "The ways of the army . . . promote a man after you arrest him."

Chamberlain was confused, did not know what Griffin was talking about. "Sir . . . I had not heard . . ."

"Right, you were on leave. When we were on the march chasing after Lee, Rice allowed his men to make camp bedding from a farmer's haystack, let them sleep above the mud instead of in it. Probably saved half the brigade from drowning. But the corps heard about it, some staff officer dusted off the regulations, and General Sykes had him arrested . . . 'molesting private property.' "

Griffin put his foot up on a stump, leaned on his knee, stared out into the trees. "It got straightened out pretty quick. Somebody at Meade's headquarters heard about it, knew the newspapers would have a carnival. We let Lee escape, so we make up for it by arresting our best officers."

Chamberlain stood, watched Griffin, the nervousness now replaced by something else—curiosity. "Well, sir . . . General Rice will surely make us proud." He felt awkward again, did not enjoy formal small talk.

Griffin said, "There's quite a few fellows who think they're the one to fill his vacancy, some of 'em deserving. Tough choice. I picked you." Chamberlain stared, waited for more. Griffin turned toward him, said, "You, Colonel. I want you to command the Third Brigade."

Chamberlain smiled, tried to suppress it but could not, looked away, embarrassed.

Griffin did not seem to notice, said, "It's not permanent, there's no promotion in rank, not yet. I did send in my recommendation. That's an issue for Washington. Doesn't really matter anyway. You might run into a bit of resistance from your regimental commanders. Some of them been around a bit longer than you. I've made it clear . . . they do understand who's in command. It's your brigade, Colonel."

Chamberlain saluted, still smiled. "Thank you, sir!"

Griffin was not smiling, returned the salute. "You earned it, Colonel. We still have a job to do, and we need the best men to do it." Griffin looked up the hill, began to move away, glanced back at Chamberlain. "You need to pick a successor to take over the regiment. Make a recommendation pretty quick. You know your men. We'll go with anybody you say, most likely. Enjoy your evening, Colonel."

Griffin climbed the rise, and Chamberlain watched him crest the hill but did not follow. He felt like laughing, remembered a year ago, standing in front of the governor, hearing the words "lieutenant colonel," the same feeling, like a small boy receiving a great Christmas present. Now he was to lead the brigade, the whole brigade. He thought of the men, above him on the hill, the men from Maine. I will have to tell them ... something, he thought. He felt a sudden dread, choosing someone else to command them. Who? How would the men respond? It should be someone from within the regiment, of course. But he could not focus, the names did not come, it was too soon. He began to climb the hill, moved in long quick steps back to the fires, to the wonderful smells of the food.

SINCE THE LOSSES AT GETTYSBURG, WASHINGTON HAD MADE great efforts to rebuild the army, and reinforcements were coming in daily. But not all the new troops were men eager for a fight. With the draft now in full force, many of these recruits were men who had avoided the first calls for volunteers; some had even been a part of the violence, the draft riots. But now they faced the reality that they would serve whether they wanted to or not. Others were substitutes, men paid to take the place of those who could afford to buy their way out of the process. Often these men were motivated only by the gold they received, and when they first experienced the constraints of discipline, or the first brush with the horror of what a fight with the rebels might bring, many simply disappeared. To the fighting units who had won the great glory and honor on the field, these new numbers added little, except for new problems, problems this army did not need. Meade and his commanders could not afford to be tolerant of this threat to the morale of the men who were still willing to carry the fight, and so, when deserters were caught, the punishment was swift and certain.

HE STOOD IN A LINE, SURROUNDED BY THE ENTIRE FIFTH CORPS. They were lined up by division across a wide field, the men facing each other on three sides of a square. On the fourth side, the open end, he could see the short row of freshly dug graves, and beside each one a simple wooden coffin. Once the troops had completed the formation, the drums began, a slow steady roll, and finally there was motion, across the field. He could see the prisoners being brought forward, the men moving in slow, jerking motions, held to small steps by the chains around their legs. Now each man was placed into position, standing beside his own grave, and then they were sat down, each on the front of his own coffin.

Around Chamberlain, men began to make small sounds, nervous, faces turning away, some looking down. Chamberlain did not turn away, stared at the five men, felt a low hot sickness in his gut.

Suddenly the drums were silent, and for a small moment there was no other sound. Now an officer began to read something, the orders, words Chamberlain could not hear. The man finished his duty, moved away, another officer shouted something, and from one side a row of riflemen stepped sharply into position. The officer shouted again, and Chamberlain could hear the metallic sound, the guns snapped to the chests. Then he heard the single word, the hard voice of the officer again: *"Aim!"* More of the men around Chamberlain turned away now, a small groan flowing through the lines. He blinked hard, felt the sickness again, rising slowly, and he clenched his fists, said to himself, No, do not turn away. Watch this. See it.

Now the officer raised his sword, and Chamberlain heard the word clearly, the only sound breaking through the deathly calm. *"Fire!"*

The sound startled them all, a sharp hard rattle, and all around him men shuddered, jumped. He had jumped as well, blind reflex, but he did not turn away, could see the impact of the lead balls in the men, the punch in their clothes, each man collapsing, falling into a grotesque heap. There was a long quiet moment, and he stared at the bodies, could see the blood now, a dark stain spreading out on the dusty ground. All around him the men began to look at the scene, the horror, and suddenly the drums began, startling them all again. There were new orders, close by, and Chamberlain focused, heard the call to march. The great example was over.

FEW OF THE MEN, EVEN THE VETERANS FROM THE OLD ARMY, HAD ever watched a firing squad, but today they had seen one, the shocking spectacle of five men shot down by their own.

Chamberlain drank a cup of coffee, poured it from reflex, did not taste the awful burn of a pot that had sat on the fire all day, left behind in the haste to fall into line. He put the cup down, looked around the camp, saw men moving slowly, some sitting now, many just standing alone. It was late in the day, and the food would come soon, but no one spoke of it, no one gathered at the fires. He thought of Ames, of Griffin, the discipline. That was what today was about, of course. They all know that, he thought. But this was something new. Occasionally this had happened before, men were shot or hanged, usually for some hateful crime, murder, the rape of a citizen. But today men were killed because they would not fight. And it had never been made into something so . . . public. He thought of the pronouncement, the Official Word, read before the executions. Of course, it was official. The army, he knew, was not like any other organization, any business. If you are here, he thought, you fight for your country, and possibly die for your country, and you are not allowed to change your mind. How odd . . . We are fighting—some of us, anyway—for . . . freedom? And soldiers are not free.

He watched his men, thought, Stop this, you're thinking too much again. Those five men . . . ran away. If they did that in a fight, it could cause a disaster. If the man standing right next to you ran away, it could cost you your own life. I just didn't think . . . we would have to be reminded of that.

He was still with the regiment, it had been just three days since Griffin had given him the change of command. He'd given much thought to who would replace him, had made a choice in his mind only this morning, and then the news had come to the camp, Ellis Spear had received a promotion to major. Before the war, Spear had been a schoolteacher, and it was rare for anyone to have something in common with Chamberlain. From the beginning there had been friendship, and Chamberlain discovered that Spear was not only there for good conversation, but had proven himself a good soldier, and a good commander as well. That made it simpler still, for Spear was to be his recommendation to General Griffin.

The men began to relax now, more were moving about. He heard small voices, conversations. A few were looking at him, and he saw sadness in some, sharp anger in others. He was suddenly very weary, thought, Maybe a short nap, turned for his tent. Then he saw Spear walking toward him and said, "This was not a pleasant day, Major."

Spear clenched down hard on a small pipe, seemed deep in thought. "Colonel, if you don't mind? A word?"

Chamberlain pointed toward his tent, moved that way, and Spear followed. They ducked inside. Chamberlain sat on the cot, pointed at the small wooden stool. Spear sat down slowly, held the pipe in his hand, stared at it.

"What is it, Ellis?"

Spear thought, looked at the ground. "Colonel . . . I'm not sure. This was a difficult day."

"You're not sure of what?"

"I'm not sure I could do that to my own men. If that's what it takes to command . . . I have to tell you that, Colonel." He paused. "I don't know if I could order a man to stand there and shoot one of his own. How do you do that?"

"We have done it before, Ellis. We do it every time we fight."

"But that's the enemy . . . it's different."

"Is it? I was raised to believe that men aren't supposed to kill each other at all. Yet, somehow, we have accepted doing exactly that. We have learned to kill men who we have been taught are our enemy. Men are dying around us in greater numbers and in ways more horrible than anything mankind has ever experienced. This war has inspired the creative minds of brilliant men to invent extraordinary weapons, new and incredibly efficient killing machines, canister, torpedoes, mines. It's a part of everything around us. The disturbing thing about today . . . what shocks us is not that we killed men in blue uniforms, but that it was so . . . *easy*. The order is given, the muskets are fired, and the army has made its point. If we do not do our duty, it could happen to us."

"Is that how you saw this today? Was it our duty to shoot those men?"

Chamberlain looked up, glanced at the dull light of the sunset reflecting through the walls of the tent. "Yes, Major. And God help us."

4. CHAMBERLAIN

OCTOBER 1863

THEY MARCHED IN THE DARK, THROUGH THE SAME FAMILIAR mud, the thick glue of the Virginia roads, the brown sludge that had paralyzed this army once before, nine months earlier. It had been late January, and General Burnside, tempted by a brief taste of spring weather, quickly moved the army up along the Rappahannock, away from the great bloody disaster of Fredericksburg. It was a good plan, move up and around Lee's flank, and even Washington had approved. But it had still been winter, and the weather turned, the hard and angry howl of wind and rain softening the roads, swallowing the wagons and the guns. The miserable army had finally been halted, then returned to the camps they never should have left. They now called it the "Mud March," and it had been the last command decision for Ambrose Burnside.

Chamberlain felt the horse lifting its legs, the effort of each step on the thickness of the road. He shifted in the saddle, straightened his back. There was no rhythm, no gentle rocking of the horse; instead, each step was deliberate and tiring. Behind him he heard low curses, small jokes about generals and mud, one man trying to start a song, drowned out by jeers. He stared out ahead, saw the light of a lantern, men pulling at a wagon, one man with a long pole, prying at a buried wheel, lifting it from the thick ooze. His men began to call out, teasing, and he heard one man say, close behind him, "Just shoot it and put it out of its misery."

He smiled, turned, could not see the man in the darkness, thought, Yes, even tonight . . . they are in good spirits, the morale is as high as it has ever been. They want a fight. We *need* a fight.

There had not been much fighting since Gettysburg, at least not for these men. The action was in the West, at a place Chamberlain had never heard of. He rolled the word around in his mind: *Chickamauga*. The Federal army was being commanded there by William Rosecrans, and all Chamberlain knew was that the rebels had driven "Old Rosy" from the field, the papers calling it a bloody disaster, a panicked rout. That Rosecrans's army was not totally destroyed was credited to General George Thomas, who held his ground while the rest of the Federal army escaped into the city of Chattanooga. Now Washington had pulled two corps away from Meade's army, sending them to strengthen Rosecrans.

Chamberlain began to think about numbers: How many are we now? Eighty thousand? Does it matter? Does it mean we are not as strong? He thought of all the fights, the reports he'd seen. The numbers were always on their side, Lee was always outnumbered. And until Gettysburg, Lee nearly always won. So, it wasn't just numbers. Then ... what? Luck? No, he thought, we needed more than luck at Fredericksburg. It was something else, intangible. Commanders. . . . He pictured Meade in his mind, had seen him several times, mostly before Gettysburg. The army respected him; no one ever said he wasn't a good soldier. But whether he was the right commander . . .

Some had said the job should have gone to Reynolds, but Reynolds was dead. Many wanted Hancock, some wanted Sickles, but both had taken bad wounds at Gettysburg, and neither had yet returned to the army. No, he thought, we will follow George Meade until he either wins the war or makes some awful mistake.

He moved closer to a cluster of lanterns, saw a row of cannon and men gathered around one broken gun, the barrel pointing up between two crooked wheels. Men were pulling it aside, and there was an officer. Chamberlain moved to the side of the road, halted the horse, said, "May we lend a hand?"

The man did not look at him, and Chamberlain waited, watched the men straining in silence, lifting and pushing. Suddenly, there was a loud crack, the groan of splitting wood, and the gun carriage collapsed completely, the wheels folding in, the cannon barrel now pointing straight up at Chamberlain. He flinched, stared at the hole, the small round blackness in the dull lamplight, and ducked away, leaned back in the saddle, felt a cold twist in his stomach. The gun was pulled off the roadway, the men still silent, the officer now moving away.

Chamberlain pulled his horse around, alongside the column, glanced back at the barrel of the big gun, felt embarrassed, thought, Well now, that wasn't such bravery, was it? He still felt the jolt, wondered,

How many men get that close, stare right into that hole before . . . Can you see it? Do you see the blast, the split-second image of death before it takes you away? He moved the horse to the head of the column, fell in alongside the color bearer, a quiet sergeant with a full black beard. Chamberlain nodded, was always polite, and the sergeant glanced at him, said nothing, had ridden beside many commanders. Chamberlain stared ahead, thought of the cannon: Maybe that's the best way; if you have to go, go out in pieces, one big blast. He'd seen too many who went the other way, the men who cried and screamed, who felt every horrible moment of their own death, who fought to hang on.

He shook his head, brushed away the image, scolded himself: Stop that.

Focusing ahead, he saw more lanterns, the dark roadway speckled in dull spots of light. He was suddenly hungry. The march had begun before they could eat, and he felt his pockets, pulled out one old piece of hardtack, put it into his mouth without looking at it. It was always better that way. He knew not to chew, let the thing get soft first, but he was really hungry now, and so he bit down, felt his mouth fill with dry crumbs. He grabbed at his canteen, put it to his mouth, felt the blessed wetness, swallowed. Now his mouth felt like wet dough, and he drank some more, washed it down. He put the canteen aside, ran his tongue around the stale taste in his mouth, thought, Wonderful, that may be all for tonight. Remember it with a smile.

It had been this way since Gettysburg, the orders coming down at odd times, a short march or a longer one. Then they would stop, there would be no orders for a while, and they'd spread out into barren fields. Always they expected to see the enemy, and there might be a small skirmish, or nothing at all, and then more orders, and they would march back again, on the same roads. Sometimes the orders were more specific, a hint of urgency from headquarters, and so they would march at night, hurried along by the commanders, the men who knew . . . *something*. Tonight they were marching north, so were they being chased? He thought of the numbers again, the missing troops, the men sent to Tennessee. Lee must know . . . maybe it was a mistake, we are too weak.

They knew Lee had sent troops to the West as well, Longstreet's corps. Of course it was a secret, but around these armies there were few well-kept secrets. The spies had brought in the Richmond newspapers, and they were amazed to see a full written account of Longstreet's troop movements, even his route of travel. And so headquarters understood that sending Federal troops west would be no secret either.

Meade was always being pushed by Washington, the impatience of a government that had expected Gettysburg to bring greater results, a quick conclusion. But Meade was still wary, knew that Lee was as dangerous as he had ever been, that Lee's army would wait for him, try to outmaneuver him. When Washington pushed Meade forward, he would only go far enough to probe, seek an opportunity. If the opportunity was not there, if Lee did not leave himself open to attack, Meade would draw away again. For two months the armies stalked each other like two cats, and now Meade was backing away again. By morning the army would reach a small river, Broad Run, and cross to the safety beyond, at the fords around Bristoe Station.

H E WAS ON THE NORTH SIDE OF THE STREAM, AND WATCHED from his horse as the last of the brigade moved across. Below Broad Run he saw a squad of blue cavalry come up out of the far woods, riding hard, moving closer to the rows of troops crossing the stream. Now he saw more cavalry, emerging from the woods farther to the right, and there were scattered shots, musket fire in the woods. His column began to break up, men falling out, trying to see behind them, the sounds rolling across the stream, and the officers began to shout, moving the men back into line.

Chamberlain watched the distant woods, could see nothing, and he yelled toward his men, "Keep moving, clear away from the water, let the column across!"

His men pushed forward, and Chamberlain felt a sudden rush of energy, thought, Yes, they *are* chasing us. Below the stream the cavalry began to dismount, officers yelling orders to form a skirmish line. Chamberlain saw that his men were well above the stream now, saw the last of the First Division crossing, and he rode back to the bank, where Griffin was splashing his horse through the shallow water, coming toward him.

Griffin pointed back to the line of cavalry, yelled, "Colonel, prepare to receive an attack! Move your column to that rise above the creek. Lee's right on our tail!"

Chamberlain turned, saw his men moving up on the ridge, said, "Right away, sir! We're there already. I'll turn them this way." He saluted, spurred the horse, climbed the short rise. The men were turned, the regiments forming a line of battle facing the stream. Chamberlain watched Griffin direct more troops into line toward his flank, and he rode forward, climbed a small knoll and saw them. Below the stream, across a wide field, two thick lines of rebels came out of the woods, advancing toward the last of the men still waiting to cross. Then Griffin was beside him, and Chamberlain watched him staring hard across the field. Griffin said, "It's A. P. Hill . . . they got up around us. They're trying to cut us off. But it's too late."

Chamberlain could see the rebel lines moving closer, and now there was a solid line of gray smoke and the sound of the volley. The cavalry line was being overwhelmed, and they rushed back toward the stream, closer to the mass of blue infantry. Then the rebels moved forward again, pressing the attack.

Griffin said, "Only a division . . . maybe two brigades. They don't have the strength! What the hell is going on? Where's the rest of them?"

The rebels moved closer, there was another volley, and along the stream shells began to explode, the booming of rebel guns from far across the field. Chamberlain's chest was pounding now; he heard the

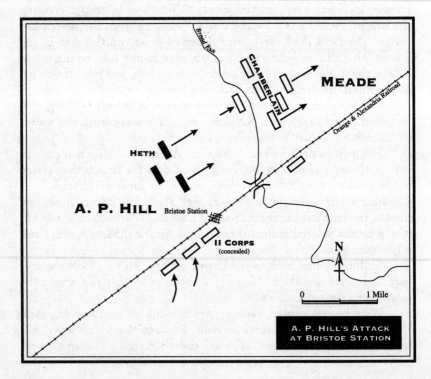

A. P. HILL'S ATTACK
AT BRISTOE STATION

whiz of a musket ball over his head, then another, closer. He looked down along the lines of the brigade, saw the faces staring out at the enemy. The musket fire was steady now, and Griffin was saying something, pointing. Chamberlain tried to hear, followed Griffin's gesture. Off to the left, beyond the stream, he saw a bright flash, but it was not cannon, there was no smoke. He leaned forward, tried to see through a row of small trees, realized it was a reflection, the sun glancing off the massed bayonets of many, many men. Griffin was still pointing, said, "It's . . . the Second Corps . . ."

Chamberlain saw it all now, the smoke from the fight in front of them clearing away in the breeze. On the far side of the stream there was a railroad cut, and the Second Corps had moved up, twelve thousand men hidden by a high embankment, unseen by the rebels. Now a mass of muskets pointed out over the embankment, and suddenly there was a sharp cracking volley, a flaming blast into the flank of the rebel assault. The smoke flowed across the field, and Chamberlain felt an odd turn in his gut, the shock of the mass of fire, of watching a whole battle line collapse at once. The rebels began to turn what was left of their line, to face the railroad cut, and some moved forward, to charge this new enemy, but there was another volley, and those lines collapsed as well. Then the big Federal guns above the stream began to fire, and Chamberlain felt the ground shake, and Griffin stood up in his stirrups, yelled, "A trap! A perfect trap!"

Abruptly, Griffin spurred his horse and rode forward, followed by his staff. Chamberlain turned, saw the sergeant behind him, holding the flag, and the man was staring grimly, silently, toward the field. Chamberlain followed the man's eyes, could see the last of the rebels moving away. The musket fire faded, the big guns quieted, and in minutes it was over. Now came the shouts, the wild yells. He looked down the lines of his brigade, and the men were cheering, waving hats, muskets held high. Then the loud voices rang out to the left, across the stream, the men behind the railroad cut. Chamberlain watched the last of the rebels fade back into the far trees, and he thought, This was more than a skirmish. We won . . . we beat them. It was over so quickly. He tried to feel the excitement of the men around him, but it was held away by his own surprise at what had happened, at how clearly he'd seen it. He looked across the field at the men left behind, a horrifying mass of rebel dead. It was a foolish attack, he thought. There was no strength. And they didn't know the railroad cut was full of infantry. Griffin was right. They walked right into a trap.

He moved his horse forward, close to the edge of the stream, saw men in blue moving out into the field, tending the wounded rebels. There were men with canteens, men with stretchers. The cheering had stopped, and now the sounds came from the field, faint and high and terrible, and more soldiers moved out to help the men they had shot down. In the distance some of the wounded were still crawling back toward the woods, pulling themselves away from a perfect disaster.

5. LEE

OCTOBER 1863

HE REACHED THE EDGE OF THE WOODS, STOPPED THE HORSE, stared out beyond the wide field. He could see the stream, the small wood buildings. He looked to the low hills beyond, closed his eyes, waited, then forced himself to look at the ground close by, the wide sweep of open grass covered with the bodies of his men.

Along the stream he saw cavalry, a squad of Stuart's men. Stuart was already following Meade's trail, the roads north, and the messages came back to Lee in a steady flow: Meade was moving away. Lee knew Meade would not stop until he reached the next good ground, would protect himself from any surprises. For a while, at least, there would be no more fighting on this field, along this stream, this place called Bristoe Station.

Troops began to move up around him, skirmishers, sent into the field to make sure there were no enemy stragglers and no lingering sharpshooters. The men began to look to the bodies, to prod and poke, to search for some sign of life, but the wounded were gone. Those who had not been able to retreat were now carried by the Yankees.

Hill was beside him, sat quietly, watching Lee, waiting. Lee spurred the horse, moved out into the field. The soldiers moved with him, spread out farther to the front, watching, focused on the far hills across the stream, the tops of trees. There was no calling out, no cheers, nothing to reveal to hidden eyes who this might be, the white-bearded officer on the tall gray horse.

The horse stepped between the bodies of the dead, and Lee looked out across to the railroad cut, saw bodies spread all along the embankment. He removed his hat, held it by his side, rubbed his hand through the white hair, thought, If there had been more strength . . . we might have pushed them out of the cut, routed them across the stream. He tried to see it in his mind, the flags and the swarm of men pushing up and over the embankment, but the image was not there. This was not a field where victory had been turned away by brilliant strategy or a crucial piece of luck. It had not been close, a decision forced by the gallant heroics of one man rising up to turn the flow. It had been a simple bloody mistake.

Lee looked back at Hill, and Hill moved his horse forward, close beside Lee. The staff stayed back. Only Taylor rode out, stayed a few feet away, on the other side. Taylor stared at the dead, made an angry sound, a low discreet grunt. Lee did not acknowledge it, knew that Taylor did not respect Hill, did not regard him as a good commander. But Taylor could never say that to Lee.

Lee had not done this often—ridden out onto the bloody fields, fields where there were so many of his men, and so very few of the men in blue. There had not been many defeats like this, one-sided tragedies. Now it was up to Hill himself to explain; not to make excuses, but to understand what he'd done, the incredible disastrous mistake.

Lee still stared ahead, heard Hill clear his throat, a small cough, heard him shift himself in the saddle. Lee knew Hill was not well, had great discomfort riding, seemed to be in pain all of the time. The pain was on his face, and in the shape of his body, a great hard weight on his shoulders, pushing him down. Hill cleared his throat again.

"General Lee, there was a lack of . . . good reconnaissance."

Lee said nothing, waited for more.

"We did not know the Yankees were in force on this side of the run. I ordered . . . I believed that speed was the priority. He was spread out . . . I thought I could catch his rear unprotected."

Lee nodded quietly, still said nothing. He understood now how this could have happened.

A. P. Hill was a difficult man to command, sensitive and easy to provoke. He carried with him a dark stain from a past that he could not escape. At West Point he had missed graduating with his class in 1846, had to wait one more year, and the reason was scandalous and embarrassing: He had built a reputation as a young man who enjoyed the parties and the houses of ill-repute, the rowdy temptations of New York, and he'd suffered from what was described discreetly as a "social affliction." The late graduation meant he'd barely made it to the fight in Mexico, a fight won by the heroism of many of his classmates, Jackson, McClellan. And even in Lee's army he had never found a comfortable command. There was the great feud with Longstreet, a dispute begun by a newspaper report in Richmond, giving Hill more credit than Longstreet felt he deserved for the good fights on the Virginia peninsula, the Seven Days battles. Their arguments and hostility grew so intense that Hill challenged Longstreet to a duel, something Lee could not tolerate. Lee had only defused the situation by transferring Hill to Jackson's command. But Hill did not perform to Stonewall's rigid and inflexible standards, and so he found himself the focus of Jackson's hot temper as well. There were more charges, threats of arrest and court-martial, a controversy that ended only with Jackson's death.

But on the field, Hill had made his reputation. At Second Manassas, his battered line held their ground against Pope's overwhelming strength, and saved Jackson's flank until the great crushing blow from Longstreet swept the Federals from the field. At Sharpsburg, Hill pushed his men on a hard forced march, arriving on the field when Lee's entire position was near collapse. His division had driven Burnside's surprised troops back across Antietam Creek, and from that moment the cry among the men was "up came Hill." He bathed himself in that, the pride of his men, and most had considered him then the best division commander in the army. Since Jackson's death, Hill commanded a much larger force, many of Jackson's troops; but since Gettysburg, and through the small nameless fights of autumn, he'd shown none of the fire that had given him his reputation. It was a crushing disappointment to Lee, and he was beginning to see how it could be a great danger to the army. Here, on this one open field, in a fight that lasted less than one hour, because Hill was in a hurry, they had lost nearly two thousand men.

"Sir, I will prepare my report."

Lee nodded, put his hat on. The sun was dropping into the tops of the trees behind them, and he knew nothing would happen for a while. He understood Meade now, as he had understood the others before him, and he could anticipate the jabs, the deep probes, Meade's way of looking for an advantage. Lee knew if there was to be a fight soon, he would have to press it. But the rolling country out in front of him, across Broad Run, was too familiar. The roads ran across more fields, up toward another stream called Bull Run, where the two great battles of Manassas had been fought. The land was stripped by the war, desolate and barren, and Lee's army could not support itself there. Where else could they go now but back, southward, to the protection of the big river behind them, the Rappahannock?

Lee glanced at Taylor, still said nothing, but Taylor knew the look, pulled his horse away and moved back toward the waiting staff. Lee took a deep breath, looked down at the bodies close around them, and Hill motioned, cleared his throat.

"Sir . . . General Lee . . . I am sorry . . . sir."

Lee looked at Hill, saw the shame, the grief in the face of this small sickly man. He felt a sudden dark anger, impatience. He looked away toward the darkening sky, gripped his anger, clamped it down, would not show it, would not lecture him. He thought, There is nothing I can say that will change this. This was a lesson from God, and General Hill must learn from this, must take this with him, and it will not happen again.

Hill waited, peered up at Lee from under the brim of the battered hat. After a quiet moment Lee said, "Well, General, let's bury these poor men, and say no more about it."

THE ARMY MOVED SOUTH ALONG THE RAILROAD, THE GREAT steel link with the north, the Orange and Alexandria. He sat on Traveller, watched a detail of men with sledgehammers, some with long steel pry bars. They knew he was watching them, and so the work was fast and without complaint, and the officers did not have to tell the men how to do their job.

They pulled and twisted, and gradually a long piece of track pulled free of the rail bed. Now more men dragged the rail to a neatly stacked pile of logs, and with one great groan they laid it on top, balancing it carefully so that each end of the rail stuck far out in each direction. There were already several more rails on the stack, and now an officer moved up, carried a small tuft of burning straw, knelt beside the woodpile, spread the flame slowly around the edges. The fire began to climb, and in a few short minutes it engulfed the woodpile completely. Lee pulled at the horse, moved away from the tracks, heard the men whooping, knew that when the fire was at its hottest, the weight of the heavy steel would begin to tell, that as the steel heated and softened, the ends of the rails would begin to sag. Then the men would lift them off the fire and push them hard against a fat tree trunk, twisting them more, so when they cooled and the steel hardened again, they could never be used for rails.

He rode toward his camp, thought of the railroad, the shipments moving south from Washington, supplying Meade's army. He felt a black anger, gripped the reins tightly, did not hear the men he passed, the bright salutes, the small cheers. He did not look at them because he knew he'd see gaunt faces, rags, bare feet. From the south, the railcars did not bring the supplies that Meade received so easily from the great factories and farms of the North. The supplies were simply not there to send, the farms depleted, the citizens of the small towns and the larger cities, choked by the naval blockade, fighting their own war of survival.

Always when he moved north, he repaired the railroads as he went, fixing what a retreating Federal army had destroyed. But now, instead of repairing the damage, Lee was creating it, destroying the tracks himself. He did not share the enthusiasm for the job that his men had shown. They did not understand, not yet, that the war had changed. The defeat at Gettysburg had cost them too much, and there would be no more invasions north. With Meade in pursuit, even a hesitant pursuit, Lee knew he could not simply make a stand or drive forward into the enemy. He had to rely on maneuver now, draw Meade into a vulnerable place, allow Meade to make a careless mistake. The only way to do that was to bring Meade south with them.

It was nearly dark, and he saw his campfire, saw Taylor signing a paper, handing it to a courier. The man moved away quickly, efficiently, and Lee climbed down from the horse, handed the reins to an orderly, moved to the fire.

There were other men waiting to see Taylor, the daily routine of the headquarters, but when they saw Lee, staring quietly, alone, into the fire, they did not approach. He watched the flames, heard nothing but the soft sound of the burning wood, did not hear Taylor send aides toward the soldiers, telling them: later. Taylor moved into the firelight, and Lee looked into the boyish face, saw the major's uniform, knew Taylor would not be self-conscious; the promotion had just been announced, and the new coat would be slow in coming, the insignia of Lieutenant Colonel.

Lee said, "Colonel, we have destroyed our own railroad."

Taylor nodded, said quietly, "Yes, sir."

Lee looked back into the fire. "We are backing away from an enemy we could have beaten. We must wait for him to come to us. We do not have the means . . . to press the attack. The men . . . we are not providing for the men."

"Sir, it is a disgrace. Richmond must be made to understand. . . ."

Lee saw the anger in Taylor's face, knew that his aide shared his frustrations. He is so young, Lee thought. He does not understand . . .

you must find the control, you must not let the darker emotions surface. Lee raised his hand in a calming gesture. "No, Colonel. Richmond cannot help us. It has been clear for some time . . . we must do with what we have. The president has assured me that all that can be done is being done. But the men do not receive shoes, the rations are disgraceful. I have begun to fear . . . it seems there is treachery. Someone in the quartermaster's office does not want us to prevail." He paused, thought, No, I should not . . . we must not be a party to rumor.

Taylor was watching him, wide-eyed, and Lee said, "Colonel, this is in confidence . . . do not speak of this to anyone. I must depend on you, as my chief of staff. You must understand the importance in not allowing the business of this army to reach beyond this headquarters. It seems that principle is not being followed elsewhere. There are those in the government who find it necessary to discuss our strategy with the newspapers. I have learned more about our troop movements in Tennessee from the Richmond papers than I have from the president." He looked up, above the fire, toward the shadows, men moving through the camp. Taylor said nothing, still watched him. Lee now looked at the young man, and Taylor stood upright, a reflex to Lee's quiet anger.

Lee said, "Colonel, from this point on I must examine any dispatch that goes to Richmond. We will have to be more . . . discreet about what we tell the president, the secretary of war. And, especially, the quartermaster general." Taylor nodded slowly, absorbing Lee's words, and there was a silence. Lee thought, He is so young . . . he may not understand the importance . . .

He suddenly felt the absence of Longstreet. Lee could talk about any subject, the politics of Richmond, the dark troubling doubts, and Longstreet would always listen, patient, watching him with sad dark eyes. Then Longstreet would always offer something of his own, might even make an argument, but always respectful, only enough to make a point. Lee knew that lately, since Gettysburg, the disagreements between them had been deeper, less was said face-to-face, that Longstreet's dark moods had taken him further away. With Longstreet now in Tennessee, Lee did not think on that, on the disagreements, the controversies about Longstreet's sluggishness. Lee had seen the newspapers, knew that many were now blaming Longstreet for the defeat at Gettysburg, but Lee would not hear that, would not support anyone who spoke out, offered an indiscreet opinion. That kind of talk was not good for the army, and he knew that Longstreet was still his best soldier, the man he would have to depend on as the war went on. The bloody fields at Bristoe Station, the image of Hill's careless attack, had driven deep into Lee. He knew he would have to rely on Longstreet more than ever now, that even if Longstreet moved a bit slower than Hill might, he would not make that kind of mistake.

Lee did not know when Longstreet might return. In Tennessee, Longstreet had taken his men into the fight with as much fury and skill as the fight had needed, had driven the Federals hard at Chickamauga. But now Longstreet was under the command of Braxton Bragg, and Lee had heard only bad reports from that command, disgruntled officers, an angry Longstreet most of all.

Bragg's only support came from the president, and so when calls began to flow in from the field for Bragg's replacement, incredible reports of incompetence and friction with his commanders, nothing changed, because Davis would not remove a man he liked. Lee thought, How can Bragg . . . manage? What must that be like, the constant grumbling in headquarters, intrigue and protests? How can any man run an army if he does not have the respect . . . if he is so far removed from his command? Good fighting generals did not have to be popular generals, but it was clear now from the reports, from Longstreet's own letters to Lee, that Bragg was neither.

Taylor was still watching him, was shifting back and forth with idle energy. There is none of that here, Lee thought, the harsh words, the jealousies of great egos. And I have this young man . . .

Walter Taylor was the most valuable officer Lee had, a fiercely loyal and protective chief of staff who alone could do what Lee did not have the strength to do. Lee's staff, among the very best, had always been small. There were many who had sought the prestigious positions, but they learned they could not bear the strain, the quantity of work nearly impossible. Taylor never complained, was clearly in charge, was always where Lee needed him to be.

Taylor was still moving, rubbed his hands together, seemed nervous. Lee knew the young man had something to say, that it would come out in a burst of indiscretion, the impatience of youth.

"Sir! Surely they must know the harm . . . we must make them understand. If the quartermaster . . . if General Northrop is responsible, sir . . . we must do something!"

Lee thought, Do something? Do . . . what? He'd grown weary of asking, of explaining the army's great needs, of calling for new troops. As each request went south, he had only felt a greater sadness. Richmond could not even send them shoes.

"What we will do, Colonel, is limit the flow of information, limit the correspondence. We will reveal what is necessary to reveal, and nothing more."

"I understand, sir. We will limit the correspondence. It is . . . most regrettable, sir."

Lee took a long breath, stared deep into the fire, felt the heat now, felt it move through him, ball up in a tightness in his chest, a dull hard pain.

"Yes, Colonel. It is most regrettable."

6. LEE

December 1863

HE WAS CLOSE TO RICHMOND NOW, COULD SEE PEOPLE ALONG the dirt roads, wagons moving slowly, some stopping briefly to watch the train. They were used to the trains now, but a few spotted him, saw the white hair and the uniform, the old familiar face gazing at them through the window, and they would wave. A few hats would go up, cheers and shouts, and later they would tell their friends that he'd been there, that they had seen him with their own eyes.

He did not respond, saw patches of snow, the mud on the roads, thought now about the winter, and the men with bare feet.

There had been one more push from Meade. Once more he'd come south, across the river, crossing at a place where Lee had made preparations. Lee had thought the place defended, but the defense did not work. Meade moved quickly and with power, surprised Lee's troops, moved across the bridge that should have been protected. It was another mistake.

Lee pulled back to the west then, beyond the edge of the Wilderness, the place where Jackson had nearly destroyed the Federal army that past spring. Lee did not think of those days, of missed opportunities, of the pain of that night, when the courier brought him the news, the unbearable image of Jackson falling from his saddle, shot down by his own men. Lee had learned that in this war there were many strokes of what some called luck, but he did not believe that, thought: God has His reasons, and sometimes the tide turns against you, but there will be a balance. If we were victorious that day, we would pay a price another day. He saw Jackson's face again, the sharp blue eyes, and he could not help it, thought, *Why?* Was it necessary to take *him?* He had asked that question often, prayed long for an answer, for some understanding, but it had not come.

Now when Meade pushed toward him, Lee ordered them to put up defenses through the deep woods, a place called Mine Run, and the dirt had flown and trees were felled. It was a great change from the earliest days of the war. When he'd first suggested the digging of trenches around Richmond, he received hoots of derision in the newspapers, was called "Granny Lee," or the "Queen of Spades." Wars should be fought by men standing straight, facing the enemy, and no honor would ever be won by men who hid behind cover. But the soldiers themselves did not care what the papers said. They had seen the horrors, the bloody reality of what that kind of honor could do to the men around them, and they welcomed the trenches. When the order came, every man sought to put his hands on a shovel.

Meade had come up close, but there was only scattered fighting, no great attack. A freezing rain had soaked them all, and for several days the two armies crouched low in the brush. Then word came from Stuart that Meade's flank was exposed, vulnerable. So it was Lee who made the decisive move, pushed his army quietly around Meade's flank. But in the dawn, when the orders came to advance, Lee's troops swept forward and found no one waiting. Meade had pulled away again, a long head start for the protection of the big river, and Lee knew he'd let Meade escape, that Mine Run had been another lost opportunity.

With Meade safely away, Jefferson Davis asked him to come to Richmond, and Lee agreed. He did not like to leave his troops in the field, but there would be no more fighting now; the winter had come hard into Virginia, and the men began to build the huts and shelters that would be their winter quarters. There was another reason Lee agreed to make the trip. Mary was there, the family had rented a small house, and Lee hoped there would be an opportunity to share the Christmas holidays with at least part of his family.

He could see the church spires, the tops of the taller houses, and the train lurched around a curve, rattled on worn tracks. The railroads were in ragged condition, overused, and there was little time or manpower to make repairs. He felt the train slow, saw more buildings and more people. Sitting back, he laid his head against the seat, thought of Mary, of the children, of the tall Christmas trees, those times long ago when he could leave his post and share the warmth of the celebration, of the church services and fireplaces, snowfalls and great feasts. He closed his eyes, felt a hard weariness come over him, and the images began to fade. But he wouldn't let them go, not yet, still tried to feel the warmth, the soft love of home.

L EE LOOKED AT THE EMPTY WHEELCHAIR, PUSHED INTO THE COR-
ner of the room, facing the wall. Mary would not use it, would
still try to get around the small house with the crutch, and he
knew not to argue. The arthritis had gotten worse, a slow deterioration
that the doctors could not stop, one arm now curled and useless.

Hearing voices, he moved into the small parlor, saw his son Custis helping Mary slowly down onto the couch.

Custis glanced up at him, smiled, said, "There now, here's Father . . . perhaps you would prefer if *he* read to you."

"No, Custis, please. I love the sound of your voice." She smiled at the young man, and Lee saw the two of them as one, so much of her in his face, the gentleness.

Lee said, "I see you are in good hands. I thought . . . maybe some tea." She looked at him now, and he waited, could not predict how she would respond to him, what her mood would be.

"That would be fine, Robert. Is there anyone else home this morning?"

"No, it's just us. A bit peaceful this morning."

Custis said, "Father, sit here on the couch. I'll get the tea."

Mary began to protest, raised her hand, but Custis was quickly out of the room, and Lee smiled, knew what his son had done. He moved to the couch, said, "Might I sit? We have not had much time alone."

She nodded, smiled now, said, "Sit down, Robert. You treat me like I'm your schoolmistress. Is this how you act around your generals?"

There was humor in her voice, something he had not heard in a long time. He sat, gently, stayed apart from her, was always careful about hurting her, knew how frail she'd become, how often the pains came. She turned to face him, and he saw the effort, leaned forward to help, put a hand on her arm.

"Thank you, Robert. It's all right."

She looked at him closely, the white hair, the lines around his eyes. He understood the changes, the absence, that when so much time had passed, the effects of the war would show in his face, and it had depressed her. He'd always held the image of her from those times when she was the Belle of Arlington, cared for by her father, spoiled certainly, and it was the memories of youth, before her pains came, that Lee carried with him.

He was the same with the children, saw them as small, scurrying about the old mansion with noisy glee. He had to make himself see them, each of them as they were now, and it was difficult. Annie had died over a year ago, suddenly and without warning, and Lee had never recovered from the shock of that, of the impact of disease. It was a reminder that God was still watching over them, that no matter how much death was brought by the hands of men, the tools of war, God would decide when each would be called away.

His son Rooney was in a Federal prison, captured while recuperating from wounds, hauled away by blue soldiers while his pleading wife looked helplessly on. Robert Jr. was still on the line, manning an artillery battery. The girls would stay away in school or with friends over the holidays, and Lee was sad to hear they would not be home, but he did not speak of it, could not complain of his children's absence when for most of their lives his own absence had been felt so deeply. Lee heard Custis in the kitchen, heard the rattle of teacups, spoons.

Mary looked away, was gazing toward the small window that faced the street, said, "He is . . . wonderful to me. It is good that he can be here."

"I am grateful for that. We are fortunate his position . . . his duty is here."

She looked at him, and he knew what was coming. "Have you heard from Rooney? Is there any word?"

He shook his head. "No . . . they won't release him. I have tried . . . it is a difficult situation. He is considered a . . . prize."

"Of course. He is a Lee."

"I will keep at it. There might still be some negotiating, we do have several important prisoners. Perhaps there will be a trade."

"Charlotte is not taking it well. She is very ill. Even the baths, the springs, have done her no good. To watch him carried off like that . . . the cruelty. I am worried about her."

Lee looked down, did not want to think of his son that way; saw the beaming face, the huge young man, always a bright smile. His eyes followed the dark pattern in the rug, the deep purple of a rose. "I will do what I can."

There was a silence, and Mary said, "So, where are you off to today?"

"The president . . . I have been asked to meet with him."

"The president . . ." She made a small frown. "Well, we must not allow the president to get lonely. He cannot seem to run this country without a Lee beside him. At least he permitted Custis to have this day at home, to spend some time with his mother."

There was another rattle of china from the hallway, and Custis entered, carefully holding a tray and teacups. "So, you are talking about me when I'm not in the room?" He set the tray down on the small table, carefully handed a china teacup to his mother.

Lee reached down, stirred at his own cup, said, "Your mother is grateful the president has allowed you to spend some time . . . with your family." He paused, knew those words held great irony for Mary, for all of them.

Custis moved toward the window, looked out into the dull gray of the morning, shook his head. "He is . . . a complicated man."

Lee waited for more, knew Custis was careful with his words. Lee said, "He carries the weight of this war, the weight of the country on his shoulders. It may be too much for one man."

Custis began to pace in the small room, and Lee could see a dark anger in the handsome face. "Father, he will not listen . . . he will not accept any help. He busies himself with trivial details, spends half the day arguing with cabinet people, legislators, even generals, about . . . personalities. He wants to fill every position, every post, by himself. It is most frustrating. I don't know what my job is, what it is he expects me to do. He says just . . . *be* there."

Lee watched him, nodded, thought, Yes, I know. He recalled the early months of the war, when Virginia first joined the Confederacy. He had been Davis's first real adviser then, understood that Davis would allow nothing to pass through his offices without his personal inspection. Davis still yearned for the fight, still kept the fond memories of the great adventure in Mexico, memories they all had. He would put himself in command of troops if he did not think it would cripple the government. Lee thought of Davis sitting in his office, hidden behind piles of papers, and he suddenly remembered, pulled out his pocket watch.

"I'm sorry . . . I must leave. The president is expecting me." He stood up, saw Mary turn awkwardly, tilting her head, trying to look up at him, and he reached out his hand, put it softly on her shoulder. "I will be home for dinner. . . ."

She nodded stiffly, put her hand on his for a brief moment, said to Custis, "Please help me up, will you. I've changed my mind . . . I don't feel like a reading right now. Maybe later . . ."

Lee stood back, let his son move close, and he helped her stand. She held herself against Custis's arm, looked at Lee, and he saw a coldness in her eyes, the change in her mood. She said, "Tell Mr. Davis . . . tell him we have lost our home, we have lost children. The longer this goes on, the more we will lose. Tell him there are too many widows . . . too many mothers missing their sons. There are enough gravestones! Tell him that!"

Lee stared at her, was shocked, had rarely heard her say anything about the war. She moved toward the hallway, and Custis moved with her. Then she stopped, looked at him again, and he saw the hard anger in her face.

"Go! Tell him!"

Lee said nothing, watched her move out of the room, stood alone for a moment. He knew he could not do as she wanted, that there would be more fighting, and more soldiers would die, and he could not think about the widows and the families. He could only carry out his duty and lead his men forward until God had seen enough, until God decided this bloody war would end.

T HEY CALLED IT THE WHITE HOUSE, AND NO ONE GAVE MUCH thought to the irony of that. This was the home of President Davis and his family, and it did not compare to the grand sweeping mansion in Washington. The name was a simple description of the home.

Since the beginning of the war, Davis had been prone to illness, some real, some imagined. As his army had absorbed the defeats of the past months, his health had worsened, the illness affecting his mind as well. He became suspicious, protective, more likely to distrust his subordinates. He began to conduct more and more of the business of the government from his own home, converted one room into an office, would often not leave the home for days at a time.

Lee approached the steps, looked up to the front door, saw it open. There were hushed voices, and three men emerged, talking quietly among themselves. Lee stopped, waited, and the men came down the steps toward him. He noticed the fine suits, silk shirts, gold watch chains, the finery of official visitors. They saw him now, and for a brief moment they stared, recognizing him. He removed his hat, and they seemed to recover their formality, moved down the steps, came past him. He nodded as they passed, and they glanced at him discreetly, but there were no smiles, no one spoke. The men moved to a carriage, and Lee watched them climb inside. There was a slap of leather, and the carriage quickly pulled away. He turned, moved up the steps, thought, *Europeans*.

He saw now that the door was still open, a soldier inside standing at attention, waiting for him to enter. Lee moved into the house, and the soldier closed the door, stiff and formal. Lee looked toward the small secretary's office, what had once been a closet, a large square hole cut in the wall so the front door could be seen. He heard commotion, saw movement in the small office, the sound of a chair pushed back, and he waited. A man came out quickly, adjusting his coat, thrust a hand toward him. It was Davis's secretary, Burton Harrison.

Harrison was a neat, dapper man. He shook Lee's hand warmly, said, "General Lee, how wonderful! How are you, sir?"

Lee smiled, had always been amused by the secretary's energy, his manic protection of Davis. "I am quite well, Mr. Harrison." He noticed Harrison glancing around the small space, self-conscious.

Harrison said, "Forgive . . . my office, General. The president insists, and so we must make do with what we have. It can be difficult—" He stopped, and Lee saw a pained look, Harrison showing displeasure at his own indiscretion. "I . . . didn't mean to suggest I am not happy here. This is the president's home. We must make do—"

There was a high squeal from Davis's office, behind Harrison. The secretary jumped, startled, and the pained look returned. "I should tell the president you are here," he said. "Excuse me . . ."

Lee nodded. There were more squeals, the laughter of children, then he heard an older voice, and the sound of heavy steps. Harrison was gone, had fled back into the small office when the door opened. Lee backed against the wall as two children burst into the hallway, squealing with laughter. Davis was behind them, bent over, the pursuer, growling like some deranged beast.

The children rushed past Lee, and Davis straightened, looked at Lee with surprise, then smiled and put a hand on Lee's shoulder, supporting himself, breathing heavily. "Well, hello General . . . excuse me . . ." Lee felt the weight of the hand, was suddenly uncomfortable, as though he'd intruded on something very private. Davis took a deep breath, and the children waited in a far doorway. Davis said, "Not now, you two . . . stay put for a while . . . the general and I have some work to do." Davis glanced into the small room, said, "Mr. Harrison, please see we are not disturbed."

Lee looked at Harrison, who nodded nervously, then jumped, startled again by the sudden cries of the children, protesting the interruption of their play. Now a maid appeared, a large round woman with deep black skin. She pulled the children quickly into their room, and Davis looked at Lee, smiled, took a deep breath. Now the smile began to fade, and Lee saw the sadness return, the dark eyes filled with sickness, the weight and gloom of the war coming over him again. Davis turned, moved into his office, said, "Come in, General."

There was no one else in the office, and Lee was not surprised, knew that by now these meetings were often private, that Davis had become unwilling to let his staff handle the affairs of running the government. Lee moved in, sat in a small wooden chair, and Davis went to the far corner of the room and closed another door, the door to the children's room and their small sweet sounds.

Davis moved to his own chair, sat behind a small desk, looked at Lee. "It's difficult ... not spending all day with them. This is perhaps ... not the best way to run a government."

Lee said nothing, could now hear small muffled sounds from the next room.

Davis said, "All morning long ... the meeting lasted for hours, and nothing ... no commitment, no encouragement. I am afraid ... we cannot expect much help after all."

Lee sat straight in the chair, said, "The ... French?"

"Yes ... you saw them?" Davis leaned forward, rested his hands on the desk. "There is no chance now. Not since the summer, since Vicksburg ..." He paused, looked down, said, "Since Gettysburg ..."

Lee could see the word was awkward for Davis, but Lee nodded, knew the mention of the place carried no blame.

Davis looked at Lee now, said, "And there was still a chance, even the English could see that we were still in control, still held on. We just had to show them ... one victory, one real smashing blow. I am certain of it ... they would still have come in, would have broken the blockade. But ... events have changed that."

Lee knew that Davis was talking about the enormous and stunning defeat of Braxton Bragg. Bragg had penned the Federals up tightly in Chattanooga, and the official reports as well as northern papers said the Federals were starving, it would be Vicksburg in reverse. It should not have taken much longer; the shroud of winter would force Rosecrans to surrender, and they all knew the pendulum would swing, the momentum lost at Vicksburg would turn their way in the West. But Bragg had grown careless, weakened his army by sending Longstreet's corps up toward Knoxville, to relieve the occupation there by Burnside's forces. And little attention had been paid when Lincoln, weary of Rosecrans, sent a new commander to Chattanooga, a name that was vaguely familiar to Lee, the man known mostly for engineering the strangle of Vicksburg. His name was Ulysses Grant.

Quickly, Grant punched through Bragg's choke hold, found a way to bring supplies into Chattanooga, and his men were not starving anymore. But Bragg was still in control, the Federal army still held tightly inside Chattanooga. Suddenly, and with complete efficiency, Grant surprised Bragg by advancing across the entire front, the blue soldiers climbing straight up the hills, first the invincible position of Lookout Mountain, not invincible after all. Then, incredibly, while Bragg's army looked down from Missionary Ridge, Grant formed his lines in the wide-open fields beside the city. The rebels had admired and applauded the parade ground pageantry, until Grant sent his massed battle lines forward, straight into the hill, the men climbing up rock by rock, protected by the ravines and cracks in the earth. Bragg had the high ground, but never counted on a direct assault, had not put his men into proper position, and so when the rebels tried to shoot straight down the hill, they had to expose themselves to the fire from the flat ground below. As Grant's men climbed the hill in greater and greater numbers, most of Bragg's army simply dissolved, pulling away from the crest of the hill. The retreat became an utter panic, a complete disaster. Now, Grant's army was in pursuit, and Bragg was withdrawing into Georgia. Davis had been forced to accept that it was time to replace him, that his friend was, after all, not the man for the job.

Davis looked at Lee, who had known this moment would come. There had been rumors, even mention in the Richmond papers that Lee would go west, take command of Bragg's shattered army. There was something ominous about Grant, something new, a deadly efficiency that the southern commanders had not faced before. To many, it was only logical that Lee be the one to confront him, the best man to face what was beginning to be the most dangerous threat. But it was not a duty Lee wanted.

Davis sat back in the chair again, rubbed his head with his hand, said, "We are not . . . in a position of strength. The Europeans know that . . . the people know that. Certainly the enemy knows that."

Lee nodded, said, "Yes, I imagine he does."

Davis still rubbed his head, and Lee saw his face twisting, feeling the pain of the headache. "General, are you the man we need? Are you willing . . . to replace General Bragg?"

Lee settled into the chair, took a deep breath and said, "I am willing to serve wherever you assign me." He watched Davis's face, the deep eyes now looking at him. Davis nodded, said nothing. "But, I believe there are others who are more suited for that command. It is not likely that the Army of Tennessee would perform well for a commander they did not know."

Davis put his hands on the desk, did not show surprise at Lee's response.

Lee said, "General Meade is still in Virginia. I believe that he is still the greater threat, certainly to Richmond. And we are still the greatest threat to Washington. The war, ultimately, must be won . . . here. The Army of Northern Virginia is familiar with my command. I do not believe they would respond well to a major change in command. They are accustomed to . . . things as they are now."

Davis smiled, said, "I should have had you here to talk to those Frenchmen. You have always been a fine diplomat."

Lee let out a breath, felt great relief. He had thought Davis might order him west no matter what he said.

Davis looked at the clutter of paper on his desk, shuffled through it, read. Lee had seen this before, knew the matter had passed, that they would now move on. Davis read from a page, rubbed one hard finger idly against his temple, said, "Well, now, General, if your army requires that you stay in Virginia, we must provide someone equally inspiring to the Army of Tennessee. . . ."

THE HOUSE WAS FILLED WITH CHRISTMAS, BRIGHT RIBBONS streaming around the windows, candles casting small shadows. He heard the voices in back, happy sounds flowing through the dark hallways, and he stopped in the dim light of the parlor, looked at the wheelchair still sitting in the corner of the room. He smelled the pine branches, sharp and familiar. He looked at the dark needles, and the smell was of the woods . . . the camps. He was suddenly very sad, still listened to the voices, stood quietly in the dim light of the room, tried to feel what they were feeling, the joy in the sounds, the holiday. But there was no holiday in the camps of the army. It was just a pause in time, the wait for the weather. They would not fight because it was impossible to move, the guns and wagons could not travel the icy, muddy roads, the men could not march through freezing nights. But it would not be long, it had never been long enough, and the roads would dry, the sun would warm them enough to move again, and there would be new fights, and new ground to cover, and places they had never heard of, villages and crossroads and small quiet rivers that would become the new horrible names they would always remember.

He moved to the small couch, sat down, felt stiff, cold, thought, I am not well. He put his hand on his chest, slid it up to his left shoulder, massaged. I do not understand . . . is it just that I am . . . old? He felt the tightness in his chest, always there now, and when it did not hurt, on those mornings when he would wake without the pain, he was grateful, gave a thankful prayer.

He thought of the past few days, the drudgery of the meetings, the arguments, men with great opinions and little understanding. He had known it would be this way, that by coming to Richmond he would be pulled into it, hear it firsthand, that men with oil in their voices would take him aside, greet him with fat handshakes, take him into their confidence, seek his valuable approval, the influence of a powerful, respected man.

There had been great debate about Bragg's replacement, and finally Davis reluctantly agreed that the best man for the job, the one the troops themselves had always followed, was Joe Johnston. It had been a bitter pill for Davis, because Johnston had never cooperated with him, had never cooperated with anyone, and they all knew that Johnston would begin it all again, would run his own show, respond selectively to orders, regard Davis's instructions as inconvenient suggestions. On the Virginia peninsula, when McClellan had come at Richmond from the sea, Johnston cut off all communication with Davis, fought the Federal invasion exactly as he saw fit. When Johnston had been wounded, Davis was forced to make a painful decision, to give up Lee, his most trusted adviser, to send him from the capital to command the army. It had been Lee who organized and equipped the new army, Lee who designed the defensive lines of Virginia, the lines that proved so crucial to the first big fight at Manassas. But Davis had still wanted him nearby, and so Lee suffered quietly in the stifling air of a Richmond office while others led the fighting. But with Johnston down, Davis had to concede that the army's well-being was as important as his own, and finally Lee was given the opportunity to command the army in the field.

When Johnston's wounds healed, he'd gone west, but his command was separate from Bragg's, one of the great flaws in the organization of the army. Johnston had not been there when Bragg needed the strength, had kept himself secure and well defended in Mississippi, against an enemy that was making the fight somewhere else. Despite all of this, Davis had been made to understand, and Lee agreed, that when it came to putting troops in the field, when there were decisions to be made that could decide where and how the battle would be fought, Joe Johnston was the best man they had left.

Lee stared at a candle flickering on the windowsill, still heard the voices, heard Mary, clearly in command, thought, I should let them know I'm home. They will be concerned, ask stern questions: Have I eaten? Is my coat warm enough? He smiled. They worry too much about me. Everyone worries too much. . . .

He tried to stand up and a sharp pain stung him, a sudden hard pinch in his throat. He sat again, stared at the candle, and the pain flowed slowly out of him, then was gone. He heard himself breathing, sat back on the couch, thought, Easy, let it go. *Thank God.*

All during the autumn the pains had come, and he'd spent many days alone in his tent. He would not discuss the ailment, not even with Taylor, and he did not tell anyone that the trip to Richmond would be for that as well, to rest, the soft comfort of home. He could never admit that to anyone, not even to Mary, and for the first few days it had helped, he'd slept well, felt stronger. But now, knowing he would return to his men, that Davis would not send him out of Virginia, the pains surprised him, coming back again. The last few nights he had lain awake staring up into the dark, talking quietly to God, feeling the motion in his chest. But even the prayers did not comfort him, and he could not stop thinking about what they still must do, how the war would go on until *he* did something, that it was *his* responsibility.

It was only a few days until Christmas, and he knew they were glad he was home, that it should be a joyous time. He stood again, slow, careful, moved toward the sounds from the kitchen. He steadied himself in the doorway, saw motion in the dark hall. Mary came out of the kitchen, leaning on the small crutch, saw him standing in the shadow of the candle. She stopped, surprised, said only, "Oh . . ." and looked at him, but they did not speak. Suddenly he could not look at her, stared down at the floor. He wanted to say something, give her something. It was always so hard.

After a quiet moment she said, "I don't need the explanation, Robert. Go . . . go on back to your army. You won't ever really be here, this won't ever be your home . . . until the war is over. We have had Christmas without you before. We will manage."

He still said nothing, felt her eyes digging deep inside him, seeing all of him, and he thought, Of course, she always knows. But there was no bitterness in her voice, not this time. He did not hear the dark anger, just the sadness, the calm acceptance of all they had missed, the family gatherings, the children growing up under the eye of their father. She had, after all, married a soldier.

She began to move away, then stopped, said, "You don't have to explain . . . not to me . . . not to any of us. If they need you to end the war, then end the war. We will still be here. We are still your family. Now, go on. They're waiting for you, you know."

She moved away, hobbled slowly down the hall, back toward their room. He watched her, waited until she was gone, then stared at the dark space, closed his eyes, saw the vast cold camp, shelters and fires, great fields of guns and wagons and horses. And then he saw the faces, the men of his ragged army, waiting for him to return, the army that waited for the command to send them forward once again, maybe for the last time.

He opened his eyes, looked into the dark, saw his faint shadow from the dim light of the candle, said quietly, "Yes . . . I know . . ."

PART
TWO

... testing whether that nation, or any nation, so conceived, so dedicated, can long endure. We are met here on a great battlefield of that war. We have come to dedicate a portion of it as a final resting place for those who here gave their lives that that nation might live. It is altogether fitting and proper that we should do this.

But in a larger sense we can not dedicate—we can not consecrate—we can not hallow this ground. The brave men, living and dead, who struggled here, have consecrated it, far above our poor power to add or detract...

7. GRANT

MARCH 1864

THE LINE MOVED SLOWLY, THERE WAS MUCH TALKING, NERVOUS anticipation. He could feel the motion, the energy of the crowd, held back by the people in front, moving only with small short steps. Gradually they drew closer to the wide doorway Now he could see into the next room, saw the pale blue walls, lit by one small chandelier. The sounds of the people began to quiet; those who had passed through the doorway were now nearly silent. He held the boy's hand, looked down, saw his son trying to see past the line of people, the glorious dresses of the women, the fine suits of the men. But the boy was too short and the crowd pressed together too closely, and so they just eased along slowly, until it was their time to enter the blue room.

He had not changed his uniform, had lost the key to his trunk, and so, had thought it might not be proper . . . and he didn't want to embarrass the boy. Frederick was only twelve, had become used to traveling with his father through the army camps, even on the march. But neither of them had ever been to see the President. He smiled at the boy, who still strained to see the adventure that lay in front of them, thought, He is used to the attention, he loves it, the son of the commander, all the officers, their wives, frittering and making a to-do around him, since the commander himself will have none of it. He thought, now, of the boy's mother: Yes, this would be for you, you enjoy this much more than I do, the receptions in great halls, shaking hands with well-dressed folks, the stifling dignity of meeting Important People. He glanced down at his uniform, saw the smudges, the worn cloth. If she were here . . . I would *not* be here. I should have taken my pistol and shot my way into the trunk, broken the lock. He smiled again, thought of her sulking, the pursed lower lip. She would definitely not approve of *these* clothes, not here, not tonight. The boy looked up at him, and he could see that part of her, the excitement in the boy's face, as they moved ever closer to the Big Moment.

He could hear small comments, realized now that people were pointing at him. Most did not know who he was, and he heard names, guesses, none of them correct. He did feel embarrassed now, began to think this was a bad idea. I should have waited until tomorrow, when the official ceremony would take place. But he had arrived early, and when the boy had heard there was a reception at the White House, the issue was settled. He frowned, thought at least he could have found a way to clean up the uniform.

Now he was in the blue room, and suddenly he could see the President, tall above the crowd, made more so by the slight bows of the people as they passed by, small greetings, careful handshakes. He was stunned by the face, the deep gray eyes, the hard lines, the sadness of a man who felt all the weight of this great bloody war, who must answer to the widows and the children, must find some way of explaining why he did this, why this war had to go on until the rebels were brought down. The tall man was smiling, saying a few words, then a brief nod and another smile. Then the eyes were caught by the blue of the uniform, and suddenly Lincoln stepped forward, moved through the startled row of silk and satin, pearls and lace, reached out a great heavy hand and beamed a wide smile.

"Why, here is General Grant! This is a great pleasure, I assure you!"

Grant took the hand, felt Lincoln's strong grip. Grant felt the warmth, the smile that seemed to spread out over him, over the room. He felt himself pulled away from the crowd, did not see them gather around now, did not feel the boy move close to his side, the attention now focused fully on this small man in the rumpled blue uniform. He stared up into the eyes, felt a sudden weight shifting onto him, more than just the eyes of the President. He felt himself smile, said, "Thank you, sir. Mr. President, sir. It is a pleasure to meet you."

He felt foolish, thought, He is the President of the United States . . . think of something to say. It had not occurred to him that he might actually *speak* to Lincoln, not tonight, had expected maybe to see him, catch a glimpse of the big man through a crowd.

Lincoln still had him by the hand, pulled Grant through the throng of people, and now they were seeing the uniform, the obvious lack of formal preparation. There were amused comments, nods of

"Yes, now here is a *real* soldier . . ." He heard his name flowing out, carried along in a small wave, "General Grant," and in the hallway beyond, the wave grew into shouts, someone began a cheer. He looked around the room, saw the faces watching him, staring.

Lincoln released him, said, "General Grant, allow me to introduce Secretary Seward."

Grant looked at the long thin face of the Secretary of State, smiling at him with the charm of the diplomat. He took the hand that Seward offered, but Seward's words slipped by, the polite formality, and Grant could only hear the rhythm of his name, a slowly rising chorus in the gathering crowd. Now Lincoln was moving him along, and Grant saw a woman, standing alone, watching him with hard quiet eyes. He was led closer, and she did not speak, watched him carefully, appraising him, and he heard someone say, "Mrs. Lincoln . . . this is General Grant . . ."

She was wearing a small hat, a strange cluster of fresh flowers, her long straight hair pulled back tightly. There was a wide-open space around her, the people did not approach her, no one stood close. He made a short bow, thought again of his uniform, felt completely awkward, thought, I should apologize.

But she spoke, and near them there were suddenly no voices, only quiet. "General Grant . . . how nice to meet you. I hear that you bring a bit less refinement and a bit more bulldog to this war."

There was laughter, and Grant tried to smile, bowed again, had no idea what to say. He glanced at Frederick, said, "Mrs. Lincoln, allow me to introduce my son, Frederick Dent Grant."

She reached out a hand, touched the boy's cheek, and the boy flinched slightly. She said, "Yes, how nice. My sons are often with their father as well. Teach them . . . show them how to be men."

Grant smiled, nodded, was not sure what she meant, wondered if it was sarcasm. There was a brief silence, and he thought, Say something . . . words, something appropriate. She was smiling at Frederick still, and suddenly she began to move away, a wide path opening in the crowd. The voices behind him began to grow again, and he turned, saw that the room was filling rapidly, the neat order of the reception line was gone, the crowd mobbing into the room. Grant felt for Frederick's hand, and the boy gripped him hard, pulled close beside him.

Suddenly there was a hand on his shoulder, and he was turned, pulled, saw now it was Seward. He followed, pushed through the noise, the hands reaching out to him, saw the tall figure of Lincoln move on in front of them. Seward moved up behind Lincoln, and

Grant followed to another room, saw it was larger, the walls light green, high white ceilings, an extraordinary chandelier. Seward led him to one side, the crowd following close behind, pushing through the wide doorway. Lincoln stopped beside a small couch, and Seward pointed, said, "General, it might be best . . . climb up here, stand on the couch."

Grant looked at Seward, said, "On the couch . . . my boots?"

"Please, General, it's all right. They seem to want to get a good look at you. It might be the only way to calm them down." Grant looked at the elaborate lace, the silk brocade, looked at Lincoln, and Lincoln was smiling, obviously enjoying the moment. Grant looked again at the couch, then took one step up, steadied himself with one hand on Seward's shoulder.

The room was larger, began to fill as well, and Grant saw other uniforms, the marine guard, the men now moving into the crowd, trying to ease them into lines. Hands were raised toward him now, and he watched the faces, saw the smiles, heard his name again. He looked down, saw Frederick beside the couch, and the boy was smiling now, was beginning to absorb the excitement and the attention from the crowd. Grant watched the marines guiding the people along, silently, gently, but the numbers and the energy were too great, and the people surged up close to him, and his name was now a single chant, the crowd calling out, *"Grant . . . Grant . . . Grant . . ."*

Beside him, Lincoln said something to Seward, and Seward leaned close to him, said, "General, when you have had enough of your adoring crowd, the President requests you join him in the drawing room."

The two men moved away, and Grant was now alone, the hands reaching up to him, a sea of silk and flowers, perfume and cigars, politicians and diplomats and reporters. He began to reach for the hands, a brief grasp for those who came close. They began to file by, but did not leave, and so the room grew more crowded, the marines began to ease away, could do nothing but stand out of the way, moved back against the far wall, watching him as well. Now the chant began again, his name, and he stared in amazement, tried to smile, thought, I am no hero . . .

There was no escape, they would not let him leave, and he shook the hands, nodded politely at the kind comments, the friendly greetings. He looked out over the faces, began to feel now what this was about, the raw enthusiasm for this one soldier. He understood the look now, something he had not noticed before, had not seen in the face of soldiers. He was giving them . . . *hope.*

THERE HAD NOT BEEN A POSITION OF LIEUTENANT GENERAL IN the army for years. Winfield Scott had been the only man since George Washington to hold that rank, and certainly no one since the start of the war had shown himself particularly worthy. After three years now, after the disastrous incompetence of some commanders, the political intrigue that surrounded others, the infighting in Washington, and the morale problems in the field, and as the casualty numbers grew more horrifying, Lincoln understood that something profound and meaningful was fading away from the people. The rebellion was bleeding more from the country than its young men. If it was to turn around, if something was to be saved out of this great war, it would fall on one man who did not speak to crowds, who did not enjoy the raw attention of an admiring public, who did not perform on the field with one eye on the newspapers.

Grant was no one's political favorite, he had not accumulated debts from men of power. He did not get along with General Halleck at all, but Lincoln had learned through bitter experience that it was not Halleck who would win the war from his comfortable office in Washington.

Grant had shown Lincoln something that the others had not. He could win . . . and he did not need to tell you he had won. If he did not win, he did not send a steady stream of explanations, excuses, he did not lay blame. And, he did not make the incessant calls to Washington for reinforcements. Lincoln had become so accustomed to hearing from his commanders how the enemy was always superior, that from the earliest days of McClellan's command, the Federal army would never be strong enough to whip their enemy. Even when there were successes, when the Federal soldiers showed their commanders that they could in fact whip those other fellows, the success was never complete, the opportunity for complete victory had never been followed up. The commanders did not seem to believe it, did not have the fire of confidence, did not appear to understand that with just a little more— another quick strike, another strong blow—those tough boys in the ragged clothes just might do as the blue army had done so often: back away. And if the blow was strong enough, and deliberate enough, it just might end the war. If Grant had his success far from the capital, far from the attention of the eastern newspapers, it was the *people* who were beginning to hear about him from the soldiers, from the men who fought under his command. He did not ride the grandest horse, he did not wear the fanciest uniform. But he had understood his army, had given the right orders, put his men in the right places. At first the names did not cause excitement in the east: Fort Donelson, Shiloh. But then came his triumph at Vicksburg, a complete and utter victory, a mass surrender of a major rebel army, and with that came Federal control of the entire Mississippi River. *Now* the papers picked up the name. When he broke out of Chattanooga, a violent clubbing of Bragg's army that swept them out of Tennessee, Grant had suddenly reversed the tide in the West. He had pulled his army together like one massive fist, cocked and ready to strike directly into the heart of the deep South. When word of this extraordinary breakthrough reached Washington, Lincoln made up his mind. If there was to be one man to control the flow of the war, he wanted Ulysses Grant.

THE MARINE HELD THE DOOR OPEN, AND HE PASSED BY, RE-turned a crisp salute. The door closed behind him, and the sounds of the crowd faded away. He had left Frederick behind, the boy now the center of attention, surrounded by the ladies. The boy had begun to charm them with the innocence and guile only a twelve-year-old knows, and Grant knew he would be fine on his own.

Lincoln sat alone at a small table, and Grant glanced around the room, saw portraits, a mantel covered with flowers, a huge silver tray lying flat on a dark table in the corner. Lincoln held out a hand, motioned to a chair, was smiling, seemed energetic, enthusiastic.

"Please, General, have a chair. I am delighted . . . truly delighted to have you here. Allow me to make good use of this opportunity . . . I have wanted to talk to you."

Grant sat, still looked around the room, felt Lincoln watching him, said, "Thank you, sir. I could have waited until tomorrow. . . ."

"Nonsense, I'm glad you came tonight. You caused quite a stir. The crowds don't respond much anymore . . . not to me, anyway. These weekly receptions have become pretty routine. This was a delight."

There was a pause, and Grant waited, did not know what else to say. Lincoln leaned forward, across the small table, and Grant felt the energy, the mind working. Lincoln stared at him, and Grant felt himself pulled forward, drawn to Lincoln's stare.

"General, there was no one else. I heard all the names, people politicking for the favorite general . . . but when it came down to it, when Congress approved the position, I considered no one else for the job. No one, not one of the men who staked their claim . . . was as deserving as you. The army gains nothing by blessing its commanders with meaningless titles. The rank of Lieutenant General *has* meaning. It belongs to only one man, and that man must understand the job he faces. I have no doubt that my choice is the right one."

Lincoln still stared at him, waited patiently for a response.

Grant said, "Thank you, sir. I hope the Secretary . . . and General Halleck agree. There are many who presently outrank me as major generals."

"Not anymore! And that is the point. Stanton, Halleck . . . you should see them scramble around here, trying to keep the details from my prying eyes. They don't feel I have any business trying to run this war. They see me as a leaking bucket, that if I am informed of anything resembling a secret, I will crow about it from the roof of the White House. There have been times, though, I admit . . . there were times when I was naive enough to have done just that. I have always made the mistake of trusting too much . . . of believing in the sincere intentions of those who profess to be my friends. It has, on occasion, been a problem."

Grant nodded, felt a smile, said, "Yes . . . I understand, sir. I may have done some of the same. It has cost me . . . I don't have much of a talent for business."

"Fortunately, it is not business that concerns us, Mr. Grant. And I *do* believe you have other talents, specifically, a talent for making a fight. And, there's the lesson, perhaps for both of us. *Make* the fight, don't talk about it. You cannot imagine . . . the volume of talk that flows around this place. Washington is like a barnyard full of braying mules . . . and that includes most of my cabinet. I'll make you a deal, Mr. Grant. You don't tell me how you plan to run this army, and I won't tell you how to run it either."

Grant sat back in the chair, looked for the smile, the joke. But Lincoln still stared at him, and he realized suddenly that Lincoln was serious.

"Mr. Grant, I have tried sometimes . . . to figure out what the army needs. I have tried to help where it seemed a great deal of help was needed. I have even made it official, sent out presidential decrees, written up special orders. Most of them have come out of frustration. And, likely, most of them have been wrong. But you cannot imagine what it is like to have all the authority to issue orders, and no power to see them carried out. But that will change now. I am giving you my word, Mr. Grant. If you take this army out and *use* it, I will give you whatever you ask for. And no one in this town will interfere. If they do, *that* is something I can control." Lincoln sat back in his chair, smiled now. "You were correct, Mr. Grant, there are a few ruffled feathers around here. Actually, there are times when I rather enjoy that . . . give some of these fine fat fellows a little indigestion. But make no mistake. There's nothing I have said to you, nothing implied in any of this, that does not carry the full power of the United States government. Tomorrow, there will be a ceremony. You will stand there and listen to me make a fool speech. . . ."

He paused, reached into his coat pocket, brought out a folded piece of paper, handed it to Grant.

"Here, that's my speech, that's what I'm going to say. I thought you should have some warning. My guess is, you don't dwell long and hard on grand public pronouncements. Neither do I. But you know they'll all be waiting for your profound thanks, how undeserving you are, all that. Especially those folks with the ruffled feathers, they'll look for you to toss them a fat piece of humble pie."

Grant opened the paper, scanned the words, was relieved to see only a few lines.

"I understand, sir. Thank you. I'll think of something . . . appropriate."

"Don't give it any more effort than you feel comfortable doing. It's not the words that mean anything. The Secretary of War will hand you a piece of paper that says you are a lieutenant general. There is a great deal of power in that . . . beyond the ceremony, beyond my speech, beyond what the newspapers make of it. How you use that power will likely determine if this nation survives. I am a great believer . . . no, let me put it another way. I have a great *love* for the Constitution. It is the thing I live for, it is the reason I sit here in this chair." He paused, then said, "The wisdom in *those* words, the power of an *idea*, how man should govern his affairs, how humanity should respect itself . . . it is what separates us from the caveman, from thousands of years of the select few making all the decisions for the rest of us. If we allow this rebellion to succeed—if we do not hold those ideas together for our children—then we sink back to the Dark Ages. We might as well send the Queen of England an apology for all the trouble we caused, ask if they will take us back. And we will deserve no better."

Lincoln leaned forward in his chair, and Grant felt the dark eyes pressing into him. He absorbed the words, felt the great weight, the enormous sadness.

Lincoln said in a low voice, "This is all so . . . new, the idea of one nation treating all of its citizens the same, that we do not divide ourselves into classes. I made a speech . . . last November, you may have read about it, the dedication of the National Cemetery at Gettysburg. It bedeviled me for the longest time . . . the first words . . . how to begin that, how to express that very thought, our *youth*. Europeans measure their history in centuries. The Chinese, my God, their system has been around for thousands of years. It is no wonder that this union, this precocious child of a country, is having such problems. There is so little to guide us, no example we can follow, we have no one to turn to except ourselves. The Constitution . . . this new idea . . . has been around for less than a century."

He paused, shook his head. "*Four score* . . . I don't usually go for the poetic."

Grant nodded, had heard of the speech, the few short minutes that so many were now quoting, had been surprised at the controversy in the newspapers, the opinions and politics swirling around that little speech like a hurricane. He thought of Washington. No, this is not where I want to be.

Lincoln looked at his hands, turned them over, flexed his long fingers, said in a low voice, "Perhaps we are simply arrogant, perhaps we have not earned the respect . . . perhaps the rest of the world should not take us seriously. But if we succeed, if we can end this rebellion and bring ourselves back together again, if we prove that this system works . . . we become a threat. What then will stop others, anywhere people allow themselves to *think*, people who do not wish to suffer under someone else's domination, who can use us for inspiration? What will stop this system from spreading all over the world? Can you imagine that, Mr. Grant? Can you imagine the power of that? I'm guessing there are many—call them what you will, kings, monarchs, despots— listening to reports of our war, staring out the windows of their enormous palaces, wondering if there is not some John Adams or Ben Franklin or George Washington somewhere out there, someone who will rise up out of muddy fields or the oppression of some small village and sweep them away." He looked at Grant, sat back in the chair, shook his head again.

"Forgive me, Mr. Grant. I am somewhat of an idealist. Some around here think I'm something of a lunatic. Comes with the job, I expect."

Grant said, "Quite all right, sir. I do understand the value . . . what we are fighting to keep. It's more than just the oath I took, or the rally around the flag."

Lincoln sat up straight, and Grant saw the flash of fire. Lincoln pounded a heavy hand on the table. "*Yes*, Mr. Grant. I have no doubt of that. I also have no doubt that you are aware that if we do not win this war—if we do not show the world that this system can *work*, that we can build a nation and manage our affairs from the power of an idea written on a piece of paper—then that idea will die out. And it must not die out. If we lose this war, something of great value will be lost with it. History will record that the idea did not work, that our piece of paper did not carry the power of a monarchy, the Constitution was not as efficient as the power of an elite ruling class, that it is acceptable for one class of human being to possess and dominate another. There is a significance to this that goes far beyond our borders, and far beyond our time."

Lincoln pushed back the chair, stood up, held out a hand, and Grant saw the hard glare in the eyes giving way to something softer, the warmth returning. Grant stood, took the hand, and Lincoln said, "And now, the matter is in *your* hands. Take good care, Mr. Grant."

T HE TENTS WERE IN THE DISTANCE, UP A LONG RISE. SPREAD around were the smaller tents of the army, a vast sea of white. Beyond, in the wide fields, the regiments were at drill, neat blue squares, flags, and the bright reflection from raised muskets. He rode with his staff now, a long cigar clamped in his mouth, the gray smoke swirling up and around the neat beard. Beside him was John Rawlins, a thin anxious man who never stopped moving, seemed to search the countryside, each turn of the road, each small rise, always alert. Grant smiled, thought, He's always waiting for something bad to happen. Grant had known Rawlins from the beginning of the war, the first organization of the regiments in Illinois. To the rest of the staff, the two men were a perfect blend—they were complete opposites.

Grant stared ahead, saw now the headquarters flag. Out in front, his security guard, a small squad of cavalry, reached the picket outpost, a small hut with no windows. A man in blue moved out into the road, then two more men emerged from the hut, watching the riders approach. The cavalry captain leaned over, said something Grant could not hear. Now several more of the guards appeared, moved into the road, all staring at Grant. There was a hushed shout, and quickly they jumped to attention, muskets hard on their shoulders. The cavalrymen moved aside, lined the edge of the road, and their captain saluted as Grant moved close. Grant saw the stripes on one sleeve, the sergeant of the guard, the man stiff and straight, and Grant reined the horse to a halt, said nothing, waited for Rawlins.

Rawlins said, "Sergeant, might we find General Meade on this road?"

The man stepped forward, still at attention, tried to keep his eyes to the front, but turned just slightly, stared up at Grant with his mouth open.

Rawlins said, "I say, Sergeant! Might we find—"

"Yes sir! Straight ahead, sir! The large flagpole . . . follow that, sir!"

They moved on, and Grant could hear the whispers now, the cavalrymen dismounting, the guards questioning, curious.

Rawlins said, "General, I will have a word with that sergeant. He should have kept his eyes to the front. We are not here to provide for their amusement."

Grant saw the large flag, a slow quiet slap against the tall wood pole, said, "This is a different army, Colonel. They are entitled to be curious about their new commander."

Rawlins slumped, said, "They think we are all backwoodsmen. That's all I hear. They think just because we come from the West, we have no . . . refinement."

Grant smiled, said nothing, thought of Mary Lincoln's strange compliment, *a bit less refinement*. "And what have we heard about them, Colonel? City boys with soft hands. It's natural, a bit of rivalry. Up to now it's been two wars, two armies, two different personalities."

"But we're not ruffians and heathens, sir!"

Grant smiled, still watched the flag. "Not all of us."

He saw the larger tents now, and men began to gather, snapping to attention. Grant stopped the horse, and an orderly stepped forward, a young private with no right arm. The man saluted with his left hand, held it, stared silently ahead.

Grant returned the salute, and the young man said, "If you will permit me, sir . . . I will take your horse."

Grant looked at the man's uniform, felt suddenly awkward, and he climbed down, stared at the boy's empty sleeve, thought, They are not *all* soft.

He looked around, realized now that many men had quietly moved closer, watching him, and no one spoke.

Rawlins stepped forward, scanned the uniforms for rank, said, "You . . . Major, this is General Grant. We are seeking General Meade."

The man was looking at Grant now, said, "Yes, sir. Welcome, sir. General Meade is back here, in his tent—"

"I'm right behind you, Major."

Grant saw Meade emerge from the tent, his wide black hat clamped down on his head. Meade stepped through the men, moved up to Grant, saluted. Grant returned the salute, saw Meade quickly scan him up and down with the look of a man whose stomach hurts. Meade said, "Welcome to the Army of the Potomac, General."

Grant nodded, glanced at the men watching him. "Thank you, General. This is Colonel Rawlins, my chief of staff." He turned to Rawlins, said, "Colonel, I wish to speak to General Meade. Introduce yourself and the rest of the staff to General Meade's people. Get acquainted."

Rawlins snapped his boots together, exaggerated formality, and said, "Yes sir! Right away, sir!"

Grant looked at him for a brief moment, thought, This may be more difficult than I thought. We have no need for posturing. He looked at Meade again, saw the same sour expression, and a small hint of impatience. Grant said, "General, might we have a word?"

Meade turned, held out an arm toward his tent, said flatly, "At your convenience, General. After you."

Grant moved to the tent, Meade followed him, and Grant stopped, looked back at Rawlins, who was still standing stiffly. "Colonel . . . at ease."

He moved into the tent, saw two chairs, a small desk. He sat in the smaller chair, leaned back, removed his hat, laid it on his knee, pointed to the larger chair, said, "General, please, take a seat. It isn't necessary for us to be . . . so formal. The air in this camp is thick enough as it is."

Meade sat, kept his hat on, said, "General Grant, this army is quite familiar with your successes in the West. Your promotion was applauded, by this command as much as anyone's. I hope you are able to do what Washington expects you to do. We all hope for that."

There was no enthusiasm in Meade's voice, and there was a silent moment. Grant said, "I assure you . . . there will be a fundamental change in the way we operate. Washington . . . the President is aware of the failure of the policy of allowing each army to operate independent of the others. There has been no coordination, no plan that involves all theaters of activity. That will change."

There was another silent moment, and Meade said, "I welcome . . . any changes the commanding general may wish to make. We have already made many changes here. I have tried to put the best men where they need to be. We have some good men in this army, the best . . . the best in the East. I am certain the general has his own strong feelings about his commanders in the West."

Grant felt suddenly annoyed. "General Meade, may we dispense with the rehearsed speeches? I don't care to be referred to in the third person."

Meade seemed surprised, glanced at Grant's hat, removed his own, put it on the desk, ran his fingers around the rim, and Grant saw something new in his face, relief. Meade said, "Then sir, if I may say—"

"Yes, General, you may say whatever you please."

"Thank you, sir. Washington has made it clear that they place little value on the ability of the Army of the Potomac to hold its own with your people in the West. There is the feeling in this camp that the Secretary, even the President, has sent you here to teach us how to fight. If my people seem a bit testy . . . it's because they don't care to be judged against your . . . against the army in the West. These men have fought some pretty hard fights. We haven't always done as well as we might have, but it is not the men. Washington must pass judgment on *my* leadership. I am prepared for that. But there has been a great deal of reorganization since Gettysburg. It has been my priority to put the best commanders where they can do the most good. We *do* have good people in this army. Good commanders are good commanders no matter where they happen to be fighting. This army sits under the shadow of Washington, and Washington can be . . . impatient. Most of what they know of your command is what they see on paper. Here, a week doesn't pass without some bloated dignitary parading through the camp asking my people how long it will take us to end this war. They go back to Washington and tell the newspapers we are sitting around doing nothing while our enemies boast of their great victories." Meade stood now, put his hat on his head, and Grant sat back, waited.

"Forgive me, sir. But if I don't . . . if you don't hear this now, you may never hear it. You may find out the hard way. The enemy here is not the enemy out West. I know something of command. Robert E. Lee is not Pemberton, he is not Bragg. No disrespect . . . your success out West is to be commended. But what flows through here from Washington, all we have been hearing is that we only need General Grant, and old Bobby Lee will turn tail. Well, sir, now you are here. Now you will find out what this army has known for a long time. It will take more than a few new corps commanders to march us into Richmond!" Meade was red-faced, breathing heavily.

Grant pointed to the chair, said, "Thank you, General. Please sit down."

Meade seemed surprised, looked at the chair and sat. Grant reached into his coat pocket, pulled out a cigar, then another pocket, moved deliberately, pulled out a small metal box, and Meade could see a piece of flint, Grant now striking it against a piece of steel. The sparks began to ignite a twist of cloth, and there was a plume of black smoke, the cloth began to burn, and Grant slowly lit the cigar. Meade watched him intently, seemed to calm down, and Grant held out the cigar, looked at it, said, "I don't know many of your people, but that will change. Some of the names are familiar, I knew some of them at the Point, some in Mexico. What I am depending on is coordination, that your army will work *with* the forces in the West. General Sherman has succeeded me in command of those forces, and I will be informing both of you what our new campaign will involve."

He stopped, saw Meade's expression change, saw surprise. "What is it, General?"

Meade removed his hat again, looked down. "Forgive me, sir, but it was my assumption that this command . . . that *I* would not be a part of your plans. It is no secret that the President has been impatient with my efforts."

"General Meade, you were in Mexico. Do you recall how rumors affected the army then?"

Meade looked at Grant now, and Grant could see the memories, Meade's own experiences in Mexico, coming back to him. Meade said, "We were cut off from the coast, from Washington, from everybody. General Scott's decision . . . to move the army inland on its own . . . we went through a different panic every night." Meade smiled now, the first change in his expression. "There were supposed to be ten thousand Mexicans waiting for us around every turn."

Grant nodded, smiled as well. "And behind us, and above us . . . Santa Anna was on top of every mountain, every water hole was poisoned, they moved like ghosts in the night."

They sat in silence for a moment, absorbed the sudden rush of memories. But Grant focused, pushed the thoughts of Mexico away, looked at Meade, and Meade was serious again, said, "I had thought the reports were reliable . . . that General Sherman would be assuming command of *this* army."

Grant was surprised, said, "Really? And where are you going? Tennessee?" Grant felt a sudden twinge of impatience.

Meade said, "I assumed . . . because of Washington's lack of enthusiasm for my performance . . . I would be relieved. I would only request . . . that you inform me without delay. Washington has always had a policy of dragging these things out, letting the commanders . . . sweat a bit. There seems to be some delight on the part of the Secretary to maintain suspense, and General Halleck has a habit of launching surprise attacks on his subordinates."

Grant felt a surge of anger, thought of Halleck, took a deep breath. "There is no surprise attack here. I have no intention of replacing you. We cannot run this army by trial and error. I know your record, I know how you command. I have no doubt you will continue to serve this army well. I have experienced the impatience of the Secretary. He makes grand judgments based on what he reads, not what he sees. And General Halleck is now . . ." He paused, had not thought of this before, of all the implications of his promotion. "General Halleck is now *my* subordinate. What pleases Washington is no longer to be your concern. What pleases *me* . . ." He paused, thought of his own words, felt the anger slip away, was suddenly embarrassed, surprised at himself. "Perhaps I should say that differently. . . ."

Meade slapped his hand hard on the desk. "No sir! You have made yourself quite clear. I am greatly relieved to hear that. We heard . . . the word was that your promotion might be . . . political. Something . . . for the newspapers to play with. I had thought, if you moved to Washington, you would probably . . ." He paused. "You would probably become one of *them*."

Grant looked at the cigar again, said, "I have been advised to maintain my headquarters in Washington. I have no intention of doing so. I had thought . . . perhaps I would go back out West, Nashville. But General Sherman knows me well, he knows what I expect of him, and he knows his opponent there. Here . . . it is different. I believe you are correct about General Lee. How we deal with *your* opponent will determine the outcome of the war."

Meade nodded, and Grant saw the enthusiasm building. Meade said, "Yes, Lee is all that stands between us and Richmond. If we can maneuver him away, move on Richmond again—"

Grant abruptly stood up, and Meade stopped, watched him. Grant tapped his hat against his leg, freeing a cloud of dust. His mind began to move, rethinking the plan he had sketched, hammered, and picked at for weeks. He paced for a moment, then stopped and looked at Meade.

"No. Our objective has *always* been Richmond. That is *not* our objective now. They are not beaten until *he* is beaten. If we seize Richmond, they will just move their government somewhere else. We will tie up our army occupying a place of small value and this war will go on for years. Richmond is a symbol, and three years ago this war was all about symbols. Symbols are for politicians and newspapers, something emotional to rally around. But if we have learned anything, it is that war is about fighting, about armies and guns and the death of men. As long as there are armies, there will be a war. I don't care about symbols. Our objective is *Lee*."

As the spring moved into Virginia and the roads hardened, Grant began to put his plan into words. In the West, Sherman would press Joe Johnston, and as in Virginia, the goal was Johnston's army, to draw him out into battle where Sherman's numbers could prevail. If Johnston were defeated, Atlanta would fall, and the Confederacy would be divided even further, the great railroad connections cut. But Grant understood that merely confronting Lee would not make Lee fight on anyone else's terms but his own, and so the plans in Virginia were more complicated. On the Virginia peninsula, a large force was assembled under the command of Ben Butler. Butler was no one's friend, had not distinguished himself as a great leader of troops, but he was a powerful political force in Washington, a man Lincoln could not afford to antagonize. If Grant did not place much value on Butler's abilities, Butler himself did, and so his influence and his ability to intimidate Washington meant that Grant had no choice but to put him in charge of a sizable command. Butler's objective was to move up the James River, pressuring Richmond from the east. If Richmond was too heavily defended, then Butler could move south of the James and assault the valuable railroad junction at Petersburg.

To the west of Lee's army, in the Shenandoah Valley, Grant assigned Franz Sigel to command a smaller force that would move south, up the valley, confronting whatever forces Lee had there. Early in the war Sigel had led the Eleventh Corps, made up mainly of New Yorkers and Pennsylvanians of German ancestry. He was a graduate of the German Military Academy, an experienced fighter who had emigrated himself because he happened to pick the wrong side in a brief revolution. He had seemed to be a natural choice to lead his former countrymen in the Eleventh, was an inspiration to the many Germans who had now taken up the Union cause. But he was undistinguished as a field commander, and he was replaced early in 1863 by Oliver Howard. It was Howard who would then carry the stain of the Eleventh, the men who would panic at Chancellorsville, collapsing from the surprise flank attack from Jackson, a failure that would always be theirs.

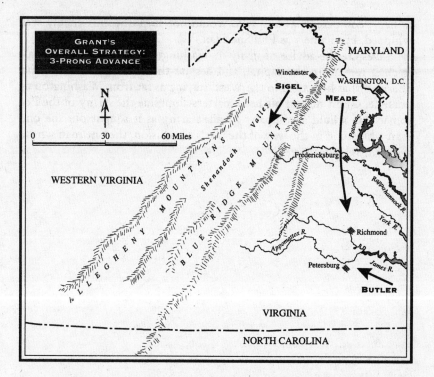

Since Howard had performed no better than Sigel, Sigel's removal had angered many of the immigrants even more, and Grant understood that Sigel's presence had value in drawing immigrants into the army. If he was undistinguished, at least he was already in place, in western Virginia. Sigel's assignment in the valley would be to prevent Lee from reinforcing himself from the Confederate troops there. If Sigel moved hard into Virginia's most fertile and productive farmland, it was a threat Lee could not ignore.

Grant made one more major change. The Federal army had never made the best use of its cavalry, and Jeb Stuart had embarrassed his blue counterparts consistently. As the war had gone on, the blue horsemen learned more about their enemy and his successes, and gradually they changed the way they fought. But the high command had still not understood fully the value of cavalry, and often they were held in the rear, guarding wagon trains or sent far off on useless raids. Grant intended to change that. In the West there was one division commander, a man who led infantry, who Grant believed could be given the new responsibility of commanding horsemen. The man had built a reputation as fiery, competent, as one who would not stop until his enemy was whipped. His name was Phil Sheridan.

Despite the advice of many in Washington that the new general-in-chief remain in the capital, and despite the advice from his friend Sherman that he return to the West, staying as far from Washington as possible, Grant moved his headquarters alongside the Army of the Potomac. He would accompany Meade's army as it sought out the one man who stood in the way of the war's conclusion, the one man whose army must be destroyed.

8. LEE

MAY 1864

THE COURIERS CAME NOW AT REGULAR INTERVALS, STUART'S messengers bringing a steady stream of information. The hard words for Stuart's failure at Gettysburg had long faded from the newspapers, and if they mentioned Gettysburg at all now, if the papers still had a bitter need to find fault, the focus was shifting more in Longstreet's direction. Stuart was the great and gallant hero, the mention of the name always painting an inspiring picture in the minds of the people, the dashing cavalryman, the plumed hat, mocking and humiliating the enemy's inept horsemen. What had flickered through the newspapers, the hint of improper behavior, a brief public scolding for the playful ride around the enemy, was forgotten now by the reality of what the new year would bring.

The papers now gave more energy to new outrage against Lincoln, whose call for seven hundred thousand *new* troops demonstrated the aggressiveness of this unrelenting man who would still send his armies into their country. There was growing frustration with the length of the war, the casual confidence of a quick victory long erased. If blame had to be placed for that, then the angry headlines and political speeches were growing openly hostile toward Jefferson Davis as well, as though Davis himself was responsible for the great disparity in strength, the increasing void between the vast power and fertility of the North and the creeping starvation and emptiness of the South.

But there were some who did not pay much attention to the rants in the papers, who knew something of tactics and strategy, who remembered Gettysburg as more than some vague and horrible disaster. The conversations were brief and private, and even in Stuart's camp the men understood that this brash and self-assured cavalier had for once let his commander down.

Stuart never spoke of it, but his staff knew something was different, noted something more serious, that he was more sober, his playful moods less prevalent. It had been nearly a year, but Stuart kept the memories fresh in his mind. His cavalry had finally returned to Lee's army late in the fight at Gettysburg, but the damage had been done, the ground chosen for them by an enemy Lee was not ready to fight, the tide already turned against them. Had Stuart been where Lee needed him to be, the fight around Gettysburg might not have happened at all; they could have kept Meade at bay, moved farther into the enemy's country, into the rich farmlands where the army could have sustained itself as long as it had to. Then, they could have struck in any direction, Philadelphia, Baltimore, and the panic in the northern cities, the reality that the bloody fields would be their own, could have put enough pressure on Washington to make the peace.

Stuart did not dwell on politics, but he had heard the talk, the bruises on his reputation. His anger at the "insults" had quickly faded. It was that one night that stayed with him, and he would lie awake staring up at bright stars, would focus on that, riding into Lee's headquarters with all the boisterous pageantry that always swept along with him. He'd expected the face of a relieved parent, the fatherly warmth Lee had shared with him since he was a cadet at West Point, the enthusiasm for the return of the favorite son, but he saw instead a hard redfaced anger, a look he'd never seen before, Lee fighting himself to hold it down. The warmth was replaced by the deep chill of disappointment. It was something Stuart would never forget.

Now, the couriers went out toward headquarters at all hours with the smallest bit of new information. Lee would never be blind again.

L EE SAT AT HIS SMALL DESK, READ THE REPORTS. IT WAS CONfirmed now, the Federal Ninth Corps, Burnside's troops, had moved east, had left their position around Knoxville and were on the trains, and very soon would add to the strength of Meade's army. He put the paper down, realizing it would be in Virginia after all. He stood, walked to the opening in the tent, stared out down the wide hill, saw his men milling through their camps, some at drill, some gathered at the fires.

Taylor, sitting at a small table out in the open, saw him, and Lee saw the line of officers and a few privates waiting patiently, the daily complaints and requests. The look on Taylor's face was a silent question: Do you need me? Lee shook his head, stepped into the open, suddenly felt the urge for coffee, moved toward the mess wagon. He saw Marshall now, the young man moving toward him, and Lee smiled as he walked; there was always something about Marshall that made him smile. He was young, nearly as young as Taylor, wore small round glasses that made him resemble a schoolboy, studious and efficient.

Marshall stopped, saw Lee focused on the wagon, said, "General, may I get you something?"

Lee said, "No, Major, quite all right. Just taking a bit of a break."

Lee reached the wagon, and the mess sergeant had a cup ready, poured a thick black liquid from a tin pot, handed it slowly to Lee and said quietly, so as not to disturb his thoughts, "Sir."

Lee took the cup and drew it up, caught the rising steam, breathed it in. The man held out a small metal box, and Lee took a spoon from it, scooped it full of the brown crystals, stirred the hard sugar into the cup. He stared at the thick swirl, slowly took a sip, felt his tongue curl at the bitterness, then glanced up at the sergeant, who was smiling, proud of his brew. Lee nodded, tried to smile, thought, Maybe . . . more sugar. The sergeant still held the box out, and Lee thought, No, we must make do . . . even the little things. He put the spoon back in the box, turned toward his tent, looked again into the cup. The men do not have the luxury of coffee, he thought, not real coffee anyway. He recalled seeing men grinding up straw and corn husks, peanut shells and tree bark, anything that could be boiled into a hot black liquid. He knew they were trading with the Yankees, that when the armies were close, the men along the picket lines would make their own quiet armistice, swapping their tobacco for coffee, newspapers for hardtack. He did not approve, but would not give the order to stop. The pickets know more than the rest of us, he thought. They are so close, and so they see it clearly.

It had taken him a long time to understand what the men on the front lines had accepted long ago. But Lee still saw the faces, knew the names, had served with so many of them, fought with them in Mexico, chased Comanches with them in Texas, had watched many of them work their way through West Point. The foot soldiers had no guilt, no difficulty killing the men in blue, no confusion about whether the Yankees were indeed the enemy. It is our sad duty, but I cannot think of them that way, Lee reflected. They are simply . . . those people.

He had believed from the beginning that there was a difference, something superior in his men that went beyond what they brought to the battlefield. But despite the poor commanders, the blue soldier had proven he would fight, and that if God gave him the chance, he would *win* the fight. Lee had finally begun to understand that the hand of God might cover more than just his army. Those boys, those other fellows, were not that different from them after all.

He thought, But God is still with us, He still watches over us, and He is still guiding us. If He is guiding them as well, if He puts the good fight in them, it is to test us, test our resolve. In the end, He will judge us for that, for our heart, for how we do our duty.

The wave of religious spirit had again swept through the winter camps. Just as the year before, the revival tents had spread out all through the army, the men gathering in great numbers before the renewed enthusiasm of the chaplains. There had been civilian visitors as well, preachers, men of great fiery oration. It was the perfect way for the men to spend the bleak winter, to relieve the boredom by the strengthening of their faith.

He looked northward, over the wide bleak fields, over distant rolling hills. It was not the same over there . . . across the river. They are such a mix of people, so little in common with us . . . even with each other. But even before Gettysburg he had been surprised, began to see something new in the spirit of the blue soldiers, the men who charged hard into his guns. He thought of the vast horror of the stone wall at Fredericksburg, how they still came, wave after wave. They do not fight for the same cause, he thought, they are not defending against an invader, they do not fight to protect their homes, but still . . . *they fight*.

He had not thought it possible that this would still go on. He'd assumed that after all the bloody fights, and so many utter defeats, those fellows would not have the stomach for this, they would simply go home. He'd thought it would come from the soldiers themselves, the men who saw the horrors, knew the fear, the panic, the sickening loss. He thought they would finally say, "*Enough,* there is no good reason for this, we are dying for fat men in silk suits who hide in clean white buildings." The blue lines would thin, the enthusiasm for the fight draining away, and with that, the Federal army would cease to be.

He had not often seen them up close, but he understood who they were. He'd seen many prisoners, thought of the faces, the bitter sadness of men who were out of the fight. Yet they do not make the fight, he thought. It is not the foot soldier who brings this war against us. They are farmers and laborers and clerks, and surely they feel just as we do, that we all have the right to be left alone. We do not threaten their cities, we do not seek to destroy their homes, we do not blockade their ports or starve their families. Yet they are still inspired . . . by what? It is not the inspiration that comes from great leadership. There has never been great leadership. It was not Meade who turned us away in Pennsylvania. We were beaten by our own mistakes, and the fight of their soldiers. Now, Washington has given them a new commander, and like all the rest, he must bring them into our guns again. But this time, they will be different . . . they will know what it feels like to *win*.

He drank from the cup again, ignored the bitterness, stared out at the camps of his men, thought, We are fighting for our independence, and that is the greatest fight there can be. Throughout the winter he had thought of his men as akin to the men at Valley Forge, the small shivering army of George Washington, praying and enduring through the misery of the elements, surviving, somehow, so they could take the fight to the enemy again. Washington had prevailed against great odds, against the better equipped army of a great empire. It had always inspired him, the great fight against long odds, the success against a powerful enemy. There is not much difference between Washington's army and ours, he mused. We are fighting, after all, for the same reasons, for the same cause. And, we *can* succeed. With the weather warming, the roads drying out, the army is rested, morale is high, and they are ready again.

He knew the First Corps was coming back, that Longstreet was already bringing them out of Tennessee, would be close very soon. That would bring the numbers back up, make Lee as strong as he would ever be. Now the reports from Stuart confirmed he was right, the fight would be *here*. But this time it could be very different, this time the Federals would be led by someone who did not put his picture in the newspapers, who did not make grand speeches. He tried to remember the face, the name a vague memory from long ago, a brief meeting in Mexico, but there was nothing that brought that back to him, nothing to separate the name "Grant" from so many others. He knew only that this man had risen to the top, that something had so inspired Lincoln that he'd given this man complete control.

He walked to his tent, saw Taylor signing papers, heard his name called, soldiers trying for some piece of personal attention, but he did not respond, moved into the tent. He looked at the latest message from Stuart, saw several more scattered on the table. Understanding what Stuart was doing, the overefficiency, he smiled, thought, General, don't wear out your horses.

He sat, moved the papers into a single pile, set the cup down, stared away at nothing. He began to think of moving the army, the new defense, the new commanders, felt relief that Longstreet was coming back. Yes, you are still my warhorse. And I will need you, and I will need General Stuart. He looked out through the opening in the tent, could see across the far fields, saw the large dark mound of Clark Mountain rising in the distance, a dull intrusion into the blue sky, thought, I should go up there, speak to the lookouts. Grant's army will not sit still for long. And we must be prepared.

He emptied the cup, felt the bitterness filling him, felt the familiar twist in his gut, the surge of energy for the new fight. He stood then, moved out of the tent, thought, If Grant is in Virginia, then he is here because *I* am here. . . .

THEY WAITED FOR HIM ON THE WIDE HILL, WATCHED HIM QUI-etly as he rode toward them, Traveller carrying him through the small trees, the trail winding between large flat rocks. He had a fresh energy, felt better than he had in weeks, had pushed the horse hard up the hill, felt the thrill of the hard ride. His staff, whom he'd left behind, were just now coming into view. He gazed across the summit of the hill, felt the coolness, saw the flowers, God's hand draped across the land in rich green patches, the new growth of spring. The horse was breathing hard, and he leaned over, patted the animal's neck, gave a small laugh.

Clark Mountain was really a large flat hill, but it loomed high above the Rapidan River and was ideal for an observation post. The lookouts themselves began to gather now, staying back behind the small group of commanders, and Lee halted the horse, dismounted, instinctively looked at the larger man, standing in front of the others.

"General Longstreet, you are looking well this morning."

Longstreet made a short bow, held a short pipe in one hand, smiled briefly. He knew Lee's moods, had not seen this one for a long while, said only, "General Lee."

Behind Longstreet, Lee saw the others watching him still, and no one would speak until he'd acknowledged them. He was used to this courtesy now, understood the formality of rank, looked to the tall thin man behind Longstreet who was moving forward gingerly on the wooden leg, stepping awkwardly across the uneven rock.

"General Ewell—"

"Sir!" Ewell snapped to attention, saluted, and Lee returned it.

Then Lee saw a smaller man, the red beard neatly trimmed, the old hat propped slightly askew. "General Hill . . ." He paused, hesitated to use the words that seemed to come naturally when greeting Hill. "Are you well today, General?"

Hill glanced at Longstreet, who did not look at him, and Lee knew this was a sensitive point, that Hill was aware of the talk in the camps of the other commanders, the longstanding feud with Longstreet never really resolved. Hill's frequent illnesses had become well-known, and many were saying it was only when the big fight was coming that he would withdraw to his cot. Hill stood straight, said, "Yes, General. I am quite well."

Lee made small greetings to the others, saw the sour expression of Jubal Early, Ewell's division commander, an outspoken and unpopular man, and more recently the man who was seen as the true commander of Ewell's Second Corps, the strength behind the weakening control of Ewell.

Ewell understood that his reputation had diminished. Under Jackson, early in the war, he'd led his division with great fire, had built affection from his men by often putting himself where a commander had no business going, right on the line, moving into the fight beside his men. The bravado had cost him a leg, and with that loss something else had gone out of him as well, something unexpected. After Jackson's death, when Ewell and Hill were promoted to inherit the divided command, Ewell had seen his first great opportunity at Gettysburg, staring down at him from the top of Cemetery Hill. Lee knew, as did the others, that Ewell had not performed, had stared up at the weak Federal defenses on the hill and done nothing. Even when his commanders had offered to assault the key position on their own responsibility, Ewell held them back, suddenly lost the great fire Jackson had always relied on. More recently, Ewell had married, moved his wife into his headquarters, and, if his strength had seemed to drain away with the loss of the leg, whatever control he still held over his staff now came from his wife. It was an odd and uncomfortable experience for his men to realize that Ewell was no longer in command, that he had served Jackson so well because he was best suited to be under the domination of someone else. With Jackson gone, many in the field knew it was now Early. In camp, the staff knew it was his wife.

Lee walked a few steps toward the north face of the hill, raised his field glasses. Hill moved closer, and Lee could feel him there, silent, trying to absorb something from him. It was painful and obvious that Hill's confidence was still badly bruised by the disaster at Bristoe Station, and at every opportunity now he seemed to hover close to Lee, seeking ... Lee wasn't sure what, but he felt the neediness, the pull at him. Lee gazed through the glasses, thought, You will have your chance, General. There will be time for amends.

The others raised field glasses as well, an exercise of respect since they had already seen what Lee was now viewing. Across the river, a vast sea of white specks, the tents of Grant's enormous army, spread out over the bare fields. It had been a familiar scene for weeks now, but there was something new, the reason the corps commanders were here, why they would meet on this tall hill. There was a swarm of activity all through the neat squares of white; slowly the neat checkerboard was distorting, the tents disappearing. Grant was preparing to move.

Lee had read reports, some from the northern papers, some from Stuart, that the Federal army was set to begin its campaign. Ewell's corps was along the river below them, guarding against a crossing that could bring Grant straight at Lee's army, but Lee knew it would not be like that, Grant would not expose himself to his army's strength. Grant had two choices. If he moved out to the left, to the west, and came across the Rapidan upstream, he could threaten to move on the Shenandoah, or cut the rail lines that fed the Confederate army. But that would take Grant far from his own supply lines, from the security of the big rivers in the east. The only other route south would be downstream, at the fords that had been used by Hooker's army a year ago, Germanna and Ely, the routes that led straight down into the Wilderness.

Lee said nothing, and the others were watching him again, already knew what the activity across the river would mean. Lee turned, gradually scanned the open ground to the northeast, then down across the river and across the thickets and dense growth of the Wilderness. He put the glasses down, stared out, thought, Yes, it will have to happen there. He did not feel an instinct about Grant as he had about so many of the others, but everything he had read, every piece of information he could find, told him that this man would not use trickery and deceit. His army was too large and too cumbersome, and so they would advance by the shortest route, the straight line. The straight line toward Richmond was down through the Wilderness. There were other reasons as well. As Grant moved south, he would be between the Confederate army and Fredericksburg, and at Fredericksburg the good roads and the Rappahannock could still provide a good supply line for the Federal troops. And if they move quickly and get below us, Lee thought, we will have a serious problem.

Lee knew he would not receive help from Davis, that the president was as concerned as he had ever been with administering the army, about promotions and transfers of officers. Davis had even moved his friend Braxton Bragg to Richmond, put the despised Bragg in the only place where those who so disliked him could not have an effect—right beside Davis as his principal adviser. The defenses of Richmond were now manned by troops that belonged to Lee's army, including what was left of Pickett's division, the force that had been so decimated at Gettysburg.

More of Lee's troops were tied up in North Carolina, even though Lee himself had information that the Federals there had already moved north, to reinforce Grant's forces on the peninsula east of Richmond. Davis's response to Lee's warnings about the new threat to Richmond was to create a new military department, with jurisdiction south of the James River. The command of all the territory below Richmond was given to the one man who had repeatedly shown a clear envy of Lee's prominence and popularity, and so could not be relied on to lend support to Lee's effort. The job was given to the man whose greatest notoriety came from commanding the firing on Fort Sumter: P.G.T. Beauregard.

Lee still stared out across the Wilderness, did not search for detail, for any landmark, because even from this vantage point, there was none. It was the same dense mass that had swallowed up Joe Hooker's army, and somewhere in those vast green thickets, along some dim trail, was the spot where Jackson had fallen. Jackson had taken one risk too many, had ridden too far forward on a night when both exhausted armies held tight to their guns, would respond with sudden manic violence to any sound. One sound had been the thundering hoofbeats of Jackson and his staff.

Lee turned his head to the north again, did not look down toward Grant's army, just out to the open sky, thought, There is no resting place . . . no sacred ground. We must do it all again, here. If Grant has the numbers, the strength, we have the advantage of knowing the ground, of knowing how that terrible bloody place can paralyze an army, the unseen enemy, the sounds of the fight echoing across the creeks and hollows, no point of reference, no way to know who is in front of you, or beside you . . . or behind you.

He still said nothing, and they began to move closer to him, expecting him to discuss the plan, what he would ask them to do. He felt a sudden lightness, felt his mind open up, stared out into the clear blue and felt like he could step out, off the hill, away from it all. He felt drawn by God, that familiar sense that God was close to them. He had felt like this before, at Manassas, when he could see the panorama of Pope's army swept from the field by his men, and at Fredericksburg, his invincible line destroying the enemy's continuing assaults. But there was also the last day at Gettysburg, when he sat on the big horse and watched his men march in those beautiful strong lines across that wide field, moving ever closer to that one clump of trees, a mile of wide-open glory, and he'd felt God beside him as he waved them forward through the smoke and brilliant flashes of light, and waited for the smoke to clear knowing they were up and over the Federal lines. But when the smoke cleared it was not like that at all, and those who had survived came slowly back across the field, shattered and beaten, and God was not beside him.

He felt a sudden shock, blinked hard, sensed the men around him again. He felt his breath choke in his throat and put his hand on his chest, focused, brought himself back to this place. He turned, saw Longstreet beside him, watching him, concern in the blue eyes. But Longstreet said nothing. Lee thought, He does not believe God was with us that day. They were his men, and he did not want them to go. But I believed they would prevail, they could do anything. It had to be something in us . . . in our will. We cannot lose that, it is what God wants from us. We must not lose faith. Grant is just another test. God is watching us to see if the will is still there. It *is* still there.

He took another deep breath, said, "General, you know this man. Will he do what we suppose him to do?"

Longstreet took the pipe from his mouth, seemed surprised at the question. "Grant? Well, yes, I don't believe Sam Grant is a very complicated man." Longstreet stared out toward the north, thought for a moment, said, "I believe there is one thing we may depend on. Once he begins to move, once he is in front of us, we had better be prepared to stay there awhile. He will not go away until we *make* him go away."

Lee said nothing, looking out to the north again, thought, If Grant is not complicated, then our job will be easier. We do not have the strength to strike him where he sits, so we must let him come to us, commit himself, at a time and place of his own choosing. But there has always been a mistake, sooner or later, with all of them. It does not matter if Grant is different from McClellan, or Burnside, or Hooker. He will make a mistake. God will provide. . . .

Lee raised his arm, pointed out to the east, toward the Wilderness. "He will cross there . . . at Ely's or Germanna. We must focus our attention there."

There were nods, low comments, and they waited, expected him to say more. But he did not feel like making plans, issuing the orders, the small details that these men would need. He felt something much larger was already in motion around them, the plan already in place, inevitable and certain. Abruptly, he turned, moved to the horse, mounted. They watched him, silent, curious, and he looked away, out toward the place where Jackson had fallen, and he felt the glare of the sharp blue eyes, knew Jackson was still there, would still help them. Yes, slow them down, General, he thought, hold them there and it will not matter if he has the numbers and the guns. It will not be a fair fight. The advantage will be ours.

9. GRANT

MAY 4, 1864

THERE WAS MOTION EVERYWHERE, HORSES AND WAGONS, GUNS and men. He rode past a row of supply wagons, each marked with the insignia of their corps, the three-leaf clover of Hancock's Second, the Maltese cross of Warren's Fifth, Sedgwick's Sixth with the St. Andrew's cross.

He passed the wagon train now, the wagons moving farther to the east, the route that would take them out of harm's way, down across the river closer to Fredericksburg. He could see the river now, the thick columns of blue soldiers crossing on pontoon bridges. He pulled the horse off the road, moved to a small rise. The staff followed, settled behind him, with only Rawlins close by.

He glanced up, saw the stark bright sky, the blazing sun. It was a perfect day, and he looked again at the river, could even see the reflection on the water, the line of troops magnified, the river sparkling with the reflections from the rows of muskets.

He was between the Fifth and Sixth Corps, watching them cross Germanna Ford. He knew that to the east Hancock was crossing at Ely's, and it was just like this, quiet and efficient, the men moving at a good pace, that they would soon be south of the river. Even Burnside was in position above them. The Ninth Corps, waiting for the order, would guard the north side of the river until the rest of them were across. Then Burnside too would move down, strengthening the army, which was already very strong. Grant thought of the numbers, nearly 140,000, the same number Joe Hooker had a year ago, but Hooker had spread them out, an elaborate plan that relied on coordination and communication, and the result was a disaster.

No, he thought, we will pass by Chancellorsville, and it will

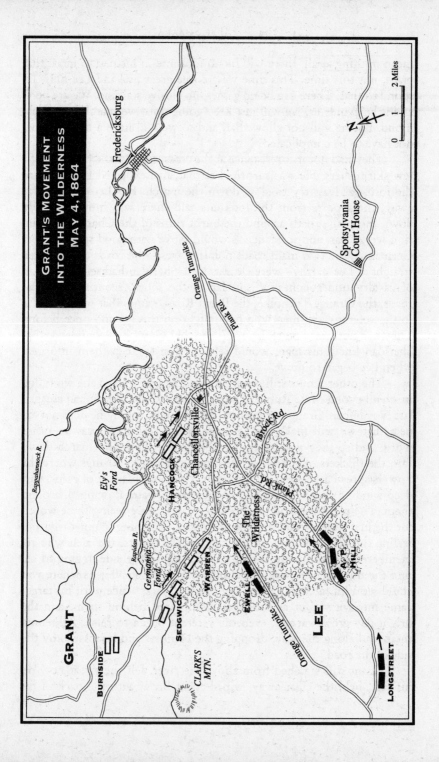

GRANT'S MOVEMENT
INTO THE WILDERNESS
MAY 4, 1864

mean nothing at all, there will be no footnote in history to mark that place, not this time. This time we are one great fist, and Lee must respond to that. There can be no games, no elusive stalking. We are here, and if he avoids us, we will just keep going until we march into Richmond. But he will not allow that, and so we will have a fight. It does not have to be complicated.

They had not met resistance at the crossings, just the potshots of a few skirmishers. He was surprised at that, had expected Lee to guard the fords, at least try to slow down the march. But Lee was still far away, the reports from the lookouts said there was simply nobody down there, the roads around the burnt ruins of the Chancellor mansion were clear, and so Hancock would move with good speed. Below Germanna, the two main roads pointing west—the roads that pointed straight at Lee's army—were clear as well. Sheridan had sent a division of cavalry under James Wilson far to the south, scouting the vital roads, the Orange Turnpike, the Plank Road, names that were familiar to the veterans, the men who had fought on this ground once before. They had not heard much from Wilson, but Grant had confidence that Sheridan knew his man, would rely on him to keep them informed when Lee began to move.

The other scouts still reported that Lee was well to the west, dug in even beyond Mine Run, the same ground where Meade had escaped last November. Grant marveled at that, thought, Surely he does not expect that we will make that mistake again? Yet there was no other word, and so they would see no rebels this day, would march down into the thickets of the Wilderness, past the small clearings where the flowers spread across the deep green in a glorious blanket of color, past deep winding creeks, the sound of the unseen water flowing all around them. The men who had not been here, who were seeing these woods for the first time, would stare up at the sky, marching in quiet rhythm, feeling the delicious heat on their faces. The others, the men who remembered Jackson, would glance nervously to the side, trying to see into the thick brush, peeking instinctively at the small gaps where you could see a bit farther, a place where a man might hide until his target came into view. But as the river disappeared behind them, and the bright day grew warmer, even the veterans began to relax, lightening their load along the way, dropping the blankets and knapsacks by the side of the road.

Grant still watched from above the river, felt the sweat now on his face, held the cigar away, wiped at his brow with the back of his gloved hand. He did not like the gloves, the dull yellow cotton, preferred the feel of the leather straps in his bare hands. They were a gift, and Rawlins had insisted they would make the necessary impression. He wore a gold braid on his hat, another change, never thought much about the uniform, but that was Rawlins again, the concern for appearances. Grant had to tell himself it mattered, that the men would look to see the dashing figure of the commanding general, and they would expect some pomp, some excess of finery. The gold braid was his only grudging concession to that. He tasted the cigar again, also a gift, the dark aroma filling him, the wonderful smoke drifting to his eyes, his nose, and he thought, Yes, there is one good thing about being the commanding general, beyond the pageantry, the ridiculous vanity, something few of them would ever understand. You *can* get the best cigars.

There was motion in the water, a row of horsemen splashing across the river, the soldiers on the bridges calling out, wet protests, some laughing. Grant watched them come, saw now it was Sheridan.

There had been comments about the appointment, this small man with the small round face. He wore a strange box hat and looked more often like an Italian street vendor than a commander of troops, but Grant knew his habits well, had seen him take his division up the hill at Chattanooga, climbing the ragged face of Missionary Ridge, and they did not stop until they were at the top, Bragg's army melting away in front of them. There had even been a question about following orders, whether Sheridan had ignored his instructions, should never have pushed his men that far up the hill; but Sheridan made no excuses, no explanations. The question quickly faded away, because Grant understood that when the fight is in front of you, and the enemy is handing you the high ground, there is great value in a commander who does not halt his men to clarify his orders. Grant never doubted that Sheridan could handle command of the cavalry corps, that nothing would be lost by the new assignment. He was a superb horseman, and was grateful to be brought east to confront Jeb Stuart.

Sheridan rode toward Grant, his men filing out neatly on either side of him. Sheridan saluted, and Grant could see he was furious. "Sir! We have been ordered . . . General Meade has ordered . . ." He was red-faced and looked down for a moment.

Grant said, "General, please proceed. Is there a problem?"

Sheridan closed his eyes, clamped down, seemed to be fighting for control. "Sir, General Meade has ordered most of my men to the east, toward Fredericksburg. There are reports that some of the enemy's horsemen have been located in that area. General Meade seems to believe that the wagon trains may be in jeopardy." Sheridan took a deep breath.

Grant motioned at him with the cigar. "Yes, so . . . what is your concern, General?"

"Sir! General Meade has us guarding the wagon trains! Surely the commanding general understands that we can better serve the army by spreading out farther to the south, protecting the roads. We have yet to locate any sizable force of the enemy, and we aren't likely to if we are sitting at Fredericksburg."

Grant glanced at Rawlins, could feel his chief of staff shifting nervously on the horse, impatiently waiting for an opening, the appropriate time for comment. Grant said, "You have something to say, Colonel?"

Rawlins tried to look surprised, said, "Oh . . . well, sir, if I may offer. A sizable portion of General Sheridan's men are already in position down below us. General Wilson is protecting our right flank. I had thought General Sheridan would be pleased that his men are, in fact, being used in valuable service."

Grant waited, wondered if the flow of words from Rawlins had ended.

Sheridan jumped in and said, "Sir, General Wilson is new to command. If it had been my decision, *his* division would guard the wagons. It is the smallest division in the corps. Now, that is not possible. General Meade insists, sir, that the bulk of my command stay to the east. He has . . . pardon me, sir, but General Meade is giving great credibility to the threat from Stuart. I have seen nothing to indicate this threat exists."

There was a silent pause, and Grant said, "General, has General Wilson located the enemy's cavalry?"

Sheridan looked down, seemed suddenly embarrassed. "I . . . don't know, sir. I have not received word from General Wilson in . . . some time."

"Well, then, until you do, I would tend to go with General Meade's instincts. He has been here before, he has dealt with Stuart before. Unless you can determine with certainty that his orders are a mistake . . . I would suggest you obey them."

Sheridan nodded, said, "Yes, you are correct of course, sir. I will send word to General Wilson to inform us of any contact with Stuart. I am convinced we will not find him at Fredericksburg. If you will excuse me, sir." Sheridan saluted, turned the horse, and the troops followed after him, thundering down to the river, splashing across.

Grant saw a row of guns now, moving onto the bridge.

Rawlins smiled, said, "General Sheridan is a might small for a job this big, wouldn't you say, sir?"

Grant did not smile at the joke, looked briefly at Rawlins, then watched the bridges again, the swaying motion of the pontoons under the great weight of the big guns.

"Colonel, General Sheridan will be big enough for all of us before this is through."

T HERE WERE FEW CLEARINGS, BUT THEY HAD FOUND ONE OPEN mound, rising above the level of the trees that spread out all around them, and he had chosen the spot for his headquarters. Meade had set up his tents nearby, and by midday the three corps were completely across the river, spread far along the roads that cut through the Wilderness.

There was a small house, long abandoned, a few pieces of furniture remaining, and Grant would use it only for meetings, was more comfortable in the tent. He leaned against a tall fat tree stump, pulled a fresh cigar from his coat. Meade's camp was slightly below him, and Grant smiled at that. Meade had clearly given thought to the elevation of the headquarters tents, and made sure he was not higher up the rise than Grant.

But it was the flag that caught Grant's attention. Meade had been given a new one, a field of deep lavender, with the stark likeness of a golden eagle in the center, circled with silver. Grant stared at it, shook his head, saw Meade now coming up the hill toward him. He thought, Let it go. Meade was never predictable, you never knew how he would react to anything. The breeze picked up, and the flag stood out straight, grand and regal. Grant couldn't resist the urge, pointed with the cigar, said to Meade, "What's this . . . are we in the presence of Imperial Caesar?"

Meade turned, looked up at the flag, and Grant saw him frown, a look Grant was becoming familiar with now. Meade carried a small folding chair, sat down, settled the chair into the soft ground. "If it is offensive . . . I can remove it."

"Not at all, it lends an air of . . . the majestic. Not sure Secretary

Stanton would approve. If he pays us a visit, I would suggest you stow it away. He would likely take it home with him." Grant put the cigar in his mouth, hid a smile.

There was activity below them, couriers beginning to arrive, breathless horsemen, the staff moving to meet them. Grant saw one officer bringing a man up the hill toward him, and the staff officer said, "General, excuse me, sir, this man has information about the enemy's position."

Grant looked at the man, had expected to see a cavalry uniform, but saw infantry, a captain. The man looked at Grant, then Meade, seemed to gulp. Meade leaned back in the chair, said, "What do you have for us, son?"

"From General Warren, sir . . . I'm to tell you that his men are halting per orders, sir, and are on the Orange Turnpike. There is no sign of the enemy in our front, sir." There was a pause. Grant saw other staff officers moving closer, the anticipation of hearing some piece of real news.

Meade said, "That's it? That's Warren's report? What about the cavalry . . . they're supposed to be on his flank."

"Uh, no sir, we haven't seen any cavalry, not since early this morning. There's nobody, sir. No horses, no rebs."

Meade looked at Grant, and Grant turned, moved toward his tent, said quietly, "General, a moment, if you please . . ."

Meade stood, said, "Well, Captain, go on back to General Warren and tell him to keep an eye out. Lee's not just going to watch us walk all the way to Richmond."

Meade moved behind Grant and they ducked into the tent. Grant sat on a small chair, pointed at another, and Meade sat down. Grant held the cigar in his hand, looked at Meade, said, "Where is he?"

Meade thought, then said, "Lee?"

"Well, Lee too. I'm talking about Wilson. The cavalry. Where are the reports?"

Meade was suddenly nervous, wrapped his fingers around his knees, gripped hard. "I will send someone down there. It is possible—in this infernal place—he is lost."

Grant watched him quietly, said slowly, "It is also possible that he has his hands full of a fight. Lee knows where we are, this is his ground. Wilson's not that good of a horseman to sneak up on him. And he sure isn't going to sneak up on Stuart."

Meade nodded, said, "We should bring the army together, tighten up. Is Burnside expected tonight?"

"He's supposed to be across the river by dark. We'll see about that, but I'm not concerned about General Burnside right now. I'm much more concerned with how far Lee will let us go before he does something."

"Mine Run . . . he must be waiting for us there."

Grant thought, Yes, General, he would like us to make your mistake again, and you would like to have a second chance. He leaned back in the chair, said, "No. He cannot afford to just wait for us. If we move on to the south, we will have slipped by him and have a clear shot at Richmond, and he will not allow that. He has to *move*, to come at us. The only question is . . . when."

Meade seemed puzzled, said, "You want us to wait for him? *Here?* Shouldn't we keep going? He *wants* us to stay here. This is the best place for him to attack."

Grant nodded. "Yes. And so we will let him. General Meade, we cannot defeat him if we cannot find him. He knows where we are, and he has three choices. He can retreat, move himself closer to Richmond and wait for us again; he can sit still and watch us go by; or he can attack. He has not built this tiresome godlike reputation by retreating or sitting still. He will come. And every time he comes, he loses more and more of his army. It is a simple case of mathematics."

Meade stared at Grant, nodded slowly and said, "But I would feel better if I knew where . . . I do not like surprises."

Grant thought now of Sheridan, but would not ask; there was no real danger yet, the numbers were too strong, the lines too compact. Lee would have to come in face-to-face, line against line, and Grant saw the faces of the commanders, Hancock, Sedgwick, Warren. This time, he thought, we have the right people, and we are ready for you. He pulled at the cigar, felt the smoke wash around his face, watched as Meade wrestled with his caution, wondered if Meade would ever understand the value of cavalry.

MAY 5, 1864

THE ORANGE TURNPIKE RAN DUE WEST, DISAPPEARED INTO THE deep woods of the Wilderness, and on both sides of the road the picket line had spread out on the edge of a wide field. They were mostly veterans, and along the tree line there was one regiment from New York, from the north country, the rugged mountains that gave their men willingly to this great army.

They could hear the birds, the first sounds of the land coming awake. One man rolled over, felt the musket, lifted it up and laid it against the stump beside him. He was young, had the smooth face of a boy, and they called him Chuckie, short for Charles. No one called him Charles but his mother. He didn't like the nickname, but he knew these men were his friends, that they trusted him, they had shared some awful bloody times. There were other nicknames as well, old Bugeye, Redleg, Hawknose. No one seemed to mind, it was all good-natured, and he knew that "Chuckie" was better than most.

Beneath him the blanket was rumpled and wet. He had kept it wrapped around him through a warm night, and so the blanket and his clothes were soaked in the raw smell of sweat. He always used the blanket, had relied on it for survival through the winter, and now as the nights gave hint of the coming summer, he would still use it. It was his shield, his protection against the drone of the mosquitoes, the small whining sounds that darted and hovered over his face. He'd spent his life in the cold mountains, and hadn't known about these strange little creatures and the misery they caused. He remembered the first one, setting down on his hand, and he had watched it, curious, not really feeling any bite, nothing like the bites of the black flies he had endured as a child. And then he'd forgotten it, and it was a day later when the bite appeared, the intense itch, the swollen redness. But there was another greater terror, a threat from below, from the soft damp ground. Months before, when his unit was in pursuit of Lee, crossing the Potomac in the steaming rain, he'd spent one hot night with his arms bare, had ignored the blanket and slept on a cool bed of damp leaves. He did not feel the slow advance of the tiny creatures from the ground beneath him, but suffered for days with the bites, a massive assault he would never forget. He had tried to see them, wondered what they looked like, always now swept the dirt with his bare hands. But they did not appear, and so he lay only on the blanket now, wide-awake, would never make that mistake again. Now he slept during the day, the brief rest stops, those days when they didn't move at all, when it seemed the generals didn't know which way they wanted to go.

He was used to the picket duty; it seemed nearly every night that he found himself out in front of the army, spread out into the woods, the first line against any movement by the enemy. It had been a while since they'd actually seen any rebs, and now most of the others had no trouble sleeping. They would use their bayonets, burrow down into a shallow pit in the ground, and the veterans joked and laughed at the new boys who slept with their muskets in their hands. He smiled, thought of that older fellow, Buchman, the woodsman, the thick black beard, the man who said he could smell the enemy. He wouldn't dig in at all, would just prop himself up against a fallen tree, seemed to fall asleep at will and wake only when the bugle sounded, the call that meant breakfast.

If they spoke at all, quiet voices in the black night, they always talked about the grouchy lieutenant. Chuckie thought about him a lot, wondered if it was just his nature to be so angry. He thought, Maybe it's something at home, a letter . . . maybe his wife has taken up with a neighbor. He did not like to think of that, none of them did; they fought to keep those thoughts far away. Chuckie rarely got letters anymore. His wife had given up asking him to leave all this, to come home. She did not understand what this meant to him, why it was important. He'd tried to explain, but he was not good with words, she would not understand, and when she stopped answering his letters, it scared him worse than anything he'd seen from the rebels. He thought about the lieutenant again, wondered, Maybe that's why he seems to be so mad all the time, and he takes it out on us, on this unit.

The unit was still in good shape, but the new faces did not erase the memory of the ones who were gone. He still recalled the early days, the excitement, the adventure of riding the long trains, the men who became friends, who learned about marching and formations and bugle calls. He made an effort to remember them, especially the ones with no families, believed they needed to be remembered. He would try to keep the faces in his mind, see them in the night sky, but it hadn't worked, because when he saw the faces, he also saw the wounds, the shattering of bones, could not keep the horrors away, the reasons why so many of them were gone.

Now, while some in the line would sneak a quick nap, and others would stare into the darkness toward the invisible enemy, he would lie on the blanket and search the dark for the little creatures that flickered invisibly above his face. He'd focus on the small high whine of the mosquito, wait for it to stop, knew now that silence meant the attack had truly begun. He would swat at his face, his ears, beating off the assault, and then the whine would begin again. He tried putting the blanket over his face, but they would still get through, no defense would work. Then he would feel a slight tickle somewhere on bare skin, the return of the strange little creatures that crawled and probed up through the leaves, moving silently onto the blanket until they found some tender place—and he'd explode into motion, scratching frantically, the counterattack.

There was a damp mist this morning, and he peeked up over the tree trunk, could see the road in the distance, disappearing up a long rise into the woods. He lay on the edge of a field, had not really known how big it was, if there were woods across the way. They had been sent out after dark, the grouchy lieutenant again ordering them into the woods. The order had come in a wave of cursing, harsh words, and angry shouts which he hadn't understood.

He used to think of the mountains, of the cool streams and fishing in the deep ponds near his home. But that had faded away with the faces of his friends. He'd begun to believe he might never leave Virginia, that it was his destiny to spend the rest of his life enduring the torture, the torment from the nightly assault of the tiny insects. He wondered if it was punishment, that he or someone in his family must have done something terrible, some unspeakable offense to God. He could not tell the others, could not talk about it at all. They teased him about his fear of the creatures, laughed that if the rebels just sent their bugs into battle, Chuckie would be the first to run away.

He could hear the others stirring now, low talk, and some were standing, arms high, the long stretch. The sky began to glow far behind him; he could see the silhouettes of the trees where the rest of the army was coming to life. He looked out again to the front, could see clearly a thick line of trees across the field, the tall grass in the field standing breathlessly still. He thought of coffee now, sniffed the air for the smell of bacon. He shifted around, felt the soreness in his feet, wondered if they would march like they had yesterday, the river crossing, then the blessed halt in the afternoon. He'd wanted to jump right into the river, they all had, but the officers pushed them hard, the march fast and urgent, and they hadn't expected to stop suddenly, surrounded by the thick woods.

Down the line, one man was pointing something out, and the voices stopped. Across the field, where the road disappeared into the trees, there was a muffled, low sound. He stared into the mist, focused, saw a horse, then more, a man with a flag. They came out of the woods, were moving straight down the road into the clearing. He felt a twist in his gut, grabbed for the musket, then thought, *Cavalry.* He remembered the lieutenant saying something . . . their horsemen were supposed to be out to the west, between them and the rebs. He felt a wave of relief, his hand shaking, and he stood, wondered about riding a horse all day, if he would ever get the chance. . . .

The horsemen kept coming forward, and behind them there was a flash, a glint of steel. He could not see clearly, heard now another sound, behind him, officers riding up fast. Men were beginning to shout, there was motion all through the trees behind him. He stared out across the field again, and now he could see beyond the horses, a heavy column of infantry coming out on the road, emerging in a thick line from the trees. Now there were shouts from across the field, and the infantry began to move off the road, the column dividing, a long line flowing out in both directions on the far side of the field. Men were beginning to move around him, the men of his unit, and someone called his name, and he still stood, watched the incredible sight of hundreds of men flowing out of the woods, the lines across the field growing longer by the second, more motion behind him, more shouts.

He turned, saw the men of his unit backing away, saw the lieutenant, ducking low, moving along the edge of the field toward him, waving at him, motioning him back, out of the field. He did not want to leave, not yet, had never been this close, had never seen the rebels so clearly. He watched the horsemen, could see them clearly now, saw uniforms that were not blue, and he felt the excitement, the moment building inside of him, and he wanted to yell, to shout, to say something to them: *I see you.*

The horsemen began to turn away, backing toward the flow of infantry, and he looked around, down the line, sought the familiar faces, but there was no one there. He could still hear the sounds behind him, thought of the lieutenant, the orders to pull back. He turned, began to step away from the stump, and something stung him, punched him down hard. He tried to lift himself up, but he could not move his arms, could not move at all. The grass was sticking to his face, and he tried to rise, to turn his head. Now he felt hands, and he was rolled over, could see the treetops, the sky, and a face above him. It was the lieutenant, holding him by the shoulders. There was no anger in the man's face, but something different, softer, and the lieutenant was saying something, but the words were faint, far away. The hands let him go now, and the face was gone. He felt himself sink slowly down into the tall grass, thought of the blanket, his shield, but this time he was not afraid, felt the soft wet ground under his back, where the tiny creatures waited.

10. LEE

MAY 5, 1864

HE HAD RISEN EARLY, WELL BEFORE THE FIRST LIGHT. HE TRIED to see the campfires where Grant had stopped for the night, and rode out late to catch some glimpse, some flicker of light. But he knew the Wilderness, knew he could see very little in any direction, not even the camps of his own men, spread behind him beyond the trees. He thought of Grant, thought, You have made a mistake, you have surrendered your advantage, you have penned yourself up in the one place I would have chosen, and now I will find a way to hurt you.

He rode Traveller through the dark, thought of coffee, but could not go back to the small fire and wait for the daylight. He was more excited than he could remember, felt the twist in his gut, felt himself breathing heavily. You knew what it felt like, when there would certainly be a fight, when the armies were very close, like two waves rolling in opposite directions, a force no one could stop. Always he'd thought of God, had prayed that not too many would die, and he rarely asked for more than that; asking for victory or the death of your enemies was not appropriate somehow. He would quote the verse, silently to himself, *Blessed be the Lord my strength, which teacheth my hands to war and my fingers to fight . . . touch the mountains and they shall smoke . . .*

He had memorized that verse years before, Psalm 144, knew somehow, strangely, that it was for *him*, that God had put those words there as a sign, words to guide him to his duty. For nearly two years now, since that rainy night on the peninsula when Davis had given him command of this army, he'd led them knowing that God was there, truly, and those few words had so much meaning. If anyone doubted that, they had only to recall the great victories, the men marching into the horror with the calm, the absolute confidence, they shared with him. It did not matter who led those other boys, or how many more there might be across the fields. God had set this all in motion, and the outcome was already determined.

He thought now of that awful day at Gettysburg. He could not escape that, knew God was there as well, and he would never understand why it had happened, had never believed it would end like that. It was still fresh in his mind, would come to him at times like this, when the new fight was coming fast, reminding him that on that one field, God had turned against them. He struggled to understand, could only guess: We were not on our own land. The invasion north had been a difficult decision, and always there was something uncomfortable, a small voice in his mind that he tried to avoid. When we fight in Virginia, we are defending our own land, and we are victorious. But we invade their land, and God takes that away. The verse came again: *Cast forth lightning and scatter them: shoot out thine arrows and destroy them . . . deliver me out of great waters, from the hand of strange children . . .*

He rode back down the Plank Road, toward his staff, could hear the motion of men in the woods around him. He stopped, listened hard, turned to the north, thought, Maybe . . . I should ride up there, see what Ewell is doing. But no, I must let them command. He knows my orders. He saw the face in the dark, the strange high-strung man, so excitable, quick to anger, and he thought, Something has been taken from him. It was something inside Ewell himself, some personal defeat that Lee did not understand. It could be the missing leg, of course, but around the camps the staff was making unkind comments about Ewell's wife, her domination of her new husband. Lee had met her briefly, and knew she was always close to Ewell now; the jokes rippled through the staff about the petticoat command. Lee tried not to judge, and his staff did not make their jokes in his presence. He did not spend much time in Ewell's camp, still preferred to be closer to Longstreet, as it had always been, even when Jackson was alive.

He knew there was another reason he stayed away from Ewell's camp. The staff consisted of many of the same people who had served with Jackson, and he knew the faces well, Sandie Pendleton, James Power Smith, the foul-mouthed quartermaster Harman. It was Pendleton in particular who affected Lee, something in the young man's face that was clear and unmistakable, the loss, the sadness that Lee had tried so hard to put aside. Pendleton had been Jackson's chief of staff, had been at the bedside when Jackson had breathed the last painful breath, and Lee knew he would carry that with him the rest of his life. Now Pendleton served Ewell, and Ewell had shown nothing of the influence of Jackson, of the fire, the instinct for moving *forward*. Pendleton knew it, they all knew it.

Lee still stared through the dark, past the small sounds close by, to the broad silence from the north. He did not like being that far away from Ewell's corps. The two parallel roads moved apart nearly three miles at this point, something he hadn't realized from the maps until this morning. Lee knew the turnpike was a good road and that Ewell was marching his men east. Lee had stayed close to Hill, down below on the Plank Road. The two roads eventually merged near Chancellorsville, then split again as they broke out of the Wilderness closer to Fredericksburg, but first they would pass right through the heart of Grant's army.

He did not know how Grant's lines were spread, only that the Federal Fifth Corps had come the closest, was somewhere near where Ewell was now marching. He did not want the fight yet, had hoped the

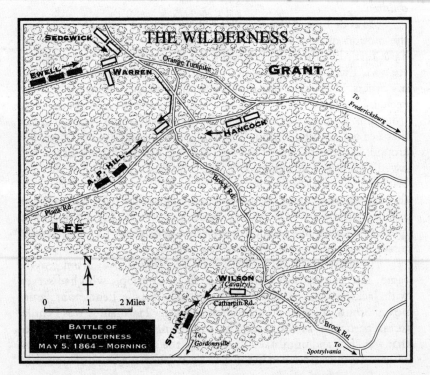

day would dawn without a major confrontation, because they were not yet strong. Longstreet was still well back, a good day's march from the place where Lee now sat, but he was coming. He'd been ordered to move out quickly, and Lee thought, This time he must not be slow.

It had been necessary to keep Longstreet farther west, since there had still been the chance that Grant might move out that way, try to cut Lee off from the valley. It would have been the wrong move, and though Lee did not believe Grant would make that kind of mistake, he could not take the risk and leave his own left flank unprotected. Once Grant had crossed the river and moved straight into the Wilderness, Lee immediately sent for Longstreet.

It was not by chance that Lee was close to Hill this morning. Hill was sick again, could barely ride a horse. The illness was more and more severe, and Lee had accepted that Hill might not be fit at all, might have to be relieved. But then Hill appeared, pained and weak, and declared himself ready for duty. Lee would not remove him if Hill said he could lead his men. And when Lee studied the lists of commanders, there was no name that rose above the rest, no one whom he felt comfortable with in that position. If Hill's corps needed a commander, Lee began to realize that he might move one step closer to the line, might have to take command himself.

The men were moving into the road now. The darkness was just beginning to break, and when they passed by him, there were small noises. Only a few men cheered or raised a hat. The woods around him were now strangely silent; there was no music, none of the jovial cursing of an army pulled out of slumber. He watched the faces, saw deadly calm, men who had done this before.

He saw Hill coming up the road, the horse brought him closer, and Hill looked very bad, the eyes deep and dark, the face drawn. Even Hill's uniform was bleak and plain, no insignia of rank, the black hat slumped down around Hill's ears. Hill said, "Good morning, sir. Fine day for a fight."

Lee nodded, said, "Good morning, General Hill. We should ride forward, if you please."

Lee nudged the horse gently and moved alongside the column of men. They rode for several minutes, the daylight growing stronger, but off the road, in the woods, the daylight did not matter, there was nothing to be seen. The road curved slightly, and suddenly there was a break off to the left, a wide field. Lee saw a small house on the far side, turned the horse. Hill followed, and the staff stayed behind, spread out in the field. They moved close to the house, and Lee reined the horse, listened hard. He stared up to the north, toward the turnpike, heard a roll of musket fire, a dull rattle muffled by the dense growth. Now there was more fire, to the west, in front of Hill's column.

Hill looked to his staff, said, "Send some people up there . . . I want to know who we are facing. Get me some idea of strength!" There were salutes, and men rode out toward the road, moving quickly away.

Lee said, "Your lead division . . . is General Heth, is it not?"

"Yes, sir. We should have heard something by now."

Hill was sweating, and Lee could hear the pain in his voice. Now Lee heard another sound, familiar, heavy hoofbeats, and a small group of horsemen came out of the trees in front. Lee saw it was Stuart.

Lee could not help a smile, saw the cape, the fresh uniform, his hat spouting a black peacock feather, one side of the brim pinned to the top, and he could not look at Hill now, would not subject himself to the amazing contrast between these two men.

"General Stuart, your appearance suggests something of a celebration."

Stuart was beaming at Lee's reception, swept the hat down in a low sweeping bow. "*Mon general*, I am at your service."

Lee dismounted, and the others followed, and Lee moved closer to the old house. Stuart bounded forward, and Lee knew the sign, knew there would be a burst of words.

"General Stuart, please report."

"Sir! You will find that the enemy has performed an admirable service. He is at this moment spread out all over the countryside. I have observed only a small force in front of this column, skirmishers mostly, but they are reinforcing. General Hill should expect to meet no more than a division at the crossroads to the east. Haste would be advisable, sir."

Lee looked at Hill, and Hill said, "We are moving to meet them. I am aware of the importance of the Brock Road intersection. I have instructed General Heth to advance as quickly as he can."

There was little enthusiasm in his voice. Hill did not have any of Stuart's energy, the tight bursts of emotion, the anger and the fire for what was coming toward them. Lee said, "General Stuart, there is musket fire in the north. Have you been in contact with General Ewell?"

Stuart turned that way, and they all listened. The firing had slowed to a small scattering of faint pops.

"No, sir. I have not been able to ride up that way. The ground between the roads is quite dense, sir. I believe the maps do not account . . ." Stuart reached into his coat, pulled out a small piece of paper, unrolled it, studied it a brief moment, then held it out to Lee. "Here, sir. The turnpike is well north of us at this position, sir. The maps show us closer together than we really are."

Lee listened for the guns again, but the sounds had faded into silence. He said, "Yes, I am aware that the maps are somewhat in error, and so we have a problem. There is a wide gap between us and General Ewell. He must not bring on an engagement before we have filled that gap. If General Grant discovers we are in two separate positions, he will cut us in two. General Hill, you must move a brigade off to the left, spread them into the woods to the north. We cannot allow any of Grant's people to cut between—" He stopped, frozen. The others were watching him, and now began to turn, following his gaze.

A hundred yards away, at the far edge of the woods, a single line of blue soldiers was moving slowly forward, had stepped clear of the thick brush. Lee felt a hard cold fist in his chest, and for a moment no one moved at all. Then, across the field, one hand went up, there was a small quick shout. The blue troops stopped, facing Lee, and there was complete silence. Lee could see their faces, saw them looking straight at him, at Stuart's striking uniform, in stunned amazement. He thought, Surely, they must know . . . they must know who we are . . . who *I* am. Lee turned his head slowly toward Traveller, thought about the saddlebag, the pistol he never wore, and he began to move slowly, heard his footsteps in the grass, looked again at the line of blue, the muskets slowly coming up, pointing toward them. He looked at the one man who had spoken, the man in charge, the hand still in the air, hanging there, could see the man's fingers balling slowly into a fist. Lee reached behind him, felt for the flap of the saddlebag, reached inside, felt the steel of the pistol, wrapped his fingers around the handle, began to pull it free of the bag, still watched the one man, the fist in the air. The hand began to move, came slowly down. The man said something, a quiet voice, and the line of men suddenly backed away, merged back into the thickness of the trees and were gone.

Now Stuart moved by him, was quickly up on his horse, and Taylor had climbed onto his horse too, moved forward, put the horse between Lee and the woods. Stuart said, "They're gone! We scared 'em away!" He began to spin the horse, yelling out, waving the hat, and now the others were all on their horses.

Lee said, "General Stuart, we should move out of this field. General Hill, I would suggest you bring your people out this way with some haste. Those men could be in advance of a much larger force. We cannot allow them to reach this place. . . ."

He saw a column of Hill's men coming forward, already moving into the field, officers shouting. One man rode up close to Hill, saluted, said something Lee could not hear. Hill pointed to the far trees, and the men began to run forward, streaming past Lee. He looked at Stuart again, and Stuart was smiling, red-faced. He said, "General Lee, the enemy has missed another opportunity! They had no idea . . . they were so close!"

Lee looked again to the trees, saw Hill's men forming a wide straight line, moving forward into the woods, and he began to let down, felt the cold shake in his hands, smiled, nodded at Stuart's excitement. Yes, they had been very close. It had been up to one man, perhaps a sergeant, one man who could have given the order to fire, but instead he'd seen the situation very differently. He may have thought his small command had made a dangerous mistake, lost in the brush perhaps, seeking out some landmark, some direction, and stumbled into the lines of the enemy. Instead of making an aggressive move, of capturing or assaulting this small group of men and horses, they had been wary, cautious. Lee glanced at the sky, said a small prayer. *You had a hand in this, it was not yet my time, thank You.*

Stuart was still watching the trees, his horse jerking about in small jumps, and Lee could feel Stuart's hot energy, the flare for the fight, the enemy so close to them, thought, No, General, we did not scare them away, it was this place . . . this infernal thicket that made them cautious. But they will go back and find their commander, and then they will return.

THEY WERE OUT IN FRONT OF HIM NOW, HAD FILED INTO THE woods, spreading into thick lines, pressing forward. There had been some musket fire, but it was not concentrated. Hill's men had not yet found the strong lines of the enemy. Lee stared to the north, to the wide gap that still yawned between Hill and Ewell, tried to hear the sounds of a fight above them, if Ewell had gone too far forward. It was still small and scattered, and Lee thought, Wait . . . not yet. He had sent word back to Longstreet again, move up *now*, and the reply had come that Longstreet was on the move, would be there by dawn the next day.

The staff was moving all around him, couriers bringing in pieces of information. Stuart was doing what he could to protect Hill's flanks, but the woods were no place for cavalry. There was nothing to be seen until you burst right into the faces of the enemy, then suddenly found yourself within a few yards of surprised infantry—men waiting for the sounds in front of them to become motion, something to shoot at.

He paced near the old house, knew what was happening, that both armies were groping blindly, thought, Grant is not moving away, or trying to get past us to the south, but is spread out in the tangle to our front. And that is where we need him to be.

There was a shout behind him, and Lee heard Taylor, turned, saw Pendleton coming out of the woods. Lee was suddenly anxious, the first word from Ewell since the distant sounds had reached them.

Pendleton saw him, drove the horse close, dismounted. "Sir . . . General Ewell sends his compliments. The general wishes to report that he has done as you instructed, sir. He has deployed across the turnpike and is now strengthening those lines, sir. The left flank is secure up toward the river, we are trying to extend the right flank in this direction. It is difficult ground, but General Early's division is in place." Pendleton was breathing heavily, and Lee waited, let him catch his breath.

"Thank you, Colonel. What can you tell me about the position of the enemy?"

Pendleton said, "Sir, the enemy is right in front of us. We have observed heavy columns moving from left to right. General Ewell . . . General Ewell will not advance unless you order him to, sir."

Lee saw the look in Pendleton's face, understood the young man would say no more than that, did not have to. Lee looked up toward the north, thought, I cannot make all your decisions, General.

He looked at Pendleton, said, "We must not bring on a general engagement until we are at full strength. But if General Ewell sees the opportunity, if the enemy is vulnerable, he must not allow those people to get past him."

Pendleton was watching him, and Lee saw something in his face: silent frustration.

"Colonel, I do not know what strength is in front of him. *He* must make that decision. Tell him he must do what the conditions suggest."

Pendleton stiffened, said, "Yes, sir, I understand."

Pendleton climbed the horse, and there was a new sound, and they all looked to the north, stared across the field past the house, felt the wave of sound roll across them, the steady high rattle of muskets, and this time it did not fade, but grew, deep and steady. Lee looked at Pendleton, said, "I believe General Ewell's decision has been made for him."

11. GRANT

MORNING, MAY 5, 1864

THERE WAS NO CAVALRY BETWEEN THE GREAT MASSES OF INfantry. Wilson's division had moved too far south, well below Lee's position, had lost themselves in the vast tangles, and finally had run straight into a heavy fight with Stuart. The sounds were hidden by the dense mass of woods, and so no one at Grant's headquarters knew that they had no screen at all, that down both roads to the west there was nothing but Lee's army, moving toward them like two hard spikes, driving straight for the exposed flanks of blue.

Meade had moved away from Grant's headquarters, the camp wagons loaded early and rolled south near a place called the Lacy house. Grant waited up near the river for the approach of Burnside's corps, still had no reason to expect Lee to be so close.

THE COFFEE WAS GONE, THE TABLES BEING CLEARED, AND GRANT moved into the tent. He had heard nothing from Meade, could now hear the low rattle of distant muskets, the occasional sharp thunder of a single cannon. He picked up his coat, the plain dark jacket, did not look at the only bit of color, the shoulder straps that carried his three small gold stars. He reached down through his camp chest, felt for the wooden box, pulled it up, opened it, saw the mass of black cigars, more gifts from the people. He grabbed a handful, stuffed them into his coat, put the box down, then paused, reached down again, grabbed the rest, stuffed them into another pocket, thought, This could be a long day.

He moved back into the sharp daylight, pulled his coat around his shoulders, pulled on his dull cotton gloves, saw the headquarters wagons moving out into the road, waiting for his order to move. Around him staff officers moved in unhurried calm, no one concerned about the sounds of the guns. One man sat at a table, writing on a thick brown pad of paper, and Grant saw it was Horace Porter. He moved that way, and the young man stood, saluted, waited for Grant to speak.

Porter was a tall, thin man, handsome, with a small goatee. He had been with McClellan early in the war, was later sent at his own request to the West, where he served with Rosecrans. When Grant replaced Rosecrans at Chattanooga, Porter had built a reputation for organizing artillery, and was ordered to Washington to sit in an office close to Halleck. But Grant remembered the bright young man with affection. Porter had recognized something in Grant that was profoundly different from the sluggishness of his other commanders, and so when Grant was given command of the army, Porter requested to join Grant's staff. Now he was the most popular man in camp, a clear contrast to the annoying perfection of Rawlins, who pecked and hovered over the whole staff.

"Colonel, have we heard anything from General Burnside?"

Porter shook his head. "No, sir, not since early this morning. He should be at the river crossings by now."

Grant looked out toward the river. "Yes, he *should* be." Grant pulled out a cigar, lit it.

Porter said, "Sir, should we send someone . . . ?"

Grant stared again toward the river. "Yes, Colonel, send another message. Tell General Burnside we are *still* waiting for him to arrive." He turned, the low roar of guns still rolling out of the trees far below. "You hear that, Colonel? The party has begun. We are in the wrong place. I do not intend to spend my day sitting here waiting for General Burnside." He puffed several times on the cigar. Smoke rolled around him, drifting away in a gray cloud. He gripped the cigar hard in his mouth, said in a low voice to himself, "This is ridiculous."

Porter leaned forward, said, "Sir?"

Grant looked at him now, said, "I have discovered something, Mr. Porter. The general-in-chief apparently is supposed to sit back and wait for people to tell him what is going on. I don't know what is going on."

He looked around, saw his horse, held by a groom, began to move that way, stopped, said to Porter, "Colonel, send word to General Burnside that I expect him to join this army at his earliest opportunity. *We* . . . are going to see just what General Meade is up to."

The staff had moved closer, heard his words, and men began to climb horses. Grant took the leather straps from the groom, climbed up as well, moved the horse into the road. The flags appeared, moved into line behind him, and he turned, saw Rawlins now, scrambling to his horse, and Rawlins seemed annoyed, always seemed annoyed, pulled away from some important task.

Grant said, "Colonel Rawlins, give the order. Advance . . ."

There were hoofbeats, and down the road a man came up fast. Grant saw a courier, tried to recall the man's name, thought, Sedgwick's man . . . Hyde . . . Colonel Hyde.

Hyde saluted, pulled out a paper, said, "General Grant, General Meade wishes me to report, sir. . . ." Hyde paused, read from the paper, "The enemy is advancing on the turnpike, and I have ordered General Warren to advance the Fifth Corps and meet him. General Sedgwick has dispatched Getty's division down to the Plank Road to confront another column of the enemy's advance. General Hancock is expected to support General Getty." Hyde stopped, looked at Grant, said, "Sir, we have a fight. The enemy is not at Mine Run as we supposed."

Grant moved the cigar in his mouth, and there was a silent moment. The musket fire was flowing up toward them now in one steady mass. Grant said, "No, Colonel, it seems General Lee was not content to watch us parade by. But if he wants a fight, then we will give him one."

H E SAW MEADE, THE WIDE HAT FLOATING ABOVE THE HEADS OF the staff, men moving in all directions, Meade's sharp voice blowing across the open yard of the Lacy house.

Grant climbed down from the horse, and Meade saw him, moved quickly, said, "General Grant, it seems certain that despite anything we may have been told, the enemy wishes us to fight on this ground!"

Grant tossed the spent nub of a cigar aside, reached into his pocket, felt for another, thought, We have not been told much of anything. He moved past Meade, looked around the open field, looked to Rawlins, said, "Right here, Colonel. I will make headquarters close to General Meade."

The staff began to move, the wagons coming forward into the yard. Meade said nothing, stared grimly at Grant as Grant moved by him. Grant moved to a freshly cut tree stump, sat down, lit the cigar. Meade motioned to an aide, and a chair was brought forward. Now a man came forward with a map, and Meade opened it, spread it on the ground, sat heavily in the chair, said, "Sir, we are engaged on two fronts. Up here, the turnpike, Warren has been ordered to press the attack. He is pushing the enemy back to his entrenchments . . . as best as we can tell." Grant looked up at Meade, but Meade did not look at him, pointed again at the map. "Down below, the Plank Road, Hancock's corps is being brought back up to reinforce Getty. . . ."

Grant said, "Brought back up? From where?"

Meade looked at him now, took a deep breath. "We felt—General Hancock felt—we were led to believe there was a considerable force of the enemy south of our flank. There was some fighting below the Plank Road. It seems . . . it was only the cavalry. General Hancock has been ordered back up to the Brock Road intersection. We did not believe the enemy was advancing there in force . . . until Getty was attacked."

Grant said nothing, thought, *The cavalry.* That's what the cavalry is for, to find the enemy, to tell us where he is moving. He felt his hands clench, was beginning to see it now. Lee had waited for him to extend on the roads in the Wilderness, had never intended to wait behind cover. Now they were spread out in a long line, fighting on two fronts. He looked again at the map, at the wide space between the two roads, said in a quiet hiss, "General Meade, how many men do we suppose Lee is sending at us?"

Meade blinked. "I don't know . . . we have heard . . . best guess is about sixty thousand. We have met Ewell's corps on the turnpike, Hill's corps on the Plank Road. We had thought Longstreet was further south, down the Brock Road . . . but he's not shown himself. Wilson's cavalry didn't find anyone but Stuart. It seems . . . our information may have been wrong about Stuart being at Fredericksburg."

Grant leaned back, looked across the open ground toward the sound of the fighting, felt the anger growing, thought, Is all our information wrong? Grant looked down to the map, said, "You haven't found all of Lee's army, General. Where's Longstreet?"

Meade looked down at the map, said quietly, "We . . . actually don't know, sir."

"Then you have not accounted for sixty thousand men. We are not facing an enemy that strong. He has to be spread out pretty thin."

"There's no one, as far as we can tell, here." Meade pointed to the space between the two roads. "We've sent some people in there, but the ground is awful. Swamps, gullies, visibility less than fifty yards."

Grant clamped the cigar tightly in his teeth, said, "If we can't see through that ground, neither can Lee. We need to punch through there. If he's on the two roads in strength, we can split his army in two."

Meade nodded, said, "Well, yes, but I thought . . . Burnside could move into that gap, protect our flanks. We're spread pretty thin too."

Grant stared at Meade, felt the man's hesitation, the caution flowing across him like a disease. "General, I would suggest you press the enemy's position. Advance your men on both roads. Order Warren to extend southward, Hancock to extend northward, until they link up in the center. Even without Burnside, we have twice the enemy's strength. If that means we are spread thin, then he is in much more serious trouble than we are. Is that not plain to you, sir?"

Meade looked at the map, stood suddenly, moved away quickly. Grant watched him, heard the sharp bite in Meade's voice, orders going out, aides writing furiously, horses beginning to move.

Grant looked down at the map again, pushed it aside with his foot, saw a fat chunk of wood, picked it up, rolled it over in his hand. He reached into his pocket, pulled out a pocketknife, began to slice slowly at the wood, small shavings curling away, floating to the ground around his feet. He stared hard at the wood, felt his anger flowing out through his hands, thought, Why can they not understand? Is it that we are too big, there is too much of this army? Are we so cumbersome that it is not possible to move effectively? He was beginning to see the flaw in the army's organization, that Meade was hesitant to act with his commander so close, and the hesitation was magnified when the enemy was watching you, waiting for it. He thought of chess, a game he had played a few times. But he was impatient, did not enjoy the game, waiting for an opponent to make a move. It was a game he could not control, could not use enough energy, could not press an attack to any advantage. He had thought, Maybe I just don't understand it. He had a mind for mathematics, but there was more to chess than simply solving a problem, and the frustration of that was too much. Now he had the feeling of being back at the board, facing an opponent who understood the game better than he did, and if the opponent did not have as many pieces, if he was missing, say, his knights, or his queen, then this should be easy. We *have* the pieces, he thought, with more in reserve. All we have to do is press him, confront him. Is this not, after all, a question of power? His hands worked the knife, the block of wood slowly getting smaller, and he thought of playing that game, of how the game *should* be played, the extra pieces you could add. . . .

Porter stood to one side, watched him quietly, saw Grant working the pocketknife furiously, saw the knife now shredding the fingers of Grant's glove, the dull yellow thread falling around Grant's feet, his eyes focused far away, staring at an imaginary chessboard.

ACROSS THE THICK MASS OF GREEN AND BROWN, OVER THE DEEP ravines and sloping hillsides, through the dense mass of trees and brush and muddy swamps, the sounds of the growing battle swelled and poured up toward the Lacy house. Along the roads that led west, the commanders sent their men into a fight against an enemy they could not see, the troops feeling their way along the rugged ground, the big guns behind them silent and useless. If the flanks were unprotected, if no coordination could be possible in the thick wood, it did not seem to give either side an advantage.

Throughout the afternoon both sides clawed carefully at each other, blasts of musket fire ripping through small trees. The men who stood and peered out, frustrated by blindness, aiming for some glimpse, for anything that moved, were the first ones cut down, never seeing their enemy. As the lines of battle fell into confusion, the men who survived the deadly whisper of the musket ball were the ones who lay flat, patient and still while leaves and small limbs rained down on their heads, clipped and sliced from the growth above them. If their officers tried to move them, prod them forward, screaming and cursing through the horrible din of the firing, it was the officers who became the best targets, their shiny gold buttons the only part of a man the enemy might see.

All day the two sides had pressed forward and pulled away, men scampering across small rises and down through sharp gullies, only to race back to where they had begun. By late in the afternoon even the officers understood that no one would win this day, that no lines would be carried, no enemy overrun. When the darkness spread over the field, both sides still lay flat, sometimes only yards apart, still firing at small sounds, at the flashes from the men firing back.

Now, between the lines, the wounded began to call out, the screams and the praying echoed through the darkness. The horror of the sounds grew in each man because there could be no help, no one could move forward. Those who could not accept that, who tried to crawl, to reach the voices, if only to take a canteen or pull a man back to the safety of a rock, found a deadly response, that someone was watching, waiting. There would come the brief terrible flash of the musket, the sharp whine of the ball, the smack of lead against tree, against rock, against bone. In the growing darkness each man began to feel that the enemy was all around him, not just the man waiting with the musket, as blind as you, but this horrible ground, the small black spaces around each man, and each man wondered why those men *back there*—with the fine horses and the hot food, polished brass and white tents—why they would send their soldiers into this terrible place.

12. LEE

LATE EVENING, MAY 5, 1864

I T HAD BEEN TWO GREAT FIGHTS, THE MOMENTUM SHIFTING BACK
and forth between the turnpike and the Plank Road. Ewell's men
had absorbed the first major push, but held their ground, the men
digging in quickly in the thick woods, a crude line of cut trees, mounds
of dirt piled as fast as bayonets or tin cups could dig. The Federals had
hit them hard, but could not move Ewell away. Soon the Federal
forces on the turnpike were scattered and groping with the confusion
of men who have lost their officers, all sense of direction swallowed by
the woods around them.

Then the great roar of the fight had shifted down to the Plank
Road, where Hill's advance eastward toward the intersection of the
Brock Road suddenly and completely reversed, a hard thrust by the
Federal Second Corps. Hancock's troops had reached the key point
first, with far greater strength, and pushed out hard against the only
enemy that came close to him, Harry Heth's division. With Hancock's
forces outnumbering Heth by nearly five-to-one, it did not take long
for Heth to find himself in serious trouble, his men clinging to whatever cover they could find. By late in the day Heth had been reinforced
by Hill's other division, under Cadmus Wilcox, and Hancock's great
strength had been neutralized by the ground, as all of Grant's numbers
had been. The assault, which had outflanked Heth on both sides, now
ground down, and as to the north, Hancock's men found themselves in
utter confusion, the momentum of their attack blunted and turned
away by the thickets and the steady response of Heth's muskets.

Late in the afternoon, Ewell had pushed out again, striking at the
jumbled mass of blue troops in front of him, but the order had to come
from Lee. Ewell was still tightly behind his makeshift wall, but Lee

could not allow the fight to swing southward with all the power Grant could bring, and so he prodded Ewell to do . . . *something*, create some opportunity. Grant had shown no willingness to move away, to leave the Wilderness, and the long lines of march were now tightened into thick lines of battle. The dangerous gap between Lee's two corps had already invited Grant to push through, and it was only the ground itself that kept the blue troops from splitting Lee's forces in half.

If Lee were to turn the tide in his favor, he would have to take every chance to strike at confusion, at disorganized regiments, at the chaos that the attacking troops had stumbled into. But Ewell had hesitated, and asked for clarification, the couriers moving back and forth between the two parts of the army in a mad rush, often passing each other on the rugged trails. Lee was seeing it more clearly than ever, that if Ewell were to do anything at all, make any decision that would show the old spirit, the orders would have to come from him. But even then Ewell pressed forward only as far as his own men could make a coordinated attack, and soon the coordination collapsed in the dense woods. Finally Ewell pulled his men back to their entrenchments, content to let the night darken the bloody ground where so many had fallen.

THERE HAD BEEN NO PAUSE, NO BREAK FOR FOOD OR REST. LEE had been on Traveller for most of the day, and he could feel the wet hide of the tired animal, his pants soaked by thick foam. He had kept close to the steady fight in front of Hill's men, but there would be nothing to see, no sign of the enemy's strength except for the sounds of their muskets, and there had been many muskets. Lee counted seven separate assaults, each one a vast wave rolling toward them from the east, and each time there were more blue troops, new units, the prisoners coming now from every division, every brigade of Hancock's enormous corps. Lee had watched Hill carefully, saw clearly that if Hill had never shown the talent for commanding an entire corps, he was still the best man the army had at leading a division. In this place, where there was no coordination and no way to even know where a corps would begin and end, where the placement of a single regiment could turn the tide of the attack, Hill had been brilliant. Lee tried to stay with him, but in the chaos, Hill had never stopped moving, guiding the smaller units back and forth through the brush, down the small trails, shifting the troops into place against the blind heavy punches of Hancock's great numbers. With Wilcox's help, Heth had held his ground, and as the light began to fade, the darkness filling the small spaces in the gloomy woods, Hancock finally pulled away, his men now flowing back behind his own fortifications, thrown up quickly along the Brock Road.

Lee was still focused toward the front, could hear the shouts of men, the sounds echoing on all sides, the same sounds that had filled these woods all day. There was a rhythm to it, the voices rolling into one long sound just before each new assault, another wave of Hancock's men striking hard at Hill's weakening lines. Only then would the voices be pushed away, drowned out by the roar of the guns, the steady chatter of musket fire. Lee expected it again, waited for it, moved the horse onto the road itself, a dangerous place, listened hard, thought, Hancock will come again, he will not stop. He's the best they have.

He felt himself shaking, gripping the leather straps hard, his chest pounding. There were scattered sharp cracks, single shots, and he strained to see, stared out toward the wide path through the trees. The smoke was clearing away, and the road was filling with blessed darkness. Now the sound of the muskets was gone, and he heard cheering, faint and hollow, but it was not a celebration of victory, but of relief, and there was no strength behind the voices, no energy, and now they began to fade away as well.

Men were moving down the road toward him, slowly, many wounded, and he saw the stretcher bearers now, and slowly the road began to fill with new sounds, faint cries, the rattle of ambulance wagons. A wagon rolled by him, moving forward, and he stared at it, breathing heavily. Looking behind him, he saw more wagons, more wounded. He tried to focus, took one long breath, let it out slowly, tried to calm the hard thumps in his chest, thought, It's . . . *over.*

There were more horses now, and he heard a voice, turned, saw Taylor, covered with dirt, his horse soaked with muddy sweat. Taylor said, "General Hill is over this way, sir. He is ill. He asked me to . . . inform you, sir."

Lee said nothing, pulled at the horse, moved slowly into the field, looked across through the last faint daylight, glanced at the far edge of the woods, where the blue soldiers had appeared that morning. Now he saw Hill's staff gathering, saw the headquarters flag. There was a tent, the dirty white canvas straightening as the tent poles were pulled tight. Hill was sitting on the ground, leaning back against a log. He was bareheaded, his dark red hair matted flat, his face black with dirt. Lee dismounted, touched the ground with stiff legs and was suddenly light-headed, unbalanced. He held the saddle for a moment, steadied himself. He felt a hand under his arm, was startled at the touch, saw it was Taylor.

"You . . . all right, sir?"

There was something tender in Taylor's voice, and Lee felt himself suddenly giving way, touched by the young man's care. He wanted to say something, to thank him. He felt his legs now, pulled himself up straight, and Taylor backed away, and Lee saw embarrassment.

Taylor said, under his breath, "I'm sorry, sir. Please excuse me."

Lee tried to smile, made a small nod. Taylor had responded with instinct, a helpful hand, and it was an awkward moment. There was no one in the army closer to Lee, and still there was a distance, a boundary clearly understood by both of them. Of course, he thought, we must not show weakness, not in front of the men. Lee turned slightly, away from Hill and the staffs, said quietly, "It's all right, Colonel. I have been in the saddle . . . my legs were a bit stiff. Do not be troubled by it. This has been a long day for all of us."

He looked at Hill now, who did not try to stand, but looked up at him with black eyes, the thin face drawn and hollow.

"General Hill, are you well enough to speak with me?" Lee moved close, leaned over. Behind him, Taylor motioned to the others, and the staffs backed away.

Hill looked at Lee, said, "General Lee, my men . . . have honored themselves. This was a day for all of them to remember."

Lee looked at the pale sickness in the man's face, thought, It has been a long time . . . there has not been much to be proud of in this command. He said, "General Hill, *you* have honored your men."

Hill sat up straight, shifted his legs, his face showing a sharp twist of pain. "Sir, I regret I am not well tonight. I am surprised . . . all day there was no problem, nothing kept me from my men. But when the fighting began to slow, it came all at once . . . like . . . a wave."

Lee straightened, said, "General Hill, you will again be of good service to this army. Rest now." He turned, said aloud, "We should all rest now. Those people will be back tomorrow, I am certain of it. We must make preparations."

He looked down at Hill again, and Hill said, "Sir, my men . . . they must be relieved. I do not see how they can hold out for another day like today."

Lee lowered his voice. "Don't worry, General. They *will* be relieved. General Longstreet will be here by morning. We will face General Grant with a fresh corps, fresh guns." He looked around, motioned to Taylor, and Traveller was led forward. Lee moved to the big horse, climbed up slowly, made a small groan as he sat, shifted his weight.

He turned the horse, his staff gathered behind, and he looked at Hill again, said, "General Hill, this army has many things to be thankful for. But we must make preparations. When General Longstreet arrives, your men will shift to the north, locate and anchor against General Ewell's flank. I will prepare the orders. We will close that open space, and we will meet those people as one solid line. Rest now, General. The Almighty has shown us we are not to be beaten, not here, not on our own ground."

Hill saluted weakly, and Lee spurred the horse, moved back to the road, past the wagons, the sounds of the wounded, past rows of big guns, crews watching him move by, hats in the air. He stared out down the road, away to the west, thought, Godspeed, General Longstreet.

THEY SLEPT WHERE THEY HAD FOUGHT, LYING FLAT ON WET leaves, on soft mud, behind a cover of old logs or the bodies of the dead. There were few shots now, most of the Yankees were gone, back to their camps, their fires, their food. But there were still skirmishers, stragglers, men who had not yet found their units, had not heard the orders to pull back. They held their muskets at the ready, would shoot at anything that moved, any sign of the enemy, and so you did not raise your head, you did not make a sound. Now, all along the lines, or what was left of lines, the blanket of darkness brought safety, and the men began to sleep, most still gripping their muskets, some holding to a new musket, taken from the man beside him who would not need it in the morning. Some crawled slowly, moving from body to body, searching for unused cartridges, maybe a piece of hardtack, a full canteen.

There were no orders. Many of the men had already found the bodies of the officers who led them, and many other officers crouched low beside these men who had done the fighting. Word had come when the shooting had stopped, passed slowly to the men who could be found: "We held the ground, we are *done*, and in the morning, they will pull us out." For now they were to stay put, stay in place, and if there was no order to dig in, to throw up a heavy defense, it would not matter because they would be replaced.

The commanders did not share the tired confidence of the men. Heth had gone to Hill, had told him the lines were in no shape for a new fight, there was no organization, but Hill was deep into the illness, sent Heth back to his camp with a sharp reminder that it was Lee himself who had told them that by dawn Longstreet would be there, and Heth's men would not have to fight. As much as Heth worried about his defenses, he understood what kind of fight his men had given this day, and so, if his commanders were confident, he would let his men rest where they were.

In front of the scattered groups of men, brushfires had begun to spread, small flickers set off by the flashes of so many muskets, and then, pushed by a small breeze, the rising crackle of the flames. Some men called it the Devil's laughter, but worse than the sounds came the thick black smoke, carrying the smells, wet cloth and burning bodies.

It had been like this before, a year ago, almost to the day, that horrible day Jackson went down. The brush and leaves had caught fire then too, and many of these men could still hear the terrible cries of the wounded, the men trapped out front, where there could be no help.

The darkness was lit now by the fires rolling through the brush in front of them, and many did not sleep, had seen this before and so could not keep their eyes away. The veterans did not fear death from the quick deadly stab of the lead ball as much as what they now saw. They prayed they would not be caught watching the slow hand, the fiery beast moving toward them, clawing along the floor of this awful ground until it swept past, burning the breath out of the men whose wounds would not let them escape.

Down the lines, one man saw motion, the shape of a head, heard the cry, crept out behind his small piece of cover, crawled slowly down a low rise, could see the boy clearly now, the face familiar, maybe a friend. Beyond the low wall of flame there was a sharp crack, but the enemy's aim was poor, the man heard the ball strike beside him, a dull punch in the soft dirt. He pulled himself around quickly, slid back to his shelter. He peeked over the rise, cursed the enemy he could not see, but the boy's face was looking back at him, and the face was reflecting the hard light of the fire, the eyes staring wildly at him, filled with the terror. The man tried not to see, lowered his head, knew it would not take long, soon would come the last sound, the boy's scream. He tried to put himself far away, think of other days, then the boy's name came to him, a sudden nightmare of memories, of marching and fighting, sharing the bad food, and now he could not look away. He eased his head up over the cover, and the boy was still looking at him, the eyes saying all he could say. There were more shots, thudding against the small mound in front of him, one ball whizzing close to his ear. He dropped down, his face in the dirt, then slowly eased his head up again, saw now the flames were jumping ahead, began to reach the boy's clothes, and the man stared with horror, could see the wounds now, the blood on the boy's pant leg. Suddenly the boy waved, yelled something. His eyes were darting around, a madness lit by the flames now beginning to swallow him, and once more he looked back at the man, begged him one last time. The man slowly slid his musket forward, lowered the barrel, sighted the small metal bead to the eyes of the boy. The boy closed his eyes, waited, and the man steadied a shaking hand, blinked away a hard tear, and pulled the trigger.

EARLY MORNING, MAY 6, 1864

LEE HAD NOT BEEN TOLD ABOUT THE CONDITION OF HILL'S DEfenses. Heth and Wilcox both knew that if Longstreet did not come, that if the morning broke over these woods, Hancock was stronger yet, and there would be no way to hold back another strong assault. But Hill would not allow them to adjust the lines, sort through the tangle of units, the confusion of command. He was insistent that these men not be disturbed, that there would be no fight for them in the morning. Frustrated, Wilcox had even gone to Lee directly, but Lee had put him at ease, shown him the latest message from Anderson, Longstreet's first division already very close now, and the rest of the corps was not far behind. Lee's confidence was contagious, and Wilcox had not pressed the point of the sad condition of their defenses, had gone back to his camp to finally get some sleep of his own.

LEE WAS AWAKE EARLY, LAY ON THE SMALL COT AND TRIED TO hear the sounds, and there was only the quiet. He sat up, put his feet out on the floor of the tent, felt the sharp jab in his knee, the stiffness of the day before. He stood, pushed his shoulders back, took a deep breath, felt his chest, put his hand on the slow rhythmic thump. The pains had not come back, not since the weather had warmed, and he was grateful for that, said a short prayer, *One more day . . . Thank You . . .*

He buttoned his coat, moved out into soft mist. There was a small fire, a coffeepot, and he was surprised to see Stuart, standing alone, staring down into the fire. Lee smiled, moved closer to the fire, and Stuart did not see him, still stared into the flames. Lee glanced around, saw no one moving, looked toward the staff tents, knew Taylor would be up soon, was always up early. Lee said quietly, "Good morning, General."

Stuart turned his head, nodded, said nothing. Lee waited, expected something more, the enthusiasm, the bright greeting. Lee was suddenly concerned, said, "General Stuart, are you well?"

Stuart seemed to focus, suddenly came alive, abruptly saluted, said, "Oh, General Lee, yes, quite well, sir. Forgive me . . . I was . . . sleeping. The fire . . . there is something in the fire. . . ." He paused, looking back down into the low flames. "Something peaceful, as though God is holding something open to you, some small bit of Himself. It is comforting."

Lee nodded, did not know what to say. He had heard that Stuart could sleep anywhere, anyplace at all, but had not thought it possible to sleep standing up.

"Yes, General, the Almighty is all around us. In everything that touches us . . ."

Stuart shook his head. "No . . . well, yes, of course, sir. But lately I have had the feeling that something has changed. It is difficult to explain."

Lee nodded, said, "Perhaps, General, since Gettysburg . . . I have seen it in some of the men, I have seen it in myself. We must not expect God to win our fight for us. This is not His struggle. He will comfort us as long as we do what is right. And everything we do cannot be right. We must remember that."

Stuart looked at him, and Lee saw something in the eyes he had never seen, a dark concern. Stuart nodded, did not seem to hear what he'd said. Stuart looked out into the deep darkness, then up at the clear sky, flecked with stars.

"They have gotten better." He looked at Lee again. "The horsemen, the enemy is getting better. There was never any doubt. We were superior, we had better riders, better commanders. If we met them head on, there was no doubt we would take the field. Something has changed."

Lee saw motion from the staff tents, the aides beginning to emerge. He leaned closer to Stuart, said, "General, you are still the finest . . ." He paused, was beginning to feel embarrassed. "You have grown better as well. You are of great service to this army, and will continue to be. Did you not confront those people yesterday, and did they not leave you the ground?"

Stuart nodded, a small smile, said, "Yes, it was tough for a while.

Wilson's division. I heard Sheridan himself was there for a while. I hear he's quite a horseman."

Taylor moved up behind Lee, and Lee turned, saw coffee cups, and Taylor hesitated, would not interrupt. Lee waved him forward, was feeling awake now, cheerful, said, "Good morning, Colonel. We're all up a little early this morning."

Taylor saluted Lee, then Stuart, and said, "Yes, good morning, sir. Allow me to pour some coffee, sir."

Lee moved aside and Taylor leaned toward the coffeepot. Stuart moved away from the fire, stared out into the dark again, said, "General Lee, if you will excuse me, I should get my men into the saddle. They may try our flank again."

Taylor held a cup of coffee out to Lee, and Lee said, "General Stuart, some coffee before you go?"

Stuart moved to his horse, climbed up, said, "Thank you, but no, sir. I suspect General Sheridan is waiting for us somewhere out there." He grinned now, suddenly reached for the gray hat, swept it down in a low bow.

"*Mon general,*" and he spurred the horse, made a quick yelp, and moved away toward the road. Lee watched him until he disappeared in the dark, could still hear the hoofbeats on the hard road, fading away.

Taylor still held the cup, and Lee took it, held the steam up to his face, breathed it in.

"Colonel Taylor, we should be hearing from General Longstreet soon. Send someone out on the road, to guide him into position. I wish us to be ready when those people make their move."

Taylor moved away, and Lee walked out into the tall grass, stared out over the open field, looked up at the great mass of stars, the small blinking eyes of God. It will be a good day, he thought. He turned, could see the dark shapes of the row of big guns, Poague's batteries, their crews beginning to gather, one man wiping at a brass barrel with a rag, sweeping away the wet mist. Lee walked toward the road, could hear more sounds, the army stirring in the woods around him. Riders were beginning to move quickly now, the first dispatches of the day.

He reached the road, looked off to the west, the black space in the woods, pictured it, the sounds, the beat of the horses, the sharp flutter of the flags, maybe a band, drums, the cheerful sound of the great advance of his strong army, and in front, the big man, the wide shoulders, and the grim expression that said only, "We are here for a fight." Lee stepped into the road, the first glow of the dawn behind him, and he could see a bit farther down the road, expected to see it even now, the great scene as he pictured it in his mind. But there was nothing there, the road still yawned wide and empty through the trees. Behind him, far into the dense woods, Hill's men lay quietly, still filled with the sleepy exhaustion of their good fight. The stars were beginning to fade away, the first glow of daylight spread out above the trees, and now there was a sound. Lee turned, felt a cold thump in his chest, and the sound grew, a great wave of shouts and cheers. It was not the sound he was used to hearing, the high scream of the rebel yell. He stared at the gray light, thought, No, they cannot come . . . not yet.

Around him men began to shout. The rest of the gun crews ran up, moving around the cannon with quick motion. He stared at the sounds, heard someone calling to him, saw Taylor, the staff, Traveller. He climbed the horse, pushed forward, moved down the road toward the sound. Now the sounds changed, a rising wave of muskets, and the hail of lead began to fly around him. He felt the horse move, pulled off the road, saw Taylor, Marshall, their faces watching him. He stood now, looked for Hill, for the commanders, and the wave of musket fire grew, volleys blending together. There were new shouts, the voices of

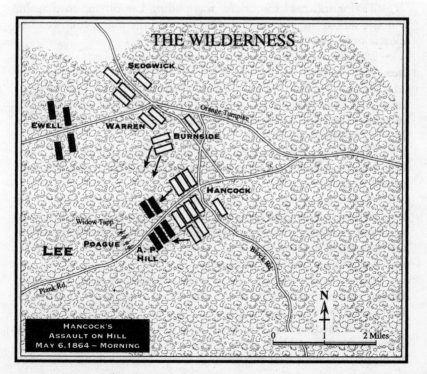

his own men, and they were coming out of the woods, moving back, away from the great blue wave that was flowing through the thick woods. He could see more troops now, on both sides of the road, no order, no lines, men running back toward him, pouring into the open field. They began to run past him, and he saw the faces, the animal fear, the unstoppable panic.

He began to shout, yelling at them to stop, saw an officer, a man on a horse, and the man looked at him, stunned. Lee yelled out, "Halt these men! Turn them around! What unit is this?"

The man hesitated, then was suddenly gone, carried in the wave of panic. There were more men on horses, more officers, and Lee saw them waving swords, some striking hard on the men who ran by them, yelling at them to stop, to fight. Lee saw a familiar face, rode forward onto the road, saw Sam McGowan, from South Carolina, older, a man Lee had always liked. McGowan was waving to the side of the road, yelling something Lee could not hear. But the men were not slowing, there was no fight in them. Lee began to feel sick, his stomach twisting.

Taylor still held the bridle, was pulling Lee off the road again, but Lee jerked the reins, and Taylor released the horse, followed Lee closely as he moved out toward McGowan.

McGowan saw him now, was red-faced, angry. Lee felt the sickness still, wanted to scream at the men to halt, could only see McGowan, wanted to reach out, grab the man hard, they were *his* men, he should have them under control. The breath slowly drained out of him, and Lee said, "General, is this splendid brigade of yours running like . . . a flock of geese?"

McGowan glanced around, still angry, raised his sword, said, "General, we're just looking for a place to form a line! These men will fight as well as they ever did!"

McGowan moved away, followed his men back into the trees behind Poague's guns. The gunners were standing ready, a man behind each gun, the lanyards held tightly, and he saw that the guns would fire right past him, and knew it was time to move. He spurred the horse, saw Poague now, shouting to his men.

Poague was watching Lee as well, waited. Lee moved his way. Poague shouted out, "General Lee, should we withdraw? What are we facing? We can't lose these guns!"

Lee turned, looked across the open ground, the trees now heavy with smoke, a thick cloud flowing forward. Lee turned to Poague, said, "Colonel, you *must* hold this ground! We will form behind you, move the men back up in support. You must not let those people come across that field!"

Poague looked out at the open ground, said, "We're ready for 'em sir. Sixteen guns. Double canister. We'll be here when the sun goes down, sir!"

Lee watched the far trees, and more volleys ripped through the air, the deadly sounds flying close to him. He heard the sharp crack of lead hitting a brass cannon, saw men beginning to fall along the guns, and then he heard shouting down the line, saw Poague pointing, could see down the road now, a thick mass of blue crowding out of the woods.

Suddenly, the guns opened up, one massive line of fire. The horse jumped, and Lee felt his heart leap in his chest. The smoke washed over him, and Taylor had the bridle again, steadied the big horse, pulled him back. Now Lee was out of the smoke, behind the guns. Across the field, all across the road, the woods came alive with the shattering impact of the hot metal. Trees flew into pieces, and now he could see the men on the road, and the great blue wave was a mass of twisted men, the wave halted, but now there were new sounds in the woods, more men coming forward, and Lee could see them on the road as well, pushing forward, over their own dead, another solid line. The guns exploded again, and again the smoke covered the field. He spurred the horse, moved farther back, saw his men gathering, a weary, ragged army, some attempt at a line, men picking up muskets dropped by the men who were far to the rear now.

Lee rode along the thin line, called out, "Form here, move up to the guns! Form here!"

The officers were gathering as well, and Lee heard the orders coming fast and clear, the orders he would have given, and now the voices were strong, the men were beginning to listen. He rode farther back, past small groups, men still dazed, breathless, men trying to find the soldier inside themselves, recovering from the shock of the massive blue wave. He saw the numbers, thought, We do not have the strength. If Hancock has sent in his entire corps . . . Poague cannot hold them back . . . we will lose the guns.

The men around him began to move back toward the fight, but the crushing wave of blue troops was closer still, the sharp sounds of lead still flew past him, men were falling all around.

Taylor yelled out, "General, please! This is not the place for you!"

Lee raised his hand toward Taylor, said nothing, was watching the guns again, the crews working with efficient speed, firing steadily,

Poague moving in and out of the smoke, directing the fire. More soldiers were coming up from the rear. Another thin line formed behind him, began to move forward, but Lee saw the first line coming back again, men still going down, and he wanted to yell again, no, do not run, but they could not stand up before the tide rolling toward them.

He saw an officer, riding hard from below the road, and the man saw him, moved quickly up, said, "General, we are being flanked . . . below the road! The enemy is extending below our right. General Wilcox is ordering the men to withdraw, but there is no order, sir. I cannot find General Heth. We don't know where his flanks are!" The man was out of breath, lowered his head, and Lee heard a slap, a dull crack of bone, and the man slumped, slid slowly off the horse. There was blood on the man's shirt, and Lee looked at it, saw the red stain spreading, the man's face looking at him, past him, the eyes not seeing.

Lee looked out past the guns again, closed his eyes, a short prayer, *Bless this man,* thought, I do not know his name. He heard Taylor again, calling to him, but thought, No, I will not move, we will fight it out right here, we have chosen the ground, God has given us this ground . . . if it must end, it will end on this ground.

The gun crews were dropping quickly now, the officers manning the pieces, the firing beginning to slow, the efficiency dropping with the loss of the men. He saw a break in the smoke, saw across the field, the road still swarming with the blue mass. He closed his eyes, said quietly, *"Thy will be done . . ."*

Behind him there were new shouts, and Taylor was yelling, manic, waving his hat. Lee turned, looked back along the road, saw the battered and beaten soldiers moving aside, lining the edge of the woods, and beyond he could see the flags, horses, a heavy column of soldiers, moving forward at a trot, the double quick. Now the men were beside him, moving past, a steady rush toward the thick smoke. He tried to see them, an officer, see who they were, what unit, and suddenly he felt Traveller jerk to the side. He looked down, saw an older man, a sergeant, and the man was pulling Traveller to the side. Lee felt an explosion of anger, yelled at the man, "Stop! What are you doing?"

Now there were more men around him, and the old sergeant looked at him, a hard grim face, said, "General Lee to the rear!"

He was still angry, thought, Who are you to suggest . . . and now all around him the men began to shout, *"Lee to the rear! Lee to the rear!"*

He glanced around, and the men had formed a tight arc around the horse, were moving him back, away from the road, from the big guns. The anger began to slip away, and he could see there was no use, no order would sway these men. He raised his hand, waved them away, saw now these were not Hill's men, did not carry the black grime of the fight. He yelled to the sergeant, "What is your unit?"

The man still pulled the horse, moved to the side of the road, said, "We're from Texas, sir. General Hood's division. Now, you just make yourself at home right here, and let us do the work. And I don't want to see you out that-aways again, you understand? I'll be back, and I expect you to be a-settin' right here."

Lee felt a sudden jolt, turned, looked away, down the road, thought, Texans . . . No, these are not Hill's men.

There were flags now, moving with the fast rush of more troops, fresh troops, and one man rode tall alongside the advance, the wide shoulders, the brim of the hat low across his face. Longstreet had arrived.

13. LONGSTREET

MID-MORNING, MAY 6, 1864

THEY HAD MARCHED THIRTY MILES IN LESS THAN TWO DAYS, and when Lee's final order came, they began the last leg at one o'clock that morning. The plan had been for them to come up from the southwest, reaching the Brock Road below Hancock's defenses, pushing northward to contain Grant in the Wilderness. But Grant had chosen the fight, had contained himself, and with Hill's corps badly outnumbered, Lee had changed Longstreet's advance, moved him up through the woods, to come in behind Hill on the Plank Road.

The men did not need to be told what lay in front of them. From first light they had heard the assault as Lee had heard it, a rolling tide of musket fire, and so their step had quickened. Now, with the smoke hanging low over the road in front of them, they began to move faster yet, the officers keeping them together. Hill's men were moving back still, and the heavy columns let the worn and beaten soldiers pass through, and there were jeers and insults, but no one believed that Hill's men were not good soldiers. If Hill was badly beaten, it meant the fight in front of them would be a test many of them had never experienced.

Longstreet reached the clearing, could see Lee now, close behind Poague's guns. The guns were still firing, the heavy thunder shaking the ground. Through brief clearings in the smoke Longstreet could see the flashes of musket fire across the field, the strong lines of the enemy, partially hidden, firing from behind the cover of the brush. Down below the road, deep into the woods, he could hear more firing, the enemy pushing forward on the flank.

He had not fought on this ground before, was staring out into the horror of the thick brush for the first time. He had not been here when they fought around the small intersection to the east, the crossroads at the Chancellor mansion, had not been here when Jackson had gone down. Lee had sent him south, to southern Virginia, a mission to send much needed supplies to the army, and at the same time Longstreet had hoped to rid the coast there of Federal troops. All that spring he had punched and struck in futile assaults on the Federal stronghold at Suffolk, and nothing had come of it but more casualties they could not afford. Lee had finally ordered him back, but the rails had been slow, and he did not arrive in time to help win the fight at Chancellorsville. Lee had prevailed with a weakened army, but the enemy then had been Joe Hooker. Now it was Longstreet's old friend, and Longstreet knew that Lee would need every piece of his strength at hand if Grant was ever to be pushed away.

His mind began to work, there was very little time. His men were advancing now close behind the big guns, the officers spreading them out into thick battle lines, and Longstreet turned, shouted to his staff, to Moxley Sorrel, said, "Major, we must not move into those woods in heavy lines. This is not the place."

Sorrel nodded, but did not understand, and Longstreet looked past him, saw Joe Kershaw, waving his sword in a high arc, spreading his men out into the woods.

Longstreet spurred the horse, moved close to Kershaw, said, "General, advance your men in a strong skirmish line, let them find their own way."

Kershaw seemed puzzled, said, "Sir, a skirmish line? The enemy will pick them apart piecemeal. Are you sure, sir?"

It was not like Kershaw to question orders, and Longstreet glared at him, had no patience, there was no time for discussion. "General, advance your men in a strong skirmish line. Follow them up with more of the same. Send them in slowly, let them make their own way. Tell them to fight on their own, not to worry about straight lines. Use the ground, the cover. The enemy will not pick them off if they cannot see them! Look at this place!"

Kershaw nodded. "Yes, sir. I will order the lines . . . regiment strength."

Longstreet looked back at Sorrel, shouted above the sounds of the guns, "Where is General Field? I want him to do the same thing, press the enemy slowly. There will be no massed charge! We must press slowly, steadily. The enemy is far outside his own defenses. Do you understand, Major?"

Sorrel saluted, stared at him, began to nod, said, "Yes . . . yes, sir. I understand."

Sorrel moved away, and Longstreet pounded a fist against his saddle. Good, he sees it too. We cannot just go by the manual here. If the enemy is firing blind, a massed assault just gives him targets. If we move carefully, move up where we can see him, then *we* will *not* be firing blind . . . and we can make them very uncomfortable.

Longstreet spurred the horse, moved closer to the big guns, looked down the road, empty now of the blue troops. The fire from Poague's guns had cleared them away from the deadly open space, but the musket fire was still heavy on both sides of the road. To the right, below the road, a bugle sounded, and Longstreet could see his men moving forward, a single line disappearing into the thickets. There was still heavy firing, some of Hill's men, the ones who did not run, still holding a shaky front below the road.

Behind Longstreet more troops were coming up, and now he saw Micah Jenkins at the front of his brigade, the young man from South Carolina, pointing his sword toward the enemy. Longstreet watched him, nodded, saw the troops moving with speed, no hesitation. Longstreet shouted, "General, over that way, follow those men into line below the road!"

Jenkins saluted, tipped his hat, moved past him. Longstreet had always thought Jenkins would rise quickly, knew he was brilliant, had led a brigade in nearly every fight Longstreet had been in. He had not been to West Point, knew only what he had experienced on the bloody fields, and Longstreet knew it was simply a matter of time before Jenkins commanded a division, or even a corps.

In the open ground above the road the rest of Field's division had begun to spread out in front of Poague's guns, and the big guns had slowed their fire. Poague would not fire over the heads of the men so close to his front. The roar of the fight came only from the muskets, and the gray line began to move forward. Longstreet could hear the deadly sounds of the minié balls all around him, and now he could see Lee again, beside the road, not far from Poague's guns.

He spurred the horse forward. The guns began to fire again, slowly, down the line, the gray troops far out in the field, Poague sending the shot and shell safely over their heads. Lee was standing up in the stirrups, and Longstreet reined up beside him, watched him, saw a look he had never seen. Lee was wide-eyed, his hair blown and wild, and now Lee reached over, put a hand on Longstreet's shoulder, gripped the gray cloth, and Longstreet saw the damp reflection in Lee's eyes. They did not speak. The sounds of the big guns rolled over them, the horses began to move about, and Lee let the hand drop, looked at Longstreet, said, "I thought . . . it was my time. I was ready to lead them, to take them across myself."

Longstreet said, "No, General, these men know what to do. They will not likely permit you to take them into *this* fight."

Lee smiled, put the hat back on, adjusted it slowly. "No, they were rather insistent. I believe, actually, I am under arrest. Some fellow from Texas ordered me . . . to stay back. He was . . . persuasive."

Longstreet laughed, looked across the field, saw the Texas flag reaching the far woods. "John Gregg's brigade . . . Hood would be proud of them. They're leading the attack."

The musket fire began to slow in front of them, the gray lines had reached the far trees. Below the road there was new firing, scattered out, but farther away, to the east.

Lee said, "The flank . . . we held the flank. We're pushing them back. . . ." He looked at Longstreet, and Longstreet nodded, knew that Lee would not say more, that it would come out later, in the reports, formal and specific.

Longstreet knew there had been disappointments before, that Lee would rarely say anything, the reproaches would be subtle, that the commanders who knew Lee well knew he would find a way to tell them silently: You did not perform . . . you will do better next time. With Longstreet, Lee had been more patient than with many of the others. Longstreet was important to Lee in ways that even Longstreet did not understand. Lee almost always stayed near him, on the field, in camp.

But at Gettysburg something changed in their relationship, the closeness strained. Of Longstreet's division commanders, Lee had always been closest to John Bell Hood, their friendship dating back to the old army, in Texas, the cavalry. But Pickett had been Longstreet's favorite, there was always humor, the good-natured insults of the man who had been last in his class at West Point. George Pickett had been Longstreet's friend since Mexico, and now Pickett was a shattered man, would never get over that horrible day, the disastrous assault that would forever carry his name. Pickett knew, as they all knew, that it was Lee's order that sent so many men across that bloody open ground, so many men who did not come back. Pickett was in Richmond now, in command of the Home Guard, and he was an angry, bitter man, who blamed Lee. Longstreet knew that somewhere inside himself, there was a small angry voice that told him Pickett was right.

Longstreet had received the reports of the fight yesterday, the couriers bringing him Lee's information, that it was Hancock again, through these woods, the same Hancock who had held the heights at Gettysburg, the strong center of the line where Pickett's division had been crushed. Pickett should be here, he thought, there would be justice in that.

Men were still coming forward, from the road behind them, and Longstreet could see the signs of men who had already been in a fight. They were Hill's men, moving back to the fight they had escaped from that morning. There were officers, leading men they had never seen. Some of the men had found familiar faces, their own units, and pieces of regiments were coming into line. They were moving past, looking now at Lee and Longstreet, and they began to cheer, exhausted and hoarse, but the muskets were held high, the hats rose up, and they moved forward to the fight.

Lee began to move his horse, rode alongside the men, and they cheered louder. Longstreet pushed the horse ahead, said, "General, if *you* would like to place these men, I believe I will retire to some safer place."

Lee looked at him, the eyes dark, the fury of the battle had filled him again, but he softened, absorbed what Longstreet had said. "Yes, General, this is your fight now."

Longstreet saluted, said, "General, with your permission . . ."

Lee returned the salute, and Longstreet spurred the horse, moved across the road, the staff following him down into the deadly brush.

HANCOCK'S FORWARD THRUST HAD BEEN BOGGED DOWN NOT just by Poague's guns, or the thin defense of Hill's unprepared men, but by the ground, by the men's own motion. As the lines went forward, they lost their connection to units beside them, there was little they could do but fire their muskets at what they believed to be the enemy in front of them. Some were able to advance faster than others, some ground was better, some had to climb down and wade through muddy swamps, and others moved around the small fires that still swept through the brush.

By the time Longstreet's men picked their way forward, Hancock's momentum had been lost. But there was no time for the Federal lines to re-form, for the officers to pull their men together. Longstreet's riflemen began to punch small holes in the confused blue masses, the men fighting on their own, one at a time, slipping carefully through the blindness to find the thick mass of blue targets. As more of Longstreet's troops found their targets, Hancock's lines began to pull back, finding their own cover, picking out targets as well. Longstreet's troops began to mass together, and the blind thickets and uncertain ground to their front slowed them as well. As the midday sun warmed the ground around them, both sides slowed their fire, dug in and kept a careful watch on the woods to their front, satisfied now to wait for something to shoot at.

H IS NAME WAS MARTIN LUTHER SMITH, AND LONGSTREET REmembered him well from West Point. They had graduated the same year, 1842, but Smith had ranked far ahead in the class, and so while Longstreet had little to say about his choice of assignments, the men at the head of the class could choose the more prestigious posts. Smith had gone on to become a fine engineer, had eventually designed the great works around Vicksburg, the works that had kept Grant's army away for so long.

Lee had spent most of his career in the old army as an engineer as well, had performed in that role as well as anyone ever had, both in peacetime and in Mexico. There, it was Winfield Scott who had recognized the value of Lee's skills and brought him to the general staff. It was a lesson Lee remembered, and so, as Smith's reputation grew, Lee would understand his value as well, and bring this man close to him.

Smith's horse was small and dark, and Smith slumped in the saddle. Longstreet rode beside him, towered above him. The men moved aside, some began to cheer, but Longstreet did not notice. He was focused on the small man beside him.

"Right through here, General. There . . ." Smith said.

Longstreet moved forward, saw the ground suddenly drop away, clearing in both directions. He moved the horse carefully, dropped down into the cut, saw out in both directions.

Smith stayed up above, said, "There you are, General. This runs all the way . . . well I expect they intended eventually to run it all the way to Fredericksburg. For our purposes, it runs east far enough."

There was no boast in Smith's voice, and Longstreet stared east, down the long straight ditch, an unfinished railroad cut. He moved the horse back up the rise, and his staff was watching him, knew the look, waited for what would come. He looked at Moxley Sorrel, said, "Major, you see what we have here? This is an opportunity . . . a bloody fine opportunity. Send word . . . pull the three closest brigades. We will move through this railroad cut until we are directly south of the enemy's flank. Then . . ." He paused, rubbed his beard, looked hard at Sorrel. "Then, Major, *you* will lead them. When they are in place, you will advance them out of the cut and attack the flank."

Sorrel's eyes were wide. "Me? You want me . . . ?" He smiled now, a wide beaming smile, looked around, saw the stunned faces of the others, looked back at Longstreet, who did not smile.

Longstreet said, "You have earned this, Major. Now, speed is critical. *Move!*"

Sorrel pointed to two of the couriers, and with a quick shout was gone into the brush.

Longstreet looked at Smith, said, "General Lee would say this is a gift from God. I would never disagree with the commanding general." He looked back toward the cut, shook his head, looked again at Smith, said, "Allow me, sir . . . to thank *you*."

The three brigades, under Wofford, Mahone, and Tige Anderson, had slipped along the cut exactly as Longstreet had foreseen. The firing along the front lines was scattered, neither side making a serious push

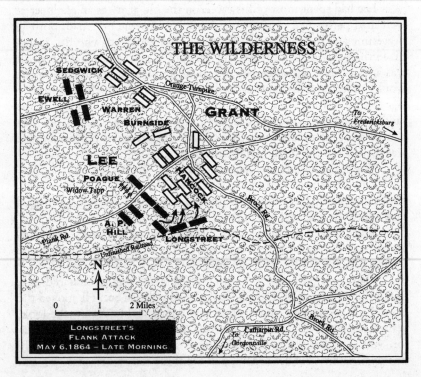

toward the other. Longstreet waited in the woods below the Plank Road, slapped one hand against the saddle, a slow nervous rhythm. The woods around him were mostly quiet, a few sharp cracks of musket fire echoing far in front. He began to move the horse forward, slowly stepping through a thick tangle of vines, then farther, across a thick carpet of small trees, cut down by the fight that had roared through these woods. He looked up at the sun, now nearly overhead, thought, We have the time, we have plenty of time. But he was not patient, did not know what was happening, if Sorrel was close, if they had been found out. He listened hard, thought, No, the enemy does not know, there would be firing, we would hear it.

The staff stayed back, and no one spoke, and he pounded his fist into the saddle again, said, "Let's go . . . !" and suddenly he heard it, the high screams, the rebel yell rolling through the woods in front of him in a terrible wave, and he spurred the horse hard, jumped it through the brush, could hear the guns now, the first wave of firing. To the left, near the road, there was another yell, and the men there began to move forward as well, clawing their way up and out of their low cover into the solid lines of blue. The attack was growing now, the woods alive with the new sounds.

Hancock's solid line was now caught in a trap, a deep V, Longstreet's men coming at him hard from two directions. Longstreet moved forward again, closer, the fire of the Yankees now cutting the leaves and brush around him. But there were not many, the musket fire was his own. Hancock's men were running, the flank collapsing completely, the panic of the surprise assault spreading along their lines. The blue troops began to flow in one great wave toward the road, each company, each regiment, carried along by the ones alongside.

Longstreet still moved forward, tried to see, thought, The road, I should send word . . . if Sorrel keeps advancing, he will cross in front of the troops along the road. He pushed the horse through the thickets, rode down suddenly into deep mud, the horse pulling itself free slowly. The staff was behind him now, and all around him men were moving toward the sound of the firing, *his* firing. The horse climbed out of the mire, and he could hear the sounds of Sorrel's advance now, closer to the road, and the firing began to slow. There were more horses, officers.

Micah Jenkins waved, rode toward him, yelled, "Did you see it, sir? Did you see it? They're gone, we pushed 'em clean out of the woods!"

Longstreet said nothing, was listening to the fading battle. He turned to Jenkins, said, "We have a problem, General! We must get these men into line, keep the assault moving forward. We're tripping all over ourselves out there!"

Jenkins stared at him, began to understand. One flank had overrun the other, the attack might have been *too* successful.

There were more horses, and Longstreet saw Smith. The engineer was breathing heavily, had lost his hat, said to Longstreet, "Sir, we can still push east . . . all the way past the Brock Road! The enemy's flank is exposed."

Longstreet said, "Push with what, Mr. Smith? Our people are crowding all over themselves. It will take too much time to sort them out."

Jenkins said, "Sir, my brigade is close by, we're in good shape . . . it won't take long. Let me pull them together, sir!"

Longstreet nodded, said, "Yes, go! General Smith, guide us to the best route. Waste no time! Let's move!"

Smith pointed, said, "This way, there's a road, a trail. We can put the troops in column up ahead, it's a short distance. . . ."

Smith moved the small horse, Longstreet followed, and now Jenkins moved up beside him. The orders had gone out, and Jenkins's men began to appear out of the woods. They formed quickly, the orders were clear. From below, more troops came forward.

Longstreet saw Joe Kershaw, shouted, "General, bring your people in line here! Whatever strength you can! Support General Jenkins!"

Kershaw saluted, shouted orders back to his aides, then turned, moved up beside Longstreet. He looked behind them, saw Jenkins's troops filling the open space, moving forward, a strong column, strong enough to turn anyone's open flank. Kershaw said, "General . . . these are Jenkins's troops? They're wearing . . . black."

Jenkins laughed, said, "Makes 'em hard to see in this place. They fade right into the shadows."

Kershaw shook his head. "Not sure about that . . . makes 'em look like Yankees."

Longstreet was moving ahead, ignored the talk behind him. He thought again of Pickett, the laughing face, thought, You would have enjoyed this, George. This is not like Gettysburg.

He thought of Grant now, had kept that away as long as he could. It had been a sickening surprise that Grant came east. Longstreet had made his move on Knoxville when Grant took command at Chattanooga, and so they had never faced each other. He had not spoken of that, how he had hoped they would not meet, not like this. They were close in the old days, and Longstreet thought often of Grant's wedding, Julia the radiant bride.

Longstreet laughed suddenly, and faces turned toward him. He ignored the men around him, thought now of Grant putting on the dress, grumbling. At Jefferson Barracks, back in St. Louis, the soldiers would perform plays, usually Shakespeare. Grant's shortness made him a natural for the female roles, and it was a distinction Grant hated. Grant as Desdemona, Grant as Ophelia. He laughed again, thought, There was always great humor at Sam's expense. And no one there would ever have believed he would command an army.

We were very young, and we didn't know much about anything. We sure didn't know much about war. Now . . . we know a great deal.

He looked back, saw the line was moving well, quickly advancing. He stopped the horse, the others rode up close beside him, the faces watched him, waiting. He said, "Gentlemen, we have upset General Hancock once today, let's see if we can do it again."

They moved forward, broke into the clear. He saw the opening, a wide trail, led the column that way. The shooting had nearly stopped, the woods suddenly quiet around him. The only sound came from the rear, the sounds of cracking brush, of men moving with deliberate steps, the grim silence of soldiers who know they are part of something important.

In front of them Longstreet saw motion, a small opening in thick brush, a glimpse of a flag, and he thought, Yes, good, more troops, saw the flag clearly now, held high by a man in gray. Suddenly the troops turned, there were shouts, and he saw flashes, small puffs of smoke. The sounds whizzed by, and he heard grunts, the cry of a horse, and then he felt the sharp pull, felt himself in the air, pulled up off the horse, then set down hard in the saddle. He heard a voice.

Kershaw was yelling frantically, "Friends! We are *friends*!"

There were more shouts, and men began to fill the road in front of them. He tried to see, but felt his head rock forward, saw the blood now, stared at the flow of red down his shirt, felt the wetness, the warmth, watched it spread slowly down his chest, thought, It does not . . . hurt.

The horse was moving still, and Longstreet began to rock in the saddle, and now there were hands on the horse, someone grabbed the reins, and he felt himself slide down, hands holding him. He was turned to one side, saw bodies, one face, saw it was Jenkins, sprawled flat on the ground, a bloody stain spreading out under his head, the face staring out at him with lifeless eyes. He tried to yell, but there was no sound, and he thought, *No . . . God no.*

They set him down on his back, and he was looking into the bright sun, closed his eyes, tried to breathe. The air would not come, and he fought for it, felt himself choking, the blood filling his throat, and he coughed, took a small breath, thought of the men behind him, the great opportunity, thought, Do not stop . . . keep them moving . . . tell General Lee . . . *keep them moving. . . .*

14. HANCOCK

LATE AFTERNOON, MAY 6, 1864

THE ATTACK ON HIS FLANK HAD EXHAUSTED ITSELF, AS ALL THE attacks had done in the thickets of the woods. Now his men were moving back to the Brock Road, to the safety of the strong defenses. He sat on the big horse, watched them come, saw not panic, but the slow dragging movements of men punched by a hard defeat. They were climbing up and over the great walls of logs, and all down the Brock Road his troops were pulling themselves together, recovering from the shocking assault. The defenses grew stronger.

It had been hours now, and there had been no attack, not even a strong skirmish. He kept his eyes to the woods to the front, thought, They will come. It's as hard for them as it is for us . . . moving in that damned place. But they surprised us, rolled us back completely. They will not just let us sit now, licking our wounds. They will come.

He had secured the flank, and back behind his left, a mass of artillery waited for targets, guns that had been silent all day. Out in front there was nothing to shoot at but the sounds, and the sounds could be your own men. Down on the left, the big guns were now in position, and if the rebels came that way, tried to make the sweep far around the flank, they would have to cross in front of the guns. No, he thought, they will see that as clearly as we do. Out in the brush, our flank was vulnerable. Back here, the flank is secure.

To the right, the woods were a mass of sounds, but they were not the sounds he'd expected to hear. Burnside had been ordered to move into the gap between the roads, to push hard into Hill's left, but there had been nothing from Burnside, no word, no sign of his men. There were sounds of a fight, but it was not strength, no massed assaults. Burnside was out there, he thought, somewhere, half his men looking for the other half, probably shooting at each other. But the woods will keep Lee from moving that way as well. Damn this place!

He moved the horse slowly along the road, still peered out toward the woods. He thought of ordering his own men forward, but no, even headquarters understood that little would be gained. He had done that already, at dawn, driven the enemy back in complete chaos, but the chaos spread to his own advance, commanders losing their own men in the thickets. By the time Longstreet suddenly appeared in front of them, the chaos was complete. Hancock's assault had become a stalemate, then a retreat, men fighting their way backward. He looked down the road, saw more men filing up and over the logs, the defense stronger still. Our advantage is here, he thought. Now it is time to wait.

Two days before, he had marched the Second Corps right past the ruins of the Chancellor mansion, the place where he'd held the rebels away a year ago. It was a memory he carried into every fight, the collapse of command, Joe Hooker suddenly losing his nerve. Hancock had been the rear guard, had held Lee at bay while the rest of the army backed away, northward, to the safety of the river. The Battle of Chancellorsville had been a complete disaster, but the defeat was not inflicted by Lee or by the rebels. Hancock's men, and the others, the great power and spirit of the Federal army, had been beaten by their own commander.

He had tried not to dwell on that, moved quickly past the ruins of the mansion, stared to the front, toward the dense woods, but those sights brought a different horror. In the small clearings, patches of burned brush, he could see the bones, men and horses, the sickening remains of the fight a year ago. The men saw it too, and many remembered this awful place, marched quietly, no one hoping for another fight on this ground. Many others, the replacements, stared at the bones and the wreckage in stunned silence, some only now understanding that the next fight could do the same to them.

The wound still bothered him, nearly every day. It had come the third day at Gettysburg, facing the last great assault from Lee's army. The musket ball struck his saddle, shattered the wood and exploded it underneath him, punching splinters and fragments up inside of him. The doctors thought they had removed all the fragments, but the pains were still there, and the wound still festered and burned, and if the doctors didn't know, he did. There were more fragments inside of him yet. He would need surgery again.

There was not much about that day he could recall. He had watched them come, a great wave of men, Pickett and Pettigrew, nearly fifteen thousand soldiers, pushing straight at his defenses. When he saw it was Pickett, he also knew it was Armistead.

Lewis Armistead commanded one of Pickett's brigades, and Armistead had been as close to Hancock as anyone before the war, a friendship that grew from the early days, Mexico, Kansas, the Seminole Wars in Florida. They had parted ways in Los Angeles, when news of Fort Sumter reached the West Coast. Much of the army simply dissolved, so many resigning, going south. He knew they would meet eventually, that there were too many in this war who were facing their friends, their brothers, across the deadly space. He had not allowed himself to feel the sadness of that. It was, after all, Armistead's choice.

He still didn't understand that, how the good men, the honorable men, could betray their oath as officers, betray their country. He had asked himself, tormented himself with the question: When this is over, will we still be friends? Will I be able to look him in the eye and not see a traitor?

Pickett's great assault had brought Armistead and his men straight into Hancock's guns, and unlike most of the shattered gray wave, Armistead's men reached the Federal lines, actually broke through, pushed across the low stone wall in one last desperate surge. But they were too few, and the men in blue too many, and Armistead fell just inside Hancock's own lines.

Hancock never saw him that day, had already gone down with his own wound. Now there would be no answers. He would never know if Armistead could still have been his friend. It all seemed so very long ago.

He moved the horse again, heard more scattered musket fire from the right, thought, *Burnside.* You're in there, somewhere. It would be nice if you would tell me where, or what the hell you're doing.

The field across the road was quiet now, the last of his men safely behind the log wall. There was a steady flow of black smoke down to the left, a brushfire moving with the breeze, rolling slowly toward the road, toward the pine of the wall. He moved that way, saw the smoke drifting across his men, a thick cloud. Men began to move out of the way, waving their arms. Some were laughing, and he heard a man say, "You boys keep a lookout. Them rebs could be hidin' in the smoke!"

He looked across the field, toward the trees, and suddenly there was a new sound, a ripple of musket fire, the high shriek of lead, dull smacks in the wall. Then the rebels were there, moving forward, and now there came the sound, the awful scream he had heard before. It was the rebel yell.

His men began to fire at the gray line, and he watched, thought, How many . . . how strong? The rebels moved closer, but the charge didn't come. They simply stopped, knelt, were trading volleys with his men behind the wall. Now the fire from his own men began to take effect, and the rebel line was falling apart. He stared, thought, This is insane. They can't just . . . stand there. It will be a slaughter.

He saw a staff officer moving along the road, coming toward him. The man reined up his horse, saluted, said, "General Hancock, we have word from General Burnside. He is moving into position on our right front. General Burnside reports he will try to assault the rebel flank, if we can only hold them in place, sir!"

Hancock stared at the man, felt a burst of anger. "If we can hold them . . . why? So he can watch? Where the hell has he been all day? Now, we don't need him, we are behind a big damned wall. The enemy is coming right at us!"

Suddenly there was a great burst of sound, across the field in the far trees. Hancock turned, saw a new wave, a heavier line of infantry emerging from the trees. The sounds of the muskets rolled all around him, the road filling with gray smoke, the hot smell of powder. Now it was a fight.

The staff was gathering behind him now, and he could hear the shouts, the men yelling at him. He jerked the horse, moved away from the wall, behind the road, thought, No, this is not the place for you to be. He moved back into tall trees, followed by the staff, saw more officers waiting for him, looks of pained relief. Well, hell, he thought. If I can't see it for myself, how am I to know what's going on?

Now a man rode quickly up behind him, a staff officer, the man ducking low. Hancock turned the horse, and the man yelled, "Sir . . . we have a gap in the lines! General Ward reports the enemy is advancing into our center, sir!"

Hancock stared at the man, watched him wilt under the hot gaze. "Yes, Captain, I can see where the enemy is assaulting! A gap? Where? Where is General Ward?"

"Uh . . . I don't know sir. When I left him, he was moving to the rear . . . with his men."

Hancock looked toward the road, thought, His men? Ward has broken? He's the center of the line. How could they have given way? He spun the horse, and now the black smoke was boiling past him. It

wasn't a brushfire anymore. It had reached the sticks and timbers of
the wall, and now a great roaring bonfire began to spread out on both
sides, sheets of flame towering above the road. Blue troops with blackened faces were streaming toward him, men with burnt clothes, a new
panic from an enemy you could not hold away.

He saw officers now, yelled, "Dammit! Get these men back in
line!" They were moving in a rush all around him, shouts and curses,
and now he could hear the sounds of the muskets, the hot lead cutting
the air around him.

He turned, yelled to his staff, "Get word to all units . . . send support to the center! Order up the reserves, to the middle of the line! Tell
the officers . . . follow the smoke! Go toward the smoke!"

Now there was a new burst of musket fire, all along the wall, and
he tried to see, thought, Yes, hold them back. Suddenly there was a
great chorus of screams, and he saw a burst of men leaping through the
flames. The rebels had reached the logs, were rushing forward through
the wall of flames. They began to flow out from the wall, and he could
see them pointing, quick aim, scattered shots. They were looking for

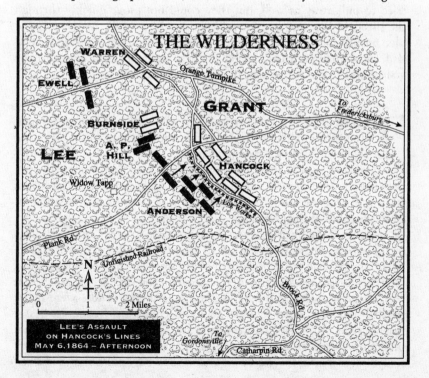

targets, began now to fire up and down the road, where the men in blue still huddled at the wall, where the flames had not yet spread.

Hancock could see the faces now, men with singed hair, blackened clothes. He spurred the horse, and the staff followed, moved farther back into the trees. The smoke was everywhere, from the fight, from the growing fire. He moved into an open clearing, took a deep breath of blessed air. On the trails behind him a column of his men was moving forward, the reserve, and he pointed, yelled to an officer, "There, double quick! They have broken through!"

The fresh troops moved toward the fire, the great crackling roar now blending with the sounds of the fight. From both directions, the Federal troops were moving toward the breakthrough, a tightening arc, containing the surge of rebels. The fight became hand-to-hand, the men in blue growing in number, too many for the rebels to push through. The break in the lines was shrinking, the rebels pushed back to the wall, to the great horror of the flames. Many gave up the fight, began to run, to climb through the fire, and those who escaped had to make the deadly retreat across the open ground. Many of the wounded tried to pull away as well, but they could not move quickly through the sheets of fire, and many could not climb the wall. As the surge of blue pushed them tighter together, those who would not surrender battled with whatever they carried in their hands, backed closer to the wall, closer to the flames that finally consumed them.

T HERE WERE SCATTERED SHOTS, A FEW REBEL SKIRMISHERS, AND then the jumbled firing from the woods far out to the right, the fight Burnside was trying to make.

Hancock moved into the road, past the men who were gathering near the smoldering wall, staring quietly at what remained. The flames were mostly gone now, but small plumes of black smoke still rose from the ashes of the great logs.

Many of the burnt timbers were not timbers at all, but the bodies of the rebels. There were bodies all along the wall, beyond the place where the fire had roared through. Many were just draped across, some in grotesque shapes. But the men focused on the smoldering ashes, that part of the wall that still held the heat, the smoke. There were many twisted and blackened figures, hands reaching up, frozen in death, reaching out, still trying to escape the fire. Some were caught in the act of climbing up, seeking the escape, their breath swept away while they struggled to reach the safety of the woods beyond. Some had been wounded, men who crawled toward the wall, only to have the flames roll over them. The clothes were mostly gone, burned away, and the men in blue stayed back, did not yet have the stomach for pulling the dead away, not like this, not when there was nothing to hold, to touch, but the burnt flesh, the charred bones.

There was a gentle shift in the breeze, and Hancock caught the awful smell, could see some of his men backing away now, some beginning to be sick. Hancock pulled his mind away, turned the horse off the road, thought, No, not here, you cannot let them see you . . . you cannot be affected by this. He pushed the horrible sights from his mind, moved the horse past more men who were gathering on the road. He turned, saw staff officers moving to catch up with him, and he thought, Tell them, keep them ready, pass the word. But he said nothing, realized the rebels were through here. This fight was over. No one over there would ask them to do this again, to charge this line. We are too strong, he thought. Nothing can be gained. He reined the horse, looked back to the road. No, they will not come again, not here. The soldiers have seen something new, a new horror, a new way to die. They have seen the face of hell.

15. LEE

LATE AFTERNOON, MAY 6, 1864

THEY WERE SPREAD OUT ON BOTH SIDES OF THE ROAD, A LONG line of trenches and piled debris, the men sitting low behind their cover. Lee saw motion down along the line, the red battle flags of each regiment, a slight wave in the fading breeze. The sun was beginning to set and long shadows spread across the road. He dismounted, still looked eastward, saw the dark smoke from the Brock Road, from that awful place where his men lay scattered, the smoke from the breastworks still rising, and Hancock's people safely behind their wall.

Faces were watching him, men were turning about, pointing at him. There were some shouts, but the men were brutally tired, and many were already sleeping. He walked off the edge of the road, into the darker shade, but there was no cool relief.

The staff waited out on the road, and Taylor followed him, moved quietly. Now even the affectionate salutes of the men faded out, and the woods were quiet. Taylor stayed a few steps back, and Lee sat on a long dead tree, punctured by many holes, colored by blood. Lee looked at the stain on the soft wood, put his hand on it, felt the wood crumble, slid his hand along, felt the rotting wood roll into small pieces under his fingers. He looked down beside the tree, to the thick mat of old leaves, saw another stain and, half buried, a man's shoe, old black leather. He reached down, freed it from the dirt, held it up in his hand, saw a hole, the sole worn through, the heel long gone. He thought, There are not many shoes in this army. This one . . . was lucky.

He did not often think of that, did not even use the word. What was luck, after all, but the will of God? He tossed the shoe aside, then looked at it again, thought, No, I should find him, he will want it. It was an odd feeling, that he must have known this man, must find him. . . .

He looked at the dark stain again, realized there might be no need. He tried to clear his mind, pull himself away, thought, You cannot do this, you cannot see them like this . . . one at a time. He stood, brushed the dead wood from his pants, thought, You can never be this close. You cannot be absorbed in the fate of each man. But you *are* closer. This terrible fight has done that, the war has done that, slowly, over time, taken the good men, the good leaders. There is something in this . . . a lesson, God has shown you that you must not forget that each of these men has his own pain, dies in his own blood, has his own soul. The line is so thin, the strong line between the commander and these men, the men who lead the charge, the men who face the guns.

He had kept Longstreet's image away until now, his mind holding instead to the faces of the men he did not know, the men who left their shoes behind. But if he did not show it to his staff, he could not keep it away from himself for very long, and so the image came to him. Longstreet's wound was thought to be fatal, but the doctors reached him quickly and the bleeding was stopped. I was not there, Lee thought, I don't know how I could have endured that. He had not seen Jackson after the arm was amputated, had been grateful for that, would not remember him as anything but the magnificent fighter, would see the man as he'd always been, not as he'd died. And now he thought of Longstreet, fought the image of the big man choking on his own blood. The staff had put Longstreet's hat over his face, to shield him from the sun, and so the men who gathered around thought he was already dead. Longstreet had heard the talk, heard them crying, lifted the hat off his face himself, and waved it at them. Taylor had been there and seen it, heard what the soldiers were saying, that it was a miracle, Longstreet back from the dead. Lee shook his head. No, he will die in his own time, in his own way. He is too stubborn to leave it in God's hands.

He looked around, the shadows filling the spaces, thought again of Jackson, and now Longstreet, both shot by their own men. He was so pleased that the fight would be *here*, this awful place, and he remembered he'd felt the same way a year ago, when Hooker had drawn himself up into these woods. But there was a difference now. Lee knew that Jackson had gone down as a price to be paid, a balance, that God would not give Lee such a great victory without something in return. This time the victory was not complete. Grant was not rushing away toward the river, as Hooker had. And so Longstreet would not die, not yet. Lee felt certain of that, the justice . . . God would be fair.

Taylor was watching him, and Lee saw him now, saw a sadness in the young man's face. He appeared pale, weakened.

"Colonel, have you any word? Anything I have not already been told?"

Taylor said, "You mean about General Longstreet, sir? No, sir, just what the surgeons said. He should survive. It is a terrible wound. When I left him about an hour ago, he was awake, but . . . his neck. I cannot think of it without feeling sick. I'm sorry, sir."

Lee nodded, said, "It is a ghastly thing . . . that we do here, that we do to each other. We are not supposed to think on that . . . it is part of the duty, of the tragedy. And there are so many . . ."

Taylor moved closer, said, "At least, sir, the general will survive. He will be back. He told me that himself."

Lee looked out past the distant line of men, looked to the gray light, fading in the small dark spaces, felt the anger rise, said, "That is what we were told about General Jackson." He pushed it away. No . . . do not question, there must be no bitterness. *Forgive me, Lord. I am weakened . . . I will not question Your will.*

He turned now, began to walk back toward the road. Taylor moved out in front, went to the horse, took the reins from an aide, held them out. Lee stopped, looked up at the others, saw Marshall, the young man staring at him through small wire glasses.

"Colonel Marshall, have we received anything yet from General Ewell?"

Marshall sat up straight in the saddle, always responded to Lee with nervousness, something Lee did not understand.

"Um . . . no sir. Just that he expects his attack to begin about . . . now, sir." Marshall looked at a small pocket watch. "Yes . . . about now."

Lee climbed the horse, moved to the center of the road, looked to the north, stared at the spreading darkness. There was no sound.

The meeting had come at Lee's request, early that afternoon, to find out exactly what was happening in Ewell's front. He thought of Ewell's explanations, still felt the small fury that had swirled inside of him, an anger he would never reveal. Ewell had done little all day, except hold the Federals in front of him tight in their lines. Both sides were aware of the other's strength, and so, as Hancock's flank was being rolled up by Sorrel's surprise from the railroad cut, and later, as the attack against the Federal defenses on the Brock Road had threatened Hancock's position, neither Warren nor Sedgwick could risk weakening their defenses in front of Ewell. But if there had been no Federal advance

there, nothing to lend support to Hancock's hard thrust early that morning, Ewell had done nothing as well, content to enjoy his strong defensive lines, while Hill, and then Longstreet, made the fight to the south.

Lee could understand a stalemate, both sides wary of making
a mistake against strong defenses of the enemy, but what had stirred
his anger was the final detail of Ewell's report. He had mentioned a
possible plan, an idea that had come from John Gordon.

Gordon's brigade lay now on Ewell's far north flank, the left
flank of Lee's entire position. Gordon had scouted out around the Federals in front of him and found that Sedgwick's lines simply . . . ended.
There was no protection beyond the Federal right, no great mass of
cavalry, no skirmish line extending up toward the river. Sedgwick's
people had not even dug trenches. The night before, Gordon had seen
it for himself, slipped quietly east, well behind Sedgwick's lines, and
watched men in blue preparing their evening meal, with no preparation against anything that might come at them from above, from the
direction of the river.

Gordon's brigade belonged to Jubal Early's division, and Early
would hear none of Gordon's plan, did not believe that a quick sweep
up and around the Federal flank would accomplish anything, and
might in fact be disastrous. There had still been the question of Burnside's whereabouts, and Lee's cavalry had no answers to that. Stuart
was focused well below, far beyond the right flank. But now, with
Burnside suddenly appearing down near the Plank Road, that mystery
had been solved.

Lee had stared at Ewell in disbelief. All day long they had known
of an extraordinary opportunity, and nothing was done about it. He
thought of Ewell, standing in front of him like some awkward flapping
bird, explaining all sides of the issue. The staff often joked about that,
but Lee had no use for it, would not judge. He tried hard, would see
only a man who had given up a piece of himself to this service, had lost
a leg on the battlefield, had earned the respect. But . . . he is not the
same man, he thought. He will not take the initiative. The order approving Gordon's attack had come directly from Lee.

He did not know John Gordon well, except that he was not a
professional soldier. He had come to the army from Georgia, an educated man who advanced through the ranks by leading infantry with
solid, quiet competence. Lee thought of Jubal Early and Early's distrust
of the plan. Early would distrust any plan that he did not conceive,
could intimidate everyone around him, and since Gettysburg, Lee had
known that Ewell was capable of allowing Early to influence him more

than was appropriate. Lee was growing weary of that. Early was vocal and openly hostile about so many things, had even made a point of protesting the presence of Gordon's wife, who had been close to her husband through many of the fights. Lee did not object to the wives being near, as long as their husbands performed their duty. Gordon had shown no sign of a problem in that area, certainly had shown nothing of the oppressive influence that Ewell's wife had brought to *his* headquarters.

He hadn't noticed the small clouds in the west, painted with the red glow from a setting sun; there was no time for the small moment of beauty, the quiet serenity. The sharp colors faded away now, the sun well below the distant trees, and what light remained was fading quickly into a gray haze. He tried to feel some optimism, that this could still work, it might be an excellent plan. If Sedgwick could be panicked, Grant might have no choice but to pull back to the east, toward Fredericksburg. With the river behind him, there might be no escape. The risk, of course, was that Gordon was wrong, that there were more blue troops behind Sedgwick, and that Gordon might be flanked himself.

Lee stared out through the dull light, thought, It has to be in our favor. Men will panic quickly in a night assault, when they cannot see their attackers. The problem is that it would be very difficult to follow up any breakthrough, to move Ewell's other forces forward in the dark. But we must take every chance. Lee clenched his fist, still stared at the silence, waiting, thought, I wish General Ewell understood that. If Gordon is wrong, at least let him be wrong moving *forward*. . . .

16. GRANT

EVENING, MAY 6, 1864

H E STILL WORKED THE KNIFE, SLOWLY, SHORT DELIBERATE strokes, the wood shavings scattered into a thick pile around his feet. The fires were growing around him now. He glanced up, saw the staff lining up with small cups, a fresh pot of coffee. He saw Porter looking at him, holding two cups, and Grant shook his head, no.

He carved the last stick into a sharp point, sharp enough for a toothpick, tossed it aside, heard a sound, a small laugh, looked beyond his tent and saw a cluster of bright colors, brass buttons, and gold braid. He was used to foreign visitors. There was always some prince or dignitary, some old soldier from the great European wars. One old Frenchman told stories of his close friendship with Napoleon, another had fought against him in some frozen field in Russia. They were usually the guests of some congressman, someone looking to show off his influence.

Their first impression of headquarters was often disappointing. Many expected their presence to be the most significant event of the day, as though there should be some elaborate ceremony. Then they would hear the guns, a sound like nothing heard in Europe, not even in the days of Napoleon, and then the wounded would flow past, wagons and ambulances filled with the screams and faint cries of the men who endured the horror of this most *modern* war. When that experience had passed, the visitors did not venture far from the tents, there was not quite as much boasting of their own heroics and how much more civilized war had once been. Even those from the most remote lands knew they were seeing the new face of war, and when they left, there was something different about them, something subdued.

Grant had no objection to the visits, but was not as cordial or open as many expected. He had little time for the ceremony of it, and often he would offend them by his lack of attention. He tried to be polite, but many spoke very little English, and if they did, and the accents were strong, he had a hard time understanding them, and it embarrassed them. Even when they were direct, a formal request for information, he'd seen their attraction to the reporters, and so there was very little he would tell them about what was happening. To them, he was just this odd quiet man, and none thought he had the flare, the great ceremonial *presence*, of the real commander. They would speak among themselves, talking about Lincoln, and smile knowingly, of course, the two men so similar, so symbolic of this young, crude country.

The group began to move away, stifled the smiles, and Grant looked down at his hands, the small knife, the dirty gloves with the fingers torn away.

Rawlins said, "They have no graciousness! They should be grateful we allow them here."

Grant looked up, saw Rawlins sipping the hot coffee from his tin cup, and said, "They don't hurt anything. As long as they stay out of the way, they add a little color to the place."

Rawlins sniffed. "But, they're so . . . *rude*! Talking about you that way, I overheard them, I know what they're talking about. It's the . . . the knife. Your habit."

Grant rolled the knife over in his hand, said, "You mean the whittling?"

"They think all of us . . . their papers describe Americans as some kind of savages, as though we have no culture, no dignity. I saw a cartoon, you, the President, and a caricature of Uncle Sam, sitting around a campfire with whittling sticks!"

Grant thought, So, that's why the laughter. I fit the image.

The Europeans had moved away, down the hill toward Meade's camp. Rawlins said, "I had better . . . keep an eye on them. They're heading toward General Meade's tent. You know how *he* is. He seems to offend them every time he speaks." Rawlins hustled away, and Grant watched him move down the hill, catching up to the bright uniforms, the elegant caped suits, Rawlins all smiles and short bows. Grant shook his head, smiled, thought, Old friend, you have a great future after this war. You're a natural diplomat.

He reached down, felt for another piece of wood, but his hand touched only the bare ground. He'd worked his way through the small pile. He folded the knife, put it in a pocket, stood, stretched, saw an officer, recognized him, one of Hancock's men. The man was running up the hill from Meade's tent, held a piece of paper, and Grant waited.

The man saluted, said, "General, sir, Major Garrett. Sir, General Meade requested I pass this along to you."

Grant nodded, felt in his pocket for a cigar. Garrett waited for a sign, some permission to speak. Grant slowly lit the cigar, said nothing.

Garrett said, "Um . . . with your permission, sir, General Hancock wishes to inform you that there is no activity in his front. The enemy has pulled back to his entrenchments. General Hancock has made contact with General Burnside's flank. But it is General Hancock's opinion that the enemy has no intentions of renewing his attack."

Grant tasted the smoke, held the cigar out, looked at it, said, "Fine. Congratulate General Hancock on a fine day's work. You are dismissed."

Garrett saluted, then smiled, said, "Oh, sir . . . I don't know if you have heard. The enemy prisoners are talking about General Longstreet. Some say he is dead. We can't be sure of that. But there is no doubt he is down, out of the fight."

Grant felt a cold stab, stared at the man with his mouth open, the cigar suddenly motionless, and Garrett's smile faded. Grant said, "No, Major, I had not heard. I want to know . . . tell General Hancock I want to know if he is alive . . . how it happened. Go!"

Garrett saluted again, moved quickly down the hill. Grant walked over to his tent, stared at the dark space inside, thought, Old Pete, you damned fool. Can't stay out of range . . . always too close. He remembered Mexico, Longstreet's wound at Chapultepec, missing the final assault because he insisted on carrying his own flag, the perfect target. Now . . . what? Someplace he ought not have been. Well, then, good, go home. Stay with Louise, have more children. He thought of St. Louis, of Jefferson Barracks. We were young and stupid, strutting and prancing in those uniforms like we were all heroes. Or would be. And the women . . . surely they saw more to us than that, the ridiculous boasting of our great military careers, of how we would all be generals someday. Did we really believe that? We surely must have convinced the women, because all of us married, right there, fought the greatest battle of our lives, fought against the will of their fathers, none of them wanted soldiers for their daughters. But it was a fight the fathers would lose, and usually it was because of the mothers. Grant smiled now, thought of his own wedding, Longstreet towering above the others, but perfect, the glory of the dress blues, young soldiers home from the great war with Mexico. But . . . if we all believed in our own glory, if we had the same dreams, if we really thought we would all be generals one day, it never should have been like this. We should not be killing each other.

He turned, saw more riders, men moving in all directions. It was near full dark, and the fires were drawing in circles of men, like blue moths around a lamplight.

He heard his name, men looking for him, messengers from the front. He still stared into the dark, saw the big man's face, the deep blue eyes, thought, I will not bear this, the fault is not mine. You made a decision old friend, a very bad decision. All of you . . . He thought of the others, the young men from the Point, all the old friends. Die for your cause, if you have to. I will do what *I* have to do.

He squinted at the firelight, saw the gathering couriers, the faces all watching him, and he clamped down hard on the cigar, moved closer to the fire. He nodded to Porter, the silent signal, and Porter motioned toward one man.

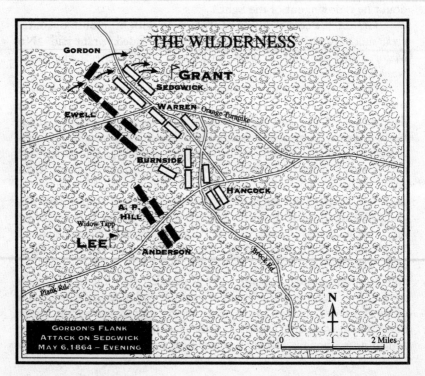

The man saluted, said, "Sir, General Sedgwick sends his compliments, and wishes you to know, sir, that the enemy is firmly in his barricades, and the general expects no more activity tonight."

There was a sudden noise from the right of the line, a roar of sound rolled up the hill, a sudden burst of musket fire, the high wailing scream of men. The officers all turned, looked out into the dark. Some began to move to their horses. Grant heard the shrill whine of a shell. Behind the camp there was a sharp blast and a wagon shattered into pieces. Now the scattered sounds of the lead balls began to zip by them, one punching the side of Grant's tent.

Grant said, "I believe General Sedgwick is mistaken."

IT HAD LASTED ABOUT AN HOUR, AND SEDGWICK'S RIGHT FLANK had collapsed. The enemy could have no grand success, the great surprise had been dulled by the darkness and the thick brush, and so the curtain was brought down on yet another assault. Grant had not seen Sedgwick, but the messages came in quick order, hundreds of blue troops captured, one brigade shattered. The panic had spread down the line, men had poured back through the headquarters, wild-eyed, running from demons screaming after them in the dark. Troops had quickly been pulled from the left, sent to stop the tide, but in the tangle of woods, men were still scattered, some were still running, and there was little anyone would do now in the pitch-darkness.

Grant was furious. Sedgwick had assured headquarters that the flank had been secured, his line re-fused, the end turned back on itself at a ninety-degree angle. But the order was never given to the right commanders, and now those commanders, Shaler and Seymour, were in the hands of the rebels. He would say nothing to Sedgwick, that would be Meade's job, to find out what bloody mistake had let the rebels get around the flank.

Meade had come up to his camp, and the couriers were still coming, most of them directed to Meade. Grant sat on the stump, listened to the reports, kept his anger tight in a thick column of cigar smoke.

He watched Meade, listened quietly. It was a younger officer, one of Meade's staff, a man Grant did not know, and he could see that the young man was clearly infected with the panic. His voice rolled through the camp, and those not moving past were stopping to listen. "Sir! The reports are that Lee is moving between us and the river. The cavalry is in Fredericksburg already! By morning we will be completely cut off!"

Meade waved his arms, yelled out, "Well, who is in charge up there? Have we no troops who can be sent? How did this happen?" Meade leaned close to the man's face, raised his voice to a full yell, "Captain, we need some answers!"

The young man paused, tried to swallow, pointed out toward the darkness, said weakly, "The reports . . . I will try to get more reports . . . sir. . . ."

Grant stood, moved close to Meade, said quietly, "The attack on our flank was small. They cannot move a large army in this country any better than we can. It has not been dark for very long, and if I recall, before the sun went down, we still had Ewell in *front* of us. I believe, if your young man here walks in a straight line down the Orange Turnpike, he will still find Ewell's troops. If he doesn't, then come back and tell me. If he does, then we will know for certain whether or not the enemy is in our rear."

There was another rider, a colonel, and the man jumped from his horse, an obvious show of urgency. He had lost his hat, his coat was torn. He stumbled toward them, said, "General Grant . . . General Meade, forgive me, sirs, but I have just come from the shooting. The enemy is moving into our flank with a large force, sir. The entire line is rolling up. Lee is circling behind the army, right back here, sir. The headquarters should be moved. You are in great danger, sir. Lee is—"

Grant held up his hand and the man froze. He turned his head, listened, thought, The shooting has stopped. He glanced at the only sound, the winded breathing of the colonel, and the man slowly straightened, also hearing the silence. Grant moved out into the light, glanced again at the winded officer, the man staring at him with wide wounded eyes. Grant said, "Colonel, you are a bit late. Your great battle has already ended. Your timeliness is noted."

He moved toward the fire, felt the anger again, said aloud, "Gentlemen . . . a word, please. General Meade, if I may speak to your staff?"

Meade said nothing, nodded dumbly.

"Gentlemen, I am growing tired of hearing about all these terrible injuries that General Lee is going to inflict on this army. If I take all your reports into account, we have the rebel army running over both flanks, in our rear, and probably surrounding Washington. I will say this once. I do not wish to hear any more speculation on what General Lee is about to do to *us*. I would encourage you to consider another point of view . . . *my* point of view. You will speculate more on what *I* intend to do, on what *this* army intends to do. Am I clear?"

There was a silent moment, firelight reflecting on the quiet faces.

He put the cigar in his mouth, moved back to his stump and sat down. The faces still watched him, and there was still no sound. He was suddenly exhausted, thought, I do not like making speeches.

The silence was broken by Meade, his voice echoing over the camp. "Anyone who does not have business here is dismissed!"

Men began to move away. Grant could see the fires clearly now, saw Meade looking at him, and Meade nodded grimly, lifted the hat slightly, moved away to his own camp.

Grant looked down, kicked through the wood shavings, saw nothing large enough to attack with the knife. He stood, moved to his tent, thought of Longstreet, said to himself, I hope you are alive, Pete. But we're coming after you again.

MAY 7, 1864

BREAKFAST WAS OVER, AND HE HAD BEEN THE FIRST TO FINISH, walking away from the tents into bright morning sun, the mist already burning away. He still enjoyed the sour taste in his mouth, rolled his tongue around, the first cigar of the day would wait a few more minutes. He had secured a box of cucumbers, and no one gave much thought to the request. The staff was always alert for the possibility of eggs, or even white flour, and the quartermasters would do what they could to accommodate them, would furnish whatever could be had for the commanding general, but the staff never revealed that the luxuries were not for Grant, but for them. He was quite happy with the cucumbers.

They had watched him in silence, slicing it into a mound of neat green circles, then pouring the vinegar over the top. Quickly, he would eat the small feast, and while the others enjoyed the smells, the roasting of bacon, the hot bread, his breakfast was done.

There had been no sounds from the front. No assault came from Ewell, and below there was no faint thunder from in front of Hancock. He knew the skirmish lines were strong, had moved out as far as they could, and the enemy was hard behind his works. To the north, Sedgwick's lines had been adjusted, pulled back slightly, turned to the right. Now a squad of cavalry patrolled up toward the river. There would be no more surprises from that part of the field.

He moved down the hill, could see a long line of wagons behind the camp, the wagons that many had said were captured, Lee's phantom success from the night before.

He was feeling restless, but better than he had since the fight began. He had actually slept, deep and long, dreams of Julia, the children. He'd woken with the bugle, jarred out of some wonderful memory, childhood, very small, riding a horse down the long narrow roads of home. It was the most comforting memory he had, being so very alone, except for the horse. He did not have many friends, had always been shy around the other boys, but after a time, when he'd learned to ride, the people in the small town had come to know him. He had an instinct, a skill for breaking the wild horses, a small boy on a great dangerous animal, holding tight and letting the horse lash out with all its anger. He would feel the horse testing him, would speak to it, and soon the animal would change. The boy could hand the reins to its astonished owner, but the boy would know the horse had no owner, and he always believed the horse knew that as well.

When he was older, at the Point, it was not his quick wit, dry humor, or skill with the lessons that made him friends, but his ability to ride. They had always thought of him as a natural for the dragoons, the cavalry, but he did not have the grades, could not choose where he would serve. The system did not reward the skill of the cadet, just the standing in the class, and his was of no distinction.

He kicked down the hill, through thick grass, and there was a sudden violent flutter, an explosion of small wings. A covey of quail blew up around him, flew away into the trees below. He felt his heart beating, laughed, heard a voice behind him.

"Where's your shotgun, General?"

He turned, still smiled, saw the bulky figure of Elihu Washburne stepping carefully down toward him, the dark formal suit out of place on a grassy hillside.

"It wouldn't matter. I wouldn't hit them anyway."

Washburne reached him, was breathing heavily. He was a large round man with long white hair streaming back from a high, broad forehead. He put a hand on Grant's shoulder, laughed through the heavy breaths, said, "No, I never knew you to show much inclination to hunt. However, your secret is safe with me."

Grant was puzzled. "Secret . . . ?"

"Your dismal marksmanship. If the men knew, might not be good for morale." Washburne laughed again, and Grant smiled.

He had asked Washburne to come along, to travel with the army on the move south and leave behind the dusty walls of the capitol. Washburne had been a congressman from Illinois for years, and it was Washburne who had seen something in this young man that the state of Illinois had sorely needed. When the regiments were organized, the first response to Lincoln's call for volunteers, there had been no one else around Galena qualified to command, to put the regiments together.

Washburne had only known him from those weeks before the real fighting began, had met him the same time as Rawlins met him. Grant's only importance to the people of Galena was that he had been in the Mexican War, but there was celebrity in that. Rawlins was consumed by the romance of it, had come to Grant with boyish enthusiasm, wanting to hear the stories, the exploits, but Washburne had seen much more. He had an instinct for character, saw beyond the shy seriousness, believed that Grant was a man who could give something to his country beyond service in a war that had long faded in importance.

When Washburne took Grant to Governor Yates, Grant had made no great impression, had left the meeting feeling there was no place for him in the *new* army. But there were sharp words behind closed doors, and the strength of Washburne's influence gave Grant his first regimental command.

It was unusual for Grant to warm up to a politician, but there was a connection between them that Grant still did not understand. Washburne was so very different from Grant's father, had seen the world, understood the great complexities of government, of power. Around Washburne, Grant spoke openly, something he did with no one else. He was the one man Grant could feel comfortable letting down the barriers that held away the old enemies, the frailties, the personal failures that no one in that camp could ever be aware of.

As the war spread, and Grant was far removed from the eyes of Washington, it was Washburne who kept his name on the desks of the important, and when the time finally came, when Lincoln made the choice of a commander for the luckless army, Congressman Washburne was given the honor of officially nominating his friend Grant for the new rank of Lieutenant General.

Washburne glanced up at the sun rising above the trees, said, "Anything going to happen today? People seem pretty relaxed."

"Not likely. Lee is back where he can do the most good, behind his works. He *wants* us to come at him now. He's been bloodied pretty bad. He doesn't want many more days like yesterday."

Washburne crossed his arms, glanced up toward the tents, said, "Do we? I hear . . . they hurt us pretty badly too."

Grant said nothing, looked at the ground. He pulled a cigar out, lit it, felt the heat swirl around his face, said, "We can afford it. Lee can't. He knows that."

"I'm not sure of that, my friend. The newspapers want numbers, and we can't give them these kind of numbers. The people won't stand for it. Mr. Lincoln wants to be reelected."

Grant looked at Washburne, seemed surprised. "Reelected . . ." The word struck him. He thought about that, had not considered . . . November. "I suppose that's true."

He stepped through the grass, slowly, felt his way along the side of the hill. Washburne moved beside him, shaky, uncertain steps.

Grant looked at Washburne's shoes. "Need to get you some boots."

Washburne laughed, said, "Boots today, then a uniform tomorrow?" Grant smiled, and Washburne said, "No, I suppose not. One thing you don't need is another politician."

There was a brief rumble, from over the hill. Washburne stopped, looked that way. "Something? Artillery?"

Grant did not look up, said, "One gun, somebody saw a ghost."

Washburne nodded. "A lot of ghosts out there. Some people say Lee's a ghost, everywhere at once, sees everything you do."

Grant looked at the cigar, tossed it aside. "Not anymore. Right now . . . he's expecting us to run away. We have always run away like a whipped colt, run until we're too tired to run anymore."

Washburne was serious now, glanced again at the camp, saw a few faces watching them from a distance, lowered his voice. "Did we lose this fight? Forgive me, General, but the word is Hancock got pretty badly hurt. . . ."

Grant nodded. "Hancock hurt them first, drove Hill's corps right out of these woods. This ground . . . you can't push out so far when you can't see. Lee was lucky, hit us with Longstreet when we were the most vulnerable. Hancock understood how it happened, said he was rolled up like a wet blanket. But Lee couldn't finish the job, didn't have the strength. Like last night—a good plan, they hit Sedgwick where he was vulnerable. But they didn't have the power to hurt us, to *really* hurt us. If Lee does not understand that now, he will very soon. Everywhere we go, he has to follow. Anytime we stop, he will either fight or lose more ground. But it will not happen here. We have done all we can do here. He is in command of the ground. If that means he won this fight, fine. It doesn't really matter. We'll make another fight. He'll have to win that one too. I don't think . . . he can keep winning with what he has left."

Washburne nodded, said, "Just remember the newspapers, the politicians. You see this fight differently than they do. If you admit you lost here, that is all that will matter. Another victory for Lee. You have to anticipate that, face the consequences."

Grant reached for another cigar, stopped, looked at Washburne. "The President told me I would be left alone."

"*He* will leave you alone. But after November . . ."

Grant thought of the politicians, all the reasons why he would never stay in Washington. He felt a sudden anger, said, "There will be no retreat, we will keep this army moving, we will force Lee to come to *us*. We already control the Mississippi, the seaports. If he does not fight us, we will capture his cities, burn his supplies, and destroy his railroads."

Washburne looked down, said, "But . . . what about Davis, and Richmond? If we focus on Lee, that is just one part of the whole. The Confederacy, the rebellion, starts with Jefferson Davis."

Grant looked at Washburne, slowly shook his head. "No, sir. Those men over there, those so-called soldiers of the rebellion, they are not dying for a government in Richmond. They do not charge into our guns screaming the name of Jefferson Davis. They are fighting for *Lee*. Lee *is* the rebellion. If he is defeated, if his army surrenders, then make no mistake, this war is over."

There was another thunderous sound, above the camp, another big gun. Grant looked that way, said, "Richmond serves one purpose. Lee must defend it. If we threaten the city, he will have to confront us. Lee will soon learn . . . we are not going away. If the newspapers and all those people in Washington must hear that, fine, I will write it down, send a letter to Stanton. You can deliver it yourself, read it to him, to all of them, make them understand what we are going to do. If it takes all summer . . . if it takes all year . . . it is only a matter of time before *General Lee* must face the consequences."

EVENING, MAY 7, 1864

ALL DAY LONG THE SKIRMISHERS AND SHARPSHOOTERS FROM both sides prodded and punched the nervous lines of their enemy. Observers were sent out, the deadly job of moving forward until they could actually see them, count the numbers, make sure the strong lines still lay in place.

By late afternoon the Federal wounded had been sent east, a long line of wagons rocking painfully toward Fredericksburg. Now the rest of the wagons, the food and ammunition, began to move, and for a time they moved east as well, but then, once the sounds of creaking wheels and bouncing timbers were beyond the hearing of Lee's look-outs, the wagons began to turn south.

The soldiers lined up as they always had, filled the road with quiet curses, the units smaller now, the lines shorter from the casualties they would leave behind. The officers tried to keep them quiet, but the grumbling was always there, rolled along the column like a dull wave. Much of it was about Grant. They were still not convinced, the great reputation had not shown them much in this place. Lee was still over there, the war was no different yet. But when the orders came to move, and the column began to ease ahead, some of the men did not need the sun to tell them direction. The word began to filter down the lines, and the grumbling stopped, there was something new about this march, something these men had never been a part of before. If the fight in the Wilderness had not gone their way—the most optimistic called it a draw—they were not doing what this army had always done before, they were not going back above the river. If they had never said much about Grant, had never thought him any different from the ones who had come before, if they had become so used to the steady parade of failure, this time there was a difference. Some wanted to cheer, but were hushed by nervous officers. So along the dusty roads hats went up and muskets were held high, a silent salute to this new commander. This time, they were marching *south*.

Well after dark, Sedgwick had pulled away from Ewell, moved back to Chancellorsville, then turned southward. Burnside followed him, taking the same route. Behind Hancock's wary troops, on the Brock Road, Warren's Fifth Corps marched quietly, and only when Warren was safely past did Hancock order his men to fall into column, away from the safety of their log wall. They would march all night, keeping tight and in line, because on the march they would be vulnerable.

Meade had given orders to the cavalry to clear the roads south, and Sheridan had sent the horsemen forward as though the job was already accomplished. But Stuart was waiting, and below the marching columns of infantry, the cavalry ran into a hard stiff wall of gray. By morning the roads were still not clear, the infantry had to slow, began bunching up, the commanders impatient with the unexplainable delay. When Stuart began finally to give way, Sheridan's troopers found themselves confronted not by a reserve force of cavalry, but by infantry. Lee had marched south as well, and if the Federals even knew they were in a race, by the next morning they knew they had lost.

The ground was much better here, the dense brush of the Wilderness fading into farm country, cut by small rivers and patches of heavy woods. Grant's objective had been to move well into the open ground. The maps showed a key intersection, convenient roads spreading to the east and south. But when the infantry could finally advance, they found what the cavalry already knew. Along the wide ridges, behind the heavy fence rows, the men in gray were preparing again, shovels and axes and bayonets throwing and pushing the dirt, cut trees piled high to their front. They formed their lines in an arc, just north of the intersection, a small village known mainly for the one landmark, the courthouse. It was called Spotsylvania.

17. LEE

MAY 9, 1864

HE WAS UP AT THREE, HAD BEGUN TO MAKE THAT HIS ROUTINE. He'd been awake even before that, staring up at the dark and thinking of Jackson. He had never understood how Jackson could come so completely awake after only a short rest, rising with perfect energy. Jackson would often call his men awake hours before the first light, order them up and into the roads before anyone could see what was in front of him. It had worked, of course, even the commanders did not need to know where they were going, something Dick Ewell had found maddening. Jackson never felt the need to tell anyone of his plans, just point them in the right direction, and soon a surprised enemy would find an unstoppable force bearing down on them from someplace where no one had ever thought the enemy would be. But Jackson himself, Lee thought, how could *he* do this, how could *he* go without sleep? Now the image was there, the sharp blue eyes, the image Lee tried not to see. God bless him, he thought. I really do miss him.

He had dressed quietly, and now walked out past the tents, would not even disturb Traveller. He stepped through a small patch of woods, could hear the sounds in front of him, the shovels. The men were working in shifts, and when one group would rest, the shovels would pass to another, and with each hour the entrenchments were stronger.

Jackson would not have done this, he thought. He would not have stopped, dug in to these long lines. The idea had come from Longstreet, and it was the fundamental difference between the two men. Jackson would have them on the road now, or be pressing them through a faint trail in the woods to strike the enemy with deadly surprise. No, Lee thought, something is very different now. The commanders, certainly, on both sides. Jackson had never faced Grant. Lee had wondered about that, especially since Gordon's flank attack on the Federal right, too weak, had begun too late. Jackson would have seen the opportunity immediately, would have stripped his lines bare, sent a great smashing blow around Sedgwick. Lee was certain of that, felt it rise up from some dark hole inside of him.

Ewell could not see that, would not act, would wait for orders. How much longer can Ewell command? he wondered. He is collapsing, not in battle, not in one great disaster, but slowly, a bit each day, becoming weaker in his mind, his resolve crumbling, falling away.

There was another kind of collapse with Hill, but the decay of that command was different. Hill could still perform with the old energy, move his troops with precision, with instinct, but then he would be gone, the sickness would simply swallow him up, and he would sit in his camp completely out of touch, no sense of a plan, his mind completely empty. Lee did not yet understand that, but had seen it with perfect clarity in the Wilderness. The first day, Hill had been perfection, but by the desperate fight on the second day, he was not even on the field. Now the sickness had grown, and Hill was out again, and Lee thought, Will he ever be back?

It was a possibility he could not afford to ignore, and so he had given command of Hill's Third Corps to Jubal Early. He knew how the men felt about Early, especially the officers, but Early was a fighter, and if his personality made quick enemies, he at least knew how to move troops. Hill accepted the change with dignity. Even he knew Lee had no choice. Early's removal from Ewell had created an opening in the Second Corps. Lee quickly promoted John Gordon to command of Early's division.

It had been an easy decision. Lee had felt some of the old enthusiasm, the confidence a commander has when he knows the army is in good hands, that the job will be done. Even though Gordon was not a West Pointer, he had already shown a talent for command and an instinct for strategy. Lee had not felt that way about anyone in a long time, except Stuart. And Longstreet.

The doctors had assured him the wounds were not fatal. Longstreet was far away now, and it would be a long time before he could return to the army, an army that could not afford to be without him. Even with all the criticism of Longstreet, the newspapers, talk of controversy and blame, there was no one Lee would rather confide in, no one with whom he felt comfortable sharing the quiet thoughts, the quiet moments. Now there was no one else.

Dick Anderson now commanded the First Corps, and if the choice had inspired no one, not even Lee, Anderson at least was dependable. Though he'd never shown anything like Jackson's fire or the rugged stubbornness of Longstreet, he had performed with the best skills of both men the day before. It was Anderson who had won the race for Spotsylvania.

Lee moved out of the patch of trees, could see the men outlined against the night sky. The dirt was flying, around him the sound of axes echoing in the woods. He saw logs, carried forward on the shoulders of tired men. The works were becoming a vast long wall, a deep trench behind, a wide ditch in front, sharpened poles and branches pointing out toward the enemy.

He walked down to the left, passed behind long lines of laboring men, and no one saw him, there were no calls, no cheers. He began to climb, a long rise, a wide hill, paused, thought of the name. They called it Laurel Hill, and now it was a great stronghold. Porter Alexander's big guns were dug in facing north and west, the crews moving slowly in the dark, the quiet work of good men, men who know how deadly

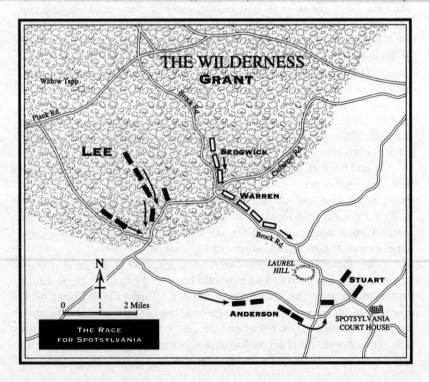

THE RACE
FOR SPOTSYLVANIA

their work could be. There were deep entrenchments here as well; Anderson had the gun positions well protected by infantry. Lee nodded, thought, Nothing will move us from *this* ground.

He began to walk back toward his camp, stopped, looked back up the rise, thought of the words again. *Nothing will move us from this ground.* There was no change greater than that, he thought. Something tugged in his gut, and he was suddenly anxious, angry. Longstreet had always believed in trenches, in hiding behind strong works. But when we won the great battles, he thought, it was because we *attacked*. Longstreet had always argued against that, and there had been Jackson to show him he was wrong. But the men . . . it was the men who began to understand. Lee thought of West Point. We learned how to fight the old way, the books were all about Napoleon, the textbooks translated from the French. But Napoleon did not have these guns. It has taken us too long to learn the lesson. Too many times we have ridden across the bloody fields, spread with the incredible horror of what these guns can do. Longstreet gave them shovels, at Fredericksburg, on the heights, and they laughed, the men thought it was not *manly*. We would stand up and face the guns. Lee shook his head. Now we do not have enough shovels. No one believes in standing up in front of certain death. There is no honor in foolishness.

He could see the tents now, daylight slowly spreading over the rolling ground toward his right flank, where Early was digging his trenches as well. He thought of Grant: We gave him no reason to retreat. Some had said Grant would move away, to Fredericksburg, toward the Rappahannock, running away from his first bloody fight with Lee's army. The rumors spread from the lookouts, excited men who came to Lee with the first reports of troop movement, clouds of dust rising from long lines of black cannon. But Lee had seen the maps, knew that the roads to Richmond came right through . . . *here.* If Grant wants Richmond, he must fight his way through these works, he thought. We must sit and wait. And if he does not come at us here, then we must find his weakness, again, we must strike out at opportunity and we must not be late or make any mistakes. He thought of the commanders again, and the tight tug in his gut returned.

None of them would talk about it, there was no hint of it even from the trenches, from the men on the front line, the men who could *see* the strength of the blue lines in front of them. But it was inside of *him* now, stirring deep in some very small place. *It is only a matter of time.* He had sent that to Davis, a response to the threat from Butler, moving up the peninsula now. The message had been clear and blunt:

Make preparations to protect Richmond, bring troops to protect the rail center at Petersburg. Davis was still seeing the army as some great organizational puzzle, departments to be moved about and manipulated. There were good defenses around Richmond, but Davis was still convinced there must be a presence at all the major points, and even minor ones, anyplace the enemy was a threat. Troops were still scattered down through the Carolinas, a weak attempt at containing a Federal threat that was as much in Davis's mind as it was in the field. But Lee's message did stir something in Richmond, because, finally, Beauregard was moving troops north, from his base in North Carolina. The movement was slow, and the troops very few. Lee had been amazed at that, felt the gut-twisting frustration that no one else seemed to share his concern for the value of Petersburg.

He knew, of course, that Davis would send few reinforcements to him. He had accepted for weeks that he would have to make the fight against Grant with whatever he had. That made the trenches, the defensive tactics, an absolute necessity, because there was nothing he could do about Grant's vastly greater numbers. But it is more than numbers, he thought. It has *always* been more than numbers. Every victory had come against superior forces. The advantage was strategy, tactics, the willingness to do what must be done to win the fight. The Federal commanders had never brought that to the field. And so he had always felt he had the edge, knew that Jackson would devour an enemy many times his size by sheer audacity.

Longstreet could be as stubborn and as vigilant as anyone those other fellows put in line against him. Even Longstreet's "slows," his seemingly sluggish movement, had been positive. Lee had thought Longstreet dangerously slow at Second Manassas, but he had not ordered Longstreet to advance, had relied on Longstreet's judgment, and when the First Corps finally moved, they drove Pope's army into complete chaos. Now, in the fight just past, Lee had to believe that if Longstreet had been in place when he wanted him, if he'd been in line against Hancock's attack, it might have been disastrous. He knew Hancock was the best they had, and his strength might have driven Longstreet back as it had Hill. Longstreet's "delay" in reaching the field might have been the one reason why Hancock collapsed. The timing, ultimately, had been perfect.

He felt the tug in his gut again, thought, If it is that, the intangible, something inside of us, something *they* do not have, then what have we lost? Who is it that I can trust to take a fight to the great numbers, and who will prevail? The name burned in his mind, the laughing face, the red beard, the ridiculous hat. Of course, he thought . . . Stuart. He smiled, nodded to himself. Yes, we still have that, *his* spirit is still in these men, and they will still look to him. He has learned along with the rest of us, he has made mistakes and gained the experience, and with that comes our ability to win this fight, *still* win this fight. But the others . . . there must still be time, they must learn. They may all rise to it, men like Gordon, Anderson, Early, but we may not have much time. And so I must do *this*, check the lines, I must be closer. I must watch over them all. I must make sure there are *no* mistakes.

He could see the staff now, moving around the small fire, and he moved toward the wagons where the food would be, felt himself sweating, his breathing short and hard. He glanced at his tent, thought of the small bed, felt the weariness crawling over him, settling down into the turmoil of his gut. He took a deep breath, tried to hold himself together, tightened the grip inside, said aloud, "No."

Faces turned toward him, but he did not see them, was staring out toward the gray light rising over the far trees, thought of Grant. Now there is *another* change. So now there will not be much sleep.

18. GRANT

MAY 9, 1864

THEY CALLED HIM "UNCLE JOHN," AND THERE WERE FEW IN THIS army who had earned as much respect from their troops as Sedgwick. If he had not shown the kind of heroism that made newspapermen happy, he had always been a solid commander, had led troops since the beginning of the war, and commanded the Sixth Corps since Chancellorsville. He was older than most, had come out of the Point in 1837, the same year as Jubal Early. A New Englander by birth, he carried none of the trappings of the "easterner," and many could not believe this rugged man was from New England. There was too much of the western frontier in him, the sharp eye of a man who has fought the Indian, the rugged exterior of a man who understands trickery, who understands his enemy.

He had served in Mexico, after winning a fighter's reputation in the first Seminole Wars. Afterward, in an army that lost many of its best men to the tedium of the frontier, Sedgwick had thrived, fought Indians wherever the action was hot, served in Utah and then Bloody Kansas, when the army found itself in the center of the worst kind of violence, citizens fighting each other over the question of slavery.

He could be gruff and profane, but the men loved him because he was efficient, because he knew how to place his troops where they would do the most good, with the least harm. He'd been up front again this morning, correcting one officer's mistake, adjusting lines of infantry that had dug in too close to the mouths of their own big guns. The men on the front lines had become wary of the rebel sharpshooters, stayed low, flinching from the small bits of lead whistling overhead, sent at them from a hidden enemy very far away. Sedgwick had laughed at them, teased one man in particular, a sergeant, who was curled into a ball on the ground. Sedgwick had stood straight, gazing out across the open ground to far trees, the cover of those men with the long rifles, was still laughing when the bullet struck him, below the eye, spun him around and dropped him onto the sergeant who still crouched low beside him.

P ORTER WAS SHAKING, AND GRANT WAITED, COULD SEE IT IN THE man's face, stung with the terrible news.

"Sir, yes, General Sedgwick was killed . . . just a few minutes ago. They're bringing the body back now."

Grant stared at the young man, said nothing. He held the cigar in his hand, looked at it, watched the ash fall to the ground, looked at Porter again, said, "Are you certain? Is he really . . . dead?" He stood, walked toward the tent, felt himself weaken, draining of energy. This is a disaster, he thought, worse than the loss of a division. He pictured Sedgwick's face, the large heavy man, handsome, graying beard. How does that happen, one man . . . just taken away? He looked back at Porter again, said, "Is he really dead, Colonel? Are you *certain?*"

Porter nodded quietly.

Grant moved into the tent, sat down on the hard bed, stared at nothing. He thought, We should tell Meade . . . but of course, Meade would know. And Meade would have to choose someone to replace him, someone to command a very good corps. There were not many good commanders to choose from.

He had hoped to hit Lee hard this morning, but the army was still moving in slow steps, cautious and clumsy. Meade wanted to assault the flanks, had sent Hancock to the west, into a ragged terrain of woods and water, while Burnside would try to move east and attack what should be an exposed flank. But nothing was happening, there was no coordination, and Grant was understanding finally why for three years this army had not won its fights.

He had watched Meade carefully, knew that Meade was still edgy about his job, still carried the insecurity that it would take only one sharp moment, one episode when Grant lost his temper, and he would be gone. Grant knew Meade was not very happy being so close to the eye of his commander, but he had not wanted Meade removed for he knew that Meade still knew his own army better than he did. If Grant had once thought that unimportant, now, at this moment, realizing the Sixth Corps needed a new commander, he understood why Meade had to remain. But there was still frustration, and he thought, I cannot get him to understand, if we are to make a mistake, let it be because we moved too quickly, not too slowly. He thought of Sheridan, and knew the two men had not gotten along, not at all, two men with strong egos and very different ways of thinking. The staff had told him this morning that Sheridan was meeting with Meade, that the staffs had gathered at a respectful distance while a violent argument boiled out of Meade's tent. He knew that if they did not come to some agreement, if Meade was stubborn enough to stick to his old ways and did not share Sheridan's understanding of cavalry tactics, he would hear about it, would have to settle it himself. He felt suddenly anxious, frustrated, tossed the stump of a cigar out through the tent flaps. Lee is right out there, waiting for us, he thought. He can move faster, because he has fewer troops to move, fewer wagons, fewer guns. All the things that give us the advantage also slow us down. And he has fewer commanders, he has control of his army. It seems . . . that I do not.

Burnside had still not moved into position, the assault on Lee's right flank delayed, the only sounds the small rattle of skirmishing. I cannot just . . . relieve everyone who doesn't perform to my standards, he thought. I cannot put colonels into command of divisions, and I cannot command the corps myself.

He moved back outside, saw Porter still standing by his small table, waiting for him, waiting for instructions. Along the road he could see wagons moving in both directions, some filled with wounded men from the fights exploding along the front lines, the uncoordinated bursts of activity. He saw one flag, the St. Andrew's cross, the flag of the Sixth, men gathered around, some hearing the awful news for the first time. He could see the looks on the faces, the shock, could hear the sounds now, one man sobbing out loud. This will take something away from them, he thought. For a while, at least, they will not fight the same way.

Lee lost Jackson, and then lost Gettysburg. But we will not lose here, not on this ground, not with these men. Every time we go at him, every good fight, even on those days when it is very bad, we bring something away, we add that to who we are, and we become better, stronger. There is something in the men who are veterans . . . they *know* they are veterans, they have seen the worst of it, some have seen the worst of themselves. Even if they have endured bad commanders, have endured defeat by an enemy none thought would be so strong or so well commanded, we are still better equipped, and by now we are better prepared.

He thought of the chessboard again. If Lee is faster, more compact, we still have the power, and we will just keep at him. If he keeps moving south, we will follow him south, and very soon he will run out of places to go. But for now he is right out there, and maybe today, or tomorrow . . . he glanced at the sky, the bright sun. The weather is ours, but the longer we delay . . .

He moved toward Porter, said, "Colonel, go to General Meade. Ask him if he has chosen a replacement for General Sedgwick."

H E HEARD MEADE FIRST, THE BOOMING ANGRY VOICE, HAD grown used to it, the voice that seemed to carry over the entire field. Usually it was aimed at a staff officer, often an innocent man who happened to bring the wrong piece of information, something Meade might not want to hear. But the voice was coming closer, and Grant sat up on his bed, wiped his face with his hand, heard another voice now, a high pitch, clear anger. It was Sheridan.

He tried to clear his head, had told Rawlins he would take a short rest, had not expected to fall asleep. He still sat on the bed, waited, listened, and the voices were close, grew quiet, small low comments, like two angry children coming to Papa, both of them right, both of them wrong.

It was Rawlins, the face appearing between the tent flaps. "Sir, forgive the interruption to your rest. We have visitors."

Grant motioned with his hand, a small wave. "Be right out. Tell them not to kill each other before I get there."

Rawlins looked at him with wide eyes, said, "I don't think it has come to that. . . ." He glanced back, then looked inside again, whispered, "But it would be advisable, sir, if you were to make haste."

Grant pulled on his boots, and Rawlins held the flap back, stood stiffly as Grant moved past. He squinted at the sunlight, saw the two men standing formally at attention, waiting for him. He reached into his pocket, felt for a cigar, but the pocket was empty. He sagged, thought, Worse yet, I am unarmed. He said, "Well, gentlemen, are we feeling the full effects of this awful day?"

Neither man spoke, glanced at each other, then Meade nodded, said, "Yes, sir. It is an awful day indeed. John Sedgwick was much loved. There is a gloom throughout the Sixth Corps, if not the whole army."

Grant nodded, and Sheridan said, "Yes, gloom. Now, sir, allow me to address you directly, if that is permissible. I do not wish to offend the chain of command." There was sarcasm in Sheridan's voice.

Grant took a deep breath, said, "You may proceed, General."

Sheridan stepped forward, his face began to flash fire, and he removed his hat, held it tightly, said, "General Grant, it is my contention that this army has been habitually misusing its cavalry. General Meade and I have quite different viewpoints with regard to the function of the horsemen. I have tried to convince General Meade that we should not be assigned such mundane tasks as guarding wagons and scouting the countryside for the general's dinner!"

Grant looked at Meade, saw the eyes expand, waited for the coming explosion.

"Dinner! I have never suggested . . . ! General, this is outrageous!" Meade puffed, removed his hat, his fist curling the brim hard in his hand. Grant raised his hand, calming, thought, No, General, don't hit him with the hat.

"Gentlemen, I have no time for this. I would like to hear something more specific, from both of you. General Sheridan, if you don't feel the cavalry is being used properly, then give me an alternative. What would be *your* strategy?"

Sheridan nodded, was clearly prepared for this moment, said in a quiet voice, "Sir, from everything I have heard, this army's cavalry has, more often than not, been turned about, confused and left highly embarrassed by the skill of the enemy in general, and Stuart in particular. From what I understand of your overall plan, sir, we are to pursue General Lee's army until we can draw him into a fight. If you will allow, I would like the same opportunity. I propose to take this army's cavalry and, instead of raiding supply depots and vandalizing railroad tracks, I would like to pursue General Stuart. If given a free hand . . ." He glanced at Meade. "If given a free hand, I will *whip* General Stuart." Sheridan put his hat on, a final punctuation mark.

Grant looked at Meade, said, "General?"

Meade glanced at Sheridan, put his hat on as well, said, "He will leave us blind. We cannot maneuver this army in the enemy's country without the use of cavalry."

Sheridan turned, said, "General, you have not allowed me to maneuver at all! You counter my orders, you place my men without consulting me . . ."

Grant felt a small headache blooming, reached again, felt the inside of the empty pocket, said, "That's it, gentlemen. General Meade, if General Sheridan says he can whip Stuart, then we should let him. If we destroy the enemy's cavalry, we will have gained an advantage that may hasten the end of the war."

Sheridan beamed a smile, saluted Grant, said, "Sir, we will move immediately! I will send regular reports."

"Send them to General Meade. You are dismissed."

Sheridan spun, moved away, began to shout instructions to his staff. Grant looked at Meade, who stared down at the ground like a scolded puppy. Grant said, "General, we must take risks. We *know* where Lee is, and for now, the cavalry's eyes are not as important as what he may be able to accomplish." He paused. "Do we have a replacement for General Sedgwick?"

Meade looked up, nodded. "Yes, sir. It was a bit of a problem . . . General Ricketts was next in line by rank. But it was always Sedgwick's preference that Horatio Wright succeed him, in the event . . . He will be adequate to the task. The men will accept him, I believe."

Grant nodded, thought of Wright, had known him in the West, a good engineer, had commanded in Ohio briefly. "Fine. I will send his name to Washington. Is that all for now, General?"

Meade nodded, saluted. Grant returned it, and Meade moved away. Grant watched him, felt the headache again, moved toward the tent, and Rawlins appeared, rushed in front, lifted the flap. Grant looked at him, said, "Colonel, you will do me a great service if in the future, before we deal with these people, you remind me not to forget my cigars."

May 10, 1864

H E HAD BELIEVED THE ARMY WAS READY, HAD THOUGHT THEY would begin a general assault all along Lee's lines. Burnside was on the left, and if Lee had strengthened his flank, Grant knew Burnside had the numbers. The ground was not difficult, there was no anchor to protect the rebels from being swept away by the three large divisions that Burnside could push forward. On the right, Hancock was still finding rough going, his forces spread over a deep creek, movement hampered by woods and the guns of Lee's left. Grant knew that Lee was responding to the threats to both his flanks, and so it was likely Lee's center had been weakened. There was still Laurel Hill of course, with the mass of big guns that commanded much of the field, but a quick strike, a hard cutting blow to the center, could break Lee's army in half. Both the Fifth and Sixth Corps were in position, and even some of Hancock's people could shift to the left and add to the strength. All they would require was a first wave, one spearhead, to make a quick thrust at Lee's position, break through, and then the vast numbers from the two corps could rush up support. By dark it could be over. The two halves of Lee's army could be rolled up in two neat packages, or at worst, Lee would be gone, a headlong rush southward toward safer ground, a confused and panicked retreat.

The plan came from one young man, Emory Upton, ambitious, egotistical, with a good eye for tactics and a good eye on his own reputation. He was not popular with his troops, commanded a brigade with his focus clearly on a greater responsibility. But if his men had no particular regard for their colonel, the commanders above had great respect for his plan.

The attack would be Upton's brigade, reinforced by four additional regiments from the Sixth Corps. Upton was explicit in his orders: there would be no firing, no stopping to shoot at the strong log works of the rebels. They would move quickly across the open ground, a tight spearhead, punching across the rebel line in one small break. Once beyond, the break would be widened, and Upton would be reinforced. Support would come first from another brigade to his left, and then, all along the front, a general assault that would prevent Lee from shifting troops to the damaged center.

The attack began with the same hopeful optimism this army had seen too many times before, and it was a failure from the first command. The troops assigned to support Upton's men were not in place. Farther along the line, the Fifth Corps faced Laurel Hill, and the men there had no enthusiasm for assaulting a nearly impossible position. Hancock's Second Corps was divided, still fumbling through the confusion on the right. Burnside was in the best position on the field, could have moved at any time toward a weak defense, a defense that was weaker still because Lee had pulled troops away, strengthening the rest of the line, something no one on the Federal side knew.

Upton's men did exactly as he had planned, ran across the deadly open field, leaping up and over the rebel trenches. The fight lasted an hour. Behind him, Upton saw the open field empty of the vast support he was to have received, empty except for the scattered bodies of his own men.

GRANT LOOKED AT THE MAP AGAIN, RAN HIS FINGER ALONG THE curving arc of Lee's lines. He made a fist, wanted to pound the table, shatter it into pieces, held his hand tight above the map, took a deep breath, let it go. He stood straight, looked at the faces watching him. No one spoke. He caught the eyes of each man, slowly, moved his stare through the group. Some returned the look, some looked away, and he thought, Yes, they know . . . the ones who will not look me in the eye, they know who carries the blame.

Most of them were there, the commanders who had failed their men. He still stared at them, and the silence lasted for a full minute, then two. He saw fidgeting now, saw Rawlins, standing to one side, nervous, shifting his weight.

"What is it, Colonel? You have something to say?"

Rawlins turned pale, hesitated, then said, "Uh . . . sir, do you have any orders?"

Grant looked back toward the assembled group, the firelight now reflecting off the polished brass, the gold braid decorating the sagging shoulders. He glanced at Rawlins, thought, They should stand here all night. He looked briefly at Horatio Wright, his first day in corps command, saw Meade, moving slowly forward, preparing for Grant's verbal assault. There were others, men who had come to headquarters with their commanders, a few Grant did not know. He glanced at the faces, said, "Any of you . . . Colonel Upton?"

There was a silent pause, and Wright stepped forward. "General, Colonel Upton was wounded in the assault. He will survive, but he is at the corps hospital."

"Keep me advised, General. He's the only one of . . . *us* who did his job today." He reached for a cigar, the last one in his pocket, rolled it over in his hand, then lit it slowly.

Meade cleared his throat, said, "General, I will forward to you General Wright's official request for Colonel Upton's promotion to brigadier general. We all are aware, sir, that he performed an extraordinary task today."

Grant held the cigar tightly in his teeth, looked at Meade, said, "Fine." He stepped toward the fire, flicked an ash out into the flames. The others began to move closer behind him, still quiet. He looked at them again, said, "Gentlemen, what do we have to do? Is it . . . too many men? Do we simply have too many men to coordinate an attack? Is it the reports, our intelligence? I was told Lee was weak in his center, only his flanks were strong. I am safe in saying, gentlemen, that Lee was most definitely *not* weak in his center." He glanced around, knew already who was not there.

"I do not see General Burnside. Smart man." He thought, No, no personalities, don't single anyone out. No one is more at fault than I am.

Warren moved up to the fire now, a small, handsome man, always dapper, a wide gold sash across his waist. He said, "General Grant, perhaps we should have . . . discussed today's plan in detail . . . a council of war perhaps."

Grant pulled the cigar from his mouth, looked at Warren, was not surprised that this would come from him, the man whose attention to detail exceeded anyone's in the army.

"General Warren, councils of war do not *fight*. They allow disagreements of opinion to affect judgment. The council of war you should be concerned with is *this* one." He tapped the side of his head. "That seems to be a problem. My decisions do not seem to be reaching all of you with enough . . . authority. I had thought we had a plan today. If we had made a general assault, struck the flanks hard, then Colonel Upton's strike at the center could have been supported. Am I correct that Upton was successful?"

Meade said, "Yes, sir. Quite successful, sir. His men broke through the enemy's line, held a gap open for nearly an hour. There was . . . failure to exploit the success."

Wright glanced at Meade, said, "General, there was not time . . . there was poor communication. Colonel Upton's plan was precisely correct, sir. We . . . did not follow it up."

Grant moved through the men, a path opening in the gathering of blue coats. He moved toward his tent, felt the frustration building, muttered to himself, "No, we did not follow it up . . . not at all."

He stopped, turned, said, "What would you have me do about that? I could court-martial all of you, but someone would insist I be on that list as well. Fine. So we will move forward, move past this. This was a terrible day. I do not want to hear how much better we may have performed if John Sedgwick was here. He is not here, and I have confidence that General Wright can handle the job. *Learn* from this, gentlemen. If Colonel Upton's plan worked, then we will use that. If those damned fortifications over there can be broken, if one colonel can take one brigade across that field, then we should consider what an entire corps could do. I have no doubt that the enemy is still where we left him today. We have given him no reason whatsoever to change that. We *gave* him a victory today. If there was ever a day an army was not served by its command, this was it. Think about nothing else . . . think about the men we left out on that ground today. The opportunity is still there . . . *Lee* is still there, waiting for us. Next time, gentlemen, we will do it right!"

19. STUART

MAY 11, 1864

THE SCOUTS HAD REPORTED THAT SHERIDAN WAS MOVING south with nearly thirteen thousand horse soldiers, three times what Stuart could bring to the field. They were spread along the roads that led straight at the heart of Richmond, in a column over ten miles long.

He had ridden all night, rested now on the side of a wide hill. He lay flat in the thick grass, stared up at a cloudy sky, the clouds growing darker, rolling in from the west. He tried to focus, to concentrate on what would happen now, the fight with Sheridan's cavalry swelling up in front of him. But he stared far away into the dark sky and saw only the sad face of his wife, Flora's eyes still digging into him, a gloom from her that he had not expected.

He had seen her that morning, could not help himself. Flora and the children were close by, guests of an estate where they all had felt safe, far behind the lines, far from the threat of Grant's army. But Sheridan's advance had changed that, and Stuart would not let duty keep him away from his family. It had been inside of him for a while now, since the first fight at Spotsylvania. He would not talk about it, but everyone close to him knew the laughter, the swagger, was gone. The staff saw it as a new sense of danger, the focus on the new enemy, that Stuart, for all his arrogance and strut, would prove he was still the best cavalry officer of the war. Now the war was changing, and the men believed Stuart was changing with it, getting down to the serious business of dealing with a serious enemy.

He didn't know what the men were seeing, had thought he was the same. But if they saw the change, it was because he was feeling it deep inside, a small black hole spreading inside of him. He had thought, it is her, it is the children, I have not seen them in so long. But it was deeper than even that, of missing his children, of holding his wife tenderly against him. He only knew it was important to see them, to leave the men and the pursuit of the enemy for just a brief time. The staff understood, of course, no one would find fault with that.

The ride had been fast and short, and he rode hard into the lush green yard of the grand house, had called out, saw the children first, the yard filling with all the children in the house, joyous cries, rushing toward this grand soldier on the fine horse, gathering around him, touching the animal. Then he saw Flora, rushing onto the porch, down into the green of the rich yard, and the tears came from both of them. It was painfully quick, he did not even dismount the horse, something holding him away, pulling him back. They touched hands, he had leaned down and kissed her, looked for a long moment into her eyes, through the tears, then rode quickly away.

He had not looked back, now wished he had, wished he'd said more to the two children. Staring at the dark gray sky, he tried to see them. We should have time, he thought, the time to sit, talk with them, smile at the playful stories. He had never let that bother him before, the war was *his* playground. He'd always thought the time would come later, gathering around the great fireplace, the marvelous stories of his great and glorious battles. He always saw a future bright with the promise of a life for his children, a life in a new South, independent, prosperous. It had never occurred to him that they could lose the war, that God would allow him to go home in defeat. He stared at the motion, the rolling wave of thick clouds, thought, No, it will never be like that. I would rather be dead. . . .

His men were in dismal condition, had ridden hard and long to catch up to Sheridan's head start. The horses had not fared well through the winter, and every man had the responsibility to do the best he could with his mount, but the grain was scarce, and the horses had to subsist on worse than what the soldiers had. If the men accepted that there was not enough to eat, the horses showed the effects, the thin weakness of slow starvation. The spring had brought new growth to the open fields, and when the men rested now, the horses at least could graze, but it hadn't been enough, the stamina was not there, there was no time. During the night, they pushed the horses hard, there was no choice, and so today neither the mounts nor the men were in shape for a hard fight.

They had thought it obvious that Sheridan was making a strong raid into Richmond—it was the largest Federal cavalry force ever assembled in one column. Stuart divided his smaller forces, sent one thrust at Sheridan's rear guard again and again. But the attacks had no power, were only a minor annoyance, and they did not stop the great mass of blue from pushing south. Stuart had taken the bulk of his force on a parallel route, shorter, to strike at Sheridan's exposed flanks, to hit him from the side, hurt him enough to slow the column, make them turn back to confront the danger from Stuart's hard blow. It would keep Sheridan occupied so Richmond could prepare, give the defenders there the time to make ready.

They were north of Sheridan's path, above a crossroads named for a long-abandoned stage stop, Yellow Tavern, only six miles from the streets of Richmond. He had sent word to Davis, asking for help from the small infantry force that crouched in the defenses around the city. But there hadn't been time, and the defenders were watching the greater danger, to the east, where Butler's advancing army was plodding forward.

Sheridan was coming from the northwest, and Stuart spread his men along the best ground, along the crest of the rolling hillsides above the intersection. The men were in a strong line, along the ridges, waiting for the long blue column to pass below them on their way down to the city. If Davis had sent the infantry, they could have slowed Sheridan enough for Stuart to hit him hard, trapping Sheridan from two directions. It might have been the only way the smaller number could turn back the great blue force. But now he understood there would be no help, there would be no infantry, that what forces he had above Yellow Tavern would be all he could throw into the fight.

He could hear the musket fire now, the feeling out, scouts from both sides pressing into the other. He sat up, saw his staff watching him, following his lead, and quickly the men were moving to the horses, the short rest over.

He had never believed it would happen this way, that the glory of all he had done, the reputation and the victories, would be overshadowed, slowly erased by an evolution he could not predict. As badly as his horses had suffered, the Federal horses had grown fatter. As his men were beaten down by the lack of supplies, by the poor food, the enemy was stronger, their equipment better. He knew about the Spencer carbines, of course, the seven-shot short-barreled rifles the bluecoats were using. It was a sad joke, the men complaining that the Yankees could load on Monday and shoot at you every day of the week. His men still used single-shot carbines, and even when they captured the new weapons, there was no way to load them. The arms makers in the South did not have the ability to produce the new-sized cartridges. But he did not see the new weapons as a turning point, as something that would turn the fight against him.

The Federal commanders had never understood the tactics, never used their cavalry to any advantage, the greater numbers, the better horses. He thought of Sheridan again, had wondered if there was anything about this man that was different, if he would bring something new, any kind of challenge, something to bring the excitement back to the glorious fight. At Spotsylvania his men had endured the repeating rifles, the stronger horses, but still they kept the enemy away, held Sheridan back long enough for the infantry to hold the important ground. Now there was no infantry, no piece of ground to hold. This would be a fight between men, one man pressing forward, one man doing everything he could to turn him away.

He climbed the horse, patted the neck, and the staff waited for him to give the order. He stared out to the west, then to the south, could see small wisps of smoke rising from the woods, from the small skirmishes. He knew his men would be falling back, the feeling out would be over very soon, and Sheridan would resume the march, push his men forward in a clear open dash down the open roads to Richmond.

He thought of Sheridan, knew only what he'd heard, the small fiery man, full of hot words and reckless tactics. There *was* a difference in this man, something Stuart had not expected. He had become so used to the rest, Averill, Stoneman, Kilpatrick, men you never saw, who did not understand momentum, the value of quickness, control of the field. Stuart was used to having a fight go his way, as though he had orchestrated it, both sides, guiding the men into line, riding through the fight itself, feeling the rhythm of the battle, the momentum, the glorious action. Even if the fight was not perfect, if his men took the worst of it, there was something to be had from the fight itself, of pushing the horses across the dangerous ground, the screams, the thunderous sounds of the battle. It was the thing he lived for, the one thing about this war that made sense of the horror, of the loss of the men around him. That they would win, that his men would ultimately destroy the enemy, was never in doubt. If his men were ever unsure, all they would have to do was watch their commander, the wide cape, the plumed hat, riding through them with the sword high, yelling at them with all the fire in his soul. They would see it in his face, in his eyes, and would share the same fire, the spirit for the fight. It was *fun*.

He knew the change had come to him at Spotsylvania. The fight with Sheridan had been grim and desperate. The enemy had not run away, had been merely *held* away, a brutal fight for every foot of ground. He could not make the glorious rides, could not spend time in the rallying of his men, the playful shouts at the enemy. There had been no time for anything but the hard and deadly fight.

He knew how well that fight had gone, what an extraordinary day it had been. He'd seen it in Lee's face, the softness, the glint in the old man's eyes. He had learned that about Lee, long ago. You would not hear the words, Lee would not tell you if you did well, but there was no mistaking the look, the small quiet nod. Only once, the disastrous day at Gettysburg, had there been something else, the anger. Even then there was no scolding reproach, none of the loss of temper, the profane violence so common from men like Ewell. But Lee's words had been very clear. Stuart had taken that with him, carried it now always, had *never* felt anything like the shock of that, the horrible aching image of Lee's disappointment. It had brought him closer to the old man than even Lee had understood, and Stuart had made a vow to himself—there would never be any reason for Lee to be disappointed; he would never see that look on the old man's face again.

Far down the rise he could see men coming out of the far trees, his own men, moving back up to the strong lines. They had been on foot mostly, hidden in the thickness of the creek bottoms, picking at Sheridan's skirmishers through heavy trees. They'd done all they could, and now it would be up to the main body if Sheridan would be stopped here. He looked to the side, along the crest of the ridge, saw long lines of horsemen disappearing into a thick wood. He thought, Yes, we can move the flank down close to the road without being seen.

The staff was behind him now, and he turned, saw Venable, said, "Go . . . to the trees . . . tell them to watch their right. They should advance in the trees as far as they cannot be seen. Tell Wickham to move at his discretion." He knew those men well, his first command, the first Virginia regiments. He nodded, thought, Yes, they will know what to do.

He glanced at the sky, saw gray clouds turning darker still, heard a distant rumble. Along the line men began to talk, the tension slipping out of them, horses moving, the violent sound familiar. But he stared to the west, above the trees, saw the brief flash. It was not cannon, but lightning, thunder, a solid black wall moving toward them, a sharp wind whipping through the trees, blowing up and over the crest of the hill. He watched the swirling of the black clouds, saw shapes, like long dark fingers, a fist curling tightly, then dissolving, then another. He stared, had a sudden rush of energy. Yes, it is the hand of God. He is here!

From below, in the direction of the tavern, his men were still moving up the ridge, and now horsemen appeared, rode up toward him. He was still watching the violence of the storm above him, and the men came close and reined the horses, watching him.

One man saluted, said, "Sir, the enemy is stopping. They're forming on this side of the road. They are not moving past."

He looked past the man, down the wide hill, and now beyond a row of trees he saw movement, a heavy column of blue. They were forming into thick lines, facing the ridge where he sat. He heard thunder again, the wind whipped around him, nearly took his hat off, and he grabbed the hat, wanted to wave it high, to shout, the glorious call to the fight, the cheer that always filled his men with the bloody fire. But the sound did not come. He looked up again, to the solid black wall blowing over the trees, the rain now soaking his men down the line. Now he saw the enemy flags held stiffly by the wind, and behind, coming up the rise slowly, a vast line of blue crawling forward, moving straight at the crest of the ridge.

"Sir, they aren't moving south anymore. They are coming right at us!" Stuart glanced at the man, said nothing, still held the hat in his hand. The rain began to blow around them now, and he felt a sudden chill, as if pulled very far away, watching this unfold from some great distance.

The blue mass began to move up the rise, and now there was new thunder, the sound of big guns.

Down the hill the high screams began to streak overhead, whistling shot hurtling past him. He heard the voices of his men now, the rebel yell rising, spreading in a wave over the ridge. His men began to return the fire, the sharp rattle of the carbines mixed with the sound of the cannon, hard bursts behind him, all along the line.

He lifted his field glasses, scanned the blue lines, stared through the wetness, searched among the flags, the long rows of horsemen, looked for *him*, thought, Sheridan is there, I should be able to see him. He should make himself seen, face me. He grabbed his sword, yelled a violent sound, felt the cold rising in his chest, looked up, his eyes blinded by the rain. Now he knew what was happening, why the raid had begun in the first place. He felt like God had opened something inside of him, a window into some perfect place, and suddenly he could see with absolute clarity.

Yes, there *was* a difference. Sheridan was doing what none of them had done before. The blue horsemen were not moving on Richmond, the prize was not railroad cars and supply lines. He put the glasses down, stared out to the heavy wave of blue, thought, You are coming after . . . *me*.

THROUGH THE SMOKE AND THE RAIN, THEY PUSHED THE LINES back and forth through the muddy fields. When there were no lines, men fought in small bunches, the horses bringing them together, hand-to-hand struggles, sword against sword, pistols blazing into the faces of men you could touch.

Many of them were on foot, the horses shot away, moving desperately to stay together, some kneeling to shoot, others lying flat in the shallow depressions, trying to load wet powder, their carbines useless in the downpour.

Stuart kept the horse in motion, directed men into line, whatever men he could rally, kept them moving to the front, to the awful confusion of the fight. He had counted the enemy flags, knew it had been only one division, Merritt's, the tough brigades of Custer, Devin, and Gibbs. Stuart held the good ground, kept the fight from pushing them too far in disorder. But there was no pause, Sheridan kept coming, moving Wilson's division into the fight, and slowly, order broke down, and over every rise, in every small depression, men found themselves in the face of the enemy, and then, short yards away, a blessed line of friends.

It lasted all morning, then into the afternoon. Stuart rode along a fence line, stopped, saw a group of his men trying to form a line, and he pointed out over a low rise, yelled, "There, advance there!"

The men saw him, one officer waving a sword, and they moved up and over the rise. On the far side a small cluster of blue soldiers were turning that way, to meet the new threat, and now smoke flowed up toward Stuart, the sounds of the volley mixed with the steady hiss of the rain.

He held the horse against the fence line, saw men moving up beside him, using the fence for protection, firing now at glimpses of blue. He glanced down, saw bodies along the far side of the fence, faces staring up, washed clean by the rain. All around him, bodies of both sides were scattered along every fence, at the edge of every rise, against every tree. But he would not look at that, yelled to the men around him, "Give it to them . . . there, over there! For your country . . . ! For the glory of God . . . !"

The men were looking toward him, more now moving up along the fence, and the wind howled around him, the cape billowing out, the red lining flashing at the enemy, a red shadow wrapping around him. He saw blue now, men stopping to aim, and around him, his men answered with a blast of fire.

He looked across the field, saw another fence, small trees, could see his men lining up behind, scattered pops of firing, small flashes in the dark rain, the men who could keep their powder dry. He saw a scattering of blue, soldiers caught in a small trap, men falling, then more blue, moving toward the fence. There was a burst of smoke, the blue mass dissolving, and Stuart raised the hat, let out a yell. Around him, faces looked up, and he saw the fire, the victory. He kept the hat high, and the men began to yell with him.

In the field before them, down a wide slope, men were streaming back toward the road, men in blue, scattered and broken, and Stuart pointed, yelled again, and there was musket fire from the fence beside him. Farther up the fence line a new wave of blue came over the rise, but it was not a line of battle. The men were running, the faces staring straight ahead, looking for the safety of their own lines. He raised his pistol, pointed it at a group of blue, only yards away, fired the pistol, fired until it was empty, felt the rage building, felt the horse move beneath him, thought, Yes, we will charge them . . . God is with us . . . God has seen the glory of our fight!

He glanced to each side, looked for officers, looked again to the front, saw men in blue moving past in a wave of blind retreat. Now one man turned, and Stuart saw the man's face, older, a face that did not have the panic of the men around him. The man's eyes focused on him now, and the man stopped moving, stared at Stuart with a black calm, the eyes cold and hard. Stuart felt a chill, could not turn away from the man's stare, the noise around him quieting, fading into the hard whisper of the rain, and it was just the two of them, alone in the swirling black of the storm.

The man slowly raised his arm, held a pistol, pointed it with a steady hand, and Stuart sat up straight in the saddle, now saw the bright flash, felt the hard punch in his stomach, his breath sucked away. The man lowered the pistol, still looked at him with the cold eyes, then turned, walked away, disappeared into the black rain.

20. LEE

MAY 11, 1864

THE RAIN FELL ALL THROUGH THE AFTERNOON, THE MEN HUD-
dled in the deepening mud of the trenches. The high mound of
dirt and timber in front of them was a solid wall of protection,
and the enemy had not come back. Many were beginning to believe
that he would not come back at all, that this ground, the massive
strength of these entrenchments, would push Grant into motion. The
fight would be somewhere else.

The engineers had designed the line, spread along the high brow
of ridges that wound through the swamps and open fields. The line extended forward in the center, pushed out around a ridge, formed an inverted U, and the engineers knew it was not the best way to design a
defense, that the U itself was vulnerable. But if the line had been
straight, the high ground would have been out front, in the enemy's
hands, and artillery could have used the hill to cause serious problems
for Lee's entire position. The soldiers called it the "mule shoe," and the
men who settled into the works in front kept a careful eye toward the
gentle roll of the open ground in front of them and to the solid line of
woods beyond. But the day had passed with only the scattered firing of
the skirmishers, the occasional glimpse of the enemy by the vigilance
of the sharpshooter. The great mass of men just sat in place, wet and
chilled and miserable.

The dark came early, flowed across the woods and fields under
the heavy weight of the clouds. They had seen this before, knew by
now that when the rain settled upon them like this, there would be no
relief. This was a Virginia spring, and the streams and swamps fed off
the storm, and the men knew the left flank was safe for now. Where
Hancock had tried to press around them, it was nearly impassable, the

creek beds roaring, pouring new water into the boggy lowlands, which now became muddy lakes.

There had been one piece of bright light, the word passed all through the men in the field. Even the men farthest from the dry tents of the commander took it with a smile, had made their own quiet salute toward Lee's camp. His son, Rooney, had come back to the army, released from the Federal hands, recovered now from the wounds. In the camp itself there had been cheering, the glad hugs and enthusiastic handshakes, but Lee had greeted his son more with relief than happiness. The homecoming was not all joy, and Rooney had brought that as well, the sadness, the grief. Charlotte had not survived the winter, could not regain her frail health, consumed by the worry for her husband. But there was no time for consolation, for the comfort of father to son, something Lee had always had difficulty showing. They all knew, with Stuart off toward Richmond, in pursuit of Sheridan's raid, Rooney would have to take command of what cavalry Lee still had close to the army.

Now word was coming to headquarters, Grant might be moving, pulling to the east. Wagons were moving on the roads to Fredericksburg, and Lee could not know if it was just a flow of wounded or the beginning of a full-scale withdrawal.

The word had gone out to the right flank, to Early's command: keep a sharp eye. If Grant was indeed moving away, retreating toward Fredericksburg, Early would be in line to pursue, could possibly strike a vulnerable Federal march. But the weather kept the scouts blinded. Little good information could be had when the men could not see through the rain and heavy mist that blew in solid sheets across the low hills.

Lee would not order any movement, not yet, not until he was certain Grant was moving more than wagons. But speed would be essential, and so he had ordered the slowest part of the army, the cannon that lined the mule shoe, to pull back and make ready to move east at the first confirmation that Grant was on the march. Along the great curving line, the men closest to the enemy, who still huddled behind the tall works, were bent low under dripping shelters made from anything they could find, choking on the thick smoke from sputtering fires. They watched in nervous disbelief as the great power of their artillery limbered up, the horses pulling the guns through the thick mud of the faint trails, taking them away, to the roads far behind the lines.

There would be little to eat, the fires could not stay lit long enough to cook the raw bacon, and so the men gnawed and chewed on what they had. There was one blessing: the rain could soften the hard-tack, wash down the taste of the stale flour. As the dark had spread over them, heads would peek over the wall, staring quietly into the blackness, at the strange noises from the far woods. As the night wore on, the noises continued, the sound of music.

Their own bands had no enthusiasm for joining in, the playful competition across the lines, each side trying to outdo the other. And so the men listened curiously, could even make out the tunes drifting across the field. Some laughed, joked about the Yankee commanders, ordering their men to play lullabies so the Yankees could sleep, some wondering about the cruelty of making the bands play in the driving rain. But the men farther out, the pickets, began to send word back to their officers, there were other sounds as well. The music would pause, small silent gaps between songs, and the new sounds would emerge, the sound of men talking, of movement, the occasional clinking of a tin cup, the stacking of muskets, a hushed order, a curse. The sounds were growing, spreading, a great mass of men marching close, gathering together. Now the music was not enough to disguise what was happening in the woods, and the men began to understand why the music had played, why it continued to play, late into the miserable night.

May 12, 1864

LEE HAD STAYED CLOSE TO HIS OWN CAMP, FEELING THE WEATHER in his bones, the stiffness, a dull ache in every step. He had waited for the old illness to return, almost expected it, knew he was very tired. But the pains had not come that way, the hot pinch in his throat, the cold stab in his chest. He had prayed for that, *Please . . .* and now he made a new prayer, thankful, blessed relief from the problems with his heart.

He sat alone, shuffled through damp papers. It is certainly this dismal weather, and nothing more, he thought. God has given us a rest, will cleanse the fields, and neither side will do much until it clears away. He stared out through the opening in the tent, saw water pouring in a stream off one side of a raised tent flap, had a sudden flash of memory, the first autumn of the war.

He'd been sent into the field for the first time, before Davis had given him command of this army. McClellan had pushed a Federal army south through the rugged mountains of western Virginia, and Davis sent Lee out to manage a bad situation, two southern commanders, Wise and Floyd, fighting for turf, for authority, and neither one able to stop squabbling long enough to fight McClellan. The place was called Cheat Mountain, Lee's first fight of the war, and it had been a failure. There was poor coordination, miserable communications, a plan that was washed away by days of weather like this, the already poor roads pulling the men down into a deep sea of mud. Lee had no experience in the difficult terrain, had devised a plan of surprise that simply didn't work, falling apart in the hands of inexperienced men in terrible conditions. There had been harsh judgment in the papers. Lee's first campaign could have condemned him to a post firmly behind the doors of his Richmond office. He did not search for excuses, kept the experience alive, would always remember the lesson: *Know* the ground, *know* the men in your command. But he had forgotten about the weather, how a good army could be held down, the morale of the men, the fighting spirit, chilled by the cold wet hand of God.

He saw movement, a horseman, heard the man calling out. He stood, felt the stiffness in his knees, saw Taylor moving toward the man, heard the voice, unfamiliar. He waited, saw Taylor turn, look at him, and Lee stepped out under the tent flap. Now more horsemen began to ride in, mud splattering on the gathering staff, and Taylor moved close, water running off his hat.

"Sir, we have reports from the Second Corps, from the mule shoe . . . the picket line reports the enemy is gathering in force to their front."

Lee saw Marshall now, speaking to another courier, and Marshall moved quickly toward him, wiping at his glasses.

"Sir, we have word from General Ewell. He requests with some urgency, sir, that the artillery be returned to his front. He says the command there reports the enemy is massing for an assault!"

Lee absorbed the words, thought of the reports earlier, Grant's wagons moving east. He felt a cold turn in his gut, looked at Taylor, said, "You see what this weather can do? I have reports Grant is moving away, now he is coming right at our center."

He stepped back into the tent, found a blank piece of paper, thought, All right, the guns should be moved back. He wrote the order, handed it to Taylor, and the young man rushed out, tripped over the tent stake, the flap shutting closed, dumping water down in a mass. Lee stood in the dark, heard the commotion, horses moving, quick shouts. It will be light soon, he thought, and we will see what General Grant has done. He felt angry, shook his head. I wanted to believe . . . he would be gone. It made sense, the strong defenses. They came at us all down the line, couldn't make us move, could only leave their dead in front of our guns. He would not do it again ... not with the weather so bad.

He thought of the men out front, huddled in shallow pits, the skirmishers, thought, They are uncomfortable, they are hearing the sounds of the enemy in motion, and they fear the worst. It makes sense. But surely, Grant has had enough ... those people have had enough. What more must we do?

The flap opened and Taylor leaned in, water dripping from his face, his hand. "Sir ... sorry, sir. I'll fix the tent."

Lee could see past him, a faint gray light, the trees around the camp thick with fog. "No, Colonel, it's time to begin the day. I'll be along in a moment."

Taylor backed away, and the flap dropped back down. Lee reached for his coat, stretched his back, felt a pain surge through his stomach, a small wave of nausea. Maybe, he thought, another day of rest, another break. If the rain lasts, nothing will happen. . . .

The flap jerked open and Taylor was wide-eyed, pointing, and now Lee could hear it, beyond the trees, toward the front of the line, a

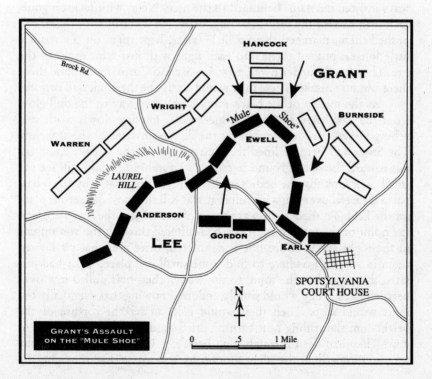

GRANT'S ASSAULT ON THE "MULE SHOE"

0   .5   1 Mile

N

solid wave of sound, rolling through the fog and the rain. He stepped out into the gray mist, and the sound was louder, the low hard growl of some great beast, growing now, into a violent roar. He felt his chest pound, saw the quick motion of men around him, horses and shouts. He stared blindly at the sound, the center of the line, beyond the small trees, toward the curving rise they called the mule shoe.

T HEY WERE THE FIRST VIRGINIA BRIGADE, HAD FORMED IN THE first weeks of the war, the first call for volunteers. Most came from the rich farmlands of the Shenandoah, and they learned how to march, to fight, to become a small piece of this great army, under the grim command of a strange professor from VMI. From the beginning, Thomas Jackson showed them something about themselves, that they could do the impossible, the outrageous, and that it was already there, inside each of them. They began to believe that, after the hard fight at First Manassas, the fight that gave Jackson the name all would know him by, but he would not keep that to himself, had always insisted the name belonged to the men. Now, with Jackson gone, each man carried the pride, the memories. He was still with them, still pushed them, marched them a little faster, kept them on the roads a little longer, pushed them into each fight with just a bit more of the fire. They fought under Ewell now, the Second Corps, but around them there was no mistake. These men would always be the Stonewall Brigade.

As the misery of the black rainy night gave way to the dull glow from the east, they began to come awake, moving slowly with stiff aching bones, bare feet frozen by the dirty rainwater of the trenches. The Stonewall Brigade lined the western face of the salient, could see out toward the open ground in front of Laurel Hill, could still see the small dark mounds, the bodies of the enemy, unreachable by the burial parties, spread over the wide hill that was still the most dangerous place on the field. To their right was the tip of the salient, the sharp angle at the point of the mule shoe. They had suffered through the wet misery of the night as the entire line had suffered, brief fires that swallowed them in smoke, nowhere to find some small dry place. Most had just sat still, resigned to the mud, to the wet clothes, hats pulled low over bearded faces. They would simply endure, knowing that eventually the rains would stop. Then they would bake under the torture of the bright sun, the stifling heat turning dried mud into choking clouds of dust. They had been through it all before, it was the *quiet* part of the war, and sometimes the silent monotony was worse than the fight, the weather showing no mercy, and these men would sit quietly, dreaming about the cool green hills of the Shenandoah Valley.

They could see the first light now, but the trees beyond the open ground were hidden, a thick fog flowed past them, a light breeze, and any man who stood, who tried to stretch the pain out of his back and legs, would feel the sudden chill, drop back down into a shivering mass.

They had heard the noises across the way, the invisible sounds of motion, of men talking, even the whispers carried across the black space. As the light began to find them, there were some who braved the cold rain, tried to see out into the field, to find some gap in the fog. Along the line there were voices now, and the men who sat huddled behind the wall heard new sounds, and they began to stand as well. There were small sharp cracks, the musket fire from the pickets out front. There was nothing unusual about that, the skirmishers always waited for the first piece of daylight, always looked for the small blue motion across the way, each wanting to fire the first shot of the day. But there was another sound, and suddenly the pickets were at the wall, climbing over in a rush, and now the officers began to shout, men grabbed their muskets, lay them along the top of the wall, pointed out through the openings in the wooden barricade, still not knowing what was happening.

Now there were hard shouts, some could see into the fog, and the sounds flowed down the line, the eyes sharp now, awake, staring through the rain. They still could not see the far trees, but they did not have to. Across the open ground a dark mass rolled toward them, a solid line, coming slowly, silent and ghostly. There were no shouts, no bands played, and no guns fired. The wave rolled steadily, closer to the barricade. They could begin to see faces now, small pieces of color, the brass of the officers, the small flutter of flags. Pieces of the wave dropped out of sight, moving down into the small depressions in front of the wall, then appeared again, closer, climbing the low hills, and finally there was sound, the orders screamed out along the line. The muskets all pointed out from the wall now, and the order echoed in the trenches: *"Fire!"*

There were scattered sounds, small pieces of gunfire. Heads began to turn, men staring in shock, most of the sounds from the vast rows of guns coming as small pops, the light crack of the percussion cap. Frantically, men put new caps on their guns, a quick aim, and again the guns did not fire. Even the most careful man had not been able to keep his musket completely dry. The thick wetness of the night had found its way into even the most secure place, and so the guns would not fire. The powder was wet.

Now the great dark wave began to make its own sounds, the neat blue mass coming apart, men running toward the wide ditch and the barriers that lay out in front of the wall. They clawed their way past the pointed sticks, others jumped up, pushed the brush down with the weight of their bodies. Men stepped on the shoulders of their friends, and now the shooting finally began, a hot rush of sound all along the line, and it came from the men in blue, men standing high on top of the wall, pointing the muskets down into the faces of the enemy. There were new shouts, a vast chorus rising along the wall, the blue wave beginning to pour over in one surge of motion. When the first volley had been fired, they did not stop to reload, but used the bayonet, and when the enemy was too close even for that, the guns became clubs, and the men stood face-to-face, punched and grabbed, wrestled and grappled. The officers emptied their pistols close to the chests of the men in front of them, the swords flew, flashes of steel cut through the damp mist all along the line. Now the shouts, the manic screaming of the attackers blended in with the new sound, the pain and panic of the wounded. The wave kept coming, and the men in gray, who had thought the wall invincible, now began to pull away, crawling and leaping through trenches, the works that spread out in all directions behind the wall. Some still tried to fight, to hold back the crushing wave, but far out beyond the wall the wave was long and deep, still moving forward, and when the rebel guns finally began to fire, and the men in blue began to fall across the bodies of their enemy, the wave did not stop, and soon the trenches behind the wall were a solid mass of blue. The gray defenders began pulling back farther, many of them no longer in the fight, men screaming in utter panic, stumbling past the men who still tried to stop the tide. But the brave were soon swallowed, surrounded. Men dropped their muskets, hands in the air, staring at the muzzles pointing at their chests, feeling the sharp point of the bayonet, staring into the black eyes of their enemy.

L EE HAD TRIED TO REACH THE FRONT, BUT THE SALIENT WAS IN Federal hands. He knew it had been Hancock, and it was not some weak thrust, a poorly coordinated attack like the one from Upton, but well timed, focused, nearly twenty thousand men pouring into the mule shoe like a great unstoppable tide. The surprise had been complete and deadly, and Lee's men, those who survived, had no choice but to pull back.

He had looked for the big guns, the great firepower he'd ordered away. Out behind the trenches he saw a few of them, but they were not there in time, could not be unlimbered fast enough. Some had even been captured, and Lee thought, It was a mistake . . . an awful mistake.

He moved the horse behind a small clump of trees, saw many men now, some still running away, some slowing, gathering, finding the strength. Hancock's men were still moving forward, deep into Lee's center, but it was disorganized. Hancock's assault had been *too* successful, the men moving farther and faster than their officers could control.

Lee moved up into the trees, tried to see, guided by the hard sounds, stared into the mist, the low wet fog. He could see small flashes of light, the musket fire, could hear the sounds, men shouting, the wounded, the panic. He clenched his fists, thought, It is the Wilderness again . . . we cannot see.

There was a new burst of firing to the right, and he looked that way, stared into the rain, could see nothing. But the new sounds were not in front, and he thought, They are still advancing . . . they are cutting us in half.

He felt a twist of cold in his gut, pulled the horse around, and now saw Marshall, wiping at his glasses, and Lee motioned to the rear, said, "Let's move, Colonel! We must do something about this!"

They splashed through deep mud, dropped down into a small trench, then up, and suddenly they were surrounded by a scattered mass of men, some running, some with the stagger of the wounded or men who have lost the fight. He stopped the horse, saw one man running, without a musket, coming straight toward him. Lee shouted, "Stop! Turn around! What unit are you? Who is in command?"

He saw the man's face, and it was not a man, but very young, a boy. The boy would not stop, ran right past him, never looked at him, and Lee could only watch him go, thought, He is so young. God help us. We are fighting with *children*.

The sounds echoed all around, there was no front line anymore, no one place where help could be sent. More men ran past him, and he fought the anger, felt the raw fury rising, and he raised the hat, shouted, screamed, "Stop! Turn and fight!"

Even the men who saw him, who heard him, did not stop. Lee felt his voice fade, held his hat in his hand, watched the men move by, chased by the terror, and he felt the rage ball up inside him, felt the helpless frustration. He shouted again, and some men slowed, heard the force in his voice, but then the terror would return, brought by others moving by, or the sound of the musket ball. They would not look at him then, would run again, and there was nothing he could say, they ran from demons he could not control.

He spurred Traveller past a small clump of trees, could see out to the open ground now, up toward the salient, could see the long wall, the fog now thick with the smoke of the guns. He saw a small block of men, a dull gray line moving forward from the left, rushing into the fight, and he yelled again, "Yes! Push them . . . !" But the line dissolved into the smoke, and now there was only a cluster of blue, emerging, dropping down into a low trench, then coming up, moving right toward him. He jerked the horse to the side, moved back through the trees. There was a wide field, an old house, and now he saw men behind him, officers in tattered gray, advancing, fresh troops. He felt a stab in his chest, saw it was a brigade, maybe more, a line of men stretching far into the trees, neat lines slowly stepping forward.

He shouted again, "Forward, move forward!" and this time there were cheers, the men hearing him. He turned the horse, moved out in front of them, pulled Traveller around, faced the sounds of the fight, began to move slowly forward, joining the line.

Now there were men on horses, a flag, and he saw the sharp uniform, a young man moving close, ramrod straight, and the man saluted, said, "General Lee, do you intend to lead my men into battle?"

Lee saw the young face, the man watching him with a curious grin. It was John Gordon. Lee said nothing, looked at the troops again, felt his chest pound, small ripples of pain, the tightness spreading all through him.

Gordon eased his horse in front of him, blocking his way, said, "General Lee, forgive me, sir, but you will not lead my men in this charge. That, sir, is my job. These men have never failed you, and they will not fail you now. This is not the place for you, sir."

Lee stared at the handsome face, and Gordon was not smiling now. He looked at the others, the staff, officers watching him, the line of men stepping past him. Now the men began to shout, waving hats, he could see the faces watching him, the voices surrounding him in one chorus:

"Lee to the rear . . . Lee to the rear . . . !"

A man moved his horse close to Gordon, and Lee felt Traveller turn, the man holding the bridle. He looked at the man, a quick burst of anger, *How dare you* . . . but the eyes were hard, the man's face grim and determined. Lee felt the breathing slow, felt suddenly deflated, empty, said to Gordon, "You are quite correct, General. The duty is yours." He pointed toward the salient, to the sounds of the fight. "We must push those people away, General."

The men were cheering again, and he pulled Traveller around, moved through Gordon's men, then turned, watched the lines move forward, the smoke now flowing across, the muskets coming off the shoulders, bayonets pointing forward. Now the sounds of the fight, the scattered bursts, began to grow, spreading out in front of him into one long chorus, the musket fire blending with the high terrifying scream of the rebel yell.

T HE MORNING PASSED, AND THE HEAVY MIST AND FOG AGAIN gave way to steady rain. Gordon's men had sealed the breach, and with their momentum taken away, Hancock's men withdrew back to the high wall, the thick protection of the dirt and logs. Early had kept Burnside back, strengthened the right of the salient, and as the afternoon wore on, the two armies faced each other only a few feet apart, face-to-face on either side of the great long barricade.

T HEY WERE SOAKED WITH THE RAIN, WITH THE SWEAT OF THE fight, and now they were back up to the wall. The numbers were very small, but they could see that, did not take time to look for familiar faces, to ask who was in command. Those who had returned, who had stayed close to the fight, knew what they had done, that the enemy had broken through, poured over their strong defense, but now they'd come back, had cleared the mule shoe of Yankees. But the enemy was not gone, was still very close, *right there*, on the other side of the wall.

What was left of the Stonewall Brigade blended together with men from other units, and the officers did not know the men around them, had given up trying to sort the companies, to find familiar faces. When they reached the barricade, they had seen the blue coats scrambling away, climbing back over the wall, and the sounds of the fight had become a roar of voices, deafening shouts. Some climbed up onto the wall, thought they would see the enemy flooding away, pouring across the field, back to the far trees. But the men in blue were still there, and if the curious man stared too long, he would be pulled over, and if he survived, he was a prisoner. As the men realized they were so close, the voices, the shouts, had risen to a frenzy. Some heard the voices from inside themselves, the boiling panic that tells you, *Run*, move from this deadly place. The sounds came from beyond the wall as well, screaming confusion. Some did run, backed away, left their muskets, splashed out of the trenches, had never been so close to the enemy, and did not have it in them to be that close now. Others responded with rage, climbed the wall, would strike out, could not stand to huddle low in the face of the men they had hated for so long. Some just crouched low, could hear the voices of the enemy, began to hear men like themselves, curious. Some yelled to the man on the other side of the logs, would call out to him, taunts, curses. But the sounds were still flowing over them, and it did not matter if that man was like you, if he was as afraid as you. If he showed himself, you would try to kill him with every part of your being. If the musket was empty, you would put the bayonet through his heart, or smash in his skull with the butt of the gun. And you knew, if you gave him the chance, if you were careless, he would do the same to you. Instinct took over, and there was only survival, the mindless anger.

There were holes in the log wall, small gaps, and men were loading muskets, passing them up to others, to the men who would wait calmly, patiently sighting down the long barrel into the opening, waiting for some flash of blue, a piece of the enemy. The musket would fire, and a fist would punch the air, *success*, the men below cheering. Some believed the enemy was beaten, hugged the other side of the wall in helpless panic, and if a man thought himself a hero, he would lead a new charge, would jump up on the wall, shoot into the faces of the men on the other side, throw the musket down, reach back for another, screaming in mindless rage, expecting the enemy to flee from the show of bravado. But the enemy was waiting as well, some chance to strike out at the rebels who had taken their success away, and so the man who would be heroic would be swept from the wall in a hail of lead.

The gaps in the logs held another danger. A man would lean too close, get careless, distracted perhaps, reaching for a new musket, and suddenly there would be the dull grunt, and the man would stare down, the red stain would spread, and the bayonet would be pulled back, disappear through the gap in the logs.

The bodies were spread everywhere, but in the trenches it was worse, because beneath your feet, in the mud that had now come over your knees, you did not feel them, you did not know what you were standing on. Some were only wounded, men who could still have been saved, would have survived if they had escaped the mud, had not been trampled, pressed down by the feet of the men who still fought.

As the night finally came over them, the men began to collapse with exhaustion, and when they finally sat, staring at the dark, they would make the sickening discovery, would feel something in the deep mud, would catch a glimpse, a small piece of uniform, or might touch something, a hand, a cold face. But there was no shock, no turning away, the emotions, the compassion, had been taken away, was drained from them. The fight had never let up, and when the darkness came, few noticed. The fight did not change because the *sounds* were still there, and the men were fighting something larger than the enemy they could see. On both sides of the wall the mass of men became something different, something beyond human. Even the hate began to fade, as did the duty, the need to fight that came from reason, from command, from intelligence. The sounds and the violence drove them further, soldiers possessed by something automatic, the darkest side of man. Those who saw it, who kept some piece of sanity, of conscience, tried to pray, to beg that this horror, this unspeakable slaughter, be stopped. But even the most devout began to feel the raw emptiness, the presence of the Beast, that God had done this, had brought these armies to this awful place, had let these men create their own hell, while He closed His eyes and turned away.

THERE WERE MEN NOW WORKING, DIGGING IN ALL ALONG THE new line, cutting straight across the base of the mule shoe. The ground was not as high, but it was a better position, more compact, defensible, easier to move troops to a new threat anywhere along the line. Lee had put them to work himself, had gathered up stragglers, men stumbling about in the confusion of the fight, some who had panicked earlier, some with small wounds, now slowly moving forward again. With the blue troops cleared out of the salient, these men became soldiers again, and Lee had guided them, put them to work with the shovel, the ax. He could still hear the fight up at the angle of the salient, but the sounds were not moving, the battle was hard in one place, and so for now the danger was past.

He would wait until late, midnight perhaps, then pull the men back from the salient, disengage from the fight and bring them into the new trenches, strengthen this new shorter line. There were horrible losses. Ewell's corps had been shattered, two generals captured, thousands of men lost as prisoners. Thousands more were flowing into the hospitals, or lay spread in a thick mass on the bloody ground. It would take days to get the units regrouped, sort out the commands. He had seen one quick report, one message to Ewell that had been sent on to him. He had stared at the paper, and when he read the words, he saw the face again, the sharp blue eyes, knew the news would spread through the army like a dark wind. The Stonewall Brigade had ceased to exist.

It was dark when he reached the camp, and he saw no one moving. The rain was still falling, and so there was no fire. He dismounted, looked around, tried to see someone, an aide to take Traveller's reins. Finally a man came forward, a shadow in the gloom, his face hidden under a dripping hat. The man saluted Lee silently, and Lee handed him the leather straps, and the man backed away, led the horse to the small makeshift corral. The rain became harder now. A gust of wind drove through Lee's clothes. He felt the chill, the shiver, could see the violent pulsing of the tents. He pulled his coat tighter, but it was soaked through, and there would be no warmth until the clothes were dry, and so he moved to his tent, still did not see anyone, knew the staff was scattered, men moving from Ewell to Gordon, from the fight in front to the hospitals behind. Still, he thought, this is . . . strange. This does not feel like headquarters.

He reached the tent, and the wind slowed, the flaps calmed, and he opened the tent, stared into the black space, moved slowly inside. He peeled the coat off his shoulders, tried to feel for the small chair, would lay it across the back, and now he heard a sound. It was a man crying. "Hello . . . who is there . . . ?"

The voice started low, and the man cleared his throat. It was Taylor. "Sir, forgive me . . . I had to wait for you. I wasn't sure where you were."

Lee began to see, caught the motion, Taylor standing up. Now Taylor flicked a match, a small glow filled the tent, and Taylor lit the oil lamp. Lee watched him, saw Taylor's hand shaking, said, "What is it, Colonel? What has happened?"

Taylor looked at him, then glanced down, put his hand on a piece of paper. "Message, sir . . . from Richmond." He slid the paper toward Lee, and Lee waited, knew Taylor would tell him more. "General Stuart has died, sir."

Lee stared at the paper, let it lie. Taylor's words were enough. He nodded, felt suddenly very heavy, his legs weak, weighed down by the wetness in his clothes. Taylor backed away from the chair, and Lee moved forward, sat slowly, his hands on the table. There was a silent moment, the whisper of rain on the tent, and Lee felt something filling him, dark and cold, felt frozen, motionless. He forced a breath, glanced up at Taylor.

The young man moved toward the opening in the tent, stopped, composed himself, pulled at his coat and said, "He will be terribly missed, sir."

Lee looked at the young man, searched for words, something to say. He thought of the stream of messages, Stuart wearing out the horses of his staff so that he would never again make the mistake he had made at Gettysburg. Even the mistakes, he thought, even when Stuart had one eye on the headlines, on his reputation, he was still the eyes of the army.

Taylor began to move, reached to push the tent flaps open, paused, said quietly, "Are you all right, sir? May I bring you something?"

Lee wanted to speak, felt the wave rising in him, fought it, pushed it away, wrapped himself hard around the emotion, said, "He . . . never brought me a piece of false information."

Taylor shook his head, and Lee saw him weaken again. The words did not help, there was no comfort. "No, sir." Taylor backed out of the tent, still watching Lee. "I am . . . terribly sorry, sir."

Lee nodded, turned, was losing the control now, the weariness taking over. The flaps closed and he was alone, stared into the dull yellow of the oil lamp. I must say something, he thought, write it down, a message to the army. They will look to me for comfort. His mind stumbled through the words, the speeches, all the letters, but there was no sense, nothing came to him. He thought of his children, the relief of seeing Rooney come back, the loss of Annie. He would always feel the guilt for not being there, not watching them grow up.

From the beginning of the war, the first time the troops looked to him as a leader, he had eased the guilt by embracing all of them, had quietly realized that he loved them all, they were all like his own children. It had come from Jackson first, the strange urgency behind the bright blue eyes, the anxious need to please, the frantic devotion to duty. Stuart had been the charmer, the boy everyone would love, who always knew the eyes were on him. Longstreet was older, serious, perhaps too serious since the fever had taken his own children away. And Longstreet had little use for Stuart's theatrics, the grand show of the uniform, the red-lined cape, the gaudy plume in the hat. But Lee knew it was all of it, all that Stuart was, the show, the spectacle, the headlines. And the cavalryman.

He still stared into the light, thought, *The army.* That is the important thing . . . we do not have the luxury of personal loss, of missing our comrades. There are too many, and I do not have the right . . . to grieve for anyone. I must plan . . . find some way to replace him. There is no time. . . .

He could not fight it. The strength slipped further away, his head began to drop down, and he put his arms on the table, rested, still looking at the light. The army, he thought, we must have eyes, we must know where Grant is going. . . .

He heard a horse outside, voices, and knew it would wait, Taylor would not disturb him now. The rain slowed, and the sounds of the battle were fading. He forced himself to think of the duty, pushed the words through his mind: I must replace him. He thought of his nephew, Fitz Lee, and Hampton, the big man from South Carolina, but his mind would not work, the names slipped away, the faces blank, unreal. He was suddenly anxious, his heart waking in his chest. He stared down at the piece of paper, the message he had still not read. He cannot be replaced. None of them . . .

He laid his head down on his arms, turned his face down, closed his eyes, and he could not keep it away any longer, the control was gone, and he began to cry.

21. CHAMBERLAIN

MAY 14, 1864

H E HAD COME BY WAY OF FREDERICKSBURG, MOVING SLOWLY
south, kept off the road by the wagons moving north. He had
often been forced to wait, could not move the horse at all, the
road narrowing, only room for the endless line of wagons, winding
through dense woods or crossing a stream. When he stopped and
waited, he heard the sounds, the voices of the wounded. He had tried
to see them at first, easing the horse up close, looking into some of the
ambulances, and the sights were always the same, the sounds and the
smells began to overwhelm him, and so, as he worked his way closer to
the army, he kept the horse to the side, let the wagons pass.

The malaria had come back, worse this time, and he'd been too
sick to even make the trip back to Maine. He was confined to a hospital in Washington, surrounded by the screaming of the wounded, and
the horror and the loneliness had been unbearable. Through the fever
he sent word to Fannie, and this time she came to him, made the rail
trip southward. It was Fannie's healing hand that finally brought the
strength back to him. If weeks in a bed began to drive him insane, what
followed was worse. Washington was swirling with official business,
the paperwork of war. The need for discipline, for policing the huge
army, had created a massive backlog of court-martial cases. Chamberlain's presence was too convenient to be overlooked, and so for nearly
two months he had endured a new confinement: court-martial duty.

Finally, after a vigorous stream of letters to the War Department,
he was allowed to return to the Fifth Corps.

He reached the camp above the bloody field at midday, and the
rain still came down, the roads flowing with thick mud. He had reported to Griffin, saw something in the man's face he had not seen

before, something dark and angry, and they did not talk, just the formality, reporting for duty.

Lee had pulled back, straightened his lines farther south. In front of the Fifth, the rebel line still included the strength of Laurel Hill, and no one in the corps believed there would be another attack here. If the army would try Lee again, it would surely be somewhere else.

His brigade, the entire army, had endured a solid week of bloody action, and Chamberlain could not just parade into the camp, announce his return as though nothing had happened, as though these men were not different now, changed by what they'd been through. It had been clear that Griffin was not the same man, and Chamberlain was curious about that, what it was, what was new. It was more than just another battle, more guns, more blood. It was something Chamberlain had missed, and the frustration of that ate at him, the selfish luxury of being sick when your own men were dying at the hand of the enemy. He walked through the camp, looked at the men, saw them one at a time, unusual. This is not like Gettysburg, he thought, or even the disaster at Fredericksburg. The men were not talking, even the music was subdued. He walked past a group of men from Pennsylvania, one man writing a letter, one reading a Bible. The faces were empty, blank, the others staring into some faraway place. He heard a low conversation, the words again, "the angle," thought, This is something I have missed, something I have to learn.

He rode toward the lines of the Twentieth Maine, felt a sudden urgency, unexpected, a small cold panic rising from all the talk of how many were gone, how bad the fight had been. Once he left Griffin, he had only one thought: *Find Tom.*

The regiment was assigned to a position along a deep trench, facing a long rise, a wide hill where the enemy's guns watched their every move. Griffin had told him about Laurel Hill, that they'd tried it, driven forward four times in all, each time leaving more men behind, spread across the terrible open ground. The last time was not as bad, the attack having not really gotten close. Warren had resisted moving out at all, but the word was that Grant had ordered them forward, to support Hancock's great burst at the salient. Warren still hesitated, had nearly been relieved of command, and the men believed it was because of them, that he would not order his men to march into certain slaughter.

He eased the horse through the boggy ground, ducked under dripping trees. He saw the flag now, the men rising, watching him, voices coming toward him. "Colonel! Colonel Chamberlain!"

He waved, felt embarrassed, did not ride into the lines of the Twentieth Maine to be applauded.

He accepted the kindness, the greetings, searched the faces, then saw the young man emerging from a large muddy hole. Tom stared at him for a moment, not believing, then ran forward, the dignity of the young officer erased by the pure glee of seeing his older brother. Chamberlain stayed on the horse, was still embarrassed, felt he was not a part of them now, as though they had moved on, left him with something still to prove.

Tom reached up to him, said, "Lawrence, you're back! I wondered if we'd ever see you again!"

Chamberlain leaned over, could not hide a smile, took his brother's hand, said, "They can't keep me away. I have better uses to this army than court-martial duty."

More men were moving closer, happy greetings, and he waved to them, still smiled. He looked at his brother, the beaming smile, and said, "Can you ride with me? Is it all right?"

Tom looked back toward the trees, and now Chamberlain heard a familiar voice. It was Ellis Spear.

"By all means, Colonel. Welcome back to Virginia. Lieutenant Chamberlain, please return by dark. We may have to move."

Tom saluted Spear, and Chamberlain smiled again, "Thank you, Colonel Spear. I'll have him home in time for supper."

There was laughter, and Chamberlain glanced at Tom's horror and was instantly sorry. The boy, red-faced now, moved toward the horses. Chamberlain thought, He will never forgive me. They will remind him to be home for supper . . . forever.

T HE VAST PILES OF LOGS AND DIRT WERE STILL IN PLACE, A FEW gaping holes, fat logs smashed into pieces, the places where Hancock's big guns had rolled up close, throwing solid shot right into the line, blowing holes in the rebel defense. All across the field there were burial parties, grim men with shovels, men with stretchers. Some were carving names, initials, into anything they could find, stabbing them into the ground beside the small mounds of fresh earth.

Tom followed him up to the wall itself. The rain had slowed to a heavy mist, the only sound the shovels of the workers. Chamberlain reined his horse, climbed up on the wall, sat high on a piece of wood, a short log, saw it had been shot to pieces, small holes all along what was left. Behind the wall there was one fat tree, lying on its side, the branches ripped away, and he looked at the base of the tree, where it had been cut down. The tree, nearly two feet thick, had been sliced through by the hail of musket balls. He stared at the white wood, could see small black spots, the lead balls that had not passed through, thought, My God . . . no one . . . how many could survive this?

Tom said nothing, stayed on the horse, stared at the grisly scene. Farther behind the wall they saw patches of dirty white, the wet shirts of coatless men who did not notice the rain, more burial parties, many more stretchers. Some carried stretchers toward the gaps in the wall, and Chamberlain saw movement on the stretchers, men in black bloody rags who had survived, pulled out alive from under mounds of corpses, men who had been thrown into the muddy bottom of trenches, stepped on and fallen on, but somehow stayed alive.

He saw a line of men alongside a deep trench, and one blue coat, an officer. The man said something, a quiet order, and the shovels began to throw dirt into the trench. Chamberlain looked down where the dirt fell, felt his stomach turn, looked away, felt himself grab at the air, a sharp breath. He had seen too much of what they were burying, a thick mass of what once were men, a mass grave of the enemy, or of friends no one could identify.

There were small pops of musket fire, to the south. Lee was still down there, skirmishers still playing the game, patiently waiting for some glimpse, picking off the careless, the men behind another strong line. The workers paid no attention, went about their gruesome business with slow deliberate steps.

On the north side of the wall, where Hancock's men had made the assault, the field was mostly empty now, the graves filled, and he saw horses, a staff, moving under a flag.

He glanced at Tom, said, "I had better get back, find out what is happening, what might happen next. General Griffin probably needs me."

He dropped down off the wall, climbed up on the horse, gazed over the long wall one more time, said, "I never believed this . . . I had thought Gettysburg was the last fight."

Tom looked down, said, "I heard that a lot, Lawrence. But this was . . . something different. I heard that these men here just wouldn't stop. The officers lost control, couldn't pull them away."

Chamberlain looked out over the field. "How could we do this again, after what we did at Gettysburg?" he asked. "How many times do we do this to each other before someone says, 'All right, that's enough'? Is there a greater meaning here, some will of God that we destroy ourselves, some divine punishment?"

Tom shook his head. "Don't know, Lawrence. Buster would say . . . it's just war."

Chamberlain thought of Buster Kilrain, the old Irishman, so different from him, and so much his friend. Kilrain was buried now on that hill in Gettysburg, the place where Lincoln himself had made that speech. Kilrain was a crusty and cynical man who carried his own reasons for fighting the war, saw this as the struggle against the "gentlemen." Chamberlain looked along the shattered timbers of the wall, the deep red stains, thought, What do gentlemen have to do with what happened here? This was not about causes or class struggle, this was about killing, about facing an enemy and tearing his heart out. Kilrain did not believe in the godliness of man, did not believe that inside of us we hold a piece of the angel. Chamberlain saw the gruff old face, could still hear the thick brogue, and said, "Yes, Buster, you would have understood this. So what happens now?"

Tom shrugged, said, "We go on till it ends, I reckon."

Chamberlain shook his head. "No, there's something more," he said. "The men who survived this have learned something new, that slaughter is acceptable, that mass killing is now routine. What does that do to us? If God is watching us, what judgment does He make now?"

He moved the horse in a slow walk, and Tom was beside him.

Chamberlain said, "You remember when Mother would read to us from the Bible? That wonderful fireplace . . . She held our attention with every word. Maybe you don't remember . . . you were pretty small."

Tom smiled, said, "No, I remember it, Lawrence. I still hear her sometimes. She loved to tell us the stories."

Chamberlain looked at Tom with surprise, said, "I wish I could . . . hear her." He paused. "Things did not turn out as she had hoped."

They rode on, did not talk, did not share the private memories now.

Chamberlain remembered her pure joy the first time he could recite the Ten Commandments, something even his father had enjoyed. Of course, he thought, there was something military about that. It was a list of rules. How important they were to her . . . how little meaning they had now. *Thou shalt not kill.* Yes, we shall kill. And before this is over, we shall kill again.

He rarely prayed anymore, had let his mother's devout hand slip away from him, had left it somewhere in his childhood. Now he closed his eyes, tried to think of some prayer, some question, some plea for divine intervention. His mind worked, words tumbling in a mass of nonsense. He opened his eyes, stared up, thought, Maybe that is how it must be. There can be no prayers, not now, not while this goes on. We have not earned the right.

He focused, told himself, All right, enough. Your brain causes you too much trouble. You are back, you are with the army again. Your brother is safe.

There were more horsemen now, men moving off to the east, more flags. He said, "Something's happening . . . too much brass moving around. I think it's time to go."

They stopped the horses, and Tom suddenly reached over, touched him, held him by the shoulder. He looked at his brother then, saw a difference in Tom's face, a sadness in his eyes.

Tom said, "Lawrence, you be careful. It would kill Mama if you didn't come home."

Chamberlain felt the emotion rising, tried to hold it away, looked down for a moment, thought, There is nothing to say. We will both do what we have to do. He could not look at Tom, no words of caution. We are different now, both of us. We are soldiers. He looked at the ground, at the dark mud, said, "Come on. It's time to go."

They spurred the horses, moved along the wall, felt the rain coming again, black clouds rolling low over the far trees. The horses splashed through deep mud, and Chamberlain glanced up at the angry sky, heard low thunder, and behind him the steady sound of the shovels.

22. LEE

MAY 24, 1864

THERE WOULD BE NO MORE ASSAULTS AGAINST THE STRENGTH of Lee's trenches. The cavalry commanders now reported directly to Lee, and it was clear from all they could see that Grant was pulling away from Spotsylvania, and again it was not to retreat. The Federals were moving south, another looping line that would take them closer to Richmond and, once again, around the rear of Lee's right flank. Since his best defense against the massed assaults came from waiting behind entrenchments, Lee had to wait, could not anticipate, could not commit his army to move into open ground to intercept Grant's movement. It was only when he knew Grant was on the march that he could leave the trenches behind.

It was much as before, since the fight in the Wilderness. Grant's march was slow, encumbered by a much larger force, many wagons, long lines of guns. Lee suffered from fewer numbers, but the one advantage still remained: he could move faster. He had one other advantage: Grant was moving on a roundabout course, while he had the straighter roads, and if he did not know exactly what Grant's objective was, he could at least plant his army in the best place to interrupt him, dig in again, the shovel and the ax now as valuable as the musket. This time the defense was formed below the North Anna River. It was strong, a difficult river to ford, made worse by the many days of rain. And it cut through the ravines and wooded land like a great brown snake, with sharp bends and high banks. By the time Grant could reach the few places where his army might push across, Lee was already in place, waiting for him.

HE HAD HOPED TO KEEP GRANT NORTH OF THE RIVER, KEEP him from coming across at all, but on the left, where the Third Corps had dug their lines, the woods between the troops and the river was already swarming with blue coats, a growing mass of the enemy.

The march to the river had been long and tense. Grant's people were to the east, and all along the way, care had to be taken that Lee was not suddenly confronted on the flank, whether by design or by accident. Hill was back in command of the Third Corps, the illness improving. Lee had welcomed his return, but it meant Early would return to Ewell's command, back to his division, and John Gordon would step down further, to command his brigade. It was a situation that required change.

HE HAD RISEN EARLY AGAIN, AND IT WAS A ROUTINE THAT WAS wearing him down. He could not eat, felt no stomach for the breakfast. He had watched the staff pick at the hard stale biscuits, scraping off the light blue mold, heard low comments, mild curses. His gut was still bothering him, and the sight of the biscuits had driven him from the table. He would wait, try to find something later, maybe a blessed gift, a local farmer offering some precious piece of his dwindling pantry.

The sun was up now, and the rain was gone; the sharp blue of the sky warmed them all. He tried to take a walk, to feel the dry air, fill himself with healing, but the churning in his gut would not go away, had driven him back to his tent.

He was on his back, staring at the blank canvas, the flaps open, the breeze billowing into the tent. He took a deep breath, then another. For a moment the cramp under his belt loosened, and he sat up, saw Taylor outside the tent, watching him.

Taylor stepped forward now, said, "General, excuse me, I have some coffee here, if it will help, sir."

Taylor held out the cup, and Lee caught the smell, strong and awful. He said, "Coffee? Are you certain, Colonel?"

Taylor looked into the cup, made a small frown. "Well, sir, it's what we've been using for coffee."

"Thank you, but I'll do without for now."

Taylor seemed relieved, backed out of the tent, tossed the contents of the cup out behind him, then turned to Lee, said, "Sorry, sir. I didn't know what else to do."

Lee smiled, nodded, then felt a small cramp return, and he took another long breath, waited for it to pass. "Colonel, we must not let word of this . . . of my condition, to reach the men. There can be no weakness now, none at all. Do you understand?"

Taylor moved closer, lowered his voice. "Of course, sir. 'The general is resting in his tent.' Anyone who has asked for you is being told that, sir."

"Very well, Colonel. Have we sent word to General Gordon?"

Taylor stood, nodded, "Yes, sir. Major Venable conveyed your request." He turned, peered out of the tent. "I will escort him here as soon as he arrives, sir."

Taylor was gone now, and Lee lay back on the cot again, slowly began to shake, wrapped his arms tightly around his waist, tried to hold the shaking away, but the chill came from deep inside him. He waited for it to pass, but the shivering filled him inside, his arms clamped hard across his chest. His mind fought it, a silent prayer, *God, please* . . . and slowly the shivering stopped, the deep knot in his gut let go. He was breathing heavily, felt the sweat now on his face, soaking his shirt. He closed his eyes, but there was no rest, his heart pounding. He thought, This is very bad, I must not allow this to interfere . . . we have much work to do.

There were voices, and he opened his eyes, pulled himself up painfully, sat up again, and Taylor was at the opening of the tent. "Sir, General Gordon, at your request."

Taylor backed away, and now Gordon stepped up, looked at Lee with concern, said, "General . . . you sent for me, sir?" He lowered his head, leaned in, tried to see Lee's face. "Are you all right, sir?"

Lee pointed to the small chair, said, "Sit, please, General. I am fine, yes. A bit of a stomach problem, nothing to be concerned about."

Gordon moved to the chair, nodded. "Yes, sir. I am sure it's just a minor ailment, sir."

Lee pulled out a handkerchief, wiped at his forehead, said, "It is of no concern, General. What is of concern is your command. I have already conferred with General Ewell, and it has been decided that your services to this army are of great value. I have prepared papers to send to the Secretary, recommending your promotion to Major General."

Gordon stood, stiff and formal, tried to hide the smile. "Thank you, sir. I have merely done my duty, sir."

Lee shifted his weight on the cot, wrestled with another cramp. "Please, General, sit down. There is more. It is not appropriate, given your service, and given your new rank, for you to return to brigade command. General Ewell also agrees that your handling of division strength forces in the last affair was admirable. We have reorganized somewhat . . . you will now command a division, consisting of three brigades, including your own. General Ewell will provide details. The Second Corps will now consist of your division and General Early's." He paused, watched Gordon slowly sit, his back straight, staring straight ahead. Lee suddenly thought of Jackson, the same posture, the man who never touched the back of a chair. But Gordon is young, he thought. He is not a professional . . . and he is not Jackson.

"General Gordon, this army needs all of its good commanders. We have lost too many. I would consider it a personal favor if you did not expose yourself to the fire of the enemy. This army must depend on your service."

Gordon said, "Yes, sir. I understand, sir. You will not be disappointed."

"No, I do not expect I will. You are dismissed, General."

Gordon stood, snapped a quick salute, moved quickly out of the tent. Lee sagged, was drained, felt weaker now than before. Gordon has the strength, he thought, the energy. So many of them had that   all of them, even . . . me. Now we will depend on the youth, the few men like Gordon who have not yet failed. He felt a wave of depression, told himself, No, have faith. One good man . . . can make a difference, can turn the direction of the war. He has already shown the fire, he knows how to face the enemy. I just wish . . . there were more like him.

H E RODE IN A WAGON, TOWARD THE LEFT FLANK, WHERE HILL was waiting. His gut was full of fire. The ailment that had punched and prodded him for days was now a full storm, and he could not even ride the horse. It could not be helped, the word had spread, and as the troops along the road watched the wagon pass, small cheers surrounded him. He felt the wagon slow, heard voices, familiar, Hill's staff. Now there were faces, helping hands, and he emerged from the wagon, his feet finding the hard ground, and he saw Hill.

Hill had come back with a flourish, had told Lee, told everyone, that his illness was gone, behind him; he was prepared for whatever faced the army. But Lee saw beyond the words, the bravado, looked briefly at the sunken eyes, the thin face. Hill was still not a well man. He felt a sudden impatient anger, turned his head, walked slowly away from the staffs. The pain in his gut was twisting into a hard knot again, and he stopped, clamped his eyes shut, thought, *Please*. Hill was beside him now, looked carefully at Lee, silent, seeing the sweat on Lee's face.

To the north, along the river, there was a small wave of musket fire, scattered thunder from big guns. Lee looked that way, knew that Grant's men had filled the woods between Hill and the river, thought, They should not be there, they should be on the other side of the river. He felt the anger again, stared hard at the sounds. Some dark place inside of him was suddenly boiling up, the control slipping away. He looked at Hill, the weakness, the frailty, one more failure, and he felt his voice rise, bursting out of him.

"General Hill, why did you not do as Jackson would have done? Those people should not be there, they should never have been allowed to cross the river. You should have thrown your whole force on those people and driven them back!" His voice cracked, the breath gone. His fists were clenched, and the sweat soaked him again.

Hill stared at him, seemed to sink down, feeling the weight of Lee's anger. Hill looked down then, said, "Sir, we did not . . . we did not learn of the enemy's crossing—"

Lee turned, was not listening to what Hill was saying, the explanation, heard only the fight within himself, the struggle for control. He held up a hand, stopped Hill in mid-sentence. "It is done. Prepare your defense, General. I must return to my headquarters."

Hill saluted, and Lee turned, saw the staff behind him, saw the faces, knew they had heard the anger, the harsh words. He moved toward the wagon, thought, I do not have time for explanation . . . this is not a time for comfort. He glanced at Hill, said, "General, we must be vigilant. General Grant is coming again."

IT WAS A PERFECT PLAN, THE ONLY KIND OF MANEUVER AGAINST THE numbers Grant was pushing toward them. The roads that led to Richmond crossed the North Anna in a place where Lee had fortified on a high knoll, a place called Ox Ford. On both sides of Ox Ford, the river curved up and away, like a wide U, and so, if Grant could not cross where Lee had his greatest strength, he would have to cross on either side. It was exactly what Lee hoped he would do, because Lee had pulled his defenses into an inverted V, both flanks pointing back away from the river. If Grant continued his advance, his army would come across the river in two separate pieces, far removed from each other. It was the kind of opportunity Lee had watched for, prayed for, and Grant kept coming.

On the left flank, where Hill's lines threw up a powerfully compact defense, the Federal Fifth Corps was advancing below the river

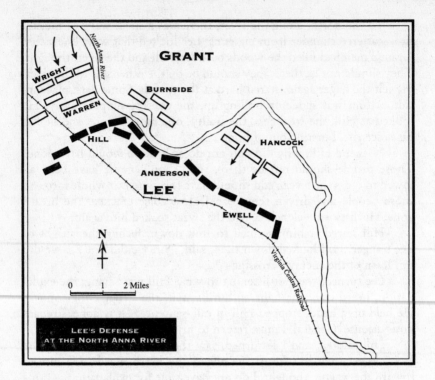

LEE'S DEFENSE
AT THE NORTH ANNA RIVER

toward them. Behind, above the river, the Sixth waited to cross as well. But the key to Lee's plan was on his right flank, downstream. Burnside was straight across Ox Ford, facing Lee's strongest position, and could do nothing but watch Porter Alexander's mass of cannon staring at them from the heights below the river. Farther downstream, Hancock's Second Corps was pushing across the river into an open area, behind which Lee had drawn half his army into a tightly coiled spring, waiting for the most vulnerable moment when Hancock's troops were spread out, a line of march led by men who stared curiously at the empty roads in front of them, a pathway south that seemed to be wide open.

H E HAD NOT RISEN FROM THE BED, THE BLANKET HOLDING HIM down in the sea of cold sweat. He could hear the sounds, outside, the horsemen moving in and out of the camp, the reports from the cavalry. Taylor would let no one see him, but he knew from the sound of the voices that something was very wrong.

His eyes were closed and he felt a small breath of air on his face. Lee looked up, blinked into focus, saw Taylor leaning over him. He tried to smile, the young man's soft concern drifting over him.

Taylor whispered, "Sir, if it is all right, I must tell you, sir. We have word from the right flank."

Lee nodded, felt the stab of pain growing in his gut again, clenched his teeth, fought it, said in a low voice, "Yes, Colonel, what is it?"

Taylor watched him, waited, saw Lee's face relax, said, "Sir, General Ewell did not advance per your instructions, sir. The attack was not made. The enemy has now entrenched. General Ewell reports that it is unlikely his attack would succeed now."

Lee stared past Taylor's face, up into the dull blankness of the tent. He closed his eyes, nodded, made a small motion with his hand, a silent command to Taylor: dismissed.

The fire tore through his mind, but there was no strength, and he could not respond to it, could not feel anger. We have let them go . . . *again*. If I had been there . . . He thought of Ewell, understood now that it was definite, as though the sentence had been passed down to him from God. Ewell is not fit. He cannot command. I don't understand, but I cannot just let him be, hope that he grows stronger, that whatever is missing in him returns.

There were more voices, Taylor still managing the couriers, and now the young man was back in the tent, crept closer, and Lee opened his eyes, looked up at him.

Taylor said, "Sir, the enemy is still across from General Hill. The troops in front of General Ewell are not withdrawing. The cavalry reports the enemy is still divided. The opportunity is still there, sir."

Lee saw the excitement in the Taylor's face, the show of enthusiasm. He said, "What time is it, Colonel?"

Taylor pulled out a small watch, and his face fell, the excitement faded. "Um . . . a bit after seven, sir."

Lee said, "It's too late. Tomorrow . . . we must try again tomorrow."

Lee felt the weakness pulling at him now, closed his eyes again. Taylor stayed close to him, waited, watching, then slowly backed away, moved out into the fading daylight.

Lee was not sleeping, felt his mind still working, and he thought of Ewell, of Hill, the two flanks of his army, both men staring out at their enemy waiting for *him* to guide them. Something about Napoleon came into his mind, odd, something he had not thought about in years, a quote from an old textbook: *To command is to wear out.* No, I am not worn-out, not yet. The army is not worn-out. He felt the fog rolling across his brain, saw the face of Napoleon. No, you are wrong. There will be tomorrow . . . *tomorrow* we will have another chance. . . .

23. GRANT

MAY 25, 1864

H E HAD MOVED FROM SPOTSYLVANIA, THROUGH THE BUSY RAIL-
road stop of Guiney's Station. The headquarters would be
near there, at least for one night, the tents spread across the
open lawn of a plantation house. The house, the land, belonged to a
family named Chandler, and the women in the house had been cordial,
polite to the commander of their enemy. He did not learn until that
evening that the small wooden building beside the grand mansion had
been the place where Stonewall Jackson had died.

As the army moved farther south he had moved the headquarters
closer to the North Anna, the tents now spread out along the hard road.
The rains had stopped, the wood at last was dry, and the troops built
huge fires, tall and roaring with great stacks of logs and brush. The fires
were not for warmth; the late spring heat had already brought the
steam up from the swamps and thick woodlands around the rivers. The
fires were a message to Lee's army, to the scouts, to the lookouts who
watched them from the tops of tall trees, who stared into the dark
night for the signs of motion, some sign of which way the blue army
was moving. The fires were their answer, a symbol of the spirit of these
men, and the message to the enemy was plain. This army was still moving south, was still coming after them.

The maps were spread across a large table, and Grant leaned low,
scanned the dark pencil lines, the positions of the troops. The reports
were all in, the staff was confident that the troop positions were accurate.
He followed the curving line of the North Anna, tugged hard at the cigar,
the smoke rolling around him. He moved now, around the table, looked
at the maps from the south, from Lee's point of view. He thought, We
are in serious trouble, we have been in serious trouble all day.

He looked up at Porter, said, "Are you certain of this? Lee's right flank is . . . here?"

Porter stepped forward, Meade easing up beside him, looking over Porter's shoulder. Porter said, "Yes, sir. We scouted all through those woods. The enemy has a strong line, has dug in down to the southeast. General Hancock's corps is directly in line to attack them, sir."

Grant nodded, thought, Yes, and that's what Lee would like us to do. He moved his hand along the map, out to the west. "How far is this? What is the distance over to the right flank?"

Porter was nervous now, sensed Grant's mood, and Meade stepped up in front of him, said, "Too far. Six miles. Too damned far. We would have to cross the river twice to support Hancock. *Twice.*"

Grant looked up at Meade, saw the agitation in the man's face, Meade now rocking back and forth. Grant looked at the map again, shook his head, thought, We gave Lee a chance . . . we made a mistake, trying to spread out on both his flanks. He had an opportunity today, a very good opportunity, and he did nothing.

He thought of the numbers, the reports from the staff. The casualties have been horrific, for us and for them, he thought. But Lee cannot absorb that, fight after fight. He is weakening, with every fight he is weakening. He has no choice but to dig a deep hole and wait for us.

He glanced up at Meade, thought, You *know* better than this, to weaken us like this, spread all over creation, facing a compact enemy. Now you want us to back away. This time you may be right. He said, "General Meade, I believe it is time for us to leave this place. Would you agree?"

Meade nodded, said quietly, hiding his words from the staff, "I thought it was not a good place . . . we should pull the army together. We can still put up a good defense. . . ." He ran his hand over the map, searching.

Grant said, "We do not need a good defense. Lee is in no position to attack us. We will pull the army together in the morning, and move on these roads to the southeast. We will be closer still to Richmond, and Lee will have to come out from behind those fat trenches and stop us." He waited for Meade's reaction, and Meade stared at the map, his face showing nothing.

Meade looked at Grant, said, "To the southeast . . . I will prepare the orders." He began to move away, stopped, and said, "Sir."

Grant moved away from the table, the meeting over. He felt a blossoming headache, thought, We are like some big stupid beast, blind to everything that does not hit us in the face. We have an enemy in front of us who is already beaten, may be beaten more than he realizes himself. Meade, Burnside . . . don't they see that?

He walked to the edge of the trees, heard music now, a tuneless mishmash of banjos and harmonicas. The fires spread all along the road, far along the wide shallow hills. *They* know, he thought, the *men* know. If I could just convince the people who give them the orders.

He walked out into the road, looked up, saw a vast sea of bright stars, a cloudless perfect night, and now he thought of Sherman. You should be here, my friend, you would know how to make this fight. But he knew that would not happen, that Sherman's war was in the West. He'd received word, Sherman had pushed Joe Johnston back toward Atlanta, was advancing slowly, deliberately, following Johnston's gradual retreat. He smiled, thought of Sherman's impatience. He is driving you mad, isn't he, General? Johnston won't fight you, he won't come out and play your game. You press him and he gives ground. But Johnston will run out of ground too, just like Lee. They cannot just keep backing away, digging more trenches. We are strangling them, slowly, and with perfect certainty. It would already be over, if . . .

He dropped his head, stared into the dark. The word had come from below Richmond, below the James River. Ben Butler's great thrust toward Richmond, toward the valuable rail center at Petersburg, had been choked to a halt. Butler had overwhelming numbers, but had allowed himself to be hemmed in by the geography of the land, by the great sweeping curves of the James River. Now his vastly superior army was trapped in a place called Bermuda Hundred, held there by a narrow stretch of land that Beauregard could seal with a small force.

He had no use for Butler, didn't know anyone in the army who did, but Butler brought great political influence to his position. To suggest Butler was not fit to command an army in the field was a subject that even Lincoln avoided. Grant thought of the great plan, the good strategy; Butler should have been such a threat to Richmond, to Lee's supply lines, that by now either Lee should have pulled back into the Richmond defenses or Butler should be right in his rear. Instead Butler had bottled up his army into an impossible place, and a few thousand of Beauregard's soldiers were the cork.

The great plan had another weak point as well. In the Shenandoah, Franz Sigel's forces had moved south with another great show of bluster and talk, had finally met the enemy, a strange mix of scattered rebel units, under the command of John Breckinridge. Breckinridge had even called out the cadet corps from VMI, throwing them straight into the fight at a small town called New Market. The boys in their new uniforms became men, leaving ten of their young comrades on the field, and Breckinridge and this strange mix of commands routed Sigel completely. The capture of the Shenandoah, the plan to deprive Lee of the crucial supplies, the one part of Grant's plan that seemed the least hazardous, was now thoroughly erased.

He looked up at the stars again. Does all that matter, after all? The war is still *here*, the enemy is still Lee. Sherman is moving on Atlanta, and he *will* succeed, there is no doubt of that. Once Johnston has been defeated, Sherman will have cut Lee off from all support from the deep South, all the rail junctions. And if *we* move closer to Richmond, Lee will have to come after us. It may take only one good fight, one more chance, get Lee out in the open. We are *so* close. . . .

THE LAND WAS SWAMPY, CUT BY SMALL STREAMS AND LARGER rivers, patches of thick woods and small open fields. It was the same land McClellan had moved through two years before, the huge Federal army having pushed hard up the peninsula, the first thrust at Richmond. McClellan had moved through this ground cautiously, had always believed the rebel army was far larger, stronger, than his, and with his caution he gave away every opportunity. The defense of Richmond had been given to Lee, the failure of the western Virginia campaign forgotten, and during the Seven Days battles, Lee had used the land, the swamps and creeks, to his best advantage. McClellan finally pulled his great army away, back down the peninsula, chased by Lee's tactics, and more, by the lost opportunities and ghosts he could not defeat.

Now Grant came into the same land, but from the opposite direction, and he had no illusions about the strength of the enemy that scrambled to intercept him, at every bridge, every crossing of the swampy rivers. The Federal army continued to push along the tree-lined roads, through the open lands that rose above the swamps, where farmers still planted and Lee's army could still find food. Here, the roads began to come together, merging into the routes that led south, straight into the heart of Richmond.

The marches had been quick and efficient, and Lee had confronted them in small skirmishes, with cavalry and whatever strength he could press hard into their path. But Sheridan's horsemen had won the race for a vital crossroads, a place where Grant had a choice, to

move on toward the city itself or slide farther to the southeast, around
the city, directly to the banks of the James River. Lee's priorities were
given to him by Davis, and he had responded in the only way that
could save Richmond. The rebels now faced Grant's numbers in a
north-south line, Grant now on the eastern side, facing west. But
Grant had captured the crossroads he'd wanted, and Lee would have to
guess where he might move next. But first there was an opportunity,
this time for the men in blue. Lee had finally come out to meet them,
extended in a line that spread out along a deep ravine, a winding stretch
of open ground and patches of woods, west of the roadways Grant had
captured. The intersection carried an English name, a type of traveler's
rest where one could find sparse shelter but no fire, no hot food. It was
called Cold Harbor.

MORNING, JUNE 3, 1864

THE RAINS HAD COME AGAIN, THE DAY BEFORE, AND THE
ground had swollen into soft mud. By dawn the rains had
stopped, but the small creeks were again strong and deep, and
the men who took their place in line were still wet and cold from the
march the night before.

They were called Heavy Artillery, had spent most of the war in
the comforts of the big forts, the strong fortifications around Washington, Norfolk, Fort Monroe. It had been a plum assignment, and most
of these men had come into the army with some influence, the power
of a family name, the favor of a politician, the means of securing the
safe posts. But Grant changed that, had not seen the need for a powerful force of troops guarding the cities from an enemy that was far
away. So the Heavy Artillery came south, marched in the footsteps of
the men of both armies, the men who had always, up to now, done the
real fighting. There was grumbling, desertion, the men who had grown
soft in the comfort of the forts now beaten down by the heat and hard-
ship of the march. But Grant wanted all the strength he could bring to
the fight, and these men would replace many of those who were lost,
the vast numbers of casualties from the vicious fights of May.

Many of the veterans gathered along the roads, whistled and
hooted at the clean uniforms, pointed and joked at the slow march of
the men whose belt line was still soft. No one welcomed these new
units to the fighting strength of the army, saw only raw numbers, not
men who would hold the line, who could be counted on to lead the
charge.

When the first order came at four-thirty in the morning, many of the men who stepped into the open ground had never seen the face of the enemy, never heard the steady roar of the great lines of muskets, the sharp whiz and dull slap of the musket ball. With the first light, the orders came down, and the men moved out in wide solid lines, flowing across a flat clear space, some slowed by the ravine, some climbing up toward a vast dense line of fire, a strong line of the enemy, protected by the quick work of the shovel. The rebel lines had been dug with the skill of men who have learned the bloody lesson, who understand with perfect clarity the value of a deep trench and a heavy dirt wall.

When the full glow of daylight had spread across the flat open ground, had lit the bottom of the winding ravine, many of the dead of the Heavy Artillery would lie beside the veterans, men who had faced the guns in every fight, the broken remains of hard men who would never flinch at the flashes from the guns to their front.

The Federal assaults were halted, and those who survived sought whatever protection they could find, moving through the vicious storm of the enemy's fire. They slid across the bodies of their friends, huddled together in small depressions in the ground, behind the shattered trunks of trees, anywhere there was blessed cover. When the orders came again, advance, resume the attack . . . the men who had marched into the slaughter and survived would not do it again. Many simply fired their muskets in the air, a show of noise for the commanders behind the lines, an angry protest at the needless disaster. They had moved across the small piece of ground into their worst nightmare of the war, a complete and utter failure, thousands of men shot down in a fight that lasted only a few minutes.

THE HORSEMEN MOVED THROUGH THE CAMP, ORDERS FLOWING out to all parts of the long line. Grant had listened to the hard wave of the first assault, the sun finally breaking through the clouds, and he had believed, from the first rattle of the muskets, this might truly be the final blow.

The reports began to come back to headquarters, and the mood began to change. By mid-morning the sounds of the fight were gone, just the occasional crack from the single musket, a small assault far to one end of the line, meaningless.

He climbed the horse now, had to see it, could not understand what had happened. In the trees to one side, beyond the tents of the headquarters, he had seen Meade, screaming like some great mad beast, a blistering tirade to some nameless officer. Grant did not ride that way, turned, moved straight toward the front, where the great burst of sounds had come, the center of the long line. He had stayed at the headquarters, would wait for it, the joyous word, the breakthrough. But after the first great wave, the musket fire had slowed. Now only faint scattered shots were heard, mostly to the north, where the fight had not been heavy, was not supposed to be heavy. But in front of him, where they should have punched through, swarmed up the shallow rise to divide and crush Lee's army, there was only silence.

He had not said anything to the staff, saw Rawlins busy with some couriers, but he would not wait, thought, Something is wrong, *again*, and this time I will see, I will be there before it is over. The anger had swelled inside of him, and he gripped the reins of the horse, stared straight toward the front line, kicked the horse hard, began to move forward.

He heard a voice, turned, saw Meade riding hard after him, thought, *Not now*, felt the anger building toward Meade, but the look on Meade's face was not what he expected.

Meade reached him, halted the horse, said, "Sir . . . it is no good. The brigade commanders report they are pinned down, cannot even pull away. The enemy has the ground, the position. Sir . . ." Meade paused, and Grant waited, had prepared himself for another tirade, listening with grinding patience while Meade puffed out in red-faced anger.

But Meade's face was drained of color, a look Grant had not seen before, shock, the look of defeat. Meade lowered his head, said, "Sir, it has been a tragedy. We lost . . . a great number. The ground is . . . it is worse than anything I have seen, sir. Begging your pardon, General. I don't know how else to say it."

Grant stared at Meade, felt a hot sickness rising, thought, If this is your caution . . . if we have stopped because you ran out of nerve . . . He fought the anger, clenched his fists, took a deep breath, said, "Can they not advance? They should have carried the fight! Lee is not that strong. What happened?"

Meade still looked down, shook his head. "They will not advance. I ordered support, but the men would not move forward. It was— forgive me sir—it was a perfect slaughter."

Grant waited for more, and Meade abruptly pulled the horse away, moved back toward the headquarters. Grant turned, looked out toward the lines, thought, This is . . . *madness*. It cannot be.

He spurred the horse, moved down a narrow ravine, heard shouts, the staff behind him. He felt the anger rising, thought of Meade's caution, the face of a man who had lost the fire. I will see this, he thought, I will know what has happened. They cannot tell me there is no fight left in these men. He spurred the horse, pushed hard through a thicket of briars, reached a trail, turned the horse, moved toward the sounds that now emerged from the woods, from the ground in front of him. He moved forward along the trail, saw now the woods were thick with soldiers. Some were walking, moving slowly away from the lines, blank faces, bloody stains on ragged uniforms. Now he saw officers, men on horses, some on foot, and one man saluted him, but most did not notice him. He slowed the horse, and now the staff hurried up behind him.

Rawlins was suddenly there, said, "Sir, what are you doing? Where are we going? Do you have orders, sir?"

He looked at Rawlins, felt his anger boiling in his brain, felt his jaw clench, said, "What has happened to this army, Mr. Rawlins?"

Rawlins stared at him, said nothing, and Grant spurred the horse again, rode down into a shallow depression, saw a vast line of blue, huddled together in a solid mass, spread out on both sides of him. Now the sounds flowed out all around him, and he could hear shouts, the voices of his men, the cries and screams of the wounded. The sounds began to grow, and he pushed the horse up a small rise, saw vast blue clusters, men crouched together, hatless, bloody shapes, faces staring up into the sky. He stopped the horse, saw a row of big guns, the crews sitting on the ground, the officers staring at him quietly. He pushed the horse past the guns, climbed a small rise, and now he could see it, spread out in front of him. The ground was like a wide flat table, a few large trees, the bark splintered, the trees stripped bare. All across the rich green of the grass lay the bodies in blue, a thick carpet, reaching across the open ground. To the far side he saw the long tall mound, the fresh dirt facing him like a dark brown wave, motionless, frozen in time. The mound spread out in both directions, hidden behind brush, snaked and curved out across a wide field, then farther, disappearing into a patch of woods. He saw a glimmer of motion, a reflection behind the mound, the morning sun now reflecting off the thick rows of bayonets. There were small gaps in the mound, and he saw movement, and across the horrible field of blue it was the only motion he saw. It was the face of the enemy.

Rawlins was beside him, and the horse was jerked to the side. He felt them pulling him back down the rise. He heard the new sounds, a

burst of firing, the musket balls flying over his head. He still tried to
see over the rise, wanted to turn the horse, but the reins were not in his
hand. He turned, thought, This is not real, a nightmare . . . But he saw
Rawlins looking at him, the reins of his horse in Rawlins's hand, and
he knew Rawlins was real, that all of it was real.

Rawlins leaned close to him, held the reins out, said in a whisper,
"Sir . . . we must leave here. We will move to the rear in good order.
The men must not see you like this, sir."

Grant took the reins, looked at Rawlins, saw the embarrassment,
Rawlins glancing about at the faces now watching them. Grant said
nothing, looked at the faces himself, and there was no cheering, no
salutes. The men huddled behind low mounds of dirt, crouched low
behind trees. The faces stared, eyes deep and dark, and he spurred the
horse, prodded gently, began to move along the trail, the eyes moving
with him as he passed by. He began to see each of them now, looked at
them one at a time, the men who made his fight, who stood up to the
guns. He saw officers, more eyes watching him, thought, Pull them together, form your lines. But the words did not come, there were no orders. There was no fight left in these men.

They moved back behind the trees, past the brush, away from the
sounds. Men were moving now, horsemen rushing with dispatches, the
business of headquarters. The staff began to scatter, the tents now in
view, and Grant halted the horse, saw a small piece of color, motion,
against a fallen tree. He leaned forward in the saddle, saw now it was a
man. The face was looking up at him, reflected the bright sun, the
man's lips a light blue. Grant moved the horse, was suddenly jostled,
the horse jumping, startled by a passing courier, an officer riding
quickly along the trail. The man's horse was kicking up a spray of mud
as he passed, and Grant felt his own horse calming, the grip of the reins
hard in his hand. He looked at the soldier again, saw a splatter of mud
on the man's face. He felt a twist in his gut, felt his throat tighten,
climbed down from the horse. Now there was a hand on his shoulder,
and a soft voice.

"Allow me . . . sir."

It was Porter, and the young man moved past him, eased down
over the upturned face of the soldier, wiped the mud from the man's
face. The man's eyes blinked, and he looked now at Grant, stared with
cold silence. Porter stood up, looked at Grant, said, "He's not going to
make it, sir."

Grant could not look away, stared at the man's black eyes,
thought, There must be something. How do we just . . . walk away?

Porter was beside him now, said, "He's done for, sir. We should go. . . ."

Porter moved to his horse, and Grant still watched the man, the eyes still held him. He had never done this before, had always stayed back, away from where the men fell, where the blood stained the ground. He could never admit that, never talked about it, but now he was facing it, could not leave this man, not yet. He wanted to say something, to ask the man . . . what? There were no words, no questions, and he moved toward the man, a step closer, saw that the eyes were not looking at him anymore, were staring ahead now into the sun, far away into some other place.

EVENING, JUNE 3, 1864

THROUGHOUT THE DAY THERE HAD BEEN SMALL SKIRMISHES ALL along the line, but there would be no great assault now.

Grant was far behind the awful place, sat alone in the dark, could still see it in his mind, could still see Meade's shock, the words "a perfect slaughter," and he could not escape the image of the one soldier, one man, the eyes that had watched him. He tried to think of his wife, of church, of Heaven. Is that where he is now? He felt angry, scolded himself, You should know about this. What is it like? He could have told you, if you had reached him sooner. You were the last thing he saw . . . in this life. Did he take that with him? Are the wounds healed now?

He stood, stared into the dark, away from the small fires. Is this what madness is, coming so close to death that it holds on to you, obsesses you? He began to walk, nervous steps, moved behind the tents, then stopped, clenched his fists. One man . . . how can you be so affected by one man? Is it because . . . you watched him die? You saw the face? How many faces lay on that field today? Is it any different because you weren't there to see it?

He closed his eyes, thought again of Julia, thought, You would know what to say, you would have the Lesson, God's comforting words for this. There are no comforting words here. Here, it is all about duty, and making the right decisions. And men must die . . . even when the decisions are the very best ones. If today was a bad decision . . . we can do no better than to make a good decision tomorrow.

The anger stayed with him all day, and the commanders had come around, bringing the explanations. He listened, said very little, absorbed just how bad it had been. This was a disaster, and after all the talk, the excuses, the maps, the numbers, it had come to him, the anger slowly replaced by something else, something much worse. He understood now, thought, You cannot blame them. It is not Meade's caution, or the inexperience of Wright, the ridiculous attention to detail that curses Warren. This is not Burnside's inept slowness or Hancock's overaggressiveness. We cannot blame this on poor coordination, or bad timing, or the curse of bad weather.

He began to move again, walked further into the dark, stared at nothing. There is no one to blame but me. This was my fight, my opportunity. He thought of Lee. He is not some demon, he made no grand strategy, no brilliant countermove. I sent them . . . I ordered them across this ground. Lee lined his men up in a straight line behind a big pile of dirt and cut this army to pieces. And I did not see it . . . I did not know it was going to happen.

He moved toward a small fire, saw men sitting in a circle. The voices were low, the faces still, eyes staring into the flame. He moved closer, saw Rawlins, Porter, others, men from Meade's staff. The tents spread out beyond, flaps open and still, for there was no breeze. There were more men sitting near a wagon, men leaning up against the spoked wheels. There was motion, a bottle, one man handing it to another, the bottle upturned, then passed along. He moved that way, and the faces turned toward him, one man holding the bottle carefully, cradling it like a small child. There were nods, small casual greetings, too casual, but he did not notice, turned, moved toward the tents. Now he saw a group of men moving slowly away from him, men disappearing into tents, staff officers, staggering slowly out of the firelight. There was a small table, a deck of cards scattered loosely, and in the center of the table, another bottle.

He stopped beside the table, stared at the cards, the colorful depictions of royalty, and knew his mind was playing with him, would not let him look at it, but slowly he saw it, fixed his eyes on the label, focused on the faint lettering. He reached out, felt his fingers tighten around the neck of the bottle, lifted it up slowly, saw the light pass through. It was nearly empty, but there was still the last good drink, enough to warm a man all the way down, the delicious burn.

It had been a long time ago, and it had been a fight he had to win. The gold rush did something to the men in California, took something away, all the lessons of home, all the rules about decency, dignity. The army was not immune, and in a place where every temptation was bold and colorful, few had been able to keep themselves away from the crude pleasures.

Julia stayed in Missouri with her family, had not made the journey, had not joined him in that amazing place, San Francisco. The loneliness had eaten at him like a disease, and the disease exposed something in him he did not understand, a weakness, and he had been consumed by it, by the numbing comfort of the bottle. He did not frequent the gambling halls, the clubs, where women offered company to a man whose family was so far away. He avoided the sounds and the lights, and so he was faced with long quiet nights, would listen to the sounds of wild streets from a dark room, trying with every piece of himself to see her face, keep her name in his mind. When it became harder, and her face faded, there was only sadness, and with the sadness came the bottle.

Julia would never know how far down he had gone, that it had been the drinking that finally cost him his job. He had resigned from the army, a choice provided by a generous commander, saving him from the humiliation of a court-martial. He always carried the weight of that—that it mattered little if he had been a good soldier, he also had a dangerous weakness. When he went back east, to his family, to life as a civilian, he made a silent vow, to her, to his children, the most important decision of his life. The weakness would never come back, would be kept away. He would always remember how his career, his life, had nearly been shattered by the bottle.

Now he moved the bottle in a small circle, swirling the brown liquid, thought of the word: *shattered*. How many men had their lives shattered today . . . how many families? He thought of the newspapers, the reporters. The numbers were already flying through the camp, thousands of casualties, and they will report that. Many men died here today because . . . I made a horrible mistake. Many men have died since this campaign began, and we have not yet brought this to a close. What right do I have to take so much from these men, without giving them something in return? I had thought . . . it would be over by now.

There was a hand on his arm, and he jumped, startled, saw it was Rawlins.

"Sir, please . . . allow me." Rawlins took the bottle slowly from Grant's hand. Grant saw Porter now, the others, men gathering slowly behind him. Rawlins tossed the bottle to another man, said, "General, if we may be of service, sir?"

Grant looked at the others, the man with the bottle, then focused on Rawlins. "Your service is noted, Colonel." Grant saw the look in Rawlins's face, the look of the one man in the camp who knew of the disease. There was a silent moment, and Grant nodded, said, "Colonel, the men may be excused."

Rawlins motioned with his hand, and the others moved off.

Grant did not watch them. He walked away from the fires, into the darkness. He heard footsteps, the crunch of leaves, a voice. "General . . . if you don't mind, sir, may I walk with you?"

Grant knew the voice, did not look at the face. It was Porter. "You have something to say, Colonel?"

"Oh . . . uh, no, sir, I just thought . . . well, sir, you look like you need some company."

Grant looked at him now, the firelight reflecting on the young man's face. He nodded, said, "All right, Colonel, suit yourself."

Grant moved further into the dark, Porter moving beside him. Grant stopped, looked at the stars, stared silently into the deep black space.

Porter said, "We lost . . . a good many men today. We haven't given out the official casualty count. Not yet. It is frightful, sir."

Grant said nothing, felt deep into his pocket, pulled out a cigar, lit it slowly, felt the smoke swirl around his face. He still watched the stars, said, "I have underestimated him."

Porter leaned forward, tried to see Grant's face in the dark. "Sir? Who, sir?"

Grant lowered the cigar, crossed his arms. "Lee. I have underestimated General Lee. That should be pleasing to some in this army. I've heard the comments from General Meade's people. I don't know anything about fighting a war until I've fought Bobby Lee. Didn't pay much attention to all that. Just talk. Now . . . maybe . . . they're right."

"I don't believe that, sir. No one does . . . not the ones who matter."

"The ones who matter, Colonel, are a long way from here. It's the people up North who matter. We can't keep sending troops home in boxes. Mr. Lincoln has an election coming up. If he can't give the people a victory, then someone else will get the chance. Likely, it will be someone who knows how to play on the people's unhappiness. Do you know what that will mean, Colonel?"

Porter shook his head, said, "No, sir."

"It means the war will end. Quickly. And if the victory is not in our hands, there is only one other way it can end. We will have to back away, withdraw the troops, and the rebels will have their country. The Union will cease to exist."

Porter said nothing, followed the small glow of Grant's cigar moving in the dark.

"There is only one way to make war, Colonel. You have to *hurt* somebody. Maybe you have to hurt *everybody*. Make them feel it, understand what it is we are doing out here. If this war is worth fighting in the first place, then it is worth winning. We cannot win unless we fight. If we fight, men will die. If more of *them* die, then we will win. It has nothing to do with cities, or government, or what is barbaric and what is civilized. We are *here*, and the enemy is over there, and if we must give the newspapers the horrifying truth, then the people will know. If Mr. Lincoln does not want me to win this war, then he can make that decision. But there is no other way to see it. If these men do not fight and bleed and die, if we do not make the rebels quit by destroying their will to fight, by destroying their army, then the only other choice is to walk away."

Porter rubbed his hand through his hair, took a deep breath, said, "I don't know, sir. The enemy is still over there. It seems like no matter what we do, we have to face those boys behind those works. It seems like . . . nothing changes."

Grant drew at the cigar, flicked the ash away. "I made a serious mistake today. We cannot just throw strength at strength and prevail. There is another way, there has to be. Lee has outmaneuvered us, outfought us. He has been a better commander than I have. Maybe he's smarter, maybe he's just luckier."

He turned, looked back toward the fires. "If we have made one great mistake, all of us, it has been that we have failed to understand *our* strength. He has guns, we have guns. He can dig trenches, we can dig trenches. So, if we cannot crush him . . . if it costs us too much to smash him with one blow . . . then we will strangle him. We will stretch his supplies until he cannot eat, we will stretch his manpower until he cannot defend. We will make them hurt, until they cannot fight."

Porter stared, wide-eyed, said, "Um . . . forgive me, sir . . . how?"

Grant looked at the cigar, tossed it down, stepped on it, the faint glow of the ash buried in the soft dirt. "South . . . cross the James. We will cut him off, from his food, his supplies. We will isolate Richmond. We will start by doing what Butler was supposed to do. We will take this army where it will hurt him the most. We will capture Petersburg. We will squeeze him and stretch him until there is no fight left in that damned bunch of rebels."

He turned, moved toward the glow of the fires, Porter following behind. He tried to think of the plan, the troops, the commanders, but in the dark, staring up into the small pieces of starlight, he saw the lone soldier again, the black eyes, staring at him. He stopped, looked to the ground, closed his eyes, pushed the face from his mind, thought, No, it cannot be like that. There is only one way . . . the only way we can succeed. We cannot allow that . . . we *cannot* see the *faces*.

JUNE 15, 1864

THEY LEFT THE CAVALRY TO SCREEN THE MOVEMENT, SLIPPED away from the disaster of Cold Harbor with the measured steps of an army that knows the enemy is still strong. They moved quickly, made their way down to the shores of the wide James River, marched calmly past grand plantations, great white mansions spread along the water, so many monuments to the glory of old Virginia. One in particular was their destination, an enormous estate called "Berkeley Hundred," the ancestral home of President William Henry Harrison. Here, there was a wharf, long boat docks that had once received royal yachts and flotillas of brightly dressed aristocracy. Now, the men of Grant's army gathered along the wide banks, waited in turn for the ferries and transports of the navy to move them across the river.

On the march, the veterans noticed something else about the sounds, the distinct tramp of marching feet, the quiet rhythm that says the wagons, the supplies, the big guns are not with us. Many had seen the great noisy columns moving away on other roads, and if they knew that Grant had slipped them quietly away from the enemy, there was still the nervous glance, the bad joke, unprotected infantry, the supplies and guns leaving them vulnerable. The foot soldiers did not know that upriver, the great columns of horses and wagons had reached another point on the wide river, Wyannoke Landing. The drivers and teamsters had stared in amazement as a pontoon bridge waited for them, a bridge nearly half a mile long, held in place in midstream by anchored ships. The wagons, guns, and nervous drivers began to cross a bridge longer than many had ever seen, the longest pontoon bridge ever built. The James was not calm, and stiff waves rolled against the bridge, bouncing the wagons, rocking the guns, but in less than a day the long columns of men and machine were across. It was an efficient march, inspired by the deep water beneath their feet.

By late in the day most of the great army, a hundred thousand men, was on the south side of the James River. The men were formed into their units, companies and regiments, brigades and divisions, and a

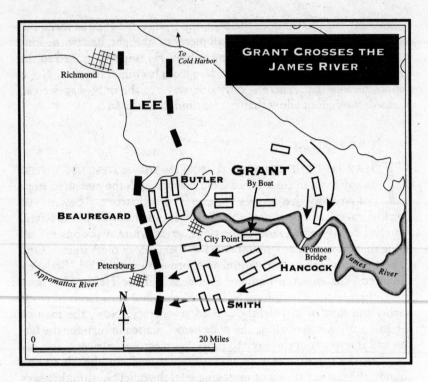

vast sea of blue spread out away from the river. As the camps began to form, the tents and fires filling the wide fields, the sounds were still muted, low conversation, a calm that surprised even the veterans. They all knew now what had happened at Cold Harbor, what had been happening to them since the first days in May, when the great campaign had begun. The massive assault that would end the war had cost this army nearly forty percent of its strength, nearly fifty thousand casualties. The reinforcements had come, rebuilt the army, brought the numbers back up, but the veterans had little respect for raw numbers, for the soft men who had never faced the guns. The veterans had seen what great numbers could mean, that when the enemy waited for you behind strong defenses, the great numbers meant a greater loss, and the hard strength of the blue army had been slowly drained away. There was quiet talk about Grant, but the veterans remembered McClellan and Hooker, Pope and Burnside, and their officers still told them Grant was the best man they could turn to, and they were coming to understand that the cost in numbers was the cost of waging war. But the blind optimism from the days before the Wilderness was gone. There was little of the excited talk of victory, of finally going home. Even the music had changed; when the army was in the camps, you did not hear the noisy clash of patriotic fever. The air echoed now with a sweeter sound, soft sad songs, songs of home and family, of God and the souls of the men who were no longer there. Even the commanders understood, you cannot force good morale, and the music reflected the mood of the army. No one gave the order, no one tried to change the spirit of the men with mindless calls for boisterous flag waving.

As the march reached the shores, when the vast winding river appeared before them, some wondered if it would be as before, two years ago with McClellan, when that huge army had reached these same shores, to load onto the boats that would take them away from the enemy, moving downriver, out of Virginia and back to Washington. Grant's boats were not taking them away, but on a short ride straight across the river. The talk stopped, and they all understood that Grant was not McClellan after all. They were still moving south, deeper into the heart of the enemy. The officers, the men who saw the maps, knew they were moving even beyond Richmond, the great prize that the politicians and newspapers seemed to value above all else. If they did not know what Grant had in mind, they knew now it was not to be Richmond, that once across the wide James, they would push on until they found the ragged army of those tough rebels. They did not yet know where the fight would be, but to the west, men were moving to meet them, filling a vast line of trenches, more deep earthworks, artillery officers gathering their men beside the big guns that had waited since the beginning of the war, guns that had never been fired, the guns defending the crucial rail center of Petersburg.

PART
THREE

...The world will little note, nor long remember what we say here, but can never forget what they did here. It is for us, the living, rather to be dedicated to the great task remaining before us—that from these honored dead we take increased devotion to that cause for which they here gave the last full measure of devotion...

24. LEE

JUNE 15, 1864

THERE WAS AN ARROGANCE TO THE MAN, AN ANNOYING POSture of superiority. Lee had heard his words, listened patiently while the young captain pleaded his case, alternating humble requests with sudden boisterous demands, and Lee knew through it all that the young man was only repeating what had been so carefully drilled into him. Lee understood that, after all, he was hearing the voice of this man's commander, General Beauregard.

"General Lee, if we do not receive the troops from your command, if we do not have your support, the general is not responsible . . . he cannot be held responsible for what will occur. The numbers are all . . . right there, plain as day, sir. What else can be done?"

The young man was pointing to the pile of papers, the neat stack he had placed on Lee's desk. Lee glanced down, did not touch the papers, leaned back in his chair, said, "Captain Paul, does General Beauregard know exactly who it is that threatens his position?"

Paul hesitated, then said, "Certainly, sir. We are facing the troops of General Grant."

"Captain, there are no Federal troops on this continent who are *not* the troops of General Grant. Does General Beauregard know *which* troops? Do we know which Federal corps?"

Lee saw the man's eyes staring at him in a dull glaze. No, he thought, he doesn't know.

Lee stood, the quiet signal. Taylor moved up, had Paul's hat in his hands, held it out to the surprised young man. Paul looked at Lee, then at the pile of paper, still had more of his presentation to make.

Lee said, "Captain, you may return to General Beauregard. Tell him we are well aware what General Grant is doing, and we are making dispositions accordingly. You are dismissed."

Paul took the hat, saluted, straightened his back, regained the arrogance, turned, brushed against Taylor as he left the tent, and was gone.

Lee sat again, looked at the papers, said to Taylor, "Colonel, we should keep General Beauregard's paperwork in a secure location. It would not be prudent to allow this valuable information to fall into enemy hands." He could not hide the sarcasm, the weariness from days of frustration.

The illness had passed, and he was actually feeling the old energy, could ride the horse now for long stretches. But there was a new illness, an old affliction that was coming back to haunt him, to infect the entire army. It was the politics of Richmond, the administrative hand of Jefferson Davis.

The James River was Davis's dividing line, where Lee's authority stopped and Beauregard's began. Beauregard had finally moved his headquarters up from the Carolinas to Petersburg, responding to the threat from Ben Butler. Butler was still tightly contained, but now the threat was much greater. Lee knew Grant was moving south, knew of the great river crossings. The word passed quietly from loyal civilians and careful scouts. It was no surprise.

North of the James, Lee had brought Grant's great numbers to a bloody halt. If Grant tried to move toward Richmond, Lee was now in his path, and Lee knew that Grant would not make another mistake like that. There would be no more opportunities like the bloodbath at Cold Harbor. Grant had only two choices: to retreat, or to move south, cross the James and isolate Richmond from below. Lee never considered that Grant would retreat, had long accepted what the papers were calling the "hammering tactics." Now he was beginning to understand something else: that Richmond might not be the target. Davis was sending Lee a stream of correspondence, needless reminders of the value of the capital, the urgency of a strong defense. The same cries were coming from Beauregard in Petersburg. He thought about the pleas, begging him to respond to an enemy that he had been facing across miles of bloody fields, an enemy he'd come to know, an army that was always there, shifting and maneuvering, moving slowly, then a quick blow, striking out and pulling away. But the indignant messages still came, and he held the anger tight inside. They called to him with outrage, as though he had no idea who this enemy was, how serious the threat. The messages were filled with predictions for Lee's benefit, as though he knew nothing about Grant and what he would likely do next.

He walked outside the tent, felt the bright sun, moved toward the horses. Yes, he thought, I will send what I can, we must move quickly. This time Beauregard is right, he is not seeing ghosts.

Beyond the command tents, faces turned toward him, and he paused beside the horse, saw the men watching him, saw the ragged clothes, the thin faces, the bones of his army. There were a few cheers, hats waved, and Lee nodded to them, reached for the reins, climbed up on the big horse.

He heard Taylor shout something, knew there would be an aide moving up behind him, that Taylor would never let him ride off alone, not anymore, not since the illness. Lee smiled at that, thought, He is like a father, stern, overprotective. And I am the son. I had thought . . . it was the other way around. He turned, saw Taylor standing by the tent, hands on his hips, watching until the aide was up on the horse. Lee moved Traveller away on the hard road, still smiled.

He did not take great pleasure in the victory at Cold Harbor. He began to think on that, on the horror of that ground, of the enemy's loss. And what did we gain? He is still there, and he will come again. Our defenses, our strong trenches . . . keep us from moving like we used to. We are slowed down by the only thing that saves us. He thought of Jackson, spoke to him: You would not have understood trenches. You would not sit still in the face of the enemy. You would press forward, mobile, fast. Lee was struck by an odd thought: that Jackson's way could have been a terrible mistake, the hard fight, pressing forward, always forward. Grant has been inviting us to come out in the open, to fight him on his terms. Jackson might have done exactly that.

He felt guilty then, never believed Jackson could have been anything but the commander this army needed. But the war had changed, the ways of fighting, gentlemen on bloody fields. He thought of the great river itself, the James. Early in the war it had been suggested the river be mined for protection against Federal gunboats moving on Richmond. The idea was cast aside with indignation, dismissed entirely for its barbarism. It was not the way wars were fought, not the way gentlemen conducted themselves on the field. That was only three years ago, but Lee knew those ideas were from another time. Now the James *was* mined, torpedoes filled with black powder. Honor had been replaced by efficiency.

He still wondered about Grant, if it was the man himself who had done this. No, he thought, there is no blame, there is only the will of God. Jackson was taken from us because it was his time. Now the war is fought by different men, many different faces. Lee knew the numbers, knew he had lost a third of his generals since Grant's offensive began. Longstreet would not return for many months. Ewell was finally sent to Richmond, given command of the city's guard, a face-saving position for a man who had once given the army so much. Hill was fit, at least for the time being, but if Lee did not think on it, the others all knew that when the next great fight came, Hill's sickness would return. No one had stepped forward, none of the names seemed to matter. Anderson was still merely competent; his greatest day would still be remembered as the race to Spotsylvania. At Cold Harbor no one stepped forward, there was no bright stroke of command. They won because the enemy had made their own mistakes, had beaten themselves to death.

He would not think of Stuart, could still not accept that; there had been no answer, no comfort. So many are gone, he thought, except . . . me. I am still here because God is not yet through with me. Lee forced himself not to ponder that, to ask why. There is only the duty. I need not understand it any better than that. When the duty has passed, there will be no mistaking it. Then God will take me as well.

He rode past the sound of running water. The thick trees around him smelled of dark spaces, rotting wood. He felt the sweat on his face, but it was not the sweat of sickness, of the fever. He still felt for it, probed for the horrible twist in the gut, but it was gone completely, and even his appetite had returned. As they had come closer to Richmond, the gifts flowed into camp again, many citizens sending the last bounty the land had given them. The packages of food were welcomed now, and he was eating regularly. He was grateful for the generosity of the people who kept their suffering to themselves, who did not have much to give, but he knew that the army was suffering more. Vegetables were almost nonexistent, and what passed for meat was either rancid or pure fat. The men were surviving on crackers and moldy flour.

Lee was beginning to understand what this meant to the fighting strength of the army. The marches were much slower now, and the work details accomplished little before the men simply fell out, exhausted, hollow eyes staring ahead at nothing.

He stopped the horse, looked back at the aide who was behind him at a discreet distance. He could hear the sounds of the army, a low echo through the woods, and he tried to hear more, was suddenly swarmed by mosquitoes, a thin cloud singing around his head, picking at his ears, his face. He waved his arm, spurred the horse again, thought, Keep moving.

He knew that Beauregard was right, after all. Petersburg was the target. If the rail center there was captured, the supplies would stop, and the symbolic buildings of Richmond would mean nothing to the starving men of this army. But Beauregard had done himself no favors, had always requested more men than the army could ever provide, was always issuing grand proclamations, great involved schemes to invade unimpeded into the North, grand impossible conquests which he would of course always lead. Now that he was facing a serious threat, the calls for troops were as frantic as ever, but Davis had heard too much of that, and Beauregard would not get his way.

The frustration came over Lee now in a wave. With Grant south of the James, he thought, Beauregard is in command. It becomes his war. That will not sit well in Richmond, and so Davis will change the departments again, shift responsibility to suit his moment, creating more confusion, more chaos.

And all the while, Grant presses forward.

LEE HAD LEARNED QUICKLY THAT GRANT HAD NOT FORGOTTEN the Shenandoah Valley. The inept Franz Sigel had been replaced, and the new threat to the South's most fertile breadbasket came from David Hunter. Lee had known Hunter from the old army, had seen a side of the man in Mexico that had not impressed anyone's sense of decency. Hunter carried a barbaric viciousness into the fight, and now into the farmlands of the valley. Moving south, his forces swept into Lexington, burned the buildings of VMI, burned the home of Virginia's Governor Letcher. The outrage was loud and direct, one more reminder that this war was no longer fought by gentlemen, but Lee knew that beyond the mindless destruction, the threat to the supply line was very real, and so he weakened his army again, sent Jubal Early with the Second Corps to push Hunter away. When Early crossed the Blue Ridge Mountains, Hunter's bravado collapsed, and the Federal troops pulled away without a fight, withdrew to the west, across the Alleghenies, the Federal commander satisfied with the damage he had inflicted on the civilians.

With Hunter no longer a threat, Early's men began to look northward, and Lee now saw an opportunity. Early would march toward Washington, repeating on a smaller scale what Lee had tried to accomplish twice before. If Early's numbers were not great enough to actually occupy the city, the threat would still shake Lincoln's chances for reelection, and certainly cause Grant to respond by sending troops, weakening his army as well.

Lee's plan was sound, but the strength was not enough. Grant sent Wright's Sixth Corps, who moved quickly, filling the great heavy defenses around Washington with veteran troops. Early reached the outskirts of Washington too late to cause any real harm.

Lee continued to support Beauregard's calls for troops to the defenses of Petersburg, and Beauregard accomplished an amazing feat, defending the city itself with a handful of troops while Grant's Eighteenth Corps, commanded by "Baldy" Smith, hesitated in front of the nearly defenseless city. Smith was to be supported by Hancock's Second Corps, who arrived on the field under a fog of confused orders. The attack never came, an attack that would have seen the Federal troops marching into Petersburg virtually unopposed. The delay cost Baldy Smith his command.

Beauregard finally strengthened the lines around Petersburg with whatever troops he could put in place, but his skill at defending the city did not save him from the wrath of Davis. Making a tactical mistake, Beauregard removed the line of troops that were holding Ben Butler's blue forces in place, allowing Butler's men to strike out at the one line of communication between Petersburg and Richmond. It was all the excuse Davis needed. Beauregard was removed, and Lee's authority to defend Petersburg was made clear. With Grant's intentions now beyond doubt, Lee moved his men south, wrapping a hard line around the city, filling the trenches and earthworks with the men who understood their duty: that no matter how much strength the enemy brought against them, they could not leave this ground. They were defending the last great lifeline of their country.

25. CHAMBERLAIN

JUNE 18, 1864

THERE WERE SIX REGIMENTS, ALL MEN FROM PENNSYLVANIA, BUT they all knew his name, this college professor from Maine, knew he would lead them as well as any one of their own. They had moved far below the James by now, marching behind the rest of the army, the men of the Second Corps, the Eighteenth. Word was already spreading, another opportunity lost, bad coordination, bad communication. Some of the staff officers had seen a furious Meade, a fiery torrent of temper launched at the unfortunate officer whose duty happened to take him to headquarters. Rumors were flying that Hancock had failed, Smith was relieved. Chamberlain had heard all of it and finally had gone to Griffin to find out the truth. Now he was back with the men, riding beside the marching column. He kept the image of Griffin with him, the anger, red-faced, explosive. Yes, the opportunity had been there, there was virtually no defense at Petersburg. But there had been confusion, hesitation—the curse of the army—commanders who could not see what lay in front of them, men who would not take the responsibility. If there was no initiative, no risk, there was no victory.

Now they were moving south, the Fifth Corps to be the left flank of the army. There had been another attack, Meade sending the center of the line against the lightly held rebel works. But the rebel lines were empty, the defenders now back to the outskirts of Petersburg, a tighter line. Meade ordered them to press on, still believing the rebel numbers were very few, but the foot soldiers saw the guns, the fresh cannon and heavy lines of muskets. The rebel works were now filling with Lee's men, the numbers rising rapidly. If headquarters did not understand what was happening across from them, then they would learn of it from the men on the front lines. There would be no mindless rush to make up for the indecision of before. This would not be another Cold Harbor.

Chamberlain heard the bugles in front, the men beginning to slow the march, moving into the deep brown grass of the fields. There were guns, distant rumbling, from the north, up where Burnside had halted, and Chamberlain reined the horse, listened, thought, No, no attack, not yet. We just got here.

The men of the brigade were nearly all sitting now, faces covered with the grime of the march, the blue of the uniforms dulled by layers of dirt. At the look of men who had absorbed the road beneath them, Chamberlain felt a smile, could not hide it. When they had crossed the James, there was a brief pause, and the men were close to the water. They did not have to be told that this might be the only opportunity they would have, and so they'd swarmed into the water, clothes and all, splashing the thick layers of dirt away, the memories of the hard marches and the bloody fights flowing away downriver. He'd sat on the big horse, watching them, heard the laughing, the pure joy, had ached to join them. It would not do, of course. The officers had to maintain some decorum, especially the brigade commander. They did not know that he'd waited until dark, just before they moved out onto the dusty roads again, and slid quietly into the water, under the watchful eye of a provost marshal—not for protection, but as a discreet lookout for Griffin, Warren, or worse, General Meade. It had been cool and delicious, and the uniform dried quickly. Now the uniforms were covered with the signs of the march again. And he knew they remembered the river.

He saw men gathering sticks, small dead trees, and fires began to dot the field, the cooks moving to the fires, the coffeepots hanging above low flames. He dismounted, moved toward the flag bearer, a huge man named Coogan. Chamberlain felt the stiffness in his feet, his legs, tried to flex the muscles. Coogan watched him, still held the flag high, the gathering place for the officers. Chamberlain approached, looked up at the bright sky. Sweat rolled into his eyes and he blinked hard, put a finger to his eye, the hard leather of the glove probing painfully, doing no good. He blinked again as Coogan held out a handkerchief.

"Here you go, Colonel."

Chamberlain took it, nodded, said, "Thank you, Sergeant." He wiped carefully at the teary eye, shook his head. "Summer in Virginia."

Coogan nodded, waited for Chamberlain to return the handkerchief, said, "Not much different from back home. Summer's always like this. We're not that far south." There was a quiet pause and Coogan said, "Sorry, Colonel. I suppose Maine is a bit farther north."

Chamberlain handed Coogan the handkerchief, was suddenly defensive. "Well, we have our summers in Maine too, Sergeant. A hard sweat does a man good . . . sometimes."

The big man was looking at him, nodded, smiled slightly. Chamberlain felt awkward, ridiculous, pawing at the stinging in his eyes. He blinked again, fought it, thought, You have nothing to prove to these men.

"Um . . . you have mountains where you come from, Sergeant?"

"No, sir, just a few hills. My family's in York, southern part of the state, near Harrisburg."

Chamberlain blinked again, the eye better now, said, "Near Gettysburg. Yes, Sergeant, I am familiar with that area."

Coogan nodded, said nothing, and Chamberlain saw the man's look, saw the respect they had all given him. No, you do not have anything to prove to these men.

He could smell coffee now, heard the sound of tin cups, men moving toward the fires. The regimental commanders were coming together, small staffs trailing behind, but they were moving slowly, without urgency. He waited for them, had nothing really to say to them, no new orders. He searched the faces, knew they were all good men, all veterans of the hard fight.

The brigade had been organized by Griffin from units that had fought far apart. Some were from Reynolds's First Corps, which no longer existed, Reynolds himself killed at Gettysburg. The 149th and 150th Pennsylvania regiments were from the old Bucktail Brigade, and the men still wore the furry tails pinned to their hats. But the pride of these men came not just from symbols, but from their good work, from the bloody fields where they'd done their job. It was the one reason that no one objected when this man from Maine was named their commander. No one doubted that Chamberlain was a man to do his job as well.

The officers saluted him. Some were drinking coffee. There were low, quiet greetings. He knew one man was missing, Major Merrick, the newest arrival, commanding the fresh 187th Regiment. He looked around, out over the fields of resting men, then saw him running toward them. Merrick was yelling, waving one arm behind him, pointing. Heads turned, there were small laughs, quiet jokes at the expense of the new officer. Merrick stumbled through the tall grass, and now the soldiers were laughing as well. He stopped, out of breath, still pointed behind him. Chamberlain waited, did not smile.

"Sir! Over there, over that rise . . . rebels! The enemy is right over there, sir, earthworks, spread on a hill . . . guns . . . cannon! We're in the open, sir!"

Heads turned that way and the laughing stopped. Chamberlain stepped forward, moved past Merrick, could see the low rise, motion, the reflection of guns. Merrick was right, they were very close to the rebel lines. He took a deep breath, thought, No one told me. Why were we sent this close? Why were we stopped right here?

There was sound behind them, wagons, horses. Chamberlain turned, saw a row of big guns moving up, men unlimbering them, quick motion from the flashes of red on the uniforms of the artillerymen. Then the guns were moving into place, pointing out over their heads, toward the rise Merrick had seen. Chamberlain moved toward the guns, looked for an officer, someone in charge, saw a man approaching.

The officer stopped, snapped a crisp salute, said, "Captain John Bigelow, Ninth Massachusetts Battery, at your service, sir."

Bigelow was a young man who carried the confidence of hard experience. Chamberlain returned the salute, said, "It seems, Captain, that we are very close to the rebel lines. We were halted here, apparently in clear sight of the enemy."

"Oh, yes, sir, I know. I was told you are serving as a screen for my guns. This is good ground, a good position, clear line of fire. But we are a bit vulnerable, if their infantry should suddenly advance. I was told you are here to protect us."

Chamberlain stared at the young man. Protect you? He turned, looked back toward the rise where the rebels were still moving into position. They can see us, he thought. They can see us right here, can see these guns. He scanned the wide field, the men now beginning to stand, all looking out toward the enemy. He saw his group of officers, standing together, and now it finally came, across the field, the puff of smoke, and he yelled, "Move! Spread out!"

They did not look at him, were watching the smoke, and now the sound came right at him, the sharp scream, and behind the guns the first blast threw up a shower of dirt. His officers began to move now, did not need Chamberlain to tell them not to stand together as one very nice brass target. More screams split the air over his head and there were more blasts behind him, the rebel gunners shooting long, harmlessly, behind Bigelow's guns. The field was filling with shouts from the officers, and the men were coming together, moving into formation. Muskets were being loaded, more shouts from the officers. The rebels always overshoot, Chamberlain thought, but they will adjust. We're too easy a target.

There were more horses now, men coming down the road from the north, and he saw the flags, saw it was General Warren, and then Griffin as well.

The shells were still flying past, and Warren yelled to Chamberlain, "Good, yes, very good. Colonel, good show displaying your men like this. You must protect these guns. We must discourage the enemy from advancing to this position, they must not believe these guns are easy pickings. Keep your men out in front, make the good show. We have two more batteries moving up along this ridge. Good position . . ."

Chamberlain moved closer, thought, *Good show?* The rebel shells now began to fall in front of them, scattering the formations, heavy showers of dirt throwing men to the ground. Chamberlain looked at Griffin, tried to keep his anger from showing as he asked the silent question.

Griffin gazed across the field, said, "General Warren, this is not a good place to defend against the enemy's artillery."

There was a sudden blast, close to the horsemen, and Chamberlain saw a man fly into the air, men now crying out. He looked at Warren, thought, We are just here to be a target? You didn't think they would shell us? We would lie here and drink coffee in plain sight . . . and the rebels would just *watch?* He felt the redness boiling up his neck, felt himself shake, holding it in. Warren looked around, and Chamberlain saw his calm expression change, something, perhaps clarity, come over him, like a window opening into a dark room.

Warren said, "Colonel, those guns are somewhat of a menace. Won't you take your men over there and do something about that?"

Chamberlain stared up at Warren, heard the calm, the matter-of-factness of the request. "Yes, sir. I believe that is a fine idea." He looked at Griffin, who closed his eyes for a moment, his own silent show of impatience. Chamberlain thought, Careful, no sarcasm, not now. He saluted, said, "General, if you will excuse me. General Griffin, with your permission, sir."

Griffin nodded, said, "Take care of it, Colonel."

There were more blasts now, the sharp screams streaking all around them, and Chamberlain moved quickly, shouted to the officers, the faces watching him, waiting for orders. Now the men began to stand, coming together into tight lines, muskets on shoulders.

Chamberlain grabbed for his horse, waved the sword, saw the lines straightening.

In a few minutes they were moving forward, pushing through the thick grass. He could hear a new sound now, the enemy answering the assault with muskets. He rode forward, saw the rebel works, bathed in white smoke now, and he yelled, waved the sword again, pushed the horse, and the smoke began to clear. The blasts and shrieks of cannon fire had stopped. Now the only sound was the voices of his men, the low growling yell of men who know they're close to the enemy. They began to move up the rise, the smoke gone, carried away by a light breath of wind. Behind the works, the rebels were pulling out, the guns rolling away with a last volley from the infantry. His men reached the works, short rows of fresh dirt thrown up around an old fence line, and climbed over, jumping down, stumbling into the empty trenches. Some fired their muskets, a last chance, and then there was a new sound, a cheer. They had driven the enemy away.

Chamberlain dismounted, saw blood, a dark stain flowing from the horse's side, a big spotted gray, the gift from the citizens of Brunswick, the horse he called Charlemagne. He stared at the blood, felt sudden shock, the horse looking at him. He reached out and touched the wetness. The ball had hit the horse's shoulder, and Chamberlain tried to convince himself, thought, It's all right . . . we can fix that. He stepped away as an aide took the reins and pulled the horse back. Chamberlain climbed the mound of dirt then, looking for the flag, for Coogan. He moved out past the fence, could see the last of the enemy flowing up a far rise, disappearing behind more works, another long row of thick dirt. His men were still cheering, and then he saw the flag, the big man holding it high, and he moved that way. Coogan was not cheering, was staring out ahead, holding the flag stiffly. Chamberlain reached him, watched the officers moving through their men.

The fight had been quick and the casualties light. The officers were organizing their troops, the smaller company flags now in place along the fence line. Chamberlain stared across the open ground toward the new rebel works. This is no victory, he thought. They were too far forward, and we just drove them back to the main lines. They were lucky to keep their guns. If we had been a bit quicker . . .

The men were quiet now, the cheering having exhausted them more than the assault. He could see them lining up in the enemy's trenches, but it was not a strong position. The best protection was behind them, since the ground in front was open, cut by small clumps of brush. Still, they were in the enemy's works, had taken the position, and if there was no great strategic gain, it was good for the men. He saw Merrick now, thought, Yes, this is good for the 187th, a shot of confidence. Merrick was following the example of the other commanders, quieting his men, taking charge, spreading them into line in the works. Chamberlain moved toward him, and Merrick saluted, beaming a smile.

Chamberlain said, "Well, Major, fine work. Now your men are veterans."

Merrick glanced down his lines, said, "Yes, sir! We are ready to go again, sir!"

Chamberlain smiled, remembered how anxious he'd been to get into the first fight, the frustration of being in the reserves at Antietam, unused, watching the rest of the army do the bloody work.

"There will be time for that, Major. Patience . . ."

Behind them he could hear the big guns moving forward, more this time, the batteries Warren had mentioned. He climbed the dirt, anchored himself with one foot on a piece of fence line, watched as the men unhitched the guns, other men with shovels throwing dirt in the air. All along the ridge shallow pits were quickly dug behind the crest, and now the guns were wheeled forward, their muzzles just above the ground.

He jumped down, moved to the horses, saw one man beside his Charlemagne. The bloodstain was dark and dry, but the wound had a small white dressing, a plug of cloth stuck straight into the bullet hole. Chamberlain moved close, stared at the dressing, then at the horse. The man said, "He's fine, sir. A grand old fellow. Take more than a musket ball to bring him down. Even got the bullet out of him . . . here." The man showed Chamberlain the flattened piece of lead.

Chamberlain said, "Good, thank you. Fine work. Yes, he's a grand old fellow. Not ready to lose him yet."

He reached out, patted the horse, reached into the saddlebag and brought out his field glasses. He moved back to the old fence, climbed up, stared out over the works, looked through the glasses. The ground dropped away in front of them, and in the low area there was a creek, winding through brush. The banks were steep, but the creek was narrow enough for a man to jump . . . if the ground were hard. He could see where the rebels had crossed, tracks in deep mud. It's swampy, he thought. They must have known where to pull the guns through, the drier ground. He lifted his gaze up the rise, saw the enemy works, motion, the sharp glare from bayonets. There were many bayonets.

The works spread all along the ridge in front of him and far out to the right, disappearing beyond more ridge lines. In front of where he stood, the enemy's lines curved away to the left, the apex of the curve pointing right at him. He lifted the glasses and gazed beyond the enemy's lines, could see church steeples, the tops of buildings. His heart jumped, the sun reflecting off rooftops. It was the town of Petersburg.

There were shouts from behind the works, the sound of a horse, and Chamberlain turned, saw a staff officer climbing over the fence, a face he did not know. The man looked around, followed the hands that pointed toward him, then moved close. Saluting, he said to Chamberlain, "Colonel, I have orders for you, from General Meade. You are to attack the enemy position immediately."

Chamberlain was trying to remember the face, wondered who the man was, then said, "General . . . Meade? What of General Warren? Excuse me, but this is not chain of command . . . um, Colonel . . ."

"Abercrombie. I come straight from General Meade. The commanding general is considerably, um, agitated that his attacks have not been carried out. Your position is the most forward of the army. You are closest to the enemy's lines. You are to attack the position."

"Alone?" Chamberlain was moved to anger again, had begun to wonder if this man was some impostor. He thought, I don't get my orders straight from General Meade. He tried to imagine Griffin's response to a breach in protocol like this, wondered if this man was a spy.

"Colonel Abercrombie, does corps headquarters know of these orders? Has General Warren been informed?"

Abercrombie glanced around, lowered his voice. "Colonel, all I know is what I was told. General Meade has expressed considerable frustration at General Warren's lack of aggressiveness. Your name was mentioned . . . your actions this morning were noted by the commanding general, and by General Grant as well. I do not speculate on General Meade's orders, but there was considerable anger behind his instructions to me."

Chamberlain thought, But we are one brigade. If we assault those works, we will receive fire from all over the field. This is suicide.

He looked past the officer, to where others were beginning to gather. He pointed to an aide, said, "Corporal, a sheet of paper?"

The man hurried forward, pulling a paper from his coat, and handed it to Chamberlain. Chamberlain stepped to the fence, spread the page on a flat board, began to write.

I have just received a verbal order not through the usual channels, but by a staff officer unknown to me, purporting to come from the general commanding the army, directing me to assault the main works of the enemy in my front. Circumstances lead me to believe the General cannot be perfectly aware of my situation, which has greatly changed within the last hour. I have just carried a crest, an advanced post occupied by the enemy's artillery, supported by infantry. I am advanced a mile beyond our own lines, and in an isolated position . . .

He stopped, looked out across the ground, then continued to write, described the ground, the enemy's entrenchments, the position of his troops. The anger grew as he wrote, and he finished the note, signed it:

Very Respectfully, Joshua L. Chamberlain, Colonel Commanding 1st Brigade, 1st Division, 5th Corps

The officer watched him, waited, and Chamberlain folded the paper, handed it to him.

"If you don't mind, take this to your commanding general, and request a response. *Respectfully* request a response."

There was a look of dread on the man's face, and he nodded. "Whatever you say, Colonel. I would suggest, sir, if I may, that judging by the commanding general's mood this morning, you can anticipate these orders will be repeated. Reports of delay have been received at headquarters with some . . . frustration." Abercrombie saluted, moved back toward his horse.

Chamberlain stared out across the open ground, could see movement in the rebel position even without the field glasses, said, "They're still filling the works."

He looked around, the officers watching him. No, be careful, he thought. Keep it to yourself. He looked up at the sun, nearly straight overhead, thought, Plenty of time. We may yet do it. It would be nice, though, if the rest of the army decided to lend a hand.

THE ORDERS CAME BACK EXACTLY AS BEFORE. BUT THE REST OF the army *would* lend a hand. Meade ordered the assault to begin at three o'clock, and included a general assault across the entire front. Chamberlain's position was closest to the enemy works, and his brigade was chosen as the focal point to begin the attack.

Warren's Fourth Division was commanded by Lysander Cutler, an old soldier who saw events very much in his own way. The Fourth was positioned behind Chamberlain's left flank, too far behind to protect it. There was time before the assault, and Chamberlain decided to speak with Cutler himself.

He rode a borrowed horse slowly into Cutler's camp, a staff of unfamiliar faces watching him with no expression. He dismounted, handed the reins to a silent aide, stood in silence, felt strangely out of place.

"Excuse me, but can someone direct me to General Cutler?"

One man pointed to a tent, the only tent, and Chamberlain thought, Why is there a tent? We've been on the march all day. This isn't the time to camp. He stepped forward, saw a sergeant standing stiffly beside the tent, and the sergeant bent low, said something quietly into the tent. Chamberlain waited, then saw the gray hair, the old man emerging slowly. Cutler stood up straight, and Chamberlain was surprised, he looked much older than the near-sixty he'd been told. Cutler stepped forward, looked at Chamberlain with impatience, as though something terribly important had been halted for this meeting.

He said, "Yes, Colonel ... Chamberlain, is it? What's the problem?"

Chamberlain glanced around, saw little motion, none of the preparation for the great fight that was about to begin.

"General, my brigade has been ordered to take the lead in the general assault. I am sure, sir, you have been told of the assault?" Cutler stared at him, said nothing. "Um, well, sir, you are on my left flank, and that flank is exposed at present. I wish to make you aware of that, sir, that when my brigade advances, we will be in some ... difficulty, if your division does not advance as well."

Cutler still looked at him, tired black eyes, a gruff gray beard. Chamberlain was becoming annoyed.

"General, with all respect, I would suggest that you could move your men *en echelon*, to support my flank, so that my men are not mown down like grass—"

Cutler lunged forward, startled Chamberlain, put a finger close to Chamberlain's face, growled his words in low anger, "You do not give me orders, Colonel. I am your senior. You will take orders from me!"

Chamberlain took a deep breath, felt the cold silence around him, the staff standing stiffly. "General Cutler, I have my orders, and I suppose you have yours. We are to work together. The entire army is to work together. You are my flank. I am also your flank. I thought it best we understand that."

Cutler turned away, began to move to the tent, said aloud, "I will know what to do when the time comes."

Cutler disappeared into the tent, and Chamberlain felt the staff begin to move again, a collective release of air. He looked around, and the faces were not looking at him. The meeting was over. He felt exhausted, angry. He had lost his patience completely, thought, Yes, I understand the orders now. General Meade, I am grateful I do not have your job.

He moved to the horse and took the reins from the aide, who said quietly, "Best of luck to you, Colonel Chamberlain."

Chamberlain looked at the man, surprised, saw the gentle seriousness in the man's eye, suddenly felt he knew him, the older face familiar, even the voice. "Thank you, Corporal. Do I know you?"

"Don't reckon so, Colonel. But I know you. Some of us . . . we just pay a bit more attention than they give us credit for. We know who the good ones are. It's not important, Colonel. You just take good care."

The man saluted, backed away, and Chamberlain watched him, still felt something familiar, even something in the man's walk, a slow calm step. The man was gone now, beyond the lines of troops beginning to move, the army slowly coming to life. He climbed the horse, tried to see the man again, then he knew, saw another old face, heard the voice in his mind, the thick Irish brogue. It was Kilrain, and he thought, Yes, Buster, there are more of you, aren't there? There are many who see beyond the orders and the flags and the stars on the shoulders. This army still has men like you, men so unlike the rest, men who know how to *think*, who see all that happens around them with such clarity. He thought, I should have asked the corporal's name. But no, it won't matter, after all. He will not survive. The thought gave him a shiver. I know it, I am absolutely certain of it. My God . . . and he knows it too. It's so clear, the calm . . . you can see it in the eyes, hear it in the voice. He will sleep soundly, while the men around him stare nervously at stars. It's the men who know they are going to die who sleep well. If you have doubts, if you are uncertain, then you are afraid. He thought of the man's words. *Take good care . . .*

H E GLANCED AT THE POCKET WATCH, THEN BACK BEHIND THE lines, to the far ridge where they had begun the day. The ground was empty, nothing moving, not one man, not one piece of blue. He lifted the field glasses, searched down to the left, back into the heavier trees, where Cutler's division should be. He tried to focus, strained his eyes, thought, Where are you? He turned, looked now to the right rear of the brigade, saw the long row of guns, waiting, as he was waiting. He looked again at the watch. It was nearly three o'clock. Well, he thought. We won't have to wait much longer.

All along his lines the men were crouched low, a last moment of rest, and he walked out in front of them, saw a solid line of blue in both directions, and they were waiting as well. Most of the faces were looking straight at him, and he was suddenly stronger, felt the power of these men, the strength of their confidence. Yes, we will do the job, he thought. These men will not stop.

The four veteran regiments were to move out in one battle line, with the 187th coming up behind. It would be an assault nearly four hundred yards wide, and if the orders were carried out, they would be supported strongly on both flanks. He'd seen the troops above them, on the right, another strong line, out in front of more big guns. They were not as close to the enemy as he was, but the flanks were secure, and there would be no mistake—when Chamberlain began to move, the rest of the Fifth Corps would move with him. He stood now in front of them, his back to the enemy, looked again down to the left flank, the empty ground. Damn that old man! He clenched his fists, wanted to shout, yell out toward the empty patch of woods. But Cutler had his orders, and he kept hearing the arrogance in the old man's words: *I shall know what to do when the time comes . . .*

He walked down toward the left flank, the exposed end of his line, looked at the faces watching him, wondered if they knew, that without support they would be hit the worst. He glanced far to the left, to a low hill half a mile away. It was on the maps, a small circle on the crude sketches of the enemy positions. The rebels called it Fort Mahone, and he'd seen it with the glasses, had seen the motion of the flags, the small black dots along the edge of the works. The fort was filled with cannon. He looked back to the men, would not see that place now, thought, If Cutler doesn't come up, those guns will have nothing to shoot at but . . . these men.

He saw their faces again. It doesn't matter to them, not anymore, not the men who have done this so many times. There are always guns. Sometimes you see them right in front of you, the sharp bright blast that sweeps away the man beside you, but more often you never see them, you only hear what they can do to you, the high scream, the sudden shattering blast, moving the ground under your feet. But none of that matters, because after all, the guns are far away, and the goal is always much closer, those men out there, the muskets pointing at your heart. That is your target, the goal. If the artillery blast takes you away, that is the hand of God, the poor stroke of Fate. But that man out there, the one looking right at you, you can never look beyond him. He turned, gazed across the wide-open ground, could see the reflection of the bayonets.

It was suddenly deathly still, no breeze, no sound at all. He stared at the enemy's works for a few seconds, then turned back to his men. The faces were watching him still, and he suddenly felt like saying something, speaking to them. He remembered Cutler's strange old corporal, looked down the rows of his own men, thought, How many of you know for certain you will not come back? He stepped closer to the line, walked slowly toward the center of the line. He felt a cloud of words building up inside of him, had to say something . . . if not for them, for himself.

"Gentlemen . . ." The word stuck in his throat, and he was suddenly angry at himself. No, these are not *gentlemen*.

"Men . . . it is close to the time. You are aware that by your successful action this morning, we have advanced well in front of the rest of the army, and so . . . they are looking to us to begin the assault." There were a few cheers, fists punched the air. He waited, continued the slow walk, saw men farther down the line beginning to stand, trying to hear him.

"We have a duty to perform here. It is not that different from the duty which many of you have performed before. You may have wondered . . . how many times, why must we do this again? We have all known men . . . friends, who have fallen on fields just like this one. And all of you know that some of us will not survive this field. If God is merciful, then it will be only a few. Look at the man beside you. Remember him, know that you are fighting together, that each of you has a part in something much greater than yourself. Think about this ground, where it is we *are*."

There were more cheers, men began to shout, *"Virginia!"*

He waited again, then raised his hand, and the shouts quieted. "Yes . . . we are very close to the end of this war. It may be today, it may be by the very action you take today, by the heroism of this very brigade, of these regiments, of the man beside you . . . of *you*. Do we know the name of this place? Will history record what we do here? Did we know that a name like Gettysburg would have such meaning? Take that with you, across this ground. What each of you does here may decide the end of the war. Think of the importance of that. If it matters to you that your nation be proud of what you do, then carry that with you. If you have a family back home, make them proud as well, take inspiration from that. But if all that is very far away, if you can only see the enemy, and you feel alone, or even afraid, then look again, now, at the man beside you. Know that he is there, and the man beside him, and the men all down the line, that what you do today may be the one great effort, the last full measure that God requires of us, to break this unholy rebellion."

Men began to cheer again, and the regimental flags began to move forward. He saw the officers step out in front, saw Coogan now, with the brigade colors, and Coogan nodded, looked at the ground beside him, a quick downward glance, a silent reminder. Chamberlain stared at him a brief moment, then felt a sudden chill, looked at his watch. It was three o'clock.

He looked down the line, both directions, drew his sword, held it straight in the air, then turned, pointed across the wide field, straight at the enemy.

"Attention . . . trail arms!" he shouted. "Double quick! *March!*"

The men surged forward, and he moved with them, Coogan by his side. He felt the wild thrill again, wanted to yell out, Yes, we are unstoppable, a mighty force! He glanced at Coogan, the big man holding the flag steadily, staring straight ahead. Now the voices spread over the field, the low growling sound, rising into one single chorus. They were moving quickly down the long rise, and he could see far off to the right, more masses of blue, the assault beginning for the rest of the corps.

Behind him, the air was shattered by the blasts from the big guns, Bigelow's battery, then more, down the crest of the hill, the other guns of the corps. The shells began to strike the works out in front of them, across the way, flashes of light, great bursts of dirt and timber. The chorus of sound from the men began to slow now, the raw excitement giving way to the hard breathing, the exertion of the charge.

He looked back down to the left, could still see the patch of woods, and there was still no movement, no sign of the Fourth Division. Cutler was still not up. He felt a rage boiling up, felt like blowing a cannon blast into Cutler's smug face. I will have him court-martialed . . . I will march into that damned tent and grab that gray beard . . .

He looked down the hill again, kept moving, pressing forward by the great flow of men around him. He began to feel something else, the quiet anticipation, the voices now silent. As they moved down the hill they all waited for it, knew it would come in a sudden shocking wave, and each man held his jaw tight, pulled his arms in tight against his sides, stepping forward in rhythm with the man beside him. And then it came, the first wave of shells ripping through the lines, solid shot rolling through the men like a hard wind, some streaking overhead, some plowing down into the ground beneath their feet. Then the hollow shells began to whistle past, a different sound, fuses timed to ignite directly overhead. But the fuses were never very good, and the blasts began to fill the air high out in front of them, bursts of fire, and then far behind them, exploding harmlessly over the ground they'd already crossed. But then would be the one good shell, the perfect timing, and the great blinding fire would shatter the air overhead, men punched down, blown away by the shock and the small pieces of iron. There were gaps in the line now, officers screaming at the men, close it up, keep it together.

Chamberlain pushed down through the smoke, could feel the impact of each shell that hit the ground around him, the rumble, the sudden shock under his feet. He looked behind him, saw Coogan, steady, still looking grimly ahead, the flag straight in the air. Chamberlain moved closer to him, waved the sword, the silent command that the men did not need.

He was close to the creek now, felt his boots slip and sink into softer ground, then sticking deep in thick mud. He pulled his feet into each step, forced his boots up and down, could see the winding ditch of the creek in front of him. It was very wet, the ground a mire, and the men began to slow, to reach the creek, some climbing down, some jumping across, stumbling, then standing again. He saw one man stopping, yelled at him, "No, keep moving . . ." But the man was reaching back, pulling another man out of the creek bed, and now more were doing the same, the men gathering now on the far side of the creek, and out in front the officers began to form the line again. Now there was a new sound, the sharp zip of the musket ball, the first volleys from the works up the hill. He tried to see, looked up the hill, across more open ground, stared into the gray smoke, great choking clouds rolling toward them, from the muskets of the enemy. How close, he thought, how much farther do we have to go? He looked out through the smoke, tried to see the faces of the men behind the works, the muskets and bayonets. If we can see them . . . we will keep moving . . .

He stood beside the creek, watching waves of his men flowing across, climbing down then up the soft banks. He looked at Coogan, to give the order, move the flag across, and there was a blast of hot air, a sudden burst of thunder in his face, knocking him straight back. He was still on his feet, the words still in his mouth, but the big man was gone, completely, swept horribly away. Chamberlain stared at the flag. It was standing upright, still, held by . . . nothing. The flag began to fall, and he jumped forward, grabbed it, looked again for the big man, the grim face, dependable. The ground behind him was a mass of churned up mud and smoke, and small pieces of blue. He stared, felt something in him turn slowly, closed his eyes, held it tight, then looked, saw more troops coming up now, Merrick's men, the 187th bringing up the rear, and he waved the flag, held it high, turned, would jump across the creek, looked up, tried to see the enemy again, a glimpse of the musket fire, sheets of red flame pouring down from the crest of the hill. He looked again for Merrick, thought of yelling, something, anything, but the sounds were deafening, and there was nothing he could say now, this was about blood and instinct and the courage of good men. And we will move up the hill . . .

He was spun around, a sharp hot sting in his side, at his hip. He felt one knee give way, and gripped the flagstaff, held himself up, looked down, tried to see . . . what? There was a rip in his pants, blood streaming out of his hip, and he felt the other knee weaken, then give way. He stabbed the ground with the sword, leaned on it, tried to stand straight, but the one leg would not hold him. He tried to pull himself up, lean his weight on the one leg, saw more blood now, on both sides, his pants legs now soaked. He let go of the sword, left it upright in the soft mud, now slowly felt the wetness, touched the torn cloth, thought, I am shot through, clean through. . . .

He let go of the flag and fell forward, his hands in the mud, and now there were hands under his arms, lifting him up, pulling him back. He looked at the faces of young men staring down at him, said, "Thank you . . . I am shot."

He tried to see across the creek, to sit up, but there was no strength, and he looked again at his side, thought, Too much . . . too much blood . . . *you are dying.*

Around him men were shouting, loud frantic voices. He lay back, the hands under his head, easing him down, and now his head was spinning, and the smoke began to drift across again, the thick gray clouds covering him, the fight still around him, the men still moving forward, fighting for each other, fighting for him.

26. GRANT

JUNE 18, 1864

THE STAFF WAS NOT TALKING. THE ONLY SOUNDS WERE THE TIN forks, the dull knives, the men hacking slowly on the hard meat of the dinner. Grant was not watching them, sat at the head of the table, listening to the soft sounds of the night, the crickets, the calling of the unseen animals as the fading light woke them to duty. He had finished his own meal, still sat at the table, staring into the dark. Down below, along the wide river, the heavy boats were moving against the landings, and he listened for that, for the sounds of wood against wood, the shouts of the officers, the sailors. He looked down at the plate, one piece of meat left, one good bite of crusty black beef. He stabbed it with a fork, held it up and looked it over, admiring it, then stuffed it in his mouth. There was a small plate of fruit on the table, grapes and berries of every kind, dried figs, and his eyes focused on the sweet dates crusted in sugar. He glanced at the staff, reached slowly out, sneaking, eased his fingers around the flaking sugar, pulled the hand quickly back toward him, the guilty pleasure held tightly, out of sight. Good, he thought, they did not see that. He stood, pushed the chair back, and the faces looked at him, the quiet broken only by the sounds of struggle with the overcooked meat.

"Gentlemen, thank you. Colonel Porter, a fine meal, fine. Thank you."

Porter nodded, had seen Grant's grab of the small treat, did not let on. He began to back away from the table.

Grant said, "No, keep your seat, Colonel. I'll have a cigar and wait for General Meade. He should be along any time now."

Porter relaxed, glanced at the closed hand where Grant guarded the small piece of dessert. Grant saw the look, moved his hand behind

his back, hiding the evidence. He moved into the dark, glanced around
at the fires, could see movement now, small sounds, a few men leading
slow horses, coffee cups and tin plates. He glanced over his shoulder,
the staff all content to stay at the table, and he slowly lifted the hand,
quickly stuffed his treat into his mouth, glanced around again. Now he
saw Porter, smiling, turning away, and he clenched his teeth, thought,
Porter saw me, Porter knows.

They always were bringing him special food. The quartermasters
seemed to search far and wide for what they assumed to be the special
tastes of the commanding general. He didn't understand that, knew
that for the last few weeks the staff supply duty had gone to Horace
Porter, the officers taking turns working with the quartermasters, and
even Porter did it, brought all manner of odd and delicate foods to the
table. Grant thought, What is it about . . . rank? Am I supposed to become suddenly strange in my eating habits, just because I am in command? Save it for the men, for the soldiers, the ones who earn it. They
eat bacon and hardtack, and my mess table is covered with amazing va-
rieties of . . . stuff. He thought of the sweetbreads Porter had found,
and it gave him a shudder. He had first eaten them when he was very
young, was not partial to the taste, the *feel* of it. Then he learned what
part of the animal it was and it made him sick. A few days earlier,
Porter had served the staff a tall plate of this odd "treat," and Grant
couldn't touch it. While the others feasted, he had sliced a cucumber.
They often found chickens, scrawny birds that had somehow escaped
the scavenging of soldiers. Grant would not touch that either, could
never stop thinking about feathers.

He was perfectly content to feed from the herds of cattle that came
from the big boats. When they had beef, which was often now, he
watched the men stabbing the bloody meat with lustful enthusiasm, and
finally he'd let them know, the subtle hint passed around. The meat will
not bleed. He would only eat it nearly burnt to a crisp, and the staff had
learned to go along; the man who liked his meat red would have to find
another table. But it was the small sweet treats that still made him feel
guilty, and he tried not to think about it, didn't really understand anyway. The food is there, on the table, he thought. If it is not eaten, it will
just . . . go to waste. But, *sugar* . . . an amazing luxury. There should be
no luxuries, not when a war is being fought, not when those men are
out there on their backs, spread out on hard dirt, sleeping so close to the
guns of the enemy. We have not earned the right, not yet. We sleep in
tents, our boots are dry, we can stand straight and stretch our backs
without a sharpshooter taking our heads off. That is luxury enough.

The taste of sugar was still in his mouth, and he began to think of coffee, then heard the horses, the commotion across the dark field. He stopped, waited, saw men rising from the mess table, and they knew as well. It was Meade.

The horses stopped, the men began to dismount, and Grant heard the greetings, the staffs talking. He watched the one man, the wide floppy hat, silent, looking around. Grant moved that way, knew Meade was there only to see him, not to socialize with his staff.

"General Meade, here. This way, if you please."

Meade moved quickly, now walked beside Grant, kept his head down, said nothing. Grant waited, knew something would pour out, always expected a flood of hot words, but Meade was quiet.

Grant said, "General, your men have done all they can do, for now."

Meade stopped, looked at him, appeared surprised. "General Grant, I am not certain I share that view. We had our opportunity, and lost it. Petersburg was in our hands, and we allowed the moment to pass. My command did not—"

"General, your command is fine. The attacks were not coordinated well, there was delay when there should have been none. It is something I have become accustomed to."

Meade was shocked, his face illuminated by the firelight as he stared at Grant with his mouth open.

Grant began to walk again, said, "General, it has been six weeks. We have not stopped moving since we crossed the Rappahannock River. Look where we are, how much ground we have covered. We are facing a beaten enemy, an army that is on the very edge of collapse. The only way Lee can fight us is behind dirt. We still have the numbers, we still have the supplies, the guns, the power. If Richmond had any strategic value, I have no doubt it would be in our hands, it would be ours. His defensive lines cannot stretch that far and be much of a defense. He knows that as well. Now we will pick our moments, select our opportunities. If this is to become a siege, so be it."

Meade removed his hat, said, "Sir, there is no excuse for our performance today. I had to issue the same order three times, to get our people to move forward. This was to be one grand assault, we should have pushed them right into Petersburg. But for every unit that went forward, another just sat there, or moved too late to do any good. Half of Warren's corps watched the other half chew themselves to pieces. The Second, Hancock . . . hell, Hancock can't even fight."

Grant stopped again, said, "How's he doing?"

"Not good. The doctors won't let him ride. The Gettysburg wounds have opened up. General Birney is now in field command of the Second Corps." Meade took a deep breath, made a low chuckle, unusual. "Hancock's still pretty mad at Baldy Smith. Wants a court of inquiry, says we should have walked into Petersburg with bands playing. I told him Smith was relieved, but it didn't help him any. He's hurting more than he lets on. Guess I'd be about as mad as he is if the doctors kept me confined to my tent. He's a fighter, no doubt. But . . . without him to give the orders, the Second is as toothless as the Ninth."

Meade stopped abruptly, had crossed a line. Grant said nothing, knew it was still a sore point with Meade, Burnside's Ninth under Grant's direct control, not a part of Meade's command. It was still a problem, as was Baldy Smith's Eighteenth, the corps that technically was still under Butler's command. But the biggest problem that day had been Meade himself, the vague orders, each corps receiving a separate command. There had been no coordination because Meade had not told them to coordinate. Grant had learned now, with these men, these commanders, the orders must be plain and simple and direct. There could be no room for discretion. The fights today had gained little, but the casualties had not been as bad as this kind of jumbled attack could have produced. Lee was now firmly in command of the works around Petersburg, most of his army having completed the move from north of the James.

Grant said, "Let it pass, General. We may have some time now, some room to breathe. The enemy is hard in his defense, and the men deserve a rest. We cannot fault the corps commanders every time a battle does not go according to plan. War is not fought on paper, you cannot draw a line with a pencil and account for what might happen. When change is needed, change is made. Who would *you* place in command of the Ninth? Of the Fifth? Is anyone ready to step into that position?"

There was a quiet pause. Meade said, "I am not especially comfortable with having my orders ignored."

Grant thought, Maybe if the orders were better . . . but no, he would not say that to Meade, knew Meade was still sensitive, still expected to be the scapegoat if anything went wrong. And he knew that some of the worst orders, the disaster at Cold Harbor, those orders had not come from Meade, but from him. Grant also understood that the army was fresh with many new troops, men who did not yet understand that the battlefield is not like the parade ground. Even the veterans were not performing like they should, and the corps commanders were learning that even the best men, the finest and most experienced units, had to take a breath sometime. This powerful army was simply worn-out.

He had seen the newspapers, the names, even those friendly to Lincoln, calling Grant a "hammer," and those who were not friendly using words like "butcher." He tried not to pay attention to that, but many of the officers did, especially after Cold Harbor. Many were questioning if there would be someone else, if that great failure would be like the failure of so many others, and would sweep Grant out of command. But Lincoln had said nothing, there had been no official blame. Grant appreciated that, that what Lincoln had told him months before was still true: *Use the army, and I will leave you alone.* He stared out through the dark, past Meade, thought, Yes, we have used this army. And we have made Lee use his more. Now it's only a matter of time.

JUNE 21, 1864

H E STEPPED ONTO THE DARK WOODEN PLANKS OF THE DOCK, watched the steamer moving closer. Behind him the staff was in their best dress uniforms, waiting along the shoreline. He held the cigar tightly in his teeth, looked up at the black trail of smoke coming from the small ship, and now he heard a voice out on the dock, close to the water, a sentry, a very young man in a sharp blue uniform. "No smoking allowed on the wharf!"

He heard another voice, behind him, Rawlins, heard the boots coming out on the wood, small coughing sounds coming from Rawlins's throat, knew what was about to happen, held up his hand.

"It's all right, Colonel. This man is quite correct. It was my order, after all. We cannot risk a fire."

Rawlins stopped beside him, and Grant glanced at him, saw him still red-faced, knew that if he'd let Rawlins confront the sentry, Rawlins might have thrown him in the river. Rawlins was choking on his own words, staring at the sentry.

"Dismissed, Colonel. Go back to the others. The man is doing his job." Rawlins stepped away, slowly, made some gesture to the sentry Grant did not see. He held out the cigar, freshly lit, and tossed it off the dock, a small hiss as it touched the water. The sentry was aware now, and Grant realized the man was shaking, staring at him with wide eyes. It was obvious he'd had no idea who this plainly dressed officer was who had intruded into his authority. But he definitely knew now.

Grant nodded, and the man saluted, a slight quiver in his hand, said weakly, "Sir . . ."

The boat was alongside the dock now, sailors moving about with ropes, pulling the boat tightly into place. The gangplank was quickly laid, and now Grant saw one man, tall above the others, stepping forward, the long legs carrying him quickly forward onto the dock. He was all smiles, the tall black hat clamped down firmly on his head, moving in long quick strides toward Grant, now holding out the wide hand.

"General Grant, it is a pleasure, sir, a pleasure!"

Grant reached out, felt his hand swallowed up, held on tightly while the lanky arm shook up and down, raw boyish enthusiasm.

"Mr. President, welcome to City Point. Welcome to the head-quarters of the army."

THE REPORTERS WERE KEPT BACK, THE STAFF GUARDING CARE-fully, and even the small bribe or promise of favor did not tempt the officers to allow anyone within earshot. The two men walked slowly along the high bluff over the river, out in front of the rows of white tents. City Point was at the junction of the two rivers, where the Appomattox flowed into the James, and at this point the water was nearly a mile across. The two men stopped, Grant pointing, and the reporters, and the staff, could only guess what he was telling the President.

The bluff was higher than even the tops of the tall ships, and Grant motioned toward one, just docked, the ropes now securing her to the wharf. "Cattle, probably two or three hundred head."

Lincoln nodded, said, "Indeed. The supply people are doing their job. I hope you agree. The supplies have been . . . adequate?"

Grant pointed to another ship, the decks piled high with brown bundles, men moving about, the piles slowly shifting to the dock itself. "More than adequate. From this place, we can keep the flow constant. The wagons can load up right at the water. We don't even have to rely on the railroads."

Lincoln nodded, said nothing. Grant turned, could see the sea of faces watching them, men scattered across the open yard of the grand estate. The big white house itself was used by the quartermasters, the headquarters tents spread out in neat lines across the open yard. Behind them was the larger mess tent, and down below, beyond the last of the staff tents, the small corral for the horses.

Lincoln still watched the ships, the activity down below. He said quietly, as though unfriendly ears were listening, "If I may ask, what of General Lee's supplies?"

Grant looked at him, surprised at the question. "We're working on that. General Lee has little to rely on *but* the railroads. That's why he's protecting Petersburg."

"Permit me, General, I know I had told you I would never ask. But I am stunned by what I see here, by the size of this effort, by the strength . . . the pure strength of your army. It is an easy thing to sit up there in Washington and forget what is happening here, the magnitude of your effort. I hope you don't hear what I have to endure, the opinions from my opposition, how easy this should be, how quickly we should overrun those rebels. I wish those men, the reporters, the congressmen . . . I wish they could see *this*, this remarkable scene, all the ships, the wagons, the men. I am impressed, General. I have to say honestly, I am impressed. I wonder, though, how strong is the enemy?"

"You mean, sir, does Lee have anything like . . . this?" He waved his arm, a sweeping gesture across the waterfront. "No, he most definitely does not. And, that is the point. I have not done as well with this army as some of your people in Washington would have assumed. I *have* read the papers. Most of them criticize you for what this army has not been able to accomplish."

Lincoln nodded, said, "I do bear the responsibility. No one lets me forget that. The victories are yours, certainly. The failures are mine."

There was something painful in the words, the signs of strain that Lincoln tried not to show. Grant looked at him, the deep lines in the worn face.

Lincoln said, "Been nominated again. Those foolhardy Republicans want me to keep at it until I get it right."

"Yes, sir, I heard about the convention. Congratulations."

"Hmm, well, don't congratulate me yet, General. There's still an election. I hear it might be George McClellan for the Democrats. He's pretty loud about a peace movement, got a bunch of people thinking we should end the war before too many more get hurt. It's the kind of talk that looks good in the newspaper. People beginning to move that way, I'm afraid. You have to give them a reason to believe this will end soon, General." Lincoln stopped, looked down, said, "Sorry, Mr. Grant. I told you I would not interfere."

There was a quiet moment, the sounds from the waterfront drifting up the rise, a light breeze now blowing across the wide stretch of water.

Grant said, "It will take time. It may only take time. This is settling down to a siege. They can't last much longer."

Lincoln looked at him, said, "How much longer? You expect this will end like Vicksburg? That would be quite wonderful, sir." Lincoln was smiling now, the enthusiasm returning.

Grant said, "I don't think it will end like Vicksburg. There's still the railroads, the rebels are still being fed. And Lee is not Pemberton. Lee is not like anyone I have fought against."

Lincoln smiled, pointed to the reporters watching them. "There's a good many of those fellows over there with the pencils in their hands who would enjoy quoting you on that."

Grant did not look. "A few generals too . . ."

Lincoln laughed, removed the tall hat from his head, ran his hand through his hair.

"Yes, we both have our crosses to bear. How long, General?"

The question was serious, and Grant looked at him again, saw the expression changed, the dark eyes looking hard into him. "We will put as much pressure on Lee as we can. We are already extending our lines around the south of the city, and as far as we extend, the enemy must extend as well. They do not have the manpower, and we do. I had hoped it would be over by now. We should have driven him out of the city by now, broken them. . . ." He glanced at Lincoln, saw a frown, knew that Lincoln did not feel comfortable hearing the details. Grant paused, said, "I don't enjoy making a siege. It requires patience. I have learned that predictions are easier made than realized. I don't know how much time it will take."

Lincoln nodded, still serious, then began to smile. "Then, General, we will exercise patience. It will be my job to convince the voters to do the same."

Lincoln stepped forward to the edge of the bluff, looked downriver, saw another ship, moving closer, and in the distance a column of black smoke, a steamer. He waved his hat in a sweep across the waterfront below.

"My God, I cannot get over this. Look at this, General! The strength, the power behind your army. It's right here, right in front of us. These ships come from every port, all the way up to Maine. The entire Union is pouring out not just its men, but its bounty. I wish they could see this, the people who doubt us, who doubt our resolve."

Grant stepped closer to the bluff, followed Lincoln's gaze, could see more columns of black smoke now, the steady flow of supplies for his army. He pulled a cigar from his pocket, began to light it, said, "There's only one person who needs to see this. If there was some way, any way, to bring him here, I'd go myself, a private invitation." Grant pulled at the cigar, the smoke flowing up and away from the river. "If he would stand right here, right on this spot, and watch those boats unloading, the supplies, the food, the guns, if he could see the reinforcements filling the docks . . . if he saw it for himself, what we are bringing to the fight . . . we would not need patience."

Lincoln was running the names through his head, the reporters who plagued him, his enemies in the press, in Washington. "One man? Who, if I may ask?"

Grant looked at him, held the cigar now tightly in his teeth, said, "Robert E. Lee."

THEY RODE OUT IN FRONT OF A COLUMN OF STAFF AND REporters, moved on the hard roads through the camps of the men. The horse that carried Lincoln was large, but not large enough, the man's legs hanging down awkwardly. Grant had not wanted to look, did not want to embarrass the President, knew Lincoln was not as comfortable on the horse as he tried to show. Some of the soldiers were pointing, Lincoln's neat black suit now covered in dust, the pants legs riding up, showing a bit of his bare leg. The soldiers seemed to cheer more at that, at the humanity, the lack of show. They were used to the spectacle of the silken dignitaries, men in perfect suits, embroidered shirts, as though posing for a portrait. But Lincoln was simply one of *them*, awkward and smiling, happy to feel their enthusiasm, and so they shared it with him even more.

They had toured through the camps all morning, and Grant now turned down a smaller road, a sudden shift in direction, guided the procession along a brief cut through thin woods. He glanced at Lincoln, saw the President ducking under a low tree limb, said, "Excuse me, sir. I thought you might enjoy visiting one of the units of the Eighteenth Corps. They equipped themselves quite well in the last fight, captured a good number of the enemy's guns."

Lincoln nodded happily, was clearly enjoying himself, said, "Whatever you say, Mr. Grant. Whatever you say."

The trees now gave way to open ground, and they rode up a short rise, then beyond, rows of tents, and now Lincoln understood, saw for himself why Grant had brought him this way. Through the rows of tents, from around the small fires, men began to move out into the road, filling it, blocking the way, began now to cheer, loud and boisterous, hands reaching out toward Lincoln, his name echoing across the camp like church bells. He touched the hands, reached out as far as he could, and Grant knew, watching them, that Lincoln had already touched each of them, all of them. It was a camp of men who had volunteered as so many had volunteered, to pick up a gun and fight and die for their country.

But there was a difference. That these men would fight, and fight so well, was a surprise to many, and many still would not believe it. But Grant saw it in Lincoln's face, there was no surprise at all, that Lincoln had believed from the beginning that war was color-blind. Grant let the horse drift to the side, let the troops move past him, a wave of blue uniforms, the sea of black faces pushing forward, the cries and the joy and the tears filling the air, flowing up and around the smiling face of the President.

27. CHAMBERLAIN

JUNE 29, 1864

HE HAD VERY NEARLY DIED. HE'D EVEN WRITTEN THAT TO Fannie, a long and tearful letter, words that came from some very desperate place, the part that fights for just a bit more time, enough time to say the right words. He was good with words, but struggled for something more, the sorrow and apology, that somehow she did not know how much he loved her. He'd told himself the letter should comfort her, but when he read it again, he knew he had written it to comfort himself, to relieve the guilt, to make a peace with her for going off to fight, and to God, for not staying closer to the Word.

The doctors had not thought it possible, the wound so severe, cutting right through him. But the surgeons agreed to try, and they spent long hours working and cutting and patching. When they took him away, loaded him on the wagon that would carry him to the hospital steamer, the men in bloody white coats had stopped their work, just for a moment, watched with shaking heads as this man was driven away, to be put on the small grim boat, set gently down among the long rows of wounded.

He did not know where they were taking him, slept through most of the trip, had to be told by a nurse, a very round woman with very bad breath, that he was at Annapolis, the naval hospital. And he would be there for a long time.

In every direction all he could see was white—white walls, a white ceiling, white sheets, women in white uniforms. Next to him there was another man, covered in more white, a man Chamberlain had yet to speak to. When the nurses came around, they spoke in whispers, and it was not because of him. He would lie wide-awake, hoping they would stop and talk to him, break the monotony. But they would only nod politely, and he'd watch their faces, the horrified stares at the bed beside him, and even the whispers would fade away. Now it was beginning to get to him. What was the matter with this man?

There was no trying to sit up or turning to one side. The wounds were still very dangerous, the surgery very fragile. If he made the effort, tried to see beyond the mounds of white that blocked his view, there would be a blast of pain, and he would apologize to himself, try to relax, let himself drift back into the soft white clouds around his head.

After a few days the pains were not constant, the sleep not interrupted, and they had stopped giving him the drugs. Now, when daylight began to fill the room, he tried to keep track of time, to measure what hour it was. His mind made it an exercise, and he told himself it might be the only way he could survive this and stay sane.

He knew it was mid-morning now, he'd been awake for a while, the room brightly lit. He had learned to watch the shadows, a picture frame on the one wall he could stare at comfortably. There was a portrait in the frame, and in the first few days in the bed, when the drugs still clouded his mind, he thought it was Dr. Adams, Fannie's father, a grim portrait that hung in their living room. The shock of that had given way to acceptance, his price for being here, for allowing himself to be wounded. But when his eyes cleared, the face had grown unfamiliar, and he was still not convinced that the painting had not been quietly switched, that the new face was someone else's punishment.

But the frame now held his attention, ornate and gilded. The morning sun cast a shadow on the wall to one side. He had not seen the window, but by now guessed how tall it must be, enough to let the sunlight hit the frame for just so long. The shadow would disappear while the sun was overhead, but sometime in the afternoon it would return, the other way, until finally it faded away with the light in the room. He even began to believe he could see the shadow move, just slightly, shifting as the sun rose and set. It was his secret, his one guilty pleasure. He was beginning to get pretty good at it; it became his game. When the nurses came around, he would ask them the time, and before they could answer, would tell them himself. By now they reacted with feigned surprise, patronizing him, and he knew that, but he also knew they had no idea how he'd figured it out. And so it was still his game.

The shadow was growing weak as the morning went on, and he heard rain. He stared at the picture frame, began to feel a small panic, the shadow fading in the dull light. Scared, he thought, My God, this game is more important than I realized. His mind began to roll over, images flashing as the daylight faded, his concentration not held by the picture frame. Hold on, he thought, what is going on?

The sounds of the rain were growing, the wind began to rattle the windows, and suddenly there was a bright flash and a sharp crack of thunder. He made a sound, a loud short scream, stared at the white ceiling above him, then heard more screams, all down the rows of beds, the storm bringing out the memories, the fear, the horrors of what brought these men to this place. He could feel his heart beating, each pulse a small stab of pain low in his gut. He heard the rain again, the soft sound above him, took a long deep breath, then another. One man was still screaming, no words, just an awful sound, and Chamberlain wanted to sit up, to say something to the man, "It's just rain, just a storm. There are no guns here."

The nurses were moving past him, and now the screaming stopped and he heard women's voices, soft, comforting, and closed his eyes, relaxing again. He tried to imagine how the rest of this place looked, had no idea there were more men in the same room with him, a row of men that stretched out . . . how far, past the one man next to him?

He opened his eyes, heard the voices of the women again, closer, and suddenly was missing her, feeling as empty and alone as he'd ever felt. Then the voices were beside him, and he blinked through damp eyes, tried to see, abruptly saw her face, her hair dripping wet, small drops of water falling on him, and he thought, No, this is a dream, like the portrait on the wall, and he cleared his mind, blinked again. He felt, then, her soft cool hand on his, wrapping around, holding him tightly. She kneeled down beside the bed, a small voice, tears. "Oh, Lawrence, Lawrence . . ."

He tried to squeeze her hand, and there was no strength, and he tried to see her, but his eyes were filled, and he closed them, felt the tears on the side of his face, heard the soft sounds of her voice.

"You're alive . . ."

JULY 3, 1864

SHE SAT WITH HIM FOR LONG STRETCHES, AND HE FORGOT ABOUT the game, about the shadow on the wall. He still could not lift himself up, the pain still waiting with every motion, and so he lay on his back. He could not see the man beside him. Fannie sat with her back to the man, sat between the beds, would only glance at him when she arrived, a brief look of horror, would sometimes say something, "Oh my," and then turn away, quickly turn her back.

He wanted to know, and some part of him already did, that even if he never saw the man, he had seen the wounds, men shot into pieces, men surviving, amazingly, pieces of them gone, taken away in a horrible moment. The arms and legs were commonplace now, but the doctors were learning, had gotten better, would now try to save men they had always thought could not be saved. It was these men who had the worst time, trying to go home, missing an entire shoulder, or hip, men who had to be carried, or would never leave a wheelchair. Or the faces, men who lost more than an eye, or some teeth. Chamberlain tried not to think on that, fought against it, the faces of scared children, what that would be like, feeling the stares, the horror of your own appearance. But the doctors were saving lives, and men were going home who two years ago would have been left for dead on the field.

And maybe that's a good thing, he thought, not just for those men, but for everyone. Take the war back home, show the citizens. He had often seen the coffins, waiting for the trains to take them home, thought, Dead men in boxes bring grief and crying, gravestones remind us of those we once knew, give us the memories, hold them for us in stone. But these men, still alive, would bring the horror of this war right into their towns, their homes; not some fading memory or sad empty space at the table.

He didn't have to see the man beside him now; the expressions from the nurses, from Fannie, told him all he needed to know. He began to feel he knew the man, and felt affection for him, the man with no voice, who never spoke, and it did not matter why. Go home, he thought, good luck. You gave as much as those who gave their lives. You have to endure, you are the living face of this war, a symbol we must look at and not turn away from. God bless you.

H E AWOKE TO HER SOFT HANDS, TURNING HIM GENTLY, AND had to force himself to relax, to let the movement come from her. The soft cloth rubbed his back, the cool dampness soothed him. Above him, a nurse waited, would help her if she had trouble. But Fannie had learned, was helping whenever they would let her. Now he was turned back, closed his eyes again, relaxed into the pillows.

"Well, what have we here, some kind of hero?"

He opened his eyes, knew the voice, and Fannie stood up, there were hugs. He tried to see, then the face leaned out over him, smiling, the rough beard, the clear blue eyes. It was his brother.

Chamberlain smiled, said, "Tom . . . how . . . you desert?"

Tom stood straight, wounded at the comment, said, "Most certainly not. I'll have you know that not only am I not a deserter, I am now a captain!"

Chamberlain wanted to reach up, to grab his younger brother around the shoulders, to feel that young energy. He lifted one hand, and Tom took it, held it for a moment, said, "We were worried about you, Lawrence, the whole regiment. Just 'cause you command those Pennsylvania boys don't mean the Twentieth Maine forgot about you. Colonel Spear sent me a message for you, said even if you ain't fit to command, there's always a place for you in the Twentieth. You can be our mascot, maybe."

Mascot? Chamberlain didn't know if he was serious or not. He glanced at Fannie, said, "I assure you, young captain, I am no one's mascot. All I need is a bit of rest, and I'll be back on the field." He looked at Fannie again, and she was smiling at him, shaking her head. He knew she didn't take him seriously, that she believed he would never go anywhere but home.

She said, "Lawrence, you have another visitor."

He heard a throat clear, and another man stepped up close to the bed.

Chamberlain saw a familiar face, said, "Well, Major Gilmore, how are you . . . my word, it's been a while."

Gilmore was smiling, said, "Actually, it's Lieutenant Colonel Gilmore, sir. The army seems to enjoy promoting men from Maine."

Chamberlain was feeling very good now, would always remember the stern face of Gilmore, the first combat veteran he'd met, the first day the regiment was organized. Gilmore had been sent to Portland to help organize and drill the new recruits, an efficient and disciplined officer who showed a subtle tolerance for Chamberlain's lack of experience.

"Colonel Gilmore, I congratulate you on your promotion." He looked at Tom again, said, "I congratulate both of you. I have no doubt the promotions were well deserved."

Tom looked at Gilmore now, made a small impatient gesture. Gilmore said, "Colonel, whether Captain Chamberlain is here with permission or not is something I cannot be certain of. However, I am here on official business."

Tom started to protest, and Chamberlain said, "For what? Who—"

"For you, sir. The Department has sent me here to read you . . . this. If you will permit . . ."

Chamberlain felt a sudden dread, thought, A discharge, they're sending me home. "Go on, Colonel, read it."

Gilmore unrolled a piece of paper, read, "To Major General George Meade, Commanding the Army of the Potomac, Major General G. K. Warren, Commanding Fifth Corps, Brigadier General Charles Griffin, Commanding First Division. Colonel Joshua L. Chamberlain, Commanding First Brigade, First Division, Fifth Corps, for meritorious and efficient services on the field of battle, and especially for gallant conduct in leading his brigade against the enemy at Petersburg, Virginia, is hereby appointed Brigadier General of Volunteers, to rank as such from the eighteenth of June, 1864. As provided by Special Orders Thirty-nine, Signed, Lieutenant General Ulysses S. Grant, Commanding."

Gilmore lowered the paper, and out across the white room there was a sudden burst of applause, a few small cheers, from men Chamberlain had yet to see. Gilmore handed him the paper, and he read it over, ran his finger over the seal of Grant's official signature.

He raised one hand, said aloud, "Thank you, gentlemen. I cannot see you yet, and I hope some of you are not here because of me."

He looked up at Gilmore, then at Tom, saw the smiles, and he read the words again, his eye now settling at the top of the page. He said, "This is addressed to General Griffin. His name is at the top. Why?"

Tom looked at Gilmore and began to laugh. Gilmore cleared his throat, leaned down, close to Chamberlain's face, said quietly, "I had hoped not to tell you, actually. You would find it out eventually. Um . . ." He stopped, and Chamberlain could see he was searching for words.

Now Tom leaned over, said with a broad smile, "Lawrence, they think you're dead!"

Chamberlain looked at the paper again, saw the order, all in the third person, not addressed to him at all.

Gilmore said, "It seems so, sir. I was told that General Grant has never promoted anyone on the field before. Ever. The first reports from the Fifth Corps seemed to indicate that you did not survive. When General Grant heard about that, he issued the promotion on the spot."

Chamberlain began to feel sick. He looked at the paper again, said, "This looks official. Can he change his mind?"

Now Gilmore was smiling, said, "Not hardly, sir. It's been

approved by Congress, by the War Department. I believe that by now General Grant is aware that you are among the living. The promotion is official. May I be the first, sir."

Gilmore stepped back, snapped a salute, and now Tom did the same. There were more voices from the room, the applause again.

Chamberlain looked up at the two men, lifted his hand, returned the salute. He stared up at the ceiling then, felt weak. It was the most exertion he had experienced in a while, and he was drained. He closed his eyes, could hear the voices of the women again, whispers, heard the boots on the hardwood floor, moving away. He felt a hand wrap around his, knew it was Fannie. She said in a soft voice, "I am very proud of you, Lawrence. My soldier . . ."

The voice drifted away above him, and now he saw one more face, the old man looking him in the eye, something he rarely did. Chamberlain still felt the piece of paper in his hand, wanted to show it to him, felt suddenly very young, very excited, remembered the question, his father asking him, "You got a chance at bein' a general?" He looked at the old face, the hard eyes, and Chamberlain smiled, said only, "Yes," and now the old face was smiling back at him, something he had never seen, and he felt the old man's hands now holding him, a tight grip on both arms, and Chamberlain said it again.

"Yes."

28. GRANT

JULY 27, 1864

H E SAT ALONE WITH THE CIGAR, A SMALL CAMP CHAIR LEANING
against a thin oak tree. He was in Meade's camp, waiting for
Burnside to arrive, but he was thinking about Sherman.

He remembered the conversation with Lincoln, he thought of it
often now, what he'd said, the phrase coming to him whenever there
were quiet moments like this one. *It is only a matter of time.*

Sherman had said the same thing, had pushed and pursued Joe
Johnston from Chattanooga all the way to Atlanta. The pursuit had
come when the good fights did not, because Johnston was skilled at retreat, at the careful maneuver, had kept his smaller army away from a
general engagement with Sherman's power. Johnston had learned the
value of the trench, the heavy mounds of dirt, and his men made good
use of the shovel. Grant smiled at that, thought of Sherman's angry impatience. He'd received a steady flow of reports from Georgia, all rip-
pling with the frustration of a commander who wanted the fight,
wanted it *now*, and Johnston wouldn't give it to him. Each time Sherman brought his great strength into line, Johnston would simply back
away, sometimes with obvious and distinct movements, sometimes
quietly in the night. But if Sherman was frustrated, he also understood
that he was in fact winning, that with the constant movement forward, the closer he pushed his army toward Atlanta, it was only a matter of time.

Grant had wondered about Johnston, just how long Richmond
would listen to the explanations of retreat. He'd read the hostile joking
in the southern newspapers, that Davis had already organized a fleet of
transport ships at Savannah, ready to receive Johnston's troops, prepared to carry Johnston's retreat all the way to Bermuda. If there was

bitterness in the humor, Grant knew that in Richmond no one was smiling, and especially not Jefferson Davis. And then the word had come. To no one's surprise, Johnston had been relieved. What did surprise Grant, and bring a smile to the impatient Sherman, was the name of Johnston's replacement. The defense of Atlanta was now in the hands of John Bell Hood.

No one questioned that as a commander of troops in the field, there were few on either side who could put the fight into his men as well as Hood. But the appreciation, the enthusiasm, for Hood's appointment, came from both sides. The most recent letter from Sherman had made Grant smile, the childlike excitement barely concealed. Sherman knew that Johnston had been relieved because Davis had heard too much of retreats. Sherman also knew that if there was one rebel commander who needed no pressure from Richmond to make a fight, it was Hood. And the one man who had pressed for a fight more than anyone was Sherman. With Hood in command of the enemy, Sherman knew he'd get his fight.

He heard footsteps, turned, saw Porter stepping slowly, quietly forward. Porter would never say anything until Grant saw him first. The staff had come to understand that when he sat alone like this, quiet, the small motion of the cigar, you did not interrupt. Unless there was urgency, they would wait for the moment to pass and for Grant to bring himself back to the business at hand.

Grant held out the cigar, said, "Yes, Colonel?"

"Excuse me, sir, General Burnside is on his way. He should be here any moment now, sir."

Grant leaned back against the tree, nodded, said, "Fine, Colonel. I'll be along shortly."

Porter saluted, backed slowly away. Grant watched him, thought, Yes, you too, Mr. Porter. You want to ride out in front, and lead men into the guns. I am sorry, young man, but it will not happen.

He thought of the others, the good staff, knew most of them were doing a fine job, would always be with him. Rawlins, of course, was the headmaster, had never dreamed of leading combat troops, probably had nightmares about finding himself actually having to look at the rabble of the enemy. Grant smiled, gave a small chuckle, thought, No, Mr. Rawlins, don't ever let yourself be captured. They'd have to build you a special prison all your own. He knew Rawlins was his guardian, the great protector, had appointed himself the keeper of his public image. Rawlins was forever watching him, a small peek through the tent flaps, a bold intrusion into Grant's private moments, something Porter would never have done. He's afraid, Grant thought, afraid of the news-papers, of Lincoln's enemies, afraid of me, of something I might do to embarrass us all. Or to embarrass *him*. He has found his purpose in life, to be a chief of staff, to be the caretaker of our good behavior. But Porter is very different, he has his eye . . . *out there*, beyond the front lines, where the adventure lies. He shook his head, stood up, stretched his back, suddenly thought of his oldest son, Fred. Yes, he would do that too, stare out past the front lines, see only the adventure, the dar-ing, the heroics. But no matter how long this war goes on, and no mat-ter how much he ever begs me, he will not get the chance. He will never see it for himself. The thought gave Grant a cold chill. He had never imagined the war would go on long enough for his fourteen-year-old son to fight. He stared into the dark, saw the boy's face, then remembered another face, at Cold Harbor, the nameless young man who had died right in front of him. No, he thought, my son will not have the chance. What we do here, what I must order this army to do . . . this will never happen again. Once this is over, this country will carry this forever, the faces, the blood, the horror. It will be the last time. It *must* be.

T HEY WERE THE 48TH PENNSYLVANIA, STRONG, HARD MEN FROM the deep coal mines back home, and some of them had been in this army since the beginning. For over a month now they dug and carried the dirt, slowly pushing farther into the side of the hill, hammering timbers into place, bracing the soft, wet dirt over their heads. The tunnel was narrow, only four feet across at the base, nar-rowing around their heads to two feet wide. None could stand up, the tunnel barely four feet tall. They did not mind the tight space, had no paralyzing claustrophobia, did not listen to the observers, men from other units who watched these dirt-encrusted men crawl into the black abyss and called them names like *moles* and *gophers*. It was the work they'd been trained to do before becoming soldiers, work none of them had forgotten. Now their colonel had convinced General Burn-side that this was not only the work they were meant to do, but a good plan for the army as well.

His name was Henry Pleasants, and he was a Philadelphia engi-neer who'd grown up in coal country. He had stood beside the steep hillside, peeked up and over to where the rebels peeked up and over toward him, measured the distance between the sharpshooters as less than four hundred feet. It had been his idea to build the tunnel, a long narrow mine, to reach out underground to the strong rebel position across the deadly space and, with enough explosive force, blow it to pieces.

B URNSIDE HALTED THE HORSE, WAITED FOR AN AIDE TO TAKE THE reins, then dismounted, moved toward Grant.
"General Grant, a pleasant evening. I trust you are in good health."

Grant returned a salute, said, "Quite well, thank you."

Burnside turned to Meade, a slight bow, said, "General Meade, a pleasure as well. Are you in good health, sir?"

Meade nodded, and Grant thought, He's still not comfortable around Meade, probably never will be. Burnside was a large man, every part of him round, and the wide face was accented by the huge tufts of beard that covered his jaw, framing his face like two handles. He was always jovial, tried to bring his own good cheer to every situation, but it was overdone, exaggerated, and he never seemed to be completely at ease. Everyone knew he carried the memories of Fredericksburg in some dark hidden place, but he never spoke of it, and Grant had rarely heard Meade speak of those days either. Now there was strain between the two men.

If there was an awkwardness to the command structure in the army, this was something far deeper, far more personal, between the two men. Burnside in fact outranked Meade, had been a major general well before Meade received his promotion. When McClellan failed at Antietam and allowed Lee's battered army to escape, Lincoln's patience ran out and McClellan had been removed. When Burnside was picked to succeed the popular McClellan, there had been little enthusiasm, but Burnside had always been cordial and polite to all. No one could think of any reason to dislike him, and he carried none of the political harshness of so many of the senior commanders. By rank, he was entitled to have his opportunity to win the war. The resulting disaster at Fredericksburg was laid directly at his feet, and no one knew the depth of his failure more than the man himself. But worse, Burnside had been in command of the Army of the Potomac when Meade's division suffered its worst loss of men. It was Meade who had broken through the strong lines of Stonewall Jackson, and if the breakthrough had been supported, the Battle of Fredericksburg might have gone very differently than the extraordinary defeat it turned out to be.

Now the Army of the Potomac was commanded by Meade, and if

Burnside tried to hide the awkwardness of their relationship by boisterous formality, Meade just let it lie. But he would never forget that while his division was fighting for their lives on that December day, this was the man who could have sent help, who had thirty thousand men standing idly by while Meade's division absorbed a fearful slaughter. The man whose inability to make the decision, to seize the moment, cost not only the lives of Meade's men, but certainly lengthened the war, and the loud joviality of the man's personality would never hide the cloud that would always follow Ambrose Burnside.

Burnside now waited, looked back and forth at the two men, and Grant finally made a small gesture with the cigar, pointed to Meade's tent, and they moved away from the fire. They ducked under the flap, moved into the darkness. Grant sat himself facing the back of the tent, the glow of the fires painting the faces of the other two men. He had long understood that their words alone did not tell the story, and he would always position himself where he could see the expressions on their faces.

Burnside and Meade both removed their hats, and Grant lit a fresh cigar. Grant said, "General Burnside, how is your plan progressing?"

Burnside seemed to inflate, his chest bursting with something Grant thought must be pride. "Splendidly, sir. Splendidly! We are ready on your command, sir! They have reached what Colonel Pleasants tells me is the proper depth. The charges are being placed as we speak, sir. All that is needed is the final coordination with General Meade's command."

Meade made a low sound, and Grant said, "General Meade, your comments?"

Meade shifted in his chair, said, "I have never placed much confidence in this plan, sir. If we are to make a breakthrough in the enemy's position, it should be done with power and with a strike of considerable force, in a narrow front. I do not see how this . . . hole in the ground will accomplish anything toward that goal. I have not changed my position on this since the plan was originally introduced. Sir."

Burnside looked at Grant, said, "Sir, what General Meade is describing is exactly the purpose of the plan, sir. A narrow front, yes, exactly. We have the troops ready, General Ferrero's division has been drilling now for weeks. When the mine is exploded, they will make a quick thrust through the opening, taking full advantage of the confusion. Once the breakthrough is made, the rest of the corps will follow them through, and with General Meade's support on either side, the breakthrough should cut Lee's lines in two. By the end of the day, Petersburg will be ours, and possibly Lee as well."

Grant leaned forward, said, "Ferrero? The Negro division?"

Burnside glanced at Meade, said, "Yes, sir. We have taken great care, they have been training for this mission in great detail, sir. I have absolute confidence that any man in that unit is as capable—"

Grant put up his hand. "General Burnside, I have no doubt about the fighting spirit of General Ferrero's division. I am concerned that this division is new to the army. They have no field experience." He stopped, looked at the small red glow of the cigar. "I am also concerned what might occur when the Negro troops appear behind the enemy's lines."

Meade said, "Yes, if they get that far. It's not a good plan, not at all."

Burnside put his hand on his face, felt the thick brush of whiskers. "Well, they are a fresh unit. But the training has been exceptional."

"Training . . ." There was an edge to Meade's voice. Grant now stood, moved to the opening of the tent.

Burnside leaned closer to Meade, said, "General, I assure you, we have the ability, the means to train these men. There is no reason they cannot perform the duty given them. Just because they are not white—"

Meade stood, his voice booming, "White has nothing to do with it, General. It is *green* I am concerned with. They are untested troops. You are trusting this entire operation to the performance of men who have never been under fire! You have four divisions under your command, three of them with experience! You have chosen the one part of the Ninth Corps that is the least likely to perform in this situation!"

Burnside looked at Grant, the confidence slipping out of his voice. "We trained them well, sir. It would be a message, show the enemy . . . it would be greatly pleasing to the President."

Grant turned now, looked at Burnside, said, "General, it is not your concern what might be pleasing to the President. And it is precisely the message to the enemy that bothers me. Their response to that message . . . might not be what you anticipate."

"Sir, what I anticipate is that the enemy will be defeated, that this plan will create a breakthrough that could end the war."

Grant absorbed the words from Burnside, thought, There is no fire, he sounds like he's reading it in a newspaper. He's not even committed to his own plan. There was a long quiet pause, the sounds of the camp drifting into the tent. The two men were looking at Grant now, and he stared past them, to the back of the tent, watched the shadows moving on the glow of the canvas. He thought, Burnside has never performed, my orders have never moved him into the kind of action we have needed. Now ... this is *his* plan, and he wants us to believe it will work without a flaw, that the coordination will happen as it must happen.

Meade made another grunting sound, said, "I am still doubtful the mine will even work. How do the miners breathe? My engineers tell me there has never been a tunnel that long, not that narrow. The powder won't burn, there's no air."

Burnside inflated again, said, "Colonel Pleasants is extraordinary. He has devised a duct system, using a fire at the mouth of the mine. I have seen it myself. The fire draws the air through the duct, from the farthest point in the mine. It's ingenious! The explosion will work, I assure you. They have split the end of the mine into a T, and I have, um ... I have authorized the placement of powder into the mine. It is ... all ready to go!"

Meade said, "It's complete? They're finished? How do they know it's far enough, that it reaches the enemy's lines? You call a cease-fire so your Colonel Pleasants could measure it?"

Burnside ignored the tone of Meade's question, said to Grant, "Colonel Pleasants has measured the distance using sophisticated engineering methods. I observed him myself. We have absolute confidence that the mine is of the correct length."

Grant had not been as hostile to the idea as Meade, had thought from the beginning that any plan was a good one if it worked. He'd heard the numbers, the amount of powder sent to the mine. Yes, it will make one *big* hole, he thought. But even if the mine worked as the miners said it would, he had the problem of Burnside. He looked at him now, said, "General, you will select another division to lead the assault. I don't see why any veteran unit cannot take advantage of a sudden break in the enemy's line and advance through it. You don't need special training for that. When the enemy recovers enough to try to contain the break, untested men could lose their initiative, and might give back whatever advantage they have gained. General Meade ..."

Meade was watching him, nodded.

Grant said, "General, you will order the Fifth and Eighteenth Corps to stand ready to advance against the enemy's positions in the event the breakthrough occurs between them. General Burnside's men may very well pull the enemy away from in front of both those corps. I don't want spectators. Your forces must take advantage of whatever occurs, of whatever weakness might suddenly open up to their front."

Meade said, "Certainly. I will see to it, sir." Meade stood up, held his hat in his hand, motioned toward Burnside. "General Burnside, if your boys do as you say, then my boys will be right there with you. You may depend on that."

Burnside stood now, clamped his hat on tightly, said, "This is splendid, gentlemen. I assure you, this will be a magnificent success. Colonel Pleasants has demonstrated the kind of initiative that the Ninth Corps has always been capable of."

Burnside looked at Grant, and Grant knew there was more.

"Sir, when do we blow the mine?" Burnside asked. "When will the army be ready to assist our breakthrough?"

Grant glanced at Meade. "If you say the mine is ready, then preparations shouldn't take long. I would say the assault should commence the morning of the thirtieth. That's three days, plenty of time to organize the assault, instruct the division that will lead the way. Make it early morning, very early. Four A.M. That give you enough time, General Meade?"

Meade said, "The thirtieth. The orders will be prepared immediately, sir."

Grant moved out of the tent, and Burnside waited for Meade, then followed him into the warm night air. Grant looked up at the stars, tasted the smoke of the cigar.

Behind him, Burnside whispered to Meade, "Um, if I may ask . . . do you . . . can you spare, say, a good-sized length of fuse?"

JULY 30, 1864

THEY WAITED IN THE DARKEST NIGHT MANY OF THEM COULD remember, stood side by side, packed together, men already sweating into their uniforms. Most of them had not made a predawn assault, at least not a successful one, and the low hum of nervous voices echoed through the web of trenches. They were Ledlie's division, the First in Burnside's Ninth Corps, and they had not known they were to lead the attack until the afternoon before. Burnside had not ordered them to the job, hadn't measured their will or their ability against his other divisions. The division commanders had debated, argued, and finally, with Burnside unwilling to make the decision, they put pieces of paper into a hat, and so it was by chance that Ledlie's men were standing in the heat of the darkness.

Their inexperience was typical of the many reinforcements to this army who had come south in recent weeks. Many of the men were from the Heavy Artillery units. For many this would be their first real fight, the first taste of crossing open ground with an enemy pointing his musket at your head. They knew of the plan of course, had been told about the mine, and how it would destroy the enemy, a wide-open gap they could burst through with ease. Their commanders had passed the word down—once the mighty blast cleared the way, it would be a simple matter to push through the enemy's position, form a line out in each direction, their backup units flooding through the gap. To those who had been here awhile, the veterans who had seen other great plans unfold, there was little talk, even when the new men wanted to know, had to know, what it was like, what would happen.

The men of Ferrero's division had heard only late the night before that they would not lead the assault they had so eagerly trained for. The Fourth Division would instead come up last, after the other divisions had completed the breakthrough. There was anger, confusion, and immediately the few reporters who kept themselves within earshot of any piece of news began to write down the comments. The mood was angry, bitter feelings about having been so well prepared, the expectations so high, the opportunity for some piece of glory, gone now by the simple decision from somewhere else, a commander most had never seen. The rumors flew easily, and most accepted what seemed obvious. These men would not lead the assault because they were black, because somewhere, someone up the chain of command did not want to give them the chance.

H ENRY PLEASANTS HELD UP A SMALL LANTERN, LOOKED AT HIS watch. It was three A.M. He glanced up at the dirty face of Sergeant Reese, the young man moving about nervously in the dark. Pleasants tried to force a smile, looked now at the somber, drawn face of Lieutenant Douty. He tried to say something, his voice choked off in the dust of his throat. He coughed, looked at the watch again, said, "It's three o'clock. It's time."

There were three fuses, each leading to a different part of the mine. They had not been able to secure long lengths of the tight hemp, were forced instead to piece together smaller lengths. The elaborate patchwork was less than a hundred feet long, so Pleasants himself would have to move far into the mine to light the end. Once lit, the fuse would burn for nearly thirty minutes before reaching the kegs of powder.

Pleasants handed the lantern to Douty, and Douty held out a hand. Pleasants took the hand, looked now at Reese, who saluted him. They had been a part of this project from the beginning, had their own experience deep in the black mines of Pennsylvania. Reese had spent more time in this hole than anyone, had directed the placing of the powder kegs, and even through the hot night had been deep inside, checking and rechecking the fuse. Pleasants knew Reese wanted the job, was eager to light the fuse himself, but this was the responsibility of command, and so Pleasants smiled now, returned the salute, leaned down into the opening of the mine, and was gone.

G RANT HELD HIS FIELD GLASSES IN HIS HANDS, NERVOUSLY FINgered them, waiting for the chance to see . . . *something*. He stared into the dark, out toward the place where the great plan was to begin. He turned, looked behind him, thought, The sun will be up soon, very soon. He looked at the watch again, saw it was nearly four o'clock. Well, that's it, let's go. He wanted to look into the glasses, had waited for it now with some excitement. He hadn't allowed himself to feel that, not yet, but here, alone in the dark, away from the staff and Meade and the dismal confidence of Burnside, Grant was feeling the churn in his stomach, the childlike sense that something truly marvelous was about to happen, something spectacular, something no one had ever seen.

He looked at the watch again, tapped it against his leg. Yes, it was working, six minutes after four. He began to move now, small steps, back and forth, impatience growing into anger. No, not this time, we cannot be delayed this time. If it doesn't go . . . nothing good can happen, there can be no assault. He stared hard into the dark, took a deep breath, thought, Why is it . . . can we not do something right even *once*?

P LEASANTS HAD RECEIVED THE URGENT MESSAGE FROM BURNSIDE, but he didn't need a commander to tell him something had gone wrong. The fuses were always slow, but they were consistent. No, there was something else, maybe the dampness of the ground. He cursed to himself, thought, No, we accounted for that, it has to be . . . they've gone out.

Douty looked at his watch, then turned to the east, said in a whisper, "Sir, the sun . . . it'll be light soon."

Reese stepped close to Pleasants now, said, "Colonel, we have no choice. Permit me, sir. I will go in."

Pleasants glanced at the opening to the mine, then looked at the young man's face. There was no fear. Pleasants handed him the lantern, said, "Quickly, Sergeant. Godspeed."

I T HAD BEEN FIFTEEN MINUTES, WAS NEARLY FOUR-THIRTY, AND Pleasants was leaning down, staring at a faint glow from far up in the mine, the light of the lantern growing brighter now. He could see the shadows, blocking the light, the movement of the men. Douty had gone in shortly after Reese. If Reese had a problem, Douty would be there to help. Pleasants stayed behind, counting seconds to himself, nervous, closing his eyes with every bit of sound, flinching at every noise that came from the mass of troops waiting in the trenches behind him.

Now he saw faces, the two men covered in the mud and dirt of the long crawl. Douty emerged first, stood upright, stretched his back, saluted, smiled. Then Reese came out, held the lantern, saluted as well. They stood side by side, and Pleasants wanted to yell, *Tell me!* He had no patience now for riddles. He leaned close to both men, did not return their salute, said in a frantic whisper, *"What happened?"*

Douty was still smiling, said, "It went out, sir. At one of the joints. We repaired it. And then we lit it again. Shouldn't be long now."

Pleasants backed away, eased up the embankment, peeked his head over the top, heard Reese climbing up beside him.

Reese said, "Excuse me, Colonel, but I'd be a-duckin' if I was you."

29. LEE

JULY 30, 1864

THEY HAD BEEN ON DUTY SINCE MIDNIGHT, REPLACING THE MEN who were there the twelve hours before. It was becoming the normal day now, half the troops manning the front lines, the best marksmen in the units sighting down their muskets, waiting for something, anything, some piece of motion. Sometimes they would fire at nothing, send the deadly message, "Come on boys, take a peek, just one look, and I'll knock your head clean off." For the men who did not fire the muskets, the duty was mostly quiet and tedious. The heat had made the covered trenches pits of hell. Some men fainted, and others just sat, stared at nothing, spent the twelve-hour duty waiting for the relief of sleep and whatever rations they would be given. The shelling would come at regular intervals, the guns firing blindly all along the line, on both sides, not at any target, but just . . . out there, across the way, a calculated guess where the exploding shell might find the enemy.

There was a new weapon now, the mortar, brought to the field by the Yankees first, but now the boys in gray had them too, and so the sport had changed. The mortars would throw a solid shot in a high arc, easily seen, and the gunners would watch it strike down hard, and if it did not bounce on solid ground, the clean miss, it had found the trench, a sudden crushing death to anyone who might be crouching low, believing himself safe.

They knew they were close to the enemy, the lines curving out slightly, the enemy's doing the same. The sharpshooters had the advantage here, could easily see the motion, and the game changed again, the tease, men sometimes testing their opponent, the hat rising slowly on a stick just to the top of the earthworks, and the answer would come, a dozen shots, more, the hat ripped to pieces. There would be laughter. Yes, fooled you, Billy Yank.

The darkness, the wet stinking mud of the covered trenches was home now, and no one had any idea when this might change. They would look for any distraction, the long hours giving way to fantasy, daydreaming, nightmares. In the long quiet times, the dark silence of the ground had given up a new sound, something very faint. The men began to gather, to lean close to the wet ground, some even dropping down and putting an ear to the soft clay. The word had gone to the officers, and most paid it little mind, the madness of boredom, but a few did come themselves, heard the sounds with their men. The word spread all along the line. The Yankees were digging!

The sounds were unmistakable now, made more so by the imagination of the men aboveground. The jokes began, Grant digging his way to the other side of Petersburg, the attack would come from the rear! Maybe a railroad, an underground train, carrying the blue army far behind them. The officers began to give the order, probe, dig down, drive the long steel pike into the soft ground. If there was a tunnel, it would be found. The men probed and stabbed, and when a pit was dug and a man lowered the few feet down, the faint dull sounds would be clearer still. The jokes began to grow quiet, the search became more purposeful, careful, deliberate.

The engineers laughed along with the best of the rumors, knew the sounds were something else, magnified somehow by the lay of the land, a rock formation perhaps, echoing the sound toward them from far away, men in blue digging their own trenchworks. It was not possible, after all, to dig a mine that far, not if you had to begin behind those lines, over there, over four hundred feet away.

Even Porter Alexander, hearing word of the strange sounds, had come easing through the trenches himself, the men standing aside, quiet, respectful. They knew this young man's name, that when it came to positioning the big guns, General Alexander was the best they had, the best on either side. Now he was there, with these poor foot soldiers from South Carolina, and he knelt down, listened to the dull sounds as the muddy faces watched quietly. Alexander heard the skepticism of the engineers, but did not laugh. He moved away with a grim silence. It did not matter if educated men said it was not possible. The enemy was digging a mine.

The gunners of Pegram's battery had heard the talk, but their duty was off to the right of the commotion, and they could not see the men with the shovels and picks searching the ground beneath them with hot frustration. The gunners still focused across the way, the four guns of the battery working with each other, the men enjoying another game, the perfect rhythm, trying to fire the guns in a quick sequence. They did not know if the work was effective, if they were killing the enemy, but the orders were plain, keep it up, adjust the range, a bit shorter, then fire again.

When the sharpshooters were quiet, the gunners were more relaxed, but this morning the Yankees were active, very active, a steady shower of lead, much more than usual. The gunners cursed, kept low. This morning there was no game with their friends, each gun fired on its own, the men waiting for the slight pause in the musket fire, then scrambling to position, loading, firing off a round. On the far right, the fourth gun, the men were flat on the ground, began to rise now, brushing dirt away, laughing. The enemy had nearly gotten lucky, and there were admiring nods, small comments, a close one, a good shot. The shell had come within a few yards of the gun pit, knocked them all to the ground. They moved slowly at first, then the captain barked the familiar command and they were up around their gun, loaded quickly, and all thought, Well, time to return the favor.

One man leaned on the wheel, waited for another man to ram the shell hard into the barrel. He jumped, startled, felt something move under his feet, then felt the gun rising slowly, the wheel in his hand now jumping, lifting off the ground. The men backed away, looked at each other, wide eyes in the gray darkness, and now the sound came up toward them from below, the earth itself rising in one massive mound. Then the mound broke, pushed skyward, the dull sound erupting into a deafening roll of thunder, a great hollow roar. To their left, where the rest of the battery had been, there was only fire and a great column of black smoke. Dirt now blew across them, the air thick with a fiery wind, knocking them flat on the ground. Above them the flames tore at the darkness, the blast carrying the earthworks, the timbers, the big guns and the bodies of men, high overhead. Slowly, the huge black cloud began to rain down on them, the roar still thundering over them, now pierced by the screams of men, the sound of debris hitting the ground around them, pieces of the guns, horses, torn pieces of men.

It was the men from South Carolina, men who had heard the small laughs and the new joke from the men who moved past them in the dark, the shift they had replaced. As they'd filed into the works, some repeated the joke, laughed that the Yankees must have given up. They had huddled low in the trenches, held their ears to the ground, some climbing down into the small pits, listening hard, possessed of a nervous curiosity. These men who had strained to hear the familiar sounds from below, who wondered why just last night the sounds of digging had stopped, felt it first, the ground lifting under them.

L EE HAD THOUGHT IT WAS A MAGAZINE, ONE OF THE CAISSONS maybe, but the sound rolled over him now in a hard wave, and he knew it was no single shell. He moved quickly. The staff was out in the open now, and he could see it, the bright horrible glow, the tall spiral of flame and smoke. The small trees to one side began to lean, struck by a sharp gust of wind, and then the smell blew past him, the choking sulfur, carried by the sudden wave of wind and thick dust. He looked around, and now Traveller was there, and he climbed up, spurred the horse hard, rode straight for the blast.

Men were moving quickly around him, officers yelling orders. Soldiers were emerging from earthworks, the lines farthest from the front, the men grabbing their muskets, surprised faces all staring toward the great sound. Lee heard a new sound then, a steady roar of cannon fire, throwing their shells right into the area of the blast, then out in both directions. The front lines began to erupt in a steady burst of explosions, flashes, and thunderous impacts. He knew it was not his guns, it was the enemy, the line had been shattered, and now the assault was on. He tried to move the horse faster, thought, They are coming, they have broken the line.

He saw a house, a group of horses, more men, and pulled up in the yard, tried to hold the big horse still, stared out, could see the chaos of motion against the dull glow of the sunrise. He heard something new, musket fire, a wave of sound reaching him now, the cheering of men pushing forward, rolling over the narrow stretch of open ground. He raised the field glasses, stared into thick black smoke, a dense cloud of dirt and debris boiling up from a vast hole in the ground, saw a long mound of dirt, ragged, uneven, the edge of the crater itself. Beyond, he saw motion, flags, then the long lines of men, moving straight at him, straight into the horrible place, the hole blown right through his defenses, right through the lines of his men.

Lee looked around, saw Taylor, Venable, the staff now with him, and he said, "We must stop them, keep them from coming through!"

He looked through the glasses again, all down the lines in both directions, tried to see his men, who was there, the response. From both sides of the crater he saw his own troops, gathering now, men stumbling in shock, some just standing and staring. But there were officers, and slowly the lines began to form, and now musket fire was echoing all around, the small flashes from far down the line. If there was no one in the center, nothing to stop the enemy from coming forward, the men on either side understood what was happening, and across the open stretch of ground they had a clear target. Now the sounds of the big guns were close, his guns, throwing their fire toward the mass of the enemy. He still tried to see, but the smoke filled the open space, different, white smoke now, the smoke of the battle, of the fire from the guns.

Men were moving on horseback, he heard voices, frantic, and one man said, "General Lee, the enemy is coming ... this area is undefended, sir. You must withdraw!"

Lee looked at the man, shook his head, said, "No ... we must not let them through!"

He turned now, saw Venable, the older man watching him, waiting for instructions. Lee said, "Colonel, go directly to General Mahone. There is no time for chain of command, we cannot wait for General Hill to pass the word. Tell General Mahone he must withdraw from the enemy in his front with great care, but he must use speed. We are in a dangerous situation here. It is my desire that he bring whatever force he can to close this gap." Venable spun his horse, was quickly gone.

The musket fire was increasing now. Stray shots whistled past him, and he pushed the horse forward. Behind him, he could hear the shouts, his staff receiving the messages, the word being passed, the army waking from a stunned sleep, recovering from the shock. He spurred the horse up a small rise, raised the glasses again, could see past the mass of destruction, the torn earth yawning open, ripped from below, piles of dirt and clay spread out in all directions. He could still see the enemy flags, saw them drawing closer together, pressed from both sides by the gathering storm of fire.

Now he could see the men on the other side of the crater, gathering together, a tide of blue, drifting down, following their flags right into the crater. The guns were still firing from far down both sides, and the blue lines that were still out in the open were falling into panic, the lines breaking up, more men moving forward, disappearing into the protection of the great hole. He could see one single gun, very close, just to the right of the big hole, and the men were firing down, an odd angle, the rear of the gun carriage raised, the barrel pointing ... *down*.

Lee stared, felt something turn in his gut, watched as the gun fired again, saw one man fall beside it, struck down, the others still moving in quick steps, then the gun firing again. He thought of the words, the horrible phrase that only a soldier understands . . . *point-blank*. He moved the glasses slightly, to the crater itself, could only see the far side, not what he knew to be down deep in the hole, a vast sea of blue soldiers, swarming right into a trap of their own making.

Closer, on the near side of the crater, a thin line of blue troops had emerged, coming up out of the hole. They were flowing down into more lines of trenches, firing out at the gray troops on both sides of them. But there were not many, not enough to push forward and sweep out on both sides, and Lee understood, thought, Yes, that was the plan, burst through, push through with great strength, then spread out, both ways, roll up the line. But it didn't work. The crater . . . they can't get out of the crater.

Now the men in blue were drifting back, pushed by growing numbers of Lee's troops, the musket fire slicing through the blue troops from all directions. Lee watched them, the ones who did not fall, saw them backing up, moving back toward the edge of the crater, then over, gone, dropping away, joining the mass of men who did not go forward with them, who did not try to climb out. Lee could see it now, most of the assaulting force had sought the cover of the great wide hole or been stopped by the hole itself, men dropping down, only to find themselves staring up at the crest of the wall of earth in front of them. Peering through the glasses, Lee could feel it, the great thrust, the momentum of the enemy's assault gone. Men were still moving past him, moving forward, forming new lines. Stronger lines. He knew it was the Third Corps, Hill's troops, the division of Billy Mahone. A few cheered him, but most had their eyes on the front, toward the job at hand, the deadly gap in the line. Lee looked again at the edge of the crater, saw the last signs of blue disappear over the edge, saw his men moving forward, closer, the enemy's thrust now contained, held together by Lee's men and by their own plan, by the great hole in the earth.

D OWN IN THE WIDE CRATER, THE MEN COULD SEE WHAT WAS happening, that they could no longer push forward, that the great plan to cut Lee's lines in two had stopped in a mass of confusion and fear. The men were crushed together in a suffocating mass, a solid sea of blue with nowhere to go. The crush was getting worse, more and more men coming forward from their own lines, guided by the deadly fire of the enemy into the only place that was safe. Some continued to fight, aimed their muskets up at the crest, waited for the face of the enemy to appear, the careless man who stood up to see the astonishing sight spread before him. But the blue soldiers who tried to fight were held back, could not even reload their guns, the growing crush of men now pressing them together into a helpless tide.

As more lines of blue came forward, those who saw the hopelessness, the chaos, tried to return to their own lines, the safety of their own works. But troops were advancing in a tight line, through the only places where the men could move, blocking the escape of anyone who tried to run. The officers could see it now, the great mistake, that Burnside had not ordered the front of the earthworks cleared of brush and cut trees, and so there was no way to get back into their own works, as long as men were still being sent forward. Down both sides of the assault the rebel muskets and big guns were all pointing now toward the center, and if the gunners could not see the crater itself, they had a clear view of the open ground behind it, the flat space between the lines. The officers who tried to stop their units from making the deadly mistake, who tried to halt their men before they reached the crater, now found themselves in the open, under the massed guns of both flanks. If a man tried to leave the crater, escape back to his own lines, the rebel muskets were ready, and if the aim was not good, it did not matter, because the blue masses were too great a target, too many to hide from the storm of lead.

As the gray troops reached the edge of the crater, some remembered Spotsylvania, the bloody angle, the horror of knowing your enemy was so close, a few feet away, and some hesitated, crouched low against the ragged mounds of dirt. There was something different this time, something more horrible, even the officers could see it slowly spread through the men. There would be prisoners, thousands . . . yes, the fight was over, the Yankees were trapped, there was nowhere they could go. Those who could see, who eased toward the crater from the sides, understood that this was something truly extraordinary, that right in front of them thousands of men waited, helpless.

But the fight was not over, and along the edge of the crater there were men who still felt the rage, who still saw the Yankee as the hated enemy, who knew only that over the crest of this hole men waited to die, and so they *would* die. Slowly, the noise of the voices rose, the cries of the fight returning. Down the line, rebel gunners were still sending their shells into the mass of blue, most still not understanding how simple a target they had. The gray soldiers could hear the sounds, watched overhead as the high arc of the mortar shell landed beyond the crest, straight down into the packed horde of blue. Now bayonets began to go over the edge, men throwing them like spears, and the ones who could see into the hole watched in horror as the faces stared up, the eyes watching the hand of death reaching right for them, slowly, too slowly, and the men were packed so tightly together that there was no getting away.

There were cries of "Surrender," and many of the gray soldiers moved to the crest, offered to pull the men in blue out and over, offering survival, escape, and many accepted the hand, scrambled out of the crater to become prisoners. But now the rebels began to see the faces of the black soldiers, the shocking reality that many had never seen up close, that those men in blue had put the Negroes into the fight. Many of the blue soldiers were surprised as well, saw the screaming mass around them swell with the men of Ferrero's division, the last troops across the field.

A few voices began to ring out, a sharp cry of anger from some of the rebels, and many of the gray soldiers stopped accepting surrender, stopped taking prisoners, would not accept that the man who was like you, the man you respected as your enemy, would fight beside the Negro, would take up arms against the men they saw as their own kind. Now it was becoming something new, it was not a fight at all, not a battle like any of them had ever seen. In the crater, the black soldiers could see it in the eyes of the men beside them, that if the white men were taken prisoner with the Negroes, the result would be barbaric, ruthless. Some of the Federal soldiers still reached out, waved a handkerchief, anything they could find, still tried to surrender, but when the black soldiers tried as well, they were struck down, if not by the musket of the enemy, then by the man beside them, by the incredible horror of blind madness.

The men trapped in the crater were sentenced to death, a decision that came not from the minds of the rebel commanders, or even the irrational fear and anger that makes wars. Those men in gray, who understood that the fight was over, could only watch in shock, friends watching friends, officers watching the men under their command, helpless to stop the rising flow of blood. The men in blue felt it as well, heard the screaming roar of madness all around them, saw their own men taken down by the bayonet, the sword, stared in utter horror as the muskets began to swing, the bayonets finding the soldier who was your comrade. The faces spread the terror, the savagery, the mindless insanity of the beast, and the men who held on to their humanity stared in utter horror as the rules of war, the last fragile string of human decency, was pushed aside by those whose blind hatred would only be fed by slaughter.

30. GRANT

JULY 30, 1864

THE LOSSES WERE STAGGERING, NEARLY FOUR THOUSAND MEN, most of them struck down in and around the crater. He had not seen Burnside, not yet, but that would come. The reports were being written, but already what was said privately was the most damaging, the personal details that could never be put into official reports.

The First Division, Ledlie's division, had simply panicked, had marched straight into the confusion of the big hole and then stopped. Jim Ledlie himself was the focus of the comments, the speculation. He was the only man in his division who knew what they were supposed to have done, but he never gave the orders, never led his men around the crater, to the side, the clear open advance into the shattered lines of the enemy. Instead his men marched straight ahead, straight into the crater itself, and Ledlie could not stop them, because he wasn't there. Grant began to hear it himself, that Ledlie had been drunk, far behind the awful place where his men went to die. This was not new, not a surprise to the other commanders of the Ninth Corps. Grant was already being told that Burnside knew Ledlie's reputation yet had still allowed the man to command the first wave of the assault.

They were riding back to City Point, another sunset, another horrible day. He rocked with the rhythm of the horse, stared ahead quietly. Behind him the staff was strung out in line, and no one was talking.

They had never heard him explode in anger. He never erupted the way Meade did, the hot words flowing hard into the pale face of the subordinate. But he was feeling it now, building inside of him, boiling up in a raw red fury. He felt his heart beating, held the reins in a tight grip in his hand, stared straight ahead. He was as angry as he had ever been. The names rolled around in his mind, the puzzle had already come neatly into place. The plan had been a good one, and he'd placed confidence in his commanders that it would be carried out, that the instructions would be passed down to the officers, that the men would know what to do, that they would in fact be *led*.

He was angry at himself because he'd allowed Meade to interfere, to criticize Burnside's use of Ferrero's division. Burnside was right, they had trained for weeks, they would have known what to do, they would not have marched straight into that hole. But if the Negroes were angry at not leading the assault, they could not complain about being left out entirely. Burnside had sent them in anyway, when it was already clear that the plan had failed, the rest of the corps massing into a hopeless tangle. If they had missed their opportunity to lead the way, they had not missed their opportunity to die.

He had heard of the decision to send Ledlie in first, the drawing of names out of a hat, and it made his eyes clamp shut. His face held the expression tight, the loud yell held down deep. *Draw names out of a hat?* It was almost comical, an army run by lottery, responsibility by the luck of the draw. But there was nothing comical about the loss of four thousand men.

Burnside will go, he thought. That was definite, the order already etched hard in his mind. He knew Lincoln would allow him to handle that any way he wanted, and if it was to be today, he would have the man flogged, drag him by the collar right into the crater, make him look at the horror of what he had done. He closed his eyes, took a deep breath, thought, No, you cannot give in to that, you cannot just explode.

He forced himself to see beyond the anger. There is the right way to handle these things, he thought, there always has been, especially for the men who have served for so long. There was nothing to be gained by public humiliation, by shaming the man. The letters would be written, sent to Halleck in Washington. Burnside would be given leave, maybe a month, with instructions that his staff could accompany him. There would be no confusion about what was really happening, and Burnside was experienced enough in command to understand that. After the leave expired, he would be told to simply wait for a new assignment. It was the most discreet way to handle the dignity of the veteran commanders. The newspapers would not jump on the story, put the name in shameful headlines, because in fact there would be no story.

He could see the river now, rode across the open ground toward the tents. The camp came to life, the aides began to move out, to take the horses. Grant ignored them, pushed the horse out toward the water, stopped at the edge of the high bluff. He looked across, saw distant trees, the hills turning dark with the setting of the sun. He heard another horse, saw Porter now, slowly moving up beside him. Grant looked at him, knew that Porter would sit quietly, as long as he did, to listen, and that if he wanted to be alone, it would just take a small shake of the head and Porter would be gone.

Grant turned to the water again, felt himself let go, a long slow breath, the anger now giving way. "Colonel," he said, "I never have seen an opportunity such as that, and I never expect to see it again."

Porter said nothing, nodded.

Grant rolled the names through his mind again, thought, No, it does no good. There is nothing to be gained by singling anyone out. The men will know, the officers will know.

He looked at Porter again, said, "It was not the men. Whatever is said about this, from the papers, from Washington, it was not the men. I believe that the men would have performed every duty required of them had they been properly led." He paused, said, "Or had been led at all."

Porter still said nothing, and they sat quietly for a long moment. Grant thought, Another horrible day, another day that could have changed everything. I cannot be there, I cannot oversee every operation, every command.

He stared at the darkening river, saw the lights now on the big ships. Down below, men were beginning to look up at him, could see the perfect silhouette in the last glow of the sunset. Some wanted to cheer, to salute him with a rowdy call. But most were quiet, gathering on the wharf, on the decks of the ships, staring at the distinctive figure, the shapeless hat, the slouch in the saddle. They watched as the dark form slowly turned the horse and moved away. They did not see him take the cigar from his pocket, and they could not hear his thoughts, already moving beyond this awful day, the new plan, the motion of the army already in his mind, the chess game in progress again.

31. LEE

SEPTEMBER 1864

I
T WAS ONE PIECE OF PAPER, A FEW SIMPLE WORDS, AND IT CUT INTO
him like the violent stab of the enemy's sword. John Bell Hood had
evacuated Atlanta. Sherman had won the long fight, the continuous
moving battle from Chattanooga.

He had been unusually candid about Hood's appointment, told
Davis that he felt disappointment in Johnston's resistance to Sherman,
that he'd thought Johnston would bring the fight to Sherman instead
of the constant retreat. But he knew Hood was not the man to lead
that army. There were none who could put the fire into his troops better than the big Texan. But he understood that Hood was impatient,
would try to please Richmond, justify the appointment by doing the
opposite of Johnston, taking the fight straight to Sherman's vastly superior army. And it was not once, but three times, three bloody fights,
Hood slamming his men into the strength of the Federal forces, until
finally there was nothing left to hold Sherman back. Now Atlanta, the
great rail center, the gateway for the crops and hard goods of the deep
South, was in Federal hands.

Lee read the telegram again, put it down. There was little in the
way of detail, no troop numbers, no count of casualties. It did not matter. He stood, moved to the opening in the tent. He saw the men moving about, Taylor at the field table, the paperwork moving through,
the business of headquarters. He watched for a long moment, thought,
It's as though nothing has changed. The war is the same as it has always
been, these boys, these good boys, holding the line against those fellows over there. But it was not the same, and it was growing inside of
him like some great sickness.

North of the James, close to Richmond, the enemy had made a

push, a brief strike, with the result that they were now that much closer to the capital. Lee had done what he could, had sent men who could be pulled from the defenses to the south, had summoned Ewell to call out the Home Guard, the cripples and boys and government clerks, to line the trenches east of the city. The Federals had not pressed it, seemed content to make the point, and the point was made clear by what happened down south, below Petersburg.

The Federals had moved west, struck out at the supply artery that stretched straight down from the city, the Weldon Railroad. There had been a good fight, a poorly coordinated assault by the enemy, but in the end it was the numbers, and Lee could not stop it, and so the Weldon was now behind Federal lines. It was one more lifeline, one more way to feed his army, cut off. But it was not from some great strategy or brilliant tactical move by the enemy, it was simply the movement of troops, the extension of the blue lines. With the threat of Richmond, Lee had to pull men away from Petersburg, send them north, and so when Grant moved his men out below Petersburg, Lee had no reserve, no way to meet strength with strength. The earthworks, the solid line of defenses, was over twenty-six miles long, and Lee's army did not have enough men to make any kind of strong defense without pulling men completely off some part of that line.

There was still a chance in the valley. Early's forces, most of the Second Corps, were still intact, the fertile farmlands of the valley still under control. Lee knew that Early was no longer a serious threat to Washington, but the valley was defended, the Virginia Central Railroad still open. It was a force of fifteen thousand men that Lee needed desperately at Petersburg, but just as desperate was the need for the crops from the Shenandoah. Lee had heard that Sheridan was now on his way there, that the vicious David Hunter was no longer in command. Lee did not know Sheridan's strength, thought, They may just stay to the north, around Harper's Ferry, keep Early contained. There is victory even in that. We must not lose the valley.

He had thought of going out, riding the horse, but the day was grim, dreary, still very hot. The lines were an unpleasant place, there was nowhere he could go and feel the pride, hear the cheers, the wide grins coming from hungry men. The front lines were like some horrible wasteland, stripped of green, of any of the beauty that had been this part of Virginia. The trenches themselves were mostly covered, protection from the constant shelling, the impact of the mortars. For miles the land behind and between the lines was barren of life, as though the men had made a new world in the misery of the underground, moved only in tunnels, through the mud and darkness that bred sickness. He would not go there now, would not see the men being carried out, disease taking many more than the guns of the enemy. He turned back into the tent, suddenly felt the weariness, the sadness. He sat on the cot, looked down, thought, Virginia. It was always . . . this is where I chose to fight. It is the only choice I could have made. Look what we have done, what man has done to God's land. There has to be a price for that. God cannot ignore . . . no, He has not ignored. Lee stared into the side of the tent, thought, There has not been one day, not since this campaign began, when there was not some fight, somewhere, when we did not have casualties. There is death every day. The hand of God.

He had been thinking about Richmond, looked at the maps, at the long lines, the miles of defense. He'd seen it clearly for a while now, thought about it again. There is no way we can keep Grant out of Richmond. It will be impossible to stop him if that is where he wants to go. He can send twenty thousand men at the city and simply push his way in. The only defense would be to abandon Petersburg, move the army north. And then . . .

He stood, began to pace, felt the anger, the frustration. I did not expect, ever, to be doing this. To just . . . wait, while the enemy decides what to do next, where the next fight will be. From his first days in command, when the army was so very strong, led by the good men, the men who would bring victory, Lee had made the fight on his terms, found the advantage. He always knew his enemy, understood where the mistakes would come, knew how to strike at opportunity. Now, he thought, we are weak, and we can only . . . respond.

He had sent a letter to Davis, a long and serious plea. There was a great untapped resource of manpower in the South still, men who had not fought at all, some by choice, some by the rule of law. But Lee knew Davis could try to change the law. The age of the soldiers was fixed, from eighteen to forty-five. That could easily be changed, lowered to seventeen and raised to fifty, possibly even higher. There were still men who escaped from the fight by employing themselves in exempt positions, noncombat jobs every army must have. There had been great resistance to arming the Negroes, but there were thousands of freedmen who could be employed as teamsters, railroad workers, thousands of jobs along the lines of supply now held by able-bodied white men the army so desperately needed. It was only a question of organizing, convincing the state governments. Lee had stressed it to Davis, how the army was losing strength every day, but if Davis ever had the power, the persuasion to energize the states to answer the call, he did not have it anymore. Many of the states saw the war now as a simple issue of survival, and if there were men in Georgia who could be brought to the fight, they would stay in Georgia, defend Georgia. Lee was beginning to understand that what had created the Confederacy in the first place, the cooperation of the states, was falling apart as well. As the losses grew, the states pulled away from the larger fight, looked to their own. Lee did not need Davis to tell him that whatever strength the army had now, in the filthy desolate trenches at Petersburg, was all the army he would ever have.

To evacuate Richmond . . . he had not yet suggested that to Davis, not with the force needed to convince him. Davis would not even discuss it, still saw Richmond as the heartbeat of the Cause, and Lee was beginning to understand that Davis was slipping, not just his physical health, but slipping further from the reality of the war. Davis was now talking about liberating Atlanta, had even written that Sherman could still be swept completely out of Georgia, his huge Federal army "utterly destroyed." Lee did not ask him how.

Lee thought of his father, Light-Horse Harry Lee, the great hero of the Revolutionary War, remembered hearing the old man talk about defending Virginia. *If you do not control the water, the ports, the rivers, the only way to defeat the enemy is to move inland, take him away from his base of supply. If you can bring him into the open, then the advantage is to the more mobile force.* The old man spoke of a time when there were no railroads. And the British were a very different enemy, did not know the land, did not know their opponent. But still, the strategy was very sound, very modern. We need open ground, we need to maneuver, to find opportunity, Lee thought. It is the only way there can still be a victory. Grant *can* be defeated, if we can fight him on our terms. He said it again, said it out loud in a low voice, *"On our terms."*

Holding on to Richmond . . . using our army to sit in one place while the enemy stretches himself slowly around us, like some great fat snake . . .

He felt suddenly like he was suffocating, moved outside, tried to breathe, but the air was no cooler. He stood beside the tent, and the faces were looking at him now.

There was one voice, one man said, "General Lee! God bless you, General Lee!"

He looked for the voice, the man's face, had to see him, abruptly felt the need for that, for the energy of the man. But now there were only blank stares, and in front of Taylor the paperwork began to move again. He still watched them, thought, Maybe I should ride out, move through the men. They always respond, there is always the spirit. He looked toward the horses, suddenly felt very weak, the hollow coldness in his chest, thought, Maybe later. It might be cooler. . . .

He looked toward the town, the church spires, could see damage, small signs that the war was there as well, that they too would not escape. He had heard about Atlanta, the fires, the destruction, thought, It was never like this, this is not the way wars are fought. You do not hurt the innocent, the people who simply get in the way. He remembered Fredericksburg, the Federals allowing the townspeople to leave, time to evacuate. It doesn't seem to matter anymore, he realized. There is no thought to the fighting, the destruction has become so commonplace, we don't even see it now.

When the Federal soldiers had looted Fredericksburg, ransacked the personal lives of the innocent, he'd been furious, outraged at the indecency, the barbarism of that. Now the indecency was simply a way of life, everything they did was barbaric. He had ridden to the crater, had to see it for himself. He was, after all, an engineer, and it was an amazing accomplishment, and he felt oddly inspired by that, thought, I would like to meet them, the men who did that. And then he had seen the hole itself, the wide rip in the earth, and packed into the bottom, the horror of what they had done to each other. He'd looked down on the scene and his mind saw a painting, small shreds of color mingled with the clay, the twists of metal. When he walked away, he felt a strange calm, thought, Yes, it was horrible, horrible indeed. But he had to tell himself that, remind himself to see it that way. There was no sickening revulsion, no outrage, no indignation at the barbarism. It was just one more scene from this war, one more horror, one more mass of death, blending together with all the rest.

32. GRANT

NOVEMBER 1864

H E BEGAN TO FEEL IT, SLOWLY, GROWING INSIDE OF HIM, NOT
confidence, not the self-assurance he had never lacked anyway, but more. It was enthusiasm, the complete calm, rising
up inside, from some very important place. He felt it every day now,
every morning when he rode out along the lines, a ride that for weeks
now had become that much longer. The army was wrapping farther
around Lee, extending to the southwest of Petersburg. Lee's lines were
now over thirty miles long. Grant would ride along the new trenches,
out along the far flank, sit and watch the workers throwing up the logs
and fresh earth. If they could not tell by looking at him, if the soldiers
did not know what was coming, he knew it with absolute certainty.
The flank would be moved again, farther, stretching Lee's ability to defend, would continue to stretch until Lee could defend no more. It was
simply a matter of time.

If there had been confidence around Petersburg, it was still a siege.
There could be little excitement in that, in knowing you were slowly
starving your enemy. The newspapers, the politicians in Washington,
had shown slight praise for a war that clearly was going to take a while
longer to end. Grant had begun to despise reporters, had grown weary
of reading the fine exploits of the rebel armies, while his own victories
were never "complete." There was not to be any satisfaction in the
North until the war simply ended. They wanted a time, a date, some
careless boast to fill the headlines. Grant knew that even Lincoln did
not expect that, had heard too much of it anyway. The progress was
slow, but it was progress.

Then came Sherman's message from Atlanta. Grant had been so
excited by that he even considered going there himself, to look into the

sharp eyes of his friend, to grab him hard by the shoulders, tell him face-to-face, "You have done something truly extraordinary." He did not go, wrote to Sherman instead, a glowing letter filled with the praises of the proud commander and the affection of the good friend. But the letter had not been enough, and the man who did not show jubilation had his army do it for him. Grant ordered a salute, fired from every big gun in every battery that faced the enemy. When the word was passed, it became a celebration that gave a thrill to every blue soldier, and across the way the rebels kept low, absorbed yet another pounding. If the sound of the guns did not carry to Washington, the spirit of the celebration did, and it did not take a message from Grant to tell Lincoln that, "Yes, now it is more than a good fight, it is more than progress. Now, we are *winning*."

There had been another salute, another cannonade. This one was for Phil Sheridan. The cavalry commander had been given charge of the fight in the Shenandoah, to deal with Jubal Early once and for all. Lincoln did not send instructions to Grant, there had been none of the needling telegrams that this army had become so accustomed to, but as long as Early was in force in the Shenandoah Valley, Washington was nervous. The more nervous, the worse it was for Lincoln, and his chance for reelection.

Grant had overestimated Early's strength, had believed the rebels to be much stronger, and ultimately, when Sheridan took command, he was given a considerable force, was able to bring nearly forty thousand men into the valley. The newspapers made great sport of the confrontation, and many made comparisons to the great Stonewall, that Jubal Early would do what Jackson had done, rid the valley of yet another Federal invasion. But Sheridan proved that he was not to be chased away, would not run from a bold attack. At a place called Cedar Creek, Early threw his fifteen thousand men against Sheridan's great force. It was a plan Jackson would have approved, an assault that depended on surprise and audacity. But Sheridan created his own legend, rallied his retreating troops and turned his men southward. Unlike Jackson, this time it came down to numbers, Sheridan finally crushing Early's smaller force. No matter how much praise and legend the newspapers tried to give Jubal Early, he was not Stonewall Jackson.

What was left of Early's forces now hugged close to the big mountains, but they were no longer a threat to Sheridan. The Federals not only controlled the valley, they began to destroy it; not the mindless barbarism of David Hunter, but the methodical and strategic destruction of the farms, the breadbasket of the Confederacy. If Lee's army was to be fed, it would not be from the Shenandoah.

THE ROW OF HEADQUARTERS TENTS WOULD BE REPLACED BY permanent structures, small log cabins. The days were shorter, had become much cooler, and the winds blowing across the wide river had made the tents an uncomfortable home. The cabins were not yet completed, but every day, the logs were dragged close, the carpenters working with clean efficiency, especially when their audience included the commanding general.

Grant was still not comfortable with patience, made the rides along the lines when the weather would allow. The men were becoming used to seeing him, and he was recognized now, as he had rarely been before. If the soldiers were not yet sure, if this plainly dressed officer with the cigar did not catch their attention, it was the young boy riding beside him who did. The lull in the fight meant that finally his family could come down, he could see Julia and the children. Fred was the oldest, and so had the honor of riding out with his father, beside him, and the troops cheered him, laughed and pointed at the boy's wide smile, his eyes wide, too, as the men emerged from the dugouts, from the camps, standing straight with the pride of good soldiers, holding the muskets and swords to their chests, a show the boy would never forget.

GRANT WAS ON HIS BACK, BUCK HOLDING HIM DOWN BY THE shoulders, while down at his feet, Jesse, the smaller boy, sat on his legs. They had been at it for a while now, and Grant was feeling the exhaustion. He looked up at the older boy, felt the strength in the boy's hands, thought, Soon, I won't be able to do . . . *this*.

He grunted, rolled over, carefully moved Jesse off his legs, then wrapped his feet around the boy, pinning him between his legs. Jesse was howling with laughter, trying to free himself, now lying sideways, pushing in vain at the trap that held him tightly. Grant looked at the older boy, and there was something strange in Buck's eyes; it was not play. Buck was still trying to pin him down, grabbing his father's shoulders hard, the face now red and angry, and Grant felt the boy's fingers clawing into him, hurting now. He reached up, held the boy's arms, pulled him away, said, "All right, easy, a moment . . . take a moment. . . ." He was breathing very hard, and the boy let loose now, sat back on the ground.

Grant released Jesse, still giggling, sat up between them, saw the opening in the tent and the face of Horace Porter. Grant laughed, said, "Colonel, you care to give it a go? I feel quite sure the fight isn't over here." Grant looked now at Buck, thought, He is not like his older brother. Fred is so much like Julia, but Buck . . . he is stubborn, a fighter. He is . . . like me.

Buck was actually Ulysses Jr., was just twelve, the second oldest, not yet old enough to ride through the camps with his father. It was a major disappointment, not helped by Fred making sure no one forgot the privilege of age. Jesse was only six, and he knew nothing of the rivalry of his older brothers, was concerned more with the daily torture he received from his sister Nellie, three years older than he, and very capable of making his life pure misery. The wrestling match with his father was a joyous relief, no matter that defeat was only a matter of time.

Grant saw Porter's hands full of papers, looked again at the older boy, said, "No, I don't believe Colonel Porter has time for a game right now. You two run outside for a moment. Buck, take your brother to see the ships. There was a new one coming in just a while ago."

The boy stood and held out a reluctant hand for his little brother, but did not hide his disappointment. He said, "All right. Come on, Jesse, I'll race you. . . ."

Buck waited for the smaller boy to run out of the tent, a respectable head start, looked at Porter, then at his father, said, "You leaving? You going away again?"

Grant said, "No . . . why?" The boy was quickly gone, the race on, and Grant pulled himself up, reached for the chair, sat down, took a deep breath. "He is . . . very serious, for a boy."

Porter moved toward the desk, set the papers down, said, "It's envy. Fred gets the attention. The oldest always do."

Grant glanced at the papers. "No, more than that. He's angry. These wrestling matches aren't a game to him. He's always trying to beat me. I see how big he is now, and I realize it won't be long and he'll be strong enough to do it. I wish he'd . . . laugh more."

Porter said nothing, began to move through the papers.

Grant looked out through the opening in the tent, said, "He's like me . . . I never really saw that until now. At his age, even younger, I wouldn't budge, stubborn, had to do things my own way. Only saw

one way of ever doing anything, and if it didn't work, I'd do it harder."
He laughed, pulled out a cigar, the end smashed flat.

Porter glanced up, smiled, looked back at the papers.

Grant leaned over, tried to see what held Porter's attention. "How's
things at the quartermasters'? Any problem feeding the family? Four kids
eat a lot."

Porter seemed surprised, said, "Oh, none, sir. Plenty . . ."

"Well, good. You be honest with me, Colonel. They make themselves too much of a bother, you tell me. No favoritism here, not in
this camp."

Porter put the papers down, looked at Grant, smiled again. "Sir,
forgive me, but I believe you are entitled . . . it is acceptable for a man
in your position to . . . do whatever you please."

Grant pulled out another cigar, saw less damage, said, "No, Mr.
Porter, it most definitely is not. You need proof of that, just ask Mr.
Rawlins. If I am not certain that something is acceptable behavior, he is
my authority on the subject. I doubt he approves of my family having
the run of the camp."

Porter looked down, tried to hide a smile, said, "Sir, Colonel
Rawlins, um . . . Colonel Rawlins is somewhat nervous by nature, sir.
He has taken it upon himself to be our protector. No disrespect intended, sir, but I do sometimes wish that Colonel Rawlins would . . .
not look so closely over my shoulder."

Grant nodded. "I share your feelings, Mr. Porter. But he is doing
a good job. Keeps the reporters away, knows how to deal with the for-
eigners. Knows the rules . . . that's it, you need someone who knows
the rules, the things you can say, things you can't, what makes headlines, what causes scandal. Never made much difference out West, but
here . . . too close to Washington."

Porter looked to the papers again, said under his breath, "He re-
minds me of my grandmother. . . ."

Grant pulled at the cigar, said, "Well then, Mr. Porter, if anything
happens to Colonel Rawlins, have your grandmother report to me
immediately."

HE WAITED, LISTENED FOR THE SOUND OF HORSES. HE STOOD
now, feeling the impatience, then sat again. He heard motion
outside, knew Rawlins was close, a quiet day, nothing to aggravate the chief of staff. Grant shouted, "Colonel, any sign?"

Rawlins was at the tent now, said, "Of . . . what, sir?" Grant looked at him, and Rawlins saw the impatience, said, "Oh, if you mean General Hancock, no, not yet."

Grant nodded, pulled at the cigar, the peak of the tent above him thick with smoke. "What time did he say . . . ?"

Rawlins looked at his watch. "Two o'clock. About . . . now, sir." Rawlins turned away, looked out beyond the tents, said, "It's a wagon, sir. And the flag of the Second. He's here."

Rawlins was gone quickly, and Grant stood again, felt anxious. He did not know Hancock well, knew him at first from pure reputation, had always heard that Winfield Hancock was the best commander in the army. It was something that Meade kept with him like a small burning wound. Meade fully expected that Hancock would succeed him when Grant's patience, or the pressure from Washington finally took Meade away from the army. But it had not yet happened, and now Hancock had sent the word, through Meade first, but then directly to Grant himself. He could no longer lead his troops.

He had requested a personal meeting with Grant, and Grant knew that it was final, that if the wounds did not heal, it could be the last meeting. What had plagued Hancock since Gettysburg, the daily grief of a painful wound, the inability of the doctors to repair once and for all the damaged groin, now became the enemy Hancock could not defeat. The wound had opened up again, so badly that he could not ride, could not be there to direct his troops. Command of the Second was given to Andrew Humphreys, Meade's chief of staff. Humphreys was an older man, an engineering genius, had led troops throughout the war with quiet ability. But Grant already felt the loss, the energy that would slip away from the army when Hancock was no longer on the field.

He moved now to the opening of the tent. A wagon? he thought. Then he saw it. Of course, an ambulance. Hancock would not do that for show, to be dramatic. The wound was serious, and he could not ride. Grant waited, saw the aides move to the rear of the ambulance, hands reaching out, and now he saw Hancock, easing down to the ground, his face pale, drawn, weak. Hancock looked at him, straightened, saluted, and Grant saw the clean white shirt, the sharp blue of the dress uniform, smiled, nodded, returned the salute.

To one side, Hancock's aide tried to assist him, and Hancock barked, "I'm fine. I can walk, dammit!" The aide backed away, and Hancock limped forward, moved toward Grant.

Grant met him with a hand. "General Hancock, it is always a pleasure."

Hancock took the hand, tried to smile, but the pain filled his face, even the short walk a strain. Grant backed into the tent, and Hancock followed. Grant pointed toward the rear of the tent, to the bed, said, "If it is more comfortable, General, please, do not hesitate."

Hancock glanced at the bed, then moved toward the small chair, sat slowly, heavily, made a small groan. "This will do, sir."

Grant sat in his own chair, saw the tight lines in Hancock's face, the big handsome man fighting the pain, holding it away. Grant said, "May I get you anything, General?"

Hancock let out a deep breath, slumped now on the small chair, said, "No, thank you, sir. I won't take up your time. I just wanted to speak to you, before I left, just a moment."

Grant nodded, waited. He had actually looked forward to this, to speaking to this man when there was no one around, when Meade was not there, when the others were not a part of it. There had always been something different about Hancock, an angry impatience, something Grant understood, something Grant held tightly inside himself. Hancock was known for his angry outbursts, but his were not like Meade's; the anger was always focused, and utterly brutal, and he would find the weakness, the mistake, wrap it with intense profanity and launch it back at the guilty man like a missile. Hancock had no tolerance for incompetence, no patience for wastefulness. And if the subject was never officially discussed, Grant knew it was the one thing that would keep Hancock from command of the army: Hancock would never put up with Washington.

Hancock leaned forward now, said, "As you know, sir, I will be leaving for the capital in a few days. I have been informed that a new command has been created. If you had something to do with that, I am grateful."

Grant nodded, said nothing. If Hancock could not lead troops into battle, Grant understood that his name alone could still be very useful for recruitment, to bring the experience of the veterans back into the service, the experience that was so lacking in the new recruits, the new draftees. There would be an official organization to these veterans, a new corps that Hancock would command. It was hoped that if the war was to last much longer, Hancock might again lead good men into a good fight.

Grant said, "I expect we'll see you back here soon."

Hancock nodded. "I would prefer it that way. I wouldn't want to miss it, not again."

Grant said, "Miss . . . the end?"

Hancock nodded painfully, his face twisted slightly. "I missed it once before, in Mexico. The final blow, Chapultepec. I was sick, damned flu, my gut tied up in one big knot. Watched my own men hit that wall, climb those ladders, watched them through field glasses. I pulled myself out of bed, climbed out on a rooftop, sat there like some groaning old woman while my boys went over the wall. I marched them all the way from the coast, all the way to Mexico City, and when the time came . . ." He stopped, and Grant could see the anger in Hancock's face, the memories. Hancock forced a small laugh, said, "Looks like . . . I may miss it again."

Grant thought of Mexico, of the bloody fights against an enemy no one thought would be so strong. "That was a good day . . . Chapultepec. My men captured a couple of guns, put them to good use. . . ." He smiled now, thought of all the faces, so much younger, and the smile faded, the names rolled through his mind, so many of them gone now.

Hancock was looking at him, said, "We've killed more of our boys ourselves . . . than the Mexicans did. Who would have thought . . ." He stared away.

Grant pulled at the cigar, said, "Did you know . . . Pete Longstreet was in my wedding?"

Hancock shook his head. "No, guess I didn't. He's back, I hear. Not like . . . some of the others. I served under General Johnston in California, ran the quartermaster department in Los Angeles." He smiled, said, "Department. Me. One man. Not much happening in southern California in those days. I watched Johnston leave, and Lew Armistead, and Dick Garnett. Going home, fighting for their damned rebellion. Now . . . they're all gone." Hancock stared at the floor for a moment, said, "I always thought John Reynolds would take command, lead us to the end." He looked at Grant now. "No disrespect, sir."

Grant smiled. "I thought so too. Always thought he was the best we had. We killed Albert Sidney Johnston at Shiloh, they killed Reynolds at Gettysburg."

Hancock nodded, said, "Too many others, Phil Kearny, McPherson. Even Sedgwick could have handled the job." Hancock was suddenly uneasy. "I didn't mean to suggest that General Meade is not—"

Grant held up his hand. "If it's all the same to you, General, I'd prefer it if this meeting was unofficial. Speak your mind. I'm going to miss you here. I'm going to miss knowing that out there, somewhere, the Second Corps is where I need it to be, that those men are doing what they're supposed to be doing."

Hancock looked down, seemed embarrassed, said, "Humphreys is a good man."

Grant said, "Humphreys is a brilliant man, maybe the smartest commander in this whole army . . . both armies. But he's—excuse me, General—he's not Winfield Hancock."

Hancock straightened, nodded slowly, said, "Thank you, sir."

There was a quiet moment, and Hancock began to move, stood up slowly, tried to stand straight, leaned slightly to one side. "Sir, I won't take up more of your time. I just wanted to say good-bye. I am in the belief, sir, that the army is in the most capable hands it could be."

Grant stood now, set the cigar aside, felt a sudden wave of affection, something unexpected, thought, There are so few . . . so many of the good ones are gone. He looked at the big man's dark eyes, wanted to say something of comfort, ease the man's pain.

Hancock forced himself upright, saluted, said, "With your permission, sir."

Grant returned the salute, held out a hand, said, "General Hancock, this command is more than grateful for your service. If you miss the end *this* time, that's not a bad thing. It means the end is pretty close."

D INNER HAD BEEN QUIET, THE CHILDREN WERE AWAY, GUESTS of the navy. It had been Fred who insisted on seeing one of the big gunboats that patrolled the James River. Grant had hesitated, but Admiral Porter was anxious to have the young man as his guest. Fred's enthusiasm seemed to wane when Porter requested that all the children join the tour.

Grant had finished dinner, thought of his oldest son, trying to maintain his fragile dignity, boarding the ship, passing by the respectful line of sailors, forced to endure the embarrassment of six-year-old Jesse holding his hand. Grant smiled, held out his cigar, thought, Not every responsibility is a glorious one.

The staff was slowly rising, formal, polite, and there were small polite greetings to Julia. Grant still felt uncomfortable with their efforts, their attention, thought, It should not be, she is here for my own selfish reasons. They should not be so concerned.

The chairs were empty now, and Grant leaned back, pulled at the cigar, looked at his wife. She was smiling, watching him, said, "Well now, that was pleasant."

He nodded, said, "You make it so. They are not usually this . . . kindly."

He stood, held out his hand, helped her from the chair. She stood, wrapped her arm in his, and they walked out into the dark, toward the river, toward the distant lights of the big boats. He moved slowly, let her steps guide him, felt her arm against him, focused only on that, on the small part of her, said, "It won't be much longer."

There was a quiet moment. They reached the edge of the high bluff and she stopped, turned to him in the darkness, said, "I believe you. But you need not worry about us. There are many kind people, we are treated so well everywhere we go. You are a very respected man."

It was an odd word to come from her, and he had not thought of that, had always felt she was removed somehow, from all of this, from the war. He thought of her family, in Missouri, so different from him. Her father still would not discuss the war, and Grant had no reason to ever try. The old man had been a slave owner, and even now it made Grant sick inside, the anger. He tried not to bring it up with her, would keep the anger hidden away—there was no point in attacking the old man, or his politics. He was fighting this war to end that way of life, and the old man was just one more reason why this war was fought at all. He looked at her still, her face illuminated by the small lights from below, thought, Yes, we need this to end, to become a family again, all of us, all the families. She is so patient.

He smiled, looked down, and she said, "What is it? Tell me."

He looked out over the river, said, "It is a fortunate thing that I am not waiting somewhere for *you* to come home. I do not have the patience. No telling what I might do. I'd probably come here and never leave, until you came with me. No. I would not make a good wife."

He laughed, but she did not, still looked at him, said, "No one is happy waiting for you to come home, for this to be over. We do what we must, all of us, all the wives, all the mothers. Everywhere I go, New York, Washington, it's all I see, in every face, every woman I meet. They even ask *me*, as though I know something, some secrets, that because my husband is in command I must know these things. They all ask the same thing: 'How long?' "

Grant reached for her hand, wrapped his fingers around hers. "What do you say?"

"To pray, to have faith, to believe in what their men are doing. It's not always the right thing to say. I have had some . . . anger. The widows, that is the hardest thing, what do you say to someone whose husband is not coming home?"

He looked down, shook his head. "I try not to think about that. It's part of my job, my duty. I make widows. I could not do that very well, talk to them, see the hurt, the tears. I must *not* do that. The war cannot have a face, or a name. I hear about people I have known, back in Mexico, or at the Point, men I have served with. I hear that they are dead, and it shocks me how hard that hits me. I can't tell anyone about that. How do I order men to their deaths if every death causes so much pain?"

She put her hand on his shoulder, whispered, "Because it is who you are. It is why God has put you here. If you did not believe that, then you would not end the war. If the deaths of so many did not bother you, you would not care if it ended. That's why you will survive this war. That is God's lesson. That's why I am patient."

He stared at her, surprised, had never heard her speak like this. She was always devout, had always insisted the children be raised with the strictest religious instruction, but he'd never heard her talk of the war before. He thought of her words, thought, If that is true, if this war, if what I am doing, is some kind of lesson from God, then God must be very pleased indeed.

They stood for a long quiet moment, felt the chill of the darkness, could hear the sounds from along the waterfront. There was a noise behind him, and he turned, saw several men silhouetted by the glow of the campfires, could hear a low murmur of energy, small quiet voices, intense whispers. He felt something cold stab his gut, said, "What is it? What has happened?"

One man stepped closer, and Grant tried to see the face, knew now from the walk, the proper step, that it was Rawlins.

"Sir, forgive the intrusion. We just received word from Washington, sir. President Lincoln has been reelected."

I T WAS LIKE A PARTY, AND IF IT MEANT THE WAR WOULD GO ON, IT meant finally that they would win. The soldiers had cast their own votes, something that had rarely been allowed before in wartime, anywhere. Grant himself had strongly advocated the vote for the soldiers, that these men were not just paid mercenaries whose vote could be swayed by a commander. They read all variety of newspapers, they understood the issues, and each man was very capable of making his own decision. The war itself was to preserve something unique in the world, the rights of men to choose their own leaders. Grant realized that to deny that right to the very men who were fighting for it made no sense at all. There had been no serious objection to that from either side of the political race, the McClellan people believing that their man had been such a popular commander with the soldiers, it could only help his chances. What McClellan did not understand, and Grant clearly did, was that the soldiers were not interested in going home until the war was won. Despite his popularity in the field, McClellan ultimately had not shown his army that he was prepared to win the war. By choosing Grant, and supporting him, Lincoln had.

The victory for Lincoln was no great landslide, and likely the vote of the vast majority of the army won him the election. Throughout the North sentiment was still very high for the war to end. In the end it was confidence that Lincoln would be more likely to preserve the Union. McClellan himself had begun to back away from an outright declaration of peace, that he would simply stop the war. It infuriated some of his own supporters, but as a military man, McClellan understood that simply ending the war meant recognizing the rights of the Confederacy to form their own country. That was a break with many of the Democrats he was supposed to represent. His commitment to the Democratic platform was consistent with the way McClellan had led his troops into battle: he went halfway.

With Lincoln's victory, the morale in the army soared, and at Petersburg the blue troops peered out at the enemy with a new sense of what was coming. There were still some, the veterans from the first disasters of the war, who might still believe that those fat men in Washington would only disappoint, that the commanders of this army did not know how to finish the job. Now the talk was more enthusiastic. Even the most cynical veterans began to see it, to believe what many were saying, that Grant and Lincoln would do the job, would see it through to the end.

33. LEE

November 1864

H E HEARD IT FIRST FROM THE SOLDIERS, FROM THE SHARP-
shooters out front. He knew it was still going on every night,
the small quiet truce, enemies meeting face-to-face to trade, to
pass along newspapers, bits of information. There was still tobacco—
the boys in gray had little else to offer, and the Yankees would still
trade for it—and each night it might be the only way his men would
get anything to eat. But now the word came back, men moving
quickly, and at first it sounded like the familiar rattle of rumors, but
then there was a newspaper. If an officer took the time to read it himself, he still moved, kept the horse in motion toward the headquarters.
The news came to Lee like a cold black wind. Lincoln had won the
election.

There had been hope that if the people in the North were listening to their own newspapers, the fiery talk from those who opposed
Lincoln, they might respond, the price for the years of blood, the
death of so many sons. Davis had believed it absolutely, told Lee that
what they'd given up in land, even now, all the cities, the rivers, the
ports, in the end would still mean victory, because the price for the
North had been the blood of so many of its young men. Davis had already been planning how to deal with McClellan, the terms of the
treaty, the independence that was so very close. Lee had not shared his
enthusiasm.

Now Lee sat alone in the tent, heard the wind howling outside,
the first hard chill, another winter rolling hard toward Virginia,
toward the army that sat low in the trenches.

With the change of seasons had come one change in command.
Longstreet had returned, the wounds not fully healed, but he would

not accept the comfort of a safe position. His right arm was still paralyzed, and he'd learned to write with the left hand. Lee smiled at that, thought, You are still stubborn, and that is what we need right now. Longstreet would command the forces above the James, protecting Richmond. Lee did not believe Grant would strike there. He believed that the small fights, the occasional strong attacks, were meant to distract him from the greater goal, the true plan. Lee understood the maps, saw it plainly, and so would stay close to Grant's real objective— that no matter how much activity the blue troops threw north of the James, they were still extending west of Petersburg. If they kept reaching out, they would soon reach the Southside Railroad, the final artery for supplies south of the Appomattox River. If the Southside fell into Grant's hands, there would be only one course left—to pull away from the capital, and from Petersburg, and move inland. The siege of Petersburg would become something else.

He stared down between his feet, thought, They must not know . . . the men must not feel this as I do. He shook his head, tried to clear his mind, glanced at the newspaper. This is a defeat unlike anything I have been through. Not one shot, not one gun, and yet it is as though we have been . . . what? If it is not a defeat in battle, utter and simple, then . . . it means that nothing will change. Grant will just continue to do what he has been doing since the spring. And we do not have the strength to stop him.

Abruptly, he stood, closed his eyes, clenched his fists. No, this is not what they expect of me. This is not what my duty is about, to sit here and brood, the luxury of self-pity.

He lifted his head, said in a low voice, "God, protect us. We do not doubt . . . we do not question Your will. . . ." He paused, searched for words. "We ask only . . . understanding. Show us the way. If it pleases You, we will do our duty, we will carry on as You have shown us the way. . . ."

His mind would not focus, the prayer was weak, wandering. No, he thought, we do not look for answers. We do what we must do. That is all He asks of us. There can be no more than that.

DECEMBER 1864

IT WAS ONE MORE INVITATION, ONE HE'D HEARD EVERYWHERE THEY had set up the headquarters. He declined of course, as he always declined, had heard it so many times, the generosity of a people who could afford little, opening their homes, their soft beds, to the commander of their army. He would always be gracious, insist that he keep to the tents, even if they were set up right by the house, right in the yard. But the cold winds were blowing hard across Petersburg, and for the first time there had been argument. It came not from the insistence of the civilians, but from Taylor, who knew what the winter could mean to Lee's health. The young man had stood up to Lee, insisted in a tone that was direct and firm. Lee had been surprised by that, but he was surprised more by the tactics Taylor used. It was a letter from Mary, scolding him into protecting himself from the harsh invasion of the cold. If Taylor did not admit it, Lee knew there was a plot, a conspiracy, and against the united front Lee was powerless. That Taylor was reinforced by the iron will of Mary Lee meant only one outcome. For the first time, Lee accepted the invitation to sleep under the dry and solid roof of a civilian home.

The family was named Turnbull, and their home had been spared from damage, at least so far, from the nightly bombardment of the city by Federal guns. The house was on a gentle hill, west of the town, the land around still scattered with the big oaks, an orchard of apple trees, the fields not yet stripped and scarred by the feet of the armies. It was not a grand estate, but a solid frame home, two stories, with a porch that faced the road, another to the side.

The first night was misery, his back settling onto the soft mattress with great protest, and he'd stayed awake, turned, looked down at the hard floor, thought, Maybe . . . down there, just move the quilt. But he endured. The second night, he slept with the soft sounds of angels, dreaming of those days, forgotten now, when Mary was so young, the playfulness, the glorious calm of the old estates, the lush green of the fields. He could hear the music, the voices perfect, the songs of God, the pure joy of the church service, then afterward, the great feasts of Sunday dinner. . . .

"Sir?"

His face was buried deep in the soft pillow, and he opened his eyes, stared dreamily into the lush white.

"Sir?"

He lifted his head slightly, saw daylight, the room lit by the early dawn flowing through lace curtains. He raised himself up, felt the stiffness, felt the age. He turned, saw Taylor standing in the half-open door, looking down, embarrassed; he would not look at Lee in his bedclothes. Lee blinked groggily, rolled over, sat up, said, "Yes, Colonel, I am awake. What is it?"

Taylor still did not look at him, said, "Forgive me, sir. We have received word . . . from the War Department . . . about General Hood, sir."

Lee took a deep breath, knew from the sound of Taylor's voice this was not good news. "Go on, Colonel."

"Sir, General Hood has been repulsed at Nashville. The reports are unclear how badly his losses were, but the army is in retreat. There is no doubt that he has been forced to withdraw."

Lee was fully awake now, said, "Thank you, Colonel. I'll be out in a minute."

Taylor closed the door, and Lee sat for a moment, looked over to the window, saw motion, and sharp wind in the trees, thought, They should have gone after Sherman. . . .

After Sherman swept him away from Atlanta, Hood insisted on gathering his army and moving north, Davis approving a plan that should have pulled Sherman up after him. Hood had been effective at harassing Sherman's supply lines, the railroads in Sherman's rear, all along the route toward Chattanooga. But Sherman let him go, focused instead on moving his great strength farther east. No one knew for sure what Sherman's intentions were, but Richmond had seen value in taking the offensive, not merely nipping at Sherman's heels. Hood continued to push northward, moved into Tennessee, finally found a hard fight at Franklin, just below Nashville, a fight that by all accounts had been a bloodbath. The Federal troops then pulled away, withdrew to the safety of the strong works at Nashville, and so Hood could claim victory. But it was costly, a disastrous loss of commanders, so many good men, struck down in front of troops that desperately needed good men.

There was value to Nashville, it was a major rail hub. If Hood had taken the city, it would have been a concern to Washington, a dangerous threat to the Ohio River. But as well as Lee knew the reckless aggressiveness of Hood, he knew the Federal commander. It was George Thomas, who had served under Lee in Texas, in the cavalry. Thomas was a Virginian who surprised Lee by staying in the old army, resisting the enormous pressure to join the forces of his home state. It was Thomas who had saved the Federal army a year ago from complete destruction by Bragg's army, allowing Rosecrans to escape into Chattanooga. By his brilliant defense Thomas had earned the nickname the newspapers loved, the "Rock of Chickamauga." If Thomas had now made a reputation for being somewhat slow to move, it did not matter.

He was already in place, in the strong fortifications around Nashville. All he had to do was wait for Hood to move up close. Thomas had been reinforced, greatly outnumbered Hood's exhausted and bloodied army, and so the results were predictable.

Lee moved from the bed, went to the window and held the lace aside. He looked out at tall trees, could see gray clouds beyond. He touched the pane of glass, felt the icy cold, a faint flow of air seeping into the room. Hood will be of no help now, he thought. If Thomas comes after him, he could pursue him all the way to the Gulf. But even if Thomas sits tight, Hood's army will have used itself up. If he has been beaten badly at Nashville, forced into a rapid retreat, it means he has lost guns, left them behind. And how many good men?

He looked up at the clouds blowing over the trees, low and heavy, the light in the room now fading, a dim gray shadow. Winter, he thought. The weather has not been too bad yet, but that will change. A good hard storm, a hard freeze, the armies will sit tight for a while. Grant may be content to just hold his lines. But Sherman . . . there is nothing in his way, he can move in any direction. If he moves *north*

Lee reached for the uniform hanging on a hook by the door and began to dress. There was a high moan, the wind swirling through the trees, and he looked out the window again, heard the panes rattle. He felt a chill, buttoned his coat, stared for a moment, saw a swirl of motion, the first wave of snowfall. Then the wind grew quiet, the snow falling softly. He knew Taylor was waiting, that outside, in the road, the wagons and the horses were moving, the clatter and hustle of headquarters. He did not move, waited a moment longer, watched the snow gathering on the window ledge and beyond, blowing softly through the tall limbs of the big trees.

CHRISTMAS 1864

MEN HAD BEEN LEAVING THE LINES EVERY NIGHT, SOME ON their own, one by one, slipping away from their posts on the skirmish line, sometimes a whole section of picket line. At first the blue sharpshooters had been wary, steady fingers on tight triggers, suspicious of the ragged enemy who approached, the same men they had sought out for so long down the barrel of the musket. But there was no treachery, no fight in these rebels who came across the line, who called out in harsh whispers, who waved small pieces of white in the moonlight. They had simply had enough. Soon, the men in blue became used to it, waited for the small sounds every night, and every night more of Lee's army slipped away, crossed over to the warm fires, the promise of a good meal.

Lee rode slowly, pulled his coat tight around him, the cold wind raising a dust cloud that swirled down through the men crouching in the shelters. He could see the faces, looking up at him from below, from the shelter of their dark holes. He saw one man stand, and Lee stopped the horse at the familiar look, the man staring up at him as the men had always looked at him. This man raised one hand in a crooked salute, and Lee could see he was shivering, his thin coat ripped at the shoulder, exposing bare skin to the wind. Lee returned the salute, the old instinct, and he wanted to say something to the man, thought, Stay low, stay warm. But there were no words, he could not speak, he felt his throat pull tightly into a knot. He raised his hand, motioned to the man, a silent gesture, sit, go back into the shelter, and the man's voice rose faintly through the wind, his arms now wrapped around his frail body.

"General Lee, I'm hungry."

Lee could not control it now, felt the icy wetness on his face, looked down into his gloved hands, wanted to say to the man, "Have faith, God will be here for us . . . God will provide." But still there were no words. He looked at the man again, the gaunt face now turning away, and Lee saw him drop down out of sight, into the shelter. Lee turned the horse, blinked hard at the wetness in his eyes, thought, They deserve so much . . . and I have nothing to give them.

He knew of the desertions, the reports came to him every morning. The numbers were growing, and he knew that through the winter the numbers would grow worse. The army was extended in a line that no army had ever held, and there were fewer men to hold that line every day.

He rode back behind the lines, close to the buildings of Petersburg. He was beginning to know many of the people who were still in the town, familiar faces, the strong-willed citizens who would never accept defeat, civilians who still cheered him. He had appealed to them to give to his men what they could, but the supplies were low for them as well, the cellars and pantries as bare as the farmland around Petersburg.

He rode into the streets now, past the destruction from the Federal bombardments, broken windows, shattered walls. But the people still came forward, faces watching him from the places that could still keep them safe, voices rising from the cellars, calling out to him.

He turned a corner, saw a wagon moving toward him, drawn by

one lame horse. The wagon slowed, and Lee saw an old woman, holding tight to the reins, and she said to him, "General Lee . . . it is a fine day, sir! It is the Lord's day!"

Lee raised his hat slightly, made a short bow, thought, Yes, we must not forget that. "Thank you, madam. Bless you. But please, it is not safe . . . the Federals may start shelling the town at any time."

The woman turned a hard eye to the east, said, "No, General, I don't believe so. Not today."

There was sound now, from a side street, and Lee saw another wagon, followed by an old man, walking, carrying a bundle on his shoulder. Now the sounds came from all sides, the people slowly moving toward the main road, wagons and carts, women, old men, children. Some moved by him, and he stared in amazement, looked now at the old woman.

She said, "Excuse me, General Lee. I got to be goin'." She slapped at the old horse, who lurched, hobbled past him, and then he saw into the back of the wagon, round bundles wrapped in cloth, and the smells rose up to him, the wonderful fragrance, warm bread. He watched the wagon move away, and the others were moving by him now, and there were more smells. He felt his stomach growl, reminded of the great Sunday feasts, the bounty of Virginia.

People still called out to him, the streets busy now. He glanced to the east, felt a stab of fear, knew the big guns were watching them, hoped the old woman had been right.

The people understood that if they had little, they at least had something, and so they gathered the small bits and scraps, the last hidden treasures, and loaded their wagons with whatever their kitchens could create. Lee moved the horse aside, watched the wagons and carts creaking and groaning past him, the people on foot smiling as they shifted their loads, nodding and greeting him, saw the faces filled with the spirit of their faith, of their cause.

He saw one man, younger, walking on a stiff leg, missing an arm, and Lee recognized the remnants of an old uniform, knew the man was a veteran, had been one of his own. The man's one hand held a package, cradled it gently, and he bowed, said, "General Lee, 'tis a fine day indeed."

Lee nodded to the man, looked at the strange bundle, saw now it was sitting on a plate. He said, "Sir, what is that?"

The man stopped, held the plate out toward Lee, said, "It's a turkey, sir. Well, it ain't a for-real turkey. My wife, she built it, so to speak. It's sweet potatoes. Don't it look like a turkey, though?"

Lee stared at the oddly shaped mass, then out to the passing carts. He felt a wave of confusion, said, "What are these people doing? Where are they going?"

The man seemed surprised at the question, said, "Why, General, sir, we're a headin' out to see the army. It's Christmas. It's time for dinner."

34. GRANT

CHRISTMAS 1864

THE LOG HUTS WERE FINISHED, AND NOW, WITH THE WIND AND the harsh wet cold settling over the army, the energy of headquarters became deliberate, patient, the business of running the army. There had been snow, then a melt, and the roads in all directions were a boggy mess. There were still those who tried to keep their routine—the sutlers, whose business would suffer from inactivity, and others, merchants or reporters, who would not always pay heed to the advisories from headquarters, ignored the requests for restricted movement on the roadways. The soldiers knew there would be no activity, that under these conditions there was no way to move men and machine. It had been this way from the beginning, and it was accepted by both sides that winter meant a grudging peace, at least for a while. There had been exceptions, of course. The Battle of Fredericksburg was the most notable, two years ago.

Now, Hood had made the same effort in Tennessee, fought against an ice storm that was as effective at stopping his army in its tracks as anything the Federals could have done. But the result hadn't had as much to do with the weather as with Hood himself. With the smashing of Hood's army, and the threat now gone from Tennessee, most of the focus would be in Virginia, and here there would be no movement until spring.

The cabin was tight and efficient, one small room in the rear, the bedroom, some privacy at least. The main room was the office and the sitting room, the tiny space for whatever important guest might require attention. At least the cabin was warm.

Grant sat quietly at the tall desk, a high cabinet divided into small compartments, cubbyholes for all manner of paperwork, orders and requests, official and informal. There were candles in each of the windows, and Julia had found pieces of colored glass so that each candle gave off a different light. He hadn't noticed, of course, and so had to absorb her gentle scolding. Now he saw the small flickers of color, dancing slowly on the dark log walls, her touch, the one bit of her feminine hand in the stark decor of the headquarters. It was, after all, Christmas.

The children stayed below, on the river, a small steamer. Most of the time Julia was with them, but came up to visit her husband when there was time, when the workdays were shorter, the nights free of the tedious detail of command. Tonight she was there, but it was very late, and she'd given up waiting for him, had been asleep for a while.

The door closed carefully, the aide backing out slowly, very aware that Mrs. Grant was sleeping. Grant sat at the desk, took the telegram apart, unfolded the paper, read it slowly, ran his finger over each word. Now he was smiling, beaming, felt suddenly like a small child. He wanted to cheer, to yell out something, to burst out into the cold night and wake up the whole army. The wire was not even addressed to him, had been forwarded from Washington, directly from the President. It was a message from Sherman, received by Lincoln on Christmas eve.

I beg to present you as a Christmas gift, the city of Savannah . . .

Sherman had done it, had cut himself off from his supplies, moved across Georgia all the way to the Atlantic. Grant was still smiling, thought of those people in Washington—Halleck, Stanton—the great outcries, predictions of disaster, how Sherman's plan would end in catastrophe, the suicide of his army, starvation, capture, desertion. Grant had refused to listen to that talk, knew Sherman too well, understood what could be gained, what a success could mean, and now what the success *did* mean.

He thought of Lincoln then, the smile on the rugged face, thought, Yes, this is your doing. If not for you, if you did not give me the authority, if it was up to those people in Washington, it would never have happened. Sherman would be bogged down somewhere around Atlanta, taking small pieces of punishment from Hood's army, and he might as well be in a prison. But now Hood was destroyed, no longer a part of the war, and Sherman's sixty-five thousand men were on the coast, healthy and jubilant, waiting for their next move. Grant stared at the last bit of flame on one of the candles, a small dot of red reflected on the window. You already know, my friend, the next move will be *north*.

The plan had been kept secret, and no one knew just where Sherman would end up, where his army, cut off from communication, would suddenly appear. There had been speculation that he would move south, toward Mobile, or even Jacksonville. Some had believed the march was just a ruse, that he still would turn and go back to Tennessee, to pursue Hood from behind. The papers in Richmond did not believe that Sherman would simply pack up and go, with little concern over Hood's great invasion northward. It was considered pure foolishness that Hood could be allowed a free hand in Tennessee, an extraordinary mistake that would surely result in a major breakthrough for the man from Texas, who everyone knew was determined to make a fight. But it was exactly that determination that gave confidence to Sherman's plan.

Hood was looking for anyone, anywhere, to throw his army against, whatever enemy he could find. Nashville was a ripe target, but Sherman guarded it with the most stubborn defender in the Federal army. Hood's invasion north was exactly what Sherman, and Grant, had hoped for. With Hood out of Georgia, moving straight toward the massed guns of George Thomas's defenses, Sherman had no one to slow him down, no force of rebels large enough to even attract his attention. The small numbers of Georgia militia, men who stayed close to their homes, could only pick and stab at this great blue wave that rolled through their state.

If neither Washington nor Richmond knew exactly where Sherman was going, it was clear that he was forsaking his own lines of supply for what he could take from the land. That was the greatest fear in Washington, that once Sherman was cut off, any delay, any obstacle, could cause him to use up whatever food was in reach. There were short memories in the capital, but not at City Point. Grant had done this before, made the march years ago, Winfield Scott's great trek across Mexico, cut off from everything but the goal in front of him. There was no difference now.

There were newspapers on the small table by the window, and he stood now, would read the one column again, the amazing hostility, the vicious attack on the army. It was not a southern paper, but one from New York. It had always been the voice of opposition to Lincoln, but this time the writing was not endless rhetoric about politics and economics, topics of interest to almost no one; this time the attacks were leveled directly at the army, and directly at William T. Sherman. Grant held the paper up to the light, read the words, focused on the amazing descriptions. The article quoted the governor of Georgia and the representatives in Richmond. They were howling mad, claimed the worst kind of barbarism was sweeping across the state, that what Sherman was doing was little more than raping the land, burning and looting the farms and towns of the innocent. Grant turned slightly, let the lamplight wash over one paragraph, one sentence in particular.

> Wars are the exclusive property of the men who fight, and should never injure the innocent civilian.

He had read that the first time with astonishment, read it now with disgust. He put the paper down. Innocent? he thought. Where is the line? Does the man who works in the munitions factory differ from the man who grows the food? Do they not both support the ability to fight a war? He knew how Sherman saw this, how Sherman had responded to the indignant civilians, the small-town politicians who protested his method of war. His response had opened something in Grant's mind, something Grant had not considered. Sherman had told them: If *you* are not affected, if *you* are not hurt by what we do, then *you* will not do anything to stop it. The war will simply continue. As long as it is just the soldiers, these barbaric men with guns who kill each other, as long as the damage is far away, the destruction and death out of your sight, then no amount of hand-wringing and moral outrage will make it end. If *you* are affected, if your farms, your crops are destroyed, your neat buildings in your perfect towns burned to the ground, then there will be a reason to stop this. War is not tidy, it is not convenient, it is *everywhere*, it has to be felt by *everyone*.

Grant had not thought of that, had always assumed you won the war by winning the battle, your guns against their guns. But now he realized that so much had changed, not just the ground, *where* the war was fought, but *how*. The horror of what was written about, the accounts of the bloody fields, the horrible numbers of casualties, were commonplace now, drifting through headquarters as another piece of the daily routine. The angry reports of Sherman's march were in the southern papers first, as though Sherman himself had somehow changed the war, brought some surprising and outrageous barbarism to this gentlemen's disagreement. Grant thought of his friend, the manic energy, thought, Yes, I have no doubt he has been efficient, completely efficient. But if he is a barbarian, then what about the rest of us?

Above the James River, Longstreet was using land mines now, on the roads east of Richmond, explosive charges that did not distinguish between who was innocent and who deserved to die. Hardee had done the same in defense of Savannah, and when Sherman's army approached, men and horses were maimed in horrific ways by hidden charges they never saw. When the weapons are that anonymous, when we can kill our enemy without ever seeing him, then how do we know who the victim might be? he thought. The guns are so good now, we can drop our shells with such precision, the killing happens with such casual regularity. Was it different when we had to look him in the eye, stare face-to-face, comparing our honor and our courage to his?

Grant had been relieved to hear the wounds had allowed Longstreet to come back. But Pete, he thought, you are my enemy. It was not supposed to ever be like that; this was to be nothing more than a conflict over whether or not you fellows could break away, be left alone, govern yourselves any way you saw fit. It was a fight over an idea, an argument over politics, a duel between gentlemen. How naive . . . Did you believe, truly believe, that there would be no blood, that the innocent would be spared? The politicians thought it would take a month, maybe two. The first troops who volunteered signed up for ninety-day terms.

He thought of Beauregard, another veteran of Mexico, another good soldier in the old army. He commanded the gunners at Fort Sumter. So they shell the fort, show us how serious they are, and expect us to . . . what? Just back away? Just allow it to happen, the country to be divided up, the Union destroyed? It seemed so long ago, a lifetime, another world.

He didn't know how much to believe of the reports, whether or not Sherman had been as vicious as many claimed. But of course, he knew what Phil Sheridan had done to the Shenandoah. If the enemy cannot eat, the enemy cannot fight. Is that any more barbaric than blasting twenty pounds of canister through a line of men? Or dropping a thirty-pound iron ball through the roof of a shelter where men sit, believing they are safe?

He went to the candles, pinched each one, then picked up the lantern, raised the glass, blew the light out. He stared out the window, saw snow now reflected in the faint light of the other cabins. He was surprised, thought, They're still awake, still at work, or, no, maybe just talk, card-playing. He watched the snow, felt the dark silence, thought of her now, sleeping in the small room. He looked toward the door, could see very little, a small reflection. What will this be like . . . when it is over? The boys especially, Fred and Buck, all the attention they get as the sons of the commanding general. It would be nice to be just . . . Father.

He thought of the last time he felt at home, like he belonged in some place, some house that was truly his. He shook his head, thought, Maybe it has never been like that. I have never been very good at anything but . . . *this*. This I know how to do. And it makes very little difference what newspapers say, or how indignant politicians become. We will do whatever we have to do to win this war. This can end, any time. There does not have to be any more barbarism, any more death, any more savagery. And if Lee and Davis don't understand that, then it will go on, and there is nothing they can do to stop us. It has never been clearer than it is right now. They cannot win. It is only a matter of time.

He moved to the door, pushed it open, slowly, a small squeak of hinges. It was very dark, no light at all from the covered window. He could hear her breathing now, soft and slow, and he stared into the dark, thought, She rather likes this, being here, so close to all this. She is very aware of my place, my status. He smiled. Yes, she is spoiled. Her father did that, and now . . . I am no better. I would give her anything . . . and I cannot say no to her. Certainly she knows that. So, how will she adjust? What will we do when there is no war, when I am not in command? Will I be able to make her happy?

He felt his way, sat down on the bed, pulled off his boots, set them quietly on the wood floor. She turned, soft motion, and he tried to see her face, his eyes searching the dark. He felt guilty, thought, No, I'm sorry, I should have been quiet. Now her hand touched his arm, her voice drifting toward him, a quiet whisper, *"Merry Christmas."*

35. GRANT

February 3, 1865

THE CARRIAGE WAS ELEGANT, ACCENTED WITH POLISHED BRASS and deep rich leather, led by the best horses that could be found. They moved through the rebel lines first, out into the bleak open ground, then, slowly winding, made their way through the Federal lines. The passengers were not familiar to the soldiers they passed, the men straining to see, officers with field glasses, men climbing on each other's shoulders for a clear look. They were well dressed, they were civilians, and they did not look to the side, did not wave or answer the shouts of the soldiers. It was a show of dignity, of grave seriousness, a clear indication of the importance of their mission. The word flew, propelled by the sudden burst of hope, and the men began to cheer, to shout and yell and laugh, slapping each other, each regiment, each line of entrenchments passing it along, the contagious joy, the raw sense of relief, of what this one carriage, carrying three nameless men, could mean.

The cheers echoed all down the lines, spread through the dark holes and frozen earthworks, the trenches of both armies. The word spread farther, well beyond sight of the carriage, rippled through the trenches like a flood of cool water. From the James River to well below the deep works around Petersburg men began to stand, to listen to the sounds, to show themselves in the deadly space where no man had dared. But the sharpshooters had laid down the muskets, joined the men behind them, waving hats, blowing bugles, beating drums. On both sides of the line the two armies began to yell at each other, a competition, who could yell the loudest, shout it out with the most passion, their voices swollen with the hope they shared with the very few who knew what the mission was about. Even the officers caught the fever, began to speak of it, spreading the great unstoppable word, and the men believed it even more, made more real by the enthusiasm of their own commanders, the men who *knew* what was happening. More men emerged from the ground, stared at each other, at the enemy across the way, some wondering still if the word was real, if the hope would become truth, if the carriage and the civilians meant *peace*.

Grant didn't know the men, didn't know many politicians at all. But the names were now familiar, and they were important. The group was headed by Alexander Stephens, a former United States congressman from Georgia, and now vice president of the Confederacy. The other men were John Campbell, a former Supreme Court justice, now the Confederate assistant secretary of war, and Robert Hunter, who had been the U.S. Speaker of the House of Representatives and was now president of the Confederate senate.

Grant *did* know why they were coming, waited impatiently as the carriage made its way slowly to City Point. He could hear the cheering following the carriage along the road, while in the camp there was no motion, everyone watching the carriage. For a brief moment the business of the army, of the war, had stopped.

The carriage was led now by a Federal escort, and the horsemen pulled to the side, formed a neat row, most eyes focused on Grant. The carriage stopped, and Grant looked at the driver, a small nervous man with huge eyes that darted about in all directions, absorbing all he saw, a man feeling very much alone in the camp of the enemy.

Grant moved forward, watched the three men climb out of the carriage, one much shorter than the others, the small man moving with difficulty under a thick layer of overcoats and scarves. The face meant nothing, but Grant thought, He's Stephens.

He moved closer as the men adjusted themselves from the ride, and the faces now turned toward him. There were smiles, and Grant was surprised, had expected . . . he was not sure, maybe . . . anger?

Stephens stepped forward, held out a hand, and Grant took it, realized just how small Stephens was, the hand feeling fragile, tiny, in his own. Grant bowed slightly, and the others now came forward, more hands, more smiles.

Grant said, "Welcome, gentlemen . . ." He paused, began to feel it now, could still hear the cheering out on the road, the men still infected by the rumor, by the hope, by the power these men carried, and all that it could mean. Grant looked at Stephens again, the pleasant smile, thought, My God . . . maybe it's true. He stepped back, more formal, made another short bow, said, "Gentlemen, welcome to the headquarters of the United States Army."

THE MEN CARRIED THE OFFICIAL DESIGNATION OF PEACE COM-missioners, and had expected to go all the way to Washington. But Lincoln would not wait for them, came by a fast steamer, and hosted the commissioners on a small ship anchored at the mouth of the James River at Fort Monroe. The meeting lasted four hours, small talk and grave discussion, bits of humor and bursts of anger. The men knew each other well, from years of political wrangling, the busi-ness of Washington, the common ground of political experience. When it was over, the peace commissioners returned by the same route they had come, and Lincoln came to City Point to see Grant.

"IT WAS NOT A WASTE OF TIME. NOT AT ALL." LINCOLN LEANED back in the chair, stared at the ceiling of the dark cabin.

Grant held the cigar in his hand, watched Lincoln, would not ask. He will tell me if I am supposed to know, he thought. Lincoln rocked forward, leaned close to Grant, said, "But I know them . . . I know Stephens. They brought me a piece of paper that came straight from Davis. Stephens wasn't happy about it, but his hands were tied." Lincoln shook his head, leaned back again, slapped his knee with his hand. "They don't seem to understand . . . it amazes me, like speak-ing to a blind hound dog. He knows what he's supposed to do. But turn him loose and he runs in circles. That's it . . . they're running in circles."

Lincoln stood now, ducked under a low beam, moved toward the warmth from the fireplace. Grant still watched him, held the cigar in his mouth, turned it slowly with his fingers.

Lincoln stared at the fire, said, "We talked about it until we beat it to death, and it still came back to one point. They don't see coming back . . . coming together as one country. That's Davis talking, holding out till the end. He still believes they can end this thing and become in-dependent. I could see it in Stephens's eyes. *He* knows better, knows it can't be like that." Lincoln straightened, looked at Grant. "One country. That's the first point, the only place to start. We end the war by reuniting. Everything else comes later. All the discussion, all the terms, come later. But Davis . . ." Lincoln looked at the floor, shook his head. "Davis has his dream, and he can't be moved. As long as Davis is in charge, all the peace commissioners in the world won't make a difference."

He leaned over, put his hands on Grant's desk, looked hard into Grant's eyes, said slowly, a grim, quiet voice: "Mr. Grant, I would have given them a blank sheet of paper, anything they wanted, any terms. All they had to do was come back to one country. Even the slave issue . . . they know there's no hope there, not even Davis believes they can maintain slavery. But . . . it was right there, on the table. It was in their hands . . ." Lincoln straightened again, held his hands together, then slowly spread them apart. ". . . and they let it go. It was . . . sickening."

Grant could see the sadness on Lincoln's face, and Lincoln moved to the chair, sat heavily, slumped down, the thin shoulders sagging. Grant could feel his mood, and Lincoln put his hands on Grant's desk, leaned forward, said, "There is only one solution, Mr. Grant."

Grant nodded, said, "Yes. Always has been."

Lincoln looked at him, shook his head. "No, not always. Reasonable men do not do this. History will not consider what we have done to ourselves as reasonable, or necessary . . . or civilized. I am very afraid that God will judge us harshly. If not all of us, perhaps then only some of us. We have paid a terrible price. This country will never recover from this war, there will always be wounds. And it saddens me, Mr. Grant, it saddens me deeply that this must still be *your* affair."

Grant nodded, stared at Lincoln in silence, at the man's great sadness. Lincoln took a deep breath, shook his head again, and there was a change in the man's face, dark, serious, and he looked hard at Grant now, the soft kindness gone from his voice.

"Mr. Grant, I must ask you . . . forgive me, I must *instruct* you. There will be no more conferences, no more meetings with commissioners. You are not to decide, discuss, or confer upon any political question. That authority rests . . . with me." Lincoln paused, rubbed his tired eyes, let out a long breath. "Your job is regrettably simple. The rebels will agree to our terms when their army is defeated. Defeat their army."

Grant nodded, said nothing, was already far beyond the events of the day. He had felt the enthusiasm, the optimism that the peace commissioners might bring something tangible, justify all the cheers, all the energetic hope of the soldiers. But that was past, and now his mind was already working, the new plan, that when the warm weather came again, the reality was grim and simple. The killing would go on.

On the front lines the joy of the soldiers was swept away now by shock. There would be no peace, the deadly spaces between the lines would remain. The men stared across the open ground, one long look at those men, over there, the men so much like them. Now they began to crawl back into their dark holes and huddle below the frozen earthworks in stunned silence. Gradually, some began to move around, reaching for the muskets, loading with slow precision, then peering up, slowly, carefully, looking for any piece of the man across the way. As it grew darker, the deep rumble shook the ground, and the men did not even notice, the sound too familiar, the low thunder, the big guns launching their terrible fire through the darkness.

36. LEE

H E HAD BEEN SHOCKED BY THE LETTERS, BY THE ANGRY OPIN-
ions spread out across the pages of the newspapers. The calls
had been loud and thoughtless, but they came from desperation and frustration with a war that was slowly destroying their country. Davis had exhausted the patience, and for a long time had been
losing the support of the state governments and the governors themselves, particularly in the deep South. But the surprise for Lee was that
his own name was so prominent, the solution, the simple answer to
what was ailing the country. As the new year had opened, the calls became louder, and Lee began to receive inquiries directly, some quiet,
secretive, as though there should be a subtle plot. Some were open, public, voices of influence, and Lee absorbed it all in stunned silence. Sentiment had grown, and the calls became clear and open. What the South
needed was a military commander, someone with absolute authority to
take charge of the fumbling incompetence of the government.

The horrible tales told by the soldiers, men who simply quit and
went home, began to grow and exaggerate, the stories about the
scarcity of food now became horrible tales, ridiculous rumors, men eating rats, even shocking reports of cannibalism. In the camps, the soldiers laughed through their hunger, shook their heads at the absurdity,
and no one thought the people back home would listen to the foolishness, surely no one would believe these fantasies. But the politicians
had used the horror for their own benefit, and the men who never had
great loyalty to Davis now blamed him for all of it, and the outcry was
tearing the Confederacy into pieces. There was only one man who still
commanded respect, even among the most radical, the most vocal enemies of Davis. Robert E. Lee.

It sickened him. Publicly he had responded with a humble decla-ration that he was not qualified to lead a nation, that for the sake of the Cause, for the country, Davis had to maintain control. But inside him-self, the thoughts would not go away, he could not escape the frustra-tion and the pain of knowing that if Davis was removed, it meant the system had not worked. But worse, he knew what the outcry meant, what the loud voices wanted from him. No one used the word, at least not to him directly, but Lee knew the definition, what the power would mean, and it was a word he hoped to never hear: *dictator*.

He did not look out the window, rocked uncomfortably in the seat, the train moving behind the lines of his men, a thin wall of pro-tection that held Grant's army away, allowing the rail line to stay open between Richmond and Petersburg. The train was crowded, filled with soldiers, men in fine suits, men in rags. He tried not to look at them, knew they were all looking at him, and he had closed his eyes, thought he'd nap, but then he would glance up, see the faces, the curious and the concerned, the shy and the devoted. There was a small group of sol-diers, bearded men who carried the dust of the field, and Lee thought, Where are you supposed to be? But he let it go, there was no guilt in their faces, and they kept turning toward him, brief smiles, nods.

He looked now at the suits, at the fat men in rich wool, thought of the politicians, the Virginia legislature. They had invited him to visit, made a great show of passing a proclamation, a call for fifteen thousand new recruits. The vote was unanimous, and there had been back slapping and the self-congratulation of men proud of the Good Thing they had done. They made a great show of presenting the paper to Lee, but his weariness had betrayed him, and he'd responded not with the gratitude of the good soldier, but a small scolding, saying, "Passing resolutions is kindly meant, but getting the men is another matter." They had looked at him with a patronizing kindness, a clear message that he simply didn't understand the ways of government. It was just as clear that they had no understanding at all of what this war had done to Virginia. Even if you brought me the men, he thought, they have to be fed. Virginia has given this war all she can give.

He glanced out the window, could see very little, the landscape barren and desolate. The train gave a sudden jolt, and voices responded, the shock of the bad track. Lee could see the signs of a fight now, bro-ken wagons, mounds of dirt, thought, Horses, at least they buried the horses. He thought of the place, could not remember the name, knew the tracks had been wrecked, briefly, but the repair had come quickly.

The faces had turned away from him, were focused more outside.

Yes, he thought, look at it, look at this land. See what we have done, what the war has done.

He could see down the aisle now. Most of the people were up on the seats, staring silently at the scenes of war. Now he saw one man, crippled, a crutch resting between his knees. Lee watched him, but a fog began to fill his mind, he was drifting off toward another nap. Now the man began to move, reaching behind him, trying to pull a coat around his shoulders. Lee's mind suddenly cleared and he focused on the man, watched as the man struggled with the coat, and Lee could see the insignia on the coat now, Virginia, the First Brigade. The man could not turn himself around, and now Lee saw that he was missing a hand, the arm missing below the elbow. The man sagged for a moment, seemed to give up, then reached behind him again, felt for the collar of the coat. Lee looked past the man, people crowding the seat across from him, on all sides, the faces all turned away. Suddenly, Lee stood, wanted to shout at them, fought to keep the words inside, "Look, look at this man! Look what he has given up . . . someone help him!" He clenched his fists, moved toward the man, and faces turned, saw him now, saw the soldier.

The soldier's eyes widened, his mouth opened, and he said, "Marse Robert . . ."

Lee reached behind the man's head, pulled the coat over the man's shoulders, then put his hand on the insignia. There was silence now, the only sound the rough noise from the wheels beneath them. Lee said, "Your unit, soldier. Tell them your unit."

The man glanced nervously at the faces suddenly watching him, then at Lee, said, "The Stonewall Brigade . . . sir."

Lee looked around, saw the eyes now staring hard at this soldier, and Lee said, "Yes, I know. God bless you, soldier."

Lee moved toward his seat, still felt the anger, thought, Yes, look at him, see him, see *all* of them.

THE TRAIN BROUGHT HIM CLOSER TO HIS ARMY, THE MEN WHO were starving, and the anger stayed hard inside him, a black burning disgust with the arrogance of all the mindless words. He'd kept it inside, hidden deep in that dark place that men in Richmond would never understand. He could not wait to leave the capital, to be away from all the talk. They are very good at talk, he thought.

When the failure of the peace conference became known, Lee was amazed at the sudden changes, men shifting their loud opinions in mid-sentence. Now they supported Davis again. That had amazed him, the sudden shift not only in the mood of the politicians, but in the papers as well. Davis had been very careful to blame the failure of the conference on Lincoln, making the most of the demand from Washington that the South accept absolute and utter surrender, total defeat, that no principles of the Confederacy would ever be allowed to continue, no sense of identity, no independence at all. Davis had brought his opposition together, maneuvered them into seeing what the peace process meant for all of them. He used skillful tactics, showing how he alone had held tight to the principles that caused the war in the first place.

Lee had seen the changes, watched the papers with amazement as they all gradually came into line, gave up their reckless calls for Davis's removal and suddenly seemed to unite against the true enemy. It was the same spirit that brought Virginia into the war from the beginning, the outrage that a President in Washington would make the rules, that the wishes, the way of life so strongly fought for, was of no consequence in Washington, and would be dismissed completely before the war could end.

Now, when the eyes came back to Lee, it was not with desperation, not to throw Davis out. It was hope, the last true hope, and Lee knew that it was Davis who had engineered it. He'd seen it in Davis's eyes, saw through the grand speeches in the capital. Davis was more sickly and suspicious of everyone than he had ever been, but he was still a political craftsman. The weight, the responsibility, had been shifted from the president's weakening shoulders. It was now up to Lee, up to the army. The politicians were united now, spouting new oratory, eloquent speeches. The newspapers filled with a different fire, now vented their wrath northward, as at the beginning of the war, calling for the utter defeat of the invader. To them it was a simple matter for Lee to carry it forward.

He could not see the crippled soldier now, the people again filling the aisle. There would be no nap, the train was coming into Petersburg. He felt his pocket, touched the folded paper, the official document. He had not even read it completely, all the flowery words, the grand pronouncements. He ran his hand along the edge of the paper, thought, I am supposed to feel a great honor. These people . . . they will read about this in the papers, and they will know why I was here, on this train, and . . . maybe they will find some excitement in that. I suppose that is a good thing.

Lee had been named General-in-Chief, now commanded all the armies throughout the South, had full authority over Beauregard, Joe

Johnston, all the rest. He accepted it with mild protest, but knew his feelings made little difference. It was ultimately for Davis's benefit. It was Davis's compromise, a concession to the loud voices. Though the opposition had united behind the government, behind Davis, the president's power was still at issue. Lee knew it had been difficult for Davis, but it was a fight he could not win, a price for quieting the voices, for securing his office. The compromise called for a piece of the president's treasured authority over the military to be taken away and placed carefully in Lee's hands.

Lee had been polite and gracious, but the title meant very little to him. His war was still right in front of him, the dismal ground around Petersburg, and he knew that as the weather improved, Grant would come after him again.

T HERE WAS NO DIFFERENCE IN THE CAMP, THE STAFF. HE WOULD allow no ceremony, moved quickly and without fanfare away from the train. It was almost desperate, the anxiety growing in his gut, to get back here, to the headquarters, to the familiar.

He had not yet changed his clothes, stood alone in the bedroom of the house, the door closed, felt the blessed quiet washing over him, the jerking motion of the train slowly fading away from his mind. He had spoken to no one, other than a brief word to Taylor. He knew the young man would understand, would keep them all away, at least for now, for a while. The business of the headquarters would wait.

He pulled the scroll of paper from his pocket, held it up in the dull light of the window. He still wouldn't read all the words, the grand formality, the gold seal splashed across the bottom. He shook his head, moved to the foot of the thick bed, rolled the paper into a neat tube, stabbed it down into his trunk.

He stood straight, stretching his back, looked toward the window, saw the wind ripping at the trees, blowing snow now, another gathering storm.

He thought of the newspaper someone had given him, the first mention of his new title. Someone had called for some elaborate—he thought of the horrible word—*coronation*, as though his new position had given him some sort of royalty. They still look for symbols, he thought. I suppose it was always that way. Wars were fought for flags. We still hold tight to that, the men still go after them, the colors of the enemy, as though that is the most important thing. If you take his flag, you take his pride, his honor.

He moved to the side of the bed, sat, looked down, realized that he was still very dusty from the trip, had put a dirty shadow on the white linens. He sagged, let out a long breath, stood up and looked at the dusty impression he'd made. I should not be here, he thought, not in a house. These people . . . so kind. But I should not be in a bed. This is the army, and I am not entitled to any more than what those boys have. He felt the anger coming back, closed his eyes, thought of those men in Richmond. Eat your peanuts and chew your tobacco, pass out titles and pronouncements. But leave the war to the men who understand it.

He glanced down at the trunk, at the rolled-up paper with his name on it, thought of the words "General-in-Chief." Is it too late for that? What does that do for these men? He would not go to the West, or the Carolinas, or anywhere else, no grand tour of his new authority. He would not gather the commanders and issue profound new orders, would not do anything differently than he had before. Beauregard was in Mississippi, commanding a department that was little more than a name on a map. What remained of Hood's battered forces had been assigned to Richard Taylor, who still held control of much of Mississippi and Alabama. Joe Johnston was without a command, and Davis would not even speak his name, the feud now complete and incurable. That is a mistake, Lee thought, it was always a mistake. Johnston might even have held Atlanta, understood what Hood did not, that you must maneuver and outwit a powerful opponent, not throw yourself at him with complete abandon. Now Sherman will have nothing to stop him, will have nowhere else to go but north, and if he reaches Virginia, we are surrounded. Johnston must be used, can still be of great value.

Lee looked at the paper again, felt suddenly awake, thought, I believe . . . I can do that. I have the authority. He smiled, thought of Davis. This will not make you happy, but it is the one thing they have given me. If I am to command this army . . . *all* of this army, then I need Joe Johnston.

He moved quickly now, opened the door, moved out of the bedroom, saw Taylor sitting at the desk in the main room of the house, said, "Colonel, I need to know where General Johnston may be reached. We must send a wire."

Taylor looked at the papers on the desk, thought a moment, said, "Um . . . sir, I don't know where he is. It might be best to ask Richmond."

Lee nodded, said, "Yes, yes, Richmond."

Taylor said, "I can wire the president right away, sir."

Lee looked at Taylor, slowly shook his head. "No . . . not the president. The Secretary of War. Send a wire to Mr. Seddon." His mind began to work, and he thought of Johnston now, was beginning to feel the old energy, that it was possible, that if Sherman could be stopped, hit him while he's strung out on the march, Grant might have to help him, pull troops away from Petersburg. Lee began to move with slow rhythm, his fists slowly clenching, thought of the message, how the wording should go, ran it through his mind, thought, Maybe it's time to play the politician. Johnston . . . no one has the confidence of the people . . . or the army, and I request he be ordered to me . . . for assignment. Yes, good. He moved closer to Taylor's desk, said, "Colonel, if you please, send a message to the Secretary of War. . . ."

MARCH 1865

WHAT WAS LEFT OF THE SCATTERED FORCES IN THE DEEP South were slowly brought together, and even the few troops that followed Beauregard came with their commander to join the odd mix that Johnston would command.

The roads were still thick with the soft mud of an early spring, but Sherman was already in motion, pushing his powerful force northward toward the Carolinas. Johnston understood what Lee needed him to do, would wait for the moment, probe and seek the opportunity, and Lee believed it would happen, that Sherman could be trapped, held in the mire of the swamplands and slowly cut to pieces. Grant would have to respond, could not just allow Sherman to be crushed piecemeal, and that was the opportunity Lee would need. There would be a weakness, somewhere, an opening in the long line around Petersburg. The response would have to be sudden and complete, but the breakthrough could be made. It might not take much, it might not require a total defeat, just a hard shocking blow. Those fellows are on foreign soil, far from home, he thought, and surely, *surely*, they have had enough of this, of missing their wives and children, of the blood and the cold and the loneliness.

He rode the lines again, felt the wind drifting across the muddy fields. The snow was melting, the roads now worse than before, but soon, very soon . . . He saw the faces again, watching him, men peering out from the soggy slop of their muddy shelters, the sickness in their faces, the rags barely hiding the signs of starvation. But still they looked at him, saluted and called out. They know it too, he thought, they feel the change, the spring. We are still here, we are still an army.

It is not up to politicians and conferences. It is right here, it is in these men. He could hear cheers now, echoing down the lines, more men rising up, pointing, and he straightened in the saddle, knew that they felt it, drew it from him; that feeling, he thought, that they are not beaten, that this is not over until *we* end it. He thought of those other fellows, across the bare soggy fields: No, you do not have *this*, you do not feel what these men feel. This is our home, this is our land. And God willing, we will make you *leave*.

37. LEE

MARCH 23, 1865

GRANT HAD NOT YET MOVED, THERE HAD BEEN NO REAL PRESsure against the defenses Lee could mount around Petersburg. There had been some activity down below, the slow and painful lengthening of the line, the Federal troops gradually pushing out to the west. Lee's lines now spread out nearly forty miles, and in many places the soldiers stood better than six feet apart, and no one had any illusion that if Grant knew *that*, if the blue troops across the way understood how thin the lines were, all it would take was one great thrust.

When he rode the lines now, it was more to the south, and he could see the effects of the lack of food, the weakness of the men. They stared at him with dark hollow eyes, and the officers would tell him, quietly, that the work details, the men who must dig the trenches, were simply collapsing.

He moved off the road, saw familiar flags, moved the horse toward the one tent, the small command post, saw faces he recognized now, men he had not seen since Gettysburg. He reined the horse, slowly climbed down, and he saw a man, a sergeant, hurry toward the tent, ducking inside. Lee waited, said nothing, could hear his aide behind him dismount. Around them it was quiet, no one spoke, no salutes, no cheers. Now there was motion from the tent, the sergeant first, and then the commander. It was George Pickett.

"General Lee. Welcome to my headquarters, sir."

There was cold formality in his voice, and Lee returned a salute, said, "General Pickett, I hope you are well."

Pickett nodded, unsmiling, said, "Yes, sir. I am quite well. My division is ready for a fight, sir." There was no change in Pickett's voice, no life in the words.

Lee felt a sudden wave of gloom, felt it pouring down all through him. No matter the rank, no matter the solemnity of the occasion, Pickett had always been the spark, the man who would make the inappropriate comment, draw the laugh from stern faces. He had always been Longstreet's favorite, exuded a bright and carefree gaudiness, in contrast to the serious warrior that was John Bell Hood. Pickett's behavior had always infected his troops; he was the most popular division commander in Lee's army, and spread a childlike charm over his men. But all that was before, and all that had been changed by Gettysburg. There was no humor in the man now, and Lee saw the eyes looking at him, looking *through* him, an empty gaze. Lee felt suddenly very out of place, uncomfortable, unwelcome. He turned to the horse, climbed up, said, "Carry on, General. We may need you before very long."

Pickett seemed to rock back, a small reaction to Lee's words, and he saluted again, said with cold seriousness, "General Lee, my men have always been where you needed them."

Lee said nothing, turned the horse, began to move, thought, He will never be the same. I cannot remove him . . . he has earned the rank, the command. But he will never be a leader. I must remember that, not to use these men in a critical place.

He rode slowly back toward his headquarters, climbed a long hill, the road straight and dusty. He was very depressed now, thought, No, do not let that man affect you this way. He is not the army, he is one man whose heart is gone, who has had the fight taken from him. We still have the spirit. We can still make the good fight.

He knew he was trying to convince himself, but what had happened to Pickett had happened to many others, Dick Ewell, even Anderson. They would not speak of it, would never say anything to Lee, yet it was there, in their faces, in the way they carried out their orders. If the men on the line gave up, drifted away, they were nameless to Lee, a small dark piece of a much larger picture. But when the spirit left the commanders, it was something he could not ignore. If any general lost the will to fight, he had to be removed. You had to treat him as though he carried a deadly disease, a disease that would infect the entire army. Ewell had been sent to Richmond, Anderson was back under Longstreet's control, north of the James.

Now Pickett has lost the will too, he thought. He felt the sadness of that again. No, give him the chance, he has always been good in the field, can still lead troops. We must not be too quick to judge. And we need all of them, every man. He thought now of Hill. He will still be there; even in his sickness, he has the fight. Hill was gone again, the illness flaring up, but his own home was close now, and so Hill would have the soft care of his family. And he will be back, he has always come back.

Lee could not avoid it now, had tried to keep it from his mind, focusing instead on his problems right here, along these lines. But it was *all* his concern now, and he could not keep it away. He could see the mound of paper, the strange and unexpected flood of dispatches and wires from Joe Johnston. The line of communication was wide open, and with Johnston that was a surprise. But there was a great difference now, and Lee knew it immediately. Johnston accepted his new command and Lee's authority over that command without complaint. Johnston's title was Commander of the Army of Tennessee, but Tennessee had little to do with what was happening now.

Lee had underestimated Sherman, his strength, and his ability to move troops. Johnston had done the best he could, had gathered the scattered remnants of whatever units could be brought to the field, Hardee and Harvey Hill's men, even some of Hood's people. But they counted barely twenty thousand troops, with a wide variety of experience and skill, and now the difference in numbers became clear. The port of Wilmington had finally fallen into Federal control, and the Federal forces there had united with the men who had marched across Georgia. Sherman's army was nearly one hundred thousand strong.

Johnston had to seek out, probe cautiously, wait for the opportunity for Sherman's army to be divided along the scattered roadways. The chance had come, and Johnston struck out at one flank of the blue force, a sharp surprising fight at a place called Bentonville. But Sherman was simply too many, and the surprise did not last. Johnston could not bring enough power to the field to sweep Sherman away. Now Johnston had to rely again on the small bites, the quick stabs at this great and unstoppable force as it gradually pushed north, deeper into North Carolina, closer to a rendezvous with Grant.

Lee could see the house now, the yard of the headquarters filled with horses, the distinct gathering of staff officers, men in clean uniforms in an army that barely had uniforms at all. He tried to see the flag, wiped at his eyes, saw the one man who stood out, stiff in the saddle, back straight, and for one brief flash it was Jackson. Lee's heart jumped in his chest, a cold hard thump. Lee had always been able to spot him, the man never slouching, never bent. It made Jackson awkward on the horse, and no one ever considered him to be a good rider. Lee would never laugh, never smile at Jackson's explanation, so serious to him, so comical to everyone else. Jackson would explain with complete precision why he sat so straight, why he never allowed himself to touch the back of even the straightest chair. He always thought it would crush his insides, that his organs would be pressed dangerously together. Jackson had a lifelong ailment, always the pains in his side, but he would not complain, certainly not to Lee. When his duty kept him away from the hot springs and the water spas, his only treatment was to stay straight upright, keep everything safely, comfortably in order, no matter how uncomfortable it made him on a horse.

Lee could see the man more clearly now, the short narrow beard, and he looked down, felt the sadness even more, scolded himself, No, do not do this. This is no time for daydreaming, for behaving like a foolish old man. If Jackson is here, he will show himself at the right time, he will give something to the fight, to these soldiers. But you will not see him at headquarters sitting on a horse.

He looked up again, saw the men watching him, and the one man moving forward, ramrod straight, the crisp salute. It was John Gordon.

THE MAP WAS DRAWN IN INK, A SYMBOL OF THE TIMES, OF JUST how long they had been in place, on this same ground. Little had changed in a very long time, and now Lee stared at the familiar lines, had listened to Gordon's plan, a concise and eloquent presentation. He looked up at Gordon, saw a tight confidence, the man completely self-assured. Lee thought, It used to be there, in all of them. He thought of the day's ride, the gloomy visit with Pickett. Gordon is not a career soldier, has not learned what so many of them have learned, how to make mistakes, how to be defeated. How strange, he thought, this man was never taught to be a commander, and now he may be the only real commander I have left. He doesn't understand that ... not yet. And that may be for the best. This is what we must give the men, this is what we must have, all through this army, if we are to succeed.

"General Gordon, your plan is very detailed. I commend you. If you are correct, and your men succeed, we may drive those people into a panic. It has been the best way, always. You may proceed, General."

Gordon saluted, and Lee nodded, his mind already moving away. Now Gordon's men filed noisily from the house, and Taylor closed the door, moved to the desk, sat, waited quietly. Lee did not look at him, moved to the front window of the house, watched Gordon and his staff mount their horses, move away into the road. Lee stared for a long moment, thought, This may be the best we can do now, it may be the only blow we can make. General Gordon believes he has found a weakness, and we cannot wait, we cannot allow General Grant to make the first move.

The cloud of dust spread out from the road, blew slowly into the few trees across the way, Gordon's men gone now. Lee turned, saw Taylor watching him, always watching him.

Taylor said, "It is a good plan, sir."

Lee nodded, moved slowly from the window, toward the soft silence of his room, said quietly, "Colonel, it is the only plan."

38. GORDON

MARCH 25, 1865

HE HAD NEVER FELT THIS WAY BEFORE. WITH JUBAL EARLY, you came to expect the harsh rudeness, the hostile response at every encounter. He had little chance to deal directly with Dick Ewell; Early had always been there, always in the way. Gordon knew that as long as Early was his division commander, he would rarely know the corps commander at all. But now . . . He thought of Lee: He looked right into my eyes, and it was as though . . . I could feel the weight, the responsibility, and the respect.

He felt a chill, the excitement had been in him all night long. It was still very dark, and he stood high up on a barricade, looked out into blackness, could barely see the outline of the earthworks across the way. It was very close, less than two hundred yards, a fat mound of dirt. He could see nothing else, did not have to, knew the place well, had studied the ground, had scouted as closely as he could, talked to the pickets, the cavalry, put together every piece of information he could about the place. He knew what they all knew, that it was just one more focal point on the long Federal line, was filled with big guns, infantry support spread out in both directions in a line that led to other forts like this one, like fat knots in a long rope. The other ones carried numbers mostly, Battery Ten, Battery Eleven, but this place had a name, a custom for the Yankees, honoring one of the fallen generals, a man killed during the slaughter at the Crater. It was called Fort Stedman.

Behind him the hill fell away, a long slope, and he turned, listened, heard nothing, not even the small sounds of men. Good, he thought. Quiet, there must be quiet. It is the only way this can work.

The field in front of him had been a cornfield, still had a few rows of standing corn, left in haste by a nameless farmer, a man long forced out by the spread of Grant's lengthening lines. The field was cut now by small trenches, quickly dug to conceal the single line of riflemen, the skirmishers of both sides, facing each other only a few yards away. There had been the occasional shooting spree here, but not lately, the men now close enough to speak out, the voices becoming familiar. There were no names, all along the line the men were simply known as Billy or Johnny, the common name for the Yank or the Reb. There was little actual contact, no truces, none of the trading of goods that had gone on before. The rebels had nothing left to trade. The talk now was brief, but there was a kindness to it, small questions, brief answers, home, family. But then someone would make a mistake, violate the unspoken etiquette, and a musket would flash, and if the ball did not find its mark, there might be an angry protest, there might even be humor, the playful warning, and none of them could forget that this was still a war, and when the time came, those boys over there would still put the bayonet into your heart.

Gordon knew that right now the Federal pickets were spread out in the field in front of him, knew that if the alarm went up, even one shot, it could alert their entire picket line, and *that* would alert the fort. If the big guns came alive, the attack would be over before it began.

He had ordered the barricades in front of his own lines to be taken apart, slowly, discreetly removed, allowing his men a clear pathway into the open field. The work was mostly complete, but there were still obstacles, and a few workers were slowly slipping by him, quiet steps, whispered voices, pulling and lifting the timbers and wire aside, clearing the open trails for his men to follow.

Close behind him, the first fifty men waited, armed with nothing more than axes, but they understood their part in this. They were hard strong men, and the axes were sharp, and their only job was to cross the field and cut a quick opening in the piled logs and felled trees that pointed out at them in front of the dirt walls of the fort.

Tight behind the fifty axemen were three hundred infantry, each group of one hundred led by a senior officer. They were veterans, handpicked men who had been hardened by battle, and so would move forward without hesitation when the fire flashed in their faces. Their assignment was basic as well. They would immediately take out the skirmishers, quietly, no shooting, and then, when the axemen had done their job, the three hundred would launch themselves straight into Fort Stedman, and there the shooting could begin. Their first goal was the big guns, not just to quiet them, but to *take* them, hold them so that the next men in line, the great mass of Gordon's infantry, could use them, turn the big guns to the side, aim their charges straight down the lines of the Yankees, in both directions. Once the main body of infantry reached the breakthrough, they could push outward, sweeping the enemy out of their trenches, pushing farther down the lines, capturing more of the batteries, more of the big guns. Those guns could be turned as well, widening the breakthrough, driving a deep wedge through the Federal line, cutting off Grant's left flank entirely, panicking the men in blue into a rout.

The three hundred-man companies had another duty. Once the breakthrough was secure, each hundred men would continue to drive straight back, beyond the rear of the Federal line, each company assaulting a fort, a nest of big guns that Gordon believed supported the main blue line. This could not be done by brute force, but only by deception. The officers understood that they would approach each of the forts, identify themselves as retreating Federal officers ordered back out of Stedman. In the dark it could be all they would need to slip into the forts, to surprise the enemy before any defense could be made.

Gordon had explained it all to Lee, every detail, every piece of this amazing plan. Lee had listened intently, had asked a few questions, and Gordon had a good answer to every one, had left nothing to chance. But now, standing alone in the dark, staring out toward the low mound of Fort Stedman, Gordon did not think on details, on conversation, did not remember anything more than Lee's face, the eyes still in his mind. Gordon had believed that he could design an opportunity to push the Federals back, away from Petersburg, shorten their lines, make Grant pull troops back toward City Point.

But there was more in Lee's eyes, and Gordon still felt that, the weight, that Lee had given him something he did not yet understand, some responsibility he did not expect. He had left the meeting with an uneasy stirring, a nervous twist in his gut, that Lee was putting too much into this plan, the hope, the need for absolute success. Gordon had confidence in the plan, would never had taken it to Lee unless he felt it would work. But he did not realize until he left the headquarters how important the plan was to the army, to Lee himself. The Old Man's image was with him now, the white hair, the grim tired eyes. Lee had not offered any suggestions, had made no changes, had given just the simple instructions to proceed. Gordon carried that away from headquarters with a great deal of pride, that he had the faith of the commanding general. Now he thought of that pride, thought, No, it comes down to more than . . . *me*. Lee believes in these men, in what this army can still do. Now it is up to me to see that this plan is a good one.

He opened a small pocket watch, tried to see the face, knew it was still early. He heard a small sound behind him, saw a brief glimpse of white, the small strip of cloth each man wrapped around his arm, the one piece of identification they would carry into the dark confusion of the enemy.

There was a low whisper, "General Gordon, the men are ready. At your command, sir . . ."

Gordon tried to see past the man, but there was nothing but the hollow darkness, and now he looked back beside the barricade, could see the dim shape of one man, the one soldier he had picked to fire his musket, the only signal to the men behind him to begin the attack. The man was waiting, climbed up on the barricade now, slowly, quietly, knew better than Gordon himself that they were both now in the open, that if there were any light at all, they would be completely visible to the muskets of the enemy only a few yards away.

Down in front, a man was carrying a long piece of timber, one of the last obstructions now removed. The man suddenly stumbled, the timber fell against the barricade, a sharp crack. The man froze, waited, and then there was a cold silence. Gordon stared down at the man, clenched his fists but could say nothing, did not have to say anything. No one had to be told of the value of silence. Gordon looked now into the dark field, felt his heart exploding in his chest, the excitement of the moment now crushed by a sudden fear, *discovery*. For a long moment there was no motion, no sound at all, even the breathing of the men had stopped.

Suddenly there was a man's voice, out in front. "What're you doing over there, Johnny? What's that noise? Answer quick, or I'll shoot."

Gordon felt a stab of ice in his gut, looked at the soldier beside him, and the man took a·deep breath, said aloud, "Never mind, Yank. Lie down and go to sleep. We're just gatherin' a little corn. You know rations are mighty short over here."

Gordon stared into the darkness, felt himself pulling together, his shoulders hunching low, bracing himself for the shot, the one horrible sound that would alert everyone on the field and end the attack.

The voice came back, relaxed, a small chuckle, "All right, Johnny, go ahead and get your corn. I'll not shoot at you while you're drawing your rations."

Gordon stared at the direction of the voice, felt a smile now, the hard knot inside of him loosening, and he wanted to laugh, looked at the man beside him, thought, A card-player, you must be a very good card-player. He leaned close to the man now, whispered, "All right, soldier. It is time. Fire your musket."

He could see the man looking at him, a small hesitation, and the man now raised the musket, pointed it first toward the voice of the enemy, at the spot where that one man had nearly ended the day. Gordon waited, felt his heart surging again, but the man did not fire the musket, raised it up now, pointed at the air, still hesitated. Now the man lowered the gun.

Gordon said, an urgent whisper, "Fire your gun, soldier!"

The man raised the musket again, and again hesitated, lowered the gun, said in a low hushed voice, "Sir, I can't lie to him. I talk to that Yank every night. It's not right, sir."

Gordon stared in amazement, the excitement changing now to fury. He could not see the man's face, thought, This is not the time. He leaned close to the man again, said, "Soldier, fire your gun! *Now!*"

The man hesitated again, then raised the musket, pointed up at the sky, said, aloud, "Hello Yank, wake up! Look out, we're coming!"

The musket exploded through the silence, the flash ripping the darkness. Now the man jumped down, moving out into the field, where the rest of the pickets lay low. Gordon could not see them, but he knew that they were already moving, fast and silent, heard only small grunts and quick shouts, the bayonet and the butt of the musket doing the deadly work. In the openings on either side of him, Gordon could feel the men surge past, a silent wave, moving as one mass, the axes held against the chests, men with one purpose, one job to do. Now he jumped down as well, began to move with them, felt himself carried along by the great surge, closer, felt himself pushed through the corn stalks. It was a short distance, and he could hear the breathing, the excitement in the men around him, close to their target, then suddenly there was the sound of axes, like a wild beating of drums. The wave had slowed, waiting for the obstructions to come down, and now the men could hold their silence no longer, and the sounds began to swell, the darkness filling with the high terrible scream, the men pushing forward, up and over the dirt walls, driven hard now by their own voices, by the sound of the rebel yell.

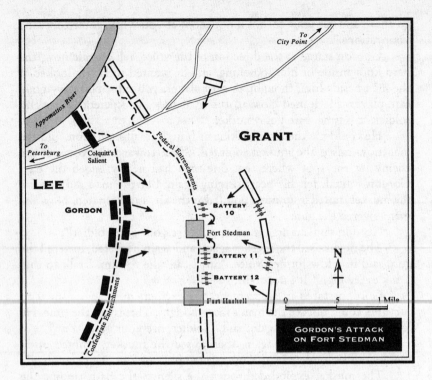

To City Point

Appomattox River

To Petersburg

Colquitt's Salient

Federal Entrenchments

GRANT

LEE

GORDON

Battery 10

Fort Stedman

Battery 11

Battery 12

Fort Haskell

Confederate Entrenchments

N

0   5   1 Mile

GORDON'S ATTACK ON FORT STEDMAN

THE GUNS WERE SHAKING THE GROUND, GORDON'S MEN NOW handling them like their own. He could not see far, but the gray dawn was slowly spreading on the barren ground, and as far as his eyes could focus, the men in blue were gone, a quick retreat away from their trenches, or swept away by the sudden blasts from their own guns. The three handpicked companies had already moved to the rear, were gone from view, and Gordon looked in all directions, felt the pure hot excitement, the hard shouts of his men still close, still filling the fort, spreading out in a widening hole in the strength of the enemy, the new ground that was now their own.

Muskets were firing all along the walls, men seeing their targets now. Some of the infantry support had moved into the fort, held there by their officers, waiting for the order to move out.

Gordon was moving forward, could see the faces of his men, the raw excitement, eyes wide, faces red. Now he saw a mass of blue, some men in white shirts. It was the prisoners, the men dazed, stunned by the sudden assault. They were slowly moving belowground, herded into a "bombproof" by the men who had been so effective at interrupting their sleep. He saw one officer, saw the star on the man's shoulder, moved that way, and the man looked at him, wide-eyed, his dirty face now full of the shock of what had happened to his stronghold, his Fort Stedman.

Gordon said, "My compliments, sir. May I know who you are?"

The man nodded formally, said, "Brigadier General Napoleon Bonaparte McLaughlen. My compliments to your operation, sir. You have humiliated a fine command."

Gordon said nothing, thought, Napoleon Bonaparte . . . ? Well, then, your namesake would not be pleased *this* day.

McLaughlen said, "If you permit, sir, I am your prisoner, and wish to remain with my men."

Gordon motioned to the shelter, said, "By all means, sir. We have work to complete."

McLaughlen disappeared into the mound of dirt and timbers, and now Gordon moved quickly toward the rear of the fort, stared out at the growing daylight, lifted his field glasses, searched for the three forts, for the men who would occupy them. He expected to hear more big guns, the men adding to the firepower that was around him, throwing the deadly charges farther down the lines, farther into the rear. He gripped the glasses, turned, swept the horizon, could see some earthworks, flashes of musket fire, but nothing like he had expected, no distinct earthworks, no clear targets for the thrust of the foot soldiers, no sign of the three forts.

There was a sudden blast behind him, the ground ripping under his feet, and he turned, saw men scattered, bodies torn, timbers and dirt smoking from the impact of the shell. Now more shells came overhead, the high screams from guns far down the line. The ground began to bounce him, more blasts against the dirt walls, then the sharp blow of shot exploding overhead. Now there were screams, men wounded, men with nowhere to go, crouching low, leaning against the dirt walls. He climbed up on the embankment, looked for the three companies through the glasses, for some sign that they had found their own big guns. Where? he thought. Where are you? What is happening?

Suddenly he could see them, men running toward him, dull shadows in the smoke, but he knew they were his men, could see the small scraps of white, the strips of cloth, and he watched them fall, cut down by fire from behind, from both sides. They began to reach the fort, the men saw him now, climbed into the fort, staggered toward him. He jumped down, could hear the whistle and zip of musket balls flying overhead, the slap of lead into the dirt.

One man saluted him, crazily, was breathing heavily, was unarmed. "Sir! We got lost, sir! We couldn't find the fort! There were Yankees all around us! The men are coming back! There's nowhere to go, sir! What do we do?"

Gordon moved past the man, climbed the dirt again, felt the sweat now in his clothes, the fever filling him, a hot sickness. Now he saw more of the men, it was almost fully light. Men were trying to hold a line, firing to the rear, but the Federal fire was coming at them from all directions, and the line dissolved. He looked down the enemy trenches, toward the next massed works, the name flashed in his mind, Fort Haskins, another strong battery, saw the bright flashes, the smoke pouring out in sharp bursts. He knew Haskins should be cleared out, the guns now in the hands of his men, but now he could see his men in line, spread all along this side of Haskins, out in the open. He watched, stared hard, thought, We did not take the big guns . . . they did not get inside. Now those men were falling away, the great clouds of smoke blowing across them, the hot shreds and scraps of metal, the deadly canister, ripping through his troops. He stared, saw glimpses through the smoke, thought, We should be *in* there, those should be *our* guns now.

All along the heavy dirt walls his men were firing outward, in all directions. The big guns still fired, but he looked around, counted, thought, Too few, without the other forts . . . if we did not take the batteries . . . we don't have enough guns.

More men poured up and over the walls, and the musket fire filled the air, his men with more of a target now, the enemy moving closer, the great numbers of Federal troops slowly closing in, tightening down on the breakthrough, the hole in their line. Gordon looked back across the cornfield, saw men moving in one direction, away, the first wave of his troops who would not stand up to the brutal fire. He did not look for more troops. There were no great strong lines of gray ready to cross the field behind him. Everyone had gone in, he'd sent everybody across. Reinforcements . . . he thought of Lee now, of the soft sadness in the old man's eyes. No, there are no reinforcements. From the low ground beyond the cornfield there was silence, no smoke, no great flashes of fire. The rebel artillery was quiet, no batteries had been moved up in support. Gordon stared back toward his own lines, thought, I did not think . . . we would need *our* guns.

More men began to run, escaping back across the open ground, jumping down and across the small trenchworks, across the bodies of the blue pickets. But few made it to the far side. The field was swept completely by the guns of the enemy. Still more men began to pull away from the trenches they had occupied, from out on both sides of the fort. They all knew there was safety beyond the cornfield, and men began to flow out in great numbers now, some dropping their muskets, some moving slowly, stopping to help the wounded. Gordon saw men rushing through the thin rows of corn, saw them suddenly swept away in a bright flash. Now the field began to burn, small fires in the trampled ground, the smoke a spreading blanket, the field alive with the movement of men, the great blasts of dirt and flame.

He felt a man pulling at him, turned, saw a familiar face, the man shouting through the noise. "Sir . . . General Lee orders you to withdraw! Your men cannot hold this position, sir!"

Gordon stared at the man, nodded, looked around again, said, "Yes. Yes, we must withdraw."

The man was gone, swept away in the flow across the field, and Gordon saw an officer, the man watching him, knowing what was coming, and Gordon said, "Find a bugler . . . someone to give the call. We must withdraw. Pull them out! Now!"

The man saluted, was gone into the smoke. Gordon turned, was suddenly on the ground, blown down by a hot rush of wind. He pulled himself up, was on one knee, shook his head, wiped the dirt from his eyes, thought, What could we have done . . . what happened? He tried to stand, felt the ground still shaking, the big guns from all sides closing farther in, driving his men away. He began to move toward the front wall, saw his men climbing out in a mass, and now he saw a man in blue, rising up from the shelter, saw it was McLaughlen, and McLaughlen stared at him, said nothing, just a polite nod, the quiet confidence of a man who understands that his army is just too many, just too strong.

39. GRANT

MARCH 26, 1865

"HOW CLOSE DID THEY COME? I HEARD MENTION THAT they turned the guns toward here." Lincoln was grim, serious, concerned.

Grant shook his head, said, "No, not close. It was probably part of the plan, throw us into confusion. A few shells landed down that way . . . nothing to worry about."

Lincoln walked now, a few long steps, stared out beyond the cabins of the headquarters, then turned, looked at Grant. "Lee cannot hold on much longer. Surely, he cannot."

Grant moved out to where Lincoln stood, glanced to the side, to the small group of reporters, the civilians who always seemed to gather around the camp when the President was there.

Lincoln caught the look, nodded, lowered his head, waited for Grant to come closer, said quietly, "Forgive me. I am still accustomed to everyone knowing my business. It is not my place to inform the rest of the world what the situation is here."

Grant smiled, said nothing, moved close to Lincoln now, pulled at the cigar, felt the smoke roll up around his face, glanced again at the people watching them, said, "No, he cannot hold out much longer. It worries me. I wake up each morning and expect to hear that he's gone."

Lincoln tilted his head, looked at Grant with curiosity. "Gone?"

"In retreat, evacuated the city. Moved his army out to the railroads, the Danville line. If he makes it there, he can move south, join his forces with Johnston. Could cause some problems for Sherman. And worse, could make this war last for a while yet."

Lincoln seemed to droop, said gloomily, "How much longer?"

"Don't know. Long enough. He can move faster than we can,

fewer men, fewer wagons, he's on friendly ground. No, I do not want him to leave. We need him right there. The attack on Stedman may have been a sign that he's about to move, put us back on our heels, throw some confusion into our position so that he can slip away, get a good head start. Can't allow that. And he can't do too much more of that. They lost nearly four thousand men yesterday, half of them captured. No, he has to do something else. General Sheridan will be here very soon. We need the cavalry, I'll send them out west, cut Lee off, cut the escape route." Grant stared out toward the river.

Lincoln looked at him, the energy coming back, the smile. "It is your game, Mr. Grant."

Lincoln turned toward the onlookers, saw familiar faces, waved, called out, began to move away. Grant looked back, watched Lincoln move toward the crowd, did not know the faces, the men and women Lincoln began to greet, the handshakes. Grant thought, They're not here to see *me*. He turned again, looked at the river, now heard quiet steps, saw Rawlins moving toward him.

Rawlins was watching Lincoln, moved up close to Grant, said in a whisper, "He's here a great deal now. Puts this place on a bit of an edge, I must say."

Grant did not look at him, said, "No *edge* here, Colonel. I invited him. I imagine this is something of a relief from what he has to endure in Washington."

Rawlins whispered again, seemed suddenly embarrassed at some indiscretion. "Oh, sir, no, I meant . . . I mean, it's as though he is looking over our shoulder, watching everything we do. I have heard it's like he was with General McClellan, same thing."

Grant looked at him now, held the cigar away, stared at Rawlins for a short moment, suddenly felt annoyed, and Rawlins seemed to wilt. Grant said, "I don't know who you have been speaking to, who has given you such good intelligence. I have very little interest in what the state of affairs was in the headquarters of General McClellan. You may rest at ease, however, about the President's spying on us. He has yet to ask me anything about my plans, my orders, or what we intend to do. And, in fact, Colonel, he is the one man on God's earth who has a right to know."

THEY CAME IN A PROCESSION, SLOWLY, EACH HORSE MOVING IN slow jerking steps, pulling their feet out of the mud one step at a time. The man in front kept his back straight, wiped now at his face, at the mud that had splashed up and over him all day. The rains had turned the roads into small rivers of ooze, and on both sides the men and the wagons went nowhere at all. But the horses could still move, and Phil Sheridan had finally come back to Grant's army.

There had been one more fight with Jubal Early, but it was quick and simple, and except for Early himself, what had once been a fine command was now almost entirely gone, buried in the hills of the Blue Ridge Mountains, or marching slowly northward to the Federal prison camps. With little to slow Sheridan down, the horse soldiers had cut a destructive swath across the railroads, canals, and communication lines that still linked Lee's army to anything west of the mountains. Now the cavalry was moving down across the James River, and Sheridan was full of the confidence of a man who knows the power he commands, who understands his own importance.

The staff watched him cross the open ground, the horse still struggling in the mud. Behind Sheridan, his escort, a dozen troopers, pulled off to the side, were already looking toward the wagons, toward the smells of coffee and bacon.

Sheridan still rode forward, finally drew up close to the cabins, dismounted, raised the hat to the staff, made a low bow. "Gentlemen, the cavalry has arrived. We are at your service!"

Rawlins moved forward, beaming, grabbed Sheridan by both hands, shook them, then slapped the small man on the shoulder, said, "Yes! Yes! A pleasure, General, indeed! The commanding general has been expecting you! Now there will be some action, yes?"

Sheridan looked at Rawlins, a hesitant smile, then let down his guard. "Yes, by God, we will see some action now! I expect to run the enemy into nothing short of complete destruction! We will press him until he can stand no more!"

Rawlins backed away, satisfied that the greeting had been appropriately respectful, and he pointed toward the larger cabin, said, "General Grant will be delighted to hear your intentions, sir! Why don't you join him? He is in his quarters now. I know he wishes to discuss your impending rendezvous with General Sherman. Yes, that will put quite a bite on old Joe Johnston!"

Sheridan looked toward the cabin, frowning, looked at Rawlins, said, "Sherman? He wants me to go to North Carolina?"

Rawlins was still absorbing the light of his small piece of privileged information, the official word, did not notice Sheridan's change of mood. "Why, yes indeed, General. First, you and General Sherman put away Johnston, and then, by God, it's back up here to finish off

Lee! A fine plan, I heard General Grant speaking of it myself! I would suggest, sir, you make yourself known to the general. He's in his quarters now. By all means, you go right in!"

Sheridan seemed stunned, glanced at Rawlins's wide smile, said, "Move south . . . to join Sherman? I do not think . . . I must say, I'm not pleased by that plan."

Rawlins's smile vanished. He saw Sheridan's expression now, and his mouth opened, hung there for a brief moment, then he said, "Oh, um . . . no, why of course, General, North Carolina . . . no, not a good idea, not at all. You must convince General Grant to reconsider. Perhaps . . . perhaps I misunderstood the general. . . . No, you should talk to him, now, right now, by all means!"

Sheridan stared at the ground, then looked at Rawlins, said, "Colonel Rawlins, I believe it is better if the general invites me in. It is not proper for me to simply intrude."

Rawlins seemed perplexed, suddenly seemed to have a stomachache, said, "Yes, I see. We should . . . inform the general you are here, perhaps he will ask for you, if he is not busy . . . or perhaps not. Oh dear . . ." Rawlins was red-faced now, felt crushed under the weight of some disastrous blunder of protocol.

Porter quietly moved up behind him, said, "Colonel Rawlins, if I may . . . General Sheridan, General Grant invites you to his quarters, if it is a convenient time, sir."

Sheridan stepped forward, angry, staring ahead, moved past Rawlins, said, "Yes, it is a convenient time. North Carolina . . ."

Rawlins turned, looked at Porter, puzzled.

Porter smiled, said quietly, "I took care of it, sir."

GRANT HANDED HIM THE WRITTEN ORDER, AND SHERIDAN READ quietly, nodded, read again, absorbed the details of the movement of the army, the great final push to the west. Grant would not wait for Lee to make another assault, would not give him the precious time to escape the widening arc of blue.

Sheridan was now under Grant's direct command, eliminating any conflict with Meade. In the field, Sheridan would command not only the cavalry, but the infantry that would move with him in support, the powerful numbers of the Second and the Fifth Corps. The cavalry would lead the way, moving quickly to the west, then north, surrounding Lee's lines, cutting through the Southside Railroad, then farther up, through the Danville as well. If the plan was carried out with speed, and with good movement of troops, Lee's army would be completely cut off from any supply. If Lee did not quit, he would have to come out from the trenches, come out and make the best fight he could. It was exactly what Grant wanted.

The order did mention North Carolina, that if Sheridan's horsemen completed their work with the railroads, he could move south and link up with Sherman. With Lee in a tightening noose, with the defeat of Lee's army so close, it was not Sheridan's choice to move away from the great spotlight, the final bow to the great theater in Washington.

"SIR! I CAN'T JUST . . . I SUGGEST ANOTHER COURSE!" SHERIDAN was red-faced, and Grant did not interrupt him. "Sir, I believe I can best serve this army in Virginia . . . right here!"

Grant looked out toward the staff, said, "General, walk with me, if you please."

Sheridan was still angry. The discussion had been brief, his protests as restrained as he could keep them. Grant had been patient, had let Sheridan blow off some steam, watched him now with amusement as he tried to hold himself together, to keep himself from crossing that line with his commanding officer. Sheridan's face was tight and dark, and Grant moved away, left him standing alone. Grant stepped across the soft ground, turned, looked back at Sheridan, a silent request to follow. Sheridan took short steps, came up beside Grant, and now they walked together, away from the cabins, away from the ears of the staff.

Grant could hear him breathing, the odd hat crushed low on Sheridan's head. Grant began to put the words together, thought of Lincoln, of the man's perfect ability to explain any situation, the humor and the homey stories that would cut through anyone's angry wall, bring down anyone's self-importance. He glanced at the shorter man, said finally, "Please, General, be at ease. I do not wish you to go to North Carolina. My orders . . . there is very little that goes on paper in this army that does not soon reach the newspapers, the eyes of Washington."

Sheridan looked at Grant with confusion. "Washington?"

"General, do you know what will happen, what will happen to *you*, if we do not succeed? We are so close, but this army has been close before, more than once. It is possible that no matter how good the plan, something will happen. Someone will move too slowly, there will be poor coordination."

Sheridan shook his head, smiled knowingly, said, "No, not this time. We have him! My cavalry alone can turn his lines—"

Grant held up his hand, and Sheridan stopped, the smirking smile slowly fading. "Lee has a way . . . a talent for survival. General, you are the best man I have for this operation. But if something goes wrong, something we cannot anticipate, it is you who will pay the price. Washington has very little patience for failure, not now, not after so long. I cannot afford to lose you to the reckless demands of politicians. The order as written says that I intend you to link up with Sherman. That is for the newspapers. It may also be for General Lee. He seems to find out about my orders as fast as they're written. I do not expect you to fail, and I do not expect that this operation will conclude with anything other than the defeat of Lee's army." He paused, thought of Lincoln again. "But I have learned something . . . I have spent a great deal of time with the President. There is something to be said for giving yourself some . . . room to maneuver. If somehow Lee slips away, if your people don't succeed, then we can say, 'Well, it wasn't the plan in the first place.' "

Sheridan looked at Grant with a baffled expression, said, "I don't understand, sir. You are ordering me to go to North Carolina, but . . . not really?"

Grant smiled, lit a fresh cigar. "That's about it, General. Welcome to the world of politics."

MARCH 27, 1865

IT WAS SHERMAN'S IDEA TO TAKE A SMALL STEAMER NORTHWARD, the journey now much shorter than it had ever been. Grant had waited for word of the arrival, finally received a wire from Fort Monroe. The boat had entered the James River and would be at City Point very soon.

He stayed away from the staff, made it very clear that he wished to be alone. They had thought it was because of the seriousness of the meeting, the hard talk of strategy, but Grant had another reason. From the first moment he received Sherman's request, from the time he'd known the tall red-haired commander was on his way, he felt the thrill, felt like an excited child, and it was embarrassing. It had been a year since he had actually spoken to Sherman, the last strategy session in

Cincinnati before Grant came east to take command. It was a year that had changed both men, had made both of them heroes, and, to some, the most horrific villains of all time.

He had been pacing along the waterfront, watched the boat move slowly up the river, and he'd stared at it, a black stare, willing it on, ordering it to push against the current faster. Finally the ropes were thrown out, the crews on the wharf securing the boat tight to the moorings. Grant waited, still paced, small nervous steps, glanced behind him, saw officers, one of them Porter, was suddenly annoyed, thought, I was specific, no greeting party. But Porter was looking toward the boat, smiling, then began to wave, and Grant turned, saw the tall lean figure jump down from the boat, a loud thump of boots on the dock. Before Grant could say anything, Sherman was in front of him, suddenly straightened, saluted with a toothy grin, a small hesitation, the protocol of rank, and Grant laughed now, held out a hand, said, "How do you do, Sherman?"

Sherman was a tall nervous string of energy, every part of him moving in some way. He smiled, said, "How are you, Grant?"

Then both men laughed, and Grant was suddenly overcome, stepped forward and grabbed Sherman by the shoulders, forgot now about the staff, watching from a discreet distance, said, "My God, Sherman, you have done a job! I never had a doubt. . . ."

Sherman put a long finger on Grant's shoulder straps, touched the center of the three stars, said, "Well, my my. Never saw those before. Hard to crowd all those stars on one shoulder. From what I see, those shoulders are holding that weight up pretty well."

Grant was still smiling, said, "It is very different here, these are good men. We've made a good fight . . . mistakes, some things we could have done better. But . . . well, come on, let's don't discuss this war now. That comes later. There's a darling woman up at headquarters who is waiting with some considerable patience to see you!" Grant turned, pulled Sherman by the arm.

Now Porter stepped forward, saluted, said, "General Sherman, welcome to City Point. It is a pleasure to see you again, sir!"

Sherman reached out a hand, grabbed Porter hard by the shoulder, shook him playfully. Porter tried to keep his composure, but the smiles were contagious, and Porter loosened.

Sherman said, "Colonel Porter, if I were you, I'd ask for some leave time. Hell, just hauling cigars for this man is duty enough!"

Sherman laughed now, and Grant felt his face turn red, could not help it, saw Porter share Sherman's good spirits, laughing now as well, throwing a quick self-conscious glance at him. Sherman began to climb the hill, looked out in all directions, turned, stared for a brief moment across the wide river, said, "My God, Grant, you have picked a spot! Hell, I could take a vacation in a place like this!" He cocked an eyebrow at Grant, then pulled Porter up the hill by the shoulder, said, "Colonel, you have to tell me the truth. Now that he's the big man, has he gotten soft? I mean, look at this place . . ."

Grant waited, watched them move up toward the camp, saw Porter turn, still self-conscious, glance back at him, but Sherman was in joyous control, pulled Porter along, the others now moving with him, and Grant began to follow, laughed himself, shook his head, thought, There is no one like him, no one at all.

T HEY HAD COME FROM THE RIVER, DINNER WITH LINCOLN aboard his small boat, and the meeting was cordial and serious. Sherman had told his tales already, captured the attention of the staff and the lucky onlookers, a great show around the campfire, glorious stories about his campaign. But with the President, Sherman was more serious, responding to a strange gloom from Lincoln. There was none of Sherman's boundless energy, the endless chatter from the mind that never slowed down. Lincoln seemed removed, spoke only of the end of the war, the slow and difficult healing process, what it would mean for the country, was already thinking far ahead.

They passed by the quarters of the staff, most in bed by now. Reaching the larger cabin, Sherman jumped out in front, pulled the door open for Julia, made another long low bow, had been doing it all evening. Julia glanced at Grant, shook her head, smiled, moved into the cabin. Now Sherman stood straight at attention, said simply, "Sir!" and Grant nodded, a quick smile at Sherman's mock show of formality, and followed Julia into a warm glow. Grant glanced at the well-stocked fireplace, a fire that had not been burning for long. Grant smiled, thought, Porter never forgets a detail.

They sat, a small table covered with maps, and Sherman was suddenly serious, leaned over, pushed one map to the side, studied it for a moment. Julia sat across from him, Grant to one side, and Sherman pointed at something on the map, then suddenly covered the map with his broad hand, looked at Julia with grave suspicion, leaned close to Grant, said, "What do you think, Grant? Can we trust this one? Might not do for the papers to find out a *woman* helped plan our strategy."

Grant smiled, knew that Julia understood the game, said, "Well, you know, Sherman, all the official documents I've ever seen always begin 'Know ye by all men present . . .' Now, in this case, I would suspect it might be better said, 'Know ye by this *one* woman,' because then all men would be certain to hear of it."

Julia huffed, said playfully, "Well, then, gentlemen, would you prefer I not be a party to all your secret planning?"

Sherman rubbed his chin, squinted his eyes, said, "Tell you what, Grant. Let's test her. See what she knows." He leaned forward, the tough interrogator, said, "Tell me, Mrs. Grant, do you know the enemy's present whereabouts?"

Julia fluttered her eyes, put her hand over her mouth, feigning the voice of the belle. "Oh my, certainly, the enemy is in . . . the *South*."

Sherman nodded, said to Grant, "All right, she can stay."

Grant laughed now, pulled out a cigar, winked at Julia, said, "You know, Sherman, I've always said that women should be entitled to vote, in fact, they should have *two* votes, and the men should stay home. That way, there would never be an argument, and no one would ever vote the wrong way."

Julia laughed, said, "And a fine plan it is." Then she stood, said, "Gentlemen, I will leave you to your manly conversation."

The men stood, and she smiled at both, gathered in her dress carefully, moved past the table, disappeared into the back room, eased the door closed.

Sherman said quietly, "My God, Grant. You are a lucky man."

Grant looked at the table, began to move the maps, said, "She is . . . the brightest star in the heavens." He held the cigar out, stared past it. "She knows what's happening. She knows it's time for me to leave. I will be moving with the army, with Sheridan's advance. It's time to go."

Sherman knew the tone was serious now, said, "Lincoln? He's going back to Washington?"

Grant looked up, said, "No, actually, he wants to stay here. He understands that we are very close, that it could happen any time. He wants to be near it all. Can't blame him."

"No. He should be here. He's earned it."

Grant was surprised, said, "Never knew you to be a fan of Lincoln's."

"No, I wasn't. Thought him a bit of a bumpkin, actually. I didn't think he understood what was about to happen, just what a war would mean to this country. He was always spinning yarns, making everything into some kind of joke. But he's changed. I saw it tonight, at dinner. He's a thinker, sees way ahead ... understands things most of those people in Washington never will. That's a great relief."

Grant nodded, felt the cigar smoke drift up between them, said, "He's no bumpkin. He has endured. We have it easy in some ways, you and me. We control our own situation, we have the power. That's what the military is all about, absolute discipline. Washington ... no such thing as discipline, as command. The government ... *our* government can't work that way. And you're right, he's already thinking ahead, already knows what we have to do after the fighting stops. There's a lot of revenge-minded people around Lincoln, a lot of pressure on him to make them *pay*, punish anyone who called himself a rebel. He knows that won't work. We're still one country. Our job is pretty clear, take the fight out of them. His job ... a lot tougher, the whole business of *forgiveness*. He has to take us forward, heal the wounds."

Sherman stood, moved in nervous motion, stalked slowly around the small room like a cat.

Grant smiled, held the cigar tightly in his mouth, said, "Sit down, General. Let me show you how we're going to end this war."

40. CHAMBERLAIN

MARCH 29, 1865

THE WOUND HAD NOT HEALED, HAD TAKEN HIM FROM THE ARMY again, through most of the winter. There had been operations, difficult days and sleepless nights, but he would not stay there, would not accept the comfort of the hospital. He'd come back finally in February, the hip still tender. But Griffin welcomed him with a wide smile, grateful to have him, and did not hesitate to put him back on his horse, again in command of the First Brigade, First Division, Warren's Fifth Corps.

With the coming of warmer weather had come the healing, and Chamberlain would not aggravate the injury by riding into battle. He could feel it every day, the strength, testing himself on the big horse, the beautiful Charlemagne, grand and majestic.

THEY MARCHED AT FIRST LIGHT, THE ROADS HARDENED NOW BY a blessed break in the rain. He kept in front, stared hard into the woods and low hills, the small stretches of dark swamp. In places, the road had been corduroyed, paved with small trees, forming a miserable carpet, an uneven platform that slowed the horses and men, stepping carefully to avoid breaking an ankle.

They had marched most of the morning now, and the sun was pushing at them from behind. He shifted his weight, tried to find a comfortable place, a part of him that had not yet taken a pounding from the hard saddle.

He could see the ground rising slightly ahead, and the ragged roadbed was smooth again. The horse stepped onto the smooth surface, moving now in the slow, gentle rhythm, and Chamberlain relaxed in the saddle, let out a breath. He could feel the pressure from behind, the men moving well. There had been no straggling, the strong pace of the march picking up even more on the good road, the packed dirt still damp enough so the dust did not yet rise behind him.

The Fifth Corps had broken camp early that morning, the orders to Chamberlain coming directly from Griffin. The word spread quickly to the men—this was not another of those exercises, some mindless drill, some poorly planned scouting expedition. Chamberlain did not have to prod them into motion. There was no grumbling about leaving the misery of the trenches. The deep earthworks had been home through the cold of the winter, but with warmer weather, long days of rain, the holes became pits of mud and misery, and when the order came to strike the camp, to load the supplies, the work had been done with a hum of enthusiasm. There was no sentiment for the camps, for the dismal place they would leave behind.

The orders were to follow the lead of Sheridan's cavalry, move out to the west, well beyond the distant spires of Petersburg. The Second Corps would follow the Fifth, and the word had spread, as it always did, the instinct of the veteran, that this move was something new, a powerful advance by a powerful army, commanded by a fiery little man who would lead them straight into a fight.

The flag bearer rode beside him quietly, a small thin man, clean-shaven, boyish. Chamberlain could not remember his name. He was a sergeant, and Chamberlain wondered about that, if the enlisted men really thought of the rank as a privilege, the promotion as something to be valued. He'd known too many sergeants, had watched too many of them die, and so something in his mind kept him away from this new man, hid the man's name in some safe place. He tried not to think on that, told himself, No, there is no plan here, the man with the flag is not necessarily doomed. He glanced to the side now, and the man looked at him with an excited smile. Chamberlain looked away, thought, He is new, has not ridden up here, at the front of the column. He still thinks it's some kind of honor. I hope he's right.

The low rise began to flatten out, and he could see thick trees on both sides of the road, the sound of a small creek. The blessed smoothness now ended, giving way to more logs, and he sat up straight, lifted himself slightly off the saddle. Out to the side he saw skirmishers falling back toward the front of the column, men pressing and forcing their way through vines and deep mud. Now men came into the road in front of him, emerging in dirty blue from the thick woods.

There was another sergeant, a dark man caked with wet mud up to his waist, and he saluted Chamberlain, said, "Sir, we're moving out into the road. The men can't push through this stuff. If you wish, sir, give us a minute, and we'll move out in front a bit further."

Chamberlain said, "Fine, Sergeant. We'll hold the column for a minute. Have your men advance. Any sign of a . . . problem?"

"Oh, no, sir. Nothing. The rebs are up thataway, for sure, to the north. Nobody down in this infernal place. This is Arthur's Swamp. We scouted it out once before. Mosquitoes as big as birds. Even the rebs stay clear. We'll move up a ways, dry ground up ahead, then spread into line again, with your permission, sir."

Chamberlain was impressed, said, "By all means, Sergeant. Proceed."

The man saluted, and now more of the skirmishers flooded into the road, moved quickly ahead, some stumbling on the roadbed. Chamberlain turned, motioned to the bugler, and the man gave a short blast on the horn, the call to halt. Chamberlain watched the skirmishers move farther away, well in front of the main column, the men who would be the first to see the enemy. He thought of their sergeant, thought, It's easy to forget that, sometimes. We are a very good army, men who have done this before, who know how to do their job, and maybe the most important of all, who know what's up there, in front of them.

Behind him there were small voices, men used to waiting. He watched the skirmishers disappear, moving off the road again, saw the sergeant look back, raise his arm, a quiet signal. Chamberlain looked at the bugler again, nodded, waved his arm forward, and there was another blast from the horn, the men beginning to move.

The horse stepped carefully, but the saddle bounced in one hard jolt, punched him from below, a shock of pain piercing up through him. He was not often bothered by the wound, But no, he thought, it won't let me forget. He tried to hold himself aloft again, a small cushion of space between him and the saddle.

Beside him the flag-bearing sergeant said, "I wonder who Arthur is?"

Chamberlain saw the man gazing into the dense woods, and he flinched from another stab of pain, said, "What?"

The man looked at him, almost apologetic, said, "I meant, sir, he said it was called Arthur's Swamp. I wonder why."

Chamberlain stared at the man, said nothing, the man turning away, not expecting an answer. Chamberlain looked into the woods, thought, A good question. Why would someone want a swamp named after him? Maybe Arthur owned the place. He pondered the possibilities. Maybe someone named Arthur came to some interesting end in this place, a piece of local folklore. He glanced at the man, began to feel a small irritation. *Now I will have to find out. Can't let a question like that just pass unanswered.* He could see the road ahead smoothing out again, prodded the horse slightly, a silent command, *Move forward, please.* He glanced at the young man, the flag slapped by a small breeze. Chamberlain said, "What's your name again, Sergeant?"

The man looked at him, said, "Arthur, sir."

I T WAS THE FIRST CLOUD OF DUST HE'D SEEN, THE ROADS UP AHEAD drying out under a high warm sun. The horses moved quickly, came straight toward him, and now he saw the flags, pulled his horse to the side, out of the road, waited, then saluted. It was Griffin.

The horses reined up, and Griffin was sweating, said, "All right, General. We have a job for you. There's a road around this curve, goes up to the right, called the Quaker Road. Take your brigade up that way, keep a sharp lookout. The enemy's flank is north of this position, and we need to know what he's up to. Keep moving north until you find him. You'll come to a creek . . . wait." Griffin pulled out a map.

A man behind him said, "It's Gravelly Run, sir."

Griffin looked at the map, said, "Yes, Gravelly Run. Take good care, General. Keep your pickets close in."

Chamberlain felt his heart thump, looked at the map as though there were some answer there, something Griffin had not told him. He nodded, said, "What do we do if we . . . find them, sir?"

Griffin smiled, pointed at the column moving past them now, said, "How many men reported for duty in your command this morning?"

Chamberlain knew what was coming, felt suddenly ridiculous for asking the question. "Seventeen hundred, sir. Just under."

"Well then, General, you can have yourself one very large dance party. Or you can drive the rebels back as far as they'll agree to go. But advise me first. Lee is likely shifting his weight, knows we're down here. You may run into half the rebel army, and even *your* seventeen hundred men might not be enough. The rest of the division will move up behind and cover your flanks. Keep me informed."

Griffin was not smiling now, and Chamberlain saluted, said, "Yes, sir. We will make contact, and keep you advised, sir."

There was a roll of low sound now, dull thunder off to the west. Chamberlain looked past Griffin, and all heads turned that way.

Griffin said, "Sheridan. The cavalry." He glanced at the map again. "Sounds like he's . . . maybe up here, above Dinwiddie Courthouse." He looked at Chamberlain. "Let's find the enemy, General! We need to know what's up that road."

Griffin spurred the horse, the staff moving away in a thunder of hoofbeats. The troops still marching in the road were watching him. Some had heard Griffin's words.

One man said, "Where they at, General? We close to the rebs?"

He spurred the horse alongside the column, glanced at the voice, all the faces now focused hard on him. He said aloud, "Eyes to the front, gentlemen. It seems . . . we're going to make a fight."

THEY HAD APPROACHED GRAVELLY RUN IN A WIDE LINE, AND there was already a scattering of musket fire from the other side, a rebel skirmish line along the creek itself, men hidden by thick brush, some firing from the thickets of small trees that lined the creek bed. He was still in the road, raised his field glasses, looked up beyond the water, thought, If their pickets are on the creek, the rest of them have to be close behind. He could hear the musket balls zipping past him, felt himself ducking, still stared hard through the glasses, laughed, thought now of Kilrain, something the Irishman always said: *You won't hear the one that gets you.* He lowered the glasses, could see the small flashes of fire, thought, No, not the best place for me to be. Pulling the horse around, he moved back to Arthur, the man with the colors, and the rest of his staff.

Down the line he saw his own skirmishers easing forward, low to the ground, protected by anything they could find. Now the firing went both ways, and he thought, Good, yes, push them back, give us some room. He rode to a small rise, wondered if they should cross the creek. Raising the glasses again, he watched for the thin line of the enemy to pull away, giving up the ground in the face of his great strength. He looked up beyond the creek again, saw a reflection, the flickering motion of bayonets, then a man on a horse. Now he could see fresh fallen trees, logs, dirt, a wide solid line. He scanned along the far side of the creek, down to the right, and saw more men, flags and the reflection of many bayonets. He felt his heart shoot into his throat, thought, This is more than a skirmish line. Yes, we have found the enemy . . . we have found a *lot* of the enemy.

He lowered the glasses, and there was a hush of silence all down the line, the troops dressing the formation, men lining up close to the men beside them.

He could hear horses, turned and saw Griffin, moving quickly. Chamberlain saluted, waited for Griffin to rein up the horse, then pointed out across the creek, said, "General Griffin, as you requested, sir . . . the enemy."

Now there were small shouts along his lines, his men reacting to the small pops of musket fire, the single shots coming from the rebel pickets along the creek. His staff began to gather close to him, the couriers waiting, the horses moving in small jerking motions.

Griffin stared through his field glasses, then smiled at Chamberlain, said, "Well, General, it seems they don't want us to cross this creek. You know what that means?"

Chamberlain absorbed the question, could still hear the sounds of Sheridan's fight off to the west. He looked toward the enemy line, then toward the scattered musket fire of the pickets. "Yes, sir. It means we should cross that creek."

T HE BRIGADE WAS SPREAD INTO LINE ON BOTH SIDES OF THE road. Reaching the creek, wide and muddy, the men began to splash across. The left flank moved first, and Chamberlain rode close behind, could hear the great roar of muskets from the right flank, the volleys aimed across the road, a covering fire for the left flank to cross the creek. Behind the low works, the rebels were returning fire, thick smoke pouring down toward the creek in great waves. He pushed the horse through the water, then up out of the creek, moved through small patches of thick brush, could smell the choking sulfur of the smoke, tried to see in front of him, steadied the horse. His men were moving forward, beyond the creek, now reaching the rebel works. He pushed the horse forward, saw the blue wave streaming over the low wall, and beyond, saw the rebels pulling quickly away.

He broke into a clearing, a straight path toward the open field beyond, could see down the line now, his men still pressing forward, the lines wavering but strong. The rebels were stopping to fire, and he could see men falling, could hear the screams now, saw one man drop close to him, clutching his throat, rolling slowly in the grass. Chamberlain stared at the man for a brief moment, saw another man break out of line, move toward him and kneel down. Then the man's sergeant grabbed him by the shoulder, yelled something profane, pulled

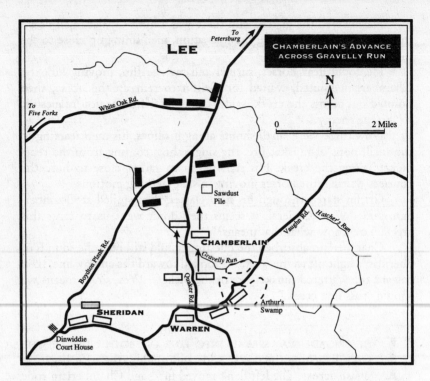

LEE

To Petersburg

CHAMBERLAIN'S ADVANCE
ACROSS GRAVELLY RUN

N

To
Five Forks

White Oak Rd.

0   1   2 Miles

Sawdust
Pile

Vaughn Rd.

Hatcher's Run

CHAMBERLAIN

Boydton Plank Rd.

Gravelly Run

Quaker Rd.

Arthur's
Swamp

SHERIDAN

WARREN

Dinwiddie
Court House

the man back into line. Another job for the sergeants, Chamberlain thought.

He moved the horse, rode to the left, a gap in the log wall, jumped over the shallow trench, could see more horsemen now, the regimental commanders, swords up, pointing forward. His men were still in motion, the rebels in chaotic retreat, no formation, pulling away on their own. The smoke was clearing, a breeze behind him pushing the white fog out before the blue wave, and he reined the horse and just watched, could hear the sounds of his men, the low cheer of soldiers who know they are winning.

Smoke now filled the patches of woods in front of them, each volley sending a blinding cloud toward the enemy. A break, a piece of luck, he thought, the wind is behind us.

He scanned the open ground, could see the wounded, the dead of both sides, some moving slowly, some not moving at all. Suddenly the name came to him, Griffin's orders . . . the *Quaker Road*. He shook his head, thought, No Quakers here on this day. They would definitely not approve.

Out of the thick fog he saw a cluster of men emerging, a slow march across the field, enemy troops moving straight toward him. Chamberlain's heart pounded and he pulled at his pistol, but then saw his own men, the muskets raised, saw that the ragged soldiers were not armed, were being herded to the rear, back toward the creek. They were prisoners. He laughed nervously, thought, Lawrence, have a little faith. As they moved by him, his own men saluted wildly, great toothy smiles. Chamberlain looked at the prisoners, saw bare feet, gaunt faces. They did not look up at him as they moved slowly by, and he thought, They do not look like soldiers, like an army. His own men were shouting out, the pride of the capture, but Chamberlain did not hear them, continued to stare at the prisoners, recalled the great long march toward Antietam, when he'd seen prisoners for the first time. They were ragged then too, torn clothes, the uniforms barely evident. But you could still see the spirit. They had marched past him then with a defiance that said, "We are your enemy, and we will *still* fight you." Now the faces stared at the ground, silent, and he thought, These men look like . . . ghosts.

The fight was moving away from him, his men still pushing forward. He spurred the horse, moved past a line of small trees, saw a wide field, farmland, could see a house now, small white buildings. He moved forward, saw a huge sawdust pile, an old sawmill. His men were in line, kneeling, firing into the thick smoke, rebels holding a line around the sawdust.

He thought, Move forward, get closer, and recalled something Griffin had said long ago, quoting the instructions, laughing, something from some military manual. *The brigade commander shall remain one hundred fifty yards behind the line.*

He could hear the musket balls of the enemy whizzing past him, high, wild shots, men blinded by the smoke, by the pressure, the strong advance of the blue line. He saw officers riding toward him, watching him, and he knew the look, men waiting for the command, making sure. He looked toward the sawdust pile, saw the enemy pulling away, yelled, "Forward! Keep pushing them!" The horsemen moved away, and Chamberlain looked behind him again, then far off to the right, thought, Yes, maybe . . . more strength, coming up on our flank. But he could only see his own men, far down the open field, the line thinning, the men slowing, holding their position.

He looked past the sawdust pile, and then the wind began to shift, the smoke flowing away, across the field. The rebels were still moving away, but he could see woods now, and along the edge, men climbing up and over a wide wall, a thick mass of logs and dirt. Suddenly, the wall erupted in a solid blast of flame, dense smoke pouring forward, and the air around him was alive with the horrible sounds, the piercing whine of the hail of lead. His men were falling all down the line now, there was no cover, no safe place, and the line began to fall apart, men slowly moving back.

The officers were screaming orders, "Hold the line," "Stay together," but the men saw what was in front of them now, what lay beyond the open field. Chamberlain saw the faces of his men, some beginning to run, close to him now, not looking at him, and he pulled out his sword, waved it over his head, felt the hot anger, yelled at one man, a sergeant, "Stop! Pull them together!"

The man looked up at him, and Chamberlain wanted to yell at him again, red rage, but he knew the face, said only, "You . . ."

It was the man in the swamp, the man in charge of the pickets. He looked up at Chamberlain, and Chamberlain saw his face change, the wild panic erased now by an angry black light. The man said nothing, but turned, grabbed a man who was running by him, pulled the man around hard and shouted into his face. Now others began to stop, to fall together, forming a new line, close to Chamberlain, some looking at him. He yelled to them, not words, some sound, thought, *Hold them*, keep them *here*, but his voice faded into hoarseness.

The men were bringing themselves into order, the line strengthening. The officers began to gather, and Chamberlain waved the sword, the silent signal. The officers moved out, still pulling the line together. Some men began to fire back toward the heavy rebel line, and Chamberlain thought, No, wait . . . too far. He could hear the officers shouting the orders to hold fire, and the firing stopped, the sounds now only the voices of the men, the brigade finding itself again, the flags spreading out, men moving to their place in line.

He watched, felt the sudden burst, the energy of pride, *Yes*, you will not brush us away! Now, from the rebel works, there was a new sound, and he stared, had heard it before, that awful scream, and men began to pour over the top of the works, the furious scream rolling forward, the line of rebels coming at them. Chamberlain felt his heart thump in hard cold beats, yelled weakly, "Hold on!"

But the blue line began to roll backward, some men breaking out, running toward the rear, wild eyes, driven hard by the panic, chased by the sounds. Some still held their position, and the orders were shouted, and Chamberlain saw his line explode into one long fire, a massive volley, a sharp blast into the rush of rebels. The rebel yell began to fade, and Chamberlain's men fired again, all along the wavering line. Now the smoke drifted away again and he could see the rebels backing away, withdrawing to their heavy defenses. He yelled, a hoarse sound, a cheer, and his men looked at him, began to understand that they had held, had beaten back the assault.

Chamberlain looked in the direction of the creek, the wide, empty ground, began to feel the heat, the raw fury, thought, We cannot hold here all day. *Where are you?*

He rode a short way toward the creek, the field scattered with his men, many wounded, some men bending low over still bodies. He glanced at the rebel line, saw men moving out in a low crouch, moving toward their own wounded, dragging men back to the works. He took a deep breath, and for one moment there was silence, a complete calm, the smoke gone, and he looked out over the open ground, could see fresh dirt, furrows in the ground. Of course, he thought, it is planting time, but that will have to wait for now. He glanced at the scattered bodies, the dead. If we bury them here, he thought, what then? Is this still a farm? Will you go on as if nothing had happened? He looked at the farmhouse, was suddenly curious, wondered about the people, thought, Probably a woman, maybe children. There would be no man, no able-bodied farmer. He would be gone, maybe dead himself, or maybe . . . right over there, behind those works. Maybe he's fighting on his own property. How odd, you could never have expected this, what must it feel like? Does it make you a better soldier?

No, stop this, he thought, trying to clear his mind. Your brain again, you still think too much. He looked down the line of blue, saw men still falling in, the quiet, the lull, now drawing them up from behind. He looked back toward Gravelly Run, thought, There are still men there, there always are some, hiding, men paralyzed by the panic. He saw troops moving near the water, the provosts, the awful duty, finding the ones who ran, and if they did not return to the line, to arrest them, haul them to the stockade. He shook his head, thought, It is always like that, in every fight. Some men will suddenly come apart, something inside of them suddenly opens up, breaks out in a blinding madness. He recalled the firing squad, the execution of the deserters, the image always there, somewhere deep in his mind. No, we will not do that, not in this brigade, not if I can help it. But if they leave this field, if they run far enough and are caught . . . then I *cannot* help it.

He saw horsemen now, flags, Griffin, let out a breath, *Finally.*

Behind the horsemen came a column of troops, men moving double-time. Chamberlain tried to see the numbers, the strength as Griffin reined up, said, "That's a strong line over there, General. We have prisoners from Anderson's division. They say more are coming, a lot more. No surprise, Lee has to move out this way, can't allow us to keep pushing north."

Chamberlain was watching Griffin's face, thought, We did not do . . . what we were supposed to do. We were repulsed.

Griffin was scanning the rebel lines, said, "Behind those woods . . . the White Oak Road. Very important, it's their main artery from this area back to Petersburg. The Southside Railroad is just above. If we can take the road . . . they have no choice but to pull back, protect the railroad."

Chamberlain absorbed the words as Griffin pulled out a map. Chamberlain thought, He doesn't seem to be too upset that we were pushed back. He felt a sudden wave of relief.

Griffin was already moving beyond what had just happened, looked again at the rebel line, said, "General Chamberlain, we need those works. If you can move the enemy out of there by nightfall, we will be in strength here. The rest of the corps is behind us, and the Second is moving up on our right. We must hold here, keep Lee from pushing us back below the creek." Griffin's voice was calm, matter-of-fact.

Chamberlain watched Griffin still scanning the map, thought, We tried once, but . . . Anderson's whole division? That means we're up against . . . maybe four, five thousand men.

Now Griffin looked at him, said, "Are you not clear about something, General?"

Chamberlain cleared his throat, said, "Sir, how close is the rest of the corps? May we expect . . . support?"

Griffin looked out toward Chamberlain's men, said, "If you can move the enemy out of those works, and hold that line for a while, you'll get all the support you need. There is no time to lose, General. General Sheridan has his hands full. We need to hold on here, keep Lee from moving any farther west."

Griffin was looking at the map again, said something to a staff officer. Chamberlain looked across the open ground, past the farmhouse, the sawdust pile. He raised his field glasses, took in the rebel line, saw flags spread all along the wall, knew each one meant numbers, strength. He thought of Gettysburg then, of that rocky hill, those men from Alabama who had come at him, trying time after time to take that hill. Now that's . . . *us*. At least here . . . it's not uphill.

He put the glasses down, and Griffin patted him on the shoulder, said, "*Now*, General!"

THEY ADVANCED WITHOUT FIRING, THE LINE FIRM AGAIN, MOVing forward quickly. Behind the works, the rebels met them with one solid volley, cutting holes in the blue line, but then Chamberlain's men were up, climbing over the cut trees, men firing their muskets right into the faces of the enemy.

Chamberlain was just beyond the sawdust pile, saw his men still pouring fire straight into the enemy's position, could hear the horrible sounds, the musket fire now replaced by the bayonet and the sword, the clash of steel, the grunts and shouts of men grabbing each other, clubbing with empty muskets, the hollow screams of men driven by the power of the beast, men ripped down by fists and feet, knives and boots.

He moved the horse up closer, pulled his pistol, tried to find a target in the swarming mass of men around him, aimed, then held up, the chaos now complete, the targets swirling together into one mass of confusion. He raised the pistol again, saw a man swinging down hard on a blue soldier with the butt of a musket, a huge man with a bearded face, eyes now looking up at him, staring at Chamberlain with the bloody fire of some terrible demon. The man smiled, staring right at him, and Chamberlain aimed the pistol, pulled the trigger, his hand jumping with the blast. There was smoke, then he saw the man still staring at him, but the eyes were different now, the demon gone, and the man slowly dropped to his knees and fell forward.

Chamberlain heard his name, saw an officer, yelling, waving him away, heard the man say something, then again, now heard the words, "Sir! Get back! Move back!"

He looked into the mass of the fight again, thought, *One hundred fifty yards behind the line* . . .

Men were swarming out on both sides of him, all along the log wall, the fight now all around him. He turned the horse, thought, You damned fool, get out of here. He spurred the horse, crouched low, saw a rebel officer suddenly right in front of him, the face of a boy, a long sword in the man's hand, and the sword went up, the man aiming for the legs of the horse. Chamberlain raised the pistol again, fired into the man's chest, moved quickly past him, did not look back, thought, Keep moving, go!

He saw staff officers now, Sergeant Arthur with the flag, and he turned, could still see the fight across the enemy's works. Men were shouting all around him, officers giving orders, some with wounds. Others now moved back, away from the fight, with bloody faces, torn clothes.

He moved the horse again, could see the woods beyond the wall, men up in the trees, sharpshooters taking slow, careful aim. Then he saw more men moving forward, coming out of the woods, more flags, rebel troops moving right into the fight, fresh muskets, and he could hear more of that horrible sound, a rising chorus of rebel yells.

His men began to climb back out of the rebel works, some crouching low, reloading muskets, some without weapons at all, some snatching up muskets from the arms of the dead. He could still see beyond the wall, a cluster of blue moving across the road, straight into the oncoming rush of the enemy. He felt a thrill, thought, Yes, move ahead. Then he saw the rebels around them and stared in horror, recalling the men who had come by him before, near the creek, and he thought, My God . . . prisoners . . . my men.

Chamberlain turned the horse, saw officers pulling their men back, trying to keep some order, pulling away from the rebel works, but there was no order, men firing blindly, more now climbing away from the enemy. He yelled, pointed, and an officer saw him, moved a few men into one small line. They loaded their muskets, the order was given, a small piece of command, and the muskets swept away a group of rebels climbing over the wall.

His men were beginning to pull away, some organization forming now, small lines of musket fire holding the enemy back, keeping them away just long enough for the blue soldiers to make an orderly retreat. Chamberlain moved away from the road, toward the farmhouse, saw his men in a neat row, kneeling, firing. He rode toward the sawdust pile, saw rebels on both sides of it now, moving forward, pressing the retreat. His men were holding their position, firing in waves, the volleys growing, blowing in both directions, the waves of smoke drifting across. He held tight to the horse, stared for a long moment, and now his men began to move back again, slowly giving ground. The horse abruptly moved forward, pulled him into a cloud of smoke, and he could see nothing, the sounds of the fight suddenly all around him again. He pulled hard at the leather straps, jerked the horse to the side, and now a deafening blast of musket fire blew past him. The horse lurched forward in full panic, dashing through the smoke. He tried to hold it back, pulled hard on the reins. He could see the works again, the logs draped with the bodies of men, and the horse now rose up, threw him back. He lunged forward, grabbed the horse's mane, gripped the thick hair, thought, Damn you, stop! Behind him, he heard shouts, his own men, more horses, heard his name, a staff officer, but the horse still bucked him.

He yelled, "Turn around!" In front of him there was a great flash of musket fire, and the horse rose again, its front legs pawing the air. He felt a hard punch in his chest, then was slammed down hard on the horse's neck. He wrapped his arms around the horse, felt a flood of wetness. The horse was running now, and he gripped the mane, his hat blown off. He could see nothing, the smoke choking him as he held tight to the mane, the blood now soaking his shirt. He could see red spreading down the horse's neck, his face pressed into it. Chamberlain thought, Oh God . . . both of us . . .

He leaned back, out of control, his hand not holding the reins, and he caught a blurry glimpse of the sleeve, the coat ripped into bloody shreds. He tried to grab the reins, could not feel his hand or flex his fingers, his face soaked by the blood of the horse. He thought, No, not an arm . . . please, God, don't take my arm. The horse jerked again, and he dropped the pistol, grabbed at the mane with his right hand, but now the horse reared back and then down, Chamberlain thrown forward, his head slamming hard into the bloody wound on the horse's neck. . . .

H E WAS STILL ON THE HORSE, FELT A HAND INSIDE HIS SHIRT, could hear voices, distant echoes of sound. He tried to shake his head, clear his eyes, felt a rag rubbed across his face, heard a soft voice.

"My dear general, you are gone."

Chamberlain opened his eyes, focused, saw Griffin's face close to his, realized that Griffin was holding him up. He tried to move, felt a sharp pain through his ribs, then looked at his left arm, saw the fingers, thick with dried blood, flexed them, flexed them again, felt a great flood of relief, said, "Well, no, not just yet . . ."

He turned, his ribs screaming, saw a staff officer, and the surgeon who had a handful of bandages and was frowning, waiting to do his good work. Chamberlain gritted his teeth, sat up in the saddle, and Griffin released him, surprised. Chamberlain looked at the horse's neck, saw the hole, the thick blood still flowing. "Is it mortal?" he asked.

The surgeon said, "No, sir, not to worry. The bullet tore your sleeve, punched through your orders book, apparently, and moved . . . around you. Came out . . ." He pointed to Chamberlain's back, touched a tear in Chamberlain's coat. ". . . right here." The surgeon was pleased with himself.

Chamberlain was suddenly annoyed, said, "No, doctor . . . the *horse!*"

"Oh, well, no, sir. The horse took the bullet before you did, probably saved your life. It passed through his neck, but just the muscle. We can patch that up as well."

Griffin was staring at Chamberlain's face, said, "Doctor . . . the blood."

Chamberlain felt his face, the crusty goo, his hair a thick mat, saw now that his shirt was dark red.

The doctor said, "From the horse, sir . . ."

Chamberlain could hear musket fire now, said, "What . . . how are we doing?"

Griffin backed away, still looking at him with horror, and Chamberlain tried to clear his brain again, gazed out toward the sounds.

Griffin leaned closer, took another look at him, said, "We are holding the line, General. A few more minutes and I'll have you a battery. Are you . . . sure you're all right?"

Chamberlain felt the tender ribs again, winced, said, "I am fit for duty, sir."

He could see the smoke now, a new volley of musket fire, thought, We're . . . still in place, they're still behind the works. He looked down at the horse, spurred it lightly, and the horse moved forward, ready for the next command. He touched the neck, and the surgeon handed him a small bandage, rolled into the shape of a plug. Chamberlain stuck the bandage into the hole, and the horse quivered, then snorted.

Chamberlain looked at Griffin, said, "General, when will those guns be here?"

Griffin turned, looking to the rear. "Anytime now. Just . . . hold on."

Then Griffin moved away, and another man rode up, sweating, his face covered with dust. He reined up, looked at Chamberlain with wide eyes, said, "General Chamberlain, we have a problem . . . on the right, sir. The enemy is reinforcing, sir." The man looked closely at Chamberlain's face, said, "Are you . . . all right, sir?"

He thought, I have to see a mirror, reached into his coat, felt the metal frame of the small shaving mirror, pulled it from his pocket, a small shower of glass falling into his hands. He said, "The bullet seems to have made another stop in its travels."

HE PUSHED THE HORSE HARD, FOLLOWED THE WAVE OF HIS MEN, the momentum now driving the enemy away on the flank. For the moment, the crisis was over. They were pressing the enemy back into the woods, and there were small works here too, fresh-cut trees. He wanted to jump the horse across, move closer to his men, thought, *One hundred fifty yards behind the line.* He stopped, looked at the horse, saw the head go down, the strength fading, thought, No, dear God . . . hang on, old man. He jumped down, turned the horse toward the rear, gave him a swat on the rump, and the horse began to move away from the fighting.

Climbing up on the works, Chamberlain saw his men firing, saw bodies everywhere. Right below him, beside him, a man was sprawled faceup against the trees, the eyes wide, ghastly. He made himself look away, jumped down and felt for the pistol, moved toward his men, and suddenly they were not men in blue. The smoke washed past him, exposing different men, wearing ragged brown and tan, men with rough beards, barefoot, screaming. He thought of firing the pistol, turned, suddenly looked at the small black hole of a musket, the point of the bayonet right under his chin. There were voices, more bayonets.

One man said, "You are mine, Yankee. Surrender or die."

Chamberlain stared at the musket, then slowly looked up at the man's face, blackened with dirt, red eyes, no smile, no emotion, just the business of the fight. The man looked at Chamberlain's coat, the dirt and blood blended into dull filth, and Chamberlain saw a moment of doubt, a small question, and said, "Surrender?" He thought of the man's words, the perfect drawl, and said to him in a voice as close as he could to the one he'd just heard, "What's the matter with you? What do you take me for? The fight's . . . thataways!"

The muskets were lowered, the men behind looking toward the works, toward their own line, where the Yankees had pushed them back. Now more rebels were moving past, the flow going forward, and Chamberlain looked at the man, saw the bayonet moving away, the man still looking at him, still not sure. Chamberlain moved then, said, "Come on, boys! Follow me!"

He reached the works, saw his own men on the far side, muskets aimed at him, then the faces, confusion, the muskets again rising toward the men behind him, the rebels following him across the works. He rushed straight at his men, thought, Dear God, let them see . . . Now they moved forward, a sudden lunge, muskets firing, bayonets clashing together, but there were too many men in blue, and suddenly the small group of rebels was surrounded, hands went up, muskets hit the ground. He looked back, saw the stunned surprise, saw the one man, his captor, looking at him. The man slowly nodded, looked to the ground, a quiet salute.

His men began to pull away from the works now. There was another lull, a breath of silence, and he moved with them, saw officers on horseback and walked that way, felt the stiffness in his ribs, the arm throbbing. The officers saw him and there were salutes, men with wide eyes.

One man said, "Sir . . . are you all right?"

He looked at the man, familiar, then recalled his name and smiled; Major McEuen. "I believe so," he said. "Tend to your line, pull them together. We're not through here yet."

McEuen turned, shouted something behind him, and now there was a horse, a heavy white mare. Chamberlain looked at McEuen, said, "Thank you, Major. I'll try to take good care of her."

He climbed up, his side ripping with the pain, and felt the ribs, the wetness. Yes, the bullet was not *that* kind, had ripped into him more than he realized, a neat tear under his shirt, his skin split around his side. He looked at McEuen again, saw the concern, and McEuen said, "You sure, sir? We can have you escorted to the rear. . . ."

Chamberlain heard the sound, the ball coming right past him, heard the impact, the sharp punch. McEuen looked at him with sudden surprise, shocked, his mouth open, now reached out a hand. Chamberlain reached for the hand, McEuen's fingertips just touching his, watched as the young man fell forward, off the horse, hard to the ground. Men were off their horses in sudden jumps, turned the young man over. There was blood now on McEuen's chest, his eyes staring away. Chamberlain closed his eyes, could not look at the face, thought, You cannot . . . you must not stop.

The right had been secured, the 198th Pennsylvania now holding the flank. He looked at the officer kneeling beside McEuen's body, saw the man was crying, thought of words, felt suddenly weak, powerless.

A horseman was coming fast, shouting, "General Chamberlain . . ." He reined, stared at Chamberlain in horror, said, "Sir . . . are you all right?"

Chamberlain nodded wearily, thought, Maybe I should carry a sign reading "Yes dammit, I'm fine!"

The man studied him carefully, said, "Major Glenn is looking for you, sir! We are holding around the road, but the major requests your presence, sir!"

Chamberlain said nothing, turned the horse, wanted to look down, one last glimpse, but he kicked with the spurs and the horse moved under him, taking him away.

He rode back along the line, saw the faces turn, watching him. As they saw him, muskets went down, the fighting stopped, a brief pause, his own men pointing, staring, then a cheer. He moved toward the center again, saw his men in line, ready, a brief lull here as well. The rebels were in their works again, the two sides pausing, licking their wounds, two weary animals making ready for the next assault.

He had not found his hat, rubbed his hand over his head, felt the hair stiff and matted thick with the blood, suddenly thought of Fannie: It is a good thing . . . no women spectators. The men began to cheer him, and he moved toward the sawdust pile. He heard his name, tried not to look at them, focused on the job at hand, on the lines of the enemy waiting beyond the works. There was scattered musket fire, a sudden sharp volley down to the left, and Chamberlain looked that way, began to ride. Another group of his men saw him for the first time, his face a solid mask of deep red, the shirt and coat ripped and still wet. He saw the faces, the horror, changing now to relief, then something else, the cheering rolling along the line as though he was some sort of horrible symbol, their own messenger of death, one horseman of the Apocalypse. Then, across the field, the open ground scattered with men from both sides, rebel troops began to stand up on the works, and he looked that way, saw an officer, sword in the air, and muskets, men raising them high overhead. The sound echoed across the bloody ground, but it was not the rebel yell, the enemy was not coming out again with a new charge. They were cheering *him*.

THE GUNS CAME UP JUST AS GRIFFIN HAD PROMISED, AND THEN the fight turned, the battery adding new weight to Chamberlain's balance. On the flank, more troops from the corps moved forward as well, men who had been delayed by the swollen waters of the distant creeks, who could not be where Chamberlain needed them. Now the rebels began to move away, withdrew from the logs and the woods behind the farm, moved to another strong line, stronger still, reinforced by more of Lee's army, a new defensive line anchored hard along the White Oak Road.

Night had finally swept the field, and Chamberlain rode slowly, felt the unfamiliar rhythm of a new horse. He'd been to the hospital, seen the men who carried the wounds, the men who might yet survive, the ones who would not. He had made a brief visit to the magnificent Charlemagne, now resting, recovering from yet another wound. He looked down in the dark, the white mane, did not know this horse's name, thought it was probably for the best: I'm a curse on horses.

The Fifth Corps had spread into position, and his brigade would now rest in the rear, men gathering in exhausted silence around the small fires, the blessed food. They were fewer now, had lost nearly a quarter of their strength. But Chamberlain had heard from the staff, then from General Warren himself. The rebel prisoners came from four brigades, a force numbering nearly seven thousand of the enemy's troops. Warren had promised him a promotion, a personal note to Washington, then rode away in the splendor of a command that today did not lose.

He is probably a very good commander, Chamberlain thought. But we could have used some help today. It could have been very different. He remembered the prisoners, watching his men marched away, thought, Where are they now? What will happen to them? He'd heard the stories, rumors and poorly written newspaper articles, sensational and dramatic, the rebel prison camps down south, Georgia, one place called Andersonville. No, don't think on that, he told himself. It is a part of it, part of it all. They will survive. They are not like the men in the hospital, the men who will go home broken, leaving something behind.

He had seen the same horrifying sight, always around the hospitals, the great piles of arms and legs, thought again of his own great fear, the shock, believing he'd lost an arm. He reached down, probed the old wound slightly, low in his gut, thought, I always believed it would be . . . in the body. If I went down, it would be there. Usually, that meant you would die. But to go home . . . missing something. He could never admit that fear, not to the men, not to anyone. He marveled at the ones who actually came back to fight, men like Oliver Howard, one sleeve hanging empty. He had heard about Ewell, and John Bell Hood, the horrific wounds, the rebel commanders still riding into the fight, thought, It *must* change them. It would change me.

He had tried not to think of the young McEuen, the body resting under a blanket, laid to one side, one awful corner of the hospital. He would have to write McEuen's father, a doctor in Philadelphia, knew that the memory would stay with him now in that terrible place, where all the memories would stay. The doctor had visited the camp the autumn before, had come to see his son's small command for himself, the pride of the father. He had put his hand on Chamberlain's shoulder, a stern request, to take good care of his boy, as though the boy's safety were Chamberlain's responsibility. Chamberlain had been gracious, smiling, assuring the old man that the boy would return a hero. Now he would have to send a letter, as he'd sent many letters. He was a master at language, at the use of words, but when that time came, when he could see the faces of the men he wrote about, the words dissolved. Nothing he could ever say, no prayers, no tales of heroics, would replace the loss of the son, or the husband. He could not help it now, saw the boy's face, and the face of his father, could see it all, the letter being read aloud, the women weeping, the father trying to comfort. Would there be blame, anger? Would he be cursed by this man, the man to whom he had given the promise? Am I responsible, after all? He stared into the dark, thought, No, the army does not think so, it is all a part of the job. But what do people in Philadelphia know of . . . the *job*?

He was still near the hospitals, could see a long row of lanterns now, wagons moving up the road. The wounded were being taken away, moved to the railroads, back to City Point. After that they would ride the boats north, as he had, to the soft white beds, would stare at blank walls and try to keep their minds alive, wait patiently for the time when they might be allowed to go home or return to the war.

He pulled the horse around, looked up at the stars, but there were no stars. The sky was dull and black, and now he could hear a slight gust of wind, felt the first drop on his face, then more, the sound of the wind now becoming the sound of the rain. He prodded the horse toward the camp, then saw a flicker of light across a wide field. He tried to see, as the rain fell hard around him, and could make out the horsemen, more lanterns, the light reflecting on the flags, the wide column of troops. He nodded to himself, understood now, had received the word from Griffin's headquarters. It would be the Second Corps, Humphreys's command, the men who had fought under Hancock. They would move into line beside the Fifth, and so tomorrow . . . he looked up, closed his eyes, felt the rain on his face, thought of the streams, the muddy roads. Well, maybe not *tomorrow*.

He rode toward the camp, thought of Sheridan, Grant, the great power of this army, knew that very soon they would move again. If they were no longer beyond Lee's flank, could not quite move as Sheridan had wanted, to cut the railroads, to wrap Lee's army up into a tight ball, they would simply drive up hard into whatever Lee put in their path, whatever defense Lee tried to make.

41. LEE

MARCH 31, 1865

THERE HAD BEEN A STRANGE AND CONFUSED FIGHT ALL ALONG the White Oak Road, the Federal troops pushing forward again. Confused and uncoordinated, their attack was made more difficult by the rain, the difficult crossings of the creeks, the small swamps and bogs that were now an impossible barrier to troop movement. Lee's men had broken the first wave of Federal assaults, sent the blue troops racing southward, back across the torrent of Gravelly Run. But he knew this was the Fifth Corps, and to the east there was help from part of the Second, and so Lee had been forced back again, the blue troops finally establishing control along the valuable road.

Lee's men still faced southward, and the White Oak Road would give no one an easy passageway. The men who had fought so well there were now in motion, moving slowly westward, lengthening their trenches. There was a wide gap between the end of the line and the critical crossroads of Five Forks, and Lee knew that the great strength below him would not just sit and wait while he made his defenses strong.

There had been a good fight to the west as well, and he'd waited for it, knew that what had happened at Five Forks was more important than the loss of White Oak Road. The sounds meant that Pickett had arrived, his division nearly five thousand strong, and linked up with Fitz Lee's cavalry, to hold Sheridan away.

Lee had spent most of the last two days along the White Oak Road, and now rode in the rain toward the dull sound of musket fire. The firing had mostly stopped, except for scattered pops, skirmishers getting in the last word. The blue troops were tight against the White Oak Road, and he knew there was nothing he could do about it for now.

He thought it strange that it would be Pickett's division, circumstance moving out of Lee's control, directed by a much stronger force—the hand of God—deciding that Pickett would be in the best position, the fastest way to reinforce the far flank. Pickett's division had been close to the trains, was able to move to the flank quickest. Lee thought hard on that, did not ask why; there was no answer. But if there is some Divine plan, he thought, I can only carry it through. He considered the man himself; he had not seen Pickett again before the move west. What will he do? What kind of fight will his men make? It will matter, after all. Pickett held the flank, the most important position on the long line.

Fitz Lee had been reinforced as well, as much cavalry as could be moved. There were now nearly four thousand horsemen, as strong a force of cavalry as Lee could still assemble. He thought of his nephew, the man who had tried to step into the shoes of Stuart, and had learned to walk with the swagger, the heroic dash, of the horseman. Fitz Lee had proven he could match Sheridan, had fought him all over central Virginia now. But this was not a fight between horse soldiers. Sheridan was supported now by two corps of infantry, forty thousand Federal troops, and Fitz Lee had only the five thousand men of George Pickett.

Traveller moved through the mud, and Lee focused down, the rain flowing off the brim of his hat. It had always been about mathematics, something he'd had to absorb from the beginning, to make the best use of the poor numbers. In front of Petersburg, facing east, John Gordon had barely five thousand men. If Grant knew that . . . but it may not matter now, he thought. Grant is moving west. The forts and trenches that Gordon held was the toughest ground, the strongest defensive position on the field. Grant would know that. No, he realized, I would do the same thing, move out this way, get around the flank, cut the railroad. We must not let him cut the railroad.

The numbers were a blur, and he thought of Davis: You have never understood. If you had used the energy, made the speeches, worked on bringing the states together, uniting their strength . . . But Davis had only alienated those who could have helped, the men in the Carolinas, Georgia. Soldiers continued to drift away, draining the numbers from the army.

He closed his eyes, listened to the rain, the sound of the horse's steps. Did it matter, after all? He had been shocked to hear the numbers from Joe Johnston, had assumed that down south there was good strength, enough force to hold Sherman away. But Johnston could not organize the mix of forces, lost many to the temptations of home, many who simply walked away. Now Johnston could report barely thirteen thousand men in the field, and Lee knew that Sherman had better than sixty thousand.

The staff had put together the best intelligence they could, estimated Grant's numbers at better than eighty thousand, more than double what Lee had left. In Richmond there were still the loud calls from the papers, from the politicians, that together Lee and Johnston could whip either one of the Federal armies, then turn in one great wave and defeat the other. He still considered that, but when the reports came from Johnston, Lee knew that if Sherman simply drove hard to the north, there would be nothing he could do to prevent him from linking up with Grant.

The letters still came into camp, mindless and boastful, advice on military strategy from men who had never seen a fight. Lee had stopped reading them, left it to Taylor to sift through the correspondence, to screen out what was important. He'd hoped to hear more from Davis, but there had been nothing of substance, no help to the army. Davis was holding on to the one piece of the Cause that meant more to him than any other. He was surrounded by it, clung to it with a failing mind, saving it to the end. Lee thought, He believes it, truly believes that if we hold Richmond, we are still winning. If I tell him, he will not hear me. Richmond is a liability, a drain on our strength. Longstreet is there, holding on with what little he can, strengthened only by old men and boys, displaced sailors and crippled veterans. And I need Longstreet here.

It was late in the day, and what fighting there had been was growing silent, held down by the weather and the exhaustion of the men. Lee knew Sheridan had been pushed back to Dinwiddie Court House, good work from Fitz Lee's horses. If we can move out that way, he thought, spread out the line . . .

He could hear the workers, the axes and shovels. He did not ride along the trenches, did not want to see the faces. Not today. The work was more difficult, the men weaker still, the rations even worse than they'd been before. They would still cheer him, but he did not want that now, thought, They cannot do this for me. They must do it for themselves, draw strength from that. I cannot be the cause.

Lee moved east, toward Anderson's headquarters, knew that beyond, between Anderson and Gordon, Hill was in place, probably the largest group of fighting men left, the Third Corps numbering about six thousand men. Hill had come back, had left the comforts of his home, the care of his wife, was now somewhere along the lines. Lee thought, Yes, we still have them, we still have good men, Longstreet, Hill. We will need the best they can give, the best fight their men have left.

He reined the horse, turned in the road, the staff gathering around him. Looking out to the west, he thought, With Pickett and Fitz Lee anchored above Dinwiddie, the lines have been stretched another six miles. All we have left to the east is Gordon.

The rain had stopped, the dull gray sky was breaking up, and now there was a glimpse of color, a sunset. Lee straightened in the saddle, pointed, the staff turning to look. Lee said, "There. It is a sign. God is still with us."

Marshall was beside him, the young man behind the round spectacles, and he said, "Yes, sir, God is with *you*, sir. Always has been."

Lee shook his head, wanted to say something, thought, No, we must not do that . . . not anymore.

There was a rider, moving up fast, coming from the west. Lee watched him, forgot about the sunset. The man splashed up, breathing heavily, his face and clothes soaked in the dense mud of the soggy fields.

"Sir, compliments from General Pickett, sir."

Lee returned the man's salute, his chest tightening, said, "Go on."

"The general reports that he was unable to move the Yankees out of Dinwiddie, sir. The general has withdrawn our forces north, to Five Forks. He reports, sir, that the enemy has not followed him, that he is in a strong position there, sir."

Lee stared at the man, waited for more, but the man sagged in the saddle, the report complete. Marshall had pulled out a map, handed it to Lee, who scanned it, thought, I had hoped . . . they could have defeated General Sheridan's cavalry. Even the cavalry would have been a major victory. Now they will have *time*. Sheridan will receive infantry support. He folded the map, handed it calmly to Marshall, felt his gut turn, his jaw tighten.

He said to the courier, "You may return to General Pickett. Remind him that the Southside Railroad is close to his rear. He must not move any further north. Advise General Pickett that he must hold Five Forks at all hazards." He took a breath, felt a hard thump in his chest, looked down, saw a dull reflection in the mud, the last splash of color from the fading sunset, repeated in a low voice, "At all hazards . . ."

42. CHAMBERLAIN

April 1, 1865

T HEY HAD MOVED IN THE DARK, CHURNING THE ROADS INTO
deep glue, then, off the roads, following the straightest line,
moving through the misery of quicksand and blind trails. The
orders from Sheridan and Grant and Meade had come in a confusing
stream, the lines of communication tangled in the web of Federal command, the structure clouded by divided authority. Grant had given
Sheridan command of the field, but where that field began was something Meade did not clearly understand. Finally, word had come, the
Fifth would march to support Sheridan, would now be under his command. But orders still came into camp from Meade, and Chamberlain
had seen Warren, watched as the small dapper man was slowly beaten
down by confusion and contradiction.

They were close to Sheridan's horsemen now, and the sunlight
was drying the roads, again. The men were eating their rations, had
been given three days of food to carry on the march from White Oak
Road. The food was not very good, not what they were normally issued. The long line of wagons mostly carried ammunition, and it was a
plain, simple message. Cartridge boxes were clearly the priority, certainly to the commanders, if not to the men themselves.

He sat on a log, finished a cold cup of coffee, stared down into the
muddy flow of a creek. Hearing a horse, he turned, saw Griffin, who
dismounted and walked slowly toward him. Griffin lifted his hat,
rubbed his face with his hand. Chamberlain noticed Griffin's belt, and
that he wasn't wearing his sword.

He began to stand, and Griffin said, "No, General, stay put.
Drink your coffee."

Chamberlain motioned with the cup, said, "Your sword, sir."

Griffin put a hand on his belt. "Lost it, all the ruckus last night. Some reb probably wearing it this morning."

Chamberlain put the cup down, quickly unbuckled his own sword, held it out to Griffin. "Please, sir, I insist."

Griffin took the sword, looked at it appraisingly, nodded, said, "Thank you. Most generous of you, General. It will be returned."

Chamberlain nodded, thought, More men will follow your sword than mine. "I will find another, sir."

Griffin sat now, and Chamberlain waited, knew there was something happening, could tell from the grim clench in Griffin's jaw that he had something to say.

Chamberlain tossed the coffee cup behind him, toward the fire, saw an aide pick it up, and he nodded apologetically, thought, I suppose I will sit here until he says it's time to move. . . .

"It's going to be a tough day." Chamberlain looked at Griffin, who said again, "A tough day."

Chamberlain nodded, thought, Well, we're sort of used to that by now.

"You know," Griffin said, "we're under Sheridan's command. And this morning General Grant gave General Sheridan the authority to do what he feels is best to maintain this command."

Chamberlain said, "Maintain . . . what do you mean?"

Griffin looked at him, said, "It means General Grant has given General Sheridan authority to relieve anyone he chooses, if he sees fit. The message was specific, actually. General Grant mentioned General Warren by name."

Relieve Warren? Chamberlain thought of the march that morning, leading his column into the open ground around Dinwiddie, seeing Sheridan for the first time. He said, "That explains General Sheridan's reaction . . . what he said this morning."

"You spoke to General Sheridan?" Griffin said.

"Yes, we marched into the fields, over there, along the road, and I saw the headquarters flag, rode over myself, and he came out to meet me. I was . . . maybe I was too relieved at getting the march over with, so I was, maybe, a bit too casual."

Griffin, smiling now, asked, "What the hell did you say?"

"Well, I offered my respects, and reported to him with the lead of the division. He asked where General Warren was. I told him, at the rear of the corps."

"The rear . . . ? I'm sure he found that amusing."

Chamberlain heard the sarcasm in Griffin's voice, said, "He was not terribly amused. He said, 'That's where I expected him to be.' He asked me what General Warren was doing back there, and I tried to explain that we were withdrawing from White Oak Road in the face of the enemy, but—"

"But he didn't want to hear all of that."

Chamberlain shook his head. "No. I don't understand his reaction. General Warren was doing the best he could last night. I had thought . . ." Chamberlain paused, thought, Careful . . . But there were too many hard memories. "I thought . . . we should still be back there. We gave up a lot of good men to take that road."

Griffin looked down toward the creek, said, "We are here because General Sheridan ordered us to be here. General Warren is not popular at headquarters, hasn't been for a long time. Maybe since the Wilderness. I have seen it myself, he often concerns himself with too many details, stirs too many pots, makes too many suggestions where they might not be welcome. And he has been slow, occasionally."

Chamberlain felt words boiling up, held it, thought, Who hasn't been slow in this army? Who can operate with commanders scattered all over the countryside, orders coming in from all directions, no one knowing what is going on?

Chamberlain said nothing, knew that Griffin was probably right, that even the troops had been through the whole range of disgust and frustration, the job in front of them plain and simple, the commands often delayed and confusing. It made things simpler to be out here, far from the main lines, from Petersburg, simpler to be under the command of one man. But Sheridan was quick to anger, reacted often by charging into the fire rather than thinking things through, had a strong eye focused on his relationship with Grant, and thus his relationship with Washington and the newspapers.

Chamberlain said, "General Warren has done all right, if you ask me."

Griffin looked at him again, with a sad smile. "I don't believe General Sheridan will ask *you*."

THE ORDERS CAME LATE IN THE DAY. WARREN'S CORPS WAS TO move close to the cavalry, to strengthen Sheridan's position. But the roads were confusing, and there were delays, communications and troop movements made worse by the dense woods and swampy ground the soldiers had to travel. Sheridan had been furious at the delays, his temper echoing along the slow progress of the men, but by mid-afternoon, the corps had finally come together. If the men did not know of the anger and frustration of their commander, they quickly understood how serious their position had become. To the north, Pickett and Fitz Lee held the intersection at Five Forks, were spread in a strong line east and west along the White Oak Road. On the east end of the line, the gap still remained, a wide space that separated Pickett from the rest of Lee's army. At the eastern end of his position, Pickett had refused the line, turned his men northward at a right angle to the road.

Sheridan's plan was straightforward, and as Chamberlain looked at the drawing, the sketches on paper, he could hear his men moving into line, horses moving past, the sound of an army pulling itself into motion. He ran his finger along the road they would march, thought, Yes, this is a very good plan.

The dismounted cavalry would assault on the left, with the three divisions of the Fifth Corps moving up on the right. The focal point of the assault for the infantry would be the right angle in Pickett's line, with Ayres's division striking right on the point of the angle. Craw-

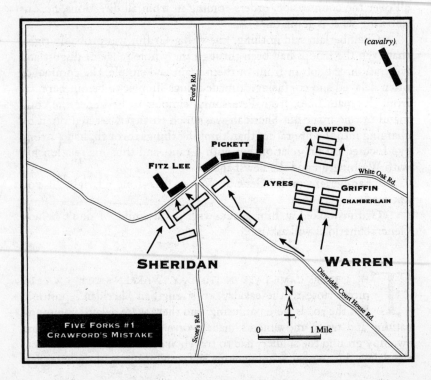

ford's division would lead, and Griffin would follow farther out to the right, moving beyond Pickett's flank, then wheeling to the left, to strike that part of the rebel works that spread to the north. With the cavalry doing the same on the west end, the sheer strength of the Federal assault should envelop Pickett and Fitz Lee's entire position, completely cutting them off from the rest of Lee's army.

They moved forward at four P.M., a quick march on hardening roads. Chamberlain rode again beside the young color bearer, Sergeant Arthur, whose name he would not forget now, had fixed itself in his mind with a strange logic. He could only see it one way, saw it every time he looked at the maps. The sergeant was named after a swamp.

He knew their right flank was vulnerable, that somewhere beyond the low hills, the rest of Lee's army was probably in motion. Griffin had warned him to keep a sharp lookout, and Chamberlain had positioned a small force out to the right, not enough strength to fend off an attack, but at least a warning. They knew now, Lee was out there himself, the prisoners had brought the news, and Chamberlain felt a pride in that, that he'd taken his brigade across Gravelly Run right at Robert E. Lee. But somewhere, locked away inside, was a small breath of relief that he hadn't known it at the time.

There were scattered shots to the left, far in the distance. Our cavalry, Chamberlain thought, out there, moving with us. He felt a thrill now, something different from before, from the assaults of the past few days. There was something about Sheridan, about going into a fight with the power, the good plan. Behind him the men felt it as well, and he turned in the saddle, looked back, saw the faces looking up at him. Men began to smile, the weariness of the march now past, the short rest and the light rations all they would need.

The maps had shown that the road they were on would take them straight at the place where Pickett's line made the turn northward. He could see out to the front now, a wide space of open ground, could see Crawford's division spread into line, moving straight ahead. There was a small bend in the road, and he was staring ahead, and suddenly there was an intersection. He pushed the horse forward, looked in both directions, a long stretch of open road, no troops, no works.

He turned, motioned to an aide, said, "Keep them moving . . . follow Crawford. I have to find General Griffin."

Spurring the horse, he moved to the rear, knew Griffin was close behind. He saw the flags, reined the horse, pulled the map out of his pocket. "Sir," he said, "it appears . . . we are crossing the White Oak Road. There's no sign of the enemy."

Griffin did not look at the map, said, "Don't worry about maps, General. Our orders are to follow General Crawford. We'll find somebody up here. They didn't just go away."

There was musket fire up ahead now, off to the right. Chamberlain turned, said, "Yes . . . there they are!" He listened to the small scattered shots, no sustained volley. Suddenly confused, he said, "But . . . that means we're on the left. The cavalry's on the left, we're supposed to be on the right."

Griffin listened, a silent pause, the shooting still scattered, far up to the right. "That's no fight, just skirmishers. Crawford's just running into some resistance from the east. Could be Lee, pushing this way. Back to your brigade, General. Keep an eye to the right."

Chamberlain saluted, saw anger darkening Griffin's face, thought, Yes, it could be Lee . . . but where is Pickett? He spurred the horse, moved up into the wide road, watched his troops still following Crawford's lines. He reined the horse, thought, If Lee is to the right, then we must be way too far east.

Suddenly, there was a roar, a massive volley of muskets, the sound rolling up toward him from the west, straight down the road. There were big guns now, the hard sounds punching the air, and he raised his hand, motioned to the bugler, the command to halt the line.

He raised his glasses, stared straight down the road, could see nothing, then made out a rising cloud of smoke, the sounds still flowing out in one great wave. He looked behind him, saw the second brigade coming up, Gregory's men, and Chamberlain yelled, "This way . . . wheel them around! We're not where we're supposed to be!"

Gregory began to move, his men flowing over the road, his lines pivoting, swinging toward the west and the vast sounds of the fight. Chamberlain moved in front of his own columns now, waved his arm, his men wheeling about as well. He glanced up above the road, could still see Crawford's division, moving farther away, and now he could see it, understood what had happened. Yes, the maps were wrong, they had reached the White Oak Road well to the right of the enemy's position. But Crawford . . . was still moving away, was moving off in the wrong direction. Chamberlain saw horsemen now, flags, could see Warren, the perfect uniform, the bright gold sash, riding hard, moving out toward Crawford. Yes, Chamberlain thought, he knows as well. Turn them around . . .

His men were in line now, facing west, and Chamberlain looked around, thought, It isn't supposed to be like this. There should be orders. I hope . . . this is the right move.

Then he saw more horsemen, Griffin, with Bartlett, the Third Brigade. Griffin was waving to him, waving the sword Chamberlain had given him, furiously waving his hand, and Chamberlain saw him pointing, the clear sign: yes, go, take them into the fight.

THE CAVALRY HAD BEGUN THE FIGHT, SLAMMING HARD INTO THE rebel front, pushing forward across the road. On the right, Ayres's division, having moved up across the White Oak Road, was suddenly blasted from the left, and moved out just beyond Pickett's flank, where it was hit hard from Pickett's line. Leading two-thirds of Griffin's division, Chamberlain could not see Ayres's fight, rode down through a shallow ravine, then up, in sight of the heavy earthworks Pickett's men had spread up to the north. The volleys were blowing down across the road, Ayres's men pushed back by the surprise, trying to hold their position. On this end of the rebel position, Ayres was the only target, and the rebel muskets ripped his lines, their big guns throwing great bursts of canister into the startled blue troops.

Chamberlain tried to see Ayres, looked for the division flags, but the smoke boiled up from the low ground, the small patches of woods down below the road. In front of him he could see big guns swinging around, the muskets now pointing into his own troops, and Chamberlain turned, yelled, *"Forward!"*

The wave of blue surged down through the shallow depression, then climbed up, and was quickly on the rebel works. Now the smoke was in front of him, the muskets firing all along the works, the sounds whistling past him. His men were climbing the walls en masse. The firing slowed, and there were the awful sounds of men against men, bayonets and clubbing muskets. He still looked for Ayres, thought, I should tell him we are here, tell him what is happening. He glanced up toward the north, could see nothing, no sign of Crawford, of the rest of the corps.

He spurred the horse, moved down a short hill, fought the smoke, climbed up on the road, moved below it. He could see small trees, thick brush, musket fire from below, the fire from Ayres's men. There were big Federal guns there now, and the sharp blasts hit the rebel works hard, shattering the dirt and logs. He pushed the horse on, searching, looking for horses, suddenly saw a different flag, a small man on a huge black horse, stopped, recognized Phil Sheridan.

Sheridan glared at him with black fury, said, "Well, by God, that's what I want to see! General officers at the front! Where's your command, where's the rest of your commanders?"

Chamberlain pointed toward the north, ducked under a sudden blast of wind, the impact of the shell tearing into the brush behind Sheridan. "Sir, General Warren is with Crawford's division. General Griffin instructed me to bring two brigades to support General Ayres."

Sheridan looked toward the north, his anger growing, said, "Ayres . . . I don't know where he is . . . but yes, take your men into the flank, good, yes! Do it! Take command of anyone you see here, any infantry! Break them, dammit!"

Chamberlain started to answer, his arm rising in salute, and there was a sudden blast close behind him, the horse bolting forward. Chamberlain regained control, then spurred the animal, was quickly gone from Sheridan. He moved now below the road, thought, No, I don't want him that angry at *me*. He saw a line of blue coming up from the thick brush, looked for officers, saw a flag. They were from Ayres's division, the Third Brigade. He moved quickly, saw a familiar face, Jim Gwyn, reined the horse. Gwyn's face was red and sweating, with a small flicker of panic.

Chamberlain said, "General Gwyn . . . what are your orders? Where is General Ayres?"

Gwyn looked at Chamberlain with relief, someone who might know something, said, "I have no orders. I've lost General Ayres . . . this brush is too thick. We're cut off."

Chamberlain could hear musket fire again, the sounds cutting the air around him, Gwyn's men now in plain sight of the rebel works. He turned, saw blue on the right, above the road, his men still fighting the rebels up close. He looked at Gwyn, saw a man waiting for instructions, thought now of Sheridan: He told me . . . take command.

"General, come with me. Bring your men forward. I will take responsibility. You shall have the credit. Let me have your brigade for a moment!"

Gwyn saluted him, still waiting for orders.

Chamberlain saw the men watching him and he yelled, "Forward, right oblique!"

Gwyn turned, repeated the order, and the blue line began to move forward, climbing up toward the road, straight into the fight where Chamberlain's men were holding a wide stronghold in the rebel works. Chamberlain moved his horse to one side, waited for the line to move by, then rode up alongside, thought of the salute, thought, He probably outranks me.

He looked farther down, saw more flags, thought, It must be Ayres. He jerked the horse, spurred it hard. He rode behind Gwyn's line, was suddenly surrounded by horsemen, Sheridan again. Sheridan was more angry than before, red-faced, waving a fist close to Chamberlain's face. "What the hell are you doing?"

Chamberlain pointed at the flags, at Ayres now riding toward them, didn't know what Sheridan was asking. Sheridan ignored Ayres, said, "You're firing into my cavalry!"

Chamberlain looked up toward the rebel lines, the fight now swelling into a new roar of sound, Gwyn's men disappearing over the wall. Chamberlain felt the heat rising in his face, looked at Sheridan, held it for a moment, then said, "Then the cavalry is in the wrong place. One of us will have to get out of the way! What will you have me do, General?"

Sheridan stared at him with wide-eyed shock, his mouth moving slowly, and Chamberlain was still angry, thought, Well, that may be the last thing I say to *him*.

Sheridan turned, his mouth still open, looked up across the field, looked back at Chamberlain again, said, "Well . . . don't fire into my cavalry!"

Now Ayres was there, and Chamberlain let out a long breath. Sheridan recognized Ayres, yelled, louder, "General Ayres, you are firing into my cavalry!"

Ayres leaned forward, looked at Chamberlain, and Chamberlain thought, I should tell him, said quickly, a short burst, "Sir, Gwyn is in on the right."

Ayres glanced up, searching, nodded to Chamberlain, looked at Sheridan, said, "General, we are firing at the people who are firing at us! I don't hear any carbine shots . . . those are muskets, the enemy's muskets. I ought to know, General!"

Sheridan's face exploded into red again. Abruptly, he jerked at his horse, rode away through the blue lines moving up from behind. Chamberlain watched him, thought, *My* cavalry? I thought it was *our* cavalry.

Ayres was watching Sheridan as well, then looked briefly at Chamberlain, said, "Fine work, General. We are back in the fight."

Chamberlain saluted. "We're in the works, sir." He turned, the musket fire slowing, said, "I would suggest, sir . . . that way."

Ayres shouted, and a bugler blew out a short command. The wave of blue began to move forward, adding to the strength, pushing into the rebel works, the fight now moving farther above the road. Ayres looked again at Chamberlain, said, "Don't fire into *my* men, General."

H E HAD MOVED PAST THE REBEL WORKS, HIS OWN MEN, strengthened by Ayres's division, now moving the rebels back. There was still a fight, small pockets of rebels, led by officers who would not retreat. The fight had become disorganized, chaotic, and as the men in blue moved forward, there were sudden bursts of fire all around, hand-to-hand fighting rolling across the line as small groups of rebels tried to hold their ground.

He moved again with his own brigade, the staff watching him with relief, men who were becoming used to the man who did not obey what they had all been trained to recite: *one hundred fifty yards behind the lines.*

The fight was in all directions now, rebels suddenly appearing out of small depressions, over low hills. Chamberlain was looking behind them, saw a mass of troops emerge from brush. His heart jumped, and he yelled, "Turn . . . prepare to fire . . . by the rear rank!" The men close to him spun quickly around, saw the rebels moving close and raised their muskets. Suddenly, the rebels began to drop their muskets, hands went up, and the hand-to-hand combat was no longer combat at all.

The rebels gathered around the raised bayonets of the blue troops, men shouting, "Surrender . . . we surrender!"

Chamberlain stared in amazement, saw many rebels now, many more than the men they were surrendering to, and the blue troops were backing up slowly, nervous, unsure. Chamberlain thought, If they see how few we are, any one of them . . . they can just pick up their muskets.

"To the rear!" he shouted, pointing. Glancing down at his men, he motioned with his hand, the urgent silent command, *spread out, move around them.* Quickly, the prisoners were eased away from their muskets, and slowly began to drift back, away from the fight. He watched them for a moment, thought, Now that was interesting . . .

The fight was still in front of him, and he could see more groups of rebels moving to the rear, escorted by the bayonets of their enemy.

He moved forward again, saw a hard line of rebels, stronger. His men were kneeling, firing into brush, small stands of trees. The volleys flew out in both directions now, and Chamberlain moved the horse forward, was surrounded by bodies, down in the tall grass, realized the horse was stepping right across many dead, many more wounded. The sounds began to rise up from the grass around him, the horrible cries that he had heard on so many fields, so many bloody fights. He still moved forward, dropped down into a shallow depression, saw his men huddled close to the ground, a long line now stopped, men holding tight to the muskets, waiting for . . . something, as though if they just held here, in this one safe place, it would end. They began to see him, and men slowly stood, watching him. He pointed up, over the rise in front of them, the strong line of rebels still in place, still full of the fight, said, "Up, move forward! It's almost done! We have broken their flank!"

More men stood, and he looked around, saw officers, a young lieutenant, and Chamberlain said, "Get them up, they want to follow you! Lead them!"

The young man looked at him, dazed, his eyes blank. Chamberlain saw the man's shirt now, saw blood, a dark stain, and the man said nothing, stared past him. Chamberlain looked beyond the man, erased him quickly from his mind, gazed out across the wide depression. There was another officer, familiar. Chamberlain fought for the name . . . yes, Major Glenn, and Chamberlain knew now, these men . . . the 198th Pennsylvania, thought, These are fighting men, there is no line anywhere they cannot cross. He felt a rush of energy. Yes, we will push, or capture them all!

He yelled to Glenn, "Major, get these men up! If you break that line you shall have a colonel's commission!" Glenn saluted, grinning, began to move, and Chamberlain thought, Yes, he always had the fire, then thought of himself, the green commander who didn't know how to do any of this, just that it had to be done. Chamberlain watched Glenn move up the hill. This is *your* time, he thought. Make your mark on these men, take them into the fight!

Glenn shouted, "Boys, will you follow me?"

There was a cheer, the men moving up the rise, a hard surge forward, and now the rebels could see their targets, and a sudden blast poured from the line of logs, but the men did not stop, rushed forward as one wave, were now up and over the low works. Chamberlain spurred the horse, moved up behind them, heard the voices, loud and strong, the sounds of the fight now swept away by the sounds of the fire in his men.

It was over in a few minutes, and he rode forward again, felt a strange pride. I can tell them . . . to do anything. We cannot be stopped! He wanted to laugh, felt alive, the excitement taking over. The job was done, the work, leading the men, commanding the brigade, now something else. He said the word to himself . . . *victory,* wanted to yell it, waved his hat, something he had never done, something from a storybook, the glorious thrill, the pure joy.

Men were falling back now, many with prisoners, small groups, then larger ones. He wanted to count them, thought, No, we will learn that soon enough. But I want to know . . .

Then he saw the wounded, men carrying an officer, and he felt something turn inside him, gripped the hat hard in his hand, saw it was Glenn. The men saw Chamberlain, moved close, lay the young man down, and Chamberlain climbed down from the horse, felt a wave of sickness, leaned over.

Glenn's face was gray as he looked up at Chamberlain. "General," said in a quiet voice, "I have carried out your wishes."

Chamberlain nodded dumbly, could say nothing, thought, I did this. I *chose* him.

One of the men kneeled down close to Chamberlain, said, "He was carrying the colors, sir. The color bearer was down, and Major Glenn . . . he took the flag. It was . . . glorious, sir."

Chamberlain looked at the man, looked past him, thought, *Glorious,* is that what this is?

He looked at Glenn closely now, the man fighting for the one breath, but the fight was past, and Chamberlain saw the soft peace cover the man's face. Chamberlain leaned low, close to the man's face, said, "*Colonel,* I will remember my promise."

He stood then, a last glance at the young man's face, turned to the horse, leaned on the saddle, thought, You *have* to remember . . . you can never forget this. This is what a soldier does, this is what you volunteered for. *You* make the decisions, *you* make the choices, you stand up to God and claim in all your arrogance that *you* are in command.

He closed his eyes, felt a great need to pray, but not here, not on ground like this, not while the fight still echoed around him. He opened his eyes again, thought, No, this is not the time, I cannot do anything but . . . what I have to do.

Crawford's division had finally come into the fight, far up the road that led north, away from Five Forks. It could have been disastrous, Crawford coming in alone, separated from the rest of the corps. But in fact it was the best place he could have been. As the rebels retreated, they ran right into the arms of Crawford's men, and so by dark there was no fight, no enemy left in front of the Federal troops. The rebels that did not find capture simply dissolved into the countryside, the scattered remnants of ten thousand of Lee's most veteran troops. The critical junction of Five Forks was now firmly in Federal

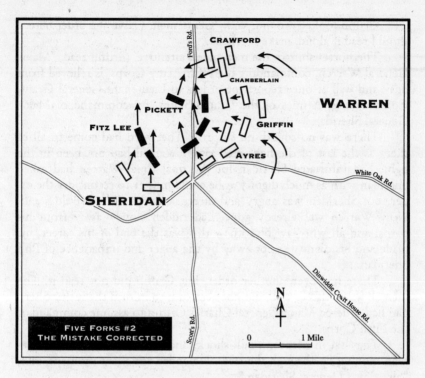

CRAWFORD

Ford's Rd.

CHAMBERLAIN

PICKETT

WARREN

FITZ LEE

GRIFFIN

AYRES

White Oak Rd.

SHERIDAN

Dinwiddie Court House Rd.

N

Scott's Rd.

FIVE FORKS #2
THE MISTAKE CORRECTED

0   1 Mile

hands, and Sheridan had no difficulty pushing up past the Southside Railroad, cutting Petersburg's last artery of supply.

By the next morning Lee's army was enclosed by a ring of blue that stretched from east of Petersburg, from the Appomattox River, southward, then out to the west, until the tightening cord wound north again and secured its flank on the same river.

In the camps the men gathered in quiet celebration, the complete victory, the crushing blow to Lee's right flank.

THEY WERE IN THE FORKS ITSELF, THE INTERSECTION THAT spread the roadways out in all directions. It was nearly dark, a last glow framing the treetops in the west. Chamberlain sat on the horse, saw the animal licking at its leg, a small hole, another wounded horse that would remember him. Griffin was in the center, surrounded by the rest, Bartlett, Ayres, Crawford. Off to the side of the road the staff officers mingled together in small conversation, low voices.

Griffin looked around, said, "Gentlemen, I have the order here. I should read it aloud, make it official."

The horses shifted, the men quiet, attentive. Griffin read, "Major General Warren, commanding the Fifth Army Corps, is relieved from duty and will at once report for orders to Lieutenant General Grant, Commanding, Armies of the United States. By command of Major General Sheridan."

There was no sound, no surprise. The word had come to all of them as the last of the fight died away. Warren had not been in the fight, had infuriated Sheridan for the final time. Warren had asked Sheridan with as much dignity as he could muster to reconsider the order, but Sheridan was angry and direct, and the order would stand. Now Warren was already gone, had ridden slowly away from his corps, and all who saw him knew this was the end of his career, his pride and his dignity swept away by the anger and impatience of Phil Sheridan.

There had been another order, but Griffin did not read it. The men all knew this as well, did not need him to inform them that Sheridan had ordered Major General Charles Griffin to assume command of the Fifth Corps.

They sat in silence, a dull shock, and Chamberlain saw a horseman moving up through the trees. He ended the silent moment, said, "Sir . . . it's General Sheridan."

The faces turned, and Sheridan rode up quickly, was smiling, filled with the glow of a man who has had his way.

"We have smashed them! This has been a magnificent day!" He paused, saw the subdued looks, said, "Gentlemen, I may have spoken harshly to some of you today. But I would not have it hurt you. You know how it is, we had to carry this place, and I fretted all day until it was done. You must forgive me. I know it is hard on the men too, but we must push on. There is more for us to do together." He looked down briefly, then around at each one of them, said, "I appreciate and thank you all."

He turned abruptly, rode away into darkening woods.

Chamberlain looked at Griffin, saw him staring in surprise, his eyes blinking, disbelieving. Griffin said, "So . . . we have learned something about Phil Sheridan."

There were quiet murmurs, then a pause, and Chamberlain ran that through his mind, thought, We have learned . . . what? That Sheridan is not a man to dig trenches, and not a man to be kept waiting? He felt angry now, thought of Warren, No, he was never the perfect commander, he would never win great battles. But he is a good man, a careful man. Sheridan is not careful. But he is different from Warren, from Meade. Yes, there is the lesson. He is *not* different from Grant.

Griffin said something, a quiet good night, and the men began to ride in separate directions. Chamberlain waited, was alone now, heard the slow sounds of hoofbeats moving away. He thought of Warren again, thought, You were a thinker. You thought too much, you took too much care. He suddenly felt he had learned something new, another lesson. Wars are not won by thinkers. He thought then of Major Glenn, of McEuen, others, Strong Vincent, Buster Kilrain. There were more, many more, and he stopped trying to recall them, thought of this afternoon, of trying to pray. No, there is no time for that, not as long as we do this. That is the lesson. This war will be won by the men who move forward, who do not stop to question what they do or what the consequences will be. It is not cause or country or the fellow beside you. It is simple and direct. The rebels were winning this war when they had men like Jackson. Now we are winning this war because we have men like Sheridan. Whether Warren's removal was justified or Glenn's death was my fault doesn't matter now. Those questions will be answered later. Now, we will simply move forward.

43. LEE

APRIL 2, 1865

Longstreet had arrived, and the last of the strong defenses above the James was coming with him, still moving into
Petersburg on the rough and battered rail line. Richmond was
now defended by little more than scattered remnants of smaller units,
cavalry and infantry, plus the home guard, the men commanded by
Dick Ewell.

Lee had heard the sounds of the fight from the west, but nothing
from Pickett. He had only the scouting reports of the cavalry, the
small skirmish line that picked at the great Federal surge on the east
side of Five Forks. He'd sent Anderson's troops farther west, at first, to
link up with Pickett, to fill the gap in the line on the White Oak Road.
But Anderson was too late, could only dig in and face the great force
that routed Pickett at Five Forks. Anderson was now the right flank.
With Pickett's men swept away, Anderson was the new end of the line.

All night Lee had heard the sounds, the skirmishers firing at his
defenses all along the line, all the way from the James River, all down
below the city. The big guns had kept up the demonstration as well,
and Lee had stayed awake, eyes wide, staring into darkness, uncomfortable now in the soft bed. By late night he knew the worst, that the
strong right flank, the force that had kept Sheridan at bay for two days,
was now gone, completely erased from the picture. With the first light
would come the new reports, what he already knew inside, estimates,
thousands of prisoners, a defeat as complete and quick as any he had
suffered.

The demonstrations meant something, and Lee had listened to a
different sound, not the usual blind bombardment. They were picking
a spot, many vulnerable places, the line so weakened that on many of

424

the parapets of the long earthworks, Lee's men stood nearly twenty feet apart. By now Grant knows what happened to us at Five Forks, knows we have stretched this line yet again, stretched it so far that at almost any place he wants to, he can drive a spear, a hard wedge of power, and split us completely apart.

I T WAS FOGGY, THE DULL LIGHT MAKING ITS WAY INTO THE ROOM. Lee sat at a long table, stared down at the smoothness, the polished wood, looked slowly up at the grim face of Longstreet.

Longstreet said, "Is anything known of Pickett?"

Lee shook his head, said, "You mean, the man? No, nothing. He could be captured. He may not have survived. His troops are scattered."

Longstreet held a small pipe, looked at it, said, "He gave it his best. Always did."

Lee leaned back in the chair, was feeling very tired, the long sleepless night dragging on him, his patience frayed, washed away by the frustration of not *knowing* He'd had doubts about the plan from the beginning, of trusting the important position to a man who wore the shroud of defeat, who had not recovered and learned and grown, who could not be relied upon, not anymore. He was angry now at Longstreet, the blind loyalty, thought, You were not here, you don't know what happened. Your confidence in General Pickett is not justified.

He clenched his jaw, closed his eyes, held it in. No, it serves no purpose. He looked at Longstreet, thought, You have always been where I needed you to be. We must think of *now*. We must move on.

Lee said, "I have not heard from him. I can tell you nothing more."

There was noise from outside, boots on the porch, and the door opened. It was Hill, the small man pale behind the red beard, moving slowly, uncertain. Hill looked at Longstreet and straightened, surprised. He said to Lee, "General, I hope you are well this morning. General Longstreet, welcome." There was a weary softness in Hill's voice.

Longstreet nodded, said simply, "General Hill."

There was a silent pause, an awkward moment, Hill still not certain he should be there.

Lee said, "General Hill, please sit down. We are grateful for your return. You look in fine form, if I may say. I wish I could respond that we are all quite fit, but I am afraid that may not be the case."

Hill sat slowly, looked at Lee, confused, said, "I am fit, sir. Thank you. It is good to be here. The men . . . my troops are full of the fight, sir. It is healing . . . to see that, to hear them salute me like that."

Lee looked down, said, "Yes, General, the men . . . there is loyalty there that still . . . impresses me. I am gratified to hear of the morale of your corps. However, our situation may not be so . . . pleasant." There was an edge to Lee's voice.

Hill glanced again at Longstreet, and Longstreet said, "General Hill, I am glad to see you here. We have serious work in front of us."

Hill nodded, seemed relieved; the conversation was not personal, there was nothing of the old conflict in Longstreet's words.

Lee looked briefly at Longstreet, nodded quietly, thought, Yes, thank you, there is no time for all of the old problems. He took a breath now, said to Hill, "Have you been along your lines this morning? Do you see any sign that the enemy is moving—"

There was a loud commotion outside, and the door burst open, Colonel Venable yelling into the room, "Sir, quick . . . something is happening, sir! We're in retreat . . . quick, sir!"

Lee jumped up, rushed outside, could see men streaming across the open ground, coming up from the defenses below. There were wagons, horses, men in the road, moving up from the far trees and the thickets to the south. He felt for his field glasses, realized he was not wearing them, turned, saw Longstreet reach for his own and hold them out to him. Lee raised the glasses, looked to the southwest, could see more troops, an organized line moving up the broad hill, well past the defensive lines that were still strong, lines that should not have given way. He focused the glasses, strained to see, could not yet tell the uniforms, the fog still holding the sunlight away.

Lee handed the glasses to Longstreet, said, "Can you see . . . ? Is that our people, a retreat? Are we pulling back?"

Longstreet focused, shook his head. "Can't tell . . ."

Lee turned to Venable. "Colonel, you must find out who those people are. Get word . . . find General Heth. I must know if his lines have been broken."

Now Hill jumped down from the porch, climbed quickly to his horse, said, "Sir, General Heth is my responsibility. If his position has been threatened, I will see to it." He spun the horse and moved quickly away, his aide scrambling to follow.

Lee looked at Venable, mounting his own horse. "Colonel," he said, "accompany General Hill! Report any news!"

Venable saluted, galloped quickly after Hill.

Lee felt the energy now fading quickly, felt a dark weariness, a black shroud of gloom, called out weakly, "General Hill . . . take good care. . . ."

THE LINES, MUDDY EARTHWORKS, WIDE TRENCHES, WERE EMPTY. The signs of the fight were all around, but there was no more fight. The men who had held these lines were far to the rear, pursued by most of the Federal Sixth Corps, Wright's men storming into the lines at first light. The men in blue, having little to slow them down, burst through the defenses, as they might have done at any time, the lines stretched thin enough that no concentrated assault could have been resisted for long.

Venable was close to Hill and the two aides, and they moved farther to the west, reached a small rise and could see the road again, a line of cannon, big guns moving slowly away.

Hill focused his glasses, said to Venable, "Colonel, those are our guns. We need them brought back . . . this way."

Venable saluted, rode quickly away. Hill scanned the ground, spurred the horse and moved down into a small patch of trees, the ground wet, a narrow creek twisting through. They moved quickly, pushed past the brush, began to climb up out of the tangle, and Hill abruptly pulled his horse up short. The two aides stopped, seeing two men in blue, muskets dragging the ground, eyes wide, exhausted.

Hill shouted, "Put down your guns. You are prisoners!"

The two aides rushed forward, but the blue soldiers had no fight, the guns slipping from their hands. Hill rode forward, looked at the two men, glanced at his aide, Tucker, who said, "General, what do we do with them?"

Hill looked at the other aide, said, "Private, escort these men back to General Lee. Sergeant Tucker, we must keep on."

THEY WERE A COMPANY FROM SOUTHERN PENNSYLVANIA, MEN who loved Uncle John Sedgwick, who now fought under a man they still didn't know and had rarely seen, Horatio Wright. They had come into the army as an alternative to life in the small towns, as common laborers, possessing the skills of handymen and carpenters. Many laughed when the shovels were passed down the Federal line, had done this work before, and by now many had used the shovels often, burying old friends and new.

This morning their good work had been with the musket, with the quick assault, but when the order came down, they looked at each other, wondered, Why now? What had changed that would make those rebs easier today than yesterday? But the order would never be questioned; the feelings about the officers would come out later, around the campfire, when they would talk more about the friends who did not come back.

They had moved forward at the first light, expected to rush into the blazing hell of the same fights they had rushed into before, but the enemy gave way quickly, without much resistance. Now the men of the Sixth Corps pushed on, chasing the rebels farther than they had before, a fast flight over the rolling fields that would eventually carry them to the railroad and beyond, to the Appomattox River.

His name was Mauk, and he was a corporal, a promotion earned for reasons he still didn't understand. He didn't know much about maps and rivers, had followed the men in front of him, as always, climbed up and over the high walls that he'd watched for months, surprised that when they reached the top there was no one there to stop them.

He had come into the army leaving a family at home, sent his pay to his wife whenever he could. He did not gamble, and if the temptation ever crossed him, he would think of the children, of the small home in the small town, and turn away from the men with the cards, the men with the bottles, and the few dollars would go home instead.

They were separated from the main body now, regiments and companies scattered all along the road, far out into the wide fields. They had moved through the old abandoned winter quarters of the rebels, and some had slipped out of line, an opportunity to perhaps find something, a memento, some piece of treasure.

Mauk stayed away from that, kept moving, a small group of men staying with him. If we keep moving, he thought, we should find the captain, find out what to do now.

What was left of his company was moving, slowly, carefully, through a small patch of damp woods, a muddy swamp. The men spread out behind him were as nervous as he was; they were behind the lines, had broken through into the enemy's ground. The main force was up ahead, somewhere, and Mauk began to scan the ground beyond the swamp, glanced into the sun, now moving higher, thought, No, not that way. He knew enough about direction to know that way was Petersburg.

One man was close to him now, and Mauk saw it was the boy, Wolford, with the freckled face of a child, who everyone thought had lied about his age. Wolford stayed close to Mauk, always, and Mauk had patience, would look out for him, pull him in the right direction, hold him down when the volleys flew thick. Mauk looked past the boy, could see toward the others now, thought they were too far apart and wanted to yell at them to close it up. But then he glanced back across the open ground beyond the trees, thought, Maybe a bit farther, stay quiet, see what might be over that rise . . .

There was a small sound, and Mauk looked at the boy, and the boy pointed, wide-eyed. Mauk heard louder sounds now, turned and saw two horsemen moving along the open hillside. He crouched low, then moved up quickly, slipped behind the cover of a fat oak tree, raised his musket. The boy came up close to him, moved against the trees as well, lower, closer to the ground, pointed his musket as well. They see us, Mauk thought. Looks like officers!

The riders slowed, then stopped, and one, the smaller man, said something to the other, and the larger man rode toward them, closer, shouted out, "Fire and you'll be swept to hell! Surrender, or I will shoot you! Our troops are here, you'll have to surrender anyway!"

The smaller man moved forward now, a thick red beard, and he yelled, "Surrender your arms!"

Mauk glanced down at the boy, said quietly, "I don't see it."

He looked down the barrel of the gun now, thought the smaller man seemed to be in command. He sighted the small metal bead on the man's chest, said to the boy, "Let's shoot them."

Both muskets fired, and Mauk saw his target fall, saw through the smoke that the other man was not hit, had grabbed the fallen man's horse, turned and rode quickly away. Mauk looked down at the boy, said, "I believe you missed."

Wolford nodded, said nothing, and they eased out from the tree, moved up the rise.

Mauk said, "Let's see what we got here. . . ."

They moved up to the still body, the gray uniform stained now with a spreading flow of red.

Mauk leaned over, said, "Look here, Wolford. Got him through the heart."

The boy was looking around, nervous still, and Mauk saw the men waving him back into the trees, small shouts, "C'mon." He backed away from the body, said to the boy, "Best be moving on. He's an officer, that's for sure." He moved away, the boy close behind, nodding now, a small piece of pride.

"Yep, got me an officer."

LEE HAD SEEN THE TROOPS CLEARLY BY NOW, DID NOT NEED THE field glasses. They were moving in a slow steady wave, and there was no mistaking that the uniforms were blue.

Longstreet was gone, off to manage the troops arriving on the trains. In the yard around the house, Lee's staff had gathered what they could, but much would be left behind. The Turnbull house was now directly in the path of the Federal advance. Lee still did not know what had happened, how the line had collapsed. He moved to the porch, stepped down toward the big horse, saw Taylor, and Marshall, carrying bundles of paper, tossing them into the waiting wagon. Lee mounted Traveller, heard horses moving quickly up the road from the west. He turned, heard Marshall say, "Sir, it's General Hill . . ."

Lee saw the familiar horse, but the rider was not Hill, and Lee was surprised, then recognized the man, thought, Yes, Tucker, Hill's aide. There were others, Palmer, Hill's chief of staff, but Lee focused on Tucker, and the man's face carried all the message Lee needed. He felt the cold stab in his chest, saw Tucker slide off the horse, waited patiently as Tucker gathered himself, looking at Lee through eyes filled with tearful grief.

Palmer moved forward now, and Lee held up his hand—no, wait—still watched Tucker, and Tucker said, "Sir . . . I am sorry, sir. General Hill is dead. We ran into some Yankees—"

Lee raised his hand again, and Tucker stopped. Lee thought, It does not matter, the details . . . not now. He closed his eyes, pushed it hard, held it away, his throat tight, the stiffness in his chest squeezing away the air. He opened his mouth, tried to breathe, fought for it, and now he looked at Tucker, at Palmer, saw tears on the face of both men, said, "He is at rest now, and we who are left are the ones to suffer."

There was a quiet moment, but down below big guns began to fire, the air overhead ripped with the screaming of shells. Lee looked at Palmer, thought, Hill's home . . . so close to this awful place. He said, "Go, now, to Mrs. Hill. Tell her what has happened. Break it to her as gently as possible."

Palmer saluted, moved quickly away.

Lee looked at Taylor, saw him toss a pile of books into the wagon, said, "Colonel, get word to General Longstreet. Since we cannot locate General Heth, I wish General Longstreet to assume command of the Third Corps."

He looked to the west, could see more lines of blue moving toward the road, the route west, said, "I hope . . . General Heth has been able to join forces with General Anderson. We may not know that for some time."

The orderlies were carrying Lee's small trunk, and Lee saw the telegraph operator now, a small thin man with tiny glasses. The man was moving across the yard, and Lee said, "Sir! Are the lines still up? Do you know if we can still send out?"

The man stopped, glanced nervously at the sounds of the enemy guns, said, "Yes . . . yes, sir. I believe so, sir."

Lee dismounted, grabbed the man by the sleeve, led him up across the porch, back into the house. The man sat at his small desk, pushed away paper, his hand now holding the brass telegraph, and he looked at Lee, waited, a silent urgency for Lee to hurry.

Lee did not look at him, thought of the words, of how the president would respond. He had thought this moment was coming for a long time, something Davis would never discuss. He believes it is the whole cause, he thought. We fight to keep him in Richmond. Lee was angry now, had often thought Davis should come out here, see for himself. There were always reasons; too busy, his bad health. So, this would be a surprise to him. Lee shook his head, looked at his watch, thought, He will be at church, at St. Paul's, and I will interrupt his morning service. A marvelous luxury, sitting in a beautiful church, the peace of a Sunday service. Lee closed his eyes, thought, There is no time for that now. There is no time for luxury.

He looked down at the small man, saw sweat on his face, the hand trembling slightly on the telegraph key. Lee put a hand on the man's shoulder, said, "It's all right . . . there's time yet. You may begin . . . 'To His Excellency, President Jefferson Davis . . .'"

T HE HOUSE WAS EMPTY, THE HEADQUARTERS NOW ON WHEELS, the wagon already moving away on the road. Lee saw Taylor and Marshall mounting their own horses, gave Traveller a light nudge with his spurs, the horse now moving across the yard. There was a sudden shattering blast, a shower of brick and wood, a shell hitting the house, and Lee glanced back, thought of the family, the generous people. This is how you are repaid. . . .

He moved the horse into the road, Taylor moving up beside him.

Musket fire could be heard now, close below the house, a new line of blue emerging from the woods, a new line of defense giving way. He stared that way for a moment, could see officers, men waving their troops on toward the house.

He looked at Taylor, said, "Colonel, this is a sad business."

T HE ASSAULT HAD COME ALL ALONG THE FRONT. EAST OF TOWN, Gordon had held away the Federal advance as long as he could. The last strongholds were now falling there as well, the men in the small forts holding on until the last desperate moment.

South of the city, Heth and Wilcox had been overrun by the Sixth, and Heth's division was now split in two. What remained of Lee's forces close to Petersburg began to move back in a tight arc around the city. But no one believed there was any reason to stay where they were. Grant's army was pushing still, and there was only one alternative. Lee gave the order. When darkness finally came, the army would move north, cross the bridges over the Appomattox and evacuate the city of Petersburg.

I T WAS A GRAND PLACE, THE MAGNIFICENCE OF STAINED GLASS, THE breathtaking soar of the grand ceiling. St. Paul's Church was usually filled by now, but there were gaps, empty spaces in the pews, many having left the city, gone to the safety of the countryside.

It was the first Sunday of the month, and President Davis sat in his accustomed pew, midway down the aisle, listened to the solemn voice flowing out over the worshippers. He did not hear the words, his mind wandering, thought now of the early days, of cheering crowds, of Varina and the children. . . .

The thought froze him, and he could not help it, glanced beside him, the pew empty. They were gone, had been sent away in a wave of tearful good-byes, had left the city only a few days before. Varina did not want to leave, did not understand why she could not be with him, and he still did not believe it would happen, but the word kept coming, spreading all through the city; the meager defense forces were called out again, manning the works that faced the enemy. They said it was real, and close, and now Longstreet was gone, had taken much of the strength with him. But Davis still believed they would be back. Go, do your job, he thought. Take care of business, then return.

Lee had continued to warn him, insisted he be ready to leave, and

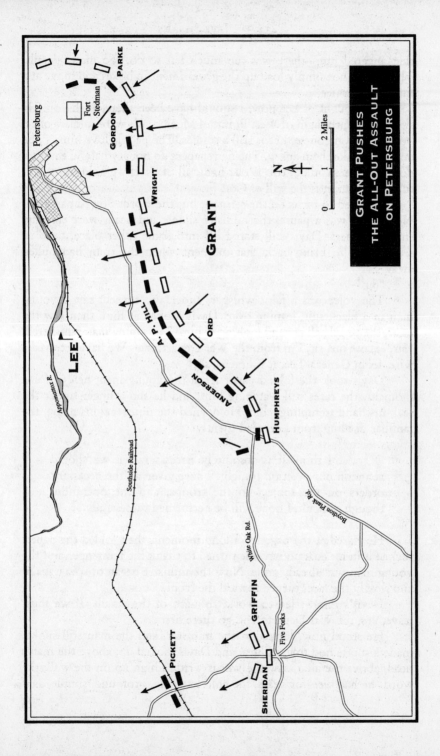

GRANT PUSHES
THE ALL-OUT ASSAULT
ON PETERSBURG

0   1   2 Miles

N

GRANT

LEE

Petersburg

Fort
Stedman

PARKE

GORDON

WRIGHT

A. P. HILL

ORD

ANDERSON

HUMPHREYS

Appomatox R.

Southside Railroad

Boydton Plank Rd.

White Oak Rd.

GRIFFIN

PICKETT

Five Forks

SHERIDAN

that angered him—there was too much left to do, too many details. They could not simply load up the government in boxes and move at a moment's notice.

He thought of Lee now: I should have been there, with you. He smiled sadly, thought of West Point, of Mexico. We were soldiers once, both of us. Of course, Lee is still a soldier. The people love him . . . he does not make them angry. The newspapers do not say hateful things. I do not understand . . . this is our fight, all of us. If we hold on, it will turn, it has to, it is the will of God.

He tried to focus on the sermon, but the words flowed past him. Now there was a pause, the minister silent, and heads were turning, small whispers. Davis still stared off into some other place, tried to see Varina, to bring back that moment when the train had pulled away. . . .

"Sir."

The voice was a faint whisper, and Davis turned, saw a young man in a black suit, leaning over. Davis looked at him, then saw the faces, the people all around looking at him. The young man whispered, "Sir, excuse me, sir. I'm from the War Department. We have received a wire, from General Lee. It is urgent, sir."

Davis took the folded paper from the young man, held it for a moment, the faces still watching him, and he slid a finger under the seal, his hand trembling, cold. He opened the note, saw his name, the familiar heading from Lee, read silently:

> . . . I think it is absolutely necessary that we should abandon our position tonight. I have given all the necessary orders on the subject to the troops, and the operation, though difficult, I hope will be performed successfully . . .

He stared at the page for a long moment, then folded the paper, tucked it in his coat pocket. He turned to thank the messenger, but the young man was already gone. Now the minister began to speak again, and slowly the faces turned toward the front.

Davis's mind tried to work, thought of the details. If we must leave, yes, the War Department, go there first . . .

He stood now, looked at the minister, and the man still spoke, made a subtle nod toward him, and Davis looked up, above the man's head, above the altar, saw the words written high up on the wall, the words he had seen for years, the gold lettering, profound, simple, as if for the first time. He understood now it was for *him*, had been sent by God as a message to him.

Peace I leave with you, My Peace I give unto you . . .

He turned slowly, his hand on the end of the pew, felt his head spinning for a moment, steadied himself, then slowly walked up the aisle. Beyond the doors of the church, in the streets, the people were already in motion, the wagons and horses weighed down with the precious memories, the symbols of home, of the cause and the country that was collapsing around them.

MIDNIGHT, APRIL 2, 1865

THEY WOULD COME FOR HOURS, LONG COLUMNS OF MEN AND horses, the guns and wagons, crossing the river on bridges that would not survive, that would be burned quickly once the army was across.

He had done this before, sat on the big horse, high above the banks of a river, watching his army move away from a disaster. He kept it hidden away somewhere, would never dwell on that, the defeats, pulling his army off the field where so many good men had been left behind. He had always remembered going north, the Potomac, the glorious marches by men who knew they were winning. Now the hidden places began to open up, and he remembered moving south, the same big river, after the horrifying day at Sharpsburg, and then, after Gettysburg, watching his battered army from a high bluff, sitting on the big horse in the misery of the rain.

Now they were moving north again, but there was no spirit in the army, the men moving in slow motion, creaking wagons pulled by weak horses. He thought of Davis, all the oratory, *the spirit of the fallen*, the bizarre notion that somehow they could energize the army by calling on the memories of all who had gone. It was a fine emotional theme for the politicians, made for a rousing speech in those places where the war had not yet come. But here, Lee thought, here the *fallen* are greatly missed, and the spirit is hard to find in the men who have lost the leadership, who have lost so much.

They did not see him, moved past under dull lamplight, faces locked forward, moving out of the city they had given up so much to protect. Many of these were Hill's men, the Third Corps, and most did not even know that Longstreet would lead them. Many had no thoughts of being led anywhere at all, that what they did now was only for their own survival.

He had heard from Anderson, finally, knew that Pickett was still with the surviving fragments of his division, that Fitz Lee could still bring horses to the fight. Lee had ordered them to move north as well, to link up with Longstreet and Gordon's men, that a good hard march would take them all to the railroad depot at Amelia Court House.

A line of wagons moved by him, and another column of troops, but there was something different about the sounds, men moving with more speed, even some voices, laughter. There was still a spark in these men, and Lee sat up straight, was surprised, looked for flags, saw now, reflected in the dull yellow of the lanterns, these were Gordon's men. He understood now, these men had not been defeated, had held their ground, held the enemy away for a full day so that the rest of the army could make it to the bridges. There is a difference, he thought. This is . . . another march. He had not thought of that—there would be some who would be happy to leave this place. Of course, there is nothing encouraging, he realized, nothing to build the spirit enduring a siege. Now we are moving out, and the enemy will have to pursue us. He smiled, thought of Gordon. The irony . . . that it would take a man who is not a professional soldier to remind us that there is still the duty, the strategy. We can still succeed. They must pursue us, and they will be vulnerable.

Amelia Court House was a forty-mile march, but once there, the Richmond and Danville Railroad could move them quickly away, southward, to link with Joe Johnston. He did not think of it as the last hope, the desperate move. It was sound strategy, might always have been, if they could have pulled out of Petersburg before. Lee thought of Davis, the pressure to preserve Richmond, thought, No, it was always a mistake. We knew there was no value, the city gave nothing to the army. This could all have happened sooner, we should have *made* it happen sooner. Now we will come together again, and there are fewer of us, but those who march, who still follow their commanders, there is still power in that. He knew that Ewell was coming from Richmond, had been instructed to go to Amelia as well. Ewell brought what remained of Longstreet's men, with as much of the home guard as were able, and even some naval units, sailors who had burned their own ships and were taking their fight across the land. Once they united at Amelia, the trains would be waiting for them, great long cars of food, and then they would be strong again, would move on the railroad toward Danville, toward North Carolina. And if Grant continues to pursue us, he thought, we will look for the opportunity, and we will hit him hard in the soft place, drive him back to these cities he holds as meaningless trophies of war.

There was a great rumble, and a bright flash of light, and he squinted, tried to see, the fiery blast shaking the ground. The men on the bridge turned, and there was a cheer. Lee thought, the ammunition, the depots. There were explosions echoing all across the town now, and far to the east the big Federal guns began to open up, a response to activity the Federal commanders could see. The sky was now streaked with bright light, bursts of red and orange, small pops and thunderous booms. There were flames now, patches of fire scattered through the town. Lee did not look at that, gazed up instead, at the billowing smoke reflecting the great flashes of light.

He thought of George Washington, his great hero, the friend of his father, thought of the statue in Richmond, the tall dark bronze, where he used to go and just sit. He had often thought of Washington, the struggle for independence, what the man had endured to see it happen. The statue will survive, he thought, they will not destroy it, even those who would burn and loot the city would not do that. I would like to see that again, take that walk along the wide street and sit in the small park across the road, and just . . . talk to him. He would understand what we are doing here, what this army must still do. We are still fighting for the same things, there is no difference now. The fight is not over until we say it is over, and these troops still have the spirit for the fight, even in the worst of times, something George Washington would have understood.

The sharp blasts from the enemy shells and the slow rumbling fires from the exploding munitions still lit the sky, and he stared up, marveled at the glory of that, thought, It looks like a celebration, Independence Day.

The echoing thunder now fell slowly into a rhythm, a steady roll of drums. He turned the horse, his mind holding the bright and terrible images, and moved away from the bridge, out on the dark road, the road filled with his army, marching again to the sound of drums.

44. LEE

APRIL 4, 1865

THERE COULD BE NO SLOWING DOWN, NO DELAY IN THE MARCH. Lee expected some pursuit, but the great Federal mass converging behind him in Petersburg was not yet on the move. On the left flank, down toward the river, Sheridan's cavalry picked and punched at him all day, but the assaults were more of an annoyance than anything significant.

They moved on roads that had not felt the marching of an army before, good roads, a network that fanned out to the west. Lee ordered the wagons and most of the artillery to move on a separate route, a parallel route above the army, so the foot soldiers would not be held back by the slow-moving horses. The goal was still Amelia, and that meant they would have to cross the river again. Once out beyond Petersburg, the Appomattox made a sharp turn northward. Amelia was below the river, and Lee sent specific word to each column of troops, to Longstreet and Gordon and Ewell, where they would cross the river, where the precious bridges should still be in place.

He rode with Longstreet's command, led a long column of troops in eerie silence. Longstreet had moved ahead, securing the crossing at a place called Goode's Bridge. Lee rode beside his own staff, a few of Longstreet's aides and a man who carried the flag of Hill's Third Corps.

He knew Gordon was behind them, bringing up the rear of the march. It was not planned that way for any good reason, except that Gordon had been farther from the bridges in Petersburg. But Gordon's men were still marching with a strong step, still carried the high morale, and so, from behind, they would prod the rest of the army forward. There were many stragglers now. The spirit of Gordon's men

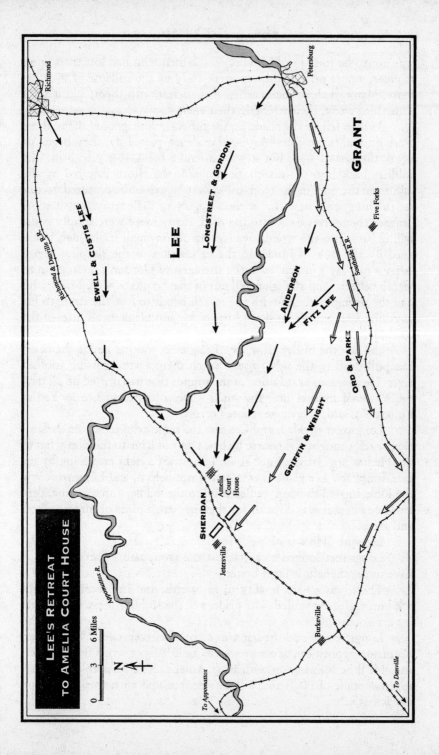

LEE'S RETREAT
TO AMELIA COURT HOUSE

N

0   3   6 Miles

Richmond

Petersburg

GRANT

Five Forks

LEE

LONGSTREET & GORDON

EWELL & CUSTIS LEE

Richmond & Danville R.R.

ANDERSON

FITZ LEE

Southside R.R.

ORD & PARKE

GRIFFIN & WRIGHT

Amelia Court House

SHERIDAN

Jetersville

Appomattox R.

To Appomattox

Burkeville

To Danville

was not to be found in Hill's corps, the men who had lost their commander, whose pride had been swept away by the collapse of their defense. Many of these men carried their defeat with them, and it took something away, their strength, their energy.

As men fell by the roadside, the others in line ignored them; there were no taunts, no jeers. As Gordon's men passed by, they began to break the line as well, but it was to lend a hand, to try to bring the soldiers back into the march. Some made the effort, inspired by the talk from the men in the road, the calls to march or be captured, to suffer the long walk or suffer at the savagery of the enemy. But if some dragged themselves back into the road, many more were simply gone, fading back into the woods, wandering off on small trails, men weakened by the lack of food and the exhaustion of the sleepless night. After a full day's march, even the strongest of Gordon's men began to feel the effects, and stragglers fell out of their ranks as well. Many who had the strength to stay with the march began to lose the strength for anything else, and so muskets, knapsacks, and blankets all littered the roadside.

Lee saw the bridge now, saw Longstreet waiting beside the river. Lee pulled off to the side, would watch them again, crossing another river. He listened, heard none of the sounds that had drifted up all day, the scattered musket fire, the small waves of cavalry. Lee looked at Longstreet, said, "Have we scouted across?"

Longstreet nodded, and Lee saw the same grim look, the dark serious eyes, thought, Of course he has, I do not have to tell him what to do. He has not changed, not at all. Longstreet's right arm hung by his side, limp, and Lee glanced at it, could not help it, and Longstreet saw the look, moved the arm, pulled it up to the saddle, a small show, defiant. Lee knew it was difficult for the big man, a piece of him now soft and weak.

Lee said, "How is it?"

Longstreet looked away, across the river, said, "Can't write . . . have to use the left. It'll get better."

There was a hard finality to his words, and Lee thought, Don't ask him again. He smiled. The pride, yes, the stubbornness. Good, that is very good.

Longstreet waved the left arm across the river, said, "We're clear, no major opposition, as far as we can tell. We got word from Anderson. He'll be meeting up with us at Amelia. He's been able to gather together some of Heth and Wilcox's people, and what they could find of Pickett's."

Lee was surprised at that, had heard nothing from below the river. He said, "Do we know how many? What strength?"

There was urgency in the question, and Longstreet looked at him, said, "Not too sure. But there's a fair number. Maybe as many as we have here."

Lee felt a charge, a spark running through him, thought, If that is true . . . we are stronger still. "Are you certain of that?"

Longstreet nodded, said, "According to Anderson . . ."

"That's very good, very good indeed. That means we have nearly thirty thousand muskets . . . and Ewell, he must have . . . several thousand." He looked at Longstreet, said, "That is very good news. I did not expect to find that much strength, once we left the city."

Longstreet pulled the small pipe out of his pocket, and both men turned, watched the column of troops moving across the small bridge. Longstreet said, "I am not sure we can call it . . . strength. I am not sure how many men can be considered effective."

Lee watched the men marching by, and there were few cheers, the men staring straight ahead, slow and mechanical. He said, "They need to be fed. When we reach Amelia, there will be time." He looked around, out toward the south, then back to the east. "General Grant should be pressing us, not just cavalry. And he is not. Surely, he can't be satisfied with just capturing the city."

Longstreet held the pipe in his teeth, said, "No, I expect Sam Grant is moving. Sheridan's not going to sit still either." He waved the pipe, pointed to the south. "They know where we're going. They have to know if we reach the railroad, if we can get to Danville, they have a big problem."

Lee nodded. "Then we cannot allow them to stop us. We must keep moving. We have a full day's march on them. Once we reach Amelia, get these men fed . . . all those people can do is chase us."

H E COULD SEE THE COLUMNS OF BLACK SMOKE, HEARD THE LOW whistle echoing through the woods, rode now up a short rise. He could see the small buildings, the one small steeple, and out to one side, a long row of great black boxes, the freight cars of the blessed supply trains.

He had sent word specifically to Richmond, sent the wire straight to the commissary commissioners—*send the rations*—and there was nothing polite or formal; it was not a pleasant request. It would be the last of the supply trains to leave Richmond, the last way out before the city fell into Federal hands. The food was warehoused there, had been slowly accumulated in anticipation of feeding troops that would still be stationed there. But those troops, Ewell's ragged mismatched command, had made the long march, six thousand men who would soon reach Amelia, joining the rest of the army. Lee had received no reply from the commissary people, but now he could see it for himself, saw another small engine, a belch of black smoke, coming from the northeast, slowly grinding to a halt at the small depot.

The word had passed back along the column, and as they came closer to Amelia, the men picked up the pace, knew that once this day's march was over, there would finally be something to eat.

Now he could hear the men moving up behind him, a low hum of voices, and he glanced back, saw them looking out at the trains, heard one man raise his hands, shout, "Praise God!" The man saw Lee, smiled, said, "Praise General Lee!"

Lee nodded, realized the man had no musket, was carrying nothing at all, and he wanted to say something, but the column moved past quickly, and there were more sounds, some directed toward him. But he did not hear, focused instead on the men themselves, felt his chest tighten, a small cold stab in his gut. He saw that many of them had shed the weight, had made the march on empty stomachs by lightening the load. Many of his soldiers did not have muskets.

The orders were given, and the men began to fill the open fields, some finding a soft place in the thick grass, simply dropping down, ignoring the directions of the officers, the call to stack arms, to stay in line. Lee moved the horse down the rise, toward the town, saw Longstreet approaching, moving slowly up the hill, away from the small buildings. Lee rode up beside him, and Longstreet was staring at him with a deep gloom, then looked at the ground, said nothing. Lee did not stop, moved on toward the depot, saw cavalry, men on thin horses, gathering along the railcars. Lee rode up toward the tracks, saw an officer sitting on a horse, looking up at one man standing in the open doorway of the car.

The soldier did not yet see Lee, said, "Yee howdy, Captain! We got all the ammunition we're ever gonna need. And not one damned thing to eat!"

Lee moved toward the officer, and the man removed his hat, said, "General Lee! Uh, sir . . . this ain't exactly what we was expectin' to find."

Lee climbed down from his horse, moved to the railcar, looked at the soldier, who stared at him with wide eyes. Lee said nothing, reached up, and the man extended a hand, helped Lee into the car. Now Lee could see the piles of boxes, the neat stacks of cloth bags, wooden crates. He took a step forward, leaned down, saw the car was packed with powder, munitions, shot and shell for the big guns. He looked at the man, said, "This is just one. . . . The others, there must be . . ."

The man was nervous now, shook his head. "No, sir. All like this one."

Lee felt a hot fire swell up the back of his neck, turned, jumped down from the car, staggered, and the captain was down now, stepped forward quickly to help him, but Lee straightened, held the man away. He felt sick, his stomach clenching into a hard knot, his throat clamping down hard. He walked to the next car, looked inside, saw the same cargo, one cloth sack split open, black gunpowder spread out on the wooden planks of the floor. He turned, leaned against the side of the railcar.

The cavalry officer said quietly, "You all right, sir? Can I get you something?"

Lee stared ahead, said, "How are we . . . we cannot feed the men. They knew that . . . and they sent me gunpowder."

The captain said nothing, saw a horseman moving through the depot, made a quick motion to the man to come forward.

Lee did not hear the man coming, and suddenly there was a hand on his shoulder and Lee turned. It was Taylor, who said, "There are no rations, sir."

Lee nodded, said nothing.

Taylor was angry, said, "It is treachery, sir! Just like before . . ."

Lee stepped away from the train, moved to the horse, climbed up, sat heavily in the saddle. He looked at the cavalry captain, said in a slow, quiet voice, "Thank you for your assistance."

The man saluted, looked at Taylor, said something Lee could not hear. Taylor moved close to the horse. "Sir," he said, "we will send out the wagons to all the farms around here. There has to be something . . . the people will not deprive their army."

Lee took a deep breath, felt the hot pain in his throat give way, and he nodded again, said, "Yes, Colonel. See to it. Spare no effort. Prepare an order . . . no, a request. We need anything that can be provided."

He turned the horse, moved through the depot, rode close to the tracks, looked into each car, all of them, could not ride away from the trains without seeing it all for himself. He did not pause, moved slowly by each one, saw that every one was filled with the tools and the fuel of war. He passed the last car, turned the horse toward the camps of the men. I do not understand this, he thought, there could have been no confusion. He thought of Taylor's word, *treachery*, but it had not been like that, not since Northrop had been removed, but what explanation could there be? No, it was just . . . a message. God has denied us. I do not understand.

He rode back up the hill, toward the field where more of the army was spreading out, the men still anticipating the relief from the weakness, from the awful emptiness. He could not look at them, at the faces, thought still of Richmond, could see it now in his mind, men in blue adding to their celebration, digging through the great warehouses stacked high with the food that could save his army.

45. GRANT

APRIL 5, 1865

H E HAD SPENT THE NIGHT IN PETERSBURG, THE STAFF CHOOSING a pleasant, modest house in the nearly deserted town. Lincoln had come to him there, a short happy visit, but was gone now, had gone back toward City Point. Grant then began the ride with his army, in pursuit of Lee's retreat.

He was west of the city, moving out on the well-worn roads, when the courier reached him, the dispatch simple and direct. Richmond was captured, had been nearly as deserted as Petersburg. The first blue troops into the city had found the last remnants of a violent and destructive departure. Some had made the decision that nothing of value would be left behind, others had simply grabbed whatever was there for the taking, and often that included liquor. Most of the citizens had fled, but they were the people who truly hoped to return. To many it was an escape from the emotion, not from the Yankees. Many simply could not bear to watch the city occupied by the men in blue. As the town emptied, the mobs had taken over, and stores, offices, and warehouses were looted. Many were burning, most from simple arson. Along the waterfront the destruction was different, the fires deliberate and necessary, the gunboats and waterfront storage sheds destroyed by the last of the rebel troops, the horrible duty of burning your own so the enemy can make no use of it.

When the Federal troops moved in, there was no fight, no opposition. The few townspeople who remained stayed mostly indoors, and in the streets there was a strange celebration, mostly Negroes, slaves and free, the people who understood as much as anyone what the fall of this city would mean.

Grant read the dispatch with regret, thought, I wish Lincoln was still here. I wish I could see his face.

Of course, Lincoln would know by now, probably knew before he did. And he knew Lincoln would go there, would have to see it for himself. Grant understood that, did not share the apprehension of some of the others, that Lincoln's life would be in danger. Yes, there could still be stragglers and deserters, men crouching low on rooftops, still determined to strike out at the enemy. If Lincoln were there, out in the open, walking the streets, he could be an irresistible target, and anything could happen. But it will not happen, he thought, because of the man himself, the message he would give to anyone who still remained, the newspaper perhaps, anyone who might represent the government of the state of Virginia.

There had been a movement already, reasonable men who looked to the future, to the mechanism for bringing Virginia back to the Union. Lincoln had encouraged that, had no intention of continuing the war when the shooting stopped, had no patience for those in Congress or the newspapers in the North who insisted on revenge, on a policy of punishment, the recklessness of a hostile relationship with those who had created the rebellion. Lincoln did not fear the streets of Richmond, especially if the cavalry and naval guard kept a sharp lookout. Grant knew Lincoln would find a way, get the message to those who held the authority, communicate that they were still part of the United States. As long as Lincoln was President, it would be as simple as that.

Grant rode farther west now, below the Appomattox River, stayed close to Edward Ord's command, the troops who had once been under Butler. The columns marched along the Southside Railroad, and all along the tracks he saw the workers ripping up one side. But it was not destruction, it was repair, adjusting the rails to fit the gauge of the Federal cars. The quartermasters had insisted, and Grant authorized the work, as long as it did not slow the march of the rest of the army. He did not believe it was really necessary, knew it was a precaution against failure. Only if Lee escaped, only if the war was to last for many months yet, would this army need the railroads.

There was no reason for him to stay close to Petersburg. The war had left that place behind, was moving away again, to a new place, new ground, where the fight would still have to be made. He had given the new orders, but the commanders already knew, the target was the rebel army, that wherever Lee went, they would go.

Much of the cavalry had moved up above the river, kept a close watch on the direction Lee was moving, but there were no surprises.

Grant knew now about Lee's disaster at Amelia, and Federal scouts and small cavalry units were following the wagons that Lee scattered into the countryside. Many were simply plucked up, the drivers captured along with their small weak escorts, and all told the same story, how they had been sent on a desperate search for food, for anything the farm country could still provide.

Whether or not Lee could feed his army, he could not stay long at Amelia. The key was the railroad, and that left only one route for Lee to follow—southwest, toward Danville.

THEY WERE RIDING THROUGH DARK WOODS, A DANGEROUS route close to the camps of the enemy. There had not been time for a formal escort, and it was not the place for it. The commotion of a large security force would have certainly brought on more attention than Grant wanted. Sheridan had sounded urgent, sent a scout in a rebel uniform across miles of open country, bringing the message straight to Grant's headquarters. The message was of troop movements, positions, but it was the last few words that brought Grant and his small escort now into the dark woods: *I wish you were here yourself.*

Sheridan was much closer to Amelia, his cavalry still on the far west of the Federal position, leading the way in the race to cut off Lee's retreat. The Fifth Corps, Griffin's command now, was spread out across the one road that ran out of Amelia to the southwest, the road that ran parallel to the Danville Railroad. Grant had left Ord behind with simple instructions: keep moving. By morning Ord's men would be at Burkeville, also on the Danville line, and so even if Lee somehow ripped through the strength of the Fifth Corps and Sheridan's horsemen, the way would still be blocked.

Grant could see small fires now, flickers of light spread out across a wide field. He felt relief, thought, Finally, we're here. But they did not stop, moved farther, beyond the vast sea of sleeping men, and Grant realized with a quick flash of excitement: Those are not our men, they are the campfires of the enemy.

There were only a dozen troopers with him, led by Sheridan's scout, a grisly looking man named Campbell. They had ridden for nearly four hours, could not stay on main roads, had to rely on Campbell's skills and his memory for faint trails in dim moonlight. Grant rode just behind Porter, the young man silent and nervous, and suddenly the small column halted, held up by the quiet hand of the scout.

Campbell rode back toward Grant, then slowly eased into the woods, his head low, probed for a long moment, then came back into the trail, moved farther back, still searching for something. Grant thought, I hope you are as good at this as Sheridan says you are. Grant could see a small movement now, saw Porter pull his revolver, discreet, ready. Grant could not see the gun in the darkness, but knew Porter held it tightly against his chest. Porter did not trust this strange man, and Grant smiled at that, had known Campbell for a long time, knew he was Sheridan's most trusted scout. He could say nothing to Porter, silence was still essential, but he thought, It's all right, Colonel. He's not going anywhere. There is no treachery here. Now Campbell emerged from the woods again, moved toward the front of the horsemen, motioned to the right, and then ducked again into the woods. The column followed, and Grant saw Porter's revolver go back into its holster. He waited for Porter to move into the woods, then gently spurred the horse and followed the rest of his escort.

The trees parted and there was a visible trail. Campbell turned in the saddle, looked back down the line, motioned to Grant and pointed ahead to a panorama of flickering light. Suddenly there were men, moving quickly out of the shadows, appearing all around them, the sharp sound of metal, weapons cocked, then the column abruptly halted. Grant could see one man looking straight at him, pointing the gun at his face, a carbine. These were Sheridan's men.

The man who blocked the trail said in a low voice, "Well, what we got here?"

There was a lantern now, and another man carried the light forward. Grant began to move the horse slowly to the front of the column, could see the first man was a sergeant, and the man said, "Well, lookee here! We got a reb escorting a dozen prisoners, or we got a dozen men escorting one rebel prisoner. Either way, reb, you must be some seriously important man."

Campbell looked around at Grant, who moved beside him, and now Porter began to move as well, and on both sides the carbines were raised a bit higher.

The sergeant said, "Whoa, easy there. No hurry boys, no one's going anywhere."

Porter said, "Gentlemen, we are here to see General Sheridan. This is General Grant's party. We are here at the request of General Sheridan."

The sergeant looked now at Campbell, laughed. "Well, now,

THE LAST FULL MEASURE 449

would *you* be the commanding general? Or are you just his chief of staff?"

There were small laughs, and now Grant leaned forward, took off his hat, said, "Good evening, Sergeant. I am entirely dependent on your professionalism as a soldier. I can offer little except that you recognize me. This is understandably . . . an unusual situation."

The sergeant moved closer, glanced at the man with the lantern, who raised the light higher. Grant leaned over farther, thought, The light, catch the shoulder straps, the stars. The sergeant looked him over, then stepped back, looked again at the rebel uniform, said, "And you would be Mr. Campbell."

Campbell nodded, a slight bow.

The man saluted Grant now, said to the men around them, "Boys, this here is General Grant. I seen you before, sir, crossing the Rapidan River. Mr. Campbell, he's another matter. Don't never look the same way twice."

The carbines were lowered, and Grant said, "Thank you, Sergeant. May we have an escort to General Sheridan?"

The man motioned with his hand, and suddenly two horses appeared, their riders climbing up. The sergeant said, "Just follow these boys, sir. Take you right to him."

The column began to move again, and Grant let out a breath, realized how tense he had been, how easily fate could have made a much different, much more deadly situation.

Porter rode beside him now, said quietly, "Forgive me, sir, I should have been better prepared."

Grant tried to see him in the dark, said, "Prepared for what, Colonel?"

"To protect you, sir. They could have been rebels."

Grant smiled, said, "Mr. Porter, if they had been rebels, we might have been able to spur ourselves around and skedaddle away, and maybe most of us would have made it. If you had done anything to *protect* me with those fellows back there, we'd be dead. Those carbines are seven-shot repeaters."

Porter said nothing, and now they were moving past long rows of sleeping men, the fading embers of small fires. Men began to stir, and Grant looked out over the ground, could see faces coming out from under blankets, a slow ripple of activity, men coming awake in greater numbers.

One man close by said, "Why, there's the Old Man! Boys, this means business!"

SHERIDAN HAD BEEN WAITING FOR THEM, CERTAIN THAT GRANT would answer the request. He'd even waited on his own evening meal.

Grant had chewed on a small piece of burnt roast beef, watched with a hidden smile as Porter and some of the others gulped down a vast pile of boiled chicken, a slab of fat beef ribs.

Now he was riding through the dark again, held a fresh cigar in his teeth, something he could not do on the long ride. But this time he was with Sheridan, and it was a short ride across a field of tobacco. Beyond the field he could see the lanterns in a cluster, a well-lit hub of activity, horses and men moving around a small cabin. Sheridan dismounted first, and the aides stepped back, almost by instinct, had observed Sheridan's hot temper too many times. Grant dismounted, and they began to recognize him. Salutes went up, small greetings. Sheridan did not answer, moved by them, and Grant followed, moved past a man who held the door open, the dull orange light barely filling the small room. Grant looked down, saw Meade lying flat on a small bed, a white shirt, hatless.

Grant moved quickly, leaned down, said, "General Meade . . . I heard you were ill."

Meade looked at him with a flash of anger, but held it, clamped it down, said, "Of course . . . yes. I am ill. I'm flat on my back, while out there Lee's army is waiting for us."

Sheridan grunted, said, "Sir, that's why . . . sir, no, I do not believe General Lee is waiting for us at all." He looked around the room. "A map . . . where's a map?"

Meade raised an arm, pointed toward a small desk, and an aide moved that way, but Sheridan was faster, pushed past the man, grabbed the paper, held it up in the lamplight, said, "Turn up the lamp, I can't see."

The aide looked at Meade, and Meade closed his eyes, said weakly, "Fine. Turn up the damned light."

Grant was still looking at Meade, sweat on his brow, the face drawn, ghostly. He said, "No. We can use this light. Lay the map out, let's have a look."

Sheridan grunted again, spread the map on the desk, said, "Lee has dug in all around Amelia. He has moved some people out this way, drawn up in a line against us. But he is not going to wait for us. He has to keep moving. General Meade has a different opinion. I will not speak for you, General."

Meade sat up now, a groaning struggle, said, "We should wait for all the troops to get up. The Fifth Corps is facing Lee now. The Sixth and Second should be here, ready to move, by tomorrow."

Sheridan said, "And we may advance toward Amelia just in time to see Lee riding away over the next hill."

Grant scanned the map, said, "General Ord will be at Burkeville by tomorrow. There is no way that Lee can use the railroad now. He is cut off from Danville. His only option is to fight . . . or keep moving. If I was in his place, I would be moving . . . right now."

He straightened, looked at Meade, who was on his back again, the small piece of strength now gone. Grant said, "General Meade, the cavalry will continue to move to the west. The infantry will divide, moving west and north. I want to cut him off, get in front of him, not just follow him. There is nothing to be gained by preparing an attack at Amelia. The fight will come when he has no choice but to face us."

Meade nodded, said nothing, and Grant knew he was resigned to it, the illness draining the argument out of him.

Sheridan was already moving toward the door, impatient, and Grant said, "General Sheridan, may I assume you intend to move your people . . . early?"

Sheridan saluted, said, "Sir . . . with your permission, we are *already* moving!"

46. LEE

April 6, 1865

THEY HAD FOUND SHERIDAN'S CAVALRY BLOCKING THE ROAD TO Burkeville, but Lee had believed Longstreet's men were strong enough to break through, to push them aside. Danville was becoming more important now than merely as the escape route. There was food there, a huge stockpile, and Lee had sent word for the trains to roll north, to bring the rations to the army.

As Longstreet had pushed down toward Jetersville, to drive off the Federal horsemen, he found not just cavalry, but infantry, the strong lines of the Fifth Corps. Scouts reported the Second Corps was moving to join them, and the Sixth was a short march away. It was clear to Longstreet, and so, to Lee, that the road to Danville was closed. The only line of march was west, the town of Farmville. There the Southside Railroad ran out toward Lynchburg, and Lee had two choices. If they could stay ahead of the Federals, the army could again turn south and try for Danville. Otherwise, they could make use of the last leg of the Southside not in Federal hands, and move the army farther west to Lynchburg.

He had camped near the home of Dick Anderson, another fine old estate that would absorb the effects of the long war. Anderson's wife and children were still there, had prepared as much of a dinner as they could for Lee and his staff the night before.

He had started the army in motion well before dawn, and once it was known that the route would have to be west, there would be no delay, no time to lose. There was still no food for the army; the wagons had come back from their foraging mostly empty. The farmers simply had nothing to give. It was the season for planting, for plowing the new fields, and whatever harvest had been stored from the previous autumn had long been exhausted. A small wagon train had escaped Petersburg, and there was a much larger train that Ewell had put into motion at Richmond, but Lee learned that the Federal cavalry had caught up to both of them, and what was not taken by the enemy had simply been burned.

The tent had been packed away, and he was pacing nervously in the yard, impatient. He saw Taylor, then Venable, coming out of the house, and Lee mounted the horse, the clear signal that it was time to move.

Taylor moved toward his own horse, said, "Sir, we have asked General Anderson's family to remain in the cellar. I told them it could be dangerous for them today."

Lee nodded, had not thought of that, could not think of civilians now. His mind was already out on the road, far out with Longstreet, with the advance of his army.

On the road, the men were already moving. He watched them, and there was no cheering, the only sounds the muffled steps of weary soldiers, their short time for sleep broken by the dull pain of hunger. We had the chance, he thought, the opportunity, a good day's start. But here, we had to stop, to wait, to see what the wagons could bring us. And it cost us a day's march. There can be no delays now, none. Sheridan has good horses, while ours drop away from their own hunger. The animals have it no better than the men.

There was a horseman, moving against the slow tide of troops, and Lee did not recognize the man, an odd sight, a neat uniform, clean, something no one saw anymore. The man had an escort, another unfamiliar face, civilian clothes. Lee sat on the horse, waited, and the officer saluted him, and now Lee could see the man's face. It was Isaac St. John.

St. John was now the commissary general, having replaced the incompetent Northrop two months before. St. John had made his reputation for efficiency by good management of the Mining and Nitre Department. Where Lucius Northrop's mismanagement had often left the army hungry, St. John's department always kept the ammunition boxes full. In the weeks before the final collapse of Richmond, St. John had done what he could to salvage something of the commissary. Lee had no reason to doubt the man's good intentions, or his capability. It was just too little too late.

St. John saluted Lee, shifted his weight in the saddle, a painful reminder that he had rarely been in the field.

Lee said, "General St. John, I did not expect to see anyone from your department." There was sarcasm in his voice, and Lee regretted it immediately. He looked down, said, "I assumed you might have accompanied the president."

St. John said, "No, sir. I am not certain where the president is, though I believe he made it to Danville. I came here . . . to find out where you wanted the rations."

Lee looked up, stared at the man in the dim lamplight. "What rations?"

"We have eighty thousand rations waiting at Farmville. I had ordered them to Danville, but when we realized the way was blocked, I sent them on the Southside out to Farmville. Farmville is about . . . eighteen miles from here, sir."

"I know where Farmville is, General. We are moving out that way now. Are you certain?"

St. John seemed surprised at the question, said, "Oh yes, sir. I was wondering if you wanted me to load some wagons and send the rations in this direction."

There was a simple matter-of-factness to the man's words that made Lee smile. St. John showed no signs of nervousness, of the strain of what was happening all around them. Lee shook his head, said, "No. Not yet. The Federals have a large cavalry force, certainly moving toward Farmville. We may be in little more than a race. If you send wagons this way, they may be captured. We will do what we can to get to Farmville."

St. John nodded, shifted his weight again, said, "I did not realize the urgency . . . I had best return to Farmville myself." He looked out toward the road, at the march of the troops. "Godspeed, sir."

Lee nodded, looked at the slow steps of the men, thought, Godspeed, indeed.

T HE CAVALRY FANNED OUT TO BOTH FLANKS, WOULD MAKE whatever stand they could against the pressure from Sheridan's horses. Longstreet's men led the march, and Lee knew he did not have to prod him, there would be no need for him to stay up front to keep the column moving. In the center, Ewell's mixed command would move behind Anderson, and behind them was much of the artillery and what remained of the wagon train. The wagons would again be sent on a parallel route, a long circling route to the north, to take them out of harm's way and to clear the road for the more rapid movement of the men. In the rear, John Gordon's troops would hold off any threat from behind, and once the wagon train was out of the way, Gordon would move up and connect with Ewell and Anderson.

Lee had ridden all along the line, tried to see into the faces of the men, to give them something, a piece of himself, some of the cheer that they always seemed to find when they saw him. But the faces were down, staring at nothing, the steps slow and plodding, and all along the road men were falling out, simply collapsing. He moved the horse carefully, the roadside littered again with muskets. There was little else, few blankets, few knapsacks remained. The men had lost all need for comforts, for any personal items that would only require more energy to carry. Without blankets the men would sleep on the ground. Without muskets they could not fight.

He had seen Heth, then Wilcox, Longstreet's commanders, holding their men together as best they could, the numbers dropping by the hour. Now Mahone passed by him, and Lee nodded, smiled, thought of the nickname, Little Billy, another of the men from VMI. Lee had promoted him on the spot for Mahone's brilliant defense after the Crater explosion, and now Mahone commanded Anderson's old division, troops that had been in every major fight since Malvern Hill.

There were some cheers now, a small number of old veterans, hard men who simply treated this as another march. Lee felt some of the energy coming back, saw hats going up, the affection as it had always been. Mahone had stopped briefly, but now was moving on, keeping his men in motion, keeping them tight against the columns in front.

Lee could see a few guns now, small field pieces, horsemen. He rode back that way, crested a small rise, saw men scattered down along the road, some crawling away, moving into the shade of tall trees. He sat straight, could hear it now, a hard roll of thunder, the sounds of a fight echoing in the east. He had expected to see the column of troops, Pickett's men, and Anderson's and Ewell's, but felt a sickness growing in his gut, looked at a road scattered with stragglers. The sounds were louder, rolling over the low hills, and he spurred the horse, began to move across the countryside, dropped down into a small gully, then up another short hill. He stopped the horse, could hear musket fire, great rolling chatter, and he spurred the horse again, rode up that way, thought, The wagon train.

He knew he was moving to the north, far above the main road, saw small creeks, swampy patches of woods. He climbed another rise, the ground falling away in front of him, a wide hill dropping down into tall pine trees, a small creek. The fight was all along the creek. Beyond, along the far rise, he could see great columns of smoke, small patches of flame. He raised his field glasses, tried to focus, saw it was Gordon's men, a rolling assault coming all along Gordon's lines. Lee stared, lowered the glasses, thought, The rear guard . . .

He turned the horse, rode along the crest of the ridge, saw officers coming toward him from the main road, saw Mahone, staff officers. Lee pointed toward the road, yelled, "Where is Anderson? Where is Ewell?"

Mahone reined up the horse, could see the smoke from Gordon's fight, said, "I don't know, sir. They were supposed to be close up behind us."

Lee felt the anger breaking through, could hold it back no longer, said, "Well, yes, General, I know where they are *supposed* to be!"

There was a small group of cavalry now, and they rode along the crest of the hill, the men staring down into the fight along the creek. Lee looked for an officer, saw a young man, a major, said, "Who is that? Who is engaging General Gordon?"

The man saluted, surprised, did not expect to see Lee, said, "Infantry, sir! Looks like the Second Corps, sir!"

Lee stared down the long slope, thought, Infantry? I had thought cavalry perhaps. How did infantry get so close to our rear . . . and where *is* their cavalry?

To the south, near the main road, there was a faint sound of muskets, and Lee turned the horse, said to Mahone, "General, ride with me. We have to find General Ewell."

They moved along the crest of the hill, and Lee saw Venable now, riding hard, waving at him. Venable pulled up, steadied himself on the horse, was breathing heavily, said, "General Lee . . . the wagons have been captured. The enemy's cavalry has broken through the column."

Lee said, "Where is General Ewell? Where is General Anderson?"

Venable shook his head, said, "I don't know, sir. I don't know if they made it across the creek. We have heard nothing." He pointed down the wide hill. "That's Saylor's Creek, sir. There has been a considerable fight there, sir."

Lee turned to Mahone, said, "I may need you, General. This way!"

They rode farther along the crest, then dropped into a shallow depression, climbed up again, and Lee reined the horse, looked down the hill, saw the creek bed snaking through a wide stand of tall pines. Out of the trees, men were flowing in a vast carpet up the hill, wagons without drivers, panicked horses dragging bridles. The men began to fall, collapsing in the open grass, mostly from exhaustion, some with bloody wounds. In the trees below, along the creek, there were scattered pops of musket fire, but the fight was past, whatever had happened to the long column was already done. Lee stared at the great flow of his men, some moving close to him now, men with wild eyes and no muskets, and he felt the horror filling him, the cold stab in his chest, said, in a low voice, "My God . . . has the army been dissolved?"

Mahone said nothing for a moment, the men now moving past them, the ones with enough strength to climb the long hill. Then Mahone shouted at the men, "Turn and fight! Stop . . . fight for General Lee!"

A few faces turned up. Lee saw recognition in their eyes, and some began to gather, to slow the panicked stampede.

Lee looked at Mahone, said, "General, I need you now. We must hold those people back."

Mahone saluted, turned the horse, said, "My men will still fight, sir!" He rode away quickly, and Lee moved down the hill, waving his hat, began to call out to the men, "Soldiers! Fight with me!" Men were moving closer, more now standing, finding their breath.

Lee saw one man holding a battle flag, the man bloody, staggering, and he moved toward him, said, "Here, son, let me. . . ." The man looked at him, dropped to one knee, said nothing, and Lee saw now the face of a child, the sharp eyes, the bright light looking up at him, and the boy released the flag. Lee held it up high, began to wave it, catching the breeze. Now more men fell into line beside him, behind him, and they began to cheer, to yell out his name. He stared below, into the trees, was ready to ride, to move in one hard wave down into the face of the enemy, drive them out, drive them away. The flag was slapping hard around him, catching a sharp gust of wind, the horse staggering to keep straight, and he thought, Yes, we will not be beaten, you cannot take this away from us!

Behind him there was a new sound, men moving over the crest of the hill, a heavy battle line. It was Mahone's men, and all along the hill came the sound of the rebel yell, high and terrible. Suddenly, someone grabbed the flag, and Lee would not let go, looked at the man with hot anger, How dare you . . . saw the face of Mahone.

Mahone still gripped the flag, gave a firm pull, and Lee felt it slip out of his hands. Mahone said, "General, this is *my* job."

THE DAY ENDED WITH THE FEDERAL CAVALRY AND INFANTRY held in check, while Gordon and Mahone slowly backed away. By dark Lee had learned the extent of the disaster at Saylor's Creek. The army had lost nearly eight thousand troops, most of them captured. Many of the commanders had made their escape. But word came to Lee that Dick Ewell had fallen into Federal hands, and then, later in the evening, he learned that most of the Richmond Home Guard had been captured. They now ceased to exist as a fighting unit, would be escorted back toward City Point, along with their commander, Custis Lee. Lee's oldest son was now a prisoner of war.

It was Ewell's mistake that gave the Federals the opportunity to cut through the column of march. The wagon train in front of Gordon had been sent on their northerly detour, but Ewell left no one behind at the intersection to tell Gordon that the wagons were changing direction, no one to tell Gordon not to follow the wagons. Without the crucial instructions, Gordon turned his column, followed the wagon train onto the wrong road.

When Ewell and Anderson slowed their march, to respond to Sheridan's assaults, they did not tell anyone in front of them, did not send word to Mahone, and so the army simply spread out, the column stretching longer, with gaps opening up, large enough for the Federal troops to cut through. The numbers were bad, the losses staggering, but Lee did not focus on that. He had to look instead at what was left, at the army he could still take into a fight.

AS LONGSTREET'S FIRST TROOPS REACHED FARMVILLE, THE blessed rations were put into the grateful hands of starving men. Lee stayed closer to the rear, moved through the scattered troops who still made their way forward. He did not want to hear numbers, had received the reports from staff officers of what was left of the commands, but would not look at them, folded the small pieces of paper and stuffed them into his coat. Most of the commanders were still close by, somewhere, but for many, for Anderson and Pickett, there were no troops left to command.

He rode slowly, thought about his son: I will write Mary. I will have to. They will not harm him, he is too valuable. There is some comfort in that. He knew Rooney was nearby, probably on the flank, riding with his cousin's command. Fitz Lee's cavalry was spread out all over the countryside, rushing to whatever crisis the Federals threw at them, were now gathering together in the same way the infantry was, finding itself, taking the head count, seeing just how much strength they had left.

Lee had seen Rooney earlier that day, and it had been all orders and tactics, the business of command. He knew Robert Jr. was probably up front, near Longstreet, pulling his guns along under Porter Alexander now, guns that could still serve the army. How odd, he thought, the one farthest from the fight, from the war, would be the one captured. Custis was a brilliant engineer, and Lee thought of that, how much alike they were. Lee himself had spent most of his early military service in the Corps of Engineers, knew that his oldest son had the talent for it, but even though Custis had gone to the Point, he was not a soldier, did not have the temperament for it. He was quiet, even shy, nothing like the boisterous Rooney.

The letter was already taking shape in his mind, but Mary would not take it well, no matter how he explained it. Lee knew Custis was clearly her favorite, and Lee was not sure why, thought, He is . . . something like me. But he has also been there, when I have not. She has learned to depend on him. He stared into the darkening trees, past the scattered movement of his men, thought, No, she has never depended on me. There has always been the army, even the early days, the duty always somewhere else, the Carolina coast, St. Louis, the Mississippi River. Then Mexico, the cavalry in Texas, and now . . . something we never could have known. No one had ever believed it would go on like this . . . four years.

It suddenly came to him that he did not know where she was, not exactly. With Richmond now in Federal hands . . . he felt the anxious turn in his gut, forced it away, told himself, No, she is safe. They have been so kind, so many good friends, looking out for her. She has always had that, from the time she was a girl. Then it was her father, now . . . it should be me.

He moved past an open field, the last of the sunlight reflecting on small pieces of motion, men coming out of the woods, still finding the road. He saw one man stop, looking at him, the man shirtless, with no hat, no musket.

The man stared, then said, "Praise God. If I ain't seen Jesus . . . I seen Robert E. Lee."

The man moved slowly away, and Lee felt himself sag, thought,

No, so profane . . . how can they do that? And yet they believe it. They have always believed it. Now look at us, look how few of us there are.

Abruptly, he reached in his pocket, had kept it away long enough, glanced through the brief reports, while there was enough light to see. He thought, The numbers are never good, never, not in any fight, on any ground. We were always up against greater strength. He already knew how many cavalry Fitz Lee had, had heard a brief report, something near three thousand. The infantry was harder to figure, and they were still finding stragglers, men still trying to keep up, dazed, starved. The best estimate was around twelve thousand, mostly under Longstreet and Gordon. There were more men than that, but the reports would emphasize *effectives*, men you could put into a fight. He did not know how many men Grant had, had heard that Ord's people were at Burkeville, and Ord had been above the James, the farthest Federal troops from Petersburg. So if Ord is here, that means . . . *all* of them are here. And that means they are slow. The thought raced across his tired mind, surprised him. They have always been slow. A very big dog, trying to catch a very small cat. He suddenly turned the horse, thought, Yes, that is one thing that has not changed. All we need is time. Even Sheridan's cavalry could only hit us in the middle, not the front.

Gordon had finally been able to pull away from his own fight at Saylor's Creek, would move now up across the Appomattox again, and Mahone would take his men that way as well. Once across the river again . . . he tried to remember the map, did not have it with him. The river is still a great barrier to Grant's people. Once we are across and can burn the bridges, we will have a very good jump on them. We can make the trains at Farmville, move on to Lynchburg.

He rode now toward Longstreet's camp, heard his name, a man calling out, a one man salute, and Lee could not see him, the darkness now deep into the trees. He waved his hat, said aloud, "Rations are at Farmville. You can draw rations at Farmville. Keep moving!"

There were small voices all around him, surprising him, men he could not see, and now he could hear them moving, footsteps in the road, and the word echoed out through the woods, far behind him on the road: *rations!*

APRIL 7, 1865

THE FEDERAL PRESSURE ON GORDON AND MAHONE MADE THEIR crossing of the Appomattox difficult, and Mahone's most important job, to burn the High Bridge before the enemy could seize it, succeeded only halfway. Mahone did set fire to the main bridge, the rail crossing for the Southside, a huge span stretching over a part of the river that was impossible to ford. But the Federal troops came on too quickly, in too much strength, and after a sharp fight, they were able to put out the fire. But worse, what Mahone had failed to do was burn a second bridge, smaller, down below, close to the water. That bridge, designed for wagon traffic, was left undamaged. Humphrey's Second Corps was able to cross immediately, keeping up the pressure behind Gordon and Mahone.

At Farmville, Longstreet camped his men on the north side of the bridges there, prepared to burn them when the last of the army could move across. But with the Federal Second Corps now on the same side of the river, Lee had to keep moving. Below the river, Federal troops under Ord were approaching fast, and so the railcars carrying the food could not stay at Farmville, could not risk being captured. St. John had to move them farther west, out of harm's way. Many of Longstreet's men were still lining up for their first rations in five days when the trains suddenly pulled away.

LEE WAS WITH LONGSTREET, PACING NERVOUSLY. HE HADN'T seen Mahone, knew that he and Gordon were doing their best to hold the Federals away in the rear.

Longstreet was sitting, leaning against a tree, smoking his small pipe. Lee stopped pacing, listened for big guns, the sounds of a fight. Longstreet's camp wagon was nearby. An aide was unloading a trunk, and it fell open with a loud clatter of metal pans.

Lee turned, said, "Quiet! I'm trying to hear!"

There was complete silence in the camp, all faces turning toward the outburst from Lee. Longstreet leaned forward, motioned the aide away.

Lee stared as the man slipped past the wagon, then looked at the faces, turning from him now, averting their glances. Lee took off his hat, rubbed his hand slowly over the top of his head, said to Longstreet, "We have done nothing right. They should have burned that

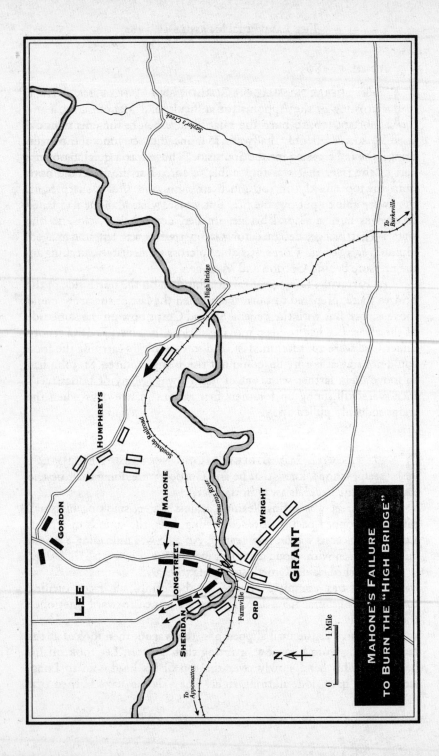

MAHONE'S FAILURE
TO BURN THE "HIGH BRIDGE"

bridge. We would . . . they should have . . ." He stopped, the words choked away.

Longstreet said, "Sir, please, sit down. Here . . ." He reached for a small camp chair, set it upright.

Lee moved to the chair and slowly sat down. Resting his arms on his knees, he looked at the ground, then gazed beyond the matted grass, staring deep into some dark place. There was a quiet moment, then he said, "If they were not on this side of the river, we would have escaped."

Longstreet nodded, said, "We have still escaped. There's nothing west of us. There's a big bunch of those boys south of the river, but they can't come across, not for a long while yet. We move quick, we can make it up to the next station, the rations will be there, and all we have to do is keep those boys behind us from making trouble."

Lee looked at him, saw a smile, thought, Something is . . . wrong with him. I have not seen a smile on him since . . . longer than I can recall. He said, "General Longstreet, your mood puzzles me. We are in a serious predicament here."

Longstreet tapped the pipe on the tree behind him, lit it slowly, said, "When have we *not* been in a predicament?"

Lee was still confused, thought, This is the man whose gloom is legendary, and now . . . with the enemy hard on us from two sides, he smiles.

Longstreet saw the look, said, "Sir, we can only do what is in our power. It is still in our power to reach Lynchburg. We might still find an opportunity to reach Danville. If we can keep moving, keep the enemy behind us . . . Gordon's men are still putting up a fight. These boys here . . . Yankee cavalry isn't going to stop them. We make it to the next station, feed them, we have a clear shot to Lynchburg. And *that* will give Sam Grant a problem."

There were horses, a small group of couriers riding into the camp, eyes searching for Lee. Lee looked up, saw Marshall step forward. One horseman saluted Marshall, said something, then reached down, handed Marshall a piece of paper.

Marshall turned toward Lee and, hesitating, moved close and held out the paper. "Sir," he said, "a message has come through General Mahone's lines, sir. It is from General Grant."

Lee took the paper, saw the wax seal, slid his finger slowly under the flap, broke the wax and opened the page. He read slowly, absorbed the words:

General:

The results of the last week must convince you of the hopelessness of further resistance on the part of the Army of Northern Virginia in this struggle. I feel that it is so, and regard it as my duty to shift from myself the responsibility of any further effusion of blood, by asking you the surrender of that portion of the Confederate States Army known as the Army of Northern Virginia.

Very Respectfully, Your Obedient Servant,

U. S. Grant, Lieutenant-General, Commanding Armies of the United States

Lee looked at Longstreet, handed him the paper.

Longstreet read it, handed it back, shook his head and said, "Not yet."

Lee looked up at Marshall. "Colonel, bring me the map. I want to see how far we still have to move to reach . . ." He looked at Longstreet. ". . . the next station, you said, General?"

Longstreet held the pipe in his mouth, said, "Appomattox."

47. GRANT

APRIL 7, 1865

IT WAS NEARLY MIDNIGHT, AND HE'D SPENT THE EVENING ON THE porch of a hotel, the only one in the small town of Farmville. The army was gathering still, and by now word that Grant was here, with them, had fueled a party, a bonfire, men cheering, singing; men exhausted by a long day's march, but not yet ready to let go of the emotion. It was clear to all of them, whether they had seen the enemy or not, whether they'd had any part in the fight, that this army was moving fast and furiously toward something momentous, something grand and joyous.

Grant sat on the porch, alongside Rawlins and Edward Ord. Men were still marching by, some coming into the town for the first time. A few were breaking ranks, moving toward the bonfire, some carrying knots of fat pine, lit now into great torches. The men were cheering Grant as they passed the hotel, and the songs were a strange mix of bad voices and disconnected melody, each unit singing something different, the sounds overlapping into a roar of noise. One group now stepped into the light, the odd uniforms of the Zouaves, the red trousers lit by the light of the great fire. They were singing especially loud, "John Brown's body lies a molderin' in the grave . . ."

Rawlins said, "Inspiring! Indeed, inspiring! 'John Brown's Body' is nearly a hymn to our boys."

Grant listened for a moment, then said, "Is that a song?"

Rawlins seemed surprised, said, "Why, yes, sir. That very song, there. 'John Brown's Body' . . . surely you know that one, sir."

Grant frowned, thought of Julia. The same thing would come from her, the scolding at his ignorance. Grant listened again, shook his head. "No, afraid not. I know two songs. One's 'Yankee Doodle.'" He paused, thought a moment, could recall some very poor harmony in a disreputable bar in San Francisco, the indiscreet words still lodged in his memory. He was suddenly embarrassed, glanced at Rawlins, said, "The other one isn't."

The Zouaves were past now, and the sounds of the great salute were winding down. Grant stood, moved to the porch rail, thought, We should have heard by now. He cannot just . . . ignore it.

There were boots behind him, and he heard Porter's voice, "Sir! Look! It's a rebel!"

Grant looked out into the dark, the dim light of the street beside the hotel. A man came out of the shadows, careful, discreet, saw Grant now, removed his hat. The man moved slowly around the porch, reached the steps and waited, still cautious. Grant could see what was left of a gray uniform, an officer.

Rawlins moved to the top of the steps, blocking the man's way, said, "Who are you, sir? Do you come from General Lee?"

The man flinched, looked at Rawlins as though expecting to be hit, shook his head, "General Lee? Oh, Lord, no. Please forgive me." He looked at the others on the porch, his eyes now focusing on Grant, and he said, "This is . . . my hotel. I am the proprietor."

Rawlins made a noise, said, "Is that a fact? You look more like a deserter to me. How did you get through? We have provost guards on all these streets."

The man smiled now, said, "I grew up here, know my way around. There's a few shortcuts . . ."

Grant stepped forward, put a hand on Rawlins's shoulder, said to the man, "What is your command? Where is your unit?"

The man looked at Grant, glanced again at Rawlins, saw Grant's shoulder straps, the rank, said, "Oh, my. Sir, my unit is . . . gone. There is no command. I didn't see much point in keeping up the fight. I heard there was a mighty lot of you fellows moving through here. I was kinda afraid . . . what might happen to my place."

Grant stepped aside, motioned for the man to move up the steps. "Welcome home, sir," he said. "We appreciate your courtesy. These are fine accommodations. No harm will come to this place."

The man seemed more comfortable now, confident, said, "Finest hotel in these parts, sir. Built it myself."

He looked past Grant, toward the front door, saw more blue officers in the lobby, men now moving past, saluting Grant. He stepped toward the door, then turned, said to Grant, "Can't rightly recall when it's been this busy . . ."

THE STREETS WERE QUIET NOW, THE TROOPS IN CAMP, THE BON-
fire collapsed into a mound of glowing embers. Grant was still
on the porch, where he sat alone. He'd tried to sleep, but it was
not to be, not yet, not until he heard something from Lee.

There was still activity in the hotel, a card game, but the sounds
had quieted now, and he heard footsteps, a low voice, "Sir?"

Grant turned, saw Porter standing in the doorway, lit from behind by the glow of an oil lamp. "Come on out, Colonel," he said.
"Have a seat."

Porter moved to a chair, sat down, said, "It might not be till tomorrow, sir. You should get some sleep."

Grant held a cigar out, looked at the faint glow. "By anyone's definition, Robert E. Lee is a gentleman, and an old soldier. He will respond.
I'm guessing he has already responded. It just hasn't reached here yet."

Porter sat back in the chair, stared at the dying bonfire. "Do you
think it's over, sir? Do you think he'll surrender?"

Two men were riding hard up the street from the east. Grant
stood, moved forward, clamped the cigar hard in his teeth, said, "We're
about to find out."

The horsemen moved closer, slowed, and one of them pointed
toward the hotel, then both saw Grant. The men approached and dismounted. Grant saw one was an officer, a familiar face.

The man climbed the steps, saluted, said, "Sir, General Humphreys
sends his compliments and wishes me to pass along to you this letter,
which was received into our lines earlier tonight."

Grant said nothing, focused on the paper, reached for it, turned
toward the light, scanned the words. He lowered the page, stared into
the dark and let out a deep breath.

Porter moved close, said, "What is it, sir?"

Grant did not look at him, held the paper out, and Porter read it
quietly.

> General—
> I have received your note of this day. Though not en-
> tertaining the opinion you express on the hopelessness
> of further resistance on the part of the Army of North-
> ern Virginia, I reciprocate your desire to avoid the useless
> effusion of blood, and therefore before considering your
> proposition, ask the terms you will offer on condition of
> its surrender.
> R. E. Lee, General

Porter looked at Grant now, said, "He's asking for terms. Sir, he's asking for terms!"

Grant looked at the courier now, said, "You men are dismissed. You may remain here, if you like, or return to General Humphreys."

The man saluted again, said, "Sir, thank you. We will return to our camp."

The man moved away down the steps, and both men mounted the horses and were quickly gone. Grant moved to the porch railing, said, "Terms . . . there are no terms." He looked at Porter. "They cannot hold out much longer. This . . . says nothing. It is no admission of anything." He held his anger, flicked the ash from the cigar. "Surely, he doesn't believe he can fight it out. He must think they can get away." He turned now, pointed out toward the west, said quietly, "I want to be sure . . . get word to General Sheridan. I want our people out there, in front of him. I want Lee's army penned up tight. This matter will be concluded." He looked again at Porter, said, "Those are my terms."

He felt the first tightening bloom of a headache, took a deep breath, moved toward the door of the hotel, said, "Colonel, tomorrow morning I will respond to . . . this. Now, I believe I will go to bed."

APRIL 8, 1865

> To General Robert E. Lee, Commanding, CSA:
>
> Your note of last evening, in reply to mine of the same date, asking the conditions on which I will accept the surrender of the Army of Northern Virginia, is just received. In reply I would say that peace being my great desire, there is but one condition I would insist upon—namely, that the men and officers surrendered shall be disqualified for taking up arms against the Government of the United States until properly exchanged. I will meet you, or will designate officers to meet any officers you may name for the same purpose, at any point agreeable to you, for the purpose of arranging definitely the terms upon which the surrender of the Army of Northern Virginia will be received.
>
> U. S. Grant, Lieutenant-General

He rode now north of the river, stayed close to the Second Corps, the tight pursuit of Lee's army. If the response came, it would likely come through those lines, the closest point where the armies met.

He'd had little sleep, and the headache had grown, erupting like some great black fire behind his eyes, fueled by a tight stranglehold on the back of his neck. He had tried to ride, to keep up with the movement of Humphreys's troops, but the movement of the horse only increased the throbbing in his head. Now he was camped at a farmhouse, could only sit and wait while his army kept up the chase.

The army was nearly equally divided, the Sixth Corps moving in behind the Second above the river, while down below, Ord's Army of the James was supported by Griffin's Fifth. Sheridan's horsemen were pushing hard, skirmishing all day with Fitz Lee as they moved closer to the most likely place for Lee to entrench. Sheridan focused on Appomattox Court House, where the river narrowed to an easy crossing, where it could no longer protect Lee from the troops below. By nightfall Sheridan's cavalry had reached the edge of the small town, and the scouts could see the great railcars that waited for Lee's army to arrive.

G RANT WAS STILL AT THE FARMHOUSE, HAD WELCOMED THE kindness of the family there, and his headache had been assaulted by every home remedy anyone in the house, or on his staff, could suggest. He lay on a sofa, stared up at the dark, could still smell the mustard from the compress that had been put on his legs. Outside, it was quiet, the family occupying a small guest house while Grant and his staff used the larger house for the headquarters.

The headache had been relentless, and he tried closing his eyes, but the pressure inside of him forced them open. He knew there would be no sleep, not while he felt like this. He stared up again, and there was a soft knock at the door. He wanted to yell, to shout, the anger at the intrusion sprouting from the flaming agony in his head. The door opened, a small crack, and he heard a quiet voice. It was Rawlins.

"Sir?"

Grant let out a burst of air, said, "Come in. I'm awake. I'm suffering too much to get any sleep."

Rawlins moved in slowly, Porter behind him, with a small candle. Rawlins said, "Sir, we have received a letter from General Lee."

Grant sat up quickly. Porter set the candle down, and Grant took the paper, held it toward the light.

General:
    I received at a late hour your note of today. In mine of yesterday I did not intend to propose the surrender of the Army of Northern Virginia, but to ask the terms of your

proposition. To be frank, I do not think the emergency has arisen to call for the surrender of this army; but as the restoration of peace should be the sole object of all, I desired to know whether your proposals would lead to that end. I cannot, therefore, meet you with a view to surrender the Army of Northern Virginia; but as far as your proposal may effect the Confederate States forces under my command, and tend to the restoration of peace, I shall be pleased to meet you at 10 a.m. tomorrow on the old stage road to Richmond, between the picket lines of the two armies.

R. E. Lee, General

Grant lowered the paper, shook his head, let out a long breath. "What does he think I had in mind . . . that *we're* going to walk away? It appears he intends to fight it out. I will send him a reply in the morning." He lay back on the sofa, closed his eyes, said quietly, "It is quite likely . . . we may *all* reply in the morning . . . with a great deal more than words."

48. CHAMBERLAIN

APRIL 8, 1865

I T WAS PURE PURSUIT, A MARCH QUICK AND STRAIGHTFORWARD. They had not seen the enemy, but the fight was all around them, the skirmishes with the cavalry, the great roar that had come from Saylor's Creek.

He rode Charlemagne again, the wound now a hard black knot on the horse's neck. They had moved most of the night, and now all of the day. There had been rain, enough to cool the men, enough to soften the roads so the wagon wheels could cut it into long furrows, the hardened ridges just high enough to break the ankles of the men who were too tired to watch their own footsteps.

He had to slow the column down. The road was clogged with another column, more wagons and guns. Ord's troops were up ahead, would share the same route for a while, and Chamberlain reined in the horse, watched as men struggled to push the wagons through a small stream. Behind him the men were in no mood for delay. Suddenly, a dozen men moved past him, toward the trouble in front, splashed down into the water, pushing the wagon up the other side. He moved the horse forward, thought, Yes, good. I suppose I should have told them to do that.

He had ridden for so long now he could not recall his last hour of sleep. The men had no patience, and when the march was slowed by the clumsy struggles in front of them, they would break ranks again and swarm past him to do whatever was necessary. Often there would be a little extra, either the removal of the horses and their drivers by force, followed by an unceremonious toss into the creek or mud, or an astounding flow of profane language. He heard it this time as well, several men yelling in delirious anger at a teamster, the man lashing at the troops with his whip. There were bayonets up now, and Chamberlain was suddenly awake, alert, thought, No, God, don't kill him. But the bayonets merely held off the driver's whip, finally knocking it away completely. The men then drifted back toward him, rejoining the column. No officer said anything, there was no reprimand, and Chamberlain thought, No, we are as tired of this as you are. We just can't do anything about it.

As they moved past him a few glanced up, and there were no smiles, and he could hear mumbled profanities, low voices. He tried to pick out the unique phrases, could not help but smile, the men scowling as they returned to their places in the line of march. A master of language, he thought, and I've never heard *that* before. I should write some of this down . . . but when on earth would I ever use it? An image flashed into his mind, and he saw the dark, frowning face of his father-in-law. Well, that would be interesting, testing Fannie's father's capacity for shock. And Fannie would respond to my eloquent use of these new phrases by . . . what? Some choice phrases of her own? No, that is not a competition I could ever hope to win.

The columns were moving again, the men behind him giving their last word to the crippled wagons on the side of the road. They climbed out of the woods, moved onto open ground, the road much better, and Chamberlain turned the horse, moved to the side, stopped and stared at the wide field.

He'd seen fields like this before, where the great fights had taken place, the violence sweeping over the ground like some horrible storm. But the violence was different now, there had been no fight here, at least no combat.

As far as he could see, there were the broken machines of the rebel army, wagons, heaps of wood and wheels, and guns as well, broken carriages, brass barrels jutting out in all directions. Now the smells began to reach him, and he could see the brown shapes, had thought they were brush and bushes, but no, it was horses, mules, mostly dead, swollen carcasses. There was some motion, animals that had simply collapsed but were still alive, many still strapped into harness, trapped by the weight and the wagons they could no longer serve.

He moved the horse, fought breathing the awful smells, thought, No, keep going. If this is what is happening to Lee, we will soon see much more.

There was another creek in front of them, and the column moved down a short hill, the road muddy again, but the creek was open, wide, with few trees. He could see small pieces of what had once been a bridge, the rest swept away, either burned or chopped to pieces by the men they were chasing.

Ord's column had already moved through, but again wagons were being pushed aside, the foolhardy who assumed the water was shallow. There was a staff officer now, one of Ord's men, directing the column of men upstream, away from the congestion and toward a shallow place where the men could wade across.

His men followed the new path, and he waited until they began to cross at the new ford. They were veterans of this now, boots coming off quickly, suspended by a high bayonet, ammunition held high as well. He turned the horse, moved back down toward the remains of the bridge, had to see why they had moved upstream. There, below, all along the muddy banks, he saw a great mass of debris, more wagons, more guns, but now he could see color too, pieces of . . . *things* in the water, scattered in the mud. There was thick brush downstream, and the creek was clogged by vast piles of something different, not pieces of the army, but of life, home. The broken carts and wagons were not all military. There were small black carriages, trimmed in gold; pieces of fine leather bridles; a broken picture frame, the painting ripped away; pots; and mostly clothes, all colors, lace and silk, hats and black leather shoes. Civilians, he thought. This is a clear picture of the chase, the panic of a people escaping from . . . *us*. He felt a sudden sadness. They must think we are something truly awful, demons. Of course, the bridges were burned by whoever got here first, protecting themselves, with no thought of who might follow. And this was what followed. On the far side of the creek the mud was a vast spread of tracks, shallow and deep, and more color, the dirty refuse of clothing, cast-off shoes and boots.

He turned the horse, moved up along the column again, splashed the horse through the water. His mind was swirling in a daze, from lack of sleep, and he realized now he was very hungry. He instinctively felt his pockets, but there was nothing there, and now he began to feel angry, thought, All the criticism for being slow, Warren's removal, the angry talk about Meade's sluggishness . . . well, somebody better write about *this*, about how we are moving now. He tried to think of distance, had heard someone say thirty-five miles, thought it was probably more.

He climbed another rise, saw a long patch of trees, a farmhouse, and movement caught his eye. He could see men now, gathered around the house, most sitting, leaning against the side of the house. He looked around, thought they might be prisoners, but there were no guards. Someone should—

In the trees close by he heard voices, then saw more of them, scattered all out in the woods, men sitting, some lying flat on the ground. They were calling out to the troops, small greetings, some weak requests, begging for food. He saw muskets then, scattered along the edge of the road, thought, It's an entire unit . . . maybe a company, different companies. He looked for a uniform, something identifiable, saw only an occasional hat, one man wearing a bent sword, a black stripe on a ripped pant leg. The faces were mostly staring out at the road, but there were others, men staring ahead with blank eyes, men close to death, or dead already. No, he thought, they don't need guards. They aren't going anywhere.

The farm was behind them now, and then there was a fork in the road, and a staff officer, another man directing traffic. Ord's people were moving away, and Chamberlain saw Griffin, talking to officers Chamberlain did not know. Griffin saw him, and Chamberlain raised a salute, felt the stiffness in his shoulder, the wound now an ugly bruise along his ribs.

Griffin said, "Take the right fork . . . keep moving, General. Sheridan's up ahead. It's getting pretty tight."

Chamberlain nodded dumbly, asked, "Where's Lee?"

Griffin leaned closer, saw the blinking fatigue, said, "Don't worry about Lee, General. You just keep your men moving on the road . . . this way. If you don't fall off your horse, General Sheridan will find you when he needs you."

T HEY FINALLY STOPPED WELL AFTER DARK, THE MEN COLLAPSING on any spot that would make a bed. Some rations made their way along the line, but waiting for food to cook meant more time awake, and so most of the men slept rather than ate. Chamberlain had slid down from his horse, given the order to the bugler, the command to bivouac. The sounds echoed down the line over the heads of men who did not need any command to sleep. Chamberlain had dropped down, spread out right where his feet touched the ground, and slept through the sound of the horse breathing right above him, finding its own rest.

He was very, very small, standing on uncertain legs, reaching up, his hands not quite reaching the tip of the icicle. Now his father was there, the

*large hand grabbing the ice, snapping it clean from the eave of the house.
The icicle was in his own hands now, and he sat in the snow, touched his
small hands to the sharp point. His father was laughing, and Chamberlain
put his tongue out, licked the icicle, felt his tongue suddenly stick to the ice,
the sudden panic, and now he began to cry, and his father's hand was on his
shoulder, shaking him . . .*

"Sir?"

The hand shook him again, and he stared up at something horrible, ugly, hovering over him, tried to clear his eyes, realized it was the
horse's nose. The voice said again, "Sir?" He tried to focus, thought,
No, don't talk to me . . . and then saw the face of the man, leaning in
close. "Sir? Orders, sir."

Chamberlain blinked hard, thought of sleep again, the snow, the
wonderful dream. "Orders? For what?"

The man stood, said, "From General Sheridan, sir."

His eyes were open now, and he sat up, bumped his head on the
horse's snout. Charlemagne was coming awake as well, snorting, a hot
wet breath on Chamberlain's face. He rubbed a hand over the wetness,
rolled over, slowly stood up, said to the horse, "Well, the orders are for
you too."

The aide held the paper out, and Chamberlain took it, could read
nothing in the dark. The man struck a match, held it in front of the paper. Chamberlain tried to focus, saw the words:

> I have cut across the enemy at Appomattox Station . . .
> if you can possibly push your infantry up here tonight, we
> will have great results in the morning.

Chamberlain looked around at the vast field of sleeping men, said
to the aide, "Find the bugler. Sound the call to rise. Let's *move*."

49. LEE

NIGHT, APRIL 8, 1865

T HEY WERE CLOSE TO THE STATION, AND EVERYONE KNEW THE railcars were waiting for them. The march had gone well, Lee staying close to Longstreet, riding with him at the head of the column as he had so many times before. He kept the memories away, tried not to think of those days, now so far behind them, when he would ride beside the big quiet man, pushing the hard power of this glorious army into a weak and badly organized enemy. It was so very different now, and it was not just that his army was so weak, so badly used up, but that the enemy was very different as well. Grant's army had never run, could never have been persuaded to leave by the sheer audacity of Lee's tactics. He thought of that now, of the fight that had been, the long siege, the chase. He wanted to believe that it was the commanders, that if Jackson had lived, or Stuart, or Rodes, or . . . so many others . . .

But it might not have been. Grant had brought something so different to those people, and whatever they had lacked before, whatever had been so terribly wrong with Hooker or Polk or Burnside, had finally been erased. Lee had always feared that, and even after Grant had been given command, he was not sure what it would mean. Always, from the beginning of his command, when Lee knew the fight was coming, when the great blue wave would slowly move forward once more, he never doubted that his army would prevail, never feared defeat. He always understood the mind of each one of those men Lincoln sent after him. He did not ever wonder about that, never asked himself if it was simple instinct, or superior military skills, or the hand of God. But now, riding in front of a slow column of starving men, he had to think of it, could not keep it away. He still did not believe that Grant had brought some strategic brilliance to the field that he could not grasp, or that his men had been outfought. But Grant had given his army something else, had propelled them forward at a horrible cost. Lee wondered about the numbers, what those boys in blue had given up. He had always believed *that* would decide the war, that the wives and the mothers in the North would not have that. But still they came, had come into his guns until his guns could not hold them away. It did not make sense, all the loss; the death of so many did not take away their spirit, but instead strengthened it, made them a better army. He had to admit that if he had underestimated Grant, it was because he had underestimated what the people in the North would allow him to do.

Lee had relieved some of his commanders, made it official, though no one else had thought it necessary. But he knew it was still the army, and there would be protocol. The commanders continued to move with the column, rode beside ragged pieces of their army, but the organization was nearly gone. Many regiments were now so small that they were grouped together with men they did not know, following unfamiliar flags. Richard Anderson, George Pickett, several others, were dismissed from command, and even if the names still drew respect from the men they had led, those men were too few. The army did not need any more generals.

Longstreet was now moved back, and Gordon's command was moved out in advance, closest to Appomattox. The greatest threat was still from the rear, from the Federals who were close behind, and Longstreet's troops were the most prepared for a good fight, now the freshest troops left in the dwindling army. If the race for Appomattox was won, it would be up to Longstreet to hold the blue infantry away. In front of them would be only cavalry. Even Sheridan could not hold his horse soldiers in line against Gordon's infantry.

There had been no delays, another hard march, and no one in the ranks thought they should stop. There was no food, except what waited for them up ahead, and the column was consumed by the forward motion, men sleeping on their feet, driven only by the slow rhythm of their own fading strength. If the rhythm failed, the men simply dropped away, fell to the side of the road. Those who remained did not notice, still moved forward because there was nothing else for them to do.

Lee had felt more energy since the morning, moved the horse along the column now, toward the front, knew that somewhere up ahead they would make some sort of camp, a place for the business of the army. Behind him some of the staff stayed close, Marshall, Venable, and Lee knew that Taylor would have the camp ready when they arrived. Traveller moved slowly, stepping carefully, moving around the men on foot, blinded by the darkness and their own exhaustion. Lee could see the ones who had fallen away, some just sitting on the side of the road, heads low, faces down. He thought, I must still rally them, say something, give encouragement. He called out, "Up, men . . . to the march!" They did not seem to hear, and he realized his voice was only a whisper, barely a sound at all. There was nothing he could say to replace what they had already given up.

Lee rounded a curve, a short rise, could see the moon, bright, bathing the open ground around him in white light. The road was still full of troops, the last of Gordon's men, pushing closer to the town, to the rail station. He spurred the horse, just a bit, a gentle prodding, and Traveller climbed the rise, another curve, reached the crest. The moon was off to the side now, and he could see his shadow, felt the coolness of the air, a slight breeze, and suddenly, far out in front, he could hear the sound of big guns.

He stopped the horse, listened, thought, It is down below, along the river, the cavalry. . . .

He looked that way, toward the south, stared into the dark, but the sounds would not let him turn away, and now he could hear it plainly. The sounds were in the west, from the one place they could not come, where there could not be anyone to block his way. He looked again to the south, thought, No, it's the wind, the lay of the land, the echo tricking me. He moved the horse a short way along the road, pulled off, moved into the wide field, crested another small rise, halted the horse . . . and now he could see the flashes of light, the sounds rolling toward him in louder bursts, sharp waves of thunder. He thought, Gordon has found them . . . cavalry, there is cavalry at Appomattox. He moved the horse quickly now, the staff following closely, his gut closed up tight in a cold ball, and he thought, They cannot be there . . . they cannot take the railcars.

MIDNIGHT, APRIL 8, 1865

THEY WERE BARELY TWO MILES FROM APPOMATTOX COURT House, a small town whose existence was defined by the railroad. The fight had quieted, a hard encounter between blue horsemen and an advanced line of Lee's artillery, big guns put into place by Porter Alexander, men who were suddenly the front line in a fight they were not expecting. Fitz Lee's horsemen, helping to guard the rear of the column, had quickly been sent up, and the fight was softened now by the late hour, the big guns holding the blue cavalry back. But they did not leave; there was nothing about the rebel line in front of them to drive them away. It was George Custer's division, men who had ridden hard for this opportunity. They had won the race, had come hard into the rail center, seen the great prize strung out on the tracks before them, and now the railcars were in Federal hands.

Lee's camp was quiet, many officers spread out on the ground, most just lying flat, staring up at the thick clouds that drifted past the moon. They were mostly staff officers, serving what remained of the command of the army. The men they served—Fitz Lee, Longstreet, Gordon—were all close around the fire, sitting on the ground themselves, faces lit by the glow, staring up at the one man who stood. Lee could not move from the fire, not yet, and they waited, patient, no one speaking. He stared down into the flames, listened to the crackling sounds, and felt the weariness, the energy of the day and of the cool night drained out of him. He turned, saw Longstreet sitting on a log, the small pipe in his mouth, watching him.

Lee looked down at his nephew, made a small motion with his hand, said, "Who is that up there?"

Fitz Lee was looking into the fire, said, "Custer. Maybe Devin."

Lee waited for more, but the young man still stared at the fire, and there were no more words. Lee was now annoyed, felt his patience suddenly fall away, said, "Cavalry? Is that all . . . just cavalry? Are you sure?"

The young man looked up at him, heard the anger in Lee's voice, glanced at Gordon, who said, "There has to be infantry."

Lee looked at him. "Do you have information? Is there something I do not know?"

Gordon said, "No, sir. But they're out there. If they're not up ahead right now, they will be by morning."

Fitz Lee nodded, said, "Probably right. Custer didn't pull away. It wasn't a probe. He meant to dig in, hold his line. He's expecting support."

Lee looked at the fire again, closed his eyes. He had not done this, not in a very long time. He did not believe in councils of war, in calling everyone together at one time. If they were alone, one on one, he could depend on honesty, could feel out each man himself, read the face, read the heart, had always felt they would open up to him. But there was no time now, and after all, it was only these three who really mattered, who really controlled what would happen in the morning. They had spent little time together, had very little in common except that they were the best commanders he had left. He thought, No, that is no accident, there is something of God in this. The weak, those with no heart for the fight, are gone, taken away by Your will. You have left me with the men who can still do this, who can save us yet. Your hand still guides us. If we are to go on, if You will provide for these men, show me . . . something, show me a Sign.

He turned, saw Longstreet, who still watched him quietly. Lee looked out to the officers spread all around them. He moved away from the fire, looked at Longstreet, then the other two, said in a low voice, "Can we break through?"

Longstreet leaned forward, took the pipe from his mouth, said quietly, "We can always break through. If it's cavalry, we can break through easily. If it's infantry, it will be a bit tougher. But we can do it."

Lee nodded, thought of the strange mood, reading the letter from Grant. Longstreet was still criticized by the papers, too slow, too much defense. Even I thought him too stubborn, he thought, and now he understands what I want, what we need to do. Maybe he always knew. Maybe stubbornness is what we need now, more than anything else.

He looked at Gordon then said, "It will have to be up to your men, General. If they are in force . . . if General Grant has infantry blocking the road . . . we may not have an alternative."

There was a silent moment, and Lee waited, could not use the word, had not thought of the word all day, but he had to see it in their eyes, if they understood what he meant—that if they could not break through, the only alternative would be surrender.

Gordon sat up, looked at Fitz Lee, said, "If the cavalry can hold the road, move them back, we can push through."

There was another quiet moment, and Lee looked at Gordon, thought, He believes that. But it is not enough. If those people have moved infantry in front of us, if they have won the race . . . we are not strong enough.

He looked at Longstreet, said, "General, we must march the men now. We cannot wait until morning to see what is in our path. Your corps must close up the ranks, hold away those people in your rear, and stay close behind General Gordon."

Longstreet was looking at him strangely, and Lee suddenly understood, thought, *Corps.* No, do not think of numbers. It does not matter that we do not have the strength. It is God's fight now . . . we will take our strength from Him.

THREE A.M., APRIL 9, 1865

THE MEN WERE MOVING AGAIN, THE ROAD A SOLID MASS OF DULL sounds, shuffling feet. The lines were compact, Gordon's men near the town, moving out into open ground. Close behind, Longstreet's troops faced to the rear, prepared to hold off anyone who came in from behind.

Lee walked away from the small camp, the moon now far to the west, settling toward the horizon. He moved out that way, stepping through soft dirt, fields that had been planted, the seeds trampled by the bare feet of his army. He could see a few stars, but only a few, small flickers of light washed away by the brightness of the large moon. He kept moving toward it, tried not to think of all this, of what was happening, of what had already happened to his army. The commanders had been enthusiastic, were ready for whatever the day would bring them. He felt a great sadness about that, moved in a soft gloom, thought, They will do their duty, as long as I do mine. Their men will follow them as long as they lead. The war can still go on, and they will still fight as they have always fought. I do not understand that.

I had thought it would never come this far, that it would pass on and be done, and we could go home, and be with our families. But Fitz believes . . . probably many others as well, we should take to the hills, keep fighting in every town, every railroad, a guerrilla war. Anyone can shoot a musket, kill someone, a soldier, a politician. You can terrorize civilians, burn crops, destroy tracks . . . but that is not what this is about. We do not fight to simply . . . destroy. There is nothing different now, nothing different from four years ago. The cause is the same, the reasons for this fight are the same. If it is meant for us to stop this, to go home, if God gives us that message, then we must listen, we must obey.

He stepped down into a shallow depression, began to climb up. It was very cool, and he pulled his coat around him, thought, We can still win this . . . we can still pressure them to give up this fight. Grant cannot just make a war against us until we are all dead. There must come a time when they will have had enough, when they will not want any more trains filled with their young men, men in wooden boxes, or worse, masses of men pushed into great scars in the earth. There has always been a simple solution . . . *stop* this, just take your soldiers and leave our land. That's all we have wanted. It should never have been up to the guns, to these men who march on that road, who must still kill their enemy, or die themselves.

He felt a great wave of grief, felt himself letting go, pulled at it, thought, No, not even here, alone in the dark, you cannot lose control. He looked up at a faint star. God is here, right here, and He will grant us what we must have. He glanced out toward the road, could hear faint sounds still, one horse, moving slowly, but he could see nothing. He walked that way, climbed slowly up a rise, thought of the men, of the great fights, the power of the army, the quiet excitement that had filled him, the victory, the cheering of the men, the loyalty, the love. He had to see them, thought, Yes, we are still an army, and we can still do this, and there is nothing but the hand of God that can stop us.

He stepped through the soft dirt, reached the crest of the low hill, looked up at faint stars, then down, all along the horizon, could see more stars, many more, and they were large and bright. He stared, confused, and his eyes began to focus, and now he could see that they were not stars, the horizon was not lit by the glow from the heavens, but by the glow of campfires, a vast sea of light spread along the horizon, a glow from a vast blue force that spread all along the west, then down toward the south, a wide arc extending far beyond where his ragged army was pulling itself together.

He stood for a long moment, stared at the horizon, felt the glow rolling toward him like some hot wind, a sickness boiling up inside of him, pulling his breath away. He knew what the fires meant, thought, They are in *front* of us now.

He looked out toward the road, toward the small town where barely ten thousand men would wait for the dawn, would wait for *him* to lead them to the desperate fight.

50. CHAMBERLAIN

Dawn, April 9, 1865

I T WAS BARELY LIGHT, THE CHILL OF THE MORNING BROKEN BY the sweat of men who had moved forward in a steady rush. They were in column again behind Ord, and this time the wagons did not slow them, there was no bogging down in soft mud. They were pulled forward by the guns, by the great hard sounds that grew louder as they moved closer, louder still with every cresting of every small hill.

Chamberlain was wide-awake, felt his eyes burning now from the drifting smoke of the field, a light haze flowing through the treetops. He watched it, thought, It is not mist or fog. It is smoke, cannon, musket fire. He was excited now, as excited as he had ever been, held the horse to the side, waving his hand, spurring his men past him. He moved the horse alongside the column, rode up in front again, saw Ord's men keeping good time ahead, thought, Yes, excellent, don't slow us down, don't get in our way.

He felt a strange energy this morning, and for the first time he did not hear the small voice, that small angry place in his mind, the voice of reason, of pure survival, that says, "No, do not do this." The voice was there in all of them, had to be, yet it was the strength in his heart, his own will, that held it away, kept it silent. He had heard the voice many times, always in the face of the guns, and he'd seen the panic, the wild faces of the men who had listened to it, whose will had been swept away by the sound of that voice. He had always feared that one day it would happen to him, feared it even as he rode right into the fight, into the vast clouds of smoke, the horrible sounds. It had angered him, his own lack of faith in himself, that no matter how often he had done this, how many of the great battles and small sharp fights, he could still give in to the panic. But once the fight was hard in front of him, once he was a part of it, the voice was always silent.

It was the same every time, after every fight. There would come the quiet moment, the blessed satisfaction, the reassurance that after all the horrors he had seen, after the painful agony of his wounds, the voice could not turn him away after all. He thought of the word *soldier*. If that is what he had become, if he'd finally learned to ignore the voice, had silenced it, then he would never run away, never hesitate to march straight into the fight.

He was still moving, could hear the sounds rolling past him, louder, Sheridan's field guns, and he scolded himself, Do your job, stop thinking. It was the first time he had no fear of the voice, and he smiled, thought, This is, after all, an adventure.

He could see a man moving back along the column, cavalry, covered in black grime, and the man saw his rank, shouted, though there was no need to shout. "Are you in command? Are these your troops?"

Chamberlain heard the urgency in the man's voice, serious, dangerous, felt his heart suddenly pounding, said, "Yes . . . two brigades of the First Division, Fifth Corps."

The man pointed away from the road, still shouted, "Sir, General Sheridan wishes you to break off from this column and come to his support. The rebels are pressing him hard. Don't wait for orders through the regular channels. General Sheridan says to act on this at once!"

Chamberlain took in the man's excitement, thought, Is he authorized? And he thought of Warren, of the fatal delay, decided, No, I don't believe I will wait. Out through the woods he could hear Sheridan's guns, a new round of firing, and he turned, saw his staff moving close, yelled now himself, "Turn the column . . . follow this man. Leave a courier behind us, tell General Crawford to keep on the road, not to follow us! Move!"

Chamberlain glanced at the man with the bugle, saw the polished brass horn come up, the sounds echoing back to his men. He looked now at the cavalry officer, and the man was already moving into the woods. Chamberlain pointed, yelled again, "There, that way. Let's move!"

THE TREES OPENED INTO A WIDE CLEARING, THE SMOKE DRIFTING toward him in great thick clouds. His men filed into line, began to move ahead in battle formation. Chamberlain tried to see, had no idea where the cavalry officer had gone, guided his men by the sound of the fight in front of him. He rode forward, felt the smoke burning his throat, the heat in his lungs, thought, Keep moving, find out what is going on.

He saw a flag, horses, moved that way, saw the great black horse and the small man. Riding up quickly, he saluted, said, "General Sheridan. I have two brigades of infantry, at your service, sir."

Sheridan stared at him with a black fire, pointed toward the sounds, said simply, "There! Smash 'em up! Smash 'em to hell!"

Chamberlain looked to the front, the smoke drifting slowly away, could see it now, a heavy line of rebels and the blue cavalry, dismounted, a thinning line, falling back, the field scattered with the fallen blue troopers. The rebels were moving forward, slowly, against the men in blue. Chamberlain thought, They cannot hold . . . they need support. He looked around at his men, moving forward in a neat line, felt suddenly ridiculous, thought, Yes, of course, that's *us*.

There was a volley from the rebels, the smoke blowing out toward him, and he spurred the horse, rode back to his men, moved close behind the line. He looked for the bugler, saw officers watching him, waiting for the word. The men could see what lay in front of them now, already knew what was coming. Chamberlain saw the man with the bugle, yelled at him, "Now! Advance!"

The men surged forward, and Chamberlain moved down the line, yelling, "Forward, advance!" But the men were in a good hard line, and there was no wavering, no hesitation. He could see more infantry now, Ord's men, coming out of the trees far off to the side, and they were moving as well, the officers turning them, linking up with Chamberlain's flank, lengthening the line, a solid, growing wave. Chamberlain wanted to say, "Yes, thank you," but there was no need. The movement was automatic now, the fight pulling them forward, the enemy so close, right in front of them. He looked at his own lines, reaching the base of the wide hill, saw the muskets go up in one long motion, the order going out from officers he could not hear, his officers, the volley blowing the smoke back toward the rebels.

He could see the rebel line backing away, climbing up the hill, men still firing, the line breaking up. He looked across to Ord's lines, felt a sudden odd stab in his gut, could see a solid front of blue, pushing forward. He watched them, stared at the great long line of black faces, a Negro division . . . Birney's men. They moved in flank with his own line, pushing the rebels back farther up the rise, a steady advance, the rebels giving up the ground. He was lost for a moment, the sounds now somewhere else as he watched the Negroes begin to absorb the fire of the rebels, men punched back by musket fire, some simply collapsing, opening small gaps in the line. The line tightened up then, the officers and the sergeants pulling their men together, keeping the formation tight. What is this like for them? Chamberlain wondered. What are they feeling? My God . . . this is what we are fighting for . . . at least, it is what *I* am fighting for. And I can never know . . . I will never feel what this means to them.

A hot rush shook him, nearly knocked him from the horse, the sudden blast of dirt behind him, and the horse jumped. He focused, thought, Lawrence, your brain again. Back to work.

He could see his men climbing up the rise now, the rebels pulling away still, back along the crest of the hill, some moving beyond, out of sight. His men were in pursuit, yells echoing where the sounds of musket fire had stopped. He rode up close, thought, No wait, we don't know what is over the hill.

He waved the sword, a silent signal to hold them up, to wait. Now there were horses coming up from the flank, flags, and he looked at the man in front, arms waving, a man he didn't know. He turned that way, saw two stars, thought . . . Ord. Chamberlain saluted, waited.

Ord shouted at him, "General, keep your men off that crest. They will be exposed to fire!"

Abruptly, Ord was gone, the horses thundering away. Chamberlain stared at the cloud of dust, turned, looked up toward the crest of the hill. Exposed to fire? he thought. Isn't that what we're supposed to do? He thought of Sheridan: I do not believe those would be General Sheridan's orders. The words came to him again: *smash 'em up.* No, I believe General Sheridan would rather we advance. He sagged slightly, thought, *Generals.*

He saw the bugler watching him, the line now snaking along the side of the hill, the officers in front, pulling the men together, straightening the line. He nodded to the bugler, said, "Now . . . advance!"

The men began to move again, the line flowing forward, and then they were on the crest. He rode up quickly, thought, Careful, be ready to order the retreat.

The ground fell away in front of them, revealing a wide valley. He saw the small town, a scattering of buildings, a small line of trees snaking through the valley, the river now only a small stream. He reined the horse, heard the sound of one shell, the explosion ripping the ground in front of his line, another streaking overhead. Then there

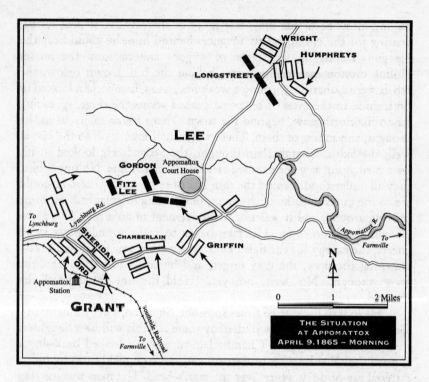

THE SITUATION
AT APPOMATTOX
APRIL 9, 1865 – MORNING

was a sudden breath of silence, and he stared in amazement, felt himself drawn forward, out across a vast field, short rolling hills, small trees. Below the wide hill, spread across the valley, was a mass of guns, wagons, and men; ragged lines, pulling back, drawing up into a defense. He thought, It is a division, and we're exposed. But there was no firing, no organized formation. Many of the guns were parked, neat squares, many of the wagons had no horses, and the troops were not gathering for a fight, were not gathering at all. He could see men sitting now, some standing without muskets, a few staring up the hill at the men in blue with a look he'd never seen before. Then he understood what lay across this small valley in front of him. It was not a division, it was not even a fighting force at all.

It was what remained of Lee's army.

HIS MEN BEGAN TO MOVE FORWARD, SLOWLY, ON THEIR OWN, and there was musket fire, scattered, men crouching low. He could see more of the Fifth Corps now, Crawford's men, pulling into line beside him, saw more of the cavalry, swords raised, waiting for the command to advance. Behind him, he could hear the big guns rolling up, the rattle of wagons and caissons, the horses pulling cannon into position just behind the hill. Down below, the rebels were gathering, forming a weak line, and Chamberlain looked to both sides, to the mass of blue that snaked across the ridge, spreading far to the north now, beyond the town. There are so many of us, he thought, and so few of them. There were small sounds off to the east as well; the Sixth, Chamberlain thought, the Second. He looked to his own men again, saw the stunned faces all along the line. No one spoke, they all understood. Behind the thin line of rebels below them he could see to the muddy banks of the river, men sitting in great masses, some moving around, and it was not the movement of an army. There was no command, no order. His men began to make sounds now, small cheers, the energy for the fight. He rode forward, saw them wide-eyed, watching the prey, the easy target, and he could feel the surge, the fever, thought, No, wait, not yet. "Hold the line, hold here!" he shouted.

He looked back, tried to see someone, Sheridan, Ord, thought, My God, if we attack . . . we will destroy them . . . this will be a slaughter.

Seeing a man point, Chamberlain turned and looked back down toward the rebel lines. A horseman was moving quickly up the hill, a tattered rag of dirty white over the man's head. The man was moving right, then left, and Chamberlain thought, He is looking for . . . someone in command. He is looking for *me*.

He rode forward, and the man saw him. Chamberlain could see the Confederate uniform, an officer, the uniform ragged but intact, and he thought, He is not combat . . . he is a staff officer. The man moved up the hill close to him, stopped, dismounted, held the ragged white cloth in front of him, looked nervously at the blue line. Chamberlain glanced at the muskets of his men, and no one was pointing their gun, there was no threat.

The man said, "Sir, I am from General Gordon. General Lee desires a cessation of hostilities until he can hear from General Grant . . . as to the proposed . . . surrender."

Chamberlain absorbed the man's drawl, could see the pain in his face, and now the word began to fill him: *surrender*. Close to him, the men who heard the man's words began to yell, to cheer, and the word proceeded to flow down the line, the voices growing louder. Chamberlain felt his stomach twist, thought, Can I do this? He thought of his own words now: There has to be the right thing to say. The officer watched him patiently.

Chamberlain said, "Sir, that matter exceeds my authority. I will send for my superior." He felt instantly foolish, the cold words of command, the formality. The man nodded slowly, understood, and Chamberlain turned, saw one of his aides, the man staring wide-eyed. Chamberlain waved him forward, said quietly, "Go to General Griffin. Find him. *Now!*"

He looked at the Confederate officer again, could see the dignity, the sadness, the man doing his painful duty. He thought, I should say something appropriate. . . . What is appropriate? How many times are we in this position? He removed his hat, at least a bit of courtesy, said, "General Lee is right. There is nothing more he can do."

The man nodded slightly, said nothing. Chamberlain's men had quieted, were all watching the officer, waiting. For what, he thought, something else? He looked out past the man, down the hill, out over the small valley. Out of the odd silence, there was a sudden sharp blast from down below, one gun hidden in small trees, and he heard the shell, the hard shriek. Down the line there was a quick rush of sound, a small blast, and he saw a man go down, falling from a horse. Men were gathering, and Chamberlain spurred the horse, moved that way, quickly dismounted. The men cleared away, and he saw a young officer, thought of the name . . . Lieutenant Clark, from New York. There was a hole in the man's chest, blood everywhere, and someone yelled for a doctor, but Chamberlain saw there was no need. He backed away, felt suddenly sick, turned from the horror.

The man in gray walked toward him, toward the body of the young lieutenant. The man said nothing, and Chamberlain looked at him, wanted to feel anger, to scream at him, the words hot in his mind, *This is your truce?* But the man kneeled down, lowered his head, and Chamberlain could see he was saying something, a quiet prayer. He stepped forward then, close to the man, thought of the word again, *surrender*, said quietly, "Pray that he is the last."

51. LEE

MORNING, APRIL 9, 1865

THE FIGHT HAD GONE EXACTLY AS THEY HAD PLANNED, GORdon striking hard at the blue cavalry, supported by Fitz Lee's horsemen. They had pushed Sheridan away at first, and for a brief time the road was open, escape possible. But Lee had seen it himself, the sudden ring of blue coming over the low hills, emerging from the woods, and very soon Gordon's men were fighting an enemy on three sides, and Fitz Lee's men became separated from the infantry, cut off out to the west. Gordon sent for help, requested in urgent terms that Longstreet come forward, turn his men to the front, but Longstreet was still holding a weakening line against the hard advance of two Federal corps.

The couriers had moved in and out of camp, the situation growing more clear. All along the front lines men were waiting for the command, to strike out again, to do whatever it would take to drive the enemy away. Lee had spoken to many, sorted through details of what they knew, of what they felt. Some still wanted to fight it out; if the mass of blue was too strong, the army could be divided, scattered into the hills, continue the war by any means. He was surprised at that, knew the passions were still high, but the talk of scattered resistance would only serve the needs of the soldier, of the men who would not end the fight. It would be devastating to the civilians, with the likelihood of brutal reprisals from Federal troops, and to the towns that would have to be occupied by force and governed by martial law. He listened to the passion, but had been firm and clear in his own mind. There could be no end to the blood and the death, and there could be no hope for a just peace, unless the war was stopped.

He had sent for Longstreet, who rode up now, trailed by a flag bearer and one other man, Billy Mahone. They dismounted and walked up the rise to where Lee waited. Lee stood straight, felt the tightness around his waist, the stiffness in the fresh uniform.

He had dressed early, searching through the trunk for the last clean one, and the one he rarely wore, reserved usually for the formality of Richmond. The uniform had not been worn in a long while. He had run his hand through the trunk, searching, finally felt the softness of the silk, an afterthought, had thought, No, too much, but then he put it around his waist, the red silk sash he'd always left in the trunk. The sword was a gift from the state of Virginia, would never see combat, was meant for some glorious ceremony, gold-trimmed, with a carved hilt and an elaborate scabbard. He'd never thought it would be worn, had even been embarrassed to receive it, but now it was there, hooked to his belt, a part of him.

He watched Longstreet move up the hill, taking long slow steps, and then he could not look at him, turned away, felt a sudden wave of sadness. Longstreet's right arm still hung low, the effects of the wound. He stopped, waited for Lee to speak.

Lee still would not look at him, said quietly, "There are heavy troop concentrations blocking our way west. General Gordon has not been able to break through."

There was a quiet pause, and Longstreet moved closer, looked past Lee, toward the sounds of scattered musket fire, a fading battle, said, "Sir, may I ask why you are dressed . . . this way?'

Lee still looked away, the voice still soft, said, "If I am probably to be General Grant's prisoner, I thought I should make my best appearance."

Longstreet let out a deep breath. "Is there nothing left? Surely, there is an alternative."

Lee looked at him now, saw the grim anger in the man's face, the look so familiar. "Do you have a plan, General?" he asked.

Longstreet looked down, and after a moment, said, "Is there anything to be gained by throwing this army forward . . . by making the sacrifice of these men? Can we gain some advantage . . . elsewhere?"

Lee thought of Johnston, and the numbers flooded his mind again, the vast strength that Grant could now send anywhere there was still a fight. He shook his head. "No."

Longstreet stared at him hard in the eye, and Lee felt it, the old power, the cold stubbornness. Longstreet said, "Then, your situation speaks for itself."

Lee nodded, looked back toward Mahone. "General, do you have a view . . . something to add?"

Mahone appeared nervous, moved forward slowly, glanced at Longstreet, said, "Can we not . . . continue the fight, sir? My division is still fit."

Lee looked at the young man, nodded, said, "How many men, General? Four thousand . . . perhaps more?"

Mahone seemed to energize, a show of enthusiasm, "Yes, sir. Absolutely, sir! Four thousand good men!"

Lee could not hide the sadness, looked at Mahone with tired, heavy eyes, thought of the numbers, carried them in his mind like some great wound. Mahone's faith in his division did not change the fact that Longstreet had barely eight thousand men holding the line in the rear, and after the fight this morning, Gordon had far fewer than that. The cavalry could not even be counted, but Lee knew that if his nephew had as many as two thousand troopers, he would be fortunate. He did not know the Federal numbers, but he knew who they were, and at least four corps plus Sheridan's cavalry meant he was outnumbered easily five to one. Lee raised his hand, pointed, motioned to the south, the west. "Do you know how many of those people are out there?"

Mahone thought for a moment, stared at Lee, absorbed his mood, and the young man's energy began to slip away. He glanced at Longstreet, said, "I do not suppose . . . we have enough."

Lee turned away, looked again to the west, out beyond the road that was now held tight inside the hard blue line, thought, It could have been . . . it could have taken us away. He wondered about that, if there were still a chance to escape, to take the army farther west, to take himself away from all of this, from the fight, from the death of his men. God had always been here, he thought, always . . . I felt Him. If He is here now, then I must do what He wants me to do. He thought now of the night before, some sign, some message that would lead them, but the message had come bathed in the hard blue of the enemy that was closing in all around them.

He looked at Longstreet now, felt a cold darkness in his chest, said, "There is nothing for us to do. It is time for me to go to General Grant, and accept the consequences for my acts."

He looked back down the hill, saw staff officers waiting, watching him, and he motioned them forward, his hand resting on the sword. He rubbed his fingers slowly on the scabbard, gripped the hilt, felt the cold weight growing inside of him. This is the message, he thought, this is the only path. He looked at Longstreet, felt the tears, had no strength to hold it away, his hand shaking now, the fingers letting go of the sword, said, "But I would rather die . . . a thousand deaths."

EARLY AFTERNOON, APRIL 9, 1865

T HE MESSAGE HAD GONE OUT TO GRANT, WRITTEN FOR HIM BY the young man in the round spectacles, the nervous hand of Charles Marshall. He had no idea where Grant was, had tried to reach him through the lines in the rear, as he had before, but there was no reply, and without a cease-fire, without the entire Federal line accepting a truce, there could be a new assault at any time.

It was the sheer bulk of the Federal forces that had slowed communication, the message passing from one front to the other. The dispatches were now flying back and forth, confused, uncertain, no one taking responsibility for ordering a truce. The word finally came that Grant had been on the move, the long ride down across the small river toward the town, from the rear of the army forward, to Sheridan's front.

Lee sat on the ground, leaned back against an old apple tree. The shooting had stopped, a fragile truce in effect, but still he had not heard from Grant. Around him, the staff had spread out, guards posted, holding the soldiers at a distance. Word of the truce had spread through his men as well as the Federals, and order was breaking down, men looking for him, to protest, to beg for the chance to fight on.

He did not hear it, the sounds of men from across the open ground, calling him, the anger, sadness, tears. He was thinking of Mary, of a letter, months before, while they were still in Petersburg, before the winter had ended. There had been such optimism, the energy for the new spring, for what would come, and the letter had been forgotten, pushed aside by the great flood of words and papers that came with the operation of the army. But now the letter came back to him.

I . . . shall endeavor to do my duty and fight to the last.

He imagined her reading the words, shaking her head, the mild scolding, her sad acceptance that yes, he truly believed it, truly believed the war would still go on, *must* still go on. Now, it would not, and already he was trying to understand that, what it meant.

He thought of Lincoln, had never imagined he would ever see him as . . . President, the commander-in-chief. Of course, Lee would not be in the army, would probably become a prisoner. And Davis . . . he realized now he had no idea where Davis was, or what might become of him. He ran names through his mind, his own staff. Taylor had taken a brief moment to be married, just as the defenses of Petersburg collapsed. Lee shook his head, could not help a smile. Taylor was the most vocal on his staff about continuing the fight, was ready to pick up a musket himself. He thought, No, young man, your life is beginning, something new, something worth going home to. They have that, the young ones. That is where the passion belongs, to yourselves, to creating a new life.

He heard horses now, looked up, saw past the men around him, to Longstreet, riding in a slow rhythm, both hands holding the reins, the good show for his men. Longstreet would still do that, he thought, still not let the weakness show. Lee pulled himself up, waited, and Longstreet dismounted, moved through the staff, saluted awkwardly with the left arm.

Lee said, "We are still waiting, General."

Longstreet nodded, held the pipe in his teeth, looked around, focused across the open ground, and men began to point. Longstreet said, "There . . . a flag of truce."

Lee followed his gaze, saw three men, two of them in blue, and they rode up fast, reined up beyond the cordon of troops. Lee felt a thump in his chest, moved forward, and the guards parted. Lee saw the Federal officer, a brigadier general, one star, and glanced at the man in gray, who saluted him. The third man took the three horses, stayed back. The Federal officer moved up, faced him, nervous, made a bow, removed his hat, said, "General Lee, I am General Babcock . . . of General Grant's staff. I have a letter for you, sir."

Lee took a deep breath, said nothing, nodded, reached for the paper that Babcock now held out. He stared at it for a moment, and opened the envelope.

General R. E. Lee, Commanding C.S. Army: Your note of this date is but of this moment (11:50 am) received. In consequence of my having passed from the Richmond and Lynchburg Road to the Farmville and Lynchburg Road I am at this writing about four miles west of Walker's church, and will push forward to the front for the purpose of meeting you. Notice sent on this road where you wish the interview to take place will reach me.

Very respectfully, your obedient servant,
U. S. Grant, Lieutenant-General.

Lee folded the letter, glanced at his pocket watch, pulled out a small stub of pencil, wrote the time on the envelope. It was one o'clock. He looked at Babcock, said, "General, I am concerned that the truce . . . will not hold. Can you see that General Grant's people be instructed to observe the truce until . . . our business is concluded?"

Babcock nodded, said, "Certainly . . . absolutely." He felt his pockets, and now Marshall was up beside Lee, handed a pad of paper to Babcock, who said, "Thank you . . . um . . ."

"*Colonel*, sir."

Marshall backed away, and Lee did not look at him, heard the hard emphasis on the word, the pride of the young man still intact.

Babcock felt his pockets again, and Lee now held out the pencil. Babcock smiled weakly, said, "Thank you, sir." He wrote something Lee could not see, and Lee waited, patient, now sensed Longstreet beside him. Babcock said, "There . . . sir, if you will have someone deliver this to General Meade's command, there should be no further hostilities from that part of the field. General Grant is up ahead, and I assure you, sir, that the truce will be observed there."

Taylor now moved up, and Babcock's note was carried away quickly. Lee reached into his pocket, pulled out a folded map, the sketches of roads, troops movements, thought, I suppose this should stay here. He reached out, handed it to an aide, now turned to Babcock, said, "I suppose, General, we should be on our way. Do you have some preference? General Grant is not specific."

Babcock made a short bow, said nervously, "I thought, sir, in the town, we can find a location that is suitable."

Lee said nothing, moved toward the horses, took Traveller's reins from an aide, reached up to the saddle.

Now Longstreet was beside him, said, "Honorable terms . . . unless he offers us honorable terms, we can still fight it out."

Lee stared out to the west, thought, No one here knows General Grant as well as you. He climbed up to the saddle, said, "Do you believe that will be a problem?"

Longstreet thought a moment, shook his head. "No, I don't. Sam Grant will be fair."

Lee spurred the horse, moved toward Babcock, who was climbing on his own horse. Lee glanced around, all the men now looking at him. Seeing Taylor, he said, "Colonel, I wish you and Colonel Marshall to accompany me."

Lee saw another man, recalled his face, Hill's man, the message brought to him on that awful day just a short week ago. Lee said, "Sergeant Tucker, will you accompany us as well?"

Tucker seemed shocked, said, "Yes . . . certainly, sir."

Marshall was on his horse, and Lee saw Taylor, standing close to the apple tree. Taylor was not moving, stared down at the ground, and Lee said, "Colonel Taylor . . . are you ready?"

Taylor looked up at him, and Lee saw the tears. Taylor said, "Sir . . . please, I ask you not order me."

Lee saw the pain, the sadness, in the young man who had been so close, such a part of the army, of Lee himself. Taylor sat now, his head in his hands, quiet sobs, soft sounds.

Lee watched him for a moment, fought it himself, said, "Very well. Colonel, you may remain here."

He turned the horse, nodded slowly to Babcock, and they began to move out across the field.

He could see the town in front of him, the small buildings, the courthouse. They rode out through the lines of his men, men who called out to him, as they always had, the men who never held anything from him, from the fight, from their affection for their commander. He moved through the lines, would not look at them, could not bear to see it in their faces. The sounds were enough, the cries, the sadness, the long years now suddenly closing in, the great long fight now passing, drifting out of them, the last piece of strength, the last emotion from the hearts of his men, pouring out across the field. Then the soft sounds were behind him, following him, inside, staying with him. He could not keep it away, held the sounds hard, tried not to show what it meant, the pain that was gripping him, pulling him back toward them.

He looked up, above the rooftops, looked into a vast sky, imagined the face of God, sad, forgiving . . . and now he saw them, the images on the clouds, the cold steel in the face of Jackson, the laughing playfulness of Stuart. They were his boys; more, they were his sons, and now the tears came, the sadness overwhelming him, the grief for a part of him that was gone forever.

52. GRANT

AFTERNOON, APRIL 9, 1865

HE REACHED SHERIDAN'S LINES, RODE PAST MEN WHO HAD already heard the news. They cheered, wildly at first, but he did not respond, moved quickly, held a cigar tight in his teeth. He was still not sure, could not really know if this was not some ruse, some deception. He had run that through his mind, that for Lee's army, it was the only way, the only escape. If they catch us resting, a lapse . . . but he thought of the letter, the last note from Lee, had read it through the hot cloud of the awful headache that had still tormented him. The letter echoed now in his mind, the cool blessed words.

> I ask for a suspension of hostilities pending the adjustment of the terms of surrender of this army . . .

After he read it the first time, the headache suddenly vanished, the violent fist gripping the back of his neck releasing him, as if chased away by some marvelous miracle. No, he thought, it is genuine, it is not deception. I have to believe that Lee is, after all, an honorable man.

They had ridden hard, along dusty trails and hard roads, the staff trailing out in a long column. He could see flags now, turned the horse, rode toward a group of officers, men who were waiting for him. He reined the horse, saw the faces, the expectations, then he saw Sheridan.

He dismounted, and Sheridan was quickly in front of the others, saluted, said, "General Grant! We should resume the assault, sir! I respectfully request that my men be allowed to finish this job, sir!"

Grant was surprised, said, "General, did you not receive a request for cease-fire?"

Sheridan made a grunt, said, "Oh, yes, I received it. Time enough for the rebels to strengthen their position! Five minutes, sir, five minutes, and this will be over. We have them right in front of us. The boys are itching to go. It will be short work. I guarantee it, sir!"

Grant glanced at the other officers, saw some men with Sheridan's fire, nervous motion, but there were others, sad frowns, small glances at the ground, men who did not share Phil Sheridan's eagerness for an easy fight. Grant said, "Are they moving troops? Have they shown any signs of advance?"

Sheridan shrugged, said, "Not that we can tell. But you know how they are, sir. Give them an opening—"

Grant shook his head, put up his hand, stopped Sheridan's words, said, "General, your precautions are noted. Have you not received something from General Babcock, some word of a meeting with Lee?"

Sheridan's face now fell into a gloom. "He is supposed to be . . . in the town. I didn't believe it, not sure I believe it now. But the message came for you to proceed at General Babcock's request."

Grant chewed hard on the cigar, thought, You would wait until you killed them all before you told me? "General Sheridan, you may accompany me. That should relieve your fears about the enemy's intentions."

Grant climbed the horse, glanced at Rawlins, Porter, the others, and said, "Gentlemen, let's find General Lee."

T HEY SLOWED AS THEY MOVED PAST THE HOUSES, THE SMALL buildings, storefronts. Along the hill in front of him, he could see the solid blue line, the sun reflecting off the bayonets, the men spread far out around the town. In the shallow valley below, he could see a line of rebels, and behind, the mass of dull gray, wagons, guns, all that was left of Lee's army. He heard Sheridan behind him, small comments, thought, Yes, five minutes, and the blood would be on our hands for all time.

He saw a man, ahead, waving, the clean blue uniform of an orderly, the man saluting now. Grant reined the horse, the men behind him slowing, the horses bunching up. The man was nervous, saluted again, seemed suddenly overcome, stared open-mouthed at the collective power of the men on the horses.

Grant said, "What is it, son?"

The man pointed, a house to the side of the road, a pleasant brick home, two-story, a small open yard, said, "There, sir! I am instructed to direct you . . . there!"

Grant saw three horses now, riderless, beside the house, and a man holding the reins, wearing a ragged gray uniform, a sergeant. He rode into the yard, dismounted, suddenly felt his hands sweating, looked at the front entrance of the house. It was quiet, with no one guarding the door. He stepped forward, reached the steps, stopped for a moment, turned, looked at the men behind him, thought, maybe . . . I should go alone, but no, it does not matter. They have earned it. This is something we will tell our children about. Say something to them, he thought, keep it dignified, quiet. But he saw the faces, and no one was smiling. He scanned the solemn faces, the weight of the moment keeping them all quiet, and even Sheridan removed his hat now. Grant turned, walked slowly up the steps, the sound of his boots echoing through the quiet of the house.

He passed through the door and into a hallway, did not wait. He saw Babcock off to the left, a warm room, dark, and Grant moved to the doorway, stopped, looked at three men, all standing, waiting for him.

Babcock saluted, and Grant nodded, returned it with reflex. Then he straightened, removed his hat, stepped slowly into the room. He could not help but stare at the calm dignity, the grace, of the man in the gray uniform facing him, straight and tall, the white beard not quite hiding the firm jaw, the dark weariness in the man's eyes.

Babcock said quietly, "Sir . . . General Grant, may I present . . . General Robert E. Lee."

Grant made a short bow, and Lee's expression did not change. Grant realized now how well Lee was dressed, saw the red silk, the extraordinary sword. There was a quiet moment, and Grant felt something odd, something he did not expect, thought, How difficult this must be. What would this be like if it were *me*?

He moved closer, held out a hand, said, "General Lee, thank you for meeting with me."

Lee did not smile, took the hand, a brief, firm grip, said, "General Grant, it is my duty . . . to be here."

Grant heard footsteps behind him, saw officers slowly filling the room, lining up along the wall. Lee glanced at them, and Grant thought, Familiar faces, surely he knows some of them. He looked now at Lee's aide, a young thin man in small round spectacles.

Lee caught the look, said, "General, may I present Colonel Charles Marshall."

Grant nodded, and Marshall made a short bow, said quietly, barely audible, "Sir."

The room was quiet again, the officers now still, and Grant began to realize what he was wearing. He glanced down, saw the mud on the boots, the dust on his clothes, was suddenly embarrassed, wanted to say something, realized he still held the cigar in his teeth. He slowly raised his hand, removed the cigar, said, "I hope you will forgive my appearance. I have ridden all morning to get here. There has not been time to change. . . . I'm not even certain where my trunk is, at the moment." He tried to be casual, relieve the tension, the quiet strain in the room, but no one spoke.

Lee simply nodded, said, "Quite all right, sir."

Grant could not take his eyes from Lee now, began to feel a growing sadness, did not know what to expect, thought, How would we ever know? We will never be in this position again. Lee's face still was hard, firm, and Grant looked for something, some sign, but could see now, thought, No, he will give nothing, he is holding it all in. Is this his way? Or perhaps he believes this is what men must do, something about gentlemen. Grant's mind was beginning to move now, a swirl of frustration.

"General Lee, I recall seeing you in Mexico. Perhaps you remember me? I was with the Fourth Infantry, a captain."

Lee shook his head slowly, said, "No, I don't recall. The Fourth . . . good unit. They were all good."

Grant thought, Of course, how would he know me? How many officers did he meet? He was General Scott's chief of staff. "Yes, all good men. It was a good fight. General Scott was, um . . ." He ran out of words now, frustrated again. What can I say to him about General Scott that he does not know? He glanced around, saw his men watching him, was impatient now, thought, I have never done well at this sort of thing, not even with Lincoln.

Lee now looked to the side, focused on a small oval table, said, "Perhaps, General, we should discuss the matter at hand. I have come to meet you in accordance of my letter this morning, to treat about the surrender of my army. I think the best way would be for you to put your terms in writing."

Grant nodded, scanned the faces, saw Ely Parker, his secretary, a pad of paper, an order book emerging from the young man's blue coat. He felt relieved now, the small talk was past, and he said, "Yes, I believe I will."

Grant moved to a small table, sat, put the cigar in his mouth, stared at the blank paper in front of him. There was quiet motion behind him, and a pencil was placed on the table. Grant picked it up, gripped it hard, stared again at blank paper, thought . . . words. I am not good with words. What is it we want? Then, tell him. He suddenly began to write, did not think, felt his mind pouring out on the pages. He kept writing, the only sound in the room the scratching of pencil on paper. He paused again, saw Lee quietly moving across the room, sitting now at the oval table. Lee's sword bumped the floor, and Grant stared at it, thought, Yes, there will be none of that, the stuff of newspaper stories, the ridiculous dramatics of handing over the swords. He wrote again, another page, then stopped, glanced back at Parker, who stood close behind him.

Parker leaned forward, and Grant held up the book. Parker read quietly, pointed to a word, and Grant frowned, of course, spelling too. He scratched at the word, corrected himself. Parker made a silent nod, and Grant put the book down flat again, took a deep breath. Then he stood, with the book, moved across the room and handed it to Lee.

Lee put the book on the small table, pulled a pair of spectacles from his pocket, wiped them slowly with a handkerchief.

Grant stepped away, nervous again, felt like a student, his words put before the grim judgment of the professor. He scolded himself, It's fine, it's simple, and it's what I want. He is taking his time, of course, give him a moment.

Lee now raised the book slightly off the table, and read.

Headquarters, Armies of the United States
Appomattox Court House, Va., April 9, 1865
General R. E. Lee, Commanding C. S. Army
General:
In accordance with the substance of my letter to you on the 8th instant, I propose to receive the surrender of the Army of Northern Virginia on the following terms, to wit: Rolls of all the officers and men to be made in duplicate—one copy to be given to an officer to be designated by me, the other to be retained by such officer or officers as you may designate; the officer to give their individual paroles not to take up arms against the Government of the United States until properly exchanged, and each company or regimental commander to sign a like parole for the men of his command. The arms, artillery and public property are to be parked and stacked, and turned over to the officers appointed by me to receive them. This will not embrace the side-arms of the officers, nor their private horses or baggage.

This done, officers and men will be allowed to return to their homes, not to be disturbed by United States authority so long as they observe their paroles and the laws in force where they may reside.

Very Respectfully,

U. S. Grant, Lieutenant-General

Lee nodded slowly, said, "Your concern for the dignity of the officers, their private property . . . this will have a positive effect on the army." Lee paused, hesitant, then said, "I must mention . . . in our army, the cavalry and artillery men own their own horses. May I request . . . that they be allowed to retain their animals?"

Our army, Grant thought. He must still believe that—that we are not one country. He said, "Under the terms as I have written them, no, they may not."

Lee looked down, and Grant saw the first emotion, Lee closing his eyes, a small glimpse of sadness. Grant watched him straighten, could see Lee fighting himself, holding the calm.

Grant thought, How important is that after all? Those men will go home now, back to the small farms, the land they will need to work to survive. He said, "I suppose it will be acceptable. I will instruct my officers to allow any man who claims a horse or mule to be allowed to keep it."

Lee looked at him with tired relief, said, "That is very kind of you, sir. It is planting season, and these men will need their horses." Lee paused, looked down at the book, said, "It will no doubt . . . be a long winter for many of them."

Lee handed the book to Grant, who turned, gave it to Parker and said, "Colonel, you may copy this in ink."

Officers now were moving outside, some leaving the room. Faces appeared in the doorway, briefly, and were gone. Now new faces appeared, to catch a quick glimpse of Lee, of the event in this modest house.

Grant reached for a chair, pulled it closer to Lee, sat now, said quietly, "General . . . I am aware of the lack of supply . . . of the difficult situation your men may be in. May I offer to assist?"

Lee straightened in the chair, nodded slowly, said, "Your cavalry has been most efficient. We have not had rations for . . . some time."

"If I may ask, General, how many rations would you require?"

Lee shook his head, and Grant saw the eyes close again. Lee said, "I am not entirely certain. Twenty-five thousand perhaps."

Grant turned, looked at Sheridan, said, "General, can you provide twenty-five thousand rations to General Lee's men?"

Sheridan seemed surprised, said, "Twenty-five thousand? That many? Why do they need—"

Grant glared at him. *This is not the time.*

Sheridan absorbed the silent message, said, "Uh . . . yes, sir. It is not a problem. We will make the arrangements."

Grant said nothing, turned to Lee, and Lee now looked up at Marshall, who still stood close behind him. Lee said, "Colonel, you may prepare a response to General Grant's letter."

Marshall sat now, pulled a pad of paper from his pocket, wrote a few lines. Grant waited as Lee read the words and said, "Colonel, it is not necessary to say 'I have the honor to acknowledge the receipt of your letter of such a date.' He is right here. Just say, I accept these terms."

Grant wanted to smile, but there was tension in Lee's voice, the guard coming down just a bit. Marshall wrote again, and Lee scanned the letter, then slowly handed it to Grant.

> Headquarters, Army of Northern Virginia
> April 9, 1865
> Lieut.-Gen. U. S. Grant,
> Commanding Armies of the United States
> General:
> I have received your letter of this date containing the terms of surrender of the Army of Northern Virginia as proposed by you. As they are substantially the same as those expressed in the letter of the 8th instant, they are accepted. I will proceed to designate the proper officers to carry the stipulations into effect.
> Very Respectfully, your obedient servant,
> R. E. Lee, General

Grant looked at the heading, thought, So, this house is now the headquarters of *both* armies. Grant looked back at Parker, who handed him the permanent letter, and Grant read it carefully, leaned down, took the pen from his secretary and signed his name. He moved across the room, handed the letter to Lee. Lee now took Marshall's letter, read it again. Grant watched him, saw Lee staring at the letter but not reading, was staring beyond, past the page, perhaps past this room in this simple house, out past all the men and guns and the horror of the past four years. Grant waited, would say nothing, felt the sadness coming again, the room very quiet now, the men understanding what was happening, what this moment meant. Lee blinked hard, took a pen from Marshall, read the letter one more time, the acceptance of the terms, the surrender of the army. Grant saw the pen shake slightly, saw Lee clench his fist, then slowly Lee signed his name.

GRANT STOOD ON THE PORCH, AT THE TOP OF THE STEPS, AS LEE and his aides moved away, the horses out on the road. The yard was full of men in blue, officers, men who had known Lee from years before, West Pointers, who had hoped to speak to their former superintendent; old soldiers, veterans of Mexico, or from Lee's cavalry command in Texas. Grant watched him move out of sight, looked across the yard, up the long rise, saw the flags, Ord's command, and the cavalry.

Suddenly, a big gun fired, a hollow blast, no shell, just a show of fireworks, and now the word was out all across the field, the men hearing from the officers that it was official, that it was *over*. Muskets began to fire, the voices drowned out by more big guns, and the men in the yard began to cheer as well, right in front of him. The depression, the sadness, still hung over him, and he began to feel the anger, the slow rage filling him. Rawlins was there now, grabbed his shoulder, said something loud, some boisterous cheer. Grant glared at him, looked out at all of them, and above him, on the hill, another big gun opened up, a spray of fire blooming from the barrel. In the yard he saw a man with a bugle, caught the man's eye, motioned for the man to come close, said quietly, "There will be none of this. . . ."

The man did not hear him, stepped up close, smiling, a toothy grin, said, "Yes, sir? Orders, sir?"

Grant stared at the man with grim anger. The man's smile vanished, and Grant said, "Stop this! Blow the call to formation! To inspection . . . anything! There will be *none* of this!"

Now Sheridan was beside him, heard the order, and he was suddenly down the steps, the orders flying. Then men were on horses, moving away in all directions.

Grant moved into the yard, mounted the horse, sat for a long moment, waited, and the sounds began to quiet, the guns did not fire. He was still angry, thought, This is not a celebration . . . there is no dignity, no honor, in humiliation. They do not need to be told they are beaten, they do not need us to tell them *we* have won. He began to move, and the men were quiet now. There were still a few cheers, a few hats waving, but around him men were watching Grant move past, and they began to absorb what was in his face, began to understand. Some were looking down across the fields, toward the camp where the men of Lee's army were lining the road, sad low cries, men gathering now around their leader as he rode slowly back into their lines.

Grant moved the horse in a slow rhythm, thought, I have learned something today, something about dignity, about the power of that, what it means to have respect from your men. He is . . . the *symbol*, he carries it with him . . . everything those men fought for. Even in defeat, even now, he still has the dignity. It is no wonder they fought for him. He had thought of that often, not just the strategy, the frustration with Lee's military mind, but the other, the intangible, They have followed him until they simply could do no more. If we had not . . . subdued them, they would still fight, no matter how few their numbers, whether they had food or guns or nothing at all. You cannot ask for that, you cannot order it. You just go about your work and your duty with absolute honesty, you fight for something you believe in without any other motive. Lee simply did not believe he was ever wrong, or would ever lose.

He thought now of the others, a long list of familiar names, thought, This army, any army, is filled with men who stake their claim, who plan their own place in history. But there is no honor in that—because their name reaches the newspaper does not mean they hold any special power, anything to be respected. You don't create honor, it creates you. I saw that today, I saw it in the man's face, in the eyes, in the man's heart. We prevailed on the field, we defeated his army . . . but we did not defeat *him*.

He looked up along the rise, saw the flags of the Fifth Corps, thought of Griffin and Warren, controversy and conflict, men who deserve the honor and men who don't. Now he stopped the horse, thought for a long moment, remembered one name, the commander who had been wounded . . . thought to be dead, the man who came back, who always came back, the man Griffin always spoke of. Grant tried to picture the man's face, but it was not there, just the name, and something came to him, stuck in his mind. The man was not a soldier, not a West Pointer, had come to the army from a college somewhere in Maine. But he was always there, in front, the hot places, had become a soldier by earning it, not by pronouncement or politics or simple good luck. Grant thought, Yes, that's what we need, not a professional, not someone who is just performing another duty. We need someone who will go back home to his family and tell them how important this is, what we have done here, what it feels like to be here.

He still tried to see the face, remembered something Griffin had said, something about words, language. Grant thought of the surrender document, the struggle for the right words. No, I don't want another military man, I want someone who can tell the people . . . who can use the right words. He turned now, saw Porter, pointed up the hill, said, "The Fifth Corps, go up there, find General Griffin, get word to him that I have chosen the man I want to receive the arms of Lee's men."

Porter moved up beside him, pulled out a crumpled piece of paper, a pencil, said, "Yes, sir, uh . . . the name, sir?"

Grant looked up the hill, said, "Brigadier General Joshua Chamberlain."

53. CHAMBERLAIN

APRIL 12, 1865

I T WAS GRAY, DREARY, AND THE ROADS WERE STILL SOFT FROM THE
rains of the past two days. He had received the order from Griffin,
still did not truly believe it, that *he* would be singled out, or even
remembered at all by the commanding general. But Griffin had been
clear and direct, and there was no ceremony, no dramatics. Chamberlain had thought, All right, but not just the brigade, it should be all of
us, the division, the corps, maybe the whole army. It was not possible,
of course, much of the army was already breaking camp, moving away.
But the First Division, Griffin's old command, would remain around
the town, and Chamberlain had insisted, had been as firm as anyone
could be to Charles Griffin, and Griffin had no objection at all. The entire division would line the road, both sides, would be a part of it, of
the ceremony none of them would ever forget.

He was on the horse, still wore the same coat, had been embarrassed about that, poked his fingers through the holes, neat and round,
punched by the musket balls of the men he would see today. No, it is
all right, he thought. No one will notice. And if they do, I suppose that
is all right too.

There had been some low voices, nervous talk down the line, and
in the distance they could see the rebel camps, the tents coming down,
the flags lowered. He could hear their bugle calls, felt the sound in
some uneasy place, a sound he had heard before, but the notes were different now, slow calls to order, to formation. The men far down the
line could see movement on the road now, the gray column in motion,
and a low murmur spread up the road toward him. He felt his gut
churn, felt the hard thumping in his chest, and finally he could see
them coming up the long hill, marching toward him.

They were led by an officer on horseback, and Chamberlain watched him, the back straight, the uniform clean, as clean as could be in the mud of the camps. The man's face was trimmed by a short beard, a neat point below his chin. Chamberlain saw nothing else now. If this man was in front of the column it was for a reason, a choice made not by chance but by something in the man himself. The horse was moving slowly, with steady steps, and the man was now close to him, looking straight ahead, the eyes cold, dark, accepting the challenge of the moment, and Chamberlain could see it all, the sadness, the courage. He did not know all the flags, how to identify all the gray units, or even how many units were still a part of Lee's army. He saw the red banner, held by another officer, behind this one commander, and now the name came, the recognition of one of Lee's best. Chamberlain felt a sudden rush of excitement: John Gordon.

Gordon moved past him, then reined the horse, and now Chamberlain saw the first of the foot soldiers, felt a small shock, the lines neat, the men marching straight, upright. But their uniforms were rags, pants torn, feet bare. The officers had some faint symbols of rank, but the coats were faded, sleeves frayed. Even the horses were gaunt, bones held together by raw patches of hide. The column was halted, and there was a quick shout. The men stood at quiet attention, and for the first time he could see the faces. They stared hard at the men who faced them a few feet away, who might have faced them on different ground in some very different place. The faces were thin, drawn, rough, and Chamberlain thought, These are the ones who still would fight, the ones who did not fall away, did not lose the strength, who are here now because it is their duty to be here.

There was another quick shout, and the men drew their bayonets, fixed them in one motion down the line, and for one brief moment he had a stab of fear, thought, How many times . . . and they know it too, they know that when the bayonets went forward, we would be close, we would look straight into the eyes, and the better man would win. The word stuck in his mind. No, not *better* . . . there is nothing in that here, this has not been some contest, some test of resolve. Look at these men, look at the faces, the strength in the eyes. They are, after all . . . *us*.

There was another order, and the men stepped forward, began to stack arms, making small pyramids, the bayonets pointing up, locking together. Then cartridge boxes were unhooked from belts, some from pieces of rope, some pulled from pockets. Slowly the boxes were piled beside the muskets, and the men backed into line, waited for the next command. He saw the smaller flag, had not really thought about that, had focused still on the bayonets, on the dull steel he'd seen too many times, but now one man stepped out of line, held the flag above him for a moment, and Chamberlain saw the man was crying, the flag slowly coming down, the man draping it carefully on the points of the bayonets. The man's head dropped and he let go of the staff, moved back into line. Suddenly, several of the men broke ranks, hands went out, small sounds, and now, loud sobs, the hands were touching their flag, men dropping down, kneeling. No one spoke, there were no orders, then slowly the men began to stand again, helping each other, moving back into line.

The line was straightened again, with a quiet look from an officer, the men standing at attention. The faces were fixed again, men fighting for control, for the dignity of the moment. There were still tears, small sounds, faces staring across to the men in blue. Then Chamberlain heard the low sounds beside him, behind him, could hear the quiet respect, the sadness coming from his own men. He looked at Gordon again, who stared ahead, waiting for the appropriate moment, waiting to move on, to bring on the rest of the column, the regiments, the brigades, passing the entire army along this road, every unit repeating the ceremony, with more stacks of arms, more bayonets, more flags.

Chamberlain glanced to the men beside him, saw his young sergeant, the man with the flag of the Fifth Corps now, the red Maltese cross. There was another man beside him, another flag bearer with a larger flag, the stars and stripes, the flag of the army, of the Union, and the flag was fluttering in the slight breeze. Chamberlain saw the faces again, the men in the road looking up at the flag, thought, Yes, it is still yours . . . it has always been yours. Despite all you have done, all of the death and the horror, the anger and the hatred. You have proven you will fight and die for something that you believe in. That is exactly what this flag means, has always meant.

He saw more faces looking up, drawn by the slow wave of the flag. There were still some angry glances, the fight not yet out of all of them, and Chamberlain thought, Well, that might be a good thing. It will take another kind of fight, a different strength now to pull us together, to mend what this war has done. They still have the strength, the will, and there is great value in that, for all of us, for the country, for the future. We are blessed by that, we are blessed that we can welcome them back, that we are all again under one flag. I salute you . . . no, we will *all* salute you.

The words came into his mind, and he did not hesitate, said in a loud voice, *"Carry . . . arms!"*

Men were looking at him, surprised, small voices, and he looked to the side, stared hard at the officers closest to him, would not repeat the order, knew they had heard it, knew they understood. Now the order echoed all along the line, all down the road.

They all knew what the order meant, that the killing anger, the hatred, the blind violence of the beast was gone, and the men who stood face-to-face were brothers after all. Now the order was obeyed, and the men in blue held their muskets up to their chests, the quiet salute, the show of respect.

Gordon was looking at him again, his face changed now, the eyes soft. Slowly, Gordon raised his sword, held it high, then dropped it down, low by his side, the point of the sword to the toe of his boot, the response, the soldier's salute.

54. LEE

APRIL 12, 1865

Headquarters, Army of Northern Virginia
General Orders: No. 9

After four years of arduous service marked by unsurpassed courage and fortitude, the Army of Northern Virginia has been compelled to yield to overwhelming numbers and resources. I need not tell the brave survivors of so many hard fought battles, who have remained steadfast to the last, that I have consented to this result from no distrust of them; but feeling that valor and devotion could accomplish nothing that could compensate for the loss that must have attended the continuance of the contest, I determined to avoid the useless sacrifice of those whose past services have endeared them to their countrymen.

By the terms of this agreement, officers and men can return to their homes and remain until exchanged. You will take with you the satisfaction that proceeds from the consciousness of duty faithfully performed; and I earnestly pray that a Merciful God will extend to you His blessing and protection.

With an unceasing admiration of your constancy and devotion to your country, and a grateful remembrance of your kind and generous consideration for myself, I bid you all an affectionate farewell.

R. E. Lee, General

He had stayed in camp until the surrender was complete, could not yet leave until the business of the disposition of his men was concluded.

He had ridden well beyond what remained of the camp, saw many of his soldiers still scattered about, and many of the men in blue, small groups, larger gatherings, some from simple curiosity, some old friends, veterans of another time, when they had served for the same cause.

He did not ride with the column, would not be a part of the ceremony, had made the excuse to himself, No, it is not necessary, my own surrender is already past.

But he knew it was far more than that, that after all, he would have been more of a disruption than support, that the men would have still rallied around him. The emotion of that, of seeing the flags go down, the faces of the men, would have been more than he could have endured. Already now his mind was moving on, as it always had before, to the great bloody fields. It never could be any other way, not for the commander, not for the man who ordered the men to go forward, to march into the guns. The death of the soldiers could not stay with you, haunt you, you could not hold the faces in your mind. The memories of all the horror, of what had happened to each man, each part of his army, all of that had to be put away somewhere, locked into some deep place. It had always been that way, and it would be that way now, leaving this behind, moving on, to the next place, the next duty, the new responsibility. When he moved the horse out onto the road, heading east, toward Richmond, he tried to convince himself this was no different, that he had already moved past all of this, was guided by the hand of God toward another destiny.

Taylor and Marshall rode with him, and they led a small headquarters wagon, the last of the personal effects. There had been no fanfare, no parting speeches, just the simple text of the General Order that Marshall had penned for him. He hoped to just slip away unnoticed, had absorbed all the overwhelming sadness that he thought possible, the pain of the men, the suffering in their bodies, now, in their hearts. He could not look again at the faces, could not hear the sounds, but he began to see it would not be that simple. All along the road, they began to gather, waiting for him, lining both sides, all out in front of him.

General Gibbon had sent a squad of blue cavalry, an escort, some measure of security for Lee's return to the capital, but Lee declined, knew that in this country, riding through this land, there was no threat, no danger, that there was no place on earth where he felt more at ease. But his own men were changing that, and the sounds were all around him now. He tried not to see, to just take himself away from it, but it was not to be. Finally, he began to acknowledge them, a glance, a small nod, a lifting of his hat.

They were letting it all go, holding nothing back. There was no need for the dignity of the ceremony now, for the decorum of the military. They were all veterans, some showing the effects of the hard march, many marches, but now there were no officers to hold them in line, and as he passed by them, they seemed to just come apart, men collapsing along the road as he passed, whose tears now soaked the ground they had given everything to hold. There were still the wounded, men in bandages who could only reach up with one arm, others who simply stood and stared, whose bodies were used up, their minds a fog of fatigue and hunger.

Some were calling out in anger, and he had expected that, and it burned into him worst of all, the men who still wanted to fight, who would blame him for giving in, for taking that away. They will understand, he thought, they will have to. He wanted to speak to them. If there had been one speech, something to leave them with, it would not have been some inflammatory call to the Cause, that they should keep the fire blazing for what they had fought for, as though, maybe, one day, they could do it all again. No, he thought, I can never say that, it is not in me to do that, not anymore. He had tried to move beyond the sadness of that, fought it with every sound he heard, every voice calling out to him. They need more than I can give them, they need more than words. There must be a healing, to move them forward, as I must try to move forward. You must put all of this . . . emotion, all this energy, toward home, to rebuild your lives, go back to the families that so desperately need you, the towns and states that need your strength. You must understand . . . there can be no other way, the Message is so very clear. It is the will of God that we bring ourselves back peacefully into one country.

As he moved farther from the camps, there were fewer men, and the cheers and crying began to fade. He kept his mind busy with memories, not the grim painful ones, but strategy, things that might have been done differently. But he had little energy for that. It was the sadness that came back, that would not leave him be. He tried to remember the beginning, the enthusiasm, his own doubts about what a war would do, how long it could last. But his mind was drifting, and he could not think of four years, of how long that was, what had been taken from him, from them, from the ones who had survived. The dead were in that wonderful place, and he thought of that, how many times God had nearly taken him, the sounds of the guns, the musket balls so close. But He did not take me, He left me for . . . this. He left me to take all of this home . . . and perhaps that is my destiny . . . my punishment. Perhaps I am to atone for this, that the memories must continue, the horrific numbers, the faces of all the souls who are now at rest. So many of us are with Him now, so many died for something they believed in, an honorable death, and after all, is that not what God rewards?

The thoughts began to run together, the weariness of the last few days now complete. There will be time for this, he thought, time for reflection. But . . . not now, I cannot do this now.

He moved through a stand of trees, could see a farmhouse beyond, an orchard, thought, This year, there will be a bounty, there will not be an army to feed. The land will heal, will become fertile again, God will give us that. The plague is past.

He knew Mary was in Richmond now, a modest house provided by the generosity of friends. He did not know if they would stay there long, if there would be some life for them in the city. He knew that many of the troops would gather there, men who had nowhere else to go, whose homes had been destroyed, whose businesses were gone. I can help them, I suppose. I can do little else. They have given so much to me.

He still had not heard from Davis, knew he was somewhere south, Danville, or maybe farther down. Sherman's army was still looking for a fight with Johnston, and Lee knew there would not be much of a fight now. Johnston understands what all good soldiers understand, he thought. There must come the time when you simply stop the killing. They do not teach that at West Point, it is something a commander feels inside of him. Death is necessary, it is a part of war, of anything worth fighting for. But to butcher your army just so they can fight again tomorrow . . .

He had seen Grant briefly again, a small conversation, polite, cordial. Grant understands as well, he thought, what must happen now, what this country must begin to do. He had been surprised at first, Grant's sincerity, nothing of the madness, the cold anger that many in Lee's army had believed. No, he is no demon, he has been simply and utterly efficient. Once the war became the great horror, what so few had ever understood would happen, once these two great armies brought all the power and passion to the field, there could be no other way to resolve it. The foolishness of the politicians, the fat men with their fiery oratory, their hot words, igniting the people into believing this was the only way . . . once that happened, the die was cast. How few understood that, especially in the beginning. But Grant did understand.

He did not know where Grant was now, thought, Probably on his way to Washington. He deserves all they can give him, all the recognition, the cheers, the celebration. *To the victor go the spoils. . . .*

He thought of Lincoln too, as he had before. There is only one President now, only one country. To some, that will never be, the wounds will not heal quickly. But Lincoln will do much . . . he will try. It is in the man, in everything he has said. He wants this to be behind us . . . *with malice toward none* . . . We can hope for nothing else. As long as he keeps control, keeps the angry voices at bay, those who would seek any excuse to punish, to bring down revenge on us, then the wounds can heal.

The sun was setting behind him now, the gray sky opening a bit, the clouds now bright with color. He did not look back, let Traveller carry him at his own pace. He stared ahead, his mind drifting away, moving far beyond the desolate land around him. He closed his eyes, rocked gently with the motion of the big horse. Yes, there is still time. His mind began to fill with the soft smells and joyous sounds, of lush fields and cool green hills, the voices of children, the memories of all he had missed, all that he had left behind. He was going home.

55. GRANT

APRIL 14, 1865

H E HAD BEEN IN WASHINGTON FOR TWO DAYS, MOSTLY THE
official business of the army, but much of the detail could be
handled by the various commands, the men in the white
buildings. He'd been offered a chance to pass through Richmond, to
see the last remnants of the great prize the army had been told so much
about. It meant little to him when he took command, and it meant
little to him now, and so he felt no need to parade through the destruction, felt no sense of pride or accomplishment that a city lay in ruins.

Wherever he went in the capital, crowds had gathered. There was
nothing secret about his return to the city. Since the word of Lee's surrender reached Washington, Lincoln himself had spent much of his
time waving to the great flocks that spread into the streets beyond the
White House, and now, knowing that Grant had arrived, the crowds
were even more enthusiastic. Grant had to move with an escort, could
not hope to travel anywhere in the city without a large mass of blue
clearing the way. They all wanted to give him something, if only their
absolute attention to anything he might want to say, any small speech.
When he could ignore them no longer, when the voices swelled loudly
enough that he had to wave, even a brief nod, a tip of the hat, there
would be a loud cheer.

Now, in the sudden quiet of the White House, the first quiet moment all day, he felt the relief, safety behind thick walls. He waited in a
small sitting room to see the man who'd given him so much, the patience and faith that had allowed him to press the fight to its conclusion. He remembered his first visit, the hesitation, the embarrassment,
the grand portraits, the artifacts, the history of his country symbolized
so deeply in that one place.

He could hear voices behind the great door, laughter, then the door opened and two men in fine wool suits came out of Lincoln's office, filling the quiet space in the small room. Grant stood out of polite instinct, and now they saw him, one man staring as if paralyzed by his good fortune.

"You're . . . General Grant! My word, sir, it is a pleasure! Have you seen the crowd? Have you, sir? You must go to the window, say a few words! The President has been speaking to them all day, I'm sure they would be thoroughly excited! Indeed!"

Grant waited for the rush of words to pass, had no idea who the man was, tried to smile, thought, Yes, this is Washington. "Thank you," he said. "Perhaps I will address the crowd later."

"Ah, well then, I am certain they will wait for you! No one in this town can draw the audience you can, sir! You, sir, are the topic of every conversation!"

Grant nodded politely, said, "Thank you, you're very kind." He looked beyond the man's beaming, bobbing face, saw Lincoln standing in the doorway with a weary smile.

Lincoln said, "Mr. Grant, if you please?"

Grant moved forward, gently pried himself past the two men, said, "Excuse me . . . the President . . ."

The men watched him go, the other man now reaching out, grabbing Grant by the shoulder, a hard grip, said, "Good show! The stuff of Presidents!"

The other man slapped his friend's back, said, "Yes! Absolutely fine idea! Washington has a way of finding the best men!"

Lincoln waited for Grant to move by him, closed the door, the voices of the two men still echoing their enthusiasm. Lincoln moved around behind his desk, sat down heavily, shook his head, said, "Please, have a seat, Mr. Grant. Forgive the show of . . . hero worship, if I dare call it that. They're quite right, you know."

Grant sat, saw past Lincoln, an open window, could now hear the sounds of a crowd. He absorbed Lincoln's words, said, "Right . . . about what?"

"Presidential, Mr. Grant. We love our heroes. Generals have a way of getting out the vote: right from the beginning, Washington, Andrew Jackson, Zachary Taylor. I have no doubt, if you were to make it known, you could walk right in here and take up shop!"

Grant was suddenly uncomfortable, said, "Why? I mean, sir, excuse me, but my place is in the army. This place, this city, has never appealed."

Lincoln sat back, smiled, "Ah, but that's why it would work. You're not a Washington man, you're a hero! Here, look outside . . ."

Lincoln turned in the chair, motioned Grant toward the window. Grant stood, thought, I don't really want to make a speech, moved reluctantly behind Lincoln, took a small peek over his shoulder, and now the sounds outside exploded, loud cheers, calls of *"Grant! Grant!"* Lincoln stood, backed away, and Grant was fully in view now, saw a sea of faces spread all across the White House grounds, all down the street. He stared, amazed, thought, This cannot be, not for . . . me? He raised his hand, a small self-conscious wave, and the noise exploded again, louder still. He backed away, stared toward the window, said, "This is . . . strange."

Lincoln, in his chair again, laughed. "Nothing strange about it. They even cheer *me*. Haven't heard that in a while. I admit I can't help but say a few words, the instincts of a politician, I suppose. These are happy days, Mr. Grant. We have been through the most dreadful time in our history. And we have survived. The rule of law, the Constitution, has prevailed. And that's not just from a politician. Look at those people, look at the newspapers. This is one big celebration!"

Grant sat again, said, "I'm not sure about that. There's some rebels still holding out, Richard Taylor's people, Kirby Smith. May take some time yet."

"Those are details, Mr. Grant. If I may, allow me to pass along a secret. Several of the states are already in contact with us, trying to work out the transition back into the Union. That will spread. Once the southern politicians understand that it can be a simple matter, that there is no restitution, that this is not about punishment, that we in fact welcome all the states with open arms, there will be no long-term problems . . . the Union will become one again."

Grant thought a moment, said, "I have a hard time believing it will be a simple matter. There has to be some bad blood, some open wounds. What about Jefferson Davis?"

Lincoln frowned. "Ah, Davis. If only I could do something about that. He doesn't have to be captured, you know."

Grant was surprised, said, "Of course . . . I mean, sir, I would think his capture is a necessity."

"From your point of view, I understand that. Consider this, Mr. Grant. If he is caught, he will be tried, and convicted, and possibly hanged. Then he becomes a martyr. That's how wounds stay open. The best thing that can happen is if he simply . . . disappears. I would not mind if he, say, crossed into Mexico, maybe found his way to Europe. He no doubt has friends who would expedite all of that. I can't suggest this publicly, of course . . . you understand that, don't you, Mr. Grant?"

Grant nodded. "Yes, I suppose so. But I can't tell my people to just . . . stop looking for him."

Lincoln stroked his chin, rubbed his beard. "No, of course not. But unofficially, Mr. Grant, it would be better all around if he simply . . . left. Solves another problem too. Anyone who still thinks the Confederacy should continue can follow him. Take a lot of starch out of the fire breathers in the South. A government in exile is better than a government coming to its end on a gallows."

Grant shook his head, said, "Never thought of it that way. That's why I'm not suited for this office. Intrigue . . . the intrigue behind closed doors. Forgive me, sir, but this job is in the right hands. My job is much simpler now."

Lincoln nodded, smiled again. "So, I understand Mrs. Grant is here as well?" Lincoln had changed the subject, and Grant felt a small sense of relief.

"Yes, sir, she's at the hotel. I'll be taking her up to New Jersey tonight. We have a house now in Burlington, on the river."

Lincoln frowned. "Burlington . . . the river, yes, lovely place. Well, that's too bad, Mr. Grant. Must you leave so soon? I assumed we would see more of you. This city is positively hungry for your presence."

Grant thought of Julia, of the new home, her impatience to leave the city.

"I will discuss it with her, sir. I know she is anxious to be under way. The children are already up there." He stopped, could see the disappointment in Lincoln's face, was surprised, suddenly felt guilty, thought, Well, maybe we can stay. One more day, surely . . .

Lincoln held up a hand, said, "It's all right, Mr. Grant. Talk to her, and if you can't persuade her to change her mind, I will understand. I am well acquainted with female willpower. Please convey our invitation, however, Mrs. Lincoln and I would be delighted to have your company. And I am quite certain the people would receive you with some enthusiasm." Lincoln laughed. "You might even stop the show."

Grant did not understand, said, "I'm sorry, sir . . . show?"

"Oh, yes, Mr. Grant. We're going to the theater tonight."

THE ABSENCE OF THE CHILDREN WAS MORE THAN SHE COULD stand, and Grant sent word to the White House that his wife's impatience had prevailed after all. The train took them to Philadelphia, then they moved through the city to the wharf along the wide river, where the ferry was taking them to the New Jersey side.

It was late now, and the ferry was just slowly making its way to the far shore. He had thought of spending the night on the Pennsylvania side, waiting until tomorrow to cross the river. But the word was out, General Grant was there, and crowds had begun to gather at the wharf, the atmosphere of a party.

Now, they would find someplace to eat a late dinner, and then board a train, the last leg of the trip up to the town of Burlington, a few miles upriver.

HE AND JULIA WERE IN A SMALL RESTAURANT NOW, A SMALL piece of privacy in a hotel near the river. He'd finally allowed himself to feel hungry, sat now in front of a plate of brown roast beef. His back was to the hotel lobby, and Julia could see the faces, a growing crowd of people, straining to see him. He was cutting the hard beef, tried not to hear his name in the general murmur of the crowd, which was kept away by the efficient energy of a gracious host. Julia still looked past him, was smiling, said, "You know, Ulyss, you could go out and say something to them."

He looked up at her, his mouth working the dry meat, said, "They'd be just as happy to hear from *you*."

She frowned at him, and scoldingly said, "Now, that's not very kind of you! You are quite the celebrity. They are being quite generous. No need to be rude, you know!"

He saw her looking out toward the crowd again, thought, Yes, she truly loves this, the attention. I suppose, maybe for her, I can say something, a few words, maybe get them to go on home. He stabbed at the last piece of meat, stuffed it in his mouth, tried to think of something, words, thought now of Lincoln, the wonderful stories, at ease in any crowd. It was a talent he knew he didn't have. He swallowed the last of his dinner, took a deep breath.

Suddenly there was a man beside him, a neat uniform, but not army, something else, a courier. Grant looked at the man's face, and the man was looking down, said in a quiet voice, "Sir . . . we have a telegram for you."

Grant took the paper, saw the strange look on the man's face, something very wrong, and he thought, What could have happened? He opened it, read the telegram, stared at the paper, the words unreal, thought, No . . . this cannot be true.

Julia was waiting, impatient, said, "What is it, Ulyss? What does it say?"

He looked at her, felt a deep cold hole open in his gut, and he looked at the message again, thought, No, this is wrong, I read it wrong. But the words were clear and brief, and the message was the same. He tried to breathe, looked at her again, said, "President Lincoln has been shot."

THE HOPE, THE JOYOUS RELIEF THAT THE HORROR AND SAVagery was past, that the rebuilding was under way, was now replaced by something else, by the last shocking blow.

The last casualty of the war was not the tragic soldier, the man who fought for honor and a cause, who faced his enemy across the deadly space. It was instead Lincoln's optimism, a belief in a future made glorious by the rights of the individual, that everything planned for this nation by the men who founded it could now go forward, leading the way for the rest of the world.

The death of Lincoln ripped apart the nascent healing of a battered nation struggling to put the deep and bloody wounds behind. In the North the outrage grew, and to many it did not matter that the plot had been little more than the mindless actions of a conspiracy driven by one fanatic, a man named John Wilkes Booth. The voices of reason were swept away, drowned out by emotional cries of revenge, an emotion that would give fuel to the self-serving needs of powerful men in powerful positions. They would now take control of the weaknesses of Lincoln's successor, Andrew Johnson, could easily point their fingers into the heart of what had been the Confederacy, using the emotion and the sorrow of a nation to punish those who could too easily be blamed.

In the South the voices of reason understood that they had lost the one man who was after all not the enemy, that with the muskets stacked and the cannon silent, Lincoln was the only man with the power and the influence to put the war behind them all, who wanted nothing more than to bind up the wounds, to reunite the people into one strong voice, the voice of hope and freedom. Even in the darkest hearts, where resistance to the peace, to the Union, was still hard, it was clear that the assassin's bullet had taken away much more than one man. Now would come the angry times, a new brutality; not the guns and the blood of war, but something subtle, quiet and powerful. What had not been taken away from the southern people by the great crushing weight of the war would now be taken by a new kind of violence, a policy of reconstruction that would do everything Lincoln would not. The wounds would not be allowed to heal, the vision of the bright future would be pushed aside, replaced by a dark vision of revenge. Instead of healing, the wounds would be probed and ripped, would become scars that would never quite close, would be kept alive with anger and hostility for generations.

PART
FOUR

... *that we here highly resolve that these dead shall not have died in vain; that this nation shall have a new birth of freedom; and that this government of the people, by the people, for the people, shall not perish from the earth.*

Abraham Lincoln
November 19, 1863
Gettysburg, Pennsylvania

56. LEE

BLUE RIDGE MOUNTAINS, SEPTEMBER 1870

THEY CLIMBED HIGHER, THE HORSES MOVING WITH SLOW GRACE, up past the small trees and rocks. He led the way, knew the trail well by now, and Traveller did not need to be prodded, the big horse knowing the ground, the long trail, as well as Lee did himself.

Mildred rode Lucy Long, the mare given to Lee years before by Jeb Stuart. The smaller horse did not have Traveller's strength, but Lee knew Traveller's pace, that he would carry them slowly, the steady climb. Lee also knew that Mildred was not afraid to use the whip, that his youngest child had become an excellent rider herself.

Of all the children, he was enjoying Mildred the most now. She was finally grown, as they all were, but as she passed out of the teenage years, she became less of the spoiled aristocrat, had grown to accept life in the valley, the life her father had chosen.

It had not been easy for any of them. Lee had accepted a position that seemed to be more tedious than the quiet retirement everyone felt he'd earned. Washington College had barely survived the war, barely survived the torches of David Hunter. The college was the neighbor of VMI, and when Hunter burned the "halls of treason," the pleasant red brick buildings next door had been looted, nearly destroyed as well. What remained of the college was little more than the will of those who worked to see it survive. The man chosen to lead that campaign had been Lee.

It would have been impossible for him to stay long in Richmond. From the earliest days after the war, he'd been under siege, great long lines of visitors, former soldiers, refugees, men who just had to see him, to look upon him with teary eyes, while others brought gifts, the devotion of a people who still saw him as their symbol. He tried to be kind, but generosity had a price, wearing him down physically, and he could not endure the pressure of the public eye.

The invitation to take on the challenge of rebuilding Washington College had come late in 1865, and at first there was nothing about the position that appealed to him. But the pressure simply overwhelmed him, the political turmoil in Virginia and all through the South, the efforts to bring him out into a public forum, all the pleas for some active role in the political chaos of reconstruction.

The offer to move to Lexington began to feel more attractive for a variety of reasons. There were many young men from his old command, soldiers who needed an education to survive, men who had the youthful energy and the intellect to move themselves forward, to create a new life for their families. Lee knew there was prestige in his name, and to use that to build something of value, to lend his name to the rebirth of an institution for learning, could not be ignored. There had been criticism, surprise that he would accept the position at this shell of a school in the small town of Lexington when larger, more prestigious schools would certainly have welcomed him, had they known he was inclined. But in fact the invitations did not come from these *better* schools, but from this one struggling place at the head of the Shenandoah Valley.

There was another reality, and he thought more of Mary than himself, though it was clear to the children and to anyone who knew him well—he was aging. Mary had become accustomed to the wheelchair, and the deterioration, the crippling effects of her arthritis, had slowed. There was even relief from the pain, and if she still could not walk or use her left arm, with the lessening of the pain came the return of the spirit, the hot anger, the impatience, the spoiled little girl who took command of the household once again. Lee had never shied away from her anger before, had simply endured her jabs, her sharp comments. It was always a fair price to pay for the guilt he carried. He had not been there for her, for the raising of the children; with him, it had always been duty first, the long career in the army.

But now he *was* there, and there was time to be with her, to sit for long hours, have conversations with the children, or endure Mary's long and angry monologues about the politics of the day. That had surprised him, her sudden interest in politics, her knowledge of detail, her passion and opinions about so many of the complicated issues that swirled through the country like some blinding dust storm. There were still times when she would rant to her friends, to their new social circle in Lexington, and her views were usually the popular ones—anger at the abuses endured by southerners at the hands of the northern politicians, the carpetbaggers, those who made opportunity for themselves from the chaos and ruin of war. She would sometimes shock him with hot words, indiscreet assaults on politicians she would fearlessly name.

The move to Lexington was a difficult change for the girls as well. Mary, Agnes, and Mildred had grown up in the shadows of great plantations, great social circles. Now they were replanted in a town that did not have the bright whirl of Virginia society. Here, the men kept a respectful distance; if they actually had the courage to keep company with the girls, it would take audacity to actually court a daughter of Robert E. Lee.

The best times for Lee were the quiet times, evenings when the girls would be at some local gathering, some function, and he would sit alone with Mary. Often they would not speak at all, just look out the windows across the campus at the tall oak trees, the green lawns.

The school had built him a new residence, near the traditional home of the president, the home that had been built for the founder, George Junkin. That had been the home where Stonewall Jackson had lived, long before anyone used that nickname. It was there that Junkin's daughter Ellie, Jackson's first wife, had died, a dark memory that followed Jackson into the war, through the last years of his life. Lee had lived there for a while, but the decision to build the new residence had been a blessing for him, more than he would tell the board, the men who provided the funds. He could never escape what had happened there, could not stand in the small rooms that had been Jackson's and not feel the weight of that, the terrible emotion that still echoed in those walls.

The new home was larger, more spacious, with large windows, and Lee even added a sun porch, a patio enclosed with glass, so Mary could sit in the warmth, surrounded by the greenery outside. He'd been amazed to discover that she had a talent for painting, something he had rarely been around to see. Now he would watch her for hours, her one strong hand still nimbly creating beauty, paint on small canvases, idyllic scenes, forests and water, and scenes of young lovers, mythic celebrations, all enclosed by the beauty of God's world. She was especially skilled at faces, the small details, and he marveled at that, looked at his own rugged hands, and thought, She has paid such a price, and surely He has given her the gift, that through her one good hand will come His blessing, His beauty.

His work at the college had always been difficult, the hours long and the duties expanded as the college became healthy again. Each year the enrollment had grown. The endowment was now receiving funds from surprising sources, many in the North. He took great pride in that, but would not take the credit. The staff, the faculty, had grown as well, and all the energy was forward. Lee knew it was the effort from all of them, the dedication and labor from beyond his own small office, that had built the school's growing reputation.

He would not focus on it, but had felt the quiet illness spreading through him. The same pains and hollow weakness that had come to him during the war were never truly gone. The workload had made it worse. He'd thought often about retiring completely, but his presence was a great force at the college, and he was not yet ready to make the selfish move, give up all the good work, and the good work yet to come, just for his own well-being. Even the rides into the hills were fewer now, the discomfort of long periods on horseback something he found difficult to admit.

They reached the crest of the long hill, and he patted Traveller's neck, thought, You do understand. You were gentle today.

Many times he had come up here, on a pleasant ride past thick green woods, climbing, a long straight trail that would take him to this special place, the extraordinary view of the town and far beyond, the Shenandoah, the Blue Ridge Mountains. He often made the trip alone, but there had been something in him, a voice, caution, and now he would wait, find the right time, days when Mildred was not occupied with something more pressing than a long ride with her father.

He turned, saw the mare bringing Mildred up the last climb, and he dismounted, slowly, felt the stiffness in his back, his arms. He rubbed his hand on Traveller's nose, the horse nodding to the touch.

Now Mildred was down, said, "Oh, Papa, this is . . . wonderful. I forget about this place."

He stared out toward the long line of mountains, said, "Don't . . . forget. Never forget. This is God's place. He has led us here. This is where He wants us to come, to see His work."

She looked at him, saw a small frown and said, "Papa, are you feeling all right?"

He did not look at her, stared at a motion against the distant sky, a large bird, far away, a long slow turn, drifting. He said, "I am fine, child. I wish I could come up here . . . more often. There is no time."

The horses began to nuzzle the ground, pulling at small pieces of green, tufts of grass in the rocks.

Mildred was still watching him, said, "I wish Mother could see this."

There was a quiet moment, and Lee nodded. "I have brought her up here sometimes, in my mind. I have imagined she could ride, that she could see this. I have talked to her, right here, as though she was with me." He was suddenly uncomfortable, had revealed some very private place, looked at her, said, "I'm sorry. That was very personal. I hope I did not embarrass you."

Mildred was smiling, shook her head. "Papa, you have never seen any of us as grown. I'm not a child. Mother is very happy where she is. After all, she has you."

He nodded, knew she was right, that often when he was with his army, he would send letters home to all of them, advice, small bits of knowledge, as though they were all still children. It was something he'd always done, even in the early days, stern letters then, the absent father teaching them from far away.

He moved forward, stood out on the edge of a large rock, peered down into thick brush, saw more birds now, small flecks of color.

Mildred was rubbing the neck of the mare, said, "Are you still writing?"

He sagged, took a deep breath, turned and looked at her. "Not for a while now. It is very hard." He stared out to the mountains again, thought of Taylor, Gordon, Johnston, so many others. There was great interest in his own account of the war, and the letters were still coming, many from men he'd forgotten, commanders who looked to him to complete the task, as though it had to be from him and him alone. There were even letters from up North, from newspapermen and publishers, prompting him to tell his side of the story, a version that otherwise might never be told. He had tried, had asked many of the veterans, the commanders, to send him their own reports, to fill in gaps in the official records, or gaps in his own memory. The papers were stacked high in his study, and on those days when he had the energy, he would begin to read, to make some notes, but the energy would not last. Even when he would force the effort, taking the pen in hand and putting words on paper, something would hold him back. He would stare into some distant place, and the memories would come back, and many of the memories were very, very bad.

He thought now of the men themselves: I cannot judge them, it is not my place. If I tell the truth, there will be controversy, anger. We do not need that now. If a man was not a good commander, or if by some mistake a fight went badly, it is for God to decide the importance of that, not me. They expect me to give them some kind of Final Word, as though only I can tell the absolute truth. No, I do not want that responsibility.

He was suddenly very tired, thought, This is why . . . I come up here. It is far away from all that, from the eyes of the people. He'd received many invitations, social and political functions, places where he would certainly be an honored guest. No, he thought, they do not understand. They still want to talk about the war, to relive the great fights, the grand memories. I do not enjoy that.

Mildred was now close to him, said, "Beautiful . . . the valley."

"Yes . . . this is home. I always knew that."

Mildred looked at him, then down, hesitated, then said, "Mother still believes . . . she still wishes you would reconsider all the offers."

Lee did not look at her, knew very well how Mary felt. "Do you feel the way she does?"

Mildred raised her arms, a long stretch. "I like having you home. If you were governor, you wouldn't be home very much."

He smiled, thought, I should have had her on my staff. There was never any doubt what Mildred's opinions were. He said, "She doesn't understand. She believes that I can do some good, help Virginia get through these times. She only sees one side, my influence, my . . ." He paused, hated the word. ". . . my popularity. She does not consider that I have many enemies. There are so many people in the North who would use me as an excuse to punish Virginia. I have to stay away from that. I am no good at being a figurehead, a symbol. If I thought my presence there would be for the good of Virginia . . . but it can only do harm."

"Papa, you have always been a symbol. You can't change that."

He stared out again, tried to find the great lone bird, saw it now, soaring in soft circles, quiet, without effort, carried on the wind.

"They must go on . . . move forward on their own. I cannot help them do that. The soldiers, the people . . ." He still followed the flight of the bird, saw it move beyond the crest of a far hill, drop out of sight. He felt a chill now, a shiver that Mildred saw, and she moved close to him, put her hands on his arm.

"Papa, you don't have to convince anyone. Everyone knows how much you have given."

The chill flowed all through him now, and he pulled at his coat, his hands shaking, said, "We had better go back."

He turned, looked back, saw Traveller raise his head, the horse rested now, ready for the ride back down the long trail.

SEPTEMBER 28, 1870

T HE CHURCH WAS DOWN THE HILL FROM THE RESIDENCE, ACROSS an open lawn. It was dark early now, and he walked slowly up the hill in a steady rain, thought of the meeting, the voices of the men. He had presided over the vestry meetings for a while now, the business of managing the church, and today's meeting had been as routine as any of the others. He rarely took a strong hand at running things, let the members work out the issues for themselves, would exercise whatever authority they had granted him only when there was some impasse. The meeting today was a long one, and it was nearly seven o'clock, past the supper hour. It had been difficult for him, the damp misery of the unheated church cutting into him, his mind drifting, pulling him off into some cold angry place. When he brought his attention back to the voices, his patience had been short, and the meeting concluded as they often concluded, with the announcement of a shortage of funds. He'd seen an opportunity there, to bring the meeting to a blessed close, offered to provide funds himself, to meet the shortfall. It had given the meeting an optimistic tone, and the men filed out with good cheer, while he moved out still feeling the misery of the cold, and clenched his jaw for the uphill walk in the rain.

They were waiting for him. The supper had been delayed until he came home, and he could smell the food when he opened the door. He slid out of his dripping coat, ran his hand through wet hair, moved into the large living room, saw the dining room beyond, the girls moving into their chairs, Mary in the wheelchair. There was laughter, some joking at his appearance, and he still felt the chill. He pulled at himself, wrapped his arms tighter. Mary was watching him, said something, and he looked at her, could not hear her words. He moved toward his chair, and there was silence, they were all watching him, watched him slowly sink into the chair. Mary said something else, and he felt his mind asking . . . what? Why do you not speak up? Now Mary moved her chair closer to him, held out a cup, the steam from the tea drifting up in front of his eyes. He stared ahead, still could not hear them, felt the fog closing across his eyes, his mind now drifting slowly away. He saw them standing now, moving forward, hands touching him, the voices like small bells, echoing through the cold darkness in his brain, the darkness spreading now, covering them all.

OCTOBER 12, 1870

HE HAD BEEN AWAKE MOST OF THE TIME, HAD TRIED TO RISE from the bed, but there were always hands, and he had no strength to fight them. He was in the dining room, had thought that was strange, some odd dream, that the bed was in the wrong place, embarrassing, the privacy violated. But when his mind cleared he could hear them, understood that they'd made the large room his hospital, had seen the faces of the doctors now, familiar, men with warm hands, comforting words.

The medicine was always there, the bitter liquid, and they told him it would help, and so he took it without protest. For two weeks they told him he was getting better, would recover, something about a congestion in his brain, something the medicine would help. For the first few days he believed them, felt the strength coming back, but then would come the bad days, when he could not hear them, when the kind faces would change, showing dark concern, and he knew what they would not say to him, that it was more than a simple illness, more than any treatment could help.

When the sunlight had come into the room through the wide bay windows that looked out to the campus, he'd seen strange faces, thought he was dreaming again, but then his mind would clear, and the faces were real. Outside the house, they had lined up for days, students at first, then people from the town. As word of his illness spread, more people came, many just standing outside the window, watching the activity inside. At night the curtains would close, but the people would stay, many of them sleeping right there, on the lawn. On the good days, he had even waved to them, and they cheered him, joyous tears, kind words. He had seen uniforms, even a flag, a strange surprise, some of his army violating the law, presenting themselves to the man who was, after all, their commander. He had thought, speak to them, tell them they do not have to do this, it is all right. But he never left the bed, and so the faces never left their vigil outside the window.

Through the night, when the brief moments came, when he was awake, he could feel Mary's soft hand holding his. He felt the pains come back, the familiar tightness, the left arm, his throat filled with a dull ache. He wanted to tell them, but there were no words, no sound except the voice in his mind. He tried to see her face, could still hear the sounds flowing around him, but the darkness settled around him, began to push it all away. His mind was still working, and he tried to see through the darkness, thought, It must be . . . the face of God, but the darkness began to open, move away.

He could see new faces, panic, tears, the faces of soldiers, the great hollow sounds of a bloody fight. There was a stone bridge, a creek, red with the blood of the armies, and flowing across the bridge was a great mass of blue, pushing away everything in front of them. He saw Jackson now, the smiling face of Stuart, and they were standing still, beside him, looking at him silently, waiting for him to move, to tell them what to do. He looked around, saw the great blue wave moving close, and he looked at the commanders, and still they did not move, and now he heard a noise, a great cheer, the high scream of the rebel yell, and he turned that way, felt the horse under him, could smell the smoke, the hard sounds of the fight along the creek.

All around him now were row after row of his men, long lines of death, but back behind him the high yell was still coming forward. He looked back, over the hill, saw troops, soldiers, his soldiers, a great wall spreading out to turn away the blue wave. He waved his hat, pulled the horse up high, Yes, come forward, push them, drive them. He could see the men on horses now, the flags, saw the one man in the red shirt, and he thought, Now, do it now! The staff was there now, the face of Taylor, and he yelled, "Tell Hill he must come up!"

In one great surge his men poured down the hill, the blue wave now backing away, a furious fight, the bridge now choked with the blue mass, death spreading all along the creek, the piercing yell of Hill's men still flowing forward. He watched, still waved the hat, felt that glorious thrill of the victory, the blessing from God he never took for granted.

The battle was past now, and the field was changed, the horrible sights, the awful scenes of death were gone. He saw Hill now, and the others, and behind, there were many more faces, all still, quiet, watching him. He wanted to tell them, Fine work, victory is yours . . . but there were no words now, and the faces were all smiling at him, and now he saw strange faces, men who should not be there, who were not at that great awful fight, the struggle for Antietam Creek. There were the faces of many friends, Winfield Scott, Albert Sidney Johnston, many others, all the familiar faces, spread out in a soft white glow. He was not on the horse now, moved forward, the white mist flowing around him, and the faces began to move away. He began to follow them, saw them looking back at him, leading him farther into the mist.

Now the mist began to clear and he saw a vast field, a great tide of men, moving away. He thought, Who . . . which army . . . But there were *no uniforms, they were all the same. He watched them, felt more men now moving past him, the flow endless, the faces looking at him with a gentle calm. Some were calling to him, silent words, but he could feel it, thought, I must still lead them. He stared out above them, the bright white of the sky, thought, The face of God . . . it must be. . . . Then he looked again at the men, the endless numbers, still flowing past him, and he thought, Yes, this is the face of God . . . you are all the face of God. He looked behind him now, thought, It is time . . . I must go with them. He looked for his staff, but there was no one there, and he thought, There must be someone . . . I must tell them . . . we must go now. He turned, yelled out the command, the last breath before he moved away, marched again with his men.*

"Strike the tent!"

57. GRANT

HE HAD BEEN WRITING ALL MORNING, THE WORDS POURING from his mind in a steady stream that seemed to outpace his ability to put them down. He would pause, resting, feel his own harsh breathing, but the words pushed hard against the dam, and so his hand would move again, releasing them, an unstoppable flow.

His hand began to ache, and he stopped, sat back in the chair, laid his head back, stared at nothing. Outside, he could hear the sounds, the birds, and he looked that way, felt the tightness in his throat, and now his weariness was complete. He looked at the paper in front of him, thought, No more, not now.

He stood, a slow labor, walked to the doors that opened onto the terrace, stared for a moment, could see the birds now, flutters of motion, and below, the road, blessedly empty, no traffic, none of the people who had gathered earlier that morning.

It had annoyed him at first, people coming just to watch him, to stare at him, his private moments. There was kindness in that, he knew, but it was still an intrusion, and the sickness took away his patience. When he needed the break from the work, from the writing, he would go outside, settle into the soft chair, listen to the birds. If there were onlookers, they were respectful, usually quiet, would not disturb him, but he always knew when they were there, and that was disturbing enough.

He'd wondered at first why they came, thought they might be reporters, or old soldiers, someone who knew him once, maybe a long time ago. But he never saw a familiar face. They had the odd habit of just standing, watching, giving a wave, a small greeting. Then it had occurred to him: they are waiting for me to die.

The first pains had come the autumn before, a sudden shock, an assault on his throat from nothing more than eating a piece of fruit. He felt a sting, thought it was an insect, a bee, and swallowed, fighting back, had bathed his throat in cold water, but the pain had not gone away. Julia insisted on doctors, but he would have none of that, had little faith in anything they would do. But Julia had her way, always had her way, and the doctors had come to him with that look that carries its own message. He had cancer of the throat.

Julia would not believe that, sought more doctors, some assurance that it was curable, but Grant did not cooperate, would not be the subject of experiments. He could feel it inside, the disease kept a hold on him every day, always announced its presence. He eventually began to weaken, and then he knew what was happening, that there would be very little time, and that he had one very important job to complete.

The memoirs had not been his idea, but when the offer was made, it seemed to be a miracle. After eight tumultuous years in the White House, after a two-year journey around the world, his gift to the patience of his wife, he had in fact been nearly destitute. He'd been approached to write some articles, a piece for a magazine, and was surprised to learn there was an audience for the stories, for his memories of the war. He was never a writer, had never even thought of putting words on paper, nothing but what came with the job. They paid him anyway, a pleasant surprise, and he'd begun to enjoy it, going back, searching through some of his old papers, the familiar names and places, and even the bad times, the grim fights where many good men were lost.

It had never occurred to him that anyone would pay to read the story of his life, that there was anything about his life that was inspiring, or even interesting. But the numbers had been presented to him, a guarantee of half a million dollars; that if he could produce the memoirs, it would ensure the financial well-being of his family. The articles, brief and to the point, had been fun. Now there was something added—a responsibility. The writing had taken on an urgency because, he knew, more than anyone else, he was running out of time.

The money, the financial security, was inspiring certainly, but there was something more, a growing friendship with the publisher, Samuel Clemens, an unexpected benefit of the simple business deal. That was a new experience for Grant, because his business deals almost always went bad. Through his entire life, the most painful lessons, his faith in man would be shaken not by success or failure on the battlefield, but by how men behaved in business dealings. It was a lesson he still could not accept, not completely, and he still wondered about the criticism he'd received, how naive he was. He had always been too eager to trust, believed that everyone would accept responsibility the way he did. It was simple and logical. If you trusted someone with doing their duty, to do a job, it did not matter if money was involved, the job would be done.

During the last half of his presidency, he had clearly shown too much blind faith in those who worked in his administration. His failure to understand and then to stop the corruption around him had not only been a severe embarrassment, but would haunt him for years after his term expired. It was as it had always been, on the fields of Virginia, or in the white halls of Washington. If he was told the job would be done, he simply believed it.

The memoirs could only be handled by him, and even if he had use of a secretary, someone to correct his spelling, his poor grammar, the words still came from him. His fading energy only gave him a few hours each day, but it had been enough so far. Clemens was confident that he was very close, that in a few weeks, or maybe days, the final pages would be written.

Clemens came more often now, and the visits were more social than professional. He would wait for Grant to complete the day's work, then they would sit and talk, as much as Grant's voice would allow. As weak as he was, as much discomfort as his voice gave him, he enjoyed the visits. It could be wonderfully entertaining, because Clemens himself had no problem filling the quiet spaces with his own words, was a man who did not even require an audience, seemed perfectly happy just speaking out loud, entertaining himself as well as anyone who might be around. Clemens had done a good bit of writing himself, great literary treasures, and Grant always enjoyed hearing about that from a professional, the magical process, where the words came from. He'd always been astounded that this man would actually pay him to write the memoirs, was honored now by the man's friendship, the man most people knew by the name of Mark Twain.

HE MOVED OUT ONTO THE TERRACE, PEERED OVER THE BALcony, still saw no one on the road. He was grateful for the privacy, moved to his chair, eased himself down. The birds chattered at him, annoyed by his presence, and he sat still for a moment, had come to know that if he sat quietly, did not move, they would soon forget he was there.

He could hear a carriage now, the birds suddenly fluttering away. The carriage slowed, stopped in front of the house. He didn't hear voices yet, listened for the sound of the bell outside the front door. He knew Clemens was supposed to come today, and he'd drawn energy from that. Even the writing had gone well, faster, stronger. He heard footsteps, thought, Please . . . no one else, no reporters, no well-wishers. The bell rang, one sharp clang, and he could hear sounds in the house, Julia moving toward the door. It opened, and he heard her voice, the flirtatious delight, and thought, Thank God, it has to be him. He relaxed then, knew what would be next. Staring out at the trees, he saw the birds gathering again, and then the terrace door was opening. Immediately, he could smell the cigar.

"Still drawing inspiration from those damned birds, eh?"

Grant smiled, and Clemens was now in front of him, the playful teasing a mask for the man's eyes, examining Grant with dark concern.

Grant said nothing, held out a hand, which Clemens took, and then Julia was there, holding a bright cluster of flowers. She said, "Look, Ulyss, he brought more flowers. I must say, Mr. Clemens, you do know how to charm a household."

Clemens winked at Grant, said, "My dear, it is not the household I aim to charm. It is the occupants. And, given that one of them is this fellow here, it is safe to say that my aim is toward his better half."

Julia made a short bow, said, "Mr. Clemens, your aim is accurate."

There was a pause, and Clemens blew a cloud of cigar smoke toward Grant, then made a great show of extinguishing the ash, tapped the cigar on the railing, slid the cigar into his coat pocket.

Julia made a short nod, said sternly, "Thank you, Mr. Clemens. Now, I will go put these in water, and leave you two alone."

When she was gone, the door closing, Clemens sat down next to Grant, peeking around toward the house, the same game played with every visit. He retrieved the cigar, lit it again, and leaned back in the chair.

It was a simple pleasure for Grant now, the wonderful smoke. He could not enjoy his own cigars anymore; the gentle warmth that he'd enjoyed for so long was now a scorching fire in his throat. Julia was considerate of that, had thought it was insensitive of men to smoke around him, a cruel tease. Usually, she was right, but she did not understand that Clemens knew it as well, would smoke only what he knew were Grant's favorites. If Grant could not enjoy the pleasure of smoking himself, Clemens would do it for him. If the men thought themselves clever, like two boys in some guilty misbehavior, they did not know that Julia understood the game as well. As the cloud rolled up between them, and Grant would absorb what he could of the glorious smoke, she would wait, then move up near the door, watching the two men enjoy their small victory over her stern discipline.

They sat for a moment, and Clemens said, "The voice . . . all right today?"

Grant nodded, said, a low scratchy growl, "Not too bad. They want me to take the morphine to help the pain. But it fogs up my brain. Can't do that."

Clemens nodded, blew another cloud of smoke, said, "You're very close. How far you gonna take it?"

Grant shook his head. "The war. I don't see how I can go—"

Clemens held up his hand, said, "The war is fine. Good stuff. That's what people want anyhow. Hard to get anybody excited about eight years in the White House. Anticlimactic." He laughed. "Even *your* White House."

Grant nodded, thought for a long moment, said, "I never would have done that . . . if Lincoln had lived."

Clemens nodded, blew smoke. "You wouldn't have *had* to. You may have saved the country, your enemies notwithstanding. We were out of control. Could have been anarchy. Too bad . . . you could write a lot about that. Teach some people a few lessons."

Grant shook his head no.

Clemens realized what he'd said, knew well that there would be little time. He said, "No, it's not important. Stick with the war."

Grant stared at the birds again. "I had thought, maybe the trip . . . write about that, what it was like . . . especially for her. She was in her glory."

Clemens glanced back toward the house, said, "Never known a woman to be so suited for a man. Pardon me, General, but if not for her, I doubt this visit would be near as interesting."

Grant smiled, closed his eyes, was feeling very tired now. He said slowly, "If I did nothing else, I made her happy. All the attention, the ceremony . . . the gowns, the parties. Everywhere we went, she had to tell the world who I was. Didn't matter much what I wanted." He paused, took a deep breath, tried to relax his throat.

Clemens was looking at him now, said, "Take it easy, General. Save your voice."

Grant shook his head. "No, it's all right. I was just thinking about her . . . anger, if something came up, some crisis, and we had to cancel a social event. She took it as a personal inconvenience. I would like to have written that . . . spent more time writing about her, about our lives. There is so much . . . I have been so blessed."

He closed his eyes again, and Clemens sat back, said, "Maybe, General, she'll do that herself."

JULY 19, 1885

HE HADN'T SLEPT, HAD BEEN UP MOST OF THE NIGHT WRITING. He was beginning to feel a small panic, the first real fear; there was so much left unsaid. It was not death. He had accepted that long ago, even when the doctors were telling Julia that he was recovering. What he feared was the weakness, losing the concentration, the flow of words, the memories. The fear gave him energy, and when the nights were sleepless, he would move himself to the small lamp in their room, where the pad of paper always waited, and would take up the pen again.

He'd been thinking too much of her, remembered Clemens's words, *the war is enough,* but she was there, always, and the memories began to fall together, confused, a jumble of thoughts. He kept an image of her, someplace in Europe, someone allowing her the privilege of trying on crowns, great jeweled headpieces, and her pure joy, the giggling pleasure, and he thought, Yes, she could have been a queen . . . as if there was any more scandal about me the newspapers needed for their editorials.

He focused on the paper again, blinked hard at the dull lamplight. There had been so many details, so many names, the numbers, and now there was little of that. He'd tried to think about how much he'd already written, some way to bring it all together. He drifted off again, thought now of the people, the crowds outside the house, the kindness. There had been hopeful, supportive letters, even telegrams, from all over the country, every state. Some had come from Confederate officers, men who faced him across the bloody fields, and that surprised him at first. But now he understood, it was more than concern for him, for one man, one old soldier, and it was more than the formal show of respect to a former President. The wounds were healing and the uniform did not matter now. All the old soldiers had a common bond, having been through the great horror. There had been great difficulties, great controversies, anger, abuse, injustice, but that was past, and the country was moving on again, strong, united, prosperous. The letters were thanking him for that, and even if he knew better—that his role was one small part—the sad reality of his illness inspired them to reach out, to thank him.

He understood now, in the dull lamplight, stared at the paper, thought, We have learned, we are moving into a new time, and all of us know what we must not ever do again. He wrote now, thought, There is nothing else I can give them, no wisdom, no comfort. It is only a simple request, the hope I can leave to all of them, to their children, to their future.

"Let us have peace."

58. CHAMBERLAIN

GETTYSBURG, PENNSYLVANIA, SPRING 1913

H E HAD COME BACK HERE MORE TIMES THAN HE COULD REMEM-
ber, would walk the same ground, the same hills. He would
find all the special places, stand where Lee stood, watching
Pickett destroy his division, wander through Devil's Den, marvel at
the huge rocks, wondering how anyone could have fought a battle
there. He would find the place where Reynolds went down, a very
good man taken away from a war he might have changed, even before
Grant. He'd walk through the cemetery, stand in the place where Lincoln had made the speech, read the words, or say them quietly from
memory. He wished he had met Lincoln. How curious a man, nothing
to ever indicate he was a master of language, had the brilliant use of
words. It was a subject Chamberlain knew as well as anyone, and he
still marveled at the simplicity of this one small speech, the finest piece
of oratory he had ever seen.

He would cover as much of the battlefield as his time allowed,
and always save that one place, that special place, for last. He had to
prepare for it, would make the long walk up the long rise, climbing
along the crest of the rocky hill, as he had fifty years ago, on that one
horrible day. Here, he did not wander, knew exactly where he was going, would ease along the trail made first by his men, now made by
generations of visitors. Finally he would come to the big rock, the
smooth flat surface, his own private place, would stay for long hours,
staring out at the distant trees, the thick woods, his mind hard at work
on the memories, the magic of the ground.

There would be a celebration of the fiftieth anniversary of the
battle, and in Maine there was no one who could better represent the
old veterans, the last survivors of this extraordinary place, than Cham-

berlain. As with every event, there had to be planning, arrangements, conveniences prepared for the fragile soldiers. They were, after all, fifty years removed from the battle.

It had been a long while since his last visit, several years, and it was the pressure from the organizers, from nameless committees, all the attention surrounding the anniversary, that brought him back even now. It would be difficult this time, something he would not explain to anyone else, and it had nothing to do with his age, with any physical problem. This time there were different memories, more than the fight, the horrible thrilling memories of that one day. This time he would bring the memories of Fannie, would remember walking the hills with her, telling her all the stories.

That he outlived her was the most painful experience of his life. She had been through terrible times, her health slowly failing over the years, her eyesight gone completely, and finally, in 1905, the end had come. But for years, even when her health was poor, the blindness nearly complete, she would still come here, hold his arm, move slowly with him through the trees, the small paths through the rocks. If it was a painful ordeal, she would never tell him that, knew how important this was to him, to be here, to share all of that with her. He knew it was a test of patience, the tolerance of a woman who had lost most of her tolerance. Their life together had been long and, more often than not, difficult.

After the war, he'd come home to a hero's welcome, and his immediate popularity had handed him the governor's chair, to which he was elected four times. But Fannie did not go with him to the capital, would not be a part of that, and the job was, after all, a job. He had never really understood her anger, what she was missing in her life, why she seemed to be so unhappy. He struggled with the balance, his responsibility to her, and the responsibility he could never seem to escape, to the people, to his state, and later, to the college.

When he came back to Brunswick, it was not to the quiet privacy of home, but more public attention, the presidency of Bowdoin, a notoriety he accepted and she did not, and it was a burden that would follow them to the end. If his private life was overshadowed by the bright spotlight of his fame, that was an observation made by others, never by him. To her last days, he loved her as he had in the first days of their courtship, the young scholar in agonizing pursuit of the girl whose aloofness kept him just far enough from her heart, just far enough so the pursuit would stay glorious. Throughout fifty years of marriage, the pursuit had still been glorious.

The walk was not simple now, not to a man of eighty-four, but he would not let anyone come with him. The reunion organizers were gathered near the copse of trees, conducting their meeting around the high-water mark, the flat ground near the center of the field. It was the most obvious place, flat open ground, where the cameras could get the best shot, where the old men would have the least difficulty. But he had been through these meetings before, already understood what would take place, what the ceremony would involve, the little speech he would be expected to make. It would be an emotional experience for everyone who saw it.

As at every reunion, the Confederates would make the trek, come across the open ground where Pickett and Pettigrew had led the disastrous charge, and they would slowly climb the long open rise, moving closer to the copse of trees, the low stone wall where Armistead had fallen, where the tide of the war slowly turned them back. Along the wall, the old Federals would wait for them, along the same line where Hancock held, where the firepower and strength had been too great. The two sides would come together with hands held out, arms reaching to arms, old men now lost in those days, some crying out loud, some holding their dignity in some quiet place. They would remember their friends, the men whose blood was still in that ground, and they would speak of it all, the memories, the tearful sadness, cleansing themselves again. There would be many fewer than the last time, and they would look at each other with the soft sadness of age, knowing that if there were another reunion, there would be fewer still.

He had made the simple request, a lone walk, had to be firm with the volunteer, a giggling woman who insisted on escorting him. He would have no one with him, and moved away with purpose, a show of strength, of good legs, leaving the disappointed woman behind. Now his legs were stiff, his breathing hard, and he sensed the soft green around him, the air damp with the spring. He walked with slow purpose, saw a sign, something new, a small wooden plaque: LITTLE ROUND TOP.

He was alone, there were no onlookers, the attention focused back at the center of the great long line. He stopped, took a long breath, felt the pains, small reminders, and he blew out a hard, disgusted breath, said aloud, "Go on, old man!"

He climbed again, found the small trail he'd used before, and now he was among the big rocks, stepping carefully, his focus on that one familiar place, where he could sit, finally, and stare out across the peaceful ground.

He felt his legs, the soreness, thought, How many of the old veterans will come up here? He could see out over the peach orchard, the wheat field. He thought of the old men, the reunion, how many stories, where they would go. He could see the great rocks in Devil's Den, thought, There, they will certainly go there. After the ceremony, old men will lead their grown children and impatient grandchildren, will point at the special place, tell the stories. The children will shake their heads, had heard it many times before. But up here there will not be many, too hard a climb for so many old legs. He felt a pride in that, how he could still come up here, the difficult climb. But then he thought, If they do not come . . . the children might never know. Someone has to tell them what happened here, what we did, how important this was. They cannot forget. He looked to the left, toward the bigger hill, Round Top, looked down into the thick green woods between the hills. Right there, he thought, it was right there. We held the rebels away, and it was important. We must not lose that, can't forget about that. How different it might have been, if not for those men from Maine.

He had grown accustomed to the attention, the individual fame. They had finally awarded him the Congressional Medal of Honor in 1893. He'd humbly accepted it, knew they had to put one man's name on that piece of paper, to identify the great deed with a man, to have someone to make a speech, to go to these reunions. But he knew better than any that it was not the generals, not some singular work of genius or valor. If the men, the privates, the men with the muskets, did not want to go forward, there would be no great fights, no chapter in the history books, no generals to wear the medals.

He still recalled the names, the men who died there, and he'd been adamant about the monument, that the piece of marble would not be some generic statement about location, but would name them, all of them. In all the fights that came after, it had never affected him quite the same way, and he wondered about that, thought, Maybe when I was wounded, I started worrying more about *me*. But, no, maybe there were simply too many to remember. He thought of his promotions, the larger commands, had always wondered if learning how to lead a large group of men meant learning how to be a better fighter. If my regiment made the good fight here, and my brigade made a good fight at Petersburg . . . yes, then that's probably true. If the war had gone on, they might have offered me a division, and sooner or later I could have had Griffin's job. . . .

He did not like thinking of Griffin. If he missed the men in his

SHAARA

command, Griffin was the only one above him who left a painful hole. Griffin had not lived long after the war, had gone to Texas, where he was killed by yellow fever. Texas was a long way from Maine, but Griffin's attachment to Chamberlain was stronger than Chamberlain himself understood. The package came one day in 1867, the dying man's request, and Chamberlain was astonished to receive Griffin's hat, and the sword, the same sword Chamberlain had given him at Five Forks. Of all the artifacts of war, it was the most cherished possession Chamberlain had.

He thought of their last meeting, Griffin's disappointment that Chamberlain would not stay in the army, would not accept a peacetime command. He had tried to tell Griffin, "I'm not a soldier," and Griffin actually shouted at him with raw frustration, told him, "You are the finest soldier I have ever known." It was a compliment that meant more to him than he would have expected, because somewhere, deep inside himself, he knew it was the goal, the reason he'd gone into the army in the first place. There was nothing he'd ever done that mattered as much as that, as leading men into the guns. Picturing his father, he thought, Yes, you were right after all. You knew it from the beginning. I should have gone to West Point.

He had thought often about that, the need for the fight, all of that business about the nature of man. He'd tried to discover something about religion, all the different theories, had traveled through Europe, had even been to Africa, the Mideast, to try to learn about other wars, to see for himself if there were differences. He'd wondered, Was it something unique about Americans that makes us fight? Was it inevitable, something in our nature, something about the pioneer spirit, that if there is no enemy in front of us, we will find an excuse to kill each other? But, no, he thought, we are not that exclusive, it is not just us, it is *all* of us, it is the history of man.

He had always believed in the Divine Light, the lesson from his devout mother, that all men held a piece of God somewhere inside, that always, given the chance, that small piece of goodness would prevail. Even after the war, when the country was exhausted, the great wounds still open and bleeding, he had expected the kinder instincts to prevail. But the cruelty, the inhumanity, did not stop with the great fight. He could still see the Irishman's face even after fifty years, the cynical disgust, Buster Kilrain's bitter words, *Where have you seen the divine spark in action?* Perhaps, Buster, it just takes . . . time.

For a long time he had believed, hoped, that surely mankind would learn from that war, would carry the lesson into the future. Our war was different, after all, he thought. Something new, something besides the amazing bloodshed, the horrible efficiency of the weapons. This time, there were *pictures*. If the lesson had never been learned by hearing the stories, or by studying numbers, or even walking among the small white gravestones, this time we could gaze at great thick books, awful collections of photographs. If we start to forget, then *look*, *see* it, the blood, broken pieces of men, the horrible things we can do to each other. That should be enough.

He shook his head. But it is not enough. The rest of the world seems to pay no mind to our lesson, and the guns are still getting better. If God is in us all, then Buster was right. We are killer angels.

It bothered him feeling this way, the cynicism, losing faith. He knew he had not truly felt this until Fannie had gone. He thought of her now, had known he could not keep that away, could not sit up here on this big rock and not have her beside him. It was nothing like the wounds, or the aches of old age; it was a soft pain, spreading all through him, filling his mind. He stared away into blue sky, thought, I don't know how long I will live . . . but I will never lose this. I will miss you always, always in the quiet moments.

He pulled himself back, his brain working again, distracting him, easing away the sadness. He looked down into the thick green, where the men from Alabama had tried to push past the men from Maine. He had thought of it every time he sat here, on this one flat rock. What might have been, what if he'd given way, what if the Twentieth Maine had turned and run away? There were great debates, academic exercises that Chamberlain had attended too often, and the scenarios were always dramatic and profound. Often it began with a discussion of the great Stonewall, if he had been here, on this ground. Chamberlain enjoyed the speculation, kept his thoughts quiet, thought now, Stonewall would have been . . . over there, the far end, Cemetery Hill. Right here, the fight might have been no different. It would still have been up to us. But if we had let them through here, things would have been very different indeed.

He had heard all the theories, if the South had won, how the nation would be split into thirds, the North, the South, and California; how there might have been another war to decide just where the boundary would be out West. There were always Texans talking about their state as a separate country. And the South . . . he thought of Europe, of all the small countries, hot boundaries, small angry kingdoms, quick to fight. It could have become . . . the kingdom of Alabama, the Grand Duchy of Virginia.

He felt a headache growing, tried to pull his mind from all of that, shut down the machine in his brain. You do that every time, he thought, you can never just . . . sit. He remembered Fannie's grim patience, holding his arm while he explained it all to her, the explanations she had certainly heard before. He was feeling the sadness again, thought, How many times will I come back here? How many times will I still have to sit here? What, after all, am I waiting for?

He didn't know if his children would come to the reunion, even to support him, to endure the great speeches, watching the sad old men. He hoped Daisy would come at least, and bring her children. There is value in that, that if my stories and all the newspaper clippings mean very little, they should at least come to this place, walk this ground. It was different with Wyllys, his son never quite finding his place in the world. Chamberlain had tried to help him, had even gone to Florida for a business venture that Wyllys involved him in. It had come apart, as much of Wyllys's life had come apart, and Chamberlain thought of that now: It is my fault, my doing. He has a lot to live up to, the name, the famous father. He doesn't have to prove anything, not to me, but he will never stop trying.

Down below, there was a noise, loud, and he looked out over the rocks, saw black smoke, an automobile, full of straw hats and colored dresses. The car growled and sputtered along the road, moving toward the town, and he thought, *There* is something new, something for the old soldiers to think about. What of armies without horses?

He stood now, slowly, eased the stiffness in his legs. The noise of the auto was still in his mind, the jarring distraction, and he thought, Enough of this. It's time to go.

He moved back along the trail, stopped, paused briefly, saw a tall thin tree where no tree had been. Beside it was a rock, small, flat, oddly round. He moved over, stepped up on the rock, looked out toward the larger hill, Big Round Top, and knew it was one of those places he had stood, watching them, watching the enemy roll up the hill in one screaming tide. He looked across the ground, saw more of the rocks now, knew they had always been there, and he remembered now, this rock, he had done this every time he came up here.

All right, Lawrence, he thought, enough. But something held him, something different this time, and he told himself, No, wait, don't leave, not just yet. It came out of the ground, the rocks, through the deep green of the trees, all around him, the sight of his men, the sounds, the smells. He closed his eyes, and he was swallowed up in all of it, his men, holding them back, holding the line, the smoke and the cries, the horrible sight of his men dropping away, struck down. He could hear the screams and the sounds of the muskets, could smell the hot burn of the smoke, saw the terror in their eyes, and now he felt it, his mind opening to the marvelous memories, the pure raw excitement. If this was the last time, if he could never come back, he knew, seeing it all again, it was the most alive he had ever been.

JOSHUA LAWRENCE CHAMBERLAIN DOES NOT ATTEND THE FIFTIETH Reunion at Gettysburg, is stricken with illness. On February 24, 1914, he dies in Portland, Maine. He does not live to see the events that will follow six months later, when, across a wide ocean, another conspiracy, another assassination, will shatter the peace. Once again a glorious army will march with banners unfurled, the colorful flags slapping in the brisk wind. This time it will be the French, and they will still remember the ways of Napoleon, still march in neat lines, a grand parade, officers leading their men, energized by the lust for the glory of war. They will not march into the rifled musket, but something new, the ever-changing technology providing a weapon even more deadly, more efficient. This time, the glorious charge will take them straight into the machine guns of the Germans. The Great War will last another four years, and again the blood and the numbers will horrify the world. And again they will not have learned.

AFTERWORD

"War is for the participants a test of character; it makes bad men worse and good men better."

— JOSHUA LAWRENCE CHAMBERLAIN

"It is history that teaches us to hope."

— ROBERT E. LEE

JULIA DENT GRANT

Regarded with great affection, she seems born to the attention that surrounds her husband's amazing career. Pious yet charming, her White House years leave Washington with a clear image of the perfect social hostess. She writes her memoirs, an odd mix of touchingly affectionate descriptions of her romance with her husband and a strident attack on the myths that surrounded him, including his presumed difficulties with sobriety. Her focus, and thus her personality, is revealed with charming clarity, as much of her reminiscences concern their two-year journey through the capitals and palaces of the world. Her book is not published in her lifetime, and only reaches a public audience in 1975. She dies the dignified widow of an American hero in 1902.

THOSE WHO WORE BLUE

MAJOR GENERAL WILLIAM TECUMSEH SHERMAN

A man with few friends in the press, his reputation for eccentric behavior continues. He is often accused of insanity, or at the very least, a brutal insensitivity to human life. But the few who know him well understand that this is a man with a deep respect for excellence, and a man of high intellect—in 1859 he founds what later becomes Louisiana State University. Promoted to Lieutenant General in 1866, and then Full General in 1869, he succeeds Grant as general-in-chief of the army. He thus is blamed or praised for the army's behavior during the great Indian conflicts throughout the expansion of the American West during the 1870s. Despite a notorious disregard for criticism, he wearies of controversy, and retires in 1884. He dies in 1891, a week after his seventy-first birthday.

Major General Philip H. Sheridan

A man who likely would have faded into obscurity without the opportunities provided him by Grant, he continues to invite controversy for his brusque manner and hot temper. The month after the Appomattox surrender, he is assigned to Texas, to confront the supposed threat from Mexican Emperor Maximilian, brought to power as a puppet of the French, who support Maximilian with French troops. Sheridan's force of nearly fifty thousand men is a successful deterrent, and the French pull out of Mexico, leaving Maximilian to the angry Mexican citizenry. Sheridan is made military governor of Texas and Louisiana during Reconstruction, but displays such brutality to the civilian population, he is recalled to Washington after a short term of office. Promoted to Lieutenant General in 1869, he later travels to Europe and represents the U.S. as an observer in the Franco-Prussian War. In 1884 he succeeds Sherman as general-in-chief of the army, and dies four years later at age fifty-seven.

Brigadier General John A. Rawlins

Grant's conscience, if not his tormentor, he is still Grant's close friend, and remains close after the war. Seen by many as a hypochondriac, his suffering becomes real, and he contracts the tuberculosis that had previously killed his wife. Still with Grant, he accepts the cabinet post as Grant's first Secretary of War, but his failing health causes his term of office to be brief, and he dies in mid-1869. It is a letter to Grant, written by Rawlins early in the war, that lends the most credence to Grant's supposed drunkenness. The letter, which Grant never saw, is made public in 1891, and in part reads, "I find you where the wine bottle had been emptied, in company with those who drink, and urge you not to do likewise." The message reflects the hovering attention to detail and proper protocol for which Rawlins was well known, and includes the additional note, which is often ignored by Grant's enemies, that this advice was "heeded, and all went well." There is no evidence whatsoever that during any campaign where the safety of the army was an issue, or during any time when Grant's decision-making was critical, was Rawlins's commander ever indulging in the destructive practice that affected the abilities of so many men of both armies.

MAJOR GENERAL WINFIELD SCOTT HANCOCK

Grant describes him as "the most conspicuous figure of all the general officers who did not exercise a separate command," and the man whose name was "never mentioned as having committed in battle a blunder for which he was responsible." Hancock still, receives the deepest respect and affection from his subordinates, but the nagging wound keeps him from returning to active command of troops in the field. At the end of the war he is officially Commander of the Department of West Virginia, and has command of the Middle Military Division, the position originally created for Sheridan in the Shenandoah Valley. He remains in the army, and his command places him in the uncomfortable position of military executioner for the assassins of President Lincoln. Despite grave misgivings, Hancock reluctantly oversees the execution of Mary Surratt, who he believes to be an innocent victim of the conspiracy.

In 1866, at Sherman's request, Hancock is named commander of the Military Department of Missouri, and moves again to Kansas, where he had spent so much of the 1850s. His duty in Sherman's controversial Indian conflicts is short-lived, concluding with a feud with General George Custer, whom Hancock arrests. In 1867 Hancock is reassigned and succeeds Sheridan as Military Governor of Texas and Louisiana, where his sympathy for the rights of the former Confederate citizens creates enemies for him in Washington. He is eventually given the thankless post commanding the Department of Dakota. Feeling the pressure of Democrats to represent their political interests, he makes an attempt at a presidential nomination in 1868, but Grant's popularity prevents any hope of success. He assumes command of the Department of the Atlantic under the new president, still keeps his political interests alive, and in 1880 receives the nomination. But Grant's corrupt administration has shifted the mood of the country away from military heroes, and Hancock loses the election to James Garfield.

Hancock then suffers the extraordinary loss of both his children, then loses the final fight for his own health and dies in 1886.

MAJOR GENERAL GOUVERNEUR K. WARREN

The unfortunate victim of Sheridan's wrath spends the rest of his life trying to correct the record, and is supported by Joshua Chamberlain for his actions along the White Oak Road and Five Forks. Pleading his case for a Court of Inquiry, he is finally granted a hearing in 1879, which clears him of wrongdoing and faults Sheridan's judgment for relieving him from command of the Fifth Corps. But the damage is done, and Warren dies in 1882 still believing his potential for a brilliant army career was stripped away by a grave injustice.

MAJOR GENERAL HORATIO G. WRIGHT

Sedgwick's successor to command of the Sixth Corps performs with competence, though he never rises to the esteem or the affection that the men had given "Uncle John." He remains in the army after the war, is assigned Chief of the Corps of Engineers in 1879, retires in 1884. He survives until 1899.

LIEUTENANT COLONEL HORACE PORTER

Grant's most trustworthy and efficient staff officer remains in the army after the war, is promoted to Brigadier General. He resigns in 1873, returns to Pennsylvania to become an executive for the railroad. He is a frequent contributor to magazines whose audiences hunger for the "real" stories of the war, and in 1897 he writes his own memoirs, considered one of the most accurate and readable accounts of life with General Grant. He survives until 1921.

MAJOR GENERAL GEORGE GORDON MEADE

He is described by Grant as "an officer of great merit, with drawbacks to his usefulness that were beyond his control . . . no one saw this better than himself, and no one regretted it more." Meade remains in the army after the war and is named to command the Division of the Atlantic. Congress's Reconstruction policies place the military in command of the southern states, and he becomes Military Governor of Florida, Georgia, and Alabama. When Sheridan alone is promoted to

Lieutenant General, Meade vents his anger in public at both Sheridan and Washington for being passed over. He resigns his Reconstruction position, returns to Philadelphia to again command the Division of the Atlantic, and dies in 1872 of pneumonia.

MAJOR TOM CHAMBERLAIN

Joshua Lawrence Chamberlain's youngest brother remains in command of Company G, Twentieth Maine, throughout the last half of the war. After Appomattox he is promoted to Lieutenant Colonel, and for a short while serves on Chamberlain's staff at division command. When the Army of the Potomac is officially disbanded in late June 1865, Tom returns to Maine, finds little to substitute for life as a soldier. He marries his ex–sister-in-law (widow of brother John) in 1870, and tries to follow his older brother's example by joining Joshua and Wyllys Chamberlain in their unfortunate business venture in Florida. He returns to Maine, saddens his family by establishing a dismal reputation for drinking and womanizing. Those who served with him during the war remember only a man who was an excellent soldier, but his civilian life can never measure up to the extraordinary esteem enjoyed by his famous brother, and he dies in New York City in 1896, at age fifty-five.

THOSE WHO WORE GRAY

COLONEL WALTER H. TAYLOR

Lee's most loyal officer was arguably the most hardworking and efficient staff officer in either army. After the war, he settles with his new wife in Norfolk, Virginia, and raises eight children. He prospers first in the hardware business, eventually enters banking, becomes president of the Marine Bank of Norfolk. He serves briefly as a state senator to the Virginia legislature, which labors to carry the state forward through the difficulties of Reconstruction. He maintains contact with his former commander, and is one of those called upon to assist Lee with material for the memoirs Lee never writes. Taylor understands Lee's fondness for those small bits of luxury Lee himself would rarely reveal, and so the young man frequently surprises Lee with gifts from the seacoast, most notably great boxes of fresh oysters, for which Lee has a weakness.

Taylor serves on the board of his alma mater, the Virginia Military Institute, and three of his sons attend the school.

His book, *General Lee, 1861–1865,* is possibly the most insightful and least egocentric memoir of any staff officer of the war. Throughout his life he is well known in Norfolk not only as the staff officer of the South's greatest hero, but for his own quiet accomplishments as well. He dies in 1913, at age seventy-four. His obituary in the *Richmond Times-Dispatch* concludes: "Few men have been more honored in life than Col. Walter H. Taylor . . . and few are more honored in memory than he. To have lived so that all men gave him reverence to the day of his death is memory fine enough, but to have lived so that in his youth he was the trusted adjutant of Robert E. Lee sets his name apart and emblazons it. His books, his work in later years, his service to his community will live after him."

LIEUTENANT GENERAL JAMES LONGSTREET

Possibly the least understood and most maligned commander in the South, "Old Pete" was decades ahead of his time with his defensive tactics, the development of trench warfare.

After the war, he and his wife Louise settle in New Orleans, where he goes into the cotton brokerage business and later founds an insurance agency. Often blamed for the loss at Gettysburg, his close relationship with Lee diminishes after the war, and he pursues a lifelong effort to vindicate his actions, which often results in controversy, since much of his writing and explanations come after the death of Lee. There is still controversy and disagreement as to what role his ego and desire for independent command played in his relationship with Lee. It is indisputable, however, that Lee relied upon Longstreet more than anyone under his command, and no one performed in difficult situations with the consistency of Old Pete.

Proving, however, to be his own worst enemy, Longstreet writes that "we are a conquered people" and should "accept the terms that are now offered by the conquerors." Though conciliatory in sentiment, it is an unwise statement to make publicly. He becomes a Republican during Reconstruction, believing sincerely that he can better aid the South by cooperation with the powers in Congress, and thus alienates many southerners who otherwise would have supported him. He accepts a job from his friend, (now President) Grant, and in 1869 becomes Customs Surveyor for the Port of New Orleans. This further outrages many who feel that he is a direct pawn of the hostile administration. His old friend, and former subordinate, Daniel Harvey Hill writes, "[Longstreet] is the local leper of the community."

He finally leaves New Orleans in 1875 and settles in Gainesville, Georgia. Later he serves as United States Minister to Turkey, but has never had skill as a diplomat, finds the position disagreeable at best, and returns to become a U. S. marshal in Georgia. He retires from government service in 1884 and settles into a pleasant life as a farmer. In 1889 he endures disaster as his home, and many of the precious artifacts of his wartime service, are destroyed by fire, and then later in the same year, his wife Louise dies. She had borne him ten children, only five of whom survived to adulthood. He eases his grief by writing his memoirs, creating yet more controversy. His view of events is described by many as flawed, either by the passage of years or his continuing need to defend his service on the field.

He shocks friends and family in 1897 by marrying thirty-four-year-old Helen Dortch, a woman younger than he by forty-two years. Gradually, though, he rekindles the affection of many of the old soldiers, attends reunions and celebrations, and is cheered with great enthusiasm by the men who remember him, after all, as Lee's war-horse. He dies in 1904 of pneumonia, having never regained the use of his right arm; he is just shy of his eighty-third birthday. Helen Dortch Longstreet survives until 1962.

The controversy that has surrounded his name is made poignant by the fact that it is not until July 1998, 135 years after the battle, that the first monument to him is scheduled to be placed on the field at Gettysburg.

MAJOR GENERAL JOHN B. GORDON

The lawyer-turned-soldier returns to his home state of Georgia after the war, and serves two terms as a United States senator, then one term as governor of the state. Always active in Confederate causes and reunions, he serves as commander-in-chief of the United Confederate Veterans. Long after the war, after most of its participants are gone, he writes his memoirs. As with Longstreet, the accuracy of the work is criticized, and again, much is made of the span of years between the events and the writing. Some suggest there are some indiscreet motives behind some of Gordon's accounts, and so, much of his reminiscences are regarded with great skepticism. Lee biographer Douglas Southall

Freeman writes that it is often difficult "to know where General Gordon's memory ended and where his imagination began."

LIEUTENANT COLONEL CHARLES MARSHALL

The grandson of the illustrious John Marshall, the fourth U.S. Chief Justice, the young man who serves Lee so well was in reality the author of many of Lee's most famous documents, including the General Order Number 9 (Lee's farewell to his troops). After the war he settles in Baltimore and establishes a successful law practice. He is often called upon to speak at dedications to Lee monuments around the South, and continues to eloquently defend the southern cause. As the years pass, he becomes equally as outspoken in the cause of healing the wounds of the country. He speaks at the dedication of Grant's Tomb in New York, where he says, "Men who were arrayed against each other in deadly strife are now met together to do honor to the memory of one who led one part of this audience to a complete and absolute victory over the other, yet in the hearts of the victors there is no feeling of triumph, and in the hearts of the vanquished there is no bitterness, no humiliation."

He survives until 1904.

MAJOR GENERAL WILLIAM MAHONE

At the time of the surrender, "Little Billy" was regarded by many as Lee's finest commander. His troops identify themselves as "Mahone's Division" at reunions and gatherings for decades, despite the brief duration of his command. He becomes president of the Southside Railroad and prospers in the business of operating the very line that his troops had fought to defend. He becomes a United States senator from Virginia in 1880, survives until 1895.

MAJOR GENERAL FITZHUGH LEE

After Lee's army exhausted any hope of escape at Appomattox, Lee's nephew, "Fitz," insisted that surrender was not an option, and without telling his commander, led what remained of his cavalry command away from the town, intending to continue the fight as a guerrilla. He changed his mind, returned, and surrendered his cavalry at Farmville two days after Lee and Grant have met.

He establishes himself prominently in Virginia politics, becomes governor in 1885, but his greatest peacetime notoriety comes as U.S. Minister to Cuba, handling the difficult duties of diplomacy prior to the Spanish-American War. On the basis of his excellent service, he applies for and is granted commission as Major General of Volunteers in 1898, commands the Seventh Army Corps during that war. He retires in 1901, and dies in 1905.

MAJOR GENERAL GEORGE WASHINGTON CUSTIS LEE

The oldest and the only one of Lee's sons who seems destined not to be a professional soldier, the shy and self-effacing man is released from capture on orders from Grant at Appomattox. He moves to Lexington, Virginia, around the same time as his father, and becomes a professor of engineering at VMI. When his father is near death, the board of Washington College votes to allow Mary Lee lifelong occupancy of the President's Residence, which she refuses. Though qualified and certainly suitable for the post himself, the board's earnest desire to assist Lee's widow plays some role in Custis's election to the presidency, succeeding his father. Since he will live in the residence, it solves the dilemma for Mary as well, who remains with her oldest son until her death in 1873. If nepotism is a motive, it proves to bring exceptionally good fortune to the school, which is soon named Washington and Lee University. Custis serves as a much-respected administrator until he retires in 1897. He survives until 1913.

LIEUTENANT GENERAL RICHARD S. EWELL

As the successor to Stonewall, no commander in Lee's army had the opportunity for lasting fame as much as "Old Baldy." It remains a mystery why he could not rise to the challenge, though blame is often given to the dominance of his wife. His harsh temper, constant illness—real or imagined—drained all the fire of the Cause from him. After the war, he fades into obscurity, and dies in Virginia in 1872.

LIEUTENANT GENERAL JUBAL A. EARLY

"Old Jubilee" was finally relieved of service by Lee just prior to Appomattox, and he became a commander without a command. He disguises himself and goes to Texas, to bring what forces he can to assist Kirby Smith. After Smith's surrender, Early hops the border into

Mexico and continues to fight the war in his own mind. He goes to Canada, where he writes his memoirs. Finally returning to Virginia after Lee's death, he becomes embroiled with Longstreet in the controversy over blame for the loss at Gettysburg. Considered vain, ill-tempered, and vindictive, it is likely that his unfortunate behavior did much to diminish the reputation he earned with his troops as an excellent field commander. He never marries, and dies in 1894.

GENERAL P. G. T. BEAUREGARD

His unfortunate vanity and hunger for the limelight is a combination that makes enemies, and so throughout the war he was never allowed to remain long in any command where serious fighting took place. Considered an able commander of troops in the field, and noted particularly for his brilliant defense of Petersburg against extraordinary odds, he has an unfortunate talent for making ill-advised demands and exaggerating his own military situation. His single-minded need to put himself in the center of the war made his superiors uncomfortable, notably Jefferson Davis. He still offered a steady flow of grand plans and military strategies, none of which showed any rational hope of success. He was assigned to Joe Johnston's command in the Carolinas, must endure being the subordinate again, but the war ended before he could alienate yet another commander.

Afterward, he serves briefly as a railroad executive, but astonishingly, his reputation for greatness is expanded abroad, and he is offered command of armies in both Egypt and Romania, which he turns down, though with some regret. He writes extensively on his role in the war, creates considerable controversy by giving a slanted and wholly inaccurate account of his communications with Lee prior to the Petersburg campaign, putting himself in the best possible light, and harshly criticizing Lee's generalship. The articles are not published until after Lee's death. He survives until 1893.

PRESIDENT JEFFERSON DAVIS

Despite great effort, he does not fulfill Lincoln's wish that he escape, and thus fade into obscurity. He maintains some semblance of a Confederate government, traveling first to Danville, Virginia, then Charlotte, North Carolina. Johnston's surrender to Sherman turns all energy to Davis's capture, and finally, desperate and on the move, he is captured near Irwinville, Georgia, on May 10, 1865. He is imprisoned at

Fort Monroe on the Virginia peninsula for nearly two years, subjected to humiliating and inhumane treatment. But what Lincoln had feared is realized, and the publicity that begins to spread creates an uncomfortable situation for the government. Ultimately, he is simply released, and the scars that would be opened by a public trial are avoided. He travels to Europe, but feels some bitterness at what he sees as the betrayal of the powers that could have given so much aid to the Confederacy. He settles in Memphis in 1869, and accepts a position as head of an insurance company, which fails in 1873. Then he moves to Mobile, where he begins a long and bitter dispute with Joe Johnston, their wartime feud now expanding. In 1881 Davis completes his memoirs, much of which is devoted to disputing Johnston's own book. It is suggested by friends that Davis apply for a congressional pardon, to participate in the healing that has helped many of his former subordinates in their new lives. He responds, ". . . repentance must precede the right of a pardon, and I have not repented." He continues to insist that though the war showed secession "to be impracticable, this did not prove it to be wrong." He dies of malaria in 1889 at the age of eighty-one.

LIEUTENANT GENERAL RICHARD H. ANDERSON

Even before his crushing defeat at Saylor's Creek, Anderson's zeal for the Cause of the Confederacy had faded, and by the war's end he shared none of the political fire that still inspired men like Jubal Early. He returns to his family's old homestead in South Carolina, and, unlike Billy Mahone, he never makes the effort to fit himself into the new opportunities that open up in the rebuilding of the South. He settles into a difficult life as a farmer and suffers financial failure. He eventually endures humiliating work as a day laborer, earning a meager living from the sympathy of his neighbors. He dies in poverty in 1879, at age fifty-seven.

TRAVELLER

Purchased by Lee in 1862 for two hundred dollars, he is possibly the best known horse in American history. He outlives his master, but in death, as in life, the two remain close companions. Traveller is buried close beside the Lee Chapel at Washington and Lee University, which houses the final resting place of Robert E. Lee and his family.

© Marc A. Hefty 1995

ABOUT THE AUTHOR

JEFF SHAARA was born in 1952 in New Brunswick, New Jersey. He grew up in Tallahassee, Florida, and graduated from Florida State University in 1974. For many years he was a dealer in rare coins, but sold his Tampa, Florida, business in 1988 upon the death of his father, Michael Shaara.

As manager of his father's estate, Jeff developed a friendship with film director Ron Maxwell, whose film *Gettysburg* was based on *The Killer Angels.* It was Maxwell who suggested that Jeff continue the story Michael Shaara had begun, the inspiration that produced Jeff's novels *Gods and Generals* and *The Last Full Measure.* He is also the author of *Rise to Rebellion, Gone for Soldiers,* and *The Glorious Cause.*

Visit the author online at www.JeffShaara.com.